The Western Empire

Book 3
of
The Master of Fate

William Price Jr

Other Books by William Price Jr:

The Master of Fate series:
Into The Northlands
The Northern Keep
The Western Empire

The Fallen Angel series:
Fallen Love
Fallen Justice

Gwynedd Islands
Barrier Ocean
Darez
Nasinal Sea
Ironheart Province
Ironhearthaven
Velaross
Velaross Duchies
Northlands
Alvaro Dukedom
Alvaro
The Northern Keep
Kordenel Counties
Imperial Prefecture
Pelsernofia
Ulheim
Frostfront
Sylvar Vale
Dagon ay
Davenos
The City of All-Sins
Endless Sands
Daivic
Oneld
Kessia
Western Empire
Tordenia
Donograd
Warrik
Efrayim Ocean
Mediesorna

I

Wildelves Wood

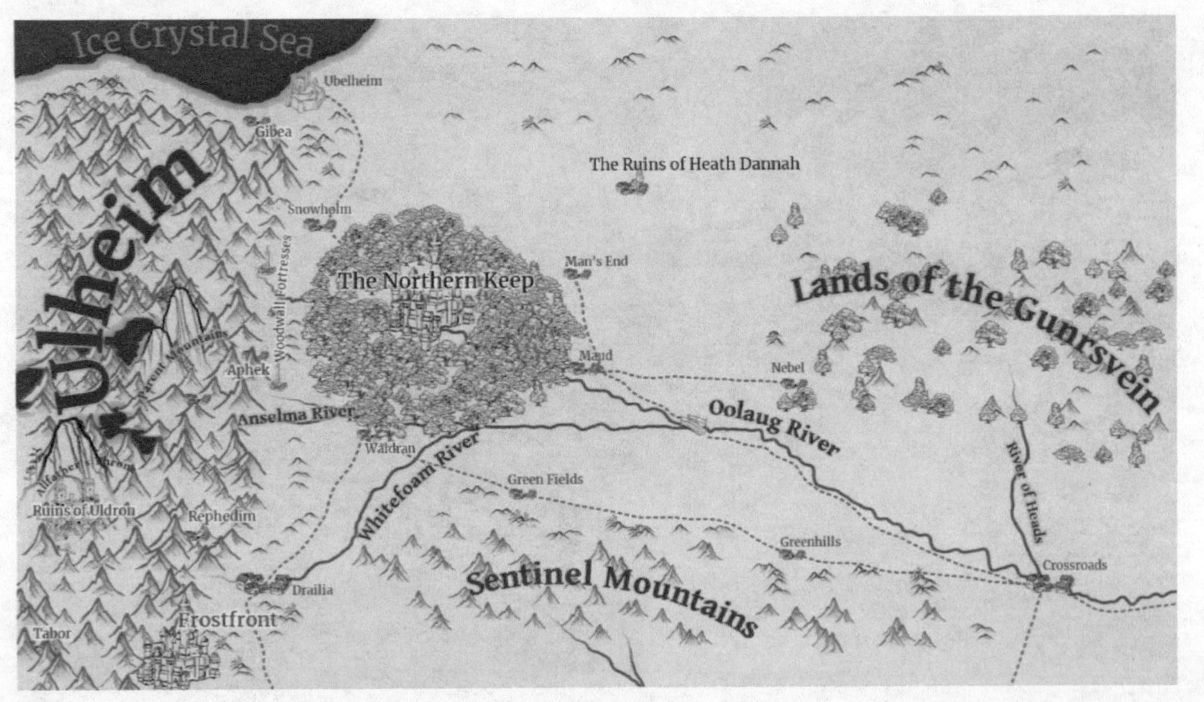

Ice Crystal Sea
Ubelheim
Gibea
The Ruins of Heath Dannah
Snowhelm
Ulheim
The Northern Keep
Man's End
Lands of the Gunrsvein
Woodwall Fortresses
Parent Mountains
Aphek
Maud
Nebel
Anselma River
Oolaug River
Waldran
Allfather's Shrine
Ruins of Uldron
Rephedim
Whitefoam River
Green Fields
River of Heads
Greenhills
Drailia
Sentinel Mountains
Crossroads
Frostfront
Tabor

Chapter 1

A soft blanket of purest white had descended upon the forest. As though the clouds themselves had lazily drifted down to rest amongst the evergreen trees of Wildelves Wood, winter had returned. The great storm that had halted all travel, commerce, and daily activity in the Northlands had at last relented. Errant snowflakes, like eager children rushing to catch up with their older siblings, still danced amongst the frost-tinged green of the ancient forest. The many pines and firs that stood together in fraternal community each bore their winter gown of with the stoicism that hundreds and thousands of winters in the harsh Lanasian Northlands teaches to all the inhabitants of Wildelves Wood. The lightly drifting snow did little to add to the forest's already-thick mantle of white, so gentle was its fall. The creatures of the Wood, having long sought out their winter dens, cared little of the weather and let the weather fall as it would. Winter had come to the great forest of the Northlands and with it, gentle serenity.

"Dirty misbegotten son of a whore!" Rogan's curse thundered across the forest with such force that the trees themselves recoiled, spilling their lacy winter coat. The knight's rage was accompanied by the ring of steel on steel, as his proven longsword, Talon, met and shattered the inferior blade drawn against him. In desperation, the seedy mercenary who had desperately thrown himself at Rogan now threw away his useless weapon and turned to flee. With another snarled oath, the prince of the Northlands dug his heels into the sides of his vicious black warhorse. Stick, sleek and powerful like all his Shamashi breed, leapt forward to pursue their quarry; the beast's own bloodlust as powerful as his rider's.

With his blinding speed, Stick needed only a few steps to overtake the mercenary. The savage warhorse raced past their whimpering foe before locking his forelegs and upturning the snow-covered turf in a sudden stop. Leaning forward and kicking out, Stick crushed the chest of his target with a vicious backwards strike of a muscled leg and a contemptuous snort. Mortally wounded, the mercenary fell limply to the upturned snow as a burst of crimson shot from his mouth and stained the frozen ground. Rogan did not bother with a second glance at the fallen mercenary, instead directing his focus on the next target.

A man who looked to be from Southern Lanasia and dressed in a weathered leather vest charged his horse at Rogan, desperately swinging his shortsword in a clumsy strike at the knight's head. Instead of his target, the Southerner caught only

Talon, as Rogan brought his longsword up to catch the attack so quickly the falling snowflakes were not disturbed by the passing of the prince's blade. The two combatants were locked for a moment, staring into each other's eyes over their crossed blades. This trial proved no different than the last as Rogan rolled his shoulder, sending the Southern mercenary's sword sliding harmlessly to the side; and in one smooth motion, the knight continued the same swing of Talon and effortlessly removed his attacker's head. Again, with no thought to the glory of his victory, Rogan instead looked to where he was needed next and acted without hesitation, spurring the raging Stick back toward the thickest batch of men who were, at that moment, attempting to surround and pull Tomas off the squire's own mount.

Despite the threat, Tomas was unafraid. His knight may be one of the paramount warriors of Lanasia, but the young man had spent months training, practicing, and learning. What's more, even as Rogan had Stick, so too did Tomas have his own bloodthirsty mount. Wielding Steelheart, the near-mythical blade of House Calonar, the young squire made several feints towards the mercenary on one side before launching a strong attack at his true target on the opposite side. The two fools who thought to attack from the young warrior's rear were defeated with similar ease by Urge, the chestnut warhorse gifted to Tomas by King Cylan Calonar during the recent Harvest Festival. The beast's brown coat blended perfectly with the fading blood scattered on the ground around him. Bred from Rogan's own Stick, Urge was every inch a warhorse, and he snorted his eagerness for more violence.

Tomas then heard his knight let out a short bark of challenge; he glanced in that direction to see Rogan and Stick thundering at another mounted warrior who had oriented on the squire and his horse. Stick charged, the aging warhorse snorting in impatience as Rogan brough his longsword to a high-ready position before swinging Talon down in a broad stroke that separated his target's head from his body. Stick thundered past the melee, drawing two of the mercenaries off Tomas and Urge. Using the distraction, the squire whirled Urge around and slashed one of his remaining attackers across the face, sending him screaming to the ground. The two pairs, Tomas astride Urge and Rogan upon Stick, then squared themselves against the last two of their attackers. Knight and squire glanced at each other even as did Urge and his own sire. Without a need for command, the warriors charged.

Tomas' target was easy to deal with, as the mercenary's skill with a blade was not much more than any common peasant; with a single flick of his wrist, the squire sent his enemy's blade spinning away, followed soon after by his head.

Rogan, though, had an unexpected complication. A startled grunt of a curse drew Tomas' gaze to his knight. There, he saw that, even as Rogan had intercepted a clumsy swing of a short blade, a second, unseen mercenary had dropped from the thick branches above and was struggling to draw a wicked-looking blade across Rogan's throat. The knight was parrying with Talon and using his free hand to hold back the blade, Stick trying his best to buck the attacker. "Little help!" the Northland hero barked.

Tomas turned Urge to aid his knight, but as fast as the fearsome chestnut warhorse was, Aebreanna was far faster. The nimble mercenary balancing atop Stick's rump and trying to murder Rogan stiffened suddenly as the iridescent patterns of a pair of Sylvai blades were imbedded into the base of his neck. Leaping from nowhere, the perfectly lithe and impossibly fast blur that was Aebreanna, the Baroness Tressalon, danced from a low-hanging branch, dispatched the threat to her friend, and spun away as though the event was nothing more difficult that crossing a street. Even as the dead man fell, a blur of Sylva motion had already retrieved her blades and landed on the horse of one of the only mercenaries still mounted. "Thanks," Rogan shouted.

At the first sign of attack, only moments ago, Aebreanna had leapt from Mayva, her nimble Sylvai pony of pure white. The spy's heavy, fur-lined cloak fell as gently as the errant snowflakes. Her form-fitting vest cradled her matronly chest and trim stomach, just as her leather leggings hugged Aebreanna's perfectly-sculpted and toned legs. Since the onset of winter, the Sylva's hair had turned perfectly white, reflecting her connection to the Winds of Magic. Normally a great, free-flowing mane, Aebreanna had, only the night before, tied her long hair into a tight braid that lashed out as she leapt and flipped amongst their attackers, very nearly a living weapon in itself. Aebreanna, renowned across the Northlands as much for her swift dexterity as for her predatory sensuality, landed on the rump of a mercenary's startled horse, opened the throat of its rider with a blinding slash that looked as much silvery water as it did metal, and had leapt off again before the somewhat portly horse could rear up and throw the dying mercenary from its back. Without missing a beat, the sultry spy flipped in the air and sent another of her many small Sylvai blades flying through the air to intercept another of the ragged-looking warriors as the man had been attempting to circle behind Rogan. Landing in front of the doomed mercenary, the terrified man had only an instant to stare into a face of unearthly beauty, to gaze into Aebreanna's opalescent eyes, burning with a passion that carried no hint of mercy, an instant after her blade lashed out. Aebreanna struck down her prey only to leap and spin, one shapely leg catching another approaching mercenary at the temple with a steel-tipped half-boot, knocking off his fur-lined cap and caving in the side of his head.

Seeing an opportunity, a tall warrior with long scraggly blonde hair that looked none too clean and the tattered smock of a runaway serf, leapt and grabbed the Sylva from behind, pinning Aebreanna's arms against her chest and planting her hard on the ground. With no leverage, braced against a Human more than a head taller than she and far broader, Aebreanna could not compensate for her lack of strength against the bulging mercenary. "Assistance would be most appreciated," she said through clenched teeth while struggling against the uncouth familiarity of the serf's touch and the rancid smell of his steaming breath.

Screaming in pain, the overly muscled mercenary flung his arms to either side and turned, revealing an Uldra waraxe buried deeply in his back. The runes carved along the curved blade plunged into the now-gaping wound, almost as though they were eager to bury themselves further. The blond mercenary managed to take two steps before falling to the ground, dead before he hit the snow. Looking up at the bearded face of her rescuer with more than a little resignation and a thinly veiled sneer of contempt, Aebreanna briefly nodded her head in gratitude.

Beraht planted a steel-shod boot on the head of the dead mercenary with enough force to crack the snow-covered stone, pulling his treasured waraxe free with his gloved hand and resting it on the shoulder of his scalemail armor in the customary Uldra display of indifference to a defeated enemy who had offered little challenge. The mountainous barbarian shrugged in response to his comrade's gratitude; the thanks of a Sylvai, after all, even one of whom Beraht did not think less than dirt, meant very little to a trueborn son of Uldron. His Sylva companion gestured over Beraht's left shoulder. "An attacker seeks your attention," she pointed out as said mercenary leapt onto the Uldra's boulder-like shoulders, roaring a battle cry that did absolutely nothing to impress its intended target.

The Uldra barbarian threw a look of pure contempt over his shoulder at the struggling mercenary before bucking his massive hip, throwing the weakling Human over his shoulder. The fool hit the ground and never had a chance to recover; Beraht reversed the waraxe and, using the blunted end, smashed the screaming man's head like a rotten melon. Tomas idly recalled from his lessons as a schoolboy that, for the Uldra, death by the blade was granted only to those who deserved it. Another mercenary, this one at least having enough courage to face the Uldra directly instead of trying to sneak up from behind like a weakling Sylvu, growled his best challenge and charged, kicking up snow and swinging something that would have been much better suited to chopping wood than fighting battles. Beraht caught the woodcutter's two-handed swing with his left hand and then head-butted him, driving the noseguard of his Druug-horned helmet deep into the man's face. Unsurprisingly, the soft-boned Human could not survive such an impact and fell. The Uldra did not let the Human fall into darkness with a tool and threw the axe away, finding one of the nearby mercenary's swords and taking it away, absently killing the screaming Human, and setting down the proper weapon beside the brave little woodcutter.

Tomas could not afford to divide his attention across the small battlefield to keep checking on his friends, being occupied by a final opponent. He caught a longsword with Steelheart, the shining blade catching and amplifying the dim light of the forest's morning. This move, though, cost him leverage, and Tomas fell with his attacker looming over him. The squire could almost hear his knight's sharp rebuke, "Never get into a pushing contest with a sword. It's for stabbing and slashing, not shoving." The moment the ground reached up for him, the young squire rolled as Rogan had taught, not only dodging a follow-up strike from his attacker, but also knocking the mercenary off his feet.

Tomas recalled a lesson from only a few weeks past. He was lying on the ground with Rogan pinning him from above. "A lot of fights end up here," the knight had said. "Do your best and move fast, but sometimes you end up on your back. It's important to know what to do, once you're there."

The squire continued his roll, putting distance between himself and his opponent and staying mindful of where Steelheart's sharp edges were. Tomas regained his feet and spun, seeing the mercenary doing the same. The two warriors approached wearily, their weapons held low. Tiring of his opponent's lack of aggression, the squire shot forward and launched a quick stab on his right before pivoting and slashing Steelheart low, making space between them. A snarling roar caught them both by surprise and the mercenary turned to face Urge. The chestnut warhorse had clearly tired of his rider's inexperience and lunged in; he reared, flailing his forelegs at the screaming mercenary, who was crushed.

Tomas sighed and stared at his unruly mount. "I had him."

Urge snorted his contempt and continued stomping the dead man into the frozen earth.

Rogan thundered up, reining in Stick mere feet from Tomas. The knight looked around after sparing a glance to make sure his squire was unharmed. "Wasn't there one more of these guys?" he asked.

"Die, Eigenhard!" The mercenary in question held a shortbow in his hands with an arrow knocked and pointed at the prince. Before he could let fly, however, Beraht's waraxe spun through the air, slamming into the last mercenary's chest and sending the dead man rolling to the ground, his arrow soaring into the mist-shrouded branches.

The Uldra barbarian stomped across the road Rogan and Tomas stood upon, brushing a few loose flakes of snow off his massive cloak and muttering to himself. "Blasted, good-for-nothing amateurs taking up my time," he grunted, pulling at the collar of his armor and releasing gusts of steam into the winter air. "Better off sitting around listening to Sylvai break wind than fighting these weaklings."

"Where's Aebreanna?" Tomas asked, wiping the sweat from his brow that was already crystallizing in the bitter cold.

"I am here." The beautiful Sylva drifted forward from the pack animals with the usual swish of her sensual hips, settling her fur-lined cloak back across her slender shoulders. "I am unharmed."

"Well, that was exhilarating," the young squire remarked, cleaning Steelheart with the oiled cloth he carried in his saddlebag before returning the blade into its sheath. "There's nothing like a good fight to help breakfast settle."

Rogan wiped his own blade down, looking his squire up and down while doing so. Though it may have been his imagination, Tomas thought he knight was breathing a bit heavier that the squire, taking just a little longer to recover from the small battle. "Before you get too full of yourself," Rogan growled, "you might want to think about how bad you fought this little adventure."

"What do you mean?" Tomas demanded, looking around at the dead mercenaries. "They're dead and we're alive. I'd call that a win."

"And you'd be right," the knight confirmed. "Except the team won this fight, not Tomas Fidelis all by his little lonesome. All Tomas Fidelis managed to do was get pulled out of his saddle by an amateur and damn near split down the middle." Rogan sheathed Talon and dismounted, pulling free the leather headband that held in place his long red hair. "He had to get saved by his horse… again."

Urge snorted his agreement. Stick gave a reminding bump of his head to Rogan's shoulder, which the knight chose to ignore.

Tomas looked down in sullen disappointment. The young man had thought that his skill had brought victory, but his mentor's harsh words quickly and efficiently deflated his swollen ego before it had even managed to fully inflate. Seeing this, Rogan replaced his headband, taking care to ensure the Uldra rune was centered, and crossed to his squire, putting a comforting hand on his squire's shoulder.

"Don't get me wrong, kid," the Northlands prince said in a low voice. "You did good. But never let a victory go to your head. There's always something you did wrong, something you can improve."

The squire nodded at his knight's words. "You're right, Rogan. Sorry."

"Nothing to be sorry about, kid," the knight assured him, putting a hand on his apprentice's shoulder. "Like you said, we're alive, and they're dead."

"Oh, stop. I'm getting emotional." Beraht's rough voice, never a source of gentle reassurance, hit them with solid reality. "I hate to bother you two just when you're about to hug, but there's probably more of these mercs around here."

Rogan straightened and turned to remount Stick. "He's right. Let's move." Tomas nodded and mounted Urge.

Beraht looked at Rogan and shook his head. "I meant we should hunt them down and kill them, not leave," he muttered. The mountainous Uldra looked down at the diminutive Aebreanna as she walked her Sylva pony past him. Despite her being mounted and he standing, still the lumbering barbarian towered over his deceptively frail-looking friend. "What's wrong with Humans?" he demanded of her.

Aebreanna just shrugged.

"How many is that now?" Tomas asked as they continued their trip west. "Three, four?"

"Four," Rogan confirmed.

"We're barely a week from the Keep, and we've already been attacked four times by mercenary bands from as far south as Alvaro and as far west as Kessia."

Beraht laughed and spat, his massive shire horse, Sus, snorting agreement. "Yeah, it's a shame they decided to split up. Maybe if they'd hit us all at the same time, we could get a decent fight."

Rogan shook his head. "Or killed before this mission really got started," he countered.

The brutish Uldra shrugged. "What's the point of fighting if you know you're going to win?" he asked. "There's no fun if there's no danger."

Aebreanna pulled the hood of her cloak up to shield from the cold breeze that was stirring in the branches overhead. "Well, I, for one, am appreciative of their division," she insisted. "A little boredom is far preferable to slow and painful death and dishonor at the hands of mercenaries and slavers." As always, it seemed the sensual Sylva's breath steamed with greater thickness when she spoke than any of her companions, as though Aebreanna's body burned with a greater heat than that of her friends.

"You Sylvai are so afraid of getting into a decent fight!" Beraht barked leaning towards her and causing his massive shire horse to stumble. "It's no wonder there's not a single decent warrior among you!"

"As I recall," the spy sniffed, "more of the enemy died at my hands than yours."

At the thought of being upstaged in battle, especially by a Sylva, the Uldra barbarian lost his grip on what little civility he possessed. "The only reason that some woman…"

"*Sy'lva,*" Aebreanna calmly corrected, absently grooming the heavy mane of her small pony. Mayva flicked her tail dismissively at Beraht's Sus when the lumbering shire horse drew too close.

"The only reason some female would beat me out of a kill count is because I was a too busy saving your flabby Sylva butt… AGAIN!"

Aebreanna primly pushed back her fur-lined cloak to reveal the generous curves of her body, conforming perfectly to her pristine pony and exquisitely-crafted silvery-grey saddle. Mayva moved with her rider, the two a flawlessly-synchronized pair. "Firstly, my proportions are worthy of song and sacrifice." She closed her cloak again. "And secondly," she sniffed, "you certainly took your time in accomplishing the minor task of offering assistance. No doubt the weight of your filth and bulging girth slowed you."

"Oh, I'm soooo sorry that I wasn't at your beck and call!" the Uldra barked with as much sarcasm as he could manage through his rage, his shaggy brown shire horse snorting at the pony of pure white. "Please forgive me for not staying at your side like a dog!"

"You are forgiven," Aebreanna replied primly, tossing a small chuck of dried beef at Beraht, who caught the treat in his mouth. "But try to do better next time. That pig had wandering hands that I fear will leave a stink on many of my more tender areas."

Beraht laughed derisively as he savored his treat. "Oh, please, like you haven't slept with worse." Sus neighed mockingly.

"What exactly are you implying?" the Sylva demanded as her Mayva snorted at the shire horse. "Of all people, you, I think, have the least right to bring into question a person's sexual predilection or history. I, for one, have never awoken after a night of drunken revelry in a pigsty."

"Oh, oh! One time! One time that happened!"

"Once was more than enough for someone who never bathes!"

By now, both Rogan and Tomas had pushed their horses far enough ahead of the dueling companions that the two Humans could almost hear each other over the yelling. Rogan winced at one particularly shrill accusation from Aebreanna. "You know," the knight observed, "it's no wonder these damned mercs keep finding us with those two going at it like that all day, every day."

Tomas glanced over his shoulder as the pair continued their traditional racial animosity. "Have they always been like that?" he asked.

"No," Rogan shrugged. "They used to really hate each other."

"Would it do any good if we gagged them?" the squire asked, Urge snorting his agreement.

The knight shook his head. "Doubtful. Aebreanna's been tied up so often that she can slip through just about any bonds we could put together, and Beraht would just chew through any gag."

"Will they keep this up for the whole trip?"

"Probably," Rogan shrugged. "Of course, there's always a chance one of us might get killed."

Tomas nodded. "Well, there's something to look forward to at least. How long did you say it will take us to get to Ulheim?"

"A week, if the weather holds. Two or three, otherwise."

"Joy."

Chapter 2

For the first time since the sorceress Vara had unleashed her arcane fury upon the Northlands, fragile warmth once again cast its glory upon Wildelves Wood. As though God Himself was blessing the beginning of their journey, rays of gentle sunlight filtered through the thick canopy of trees under which their team traveled. Each member of their small company took great comfort as they briefly passed from the shaded chill of a tree's shadow into daylight's caress. The sun shined down on the forest standing eternal vigil around the Northern Keep and pushed back the unnatural chill through which the adventurers now forged.

Although the Northlands were renowned for long and fierce winters, from the moment of its arrival, the forces of good King Cylan Calonar had known that no natural force could have been behind this storm's creation. The Harvest Festival had not even been a day passed, their victory over the Death Mage Anninihus still fresh, and the wounds from that vicious battle still raw, before dark clouds had thundered out of Ulheim like an avalanche in the sky. With the first hints of winter weather barely showing around the Northern Keep, Vara's Storm, as it had come to be called, released its fury on the Northlands.

Tomas shifted Steelheart as he rode, trying to find a comfortable position for the weight of the legendary blade of House Calonar. Despite the intense training he had received over the past several months, he was still unaccustomed to the feel of the sword now riding at his hip. That, and the terrible burden of its responsibility. Tomas was but the next in a line of heroes who had carried this weapon into battle against the worst evils to plague Lanasia.

"Problems, kid?" Rogan asked.

The squire glanced at his knight. "Not really," he replied. "I'm still just trying to get used to it."

Rogan nodded, his long red hair bobbing with the movement against the restraint of his leather headband. "Trust me, it gets so that you only notice your weapon when it isn't there." The knight patted his own Talon with a callused and weather-beaten hand. "These get to be more a part of you than most people think."

The squire grunted and once again adjusted Steelheart. His young heart sang with the thrill of the quest, of riding off on an adventure just as the legendary Heroes of Fate once had. Even more, Tomas bore the same weapon as had Cylan Calonar, the last living member of that epic group that had saved Lanasia and even the world again and again. The young man was squire and apprentice to Prince Rogan Eigenhard, heir to House Calonar. Still, the weight was real, both physical and emotional. When Tomas made another adjustment to Steelheart, his hand lingered against the flawless white ribbon tied around the scabbard. He could not hold back another sigh.

Rogan noticed this and sighed himself. "A cold road is no match for a warm bed." The knight glanced at his squire. "And a warm embrace from the woman you love."

Tomas grimaced. "But you still ride," he pointed out.

"Kyla understands," the knight shrugged. "And so does Mary."

The squire nodded. "It's one thing to understand here," he pointed to his head. "This is something else," he said with a point to his heart.

"Yeah." Rogan looked directly at his apprentice. "Just remember that she's the reason you're out here."

"What do you mean? I thought we were… I don't know… fighting for the people."

"We are," Rogan shrugged again. "But really, we aren't. Never fight for causes, kid; they'll always disappoint. Don't fight for a flag or a kingdom or a cause. Fight for a person."

"So, you fight for Kyla?"

The knight nodded. "And you fight for Mary. Every time you and I ride out; every life we have to take, every evil we defeat, every wrong we put right… we're doing it to keep them safe."

They were quiet for a while, riding through the Wood at a steady canter and occasionally noticing a particularly heated exchange between Aebreanna and Beraht. Finally, Tomas shifted Steelheart again and pursed his lips.

"I know that look," Rogan pointed out. "What's eating you now?"

"Just thinking about Vara," the young man replied. Tomas looked over at this knight, friend, and mentor and not for the first time wondering if the many scars decorating the Northlander would one day rest on Tomas's own body: the price of a life of battle and quest. Already, his shoulder bore a terrible scar from a battle against the Death Mage's blasphemous creations, one no magic had been able to erase. "Just running through how little real information there is on her."

The prince nodded. "As much as everyone thinks they know, there isn't much anyone really knows. Just stories, myths, and a lot of fears."

"My mother used to warn me that if I ever told a lie, Vara would steal my soul."

Rogan grunted. "My family pretended not to believe in 'peasant myths,' but we all knew the stories. There was a nurse that told stories to me and my cousins about how Vara would sneak into villages during the night of the Festival of the Dead. Unless you put out something to scare her away, she would steal the youngest, most innocent child she could find, replacing it with a demon she summoned from Underworld."

"That's a nice children's story," Tomas muttered.

The knight shrugged. "Scary stories are part of the Festival of the Dead. Guess you could say it's tradition to give children nightmares."

"We never celebrated it," the squire replied. "In Pelsemoria, the festival was another 'pagan ritual' the Church frowned on."

"Pretty popular in the Northlands," Rogan pointed out. "As long as the nights are up here, most people want to make sure the dead stay happy."

"Your conversations are truly fascinating," Aebreanna noted from behind the two warriors. "Most especially the way they wander from one pointless topic to another,"

Tomas glanced back at their Sylva companion. Each time their path emerged from the shadows, into a beam of golden warmth, Aebreanna lifted her delicate-seeming face, her opalescent eyes closing and a soft smile flittering upon her full lips. Tomas tried not to stare at her, wishing to respect her privacy as Rogan so often advised, but the Wyrdmark was a startling thing. He had read of it, of course; all the children of Lanasia knew that some very few Sylvai were born with it, their appearance changing with the seasons. This knowledge, though, paled against the reality. In the autumn, Aebreanna's thick mane was a deep auburn. Her opalescent eyes carried a hazel sheen. In one night, though, that changed, the same night Vara's Storm had forced an early winter upon the Northlands. Besides the nearly luminescent mane, her eyes now had an azure glow. Her complexion, already fair, had become porcelain, reflecting the pure snow around them., and matching the flawless white of her Sylvai pony.

Noticing the squire's stare once again, Aebreanna tried to smile. "We daughters of the Wyld share in our mother's seasonal changes," she told him.

Tomas blinked, forcing away the deep-seated prejudice of his upbringing. The Church called it the Witch's Mark and, for centuries, had burnt any Sylva possessing it. "I'm sorry, it's just…"

"As I have said," her words were forced and overly-neutral. "I do not enjoy discussing the… nature of my inheritance." Mayva muttered a dark warning.

Stick nudged against Urge, just as Rogan nudged his squire. The subject of Aebreanna's family was a delicate one. All of House Calonar knew not to explore the subject.

The Sylva pushed her furred hood back, exposing the thick mane of perfectly white hair spilling past her slender shoulders. After the morning's battle against the mercenaries, Aebreanna had decided to let her locks fly freely. Her lustrous mane seemed almost to glow in response to the sun's reemergence. "As I was saying," her tone communicated her unquestionable intent to change the subject. "In each instance that either of you boys approaches a topic of conversation that is either uncomfortable or unpleasant, you manage, with no coordination, to adjust the course of that conversation onto something that is not only harmless but also quite likely to evoke fond memories of childhood, bringing to you both a sense of safety and comfort."

Both knight and squire were silent for a moment. "Was that all one sentence?" Tomas finally asked.

"It was," she replied calmly. "Did I lose you?"

"No, I think I got it all."

"Well, she lost me," Rogan muttered.

"As so often occurs when the conversation changes from violence to nearly anything intellectual," the sultry baroness smiled.

The knight leaned towards his squire. "That was an insult, right?"

"Yeah. But she also managed to compliment you on your knowledge of war at the same time."

Rogan settled back into his saddle. "Well, what do you know about Vara?"

Aebreanna took in a deep breath of the crisp air, her warmer-than-Human body generating a heavy mist as she exhaled. She smiled as she so often did at the smells of the forest and winter surrounding them. "Not much more than any of you, I am sorry to say."

"You mean there are some things even Rashid doesn't know?" Tomas asked, genuinely surprised.

"While my husband's prowess at intelligence gathering is matched by none, there are, unfortunately, some facts stubbornly shrouded in mystery."

"You *kazik* think you know so much!" The deep and gravelly response came lumbering out of his heavy braided beard. "The Uldra know plenty!"

Tomas smiled at their barbarian friend. Beraht had grown increasingly irritable, more so than was normal for the irascible warrior, since their entrance into the forest. Even the repeated attacks launched against them by the mercenaries had done little to lighten the barbarian's mood. While the whole world knew the Uldra were uncomfortable amid trees, preferring the open sky of their mountains, Beraht took that distaste to an extreme. "So, great *Uldrakey*, will you share with us lowly *kazik* what the *Uldra* know of *Varabatmavet*?" the squire asked.

Rogan looked at this squire in surprise. "You speak Uldric?"

The young man shrugged. "Well, it's been a long time, but I learned a little during school. In Pelsemoria, we were supposed to learn one of the dialects of the Republic, but a few students were allowed to study either Sylvai or Uldric. I chose Uldric."

Aebreanna raised a Sylva eyebrow at Tomas. "I must admit a burning curiosity," she admitted. "Why would you choose the brutish grunting of the Uldra tongue when you had the chance to learn *Sy'lva'n* music?

The squire shrugged. "Well, for one, learning Uldric only took two years. But learning even basic Sylvai took more than a decade."

"The barbaric mountain clans may be content with their grunts and belches to convey what passes for thought," she sniffed. "But the *Sy'lva'n* know that language is thought given expression and thus deserves the same depth as that of the *Sy'lva'n* mind."

"You said, 'for one,'" Rogan pointed out. "What's the real reason?"

Tomas smiled. "You can't speak Uldric without learning the curse words."

Rogan laughed uproariously, while Aebreanna looked at Tomas with clear disappointment in her azured opalescent eyes. The squire just shrugged. "I believe we were about to be educated as to the mythical knowledge of Vara by our lumbering companion," Aebreanna pointed out, looking back at where Beraht rode as usual with the pack animals.

"Huh?" the Uldra asked.

"What do your people know about Vara?" Tomas translated.

"Oh. Well, for one, we know better than to go looking for her."

Rogan wiped his mirthful tears away. "Can't be helped," he pointed out. "We've got to know why she attacked the Keep."

"Attacked!" the barbarian spat. "She made it snow; big deal! That's no attack. Fire's an attack! Blades and blood and glory, that's an attack!"

"Aebreanna regarded her towering, hairy companion with resignation. "Do you have any appreciation for just how great an effort is required to harness and unleash a storm of even the most minimal potency?" she demanded.

"... Yes?"

The spy threw her arms up in frustration.

"So what do the Uldra know about Vara, Beraht?" the young man asked.

"She's evil," the warrior answered, making a gesture in the air to ward off dark spirits. "After she got done putting you Humans in your place, she headed into Ulheim."

"Why into the mountains? I wonder," Aebreanna mused.

Beraht laughed. "After getting done with Human blood, she probably wanted something stronger! Anyways, she reached the mountains and hunted down every stinking grey-skin pack, killing its bull and any Druug that tried to fight her."

"I've heard that legend," Tomas admitted. "She spent a century killing any Druug that showed the slightest strength until they all worshipped her as a goddess of death."

"They still do," the Uldra added. "To this day, the Druug worship her and guard her lair."

"You mean that, to reach Vara, we might have to fight our way through hundreds of grey-skins?" Rogan demanded.

Beraht shook his head. "They guard her lair from wild animals, other packs, and the Uldra. Anyone else is welcome to enter her home and be destroyed."

"Are the Uldra hunting her?" Tomas asked. "A little help would probably be a good thing."

Again, the barbarian shook his head. Beraht took off his helmet briefly to scratch his thick mass of coal-black hair and adjust the purple headband he always wore before replacing his traditional headgear. "The clans won't go anywhere near Vara's mountain."

"Why?" Aebreanna asked.

The warrior just shook his head firmly, a slight tremor going through his callused hands as he again made a sign in the air to ward off evil. Aebreanna and Rogan looked at Tomas.

"Vara knows Soul Magic," the squire said tersely.

"*Averat!*" Beraht's oath shot through the air.

The others were silent then, clearly shocked with their friend's fear. No other explanation was needed, though. The entire world knew of the Uldra fear of Soul Magic, one of the forbidden arcane forms. Developed during their Uprising by Kelinva, the Xeshlin's insidious Dark Empress, Soul Magic was meant to combat the brutal violence of the Uldra by manipulating their very souls. The power unleashed was so heinous, so evil, that its practice was forbidden and all records of its development were destroyed. The magic was so reviled by everyone that Kelinva and all who followed her were cursed, creating their hated race. In the centuries that followed, only a handful of practitioners had ever claimed even a limited knowledge of Soul Magic, and each was counted among Arayel's greatest villains.

"How do you of know this?" Aebreanna asked Tomas.

"I used to sneak into my father's study when he was away and read the briefings he received about potential threats to the Emperor."

Rogan laughed. "Guess that's just one of the fringe benefits to having a dad that was commander of the Praetorians."

The squire nodded. "About a year before the Madness, my father received a briefing on adepts who could threaten the Imperial Family. I looked through it one day while he met with the Emperor."

"What other adepts were in the briefing?" Aebreanna asked.

Tomas shrugged. "I don't remember for sure. Cylan Calonar was considered the greatest threat, of course. Cyras Darkholm was another, but the Praetorians could never decide if the Trickster Mage was real or a legend. Same with the Shadowed Mage, Fak'Har. Vara only stands out in my memory because of the stories my mother used to tell me."

"You remember anything else of interest?" Rogan asked.

"Not much. The Arcane Guild didn't know very much about her, or at least, they didn't tell much to the government. About the only facts were that she was definitely female, probably Sylvai, currently living somewhere in Ulheim, knows at least a little Soul Magic, and one other thing."

"What's that?"

Tomas looked steadily at his knight. "She wants, more than anything else, to be left alone. The quickest way to make her angry is to disturb her peace."

"Well, like it or not, we're going to find out why she attacked us."

Tomas had trouble believing that Wildelves Wood was the same forest he had come through on his journey to the Northern Keep. Upon first entering the Wood with Rogan all those months ago, the young squire had felt as if the trees themselves were pushing into him, threatening to overwhelm him with their size and the weight of their years. Everywhere Tomas had looked, he could only see potential threats, each shadow hiding a Sylvai bowman, ready to leap out and riddle his back with arcane missiles. The silence of the forest, compared with the constant background rumble of the city, was crushingly oppressive. The squire shook his head at the memory of how he had trembled in fear of the mysterious Sylvai and their wood.

That was then, before the life-changing time Tomas had spent in the Northern Keep with its many interesting people. Now, as the squire rode beside his knight, Rogan Eigenhard, the man he had once swore to kill, Tomas found himself almost completely at ease among the trees. In fact, the young man frequently found himself smiling and absently rubbing a finger against the golden rose that was pinned, as always, on his collar against the pulse of his throat. Although good sense told him otherwise, Tomas had the distinct impression that he could feel the life of the forest around him, perhaps even hear the trees and animals talking to him, telling him their secrets.

Seeing the look on his squire's face that betrayed his deep thoughts, Rogan snapped his fingers in front of Tomas's eyes, trying to bring his apprentice back to reality. "Hey, kid, you in there?"

Without blinking, Tomas shifted his gaze to the knight. Again, Tomas had the distinct impression of someone or something whispering to him. "Of course," the squire replied in a mellow voice. "You and I will not part company for some time yet. We still have much to do together."

"What in Underworld are you talking about?" Rogan demanded.

Blinking suddenly, not remembering just what he said or why, Tomas looked around. "What was I saying?" he asked.

Rogan leaned back a bit in his saddle, unconsciously putting some distance between himself and his squire. "Kid, I understand the last few months have been stressful, but I need you here for what we're going into."

Tomas looked back into the woods, feeling again the sense of welcoming that seemed to emanate from deep within. "Can't you feel it?" he asked.

"Feel what?"

"The trees. The hills. Everything around us. Even the air. Everything out here seems to be alive."

Making a big show of looking his squire over, Rogan hummed as a physician does, right before the bad news is delivered. Tomas finally snapped, "What?"

"Well," the knight drawled, "you don't seem to be developing shiny eyes, but if I didn't know better, I'd say you were turning into a Sylvu."

Perfectly mimicking Rogan's movements, Tomas also hummed and said, "Well, you don't seem to be developing pointed ears, but if I didn't know better, I'd say you were turning into a jackass."

Rogan laughed. "Better," he said. "So really, what's bugging you?"

Tomas shook his head. "I don't know. The last time we came through the Wood, I swear I could feel hostility from everything. This time, it feels like something, or everything, around here is calling to me, welcoming me." Worry obviously showed on Rogan's face, since Tomas shrugged. "Don't worry, I'm pretty sure I'm not going insane."

"Losing oneself in the power of these trees is a simple, even desirable thing," Aebreanna remarked from behind them. "Along with the forests resting to the north of Pelsemoria and those in our Vale, these trees are the greatest source of power from the days when my people lived beneath the shade of the Eternal Forest."

"Was Wildelves Wood a part of the Eternal Forest?" Tomas asked.

The beautiful spy gently shook her head. "Our histories say that, on the day Nassinalia was destroyed and the Eternal Forest retreated into Otherworld, this forest sprang up, absorbing what little remained of our ancestral homeland so that it would not be forever lost."

Rogan fished for a small portion of trail rations from his saddlebag. "Stories say that King Cylan had a vision the day before he met and joined the Heroes of Fate," the knight added. "Supposedly, he was riding through the Wood and he saw that a great city would rise in its center, both protecting and being protected by the trees."

Tomas looked at his knight. "You don't believe it?"

The knight shrugged. "It's a good story, but the King has never confirmed it. Besides, the location of the Northern Keep is less likely to have come from some mystic vision, and more from the fact that any army trying to attack it would suffer massive losses from the Sylvai that live here. And that's before it could even attempt an assault on the city's walls."

"Are there any stories of the King's early years you do believe?" Tomas asked.

Rogan swallowed a piece of tack and drank from his waterskin. "Only the ones that someone has confirmed to me personally," he replied.

"Didn't you spend months trying to convince me all those stories were true?"

"No, I was trying to convince you that all the stories you'd heard from everyone else were wrong."

"That is an interesting distinction," Aebreanna noted.

Tomas looked at his knight. "So you don't believe the stories about King Cylan's early years. You don't believe in the stories of the Teachings. You don't believe in the legends of the Sylvai Empire or the Republic's founding. What do you believe in, Rogan?"

Rogan looked at the trees overhead and around at the plants that surrounded them. "Over the years, I've seen many a strange thing. I've seen ancient gods and evil spirits. I've seen wizards twist reality. I've seen tyrants overthrown, and I've seen rebellions crushed. I've heard storytellers tell versions of events that I was at personally, and I've even met a few legends.

"I have no doubt that there is a God out there, kid. I have no doubt that there are things older than Humans or Sylvai or Uldra, and I know that they're hungry to come back. The thing is, I also know that the stories we know about God and everything that isn't flesh and blood are told by men and women that weren't there personally. Every generation puts their own personal slant on the stories of the past."

The knight looked at his apprentice. "You ask me what I believe in, kid. I believe in you. I believe in Beraht and Aebreanna and everyone at the Keep. I believe that there are evil people in the world, and that they want nothing more than to see House Calonar destroyed forever. And I believe that we'll meet these people and creatures head-on every time they raise their heads."

Tomas blinked. Then could only, "Amen."

Chapter 3

The next day, Tomas and Rogan chatted, as was becoming their custom when violence did not interrupt, on nothing of any great importance. The two Humans found interest in comparing the theoretical knowledge the squire had gained thanks to his education in the old Republic capital against the knight's practical experiences in traveling the world. They passed many hours and miles with such discussions, pausing only when some random comment would once again set Aebreanna and Beraht arguing. The Human men would likely have continued so, had not a sound deep in the forest drawn everyone's attention. Without a word, Tomas and Rogan drew their swords as Beraht readied his Uldra waraxe and pushed his towering shire horse around to the far side of their pack animals. Aebreanna dismounted from her pony and vanished into the mist-shrouded trees to investigate the disturbance.

The three warriors waited for the return of their Sylvai friend, watching for any sign of threat. Tomas tried to still himself but felt his hand tremble as it held Steelheart. "Steady," Rogan said softly, seeing his squire's agitation.

"What could it be?" the young man asked in a low breath.

"We'll find out soon enough," the veteran replied.

After an eternity of waiting, Aebreanna emerged from the surrounding trees and gestured for the warriors to lower their weapons. Complying, Rogan asked with a glance what was happening. The Sylva guided their eyes further down the road with a wordless gesture. Beraht joined the two Human warriors as they saw the source of the disturbance. At first only a few pinpoints of light were visible in the mist of the forest; these points of light were soon revealed to be ornate wooden lanterns held on long poles. Gradually, following the lanterns down through winter mist to the hands that held them aloft, Tomas was finally able to discern what it was that approached. A column of figures, deeply hooded and robed against the persistent chill in the muted tones of the winter wood, moved slowly across the road ahead of them, vanishing deeper into the trees beyond.

"Who are they?" Tomas asked in a soft voice.

"Sylvai," Rogan answered.

"The local *Fur'lya'cel'lan*," Aebreanna added, moving to her pony.

"The what?" Tomas asked.

"More shiny-eyed mystics," Beraht grunted.

"I don't understand," the young man admitted.

Rogan sheathed his sword. "They're the clergy of the Sylvai, kid, probably from all the nearby villages. They're performing a ritual. Nothing that involves us."

"Speak only for yourself, Rogan," Aebreanna said. The spy had lowered her head as the small procession passed from view, showing a deep respect that Tomas had not thought the sultry Sylva capable of. "To some, this will be a night of extreme importance." She handed the reins of her white pony up to Beraht, an act about which Mayva appeared unenthused.

"We don't have a lot of time to waste, Aebreanna," the knight pointed out.

The Sylvai threw an arch look at her friend. "Would you consider it a waste for our young companion to attend to his religious duties?" she asked pointedly.

Rogan raised his hands in surrender. "I know better than to argue once you've made up your mind. We'll pitch camp near here and wait for you." The knight dismounted and began breaking through the heavy snowdrifts beside the road to clear a path for their horses toward a suitable campsite he had spotted beside the nearby creek.

"What's going on?" Tomas asked.

"Like I said, kid," the knight huffed to his squire through his exertions, "Sylvai business, not ours."

"Perhaps," Aebreanna replied. "But then again, perhaps our youthful companion would find the ceremony interesting."

Rogan looked at his apprentice, pausing in his labors. "It's your call, kid. Go if you like."

Tomas dismounted. "Coming, Beraht?" the squire asked lightly as he handed the Uldra the reins to Urge.

"To some pansy, shiny-eyed ceremony worshiping bugs or bushes or some rock?" the barbarian growled. "Pass." The mountainous warrior led the horses and pack animals toward the clearing Rogan was entering.

Tomas grinned and joined Aebreanna. Gesturing for her to lead the way, the young man said, "Ladies first."

The lithe Sylva raised an eyebrow at the squire's attempt at chivalry and moved on through the trees to follow behind the column of Sylvai. Despite the nimble baroness's legendary dexterity, Aebreanna's pace was slow to match that of her people. Tomas thus had only a little difficulty in keeping up with her through the tangle of hidden tree roots and sudden depressions all covered by the uniform blanket of snow. The squire gave silent thanks for the extensive training the Sylva had given him in recent months, without which any one of the many falls he suffered during the trip behind the Sylvai mystics he and Aebreanna were following could have otherwise been disastrous.

After only a few minutes of travel, which was still enough to set Tomas's heart racing and his breath coming in hard gasps, he and Aebreanna, following along behind the Sylvai at a respectful distance, reached what the young man assumed was their destination. A large collection of stones rose above the surrounding trees, at once standing alone and yet remaining a close part of the forest. From the cluster of rocks at the center of the small grove ran a small stream only partially frozen over that flowed down through the forest where it would, Tomas assumed, eventually join with the Oolaug River. No trees or bushes grew around these stones, nor were they marked by animal droppings or fallen leaves. There was no discernable pattern or organization to the stones to suggest ancient construction. It was a place of quiet serenity and gentle power, where nature had been allowed to build as She wished, without interference, and the only noise was Tomas's hard breathing, which the squire was struggling to bring under control.

Even as Tomas formed a question to ask Aebreanna, the graceful Sylva held up a small hand, calling for silence. The young man complied, trusting that his questions would be answered in due time, and quite frankly, more interested at the moment in letting some of the cold air into the spaces between his skin and his chainmail anyway. When the squire tried to approach for a better look, Aebreanna held him back with a gentle hand on his shoulder. "*Klow'ans* cannot approach," she said very quietly.

"Klowans?" Tomas asked, not recognizing the word.

"Those who do not believe as we do."

As they watched, the Sylvai procession broke apart with each member wordlessly performing a specific task. Those who bore lanterns against the dim light of the winter's afternoon carried these small golden beacons to equal points distant from the stones and each other, carefully hooking them to the surrounding trees. Some carried small bundles wrapped in white fabric; these stood outside the stones as though waiting. Those who carried nothing moved across the stones, clearing them of any natural debris. Two of the group, the leaders Tomas guessed, climbed the rocks and faced each other. Once compete in their chores, the Sylvai silently formed a circle around the rocks. As one, the two individuals who stood upon the rocks lowered their hoods and let their cloaks and robes fall to the ground, revealing that one was male and the other female, both dressed only in brief loincloths despite the deep cold.

While Tomas looked on in fascination, the Sylvai encircling the rocks began to move slowly to the right, maintaining their distance from the stones and their perfect circle. As the Sylvai walked their circle, they softly repeated a word in Sylvai.

"What are they saying?" Tomas whispered.

"*Y'kasa'tormay'tan*," Aebreanna replied in the barest of whispers. "The name of the Goddess."

The Sylvai who carried the small bundles entered the ring, holding up their cargo. After three circuits, the Sylvai at the base of the stones stopped and faced in. At the same moment, the male Sylvu standing above stepped forward to face the female and spoke as she lowered her head, speaking in their strange, musical language.

Aebreanna whispered the translation to Tomas. "'Dark is the night as we reach this turning point. Here is a time of death, yet here also is a time of birth.'"

In response, the Sylvai surrounding the stones raised their arms and spoke in a low chant, each saying something different. Those with the small bundles placed them at the feet of the Sylva.

Aebreanna continued her translation in time with the ceremony. "'Endings and beginnings. Ebbing and flowing. A journey done. A journey yet to begin. Let us honor now the mother, the sister, the daughter. Let us give our strength and in return see rebirth. Let us trust our family to her safekeeping.'"

The lead Sylvu raised his head and spoke once more. "Behold the Lady of Light," Aebreanna related. "Daughter, mother, grandmother. Sister, wife, stranger. Old, young, unborn. Commend to her those who journey home."

The Sylvu lowered his arms, as the female slowly raised her head, spreading her arms outward and upward. The Sylvai who had placed their small bundles at her feet stepped back and joined the others. All the Sylvai dropped to their knees as the priestess spoke softly in the Sylvai language.

"Hear me," she chanted with Aebreanna translating. "Honor me and love me now and always. As Fate turns we see birth, death, and rebirth. Know, from this, that every end is a beginning. Maiden, mother, crone… I am all of these and more. Whenever you have need, call upon me and I am there."

"It's a funeral," Tomas whispered.

"I and my Lord are here," the priestess continued. "For I abide within you all. I carry with me all those who came before, and all those still to come. I shine the path home. I am she who is at the beginning and the end of all time, so may it be."

After completing her recitation, the lead priestess folded her arms again. Several moments of silence followed before the priest and priestess together reached down to the small crack where the spring originated and together retrieved a burned-out torch. The Sylvu carried the spent torch down before picking up a new one and handing it up to the waiting Sylva. The priestess placed the new torch in the same spot as the spent one had rested and, with just a hint of her magic, lit it, letting its light shine down on the small pool and the stream beyond. Once this was completed, the two Sylvai atop the stones pulled on their robes and cloaks, climbed down, and led their brethren back the way they came, taking only a moment for the lantern-bearers to collect their small beacons.

Aebreanna waited until the robed Sylvai were out of sight and then stepped forward, gesturing to Tomas to wait behind. The beautiful Sylva walked around to the small spring and knelt, removing her gloves and placing her small hands into the water to draw a sip of the nearly crystalline water.

"Is it all right if I ask a few questions?" Tomas asked once Aebreanna had returned and the two heroes began their walk back to rejoin the others. During the return, Aebreanna was much more careful to lead her Human companion along a path that was more forgiving to his less graceful legs.

"Certainly," the Sylva replied, showing her companion where to step along a wide root.

"I'm not really sure where to start," the squire admitted, his eyes locked on the spots where Aebreanna was pointing for solid footing. "That was a funeral, yes?"

Aebreanna ducked under a low branch, made all the lower with the weight of snow and ice. She nodded and sighed. "We burn our dead, much as you Adamics do, but we separate the disposition of the body with the journey of the soul."

"So burning the dead isn't the funeral, this is?"

"The burning is for the family, so that they may mourn and bid farewell." She paused and glanced back at the nearly-hidden glade. "This ritual is for the safety of the spirits as they travel to the Eternal Forest.

"Within three days, the bodies are immolated. The spirits remain until the Crossing may be performed."

"The crossing?" Tomas asked.

Aebreanna stopped and pointed up, to a break in the wintery canopy. Though clouds still dominated the sky, and the light of day was still fading, the moon shone clearly down upon Wildelves Wood.

"On the first night in which Vaeta is full and new, the local *Fur'lya'cel'lan'a* gather for this ceremony. This was the ceremony for those who fell in the gardens."

Tomas started. That battle had been weeks ago, but still lingered in his thoughts. The Death Mage had attacked a banquet held by the King and Queen to celebrate the end of the Harvest Festival. Although Anninihus had been defeated and his unholy monsters destroyed, the cost had been great. The city gardens had burned to almost nothing and dozens of House Guardsmen had fallen, with several innocent townsfolk.

"You see, Tomas," Aebreanna continued as she resumed their course to the camp. "We believe that any location in which water emerges from underground has been marked by the Goddess. These areas are holy to us, and the water itself, when drawn from this source, carries within it great power. The pool and the stones around it are a shrine."

"What about the torch?" Tomas asked.

"The light on the water from the torch is used as a representative for *Kar'lu'a*, the aspect of the Goddess with dominion over the moon. This is the beacon with which the Lady of Light guides the departed across the Veil and into the Eternal Forest."

Tomas reached out and lifted another low-hanging tree branch so that Aebreanna could pass without having to bend low. The Sylva's already-lesser height made this simple enough, and the sensual Sylvai made no protest at the young man's instinctive efforts at chivalry. "I always thought the Sylvai worshipped many different gods," the squire asked as they approached the road. "From the way you speak, it sounds like you only worship one goddess."

"There exist differing opinions," Aebreanna explained. "Some feel there are indeed many distinct deities in the universe, each with their own personality, traits, and influence over mortal life."

"But you believe differently," Tomas guessed.

The spy nodded. "I share the beliefs of my mother and her mother before her, that there are but two divine beings, *Y'kasa'tormay'tan* and *Y'fasawa'narmay'tor*, the Goddess and the God who are themselves merely the ultimately female and male aspects of the single divine presence behind creation, life, and the energy of the universe."

As the two approached the campsite set up by Rogan and Beraht, Tomas waved a greeting to his knight. "So you believe in God," Tomas pointed out. "You just believe He has different aspects."

Aebreanna smiled and shook her head. "That is not exactly accurate. This is difficult to explain without the many years of study and instruction I have received. I, and many *Sy'lva'n* like myself, believe that everything divine in the world originates from the same source, but that something so infinitely powerful and all-encompassing has different aspects that are, themselves, aware and divine. The Goddess is the mother of all things. She is at once mother, wife, and daughter to all life. From Her, all life springs, is nurtured, grows, ages, dies, and is reborn in the Eternal Forest. Thus, all the lesser aspects, which many worship as independent deities, draw their strength and power from the Goddess, as does all *Sy'lva'n*."

"What about the God?" Tomas asked. "Y'fasawa—"

"*Y'fasawa'narmay'tor*," the Sylva corrected. "The God is a part of the Goddess, as She is a part of Him. They are separate and yet, through their union, they are one. The will to live comes from the God. He gives us the desire to grow and improve ourselves. All struggles originate from the God, while we draw peace, contentment, and the clarity to invoke the Winds from the Goddess."

"It sounds like your goddess is more powerful."

Aebreanna shrugged. "I suppose that is true, in a matter of speaking. This is what we believe to be true. Just as you Adamics believe that the sum of all divine power rests within a single being."

"It's a little more complicated than that," Tomas pointed out.

"As are our beliefs," the beautiful spy replied. "As are most belief systems. One cannot have all they believe summarized in only a few words. Belief runs deeper than that. You asked before what it is that Rogan believes, and he gave you a fairly simple answer, but you must know that his true beliefs run much deeper and are much more complex."

"I had a feeling," the squire admitted.

Aebreanna stopped before the fire Rogan had built up, where the knight and his Uldra friend were preparing their evening meal. The Sylva put a light hand on her young companion's shoulder. "To truly understand a person's beliefs, you must first understand the person. To truly understand a person, you must first understand yourself. The reason religion so often leads to hatred between varying groups is often because neither side will take the time to learn, not only the nature of their opponent's true beliefs, but their own as well."

Tomas reached down for a slice of the bread warming by their campfire. "Well, I think I have a pretty good understanding of myself and my beliefs," he said.

The spy spread a small blanket from her saddlebags on a rock before sitting and beginning her meal. "Really?" she asked. "Would you have said the same thing one year past?"

The young man thought about it for a moment. "Probably," he admitted.

"Consider how much you have changed in only that small time," Aebreanna pointed out. "Our understanding of ourselves is never complete since we are never the same person from one moment to the next."

Rogan looked up from his own plate. "Then how can anyone ever really understand anyone else?" he asked.

The Sylva looked at her old friend across the small fire. "Full understanding cannot come from this side of the Veil. Once you accept that you can never really know anything, you can truly begin to learn."

Tomas sat down next to Beraht. Looking at the barbarian, the squire asked, "Does that make sense to you?"

The Uldra did not bother to even look up from his meal, seemingly more concerned with keeping the long braids of his full beard from soaking up too much of the stew. "Sylvai spend too much time thinking and not enough doing," he muttered through his food.

Aebreanna glanced up from her own plate. "I have noted the exact opposite in your malformed race."

Beraht wiped some of the excess stew from his face with the sleeve of his heavy tunic. "If a warrior spends too much time thinking instead of acting, he can get lost in his own head."

"And what a lonely place that would be for you," the Sylva said softly.

The barbarian tore off a chunk of bread and started mopping up the remains of his meal. "Thoughts are well and good, but the Allfather doesn't judge by what you think, He judges by what you do."

"That's a good point, Aebreanna," Rogan agreed. "Is it enough to spend your life only trying to understand everything? What good is a life unless it's used to accomplish something?"

Taking the time to swallow her food and wipe the corners of her sensuous mouth with a small piece of cloth, the spy finally offered her response. "Acting without full understanding of the possible consequences of one's actions has resulted in the many and varied tragedies of history."

"Maybe neither of you has the whole answer," Tomas suggested between bites. "Maybe it's not enough to act without thinking or think without acting. Maybe the trick is to find a balance between the two."

Rogan held up his cup in a mock salute. "Maybe that's why Humans run everything. We're all about finding a happy medium."

The squire held up his own cup to meet his knight's toast. "To the balance of Humanity," he proposed as both Humans drank deeply.

Aebreanna and Beraht looked at their Human companions and each other across the fire. Their responses were brief. "I very much doubt that." "Whatever."

The sultry spy rose from her seat and handed her empty plate and cup to Tomas. "As fascinating as this conversation is, I believe some rest is in order."

"I did the dishes last night!" the squire insisted.

Aebreanna regarded her young companion for a moment with a raised eyebrow. "That fact has what to do with your washing them tonight?"

Rogan stood and handed his own dishes to his squire before settling his sword belt around his waist. "I'll wake you at midnight for your guard," the knight said as he walked toward the edge of their small camp.

"I've got the dishes AND the midnight guard?"

Beraht dropped his filthy plate onto Tomas's lap. "Welcome to the team," the barbarian grunted as he flopped down on his blankets.

Tomas sat for a few minutes, looking from the snoring mound of Uldra on one end of the camp, the gentle curves of Sylva on the other, and the knight patrolling around the edges.

Chapter 4

Even shielded from the icy wind dancing through the branches far overhead, the night carried a deep, harsh cold that Tomas's cloak did little to shield him against. The young man threw yet another angry look up to where the moon made its lazy way across the night sky. Even through the thick canopy of trees, the bright glow was easily identifiable, as was the spot in the sky, near the constellation of the Shieldbearer that would mark Tomas's relief. Throughout his seemingly endless guard, circling around his sleeping friends, the squire often found himself muttering under his misting breath; the squire cursed any spirit or fate or god that might have conspired to place him in a forest on so unforgiving a night when the inviting shelter of his blankets called to Tomas with its seductive promise of springtime dreams. Only the impressions in the snow he followed behind gave the desolate young man any hope that his feet were still connected at all, as he lacked the courage to look down and see for certain. The newest hero of the Northlands wondered throughout his guard if he would ever be warm again. Tomas looked to the sky again as though with the sheer force of his will he could speed Time on her way.

Tomas tried to employ the advice of his knight on this interminable watch. He let his eyes drift, trusting to their periphery to detect movement rather than searching for points of identifiable light. He let his other senses compensate and do the major work in the darkness of the forest's night. His ears tracked the movement of nocturnal birds and distant animals. His nose communicated the familiar and would flag anything new or out of place. "Your entire body is gathering information," Rogan had told him. "Don't just pay attention to your eyes; they can lie. Let your mind accept what your body tells you, and trust when your instinct starts yelling." The squire did this, letting his thoughts drift as his senses did their work.

The squire admitted, in the corner of his mind, that much of his hatred for the night guard was for where his thoughts drifted. As his nose identified the forest, his memory recalled the scent of a delicate perfume. As his ears scanned the whispers of the Wood, his memory drifted to the melodious voice that had sung for him. As the night's breeze played across the hairs on the back of his neck, his memory recalled heated breath on his shoulder. He remembered eyes staring at him across a dinner table. He recalled soft skin and hair like silk. He replayed a dance of exquisite grace that, though performed in front of the entire city, had been for him alone.

Tomas missed his fiancée. In the months they had together, the couple had experienced so much. Mary had become a part of his soul, his entire being. Each night before sleep, Tomas thought of the day's events and longed to share them with her. During the day's ride, he would spot oddities or points of beauty, and feel a catch in his heart as he knew how much she would thrill in sharing the experience. The mission was important, of course, but Tomas struggled not to curse God or Fate or whatever power had conspired to bring her into his life, only to force him away mere days after their betrothal. Tomas sighed and let his hand drift over the white ribbon, passed from mother to daughter across generations as a gift awarded to the man blessed enough to win the love of its owner. His thoughts drifted across his every memory and fantasy of Mary, even as his body continued the guard.

At some point during his hateful walking and remembering, Tomas slowly became aware of a sound like the gentlest of whispers. It began with a soft vibration in the back of his skull that could not be distinguished from the prickling numbness on his hands and face. Over time, the sound intensified until the young man was snapped from his reverie and turned sharply, his hand going to the hilt of Steelheart and his eyes scanning the darkness that pressed in from the surrounding wall of trees. A faint glow from far out amidst the evergreens caught Tomas's gaze and drew him away from the flickering fire. The young warrior no longer felt the pull toward safety and warmth and memory, instead leaving such things behind and stalking amidst the trees, alert for any threat.

The ground was still covered in thick piles of snow, making his path difficult. Tomas stepped as lightly as he could, taking his time as he stalked through the night. Placing one foot carefully into each new point of snow-covered uncertainty, the squire never halted his movement toward the glow ahead and the whispering that threatened to numb his mind. The young warrior's grip never faltered from the hilt of his sword, and his perception of the cold around him drew back to be replaced by the cold readiness to inflict violence on a moment's notice. No real thought entered Tomas's mind as he stalked closer to his target, only the unalterable knowledge that should what lie ahead be a threat, it would not remain one for long.

The squire paused at the edge of a clearing from which the trees had retreated. There was no cover ahead other than that provided by darkness, and that was, Tomas quickly realized, disrupted by the source of the light. What he thought at first to be an omnipresent glow eventually revealed itself as hundreds, perhaps thousands, of pinpoints of light that floated lazily through the glen. Each time the young man attempted to look directly at one of the points of light, it was as though his vision blurred, bringing tears to his eyes and forcing him to blink rapidly to clear them. The whispering that had initially drawn Tomas's attention was, without a doubt, emanating from somewhere in this strange glade. The squire tried in vain to draw his perception away from the swirling points of light to find the source of the alien sound, but the hypnotic dance before him had captured his eyes and would not let them go. Curiosity, burning and undeniable, drew the squire forward.

As he remained trapped in his reverie, the young man's eyes eventually penetrated the hypnotic dance before him and discerned a shadow that, while blending perfectly with the surrounding darkness, remained somehow separated from the shadows as though the forest itself rejected its presence. Tomas focused all his attention on the figure, noticing its humanoid shape but unable so see any details through the thick shroud of darkness that the whispering figure had drawn about itself. The squire's soul screamed at him that this was a creature of evil even as his pulse throbbed against the golden rose pinned on his collar.

At last pulling his mind free of the creature's spell, Tomas grabbed the hilt of Steelheart, fully intent on confronting the evil before him. As one, the points of light stopped their lazy floating and swarmed toward the young man, spinning around him without making physical contact. Panicking, Tomas flailed about with his arms and stumbled forward, trying to get away from the assault of light and sound. Unfortunately, the squire kept stumbling forward until the snow suddenly gave way beneath his feet; and with a loud crack like that made by the shattering of bone, the thin layer of ice covering a small creek fractured. Before Tomas could do more than yelp in surprise and fear, the freezing darkness swallowed him.

Minutes passed as the squire lay in a warm vale, staring up at the morning sky. The tress swayed gently in the breeze, careful not to dislodge any of their prismatic leaves or those of their neighbors. Although no birdsong could be heard, somehow it seemed this forest had no need for it, as the music of the trees filled the empty space with a song of their own that was just as lovely. The sun, somewhere out of sight, must have been near the horizon as it had cast a bright crimson shade across the sky, draping the jagged clouds with an oddly bloodlike cast that matched perfectly the sheen of the trees. It was warm where Tomas lay and peaceful enough for an eternity of restful slumber.

Some time passed before the young man realized how wrong his situation was. Sitting up suddenly, Tomas looked about in confusion and growing apprehension. Surrounding him was an overly-warm valley filled with flowers each a different shade of red. No sign of winter could be seen as the young man stood and tried to clear his eyes, only to find that no amount of blinking or rubbing could clear his vision. A strange haze seemed to surround Tomas like a mist after a summer storm, preventing the squire from seeing clearly what lay about. The sounds of soft splashing drew the young warrior's attention back to the creek in which he had nearly drowned.

Kneeling at the opposite bank was a woman. Her pale hair hung limply in long bangs covering her face, falling all the way to the rocks upon which she crouched. Her tattered clothing, made of some material worn by hard years and long suffering, hung just as loosely upon the woman's boney frame as did her hair. It seemed to Tomas that the sun had never touched this woman's flesh, though her back was hunched and her hands scarred as though she had never seen a day free of hard labor, nor did it seem that a full meal had ever passed the woman's lips. If she was aware of Tomas's presence, she gave no indication.

Tomas cautiously approached this unknown person, carefully keeping the water between them. As he did so, the young man noticed that the woman was listlessly washing what appeared to be an infant's clothes in the clear water of the creek, humming softly and somewhat tunelessly to herself as she worked.

"Hello?" Tomas called out, not wanting to frighten her.

The woman stopped her work and raised her head just slightly, revealing sunken eyes of midnight disrupted only by tiny embers within. The squire gasped and stumbled back as the creature raised its gnarled hand and pointed a finger with four knuckles and tipped with a jagged nail covered in yellow filth at him. "Tomas Fidelis," it whispered in a ragged voice that tore at the young man's soul.

Tomas screamed and flung himself back, horrified by the creature's attention and driven to unthinking panic at her whisper. A soft hand grabbed him by the shoulder, forcing another scream from the young man. The soft hand turned Tomas, revealing Aebreanna. The beautiful Sylva tightened her grip on her young friend, locking his gaze with her own to prevent either of their eyes from straying to anything else. "We must leave!" she insisted and held up what appeared to be a small branch made of silver. The branch glowed with a soft light, forming behind Aebreanna a distortion of the reality in which she and Tomas now found themselves.

Aebreanna did not hesitate for a moment, simply dragging her young friend as she charged into the strange rippling effect. A moment of dizzying confusion shot through Tomas's entire soul as he passed though the portal before stumbling into a mound of snow in the blessedly cold forest from which he had originally come. The beautiful spy allowed her teammate a few moments to gasp and struggle with what he had just experienced before helping him to his feet. "Come," she said. "The campfire will help you."

Chapter 5

"What was it?" Tomas asked as he shivered violently with more than cold, bundled deeply in his blankets and staring into the campfire.

Aebreanna handed her young friend a warm cup of tea and sat beside him, wrapping another blanket around the squire and pressing against him in an attempt to banish the fear and cold that filled his body and soul. "It was Otherworld," she replied. "It was the realm of the *Fael*, the Hidden Ones."

"I thought it was just a myth." Tomas tried as best he could to drink the tea but could not still his hands enough. Finally, Aebreanna gently took the cup in her own graceful fingers and helped him sip at the steaming brew.

Seeing the cup emptied, the spy set it aside and began rubbing her young companion's torso. "Far better for Humans to believe that is so," she said in response to Tomas's question. "Even after thousands of years investigating the properties and inhabitants of Otherworld, my people still have little understanding of it. Often enough, we cannot even survive it."

Sitting on the other side of the small fire, Rogan watched his squire wearily. "How did he cross into Otherworld?" the knight demanded. "I thought the Guild made sure all the paths were closed."

Aebreanna did not spare a glance to the knight, instead filling Tomas's cup with the last of the tea she had prepared and helping her young friend drink it. "As far as I have been informed, all the established paths to Otherworld were secured some time ago. There exist, however, a number of points across *Ar'ay'el* through which one can gain access should the conditions be appropriate. Apparently, tonight the conditions were so."

"But how'd he do it?" the knight demanded.

"I am unsure. I found him in the vicinity of the shrine. Those places have a great deal of latent power and are a natural crossing point for spirits. He may have unwittingly tapped into the natural power of the area and inadvertently opened a pathway. I was able to tap into an already-weakened barrier point to extract him."

"How in Underworld did he 'tap into' the magic of a shrine? He's not an adept."

Aebreanna pulled Tomas's head down to her shoulder and put her arms around his body to try and ease his worsening shiver. "There is, I believe, more to our young companion than we were first led to believe."

"Th-there w-was s-s-someone else th-there," Tomas said through his increasingly violent shivering.

"Who?" Rogan asked. "What?"

"D-d-don't know. T-t-too d-dark. H-h-he w-was w-w-whispering t-to m-me." By now, Tomas could barely remain seated upright without Aebreanna's assistance, and the squire's growing weakness was obvious to his knight. "C-c-c-all-all-ing."

Rogan stood and added more wood to their fire, generating as much heat as he safely could. "What's wrong with him? A quick fall in that stream shouldn't have hit him this hard."

"Otherworld," the Sylvai spy answered. "He encountered one of the *Fael*, the denizens of that place. That, along with the crossing from one realm to another and back so quickly, has sapped the warmth of his soul."

"Is he going to be all right?"

"I do not know. If our fire and the herbs he drank cannot return his warmth, then I fear the damage was more substantial than his body can repair."

The knight looked up at the night sky and around into the darkness of the trees. "We're too far to get help from the Keep," he pointed out.

"And anyone marked by Otherworld would not be welcome in a *Sy'lva'n* community."

Rogan looked at Aebreanna with a set expression on his scarred face. "Can you help him?" he asked.

The beautiful Sylva looked up and locked eyes with her companion. They were quiet for a long time before Aebreanna finally spoke. "You know what it is you ask of me."

"If you don't, will he survive?"

Aebreanna turned her opalescent gaze to the young squire, whose lips had turned blue and breathing had grown shallow. Both Aebreanna and Rogan knew that was not a good sign. "No," the spy whispered. "His strength fails too quickly. He will not survive."

Rogan said nothing, instead standing in place and watching as Aebreanna made her decision. "Leave us," she finally said, not bothering to look away from her young friend.

The knight turned and stepped into the darkness of the woods as Aebreanna lowered Tomas to the ground, opening first the blankets wrapped around him, then his shirt. Aebreanna then opened her dress and leaned into him, words of power drifting almost silently from her lips. Rogan walked deep into the trees until he found where Beraht waited, looking out into the darkness.

"How's the kid?" the barbarian asked.

Rogan walked up to stand beside his old friend. "You remember how it was crossing to that place and back." The knight's tone betrayed his worry and the painful memories of their own experiences with Otherworld.

Beraht continued to scan the darkness. "Yeah," he grunted. "Not the best way to travel."

"And we didn't get into any trouble on our trip."

"The kid found something?"

"More like something found him," the knight replied. "Something attacked him."

"The kid get a look at it?"

Rogan shook his head slightly.

"How bad?" Beraht asked.

"Aebreanna's going to fix it."

Beraht looked sharply at Rogan and then toward the faint glow of their distant campfire. "She can't be too happy about that," the Uldra muttered.

"She isn't."

The Uldra turned back to the surrounding darkness. "Didn't she swear that she'd never use her father's gifts again?"

Rogan grimaced.

"This isn't the first time she's been forced to do this," Beraht pointed out.

"I remember."

"You think it's a coincidence that she keeps getting forced to use his power?"

The knight shook his head. "No such thing as coincidence with her father."

"She'll take it out on the kid?"

"Hope not."

A warm glow of golden light pulled the attention of both warriors back toward the campsite. It was brief but intense. Even men like Rogan and Beraht, whose connection to the Winds of Magic could be compared to any inanimate object, could feel the release of such power as that used by Aebreanna to heal Tomas.

The two veterans glanced at one another. "I guess that means it's clear to head back," Rogan suggested.

Upon their return, the two men saw Tomas bundled in his blankets, apparently sleeping comfortably. Aebreanna sat on the opposite side of the fire, huddled into as tight a ball as possible and staring into the flames with undisguised hatred twisting her beautiful face. Rogan walked over and sat beside his Sylva friend, being careful not to touch her. "Are you alright?" he asked.

"That is a foolish question," the spy snapped.

"I know," the knight sighed.

"No, you do not," she snapped again. "You have no idea what it feels like to use his power." Aebreanna held up a hand and looked at it with disgust. "I hate him, Rogan. You cannot understand how much I hate him. I have tried very hard to banish any trace of him from my soul, but every time I am forced to use his power, I can feel him in my blood. When I employ the power having his blood grants me, I must tap into the part of him dwelling within me."

"I wish you didn't have to go through that," Rogan said putting a hand on her shoulder. "I wish I could promise you'd never have to do it again."

Aebreanna covered his hand with hers. "I know," she replied. "Saying so would be a wonderful lie. Telling myself that I would never again have to feel his mind within my own would be a beautiful dream." She stood and looked out into the surrounding darkness. "Unfortunately, we both know he will continue to manipulate events, forcing me to acknowledge his bloodline in some sick attempt to demonstrate what he calls love."

Rogan looked at her and sighed. "You know, it's possible that he doesn't arrange for these problems just to get you to use his… inheritance."

The Sylva shook her head. "No, Rogan. You do not know my father as I do. None do. None can. He is a creature of deception. He is a master of manipulation and false promises. There can be no denying that my father has his own purposes, and to that end, he will continue to meddle in my life."

Before the knight could reply, Beraht turned and raised his waraxe, his beard bristling. The horses stirred, as agitated as the Uldra. Rogan and Aebreanna turned and readied themselves as well for whatever danger Beraht had sensed coming from the darkness.

Aebreanna gasped.

"What?" Rogan snapped, not taking his eyes from the spot that Beraht faced.

The Sylva dropped her blades and backed away from the source of her sudden fear, tears streaming from her opalescent eyes and all the color draining from her flawless face. "Something is out there," she gasped. "Something is watching us. Something hungers."

A hideous laughter came slithering out of the trees, sending involuntary shivers up Rogan's spine. The wind in the branches far overhead ceased in dread at the sound of the insidious joy carried in the laughter infecting the Wood. The trees seemed to steel themselves, drawing in the darkness and cold of winter as armor against the unearthly evil that had now come upon them. Even their campfire faded to nearly nothing, its cheery flame reduced to a whimpering flicker against the encroaching darkness.

The smell of blood and gore made Rogan wretch, even his battle-hardened skill failed against whatever was manifesting in the night. The horses reared and snapped the tethers holding them, bolting into the night. Even Stick and Urge, both warhorses trained to stand against the worst horrors the world could present them, surrendered against the wretched stench and the horrors it promised.

"What is it?" Rogan gagged.

"*Za'fael,*" she whispered in dread.

Rogan risked a glance back to his friend. "Can you send it back?" he asked.

The spy shook her head. "It must return of its own will," she replied.

"And I do not will it," the voice whispered in their minds, a voice filled with promises of pain and horror that would last an eternity.

Beraht stepped forward and held his waraxe high. "Show yourself, coward!" he roared.

A blur of murder shot from the darkness, enveloping Beraht and ghosting past the Uldra warrior before retreating back into the surrounding trees again and forcing the mountainous barbarian to his knees. "Did you see me?" the voice asked.

Beraht got back to his feet, freeing his eyes of the blood streaming from several fresh cuts and a growl in his throat quickly growing into a roar of righteous fury as he welcomed his enemy to return. The next strike was intercepted midair by Rogan's dagger, forcing the creature of darkness to the ground. Beraht leapt to the attack, bringing his waraxe down but meeting air as his target spun aside with inhuman dexterity. Not bothering to dislodge his beloved weapon from the ground, the Uldra warrior heaved and sent a shower of snow and stone flying at the cowardly creature before leaping again.

Their attacker vanished into the surrounding darkness, leaving Beraht swearing and beating at the snow in fury, with only Rogan's dagger resting on the ground at his booted feet. "COWARD!" the barbarian roared. "Sylvai-sucking shade! Do you fear me? By the Allfather you will stand and taste my axe or leave me to my sleep!"

"As you wish," the monster almost purred in response. The shadows all around them seemed to melt together and form a horror, at last framed by the dim light of their fearful fire. It was barely as tall as Beraht but twice as broad and covered in dark hair matted against its hide by a dark liquid that reeked of gore. Its long trunk-like arms trailed down, nearly to the ground, and ended in six-fingered hands that were far too long with extra knuckles and jagged claws that dripped blood from Beraht's wounds. A large nose and eyes of pure black could not draw attention from a mouth filled with yellowed fangs and a crown of coarse black hair that dripped fresh blood across the snow.

Rogan held Talon ready, unwilling to let his mind slip into madness at the sight of the creature they faced. Without turning from his enemy, the knight called to Aebreanna. "How do we kill this thing?"

When no answer came, the knight risked a quick glance to the terrified Sylva. Aebreanna stood frozen, her beautiful face locked in an expression of terror and her perfect body shaking in uncontrollable fear. Her opalescent eyes were lost in the madness of despair. "Aebreanna!" Rogan barked.

The creature laughed an evil laugh. "She is lost," it hissed while running a hand along its thick hide in a sensuous caress of forgotten pleasure. "The terror of the Sylvai is a pleasure I had nearly forgotten. I will savor the taste of her."

Beraht gave himself to the will of his Allfather and unleashed a roar that startled the snow from the most distant branches. Leaping at the creature that had threatened his friend, the berserker swung his mighty waraxe with all his titanic strength in a wide arc, intending to send the beast back with one blow to whatever pit had spawned it. Seeing his comrade committed to combat and with no idea how to help Aebreanna, Rogan charged forward as well, dancing around to the opposite side from which Beraht was attacking to remain outside of the Uldra's deadly arc and coordinate for his own assault. Even with his mind all but lost to his fury, Beraht remained enough of a skilled combatant that he knew how to exploit an ally in battle, and the two warriors had fought often enough together that their attacks were almost perfectly linked; when in battle at each other's side, Rogan and Beraht fought as one, and it was a rare opponent that could enduring even a second of their vicious assault.

The Zafael was, unfortunately, one such opponent. It danced between the two warriors, lashing out with its claws again and again, drawing blood from each of the veterans. It was clear within moments that this vision of horror could have defeated them with ease but instead delighted in the battle, toying with them both, inflicting painful lashes that drew blood, fear, pain, rage, and humiliation in equal measure. As the battle progressed and their wounds increased, both Beraht and Rogan could not help but be slowed. Worse, the loss of blood that weakened them somehow strengthened their enemy.

Finally, the creature ducked one of Rogan's high sword strikes and grabbed him by the throat, raising the knight into the air and slamming him into Beraht, forcing both warriors to the ground with brutal force. The monster licked the blood from its claws and turned slowly from the defeated warriors to look full on into Aebreanna's horrified face.

"It has been an age since last I tasted Sylvai blood," it whispered with a lustful leer. The creature moved toward Aebreanna with an evil grace, stepping through the snow and around the fire without moving its hungry eyes from her. Finally drawing up to within a breath of her shaking body, the nightmare drew a talon slowly across the right side of Aebreanna's flawless face, from her temple and down the cheek, bringing a line of blood to the surface. "The smell is so pure," it hissed in anticipation. "I had forgotten." An impossibly long tongue that dripped with black ichor unrolled from the Zafael's mouth and along the spy's colorless face, tasting her blood and leaving a trail of drool that fell from Aebreanna's chin to run down the front of her blouse. Its eyes suddenly widened in a shock of recognition. "You're a Tressalon!" it breathed. "It was your mothers who ended my feast!"

The monster drew more of the surrounding darkness to itself, towering over Aebreanna. "I will savor the taste of you, Daughter of Tressalon," he said in a rising growl. "I will drain you of your essence and leave you just enough to live, to spread the word that I have returned. Only after you have told your people and undone the work of your mothers will I taste all that you have to offer." The creature viciously grabbed Aebreanna by the throat. "Because of your mothers, you will be my first feast in a thousand years! You are mine forever, Sylva whore!"

The monster flung its arms to either side and screamed in pain and fury as ichorus blood gushed from its mouth to shower Aebreanna's face and a flawless blade erupted from its chest bearing the sigil of House Calonar. A renewed burst of flame and heat rose from their emboldened campfire as Tomas leaned over from behind the creature. "Don't call her a whore," the squire sneered as he put a boot in the monster's back and ripped Steelheart free. The squire spun and with one hand grabbed the gasping thing from a nightmare world around its head and heaved with all his chivalric strength, throwing the creature across his shoulder and into their rekindled campfire. The monster's ragged clothes caught fire, and it screamed in pain, desperately struggling to escape the vengeful flames.

Tomas stalked across the camp and kicked the Zafael in its middle, forcing it to the ground. "Do you want to go home yet?" Tomas demanded, raising the flawless blade of House Calonar and, swinging, severed one of the monster's legs. "Do you want to go home? Or do you want to stay here with me?" The squire swung Steelheart again, cutting off the other leg.

The creature rolled away from Tomas, using the snow to extinguish the fire and tried to crawl, leaving a trail of dark blood. Tomas easily followed the pitiful nightmare and plunged Steelheart again into its back. "I can't kill you monster, but I can make you wish for death! Now BEGONE!" The creature tried to roll over and make a grab for the young man's arm, but Tomas kicked aside the feeble attack and struck again, severing the arm. "BEGONE!" he barked. Finally placing a foot on the monster's mutilated chest, the squire reversed his blade and struck, planting a third of the steel into the creature's throat. "BEGONE!"

There was a distortion of the air and a burst of heat, and the Zafael was gone, including the pieces Tomas had claimed and the gore coating Aebreanna. The camp was quiet aside from the snap of the fire. Aebreanna collapsed to her knees and sobbed. Tomas stood, breathing heavily and staring down at the spot where the nightmare had been, until a single spot of flawless cold touched his right hand. The squire looked up and saw that the grateful forest was trying to cleanse them of the Zafael's memory in the only way it knew.

Chapter 6

"**She needs** help," Tomas insisted, glancing at where Aebreanna sat shivering beside the fire.

"From where?" Rogan demanded. "We're days from the Keep and still more than a week from the Western Forts. There's no help to be had."

"What about the Sylvai?" the squire asked.

Beraht shook his head. "None of the villages will take her in."

"Why?" Tomas demanded.

"They're afraid of that thing that attacked us," Rogan answered. "The Sylvai fought for centuries after the Disaster at Nassinalia to banish all the creatures of Otherworld, and they're terrified that one day one'll find a way back."

"So anyone who encounters one of those things is just left to die?"

Beraht pulled a cloth that had been warming in a small cup of water beside the fire and gently placed it on Aebreanna's pale forehead. "No," the barbarian grumbled. "Usually, they do some pansy ritual to cleanse the person that got attacked."

"Then why won't they do that for Aebreanna?" Tomas demanded.

"Because of her name."

"What?"

Rogan pulled his map of Wildelves Wood from his saddlebag. "House Tressalon isn't thought of very highly by most Sylvai."

"What in Underworld does that mean?"

The knight glanced briefly at the map in his hands before rolling it back up. "You've read the *Tragedy of Nassinalia*, right?" he asked as he replaced the map and drew out a water skin.

Tomas reached for his own water and nodded. "Of course, it's a classic."

"Well, the Sylvai tell the story a little different," Rogan said before taking a long drink of water. "In their version, it was a renegade House that rebelled against the Empress and tried to take control of the city. The Sylvai believe that it was because of the arrogance of that Noble House that the city was destroyed and Lanasia shattered."

"What does this have to do with Aebreanna?" Tomas asked.

"Aebreanna is the last descendant of that rebel House." The knight replaced the water skin and began gathering the rest of his things together. "The Sylvai all blame

Aebreanna's family for the destruction of what was supposed to be their greatest city and, more importantly, the Eternal Forest. The Sylvai all consider her cursed."

"Morons!" Beraht spat from where he was tying down the saddle of his shire horse. "Every one of those shiny-eyed idiots owes their lives to Aebreanna, but they're too scared to admit it! It's easier for them to blame her for something her ancestor did a thousand years ago."

Tomas stared numbly at Aebreanna, suddenly aware of why she had sworn loyalty to House Calonar, a House led by another outcast of Sylvai society. Calonar must have provided the rogue with a place in which she could belong. "So what do we do?" the squire asked.

Rogan lit two torches in their campfire before shoveling snow into the dying flames. "We go to the nearest Sylvai village and get Aebreanna some help," the knight said as he handed one of the torches to his squire and moved to the edge of their camp.

"How are we going to get to get to a village without our horses?" Tomas asked.

In response, Rogan put a hand to his mouth and let out an ear-splitting whistle that shattered the calm of the dark forest. The knight's whistle echoed throughout the trees, setting the branches to trembling and bringing a renewed hush of anticipation to the Wood. When nothing happened, Rogan again sent a high-pitched assault out into the darkness. This time, from the inky shadows, a horse called back.

"That's what I thought," Rogan muttered.

"Is that one of ours?"

Instead of answering, the knight took a half step forward and, in the unmistakable tone of command, began barking in broken Sylvai. *"Kaydar'nar'gal'a! Kal'eann'durn Fael'cy Calonar! Al'cy'fa!"*

After only a brief pause, the winter forest released a detachment of Sylvai. Each of them was lean, with little muscle on their narrow frames and long arms and legs that moved through the thick snow with such grace that not a single snowflake was disturbed by their passage. Their skin was pale, nearly as pale as their thick winter's breath, and their long hair was bound in tight braids. Male or female, each of the Sylvai had the opalescent eyes of their race, and any gender-specific qualities were so subtle as to be lost in the tight leather vests and thick woolen cloaks each wore for protection.

They were Walkers by the looks of the blades and bows they carried, both equally curved, and the woodland colors they wore to match their surroundings. Even had the warriors not betrayed their loyalties with their colors or equipment, the utter silence with which they moved, both through their surroundings and with which they communicated to one another, spoke louder than any of the words they never seemed to need that these were the warriors of the Sylvai.

Each of the Walkers, though moving with the grace of their people, were clearly terrified to approach the warriors ahead and what had transpired around them so recently. They approached leading the party's horses but did so with great reluctance.

Rogan waited until the entire group, perhaps a half dozen in all, had emerged with all of their horses from the surrounding trees. "*Et'qua?*" the knight then said.

"I lead," one of the Walkers said hesitantly in Velish.

"Which is the nearest village?" the knight demanded.

"No. You are marked." The Walker leader pointed toward Aebreanna. "And that one is *Sy'nok*. You will not go."

Rogan strode up to the lead Walker, looking for all the world as though he would walk right over top of the smaller Sylvu. The warrior held his ground until the last instant but stumbled back a step the instant before Rogan would have knocked him into the snow. The two warriors stood for several moments, staring into at each other as they stood surrounded by the bitter cold, made all the worse by the horrific chill in Rogan's eyes. The knight never blinked, nor shifted his gaze, but held his emotionless face fixed as though waiting for the target before him to decide whether or not he was friend or foe and not caring either way.

The Sylvu stood for only a few seconds before giving way and turning back to the safety of his friends. "This is for *Ayatorcelasi*," he said with the crumbling shreds of his authority. "They go to her."

Without turning or blinking, Rogan called out to Tomas. "Get the horses and mount up. Let's ride."

Clustered together in a small valley were several large cottages built of unchiseled stone with thatched roofs. Each of the homes had its own chimney, which cheerily released smoke that was laced with delicious scents of breakfast. A nearby stream that moved fast enough to avoid being completely frozen over, but still maintained solid teeth of ice on either bank, provided plenty of fresh water to the village. The Sylvai had clearly gone to no great lengths to clear the forest to build their homes, instead letting the trees grow where they would, with the homes and gardens built around the ancient evergreens. The Sylvai had built their community with an obvious effort to harness serenity, which was ironic since their entrance into the village was met by a near-riot.

Most of the night was needed to reach the village. The first hour was spent in gathering and calming their horses. Only then did the Sylvai Walkers lead them through the darkness, away from any roads or paths. As the predawn light began to filter in through the branches overhead, their approach was announced by several warriors from the many trees who were dispersed throughout the village without interruption well before they caught sight of a single cottage, and three matronly Sylvai were awaiting them at the edge of town. Before Rogan could say a single word, one of the elderly Sylvai stiffened and yelled, "*Sy'nok!*" The word was taken up by every Sylva present, each yelling at the top of their lungs that same word.

The stone houses ahead of the small party erupted with Sylvai, young and old, male and female, as it seemed the entire community emerged to encircle Tomas and his friends. Each Sylvai chanted that same word over and over, many making strange gestures with their nimble hands in an effort to ward off the evil they sensed these outsiders had brought among them. Tomas, having been the center of an angry mob before, grew increasingly agitated as the number of Sylvai grew. "Somebody say something," he nearly yelled in order to be heard over the roaring chorus around them.

"Stay calm," Rogan warned.

One of the braver Sylvai took a few hesitant steps forward with his arms raised in anger and yelling even louder, if that was possible, than the surrounding mob. The Sylvu continued to advance until Rogan turned in his saddle. The courageous Sylvu retreated to the safety of the mob that continued to chant its hatred.

Beraht's temper, such as it was, was depleted in short order. "*Tum!*" he roared in his native tongue. "*Shakra Kaziks!* You *lup khalash* will be silent, or by the Allfather I'll *tyia* all of you in *walf* for a year! Now BE SILENT!"

The Uldra's words echoed throughout the forest, bringing a sudden silence. Finally, Rogan dismounted and strode forward to face the three leaders of the village. "We have a companion that needs assistance," the knight said in a low, even voice that allowed for no argument. "As agents of House Calonar, we call on our loyal allies to help us."

Combined with Beraht's thunderous outburst, Rogan's chill words were met with an equal amount of frightened shock. The Sylvai threw cautions glances at one another for many minutes before a few of the more courageous ones began muttering in very low voices to one another. These voices were silenced, however, when Beraht threw them a murderous look.

One of the three matriarchs stepped forward, leaning on a tall staff. With her free hand, the Sylva moved a few errant strands of her flowing, grey-streaked hair from her opalescent eyes and looked up to the tall Northland knight. "Although we are warmed to be visited by one as honored as you, Heir of Calonar," she began in a lightly accented voice, "our village will not welcome one of her lineage."

Another hateful look and a low growl from Beraht silenced the mummers of agreement from the assembled villagers. Rogan glanced around at the gathered mob with a neutral expression before locking his eyes on the apparent leader of the village. "*Kar'lan*," he said, "we have no wish to upset your people, but we are emissaries of

House Calonar and are on a vital mission in service to our King. You will help us, and you will do so now."

Before the village leader could respond, a small commotion erupted from the back of the mob. The group was parting from the back, obviously making way for someone or something slowly approaching to where Rogan and his team was halted. When the crowd finally parted enough for the collected heroes to see, it was revealed that the approaching person was another Sylva, clothed in flowing robes or iridescent white and carrying a wooden staff that had a stylized wolf's head at the top. A thick golden ribbon was tied around her matronly waist, and she walked with the imperious presence of an empress. Like Aebreanna, this newcomer bore the Wyrdmark; her flowing mane was as white as her gown, her opalescent eyes had an azure glow, and her skin was like fine porcelain. Tomas thought he recognized this venerable Sylva, though he could not remember from where. As she passed by, the assembled Sylvai bowed very low to her and made many gestures of respect.

When she at last arrived to stand a few paces away from Rogan, the Sylva made a deep curtsy to the prince, which Rogan returned. Tomas again felt a shock of recognition toward this Sylva. Something about her reminded the young man so much of Alexia, his dear friend, dead now a year, that he could not help but stare as his hand went of its own volition to the golden rose that rested as always against the pulse of his neck. It was then the memory returned. This was the same Speaker who had saved Rogan and him from the Lamashti a year ago.

"By what right do you bring the *Sy'nok* among us, Heir of Calonar?" the robed Sylva demanded in a soft voice.

"The right of necessity," the knight replied. "We were attacked by a creature of Otherworld last night and need help. I would not have intruded on your peace were the need not great, but our duty to King Cylan demands we move quickly."

"What is this duty that compels you?"

"We are on a quest, to journey into Ulheim and uncover the source of the unnatural attack that has blanketed this forest in early winter."

The knight's words sent a ripple of surprise through the crowd, which was quickly silenced by a gesture from the robed Sylva. "Your cause if just, and your need is great. We shall provide you with whatever assistance we can. However, we must insist you all be cleansed of the taint of Otherworld."

"Agreed," Rogan said.

Chapter 7

Their party was separated from one another and led into different houses on opposite ends of the village. They were promised that their mounts would be well cared for, but it was insisted that they needed to be separated for proper cleansing. A single nod from Rogan stifled any objections from Tomas, though Beraht was as vocal in his unhappiness as always.

After being ushered into a house, the small group of Sylvai who had taken charge of Tomas ordered the young man to strip out of his clothes and don a simple white linen robe. The young man, although hesitant, complied and put his clothes and gear in a neat pile in one corner of the main room, though he kept Steelheart close. Within a few moments, the Sylvai returned with several items Tomas assumed would aid them in cleansing him. After arranging a series of white and green candles around a large table, one of the younger male Sylvu led the squire toward the table, upon which he was instructed to lie.

Curiosity and anxiety clashed within Tomas as the Sylvai gathered in a tight circle around him and joined hands, chanting in their musical language. A Sylva wearing a similar white linen robe entered and stepped forward, and the circle closed even tighter to compensate. Saying nothing and keeping her eyes closed tightly in concentration, the Sylva held a small polished brown stone over Tomas's head and slowly moved it down to his feet and back, all while the circle of Sylvai looked on in unblinking concentration.

Although the young squire was trying his very best to keep an open mind, after watching the brown stone passes several times from his head to his feet, Tomas began to grow increasingly impatient. "Am I supposed to be doing something?" Tomas asked softly.

The young Sylva did not open her eyes nor stop the movement of the stone. "Just be at peace and concentrate on healing," she replied.

Tomas let out a sigh and concentrated. Several more minutes passed, and the young man realized that his rear end was starting to get sore. "Look," he finally said with more than a little aggravation, "I don't know what's supposed to be happening, but is it supposed to take this long?"

The Sylva lowered her arms and looked from Tomas to the brown stone in his hands. "You are right, young one," she said finally. "It should not take this long." She sighed and sat in a chair. "I fear the disruption is worse that we first suspected."

"Disruption?" Tomas sat up.

She nodded. "The great storm was not only of ice. It disrupted the Winds themselves. Every adept has felt it; our skills have become... unreliable. Only the greatest of us can maintain focus enough to overcome the disruption." The Sylva grimaced at the small brown stone in her hand. "Even a simple purification has become unpredictable."

Tomas sat up and swung his legs over the table edge, taking some of the pressure off his protesting backside. "What, exactly, are you guys trying to do?" the squire asked.

The Sylva handed the stone to one of her fellows as the rest of the group extinguished the candles and left the room. "After invoking the name of the Lady of Light and calling on her power, we use the stone to focus our concentration as we call on our Goddess to heal your wounds and mend your aura. This is a relatively minor rite, yet still the disruption interferes."

"I didn't know my aura was torn," Tomas replied flippantly.

The Sylva smiled indulgingly. "I fear so," he said. "Whatever you encountered did considerable harm. Much more so than my meager skills are capable of mending. I fear the storm's disruption may have exacerbated an existing wound."

"So what do we do?"

"I will summon one with greater skill than mine. There is a great darkness that has attached itself to you, and as a servant of House Calonar, you deserve our best efforts to remove it."

The Sylva bowed slightly to Tomas and instructed him to remain there before following her small group out of the house. The young man wandered about the cottage, noting with surprise the solid construction and slightly alien architecture; the Sylvai seemed to have an affinity for the arch, he noted, and avoided the basic buttress at all costs, even with their staircases. From the outside, the village had the appearance of any of the poorer communities of the South, but if this house was any indication of the rest of the village, it was clear the Sylvai retained much of the architectural genius that had built and maintained their empire over the many millennia of its existence. The home was conservatively decorated with simple rugs, some few pieces of furniture, and a single bookshelf that was filled with several leather-bound tomes covered in flowing Sylvai glyphs. The house gave silent testimony to life and its simple pleasures.

A soft voice floated into the room from the open front door. "For what do you search?" it asked.

Tomas turned to see the same green-robed Speaker who had helped them a year ago and agreed to heal Aebreanna. She stood in the doorway, resting a hand on her staff and looking at the young man with curious eyes. "I'm not really looking for anything," the squire replied. "Just killing time."

The Sylva entered the house and closed the door behind. "Is that really all you think of your purpose here?" she asked.

Tomas held his hands up. "Look, I don't mean to offend, but I'm not really in the mood to talk about my inner purpose. I had enough of that over the past year."

"Did all of your soul-searching reveal a purpose to you?"

"No, but it did get me into several fights, and now apparently my aura is torn."

"That, at least, is something I can assist you with. I remember you, Final Host. You bore the mark of Fate, of the Trickster. At the time, I thought this was why the *La'ma'shti* were drawn to you. I see now, that was an error."

She sat on a chair at a small table, resting her staff against the wall and regarding him with an unwavering azure gaze. "You have changed much since our last meeting, and not at all."

"I don't know how to respond to that," Tomas confessed.

The Speaker smiled. "Few do. I am glad you experienced love This will strengthen you for what is to come."

The squire rubbed his eyes. "I'm getting a little frustrated with…"

"Old females being vague?"

"Among others."

"Prophecy is a dangerous thing," the Speaker continued. "To stop the wave, one must throw a pebble at just the right time, in just the right place. This is what *Palsilyagathalexia* intended when she placed you on this path." She gestured to the golden rose pinned to the collar of Tomas' shirt. "This is most certainly what she intended when she granted you her inheritance. I, Nora Calonar, even the Trickster Mage, can only trust in her wisdom and support her choices."

A suspicion came over Tomas. He stared at the Speaker through narrowed eyes. "I'm the reason you agreed to help Aebreanna," he deduced. "Whatever Alexia started, you're only helping Aebreanna because of that."

The Speaker nodded. "She is *Sy'nok*: accursed, outcast. She has no place here. But, she serves you and the Heir of Calonar, and… Alexia found some worth in her, had some… interest in her. So, we will help."

"Can you tell me what Alexia's plan was?"

"*Palsilyagathalexia* has cast the pebble… you. I foresee some of her design, but not all. I will not risk disrupting her wisdom."

Tomas sighed and the Speaker smiled again. "Do you trust Alexia?" she asked.

"Yes," the squire replied without hesitation.

The Speaker stood. "Then trust. And let us see about your… how did you say it? Your torn aura?" She gestured for the squire to approach, and when he did so, she lightly placed a hand over his heart and closed her opalescent eyes. "There is great sadness in your heart," she whispered. "Much more than one your age should have."

"Life's tough," Tomas replied, unnerved by her detached tone.

"Yours more so than I would have otherwise thought possible." The Speaker moved her hand slightly to the center of Tomas's chest, and a wince, as though from great pain, crossed her lined face.

"Are you all right?" the young man asked.

"Regret," she whispered. "So much regret. Pain and sadness. Your spirit is burdened by so much." The Speaker opened her eyes and stepped away from Tomas, moving to a counter where a large pitcher of water rested. "I see now why my daughter was unable to mend you," she said while pouring herself a drink. "Your wounds are much deeper than even you know."

"I think I have a pretty good idea," the squire replied quietly. "I was there for all of it, after all."

"You have acknowledged your pain, but not released it," she replied after drinking. "I fear the weight of your spirit may be what first attracted the creatures of Otherworld."

"Well, if there's nothing you can do," Tomas said, looking about for his equipment. "I guess I'll rejoin my friends."

The Speaker put the wooden cup back on its counter and turned to face the young man. "I never said there was nothing I could do," she objected. "The only question is whether you have the strength to be healed."

"I can take anything you can throw at me," the squire replied firmly. "There's little you can do that could compare with what I've already been through all these years."

The priestess shook her head. "You do not understand. I will do nothing to you. It is you who will cause yourself harm."

Tomas shrugged. "Either way. I can take it."

"Very well." The Sylva pulled a stone striped with differing shades of green from her robe, along with a very short blade. "Remove as much of your clothing as you are comfortable with and lie back on the table," she instructed as she walked around the table, producing several white candles from a cabinet and lighting them with the barest whisper of her magic.

"What is that?" the young man asked, looking suspiciously at the large stone.

"Moss agate. The stone will help you see the truth of your spirit and balance your soul."

Somewhat reluctantly, Tomas removed the robe that he had been provided but resolutely left his underclothes in place. The young man then lay back down on the hard table, silently hoping that this ritual would not take as long as the previous one.

"Close your eyes and leave them so until I tell you to open them."

Tomas did so. "What am I supposed to do in the meantime?" he asked somewhat sourly.

"Do nothing," the speaker replied. "Say nothing, think of nothing. Sleep if you wish. What follows will do so of its own accord."

Tomas sighed but tried to relax, breathing deeply and emptying his mind as Rogan had taught him. The sound of moving cloth drew his attention, and though he kept his eyes closed, his curiosity was piqued. "What are you doing?" he asked.

"Shhh," she replied. "Be at peace."

Tomas needed a great deal of effort to find some measure of peace, as the young man felt the Speaker using the softest of touches to push his feet together and pull his arms straight on either side of his body. This done, he sensed the mystical Sylva put her hands on either side of his head, only a hair's breadth from actually touching and slowly ran them along the entire length of his body before returning to his temples, this time placing her hands lightly on his skin. After a few moments that seemed to drag on forever, the Speaker moved her hands to Tomas's chest, again placing them lightly on his flesh and began speaking in a voice so soft that he could not make out the words.

A strange thing happened then. A white light seemed to rise up all around the squire, bright enough that he could perceive it despite his closed eyes. The light did not hurt but seemed actually to warm him against the omnipresent chill of winter. Tomas felt as though he was floating in the light, held as gently as in his mother's arms. The warmth of the light soaked into every part of his body, bringing a comfort that Tomas had not known since leaving the Northern Keep.

A voice called out softly from the light, and Tomas could not help but open his eyes in response. As the light gently lifted him into a standing position, the squire looked about for the source of the voice. "Tomas," it called out.

"Who are you?" the young man asked, careful not to speak too loudly for fear of ruining the peace the white light had brought him.

"Tomas," the voice called out again, this time much closer. A small hand reached out from the light, and Tomas took it in his own, gently pulling the person forward so that he could see its identity.

Cecilia stepped forward, still wearing the same patched red dress she had worn so often back home in Pelsemoria. "How?" Tomas asked, stunned at the sight of his raven-haired childhood friend. The squire had left Cecilia back home over a year ago at the very beginning of his quest.

"How?" she asked in mockery of his confusion. "You dare ask me how? Ask yourself how. Ask yourself how you could make love to a woman and then just leave her."

"It wasn't like that Cecilia," Tomas insisted, backing away from her hateful glare. "I had to leave! I had to save our people!"

The furious girl stepped forward and slapped the squire with such force that Tomas nearly fell. "Save our people? Is that why you've taken another woman to your bed?" Cecilia grabbed her childhood friend by the shoulders yelling, "You speak words of love to get between my legs and then forget me the moment you are away!?! Bastard!" She flung him away.

Tomas spun through the light, spinning in all directions. He could not tell direction or distance until he slammed into the armored chest of Rogan, who stood looking on in amusement. "Can't keep your women under control, kid?" the knight asked.

"What?"

"Is this all you've learned from me?" Rogan demanded. "You let a woman talk to you like that? You let a woman push you away?"

"What are you saying?" Tomas asked, tears standing in his eyes. "Rogan, I don't understand what's happening!"

From behind Rogan, King Cylan stepped forward and smiled. "You belong to me now, Tomas," the old wizard said. "You are a servant of my designs."

"How could you do it?" a voice demanded from behind the squire. Spinning, Tomas saw his mother, flanked by the people of Pelsemoria. "How could you?" his mother asked again. "How could you sell your soul to that monster?"

"Mother," the young man pleaded, "you don't understand! It's not like that!"

Luigino Mariano, the wounded Praetorian Tomas had saved, stepped forward from the rest of the crowd. "You willingly serve the Black Duke, don't you?" he asked calmly.

"Yes . . . but . . . you don't understand. The stories about him are wrong!"

The soldier raised an eyebrow. "Really?" he asked. "And who told you that? Them!?!"

Tomas looked back and forth, between the people of Pelsemoria and Rogan and Calonar. "I learned the truth for myself," he said finally but with little certainty. "I learned the truth of the Black Duke and his Northern Keep."

"You learned nothing!" a voice snapped. Forward stepped Father Konrad, priest and councilor to Tomas for most of his young life. "You were tested with temptation and have been proven unworthy!"

"Why, Tomas?" his mother asked in tears. "What did they give you that was worth your soul?"

From behind the young man came a scent that Tomas would recognize instantly. Mary stepped forward from behind Rogan and Calonar to stand between the two warriors. "They gave him me," she said.

"This is your new whore?" Cecilia demanded. "This is the one you took instead of me? Why?!?"

"Why?" Tomas's mother repeated. "Why?" Sergeant Mariano repeated. "Why?" Each member of the people of Pelsemoria repeated the word again and again, bringing Tomas to his knees with the weight of their accusation.

"Why?" a new voice asked, stepping up to stand directly before the kneeling young man. Tomas looked up in open-mouthed shock at the sight of his father, more than ten years dead with his mortal chest wound still bleeding. "I am murdered by evil men, and not only do you not avenge me… you swear loyalty to *my murderer!*"

Tomas scrambled away, unable to bear his father's scorn. The squire crawled as fast as his limbs would carry him until he was halted by green skirts. Tomas closed his eyes, unable to look up and see the greatest of his failures in life, the greatest of his sorrows. "Face me, Tomas." Alexia's soft voice reached out and lifted his head with a gentle and yet undeniable authority.

The young man looked up into the eyes of his dear friend, dead saving his life from the cold waters of Lake Tragedy. "I let you die," he whispered, the tears now flowing freely down his face.

Alexia knelt and took Tomas' face in her hands, staring deep into his face with her soft Sylvai eyes before placing a light kiss on his forehead. "Yes, you did." There was no accusation in her musical voice; all Tomas heard was the same warm affection that had always characterized his friend. "You let me give my life to save yours. You gave me what I wanted."

"You were more than I," Tomas insisted. "The world would have been better with you alive than me."

Alexia laughed the same bright laugh the young squire remembered so clearly, the laugh that still carried the joy of her long-past youth. The Sylva laughed again and lifted her young friend up and turned him to face his accusers. "Would it?" she asked. Alexia pointed to Mary and asked, "Would she?" The matriarch of House Calonar pointed to the people of Pelsemoria. "Would they?"

Tomas saw that the people of his home city no longer looked at him in accusation. They only looked at the young man in patient expectation. "Did you abandon them?" Alexia asked from behind Tomas. "Or do you fight, even now, for them?"

Cecilia stepped forward with tears still running down her cheeks. "Did you promise her anything other than your return?" Alexia asked. "Youth is marked by mistakes and broken hearts. Did you do anything more to her than life already had?"

"Is that an excuse?" Tomas whispered.

"No," Alexia replied. "And someday you will see her again and have to explain yourself. But why hold on to her hatred when you do not even know if that hatred really exists?"

The Sylva turned her young friend to face Rogan and King Cylan. "You have traveled far, my young friend. You have traveled far and seen much of the evil in the world. Do you really believe these men are a part of that darkness?"

"No."

"You hold on to doubt as all people do. That doubt will keep you from making too many foolish choices. But do not let that doubt darken your bright soul."

Tomas looked at Mary. "Ah yes," Alexia said with an amused smile. "Your 'incentive.' Tomas, do you really think Mary would allow herself to be used like that?"

"I don't want to think it, but—"

"But it is an amazing coincidence," the elderly Sylva finished. "You meet your soulmate at the same time you are tempted to serve House Calonar."

"Yes," Tomas agreed.

"You do not believe in coincidence, do you?"

"No." He looked at his lost friend. "I know it's not coincidence. I know you did it. You left the note. You knew, before you met me, that you'd send me to the Northern Keep and meet her."

Alexia laughed. "Of course I did!" She pulled Tomas close, close enough that her warmth suffused him. "I knew your path would be a hard one, and I knew she could lighten it.

Tomas looked at Alexia then back to his love.

"Fate," the Sylva said. "Destiny, divine will, or whatever it is you wish to call it. You were supposed to meet her. You were supposed to love her. If your path took a thousand miles or a thousand years, still you would have met her and loved her."

The squire turned to look resolutely at his father.

"You serve the man who took your father's life," Alexia confirmed. "Rogan Eigenhard pushed his sword into your father's chest, ending the agony that Tienel Greysoul's magic inflicted upon him. You serve the man who ended your father's life, but not his murderer."

Alexia turned him so that she could look into his eyes. "Your life has had enough darkness, my dear Tomas. Do not let anything darken that bright spirit. You must be the light that holds back the shadows, that traps it and sets it free. That is my design for you. No great conspiracies or plots; no great plans that fold in on themselves." Two figures appeared in the distance, one of distortion and trickery, the other of shadow. Alexia nodded towards them. "That is what they do, how they think." She put a hand over Tomas' heart. "I want you to be the light against them; a truth to their falsehoods.

"There will be enough hardship in the days and miles ahead. Do not add to your burdens with undeserved guilt. You must find peace in the things you will be needed to do."

The young man could sense reality beginning to reassert itself. Looking about in panic, Tomas reached out to cling to Alexia but found her as insubstantial as any of his other memories. Seeing his fear, the beautiful Sylva smiled. "You never have to try to hold on to me, Tomas." She pointed to the golden rose on Tomas's collar. "I will always be in that special place in your heart you opened to me. I will always be with you."

Chapter 8

Tomas slowly opened his eyes, fighting against the red soreness his tears had caused. The young man filled his lungs several times, while he tried to regain the calm resolve that had shielded his heart for so very long now.

"Do not so harden your heart once again that you lose the lessons of the *Sal'ay'cel'sa*."

"Is that what you call those visions?"

The Speaker nodded as she straightened the neckline of her deep robe. "Self-examination is one of the more difficult tasks one can attempt," the mature priestess said as she crossed the small room to retrieve her staff. "The *Sal'ay'cel'sa* makes the attempt, if not less difficult, at least less time-consuming."

Tomas sat up and rubbed his temple, trying to will away the empty feeling inside. "How long will I feel like this?" he asked in a hollow voice.

The Sylva turned and looked at the young man with a soft smile on her wrinkled face. "Hours," she finally replied. "Perhaps a day. The feeling inside will subside. Be careful you do not forget what you have learned."

"I can't see how anyone could forget something like that," the squire insisted.

You would be surprised how many people in life ignore the advice of their hearts in fear of the pain that could result."

Tomas breathed deeply several times and slowly worked to retrieve his clothes. "Well," he said, "I'm not one of those people."

"Only time will tell. Now, if you are able, the company of your friends will speed the recovery of your heart and aura."

Once his clothing and gear had been retrieved, the Speaker led Tomas across the village to another small house, much like the one in which he had undergone his own purification ritual. Unlike the cottage from which he had come, the first floor of this was just one large room, dominated by a large hearth and the traditional accouterments of cooking. Although dimly lit, the young man's eyes adjusted quickly enough that he was able to distinguish Rogan and Beraht and moved to join the two as they stood in a corner, observing the ritual being performed before the hearth.

Like they had with Tomas, a group of younger Sylvai had gathered in a circle around Aebreanna with hands clasped, chanting softly in their musical language. The Speaker did not join the circle but instead stood unobtrusively in the corner opposite Tomas and his friends, watching her acolytes as they performed the ceremony with calm attention. Within the circle of Sylvai, Aebreanna lay on a table just as Tomas had, though she showed little of the discomfort that had marred the squire's experience. Dressed in the briefest of undergarments, the beautiful spy lay silently as the same Sylva who had initially tried to help Tomas moved what the squire guessed was the same polished brown stone slowly along Aebreanna's supple curves. Only the slow rise and fall of the Sylva's breasts let Tomas know that his injured companion lived at all, so still she was.

Upon reaching Rogan and Beraht, the knight nodded a welcome to his squire and continued to watch the ceremony with a blank expression. Beraht's face did little to hide his impatience. "How long?" the young man asked.

"Hours," the barbarian replied.

"How much longer will this take?"

"Long as it needs to," Rogan answered in a tone that ordered silence better than any words could.

Tomas and Beraht remained silent as the ritual continued, and finally, after what seemed forever, the circle of Sylvai stopped their chant and disengaged, moving quietly out of the house. The Speaker briefly placed a soft hand over Aebreanna's heart and whispered softly to the Sylva. Aebreanna wordlessly rose and moved to the ladder that led to a loft above. Without hesitation, the spy climbed the ladder, out of the sight of her friends. The Speaker crossed the room to stand before the trio of warriors. "She must rest this day," she said. "And take no stressful action tomorrow. On the following day, she will be whole, and your journey may continue."

"I'm not sure we can afford the time," Rogan replied.

"Worry not, Heir of Calonar. I have given instructions to our Walkers. When the Daughter of Tressalon is ready, you will be shown the *Sy'lva'n* Paths."

"Sylvai paths?" Tomas asked.

"The locals know these woods, kid," Rogan answered. "They know the fastest routes."

"There is, perhaps, more," the Speaker confessed. "Once, our Paths crossed the world, offering speedy transit across our *Im'peri'a*. These are almost all gone now. A few remain, though, in our Wood. The Walkers will guide you to the edge of our home. We will have you at the border of our forest in a day." The Speaker moved to the door but paused after opening it. "This house has been set aside for your use as long as you remain. We will ensure your safety for as long as you remain under the shade of our trees. However, our people will not leave the Wood. The world beyond is no longer our concern."

Rogan nodded his head in acknowledgment.

"Tomorrow is *Asyas'darez'ay'iel.* You are welcome to join us."

"We would be honored," the knight replied.

The Speaker left, shutting the door behind. Without a word, Rogan and Beraht began moving to the ladder. "What's tomorrow?" Tomas asked.

"Sylvai new year, kid," his knight answered. "Like Endyear, but more spiritual. Part new year celebration, part day of the dead, part fertility ritual, part purification."

"So tomorrow we party?" the squire said, joining his mentor at the bottom of the ladder.

"Yeah. I don't like losing the time, but with the Walkers leading us, we'll make a lot better time anyway, so I guess it isn't too big a loss."

"Plus a free meal," Beraht added.

The next morning, Tomas was awoken to the sound of music. Dressing as quickly as he could without disturbing his companions and belting on his weapons despite their host's assurances of protection, the squire moved toward the exit of their cottage to satisfy his rising curiosity. At the front door, Tomas was startled to see a Sylvu dressed in thick leathers and furs against the winter's cold with his thick, immaculately trimmed gray hair bound behind his neck with a silver clasp. The Sylvu had a large drum strapped loosely over his shoulder and danced down the village's main road. As he passed by each house, Tomas saw that the villagers emerged from their homes, following behind the growing parade as the drummer made his way slowly to the center of the village, never ceasing in his dance or the playing of his drum.

"Are you going to just stand there, kid?" Rogan asked from behind, sending Tomas into the air with a yelp of surprise. "You're letting all the heat out."

Tomas took several moments to regain control of his racing pulse and shortened breath. The squire threw his knight a look of irritation and finally asked, "Do you really have to keep sneaking up on me?"

"I'm hoping someday I won't be able to," the mentor replied.

Tomas just shrugged away his irritation and led Rogan out of their house. "Is this their celebration?" the young man asked.

Rogan shook his head and started walking toward where the Sylvai had gathered. "No. This is the ceremony that starts the celebration."

Tomas adjusted his stride so that he could move alongside his knight. "Like the commencement ceremony for the Harvest Festival?"

"Where do you think the tradition came from?"

The squire paused, drawing his knight aside. "What is it?" Rogan asked.

"During my… purification, one of them said something about a disruption in magic."

Rogan nodded. "Yeah, that happened with me and Beraht," he admitted. "But the Sylvai were able to finish. Did it cause problems for you?"

Tomas sighed. "The Speaker herself had to come in and finish the ritual." He looked seriously at Rogan. "Do you think it's just them or…?" The squire glanced off in the direction of the Keep.

The knight shrugged and continued on their course. "Esha thought there was something more to the storm. It was kicking up interference in everything, but we thought that was just the weather. If it's a bigger problem, we have to trust the people back home to deal with it. We've got our job." He laughed then, ruefully. "You're going to find, kid, that when you're on-mission, the world'll constantly try to distract you with new problems. The key is to stay focused on your objective."

The two warriors entered a clearing in the center of the village in which its residents had gathered, back against the surrounding trees to watch the unfolding ceremony. The Sylvai continued to dance, now moving in a circle around what Tomas assumed was an altar, a large flattened stone that showed no sign of artificial shaping. The altar was partially covered in a bright red cloth and decorated with acorns, gourds, pine cones, and flowers of such vibrant colors they seemed to shine. A bowl of fruit rested on the altar, surrounded by what the squire assumed to be offerings of food, clothing, and small carved idols. Standing before the altar was the Speaker, dressed in a deep red homespun dress that matched perfectly the altar's decorations. The speaker chanted in the Sylvai tongue in such a way that it perfectly matched the beating of the drum, apparently calling the villagers to finally halt their circle.

No longer circling the altar, the Sylvai instead danced in place. Most rang small bells tied to their wrists and ankles or clapped their hands to match the beating of the drum as the drummer moved to stand across the spring from the Speaker. She then raised a silver bell above the altar and beat against it with a golden hammer three times, sending three deep rings echoing throughout the trees that again matched the continued drumming.

Once again, the Sylvai started dancing in a loose circle, letting their passion express itself though their motions. As the Sylvai continued to dance, most of them threw aside their cloaks despite the cold to allow the winter air touch their skin, letting the heat of their dance keep them warm. While the revelers danced, the Speaker placed the bell and hammer on the altar and picked up the large bowl of fruit before slowly moving out toward the circling Sylvai.

At some prearranged time, the dancers began to once again sway in place, clapping their hands and ringing their bells to accompany the drum beat. The Speaker stood before one of the Sylvai and, after giving the aging Sylva a piece of fruit from the bowl, embraced her and shared a brief but passionate kiss. The speaker then said, "*K'sal'eth ay'syka enimsysti vo Asyas'darez'ay'iel.*

This ceremony was repeated for each of the villagers without exception. The embrace and kiss were exchanged, and the same words were intoned after the fruit was offered to each villager in turn. "I wonder what she's saying," Tomas mused quietly.

From behind the young man, Aebreanna's soft voice reached out to caress his ears. "She is saying, 'I give thanks to the gods for their purification.'" Rogan and Tomas both turned slightly at the sudden arrival of their friends. Aebreanna stood with a hand resting on Beraht, her weariness still apparent.

"How do you feel?" Rogan asked.

"I am recovering, though not as quickly as I would prefer," the spy replied.

"Should you be out of bed?" Tomas pointed out.

"Perhaps not. However, given the opportunity, I would prefer not to miss the celebration." Leaning on Beraht, Aebreanna moved to join the circle, receiving her own offering of fruit before leading her Uldra crutch back to where her friends stood. No embrace or kiss was offered by the speaker for Aebreanna as they were for the other Sylvai present, though the words were still spoken.

After completing her circuit and giving the offering to the drummer, the Speaker moved back to the altar where she replaced the bowl and rang the bell another seven times. Aebreanna translated the Speaker's words as she said them.

"Though summer ends and winter begins, still the gods are ever with us. Though light fades and darkness descends, still the gods are ever with us. Though youth passes and age arises, still the gods are with us. Our Lady watches over us, as does her Lord."

The assembled villagers then chanted, "The Lady and the Lord give us their blessings."

The Speaker turned in a slow circle to make eye contact with all those assembled, including Tomas and his friends, with the notable and pointed exception of Aebreanna. As she did this, the Speaker said, "For our failures and our victories..."

"The Lady and the Lord give blessings," the villagers replied in unison.

The Speaker finished her turn and looked at the drummer. "How is the hearth?" she asked.

The drummer bowed his head and replied, "Warm and welcome."

"How are our homes?"

"Beautiful and open."

"What are our lives?"

"The harvest of the gods."

The Speaker waved a hand over the offerings on the altar. "While we enjoy the fruits of our labors and the gifts of the gods, let us never forget those who are not so fortunate as we," she said. "We offer here a portion of our goods, for those who journey to the Eternal Forest."

The villagers raised their hands and chanted, "So mote it be."

After this, the Speaker rang the bell three more times. A large plate of cakes was then brought to the altar and handed to her. She handed the plate to her partner who held it steady, while the Speaker took a small knife from the altar and touched its point to each of the cakes. While doing so, she said, "This food is the blessing of the gods, their grace and forgiveness. Let us partake freely and, as we share, let us remember to always share with those who are in need."

The Speaker then ate a small piece of cake before taking the plate so that the drummer could also eat. The two then walked around the circle, allowing each Sylvai present to eat a small piece of the cakes. When she and her partner were once again at the altar, they stood side by side. "As we enjoy these gifts of the gods," the Speaker said, "let us remember that without the gods we would have nothing. We would be nothing. Let us atone for our failures and aid those in need. So mote it be."

"So mote it be!" the crowd cheered.

The next several hours blurred together in Tomas's memory. The day was filled with games and songs. Feasting and dancing all attended to as though this was the last day of life for this small village. Children laughed and played along with the adults. Food was shared with family and friend alike. Even Beraht, whose Uldra ancestry was as undeniable as the mountains, was treated with welcome gaiety. Tomas danced and ate with such abandon that he lost all trace of worry. The villagers treated him as a combination of honored guest and pleasant oddity, both as an envoy of House Calonar and student of Prince Rogan, and so he was never left for company throughout the celebration. The day was a time of renewal for his young heart and a welcome relief from the stresses of recent weeks.

Tomas noticed that his knight was an unenthusiastic participant in the festivities. Rogan offered no objection or complaint, and he joined in all the ceremony and celebration. He spoke politely with the Speaker and other village elders. He laughed at merrymaking and enjoyed the food. Still, after their months training together, Tomas had learned to see behind his knight's diplomatic persona, to the man beneath. Rogan ate the food with overly-visible displays of gratitude and appreciation. He listened too intently to the complaints and concerns of the elders. He indulged the attention of the leading members of the Sylvai community. This, Tomas noted, was most especially uncomfortable to Rogan.

The Speaker's daughter and two other young Sylvai maidens, all bearing the Wyrdmark, seemed especially interested in Rogan. The jostled for his attention. They brought him gifts of food. They monopolized his time dancing. They laughed enthusiastically at his feeble attempts at humor. They whispered suggestions into his ear that made the scarred veteran of countless battles blush and beg off. Rogan was polite, but firm, often pointing to the wedding band on his finger which the knight kept as prominently displayed as possible.

As evening fell, the young squire and his companions had gathered with most of the rest of the villagers around the altar at the village center for a final feast. Beraht had spent most of the day with Aebreanna, helping her as needed and offering glares of imminent violence to any Sylvai who thought to approach her with hurtful words. Rogan had, at last, fended off the three Wyrdmarked maidens. The red decorations had been at some point replaced with ones of white and blue, marking the transition from one year to the next, and the Speaker and her acolytes had also changed their garb to match. As the heroes ate roast pork and hen, Tomas made a note of the two large torches that had been placed on either side of the altar.

"That is the *Portaira'sumar*," the Speaker answered over the music of the festival. "The Gateway."

"To where?" Tomas asked, savoring the vegetable stew.

"The Eternal Forest," the speaker replied. "During this time of the year, the barrier between worlds is at its weakest." The Sylvai mystic gestured throughout the village to where similar torches could be seen in front of a number of cottages in addition to the many bonfires that had been lighted to keep the celebrants warm against the evening chill. "We light the way so our loved ones can, if they are of a mind, travel through the portal to visit us and see that all is well among those who have yet to journey home."

Tomas washed down his food with a long drink of warm cider. "The barrier is weak?" he asked. "Is that how I… slipped through?"

The Speaker sipped from her wine cup. "Possible," she replied. "Although I do not know for certain, it seems reasonable that the combination of the time, along with your proximity to the natural crossroads, allowed for your misadventure. The Covenant Barrier grows weak at this time, after all, especially at these natural crossroads."

Aebreanna nodded. "As I suspected. I found our young friend very near to the shrine that rests outside your village."

"I would think that the Daughter of Tressalon would not risk entering Otherworld." The Speaker did not spare a glance at Aebreanna, nor did her voice carry any warmth. "After all, the arrogance of House Tressalon was what brought upon our people the Terror That Feeds."

Aebreanna blushed as several Sylvai in earshot muttered "*Sy'nok*." The beautiful spy did not look up from her food, trying with only partial success to hide her shame. Tomas began to rise with the intention of setting the villagers to right but was held firm by Rogan, who gave his apprentice a look that allowed for no insubordination. Beraht set down his cup and belched to gain attention.

"I've never heard that word before," the barbarian rumbled, his ugly face calm. "Sy'nok. What does that mean?"

The Speaker looked at Aebreanna with cold fire in her opalescent eyes. "It means 'corruption of hope,'" she answered. "It is the curse all Tressalon live under. They have been cursed by the actions of their matriarchs. House Tressalon was always arrogant and unwilling to sacrifice for the good of their people. They were always unclean."

Again, Tomas meant to rise, but again, he was held in place by his knight. Beraht just took another drink and nodded. "Yes," he mused. "They are cursed, aren't they?"

"Nothing less could be expected from those who first corrupted Otherworld and then destroyed Nassinalia," the speaker insisted.

"So it was the Tressalons that destroyed Nassinalia?" Beraht asked. "I'd heard it was Kelinva."

"The Dark Empress is only partly to blame," the Speaker corrected, "The matriarch of House Tressalon instigated the Disaster. They destroyed not only our greatest city but Lanasia itself."

"And her entire family must suffer for the mistake of one woman over a thousand years ago?" Tomas demanded harshly.

"A thousand years is but a single lifetime for a *Sy'lwa'n*," the speaker replied. "The betrayal of House Tressalon is as fresh in our memories as the destruction of Pelsemoria is to yours." The Speaker turned to look at Aebreanna. "And their treacheries were not limited to that one time. The failures of that family continue through to this generation."

"Are you accusing Aebreanna of treachery?" Tomas demanded.

The Speaker pursed her lips. "Our Empress, the last leader of our *Im'peri'a*, spoke on her final night, before she led the charge at Lake Tragedy. She said there would come a daughter of a fallen House, heir to a great legacy of wisdom and magic. This *Eann'fu'neth'way'san* would forever shut the Pathways to Underworld and at last conclude the defeat of *Ethroi'sa'kai*, banishing forever the darkness that plagues all souls."

She stared flat, empty eyes at Aebreanna. "Such a one had appeared, or so we thought. The lowest, most despised of Houses living in the city that was once the heart of our *Im'peri'a*. A daughter who was heir to not only this least of names, but to a mighty bloodline. She could have been *Eann'fu'neth'way'san*." The Speaker snorted. "Instead she marries a Human, births half-breeds, and consorts with degenerates."

Tomas was seething, and only the iron grip of his knight prevented bloodshed. "I though this whole celebration was about forgiveness, generosity, and welcome." He waved his hand around the assembled villagers, who were only pretending not to be listening. "Instead you call her a slut!?!"

The Speaker looked evenly at her guest. "Young man, our entire race has waited in breathless anticipation for the arrival of a pure-blood scion of House Tressalon who could have not only restored the honor of her family but could have also helped restore the *Sy'lva'n* people, to finally heal our wounds from the Uldra Uprising."

Tomas stared at the Speaker in open-mouthed shock. "You hate her for not being your messiah?" he demanded. "You hate her for not measuring up to some prophecy?"

"Even despite the circumstances of her birth, there was a chance, no matter how slight, that she could have harnessed the abilities of her blood to wield a great power for the glory of her people. Instead she contents herself to be a spy for House Calonar. We do not hate her, young one. We pity her."

"You envy her," Beraht corrected.

All present stared at the Uldra in surprise. Beraht took his time clearing the larger crumbs from his beard before he elaborated. "You envy her. Aebreanna was supposed to become some great, shiny-eyed prophet that led you in a big song. Instead you got her. You got a girl that stood up to the Greysoul, the one Human wizard that had you wetting yourselves. You got a girl that stood up to the Human Republic that beat *you* and helped take them down. You got a girl that has done everything you wished you could do, and you envy her so much you can't stand being this close to her." The Uldra stood. "You can't stand the reminder of how much you haven't done with your lives." Without another word, the Uldra warrior drained his cup and leaned down, effortlessly lifting Aebreanna to her feet and giving her any support she still needed as they left for the comfort of bed.

"I think that's our cue as well," Rogan noted. The knight stood and bowed slightly to the Speaker. "I'd like to thank you all for your hospitality and assistance. And please, you have to forgive Beraht. He isn't always this perceptive."

Tomas followed his mentor to their house, not trusting himself to speak. They caught up to their comrades as the mismatched pair approached the borrowed cottage. Aebreanna stood with her hand on the door to prevent her lumbering companion from entering. The barbarian looked down at her with a sneer of suspicion.

The spy sniffed lightly at the air. "Could you not at least have washed some of the stench from what can only laughingly be referred to as your clothes?"

"Don't you have a tree to hug, or have sex with, or something," he replied before pulling the door open and helping her inside.

Rogan looked at Tomas with a smile. "Isn't friendship a beautiful thing?" he asked.

Tomas looked inside where Aebreanna and Beraht were still arguing in increasing volume. "No," he replied. "Not really."

Chapter 9

"**We can** escort you no further, Heir of Calonar." Their Sylvai guides stood in a loose circle behind Tomas and his friends, the dark colors of their cloaks and armor making them difficult to distinguish from the shifting shadows of the forest.

Rogan turned Stick to face the spokesman of their escort. "I thank you for your help," he said formally. "You've made our journey much easier and given us an advantage of time that we'll not squander."

"Very poetic," Tomas muttered.

"Shut up, kid."

The Sylvu who spoke for his group stepped forward but made sure to never lose the advantage of the shadows. "Our honor is to aid you, Heir of Calonar," the Walker declared. "May your journey be free of tragedy and your return home without pause."

Rogan bowed in his saddle. "May your arrows fly true and your blades cut deep."

The Walkers slipped back into the trees, leaving no sign of having ever stood there. Try though he might, Tomas could not see a single leaf disturbed by the passage of the Sylvai warriors, marveling at their stealth and silence. Their journey had been disorienting to the squire. There was no apparent magic to the passage, no ritual or chants or great explosion of light. Instead, the Walkers had assembled around them and guided the group into a thick clutch of trees. When Tomas could see through the thick trunks and low branches, he was looking at the edge of Wildelves Wood. A journey of days, perhaps longer, had taken a moment.

Rogan gathered up the reins to his impatient warhorse. "All right," he said gruffly. "Let's get moving. The weather won't hold forever."

Tomas pulled Urge, his own powerful yet sleek mount, beside his knight. "What was with all the poetry?" he asked.

Rogan grimaced. "Sylvai love talking," he answered. "It's their favorite pastime. The best way to stay on their good side is to use a lot of unnecessarily-long sentences."

"As usual," Aebreanna interjected, "your answer, while having some small basis in fact, takes an issue that is quite complex and renders it down to a foolishly abrupt statement of only partial factuality."

"See," the knight pointed out.

"Yes," she said flatly. "Quite amusing."

"Well," Tomas said, "I would hate to have to face those Walkers in battle."

"Now you know how the Republic felt," Rogan agreed. "The Walkers are the biggest reason why the Northern Keep is so secure. Any army that goes through Wildelves Wood has to deal with the Walkers, and that would cost a lot of lives."

"Just about the only thing to respect out of the whole blasted race," Beraht insisted. "Never met a Sylvu I wouldn't mind killing a little, but those bow-slingers would be a little problem."

"Is that a hint of respect I hear in your voice, Sir Beraht?" Aebreanna's face shone with sincere shock, betraying the sarcastic gleam in her opalescent eyes.

"HA!" the Uldra's reply was brief. "I'll take on any of those scrawny tree-lovers anytime, anyplace, for any reason!"

The Uldra's rant continued for some time, still clearly audible from where the Walkers continued to monitor the progress of Eigenhard's party for as long as the trees could continue to cloak them. They were so preoccupied with their observation, in fact, that two of their number fell before any of the other five were aware of the danger. The third to fall, the largest of their group, was able to let lose a single muffled gasp of distress as he fell from the branch that had supported him, alerting his comrades of the attack.

The Walkers moved with a fluid grace and utter silence that masked the distress each of them felt. Of the four who remained, each moved as a veteran, trained and proficient in detecting danger before it could strike. The warriors moved without sound into the trees, circling each other and scanning with unceasing eyes for their attacker, covering the backs of their friends, and trusting that their own backs were covered in turn.

A flash of steel shot from the misty canopy overhead, striking one of the warriors and sending her tumbling down. When the Sylva's body finally hit the snow-covered ground far below, her three surviving friends saw the glint of small stars, forged of the noxious green steel of Davenor, protruding from the ruins of her opalescent eyes. Although no sign of it showed in the three remaining Walkers, their fear sang through the trees.

Another flash of steel shot from another direction of the thick branches overhead, this time deflected by a *Sy'lva'n* blade. "There," the veteran warrior whispered, orienting his two remaining comrades. As one, the Walkers unslung their bows, letting the momentum of their unceasing movement through the thick tangle of branches carry the weapons free of their shoulders. Each of the warriors used the precious time between leaps from one branch to the next to nock an arrow and let fly, doing so again after their powerful legs launched them into the air once more.

A flurry of *Sy'lva'n* missiles filled the air, hitting not only the point identified but the area all around. To the untrained eye, it would have appeared as though the Walkers fired in desperation, hoping to chance for their arrows to find a target and letting desperation be the only guide in their attacks. But one experienced in Walker tactics would recognize the stratagem, for each arrow was not meant to strike their attacker but to drive him. The deaths of four of their brethren would not be answered with the pointed death of an arrow; *Sy'lva'n* blood would cry out for the justice of the blade.

When at last the rain of arrows ceased and the air was cleared of falling leaves and snow, the three Walkers paused in their movement to lock their collective gaze upon that point of the ground on which their enemy should have been forced. It took moments, only a few but an eternity to the battle-ready warriors, for the avalanche of snow and broken evergreen branches to at last clear enough for sight. When finally the warriors caught sight of their attacker, even their Walker training betrayed them, and each gasped in surprised fear.

Standing tall on the ground was a *Xesh'lin*, so declared by the still-yet-ready grace of his stance and lithe power of his lean body. His eyes of burning blood looked up at the three Walkers with no hatred, no fear, only a casual weariness. His clothes, equipment, and armor were all dyed in varying shades of gray and black in stark contrast to the winter forest around him; with the alabaster skin around his damned eyes the only flesh visible on his powerful body. Held loosely in his gloved fist was the trademark of the monster of Davenor: the twin blades of green, noxious Davenor steel.

"Xaemus!" one of the Walkers gasped.

"Stand ready," their leader commanded. "Bows then blades." With the knowledge of the identity of their attacker, the single greatest killer to ever hunt for *Sy'lva'n* blood, their tactics changed, and their desperation grew. Without command, the three Walkers leapt from the branches on which they stood, letting several arrows fly before drawing their short blades and striking in perfect unison. The air filled with the dance of *Sy'lva'n* steel as the warriors hit the ground, each expecting to see the blood of the monster of Davenor. Instead, they saw only empty space.

As one, the Walkers looked up and saw Xaemus moving from branch to branch with a fluid grace that made mockery of their own. Again, without order, the three leapt, clearly intending to use the weight of their numbers to bring down the *Xesh'lin*. Try as they might, though, the Walkers could not catch up to their enemy, barely able to keep on his trail as it flowed through the trees.

Another flash of steel from above was followed by the death gasp of another Walker, his life's blood flowing freely from the huge gash Xaemus had cut across the Walker's face, carving out his opalescent eyes. Just as quickly, the monster of Davenor was gone, lost in the dense canopy.

The last two Walkers stood back-to-back on a large branch, abandoning the speed and mobility that had done naught but seen five of their number slain. Each Sylvai, male and female, scanned the surrounding space, above and below, for any warning sign of the monster's approach. The cold breeze set the limbs around them swaying, masking any movement among the snow-covered trees.

From directly above, Xaemus fell upon them in utter silence. The Walkers leapt apart and turned to attack. The monster of Davenor met each *Sy'lva'n* blade with a quick parry of his own dual-bladed weapon, bending low and cutting a deep slash against one of the Walker's legs, sending the limb tumbling down to be lost among the branches. The *Xesh'lin* ignored the wounded Walker in favor of the leader for only a moment, sending the *Sy'lvu* dancing back from a flurry of blade strikes that drew her blood from several shallow cuts. Seeing this target driven back, Xaemus again spun and casually decapitated the wounded Sylva, letting the turn continue without pause until he again faced the last remaining Walker.

The *Sy'lvu* could not afford to spare a glance to the falling head and body of his remaining compatriot, instead focusing all his attention on the monster of Davenor. His fear was a stinking aphrodisiac, one any other *Xesh'lin* would delight in. Xaemus was not any other of his race, though. The Walker's trembling was like an enticing dance, a luring bait that the darkest pits of his hellish soul lusted for. Any other *Xesh'lin* would rush in, would disarm this hated enemy of his people, and satisfy the primal urge to desecrate its flesh. This is what made Xaemus so dangerous, though. He did not yield to his people's curse. He was a creature of purpose.

Xaemus would never underestimate an opponent, most especially a wounded one. He moved toward his last target carefully, not betraying a single opening that could be exploited without his advantage. In a moment, the monster of Davenor assessed his opponent. The Walker's stance and eyes betrayed his entire life to the *Xesh'lin*; in only a moment, Xaemus knew this Walker better than his fallen lover ever could have, and he knew how to kill him.

The Walker attacked first, as Xaemus knew he would. He feinted with the blade, striking out with the bow still held in his left hand, trying to land a powerful blow behind the *Xesh'lin*'s right knee. Xaemus read this mode of attack immediately and danced back, out of range of the strike before dancing back in, sweeping his weapon up to draw his enemy's blade down, away from the face. The feint seemed to work, and the *Sy'lvu*'s blade lowered; Xaemus struck instantly for his target's neck but was surprised at the Walker's quick reaction.

The Walker had also read his opponent and, after making the strike against the *Xesh'lin*'s knee, which he suspected would not connect, had dropped the bow and reached out with his now free hand, grabbing the exposed part of the hilt of Xaemus' weapon and twisting, using the leverage gained to pry the blade free and send it falling to join the body of his lover. Hoping to take advantage of this, the *Sy'lvu* thrust his blade toward Xaemus' chest.

The monster of Davenor turned his body away from the strike, letting the blade pass in front of his chest rather than through it. Just as his opponent had done, Xaemus used the momentum his opponent had generated to grab the Walker's arm and twist, sending his weapon flying away. To Xaemus' surprise, the Sylvu surrendered his weapon without a fight, instead grabbing his opponent's arm and pulling him off balance.

The two warriors, their racial hatred for each other burning with a barely controlled fury, tumbled off the branch and fell. The trees beat at the two combatants as they wrestled with one another in the air until they were finally forced apart. The ground rushed up, but the Walker would not be betrayed by his own Wood; he reached out just in time and was saved by a soft branch that gave him leverage enough to swing up onto it. Xaemus was not to be seen.

This one was smarter than the others, learning from his mistakes. The Walker ducked at the last moment as the monster of Davenor dropped from above. This was why Xaemus had kept him for last; he was the only one who might have posed a threat. The *Sy'lvu* struck with his hands at Xaemus' head and chest. Each blow after the first was blocked and pushed aside by until finally the Walker threw a punch too far and the monster of Davenor grabbed the *Sy'lvu*'s arm. Xaemus raised his elbow and brought it down on, rewarded with the snap of bone and cartilage.

Blinded by pain and betrayed by his body, the *Sy'lvu* let loose a scream that was cut off by a quick strike to the throat. The last Walker could not see through the tears that burned his opalescent eyes as Xaemus spun under the arm he continued to hold and slashed a across the Walker's face, destroying those hated, opalescent eyes. The monster of Davenor let this worthy opponent join her comrades on the ground below and went to retrieve his weapons.

When his gear had been collected, Xaemus took to the branches again until he could see that Eigenhard and his companions were well out of range to have heard the muffled sounds of the combat and remained blissfully ignorant of his observation.

The *Xesh'lin* reached into his vest and drew out a small crystal. Holding the magical device in the palm of his gloved hand, he spoke the words that activated it and waited. Finally, a red mist rose from the crystal and coalesced into the shrouded from of his employer.

"Report," the wizard commanded.

"All is as you wished," Xaemus replied. "Eigenhard and his party have left the forest without further incident, aided by the Walkers. I have eliminated the group that assisted him, leaving no trace of their fate."

"Then everything is ready for the next phase?"

"Yes."

"Then proceed."

First Interpose

Chapter 10

Winter had returned to the Northern Keep. Vara's storm, that terrible blizzard that had fallen upon the Northlands with unexpected fury, had finally passed. Those dark clouds now rolled southwards, though a single glance west showed silent evidence that more of winter's assault would come. The jagged peaks of Ulheim held, for now, the rumbling tide of future storms, though even those great mountains could only stand firm for so long. This, Mary realized, was but a respite, a brief pause, in the hard season to come.

The newly-appointed handmaiden stood on the balcony of her princess' chambers atop Castle Calonar. The fortress-home of her liege-lord's House rose above the Northern Keep, offering Mary a wonderous view of the Northern Keep. The city was blanketed with snow; slanted rooftops, markets and plazas, fields and streets, all glistened with the reemergence of the weakened sun. Even the city's gardens, scarred by the recent battle against the Deathmage's monsters, had been blanketed, as though Nature meant to shield the people from the destruction of their beloved, natural refuge.

The city was stirring again, after having spent days sheltering against Vara's Storm. Workers struggled to clear the streets. Vendors and merchants reopened their shops. Clergy traveled from house to house, checking on the welfare of their fellow citizens. The people of the Northlands were accustomed to their home's harsh winters; and life resumed as it always would.

The cold breeze stirred Mary's long hair. The chill was not unpleasant, for the handmaiden was a child of the Northlands. Winter was not the great enemy to her and her countrymen that it was to the people of the South. She was not bothered by the cold; rather, she welcomed it. This was the season of family, of friends and… lovers.

No, the cold was not what chilled Mary's heart.

In the days since the departure of Tomas and Prince Rogan, Mary had spent more and more of her time on this balcony. As Princess Kyla's new handmaiden, and with their shared sadness at the absence of their loves, the two women had drawn to one another, both giving and gaining comfort in their shared sadness. Mary had been granted Tomas' quarters; as his betrothed, she had a duty to maintain his property, his effects, and his home. Despite this, she spent much more time here, with her princess. Kyla, though publicly strong and independent, a radiant beacon of hope to the city, privately suffered during her husband's long absences. Only behind the closed doors of her private quarters could Kyla let go of her public mask. Her husband was away on quest, her father was slowly dying from some mysterious poison, her homeland was under threat from an unknown evil, and she was pregnant with her first child. The princess often insisted on her new handmaiden's constant presence, sharing meals together, attending governmental and religious functions together, and even sleeping in the same bed. For her part, the newly-appointed handmaiden was not averse, despite the delay in her role as an archivist for House Calonar.

Mary had studied for years in the archivist's trade. House Calonar provided opportunities for all children to attend school, learning letters and figures. Her father had insisted, despite the needs of their farm, that his daughter attend and learn. Mary had taken to writing and histories as though born to it. Her father dedicated much of their family's limited money to locating books for his only child. Her mother had petitioned Princess Kyla for assistance in securing Mary a place at the new university in the Northern Keep, a request the loving first daughter of House Calonar had granted. As a culmination of her studies and her service to the ruling family of the Northlands, Mary had been appointed an archivist for the Noble House.

But then their men went on quest.

Princess Kyla had made no request, no command rescinding Mary's appointment. But this strong, public showing had lasted only days. Mary lived in Tomas' quarters, close to the princess. Mary could not help but observe the sorrow behind Kyla's shining pearlescent eyes. Days had passed since her betrothal to Tomas, such limited time for them to take joy in one another. Mary knew the sorrow her princess felt, for her heart also was burdened with loneliness.

The Princess had objected, of course. She was selfless in the extreme and knew of Mary's anticipation for her new duties as House Calonar's newest archivist. Princess Kyla had even tried ordering Mary to her new tasks. For her part, Mary had curtsied, said, "Yes, your Highness," and then assumed the role of handmaiden to the first daughter of Calonar.

Standing on the balcony of Kyla's private quarters, Mary's thoughts often drifted to her missing love. Her eyes shown with unshed tears as the handmaiden fought against an aching despair. In her duties as the princess' companion, her personal attendant, Mary kept her own sorrow locked away, buried so deep that even the mystical first daughter of Calonar could hardly sense it. Instead, the handmaiden absorbed Kyla's sadness, fear, and worry. She held her princess when the tears came. She laughed at her attempts at good humor. She accompanied her for all official functions and responsibilities. But, in the silence of her own soul, in the quiet moments outside her duty, the handmaiden to Princess Kyla looked out on the snow-covered capital of the Northlands and felt so very, very alone.

The view from the chambers of Princess Kyla were spectacular, to say the least. Situated as it was on the top of a great escarpment at the center of the Northern Keep, Castle Calonar provided an excellent vantage point for the viewing of the surrounding city at any level, but from the highest floors where the royal family lived, the sight was truly spectacular. No doubt, the young woman thought often to herself, the reverse view from the ground up to the mighty fortress, rising as though to touch the sky, would be all the more impressive to any enemy that thought to breach the incredible defenses of Castle Calonar. Even beyond the impressive physical walls of the castle, in the center of the mighty fortress rose a single tower, higher than all others. The tower seemed to look out over the whole of the Northlands, standing eternal vigil over its people against anything that would threaten the peace that House Calonar had struggled for so long to create.

A high-pitched but very brief squeak of discomfort drew Mary's attention back into the room. Currently, Kyla was lying back on her great canopied bed with the front of her dress open. The Queen sat beside her daughter with a strange implement plugged into an ear at one end and widened out into a cone at the other. This end Queen Nora had placed against her daughter's bared chest, and it seemed to Mary that the ageing queen of the Northlands was listening to something.

A sudden burst of frigid air lunged through the open balcony doors, as though reaching for the first daughter of Calonar. Queen Nora glanced at Mary, and the handmaiden instantly obeyed the unspoken command, shutting and latching the doors against the sudden assault against her princess. Her Majesty had ordered the doors open to allow a few moments of fresh air, but moments were all that could be allowed against the brittle winter. Vara's Storm had passed and a brief thaw had begun, but still the Northlands remained under siege; the Speakers all believed this season would be a long, hard one.

Mary's mother was in their home town of Snowholm, some leagues to the north. A secret whisper deep in the handmaiden's soul suggested spending the winter there, as Tomas quested with Prince Rogan. A shadowy corner of her heart reminded Mary of family and home and love. This temptation, though, found no purchase against her duties to House Calonar and its first daughter. The King himself would have released Mary from her duties, of course; good King Cylan had not a single unkind bone in his frail body. The handmaiden knew that, if she asked, the King and his gentle queen would let her return home; but like Mary, Kyla was also missing the man she loved, and with Lord Calonar's poisoning and the Queen's constant efforts to maintain his health, the Princess had assumed not only her husband's duties, but those of the entire royal family.

Queen Nora was assisted by Ilse, the priestess of the Harvest Mother who, despite having completed her novitiate only in the past year, had been chosen by Nora to aid in the care of Kyla during her daughter's pregnancy. Ilse and Mary had arrived at the

Keep in the same season, and grown quite close in the ensuing years. They were quite a study in contrasts, these two young women. Whereas the handmaiden was nearly as tall as a man, Ilse was much shorter, only a little taller than the average Sylva. The physical requirements of her duties and her upbringing on her father's farm had granted Mary a solid body and softspoken muscles, whereas Ilse seemed as frail as a spring breeze. These deceptive appearances were emphasized by their typical clothes; Mary wore the traditional Northlands dress, with its white blouse and her favored green apron, with her betrothal now tied at the right, while Ilse wore the undyed wool robe that made the priestess seem even smaller than she really was. Mary's friend never wore cosmetics or jewelry, while the handmaiden herself was often well-adorned, her princess being almost fanatical in wanting to enhance Mary's quiet beauty. They had both seen the same sixteen winters, and shared similar backgrounds as the daughters of peasant farmers, granted the hope of a better future by House Calonar.

Mary had watched the two priestesses, Ilse and Queen Nora, as they examined the princess. Normally, especially for someone as important as Princess Kyla, the two clerics of the Harvest Mother would have employed their magic. This could not be, though. Mary glanced back out the glass doors blocking Kyla's balcony. Vara's Storm had not only been a terrible blizzard, incapacitating the Northlands for weeks, but it had also disrupted the Winds of Magic. Since the storm's passing, Parden Esha, Cardinal Tain, and the Queen herself had all reported their inability to control their respective powers. Magic was still present, of course, but nearly uncontrollable. Thus, the Queen had begun employing new Uldra technologies in her care for Princess Kyla.

After a few moments, Nora motioned for the princess to sit up and fully remove the top of her northland dress. Seeing this done, the Queen placed the strange device against Kyla's back. "Breathe," the mother commanded the daughter. Even before the King's coronation, the people of the Northlands had long considered his wife the mother of the Northlands. Queen Nora's kindness and loving devotion to the people under her husband's protection made her beloved by all, second perhaps only to the King's aunt, the Lady Alexia. Despite this near-worship by the people, however, the Queen never commanded or asserted her tremendous authority and influence, instead softly asking and politely thanking. Even the servants who attended the aging Lady of House Calonar would have been hard pressed to name a single instance in which Queen Nora had given an order or even raised her voice. The exception to this gentle nature, however, was in her treatment of those under her medical care.

The Queen moved the strange, Uldra instrument to another part of her daughter's back. "Again," she instructed. Her typical gentleness and quiet tenderness were never to be seen when she was tending to a patient. The Queen gestured to Ilse, and the younger cleric held a similar device to her own ear, while pressing the conical end to Kyla's abdomen. Although grateful for the loving care they received under the High

Priestess of the Harvest Mother, all of Queen Nora's patients would unanimously agree that health was infinitely preferable to the stern and inescapable commandments of the Lady Calonar when caring for the sick and injured. Queen Nora would do anything to return a person to health, no matter how uncomfortable or embarrassing a treatment may become.

Princess Kyla rolled her pearlescent eyes in slight frustration but complied with her mother's instructions. "I really don't think all this is necessary, Mother," she insisted.

"Really?" the mother asked her daughter in mock surprise. "Well, if you don't think it's necessary, then it probably isn't." Lady Calonar handed the instrument to Ilse, her smiling assistant glancing at Mary while she put the strange Uldric devices in a large bag. The Queen stood as though to leave, motioning for Ilse to collect the rest of their strange Uldric implements. "After all," Lady Calonar added, "you would know much more about pregnancy than I would. It's not as though I have gone through several myself and officiated at dozens more over the many more years I have been alive than you."

"Yes, Mother," Kyla sighed in capitulation. "You're right. I should listen to you. Let's finish the examination."

"Actually, we're done," the queen said. "You can put your clothes back on."

"I'd rather not," the princess said, making a face and gently running her hands along her breasts. "You wouldn't believe how sensitive my nipples have gotten."

Nora glanced at her daughter as Ilse collected the various tools and instruments. "No," the queen and mother murmured, smoothing the front of her simple green dress. "I don't suppose I would."

Mary had noticed that, despite her status as Queen of the Northlands and Lady of House Calonar, Nora rarely wore anything more fanciful than the simple dresses common to most women of the Northlands. Today she wore a green blouse and skirt with a light blue apron, tied at the right. As always, no crown or jeweled ornament of any kind decorated the Queen's head; she did not even put in a fashionable braid, preferring to allow her graying blond hair to flow freely down her back.

Kyla rolled her pearlescent blue eyes, the most obvious inheritance from her Halvan father. She stretched out on her bed with a warm smile that seemed to beat back the cool air.

"You'll have to adapt to that sensitivity, dear," the queen added, helping her daughter dress. "It should pass in a few weeks." She paused, a knowing smile fluttering on her lips. "Until, of course, you start nursing." Queen Nora motioned to Mary, who brought a blanket forward. "Also, with the weather going sour on us, you'll have to take more precautions." Mary settled the blanket over her princess' legs and abdomen.

"Traitor," Kyla grumbled.

"Highness," Mary replied neutrally.

Nora motioned for Ilse to put the medical bag away and asked Mary to bring tea. The queen crossed the bedchamber to a large table beside the fireplace and sat in one of the deeply upholstered chairs surrounding it. Ilse hurried to put her mentor's bag near the door and stand behind the high priestess. "The beginning of a pregnancy can be dangerous because the mother feels so good," she said. "For the first stage of the pregnancy, the mother feels few, if any, of the more annoying side effects of being gravid, aside from morning sickness, and often continues with her life as though nothing were different. But even at this stage of the pregnancy, the child can be hurt. The child can become sick, especially if the mother takes ill."

Mary poured cups of tea and passed them to the various women, making sure to include in Kyla's the herbal ingredients commanded by the Queen. "You're almost as bad as my mother," the princess muttered somewhat sullenly, taking the cup.

"I live only to serve, your Highness," Mary replied with a smile and glint in her eyes.

"I'm afraid you'll just have to get used to people trying to take care of you, *Kasaya*," Queen Nora said. "It comes with expecting a child."

"Well, it's annoying!" Kyla insisted. The princess sat up and stretched "It's not like I can't still get around on my own."

"See the blessing that Rogan's quest has granted you, *Kasaya*."

Kyla stared over her teacup at her mother. "What?"

"If your dashing prince was here, then he would be even more insistent on helping you than any of us have been. He would also get so overprotective of you that you'd think yourself a prisoner."

Mary sat on the bed, beside her princess. Kyla leaned against her handmaiden. "Was the King like that during your pregnancies, your Majesty?" Mary asked, sipping at her own cup of tea.

"Oh my, yes," the aging queen laughed. "During my first pregnancy, I thought he was going to lock me in Cyras' tower and throw away anything sharp." She sipped at her tea. "Each man has his own peculiarity, but for the King, it was tripping."

"Tripping?" Kyla asked.

"He was terrified I would trip over something and land on my stomach, hurting little Kyle in the process."

"Did you know it was going to be a boy?" Mary asked.

The queen smiled. "Even without my Truthsight, I would have known. I couldn't get enough meat and cheese, but I never got any heartburn. Plus, you would not believe how good my hair looked." She ran a hand somewhat ruefully through her greying blond locks. "You girls just never gave the same lustrousness."

"So," Kyla asked, "it's not all bad?"

"Well," the queen smiled, "your father certainly appreciated how large my breasts got while I was pregnant with your brother."

"Mother!"

"You have to take the good with the bad, *Kasaya*."

The princess rubbed at her swollen feet. "Well, there's plenty of one," she grumbled.

"At least it only lasts nine months, your Highness," Mary said.

Queen Nora shook her head. "Actually, it will be some months longer than that."

"I'm sorry?"

"Like her father, Kyla is Halvan. Halvan pregnancies last a little more than a year."

"Oh my," Mary breathed.

The queen laughed softly. "Yes, I was rather surprised myself, Vaeta waxed and waned nine times with no labor. I was almost beside myself with worry by the time I finally delivered."

"Nobody told you?" Kyla asked.

"Who could?" the queen countered. "Halvans were exceptionally rare during the days of the Republic, rejected by the Sylvai and Human communities, and openly hunted by the Church. Most had to live in hiding or, like your father, travel the wilds to survive. Mine was the first Halvan child my village had ever seen." Queen Nora sighed then, her eyes going distant. "Fortunately, Alexia arrived a few weeks before I delivered. She had knowledge of Halvan pregnancies."

"Are you sure the child will be a Halvan, your Majesty?" Mary asked. "After all, the Princess may be, but the Prince is fully Human." She glanced at Ilse. "Must a child born to a single Halvan parent be Halvan?"

The priestess shrugged. "There are few records and little direct evidence," the priestess admitted. "But one would think that the child could be fully Halvan, fully Human, or some mixture of both."

Queen Nora was quiet for a moment. "I have seen it," she finally replied. "Kyla's first child will be a Halvan boy."

"First," Kyla said with a roll of her soft pearlescent eyes.

The queen smiled. "Oh yes," she said. "This will not be your only pregnancy."

"Do you know how many?" Mary asked.

Nora shook her head. "I'm afraid it doesn't quite work that way, dear," she replied. "Looking into the future rarely gives one a perfect view of what is to come."

Mary leaned forward with deep interest burning in her eyes. "What's it like?" she asked intently.

The queen was quiet as she tried to find the words to describe what her Truthsight showed her. "It's hard to explain," she admitted. "I've had the Truthsight for so long now. It's much like trying to describe color to someone who's been blind since birth.

"Imagine you are standing in a river. The past is behind you, the future in front, and the river is flowing forward. Ahead, the river forks in an infinite number of places. Some of the tributaries are larger than others, which means you are more likely to go down one of those. You can look forward to try to see what is to come, but any motion on your part could send you off into another fork that you never looked down. So the best you can do is look ahead as far as you can see and pick the most desirable course, then pray nothing happens to send you off in some random direction."

"And you must also be careful that your actions, or the actions of others, do not send you off that course," a deep voice floated on the air from the open doorway. Standing there was the royal Spymaster Rashid, looking as perfectly male as only he could with close-fitting tunic and trousers dyed dark colors and his perfectly styled dark hair swaying in a breeze that seemed to follow the sensual spy wherever he went.

On the baron's heels came Chandra, the nearly invisible woman who was Rashid's most trusted agent, dressed as always in inconspicuous clothing and with her short brown hair somehow managing to cover a fair part of her face. Mary never knew what to think about House Calonar's most senior agent, since Chandra rarely spoke to anyone other than Rashid and the other members of the intelligence service. Despite her silence, when the spy did choose to voice her thoughts, those observations were given great weight by Rashid and the other members of the King's Advisory Council. Chandra had a plain, unassuming face and effortlessly blended into the background of any situation, and the woman's dark eyes saw everything.

Mary stood and bowed to the Baron Tressalon. "You speak as though from experience, my lord Baron," the young woman said.

"Unfortunately, only a passing familiarity," the nobleman sighed in mock sorrow. Rashid waved Mary back into her seat beside Princess Kyla and took a chair Chandra brought in from the adjoining room to sit down across the small table at which his queen rested. The baron also took a stack of parchment from Chandra, letting his aide cross the room and stand against a far wall with her arms crossed. "Her Majesty and I have tried, on occasion, to use her talents to neutralize threats before they appear, but it never seems to work."

"Oftentimes, if a threat is meant to appear, it will do so in one form or another regardless of our actions," the queen explained, nodding a reply to Rashid's perfectly fluid curtsey.

"So much the better," a gravelly voice that possessed none of the musical tones of the spymaster's tumbled in behind the olive-skinned baron. General Killdare, the ugly old soldier who had been in service to House Calonar longer than any other Human, entered and made a choppy bow to his queen before sitting down beside Baron Tressalon in another chair brought in from the next room. The iron-haired veteran looked as he always did, unhappy with everything and everyone around him. The scarred warrior drew his aide into the room with a quick jerk of the head. Captain

Klug Rainer bowed low to the Queen and offered a number of parchments to his commander before withdrawing some distance without comment. To Mary, this seemed unnatural since the jovial captain was known throughout the Northern Keep as a man of constant whimsical comments in any situation and never seemed impressed by anyone's rank, especially his own. Rainer would offer his wit to any and all regardless of the situation. It wasn't until Mary saw the tall officer move to a corner with Ilse that Mary recalled that he was, in fact, the priestess's father. No doubt the two wanted to take advantage of the opportunity to visit since their respective duties probably left few opportunities for family.

"You have a problem with prophecy, General?" Kyla was asking.

"I have a problem with acting against someone for something they might do rather than something they did do."

"The General is a firm believer in free will," Rashid smiled.

"What brings you here, gentlemen?" Queen Nora asked.

"Updates, your Majesty," Killdare replied, scanning through the parchments in his hand.

Rashid nodded. "With the King ill, and Prince Rogan on another of his adventures, the general and I thought it best to relay all relevant information to you and our lovely princess."

"And we may need some official decisions," Killdare added.

Kyla sat up straighter, a mask of noble wisdom descending onto her beautiful face. Mary crossed the room and accepted Killdare's dispatches, returning them to her princess. "Is there anything threatening?" she asked, quickly scanning the documents.

Rashid shook his head. "Quite the opposite, your Highness."

"After Anninihus's attack," Killdare added, "the Wood has been quiet as a tomb."

"We expected that for a few weeks," Rashid said, rising to pour some wine for himself and Killdare from a crystal decanter on a small table near the door. "The blizzard effectively shut down most of the Northlands. Now that the weather has warmed somewhat and the roads are, if not comfortable, at least passable, we expected at least some minor increase in incidents." The baron returned to his seat.

Kyla held up one of the reports with a fearful look on her face. "General, what is this about missing Walker teams?" she asked.

"A number of them went missing at nearly the same time Rogan left the city," the old veteran replied.

"An interesting coincidence," Queen Nora mused.

"You know I have little faith in coincidence, your Majesty," Rashid said. "I've already dispatched someone to acquire more information."

"You may want Parden Esha to help," Mary said, then bit her lip for speaking out of turn.

Seeing Mary's blushing at her embarrassment, Princess Kyla put a hand on hers in instant forgiveness and reassurance. "It's a valid point and a good suggestion," she said before turning back to the spymaster. "Esha would be able to at least tell you if the Walkers are alive."

"Not lately," Killdare grumbled.

"I've already made the inquiry," Rashid said patiently. "Despite the disruption in magic caused by Vara's Storm, Esha and her acolytes might still be able to learn something."

The general snorted. Although Killdare regularly employed adepts in his operations, the veteran's impatience with anything mystical was well known.

"It costs us nothing to ask," Rashid insisted evenly.

All eyes turned at another arrival. Ward stood, as though having just appeared, in the doorway to Kyla's sitting room. Mary was always taken aback at the size of the Archaeknight leader. He was massive, nearly as tall as an Uldra, but more evenly muscled. Despite his incredible size and imposing strength, the commander of House Calonar's elite bodyguard moved with an impossible grace. His every step was silent, except when he wished to be heard. Hailing from the mysterious continent of Maka, Ward had the dark, bronzed skin of that land, with hair the color of night and eyes to match. The only disruption of this coloring was the crossed-diamond sigil of House Calonar tattooed over his left eye. "We're ready," he said in a voice and mysterious as a forest.

The chief Archaeknight gestured behind him and a young man stepped forward. He was tall, though still nearly infantile compared to the towering leader of House Calonar's elite bodyguards. The new arrival was lean but powerful, his tanned body speaking of a life of physical effort, of capable endurance. His sandy hair was cut short, in the style of the House Guard, and he stood at rigid attention in the presence of so many of the Norther Keep's leaders.

"This is Lukas," Ward said. "He's our newest inductee and has just begun training."

"One of mine?" Killdare asked, noticing the young man's military bearing.

"Yes sir," Lukas said, his eyes locked forward. "Formerly of the 3rd Battalion, 2nd Brigade."

"You were at the gardens," Rashid noted.

"Yes, sir."

"He saved quite a few civilians," Ward said. "Risked his life covering the retreat and then stayed to help the Prince evacuate survivors. That's when I noticed him." The chief Archaeknight nodded his head towards Kyla. "He's not inducted or fully trained, so I'm leaving him behind, assigned to the Princess."

"How many are you taking?" Queen Nora asked.

"All," Ward replied with a grimace. "The King has ordered me to take all seven Archaeknights in the city and gather the others on my way." His tone, though even, could not mask his displeasure with the order.

"Not the King's order," Queen Nora said as she sipped her tea.

The Archaeknight leader straitened in surprise, then crossed the room and knelt in front of his queen. Despite dropping to one knee, still he was higher than the seated Lady of House Calonar. "I still don't like it, your Majesty," he argued not for the first time. "Our duty is to the Royal Family. Our place is here, protecting you. Especially now," this he said with a glance to Princess Kyla.

Queen Nora shook her head. "It must be," she assured the chief Archaeknight. "Rogan will need you in Tordenia, and for his journey home."

Ward bowed his head and stood. Mary had noticed that the Archaeknights would voice their objections, but once a command was given in any form by a member of House Calonar, their obedience was immediate.

"What's your plan?" Rashid asked.

Ward glanced at the spymaster. "I'll need to travel to Ironheartshaven to collect the others. I'll assemble the team on the way and take ship there." He looked back to his queen. "We'll need half a year to reach the Western Empire."

The Lady of House Calonar nodded. "You'll arrive in time."

"Why not call ahead and have your team meet in Clayton?" General Killdare suggested. "Save some time?"

Ward shook his head. "The storm has blocked our communication," he replied. "We'll have to do it the old-fashioned way."

"Has there been any progress in overcoming the mystical disruption?" Queen Nora asked.

Both Rashid and Killdare shook their heads. "Esha reports none of her students can safely tap into their powers," the spymaster said. "The Tower Mistress herself and maybe two or three of her strongest can use the most minor of their spells."

"The caravans are moving again?" Kyla asked as she noted the report.

General Killdare nodded. "The merchants waste no time in moving. The blizzard caught several of them by surprise. When the snows eased up, most of them started for home, and our supply convoys are again on the move."

"As we will be," Ward said, moving towards the door.

"This raises a somewhat delicate issue, by the way," Rashid added.

Killdare nodded towards the dispatches in Kyla's hands. "With the convoys moving, especially out to the Woodwall Fortresses, there's been an increase in attacks."

"It happens all the time," Chandra noted. "Those convoys are always being hit by bandits. That's why they take guards."

Rashid leaned back in his chair, steepling his fingers. "True," he said softly. "Once the convoys leave the Wood and the protection of the Walkers behind, they often get attacked. But a few things seem odd."

"Which are?" Kyla asked.

"These new attacks are happening inside the forest," Killdare pointed out. "And the bandits are only hitting our convoys. The civilian, non-Northland merchants are being let through without incident."

Rashid nodded and glanced at Chandra. "What do you think?" he asked.

The agent shrugged. "More data."

Rashid stood and finished his wine. "Agreed," he said. "We'll try to gather more information and meet again later this week, your Highness," he said with another florid bow to Kyla.

The princess nodded. "Thank you, Rashid, General." She looked at Ward, and Mary noticed her once again fighting to control her emotions, to keep them out of her shining, pearlescent eyes. "Good fortune in your mission," she said to the chief Archaeknight.

War bowed to her. "I'll bring him back in one piece, your Highness." The leader of the Archaeknights glanced at Mary. "The Prince, and his squire."

Kyla held her handmaiden's hand. As the servants of House Calonar began filing out, the princess noticed something and held up the last of the reports. "Also, I'm seeing these reports of Esha's apprentices exploding. Would you tell the Parden to suspend her experiments until the effects of Vara's Storm have passed?"

Chapter 11

"Mary?" Princess Kyla called out from the darkness of her bedchamber.

Night had fallen. Vaeta shown through the last of the heavy clouds that doggedly refused to leave the Northlands. The moonlight cast everything in a pale, almost ethereal glow

"Mary?" Kyla called out again.

"Here, your Highness," the handmaiden called out from the balcony.

Kyla gathered her dressing gown closer around herself and stepped out to join her handmaiden. The princess had been unable to sleep through the night since the departure of Prince Rogan and his team. No doubt, having awoken and found Mary not in bed beside her, she had come looking. Mary had also awoken, the gnawing emptiness in her chest had roused the handmaiden. She had stood, her arms held close about her chest, for some unknown eternity on the balcony, her eyes filled with unshed tears and her fears replaying all the tragedies that seemed certain to befall her Tomas.

Without a word, Kyla crossed to the edge of the balcony where Mary stood, looking out on the white-capped city below, and put her arms around the young woman, enveloping them both in a heavy blanket. The princess pressed her head against Mary's shoulder, saying nothing.

"I miss him so much," Mary finally whispered.

"I know," Kyla replied, gently turning them back. She led her friend back inside to the warmth of the fire and closed the doors behind. "It's always hard when they have to go away."

Mary sat on the couch Kyla led her to and drew her knees to her chest. "Does it ever get easier?" she whispered.

Kyla sat down beside her friend and again put her arms around the girl, wrapping them as tightly as possible within the comfort of the heavy blanket. "Do you want me to lie to you?" she asked.

Tears again fell, and Mary shook a little with some lonely sadness, but mostly with aching fear. "What if something happens?" she asked in a very small voice.

The princess gently, but firmly, drew Mary's gaze to meet her own with a small hand. "You can't ever let yourself think that," she said. "They are fine and will be fine."

Mary sniffed loudly and shook her head. "We had such little time! It's not fair that he had to leave."

Kyla reached over, fetched a small handkerchief, and handed it over to her friend. "Trust me," the princess replied. "It doesn't matter how much time you have. It's never enough.

The young woman took the handkerchief and waved it in the air. "I swear if I could get my hands on that stupid Balshazzar . . . I'd . . . I don't know what I'd do!"

Kyla sighed and rested her small head against her friend's shoulder. "Then it might be better that we sent the men," she said sagely. "If you and I had gone to the Western Empire, there's no telling what we would have done to him."

"It's a wonder I put up with him!" Mary snapped suddenly. "I knew he wasn't going to stay in the Keep forever, and I still…"

"I was saying a lot of the same things after Rogan and I were betrothed, and he had to leave to rescue Aebreanna."

Mary flushed, and more tears welled up in her eyes. Kyla noticed this and softly brushed a stray lock of hair from her friend's face. "What is it?" the princess asked.

"They're going to be alone for so long," Mary replied. "They're going to be off on some great adventure so far from here for so long."

"Stop," Kyla commanded. "Don't let your thoughts go there."

"But Baroness Tressalon is so beautiful and so—"

"But she wouldn't," the princess replied firmly. "She and Rogan have been alone together on countless missions, and I know that they've never done anything like that."

"But how do you know?" Mary demanded.

Kyla leaned back, pulling Mary with her. The princess rested her small head on Mary's strong shoulder and sighed. "You just have to trust that Tomas would never betray you."

"If he's smart, he won't," Mary said grimly. "If he did I'd . . . I don't even know what I would do! But it would be bad."

Kyla smiled an evil smile. "I can think of a few things," she said with a wicked laugh.

"He might like those," Mary replied, smiling despite herself.

"That's the problem with men," the princess said, rising and pouring her friend a glass of water and drinking a large glass herself. "They get so confused when they're being punished and start to like it after a while."

"Men are stupid," the young woman declared, taking the water and sipping from it.

A knock at the door drew Kyla's attention away. "What is it?" she demanded.

Lukas the Archaeknight trainee Ward had assigned to the Princess' protection, entered. "Your Highness?" he asked cautiously.

"Lukas," the princess said exasperatedly. "Can't I go ten minutes without you checking up on me?"

The young soldier thought about his princess' question and finally answered, "I don't think so, your Highness. Of course, miracles can happen." Since assuming responsibility for Kyla, Lukas had not only tasked the dozen soldiers under him to their specific duties, but also taken charge of the princess's daily schedule and declaring himself the final arbiter of not only who would be allowed an audience but also where Kyla could go and when. Only once did the princess put her foot down and try to issue a contrary order, to which Lukas simply replied, "Yes, ma'am," and proceeded to ignore the order.

"What do you want?" she demanded.

"I heard voices and wanted to make sure everything was alright."

"We're fine, Lukas," Kyla insisted.

"Also nearly naked," Mary pointed out. drawing the heavy blanket further around the two women. Although both wore dressing gowns and caps, Mary had grown uncomfortable around Lukas. The young man was infinitely courteous and even deferential to Kyla and her handmaiden, excepting where their protection was concerned. He was professional and implacable and self-sacrificing in the extreme. Mary had no obvious, overt reason to be uncomfortable with Lukas' presence, yet still she found herself avoiding him, even the contact of his eyes. With her Tomas leagues away, she found herself especially uncomfortable with this man being near while she was in any state of undress.

Kyla glanced at Mary and nodded. "I don't want you just barging in her anymore, Lukas," she commanded.

"Yes, ma'am," the bodyguard replied. He turned to leave but paused. "Oh, since you're awake anyway, Highness?"

"Yes?"

"The Queen said you needed more rest in the morning, so I took the liberty of cancelling your meeting with the Merchant's Guild representatives."

"Lukas," Kyla said in a low growl. "You are not my clerk. You will not adjust my schedule to suit your whims."

"Yes, ma'am."

The princess rolled her pearlescent eyes. "Don't just 'yes, ma'am' me!" she said with rising heat. "You will not change my schedule without first speaking to either my clerk or Mary! Is that clear?"

"Yes, ma'am."

Now the princess was growling. "Dammit, Lukas!" As though to emphasize Kyla's indignation, a small explosion echoed up from the city.

Mary glanced towards the balcony. "I though you ordered Parden Esha to suspend her experiments?"

"I did," Kyla snapped. Her eyes flashed to Lukas, who was maintaining a bland neutrality. "I think people are getting a little too comfortable with ignoring me."

"Yes, ma'am."

"In the morning, I'll have breakfast with Mary, and we'll meet with the Merchant Guild. When I get done, Mary and I'll go to the Temple for a bath." The princess leaned conspiratorially towards her handmaiden. "Then we can talk more about our stupid men."

Lukas cleared his throat. "Actually, your Highness—"

"Oh, for Goddess's sake!" Kyla snapped, another explosion from Esha's tower seeming to agree with the irate princess. "I want to take a bath with my friend, and that's exactly what I'm going to do!"

"Then I'll arrange a proper detail to clear the temple before you get there, your Highness."

Kyla dropped her head in her hands with an aggravated sigh. Mary put a comforting arm around her princess's shoulders.

II

Ulheim

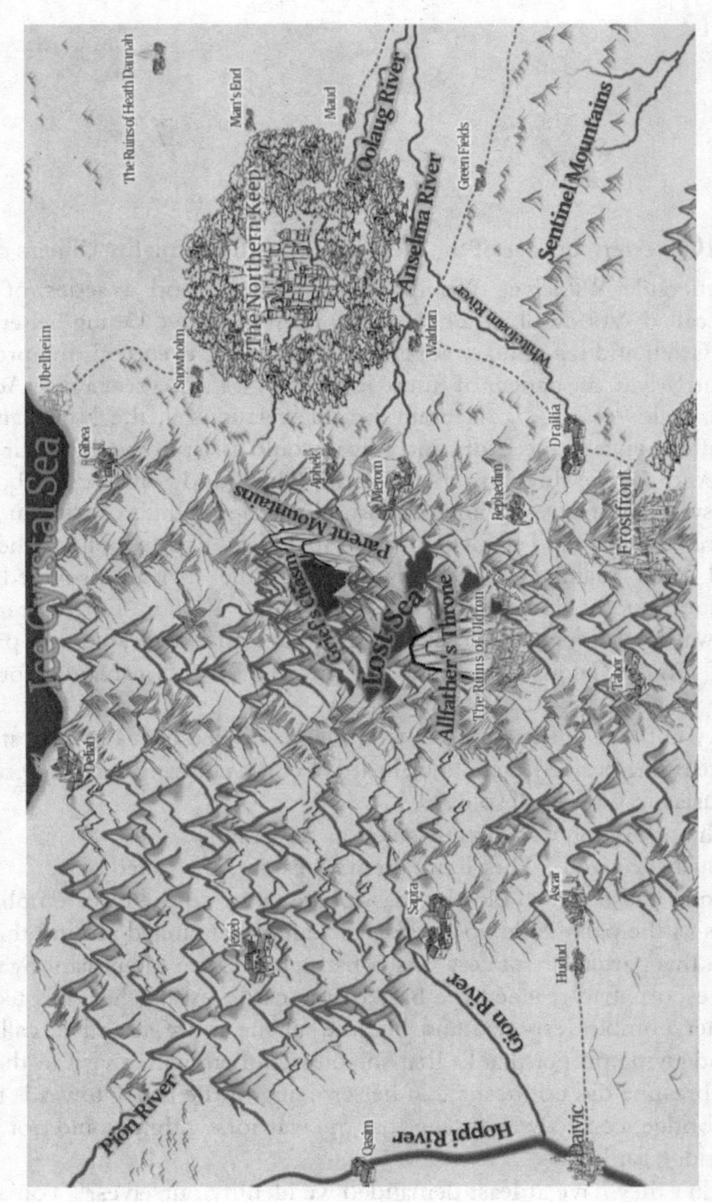

The Ruins of Heath Daunah
Man's End
Maud
Oolaug River
Green Fields
Sentinel Mountains
The Northern Keep
Anselma River
Whitelam River
Wahran
Drailla
Frostfront
Ubelheim
Snowsholm
Gihea
Aphek
Merom
Rephedim
Ice Crystal Sea
Parent Mountains
Grief's Chasm
Lost Sea
Allfather's Throne
The Ruins of Uldron
Tabor
Deliah
Jezeb
Sapta
Ascar
Huabul
Gion River
Pion River
Hoppi River
Qesm
Baivic

Chapter 12

On the western border of the Northlands, with the mighty Ulheim on one side and the venerable Wildelves Wood on the other, stood a series of fortresses collectively called Woodwall. After an invasion by a massive Druug helter years ago, good King Cylan and his military advisors realized that, even with the protection of the Uldra and Sylvai, the danger of future incursions was too great a risk. Additionally, King Cylan, in his efforts to maintain amiable relations in the Northlands, hoped having a buffer between the Uldra and Sylvai would assist in cooling their traditional animosity. And so, the three groups: Human, Uldra, and Sylvai, contributed to the raising of a system of fortresses and outposts along the foothills of Ulheim. The Uldra designed the system and provided raw materials and supplies, the Humans constructed and maintained Woodwall, and the Sylvai provided constant communication to the Northern Keep. Thus, the Western Fortresses became a reliable bulwark, an impenetrable line held by the most dedicated and professional warriors of House Calonar, ensuring the safety of the Northlands for an entire generation.

"Don't you think this is a little much?" Tomas yelled to his knight, straining his voice despite riding beside Rogan to be heard over the cheering, whistling, and waving of the enthusiastic Woodwall soldiers.

All of this adoration was directly solely at Aebreanna.

Rogan just shrugged. "They'll tire themselves out," he called out.

Aebreanna had taken to blowing passionate kisses to the most emphatic of her worshippers as the party rode up the narrow ramp that circled around the steep hill upon which this particular fortress was constructed. Once the radiant Sylva and her road-weary escorts had reached the base of the castle's walls, her devoted admirers could see her humble response and became all the more attentive, calling to the baroness and giving proper thanks that she blessed them with a visit to their humble fortress. Aebreanna did not hesitate in her crossing of the bailey towards the castle's raised drawbridge, correctly assuming that the warriors within would not hesitate to lower the bridge for her.

"Shouldn't they have at least demanded we identify ourselves?" Tomas yelled as the drawbridge bowed low to Aebreanna and her attendants.

"Do you honestly think there's anyone on that wall that doesn't know who we are?" Rogan yelled back.

"Still," the squire argued, "we could be disguised or something. What about security procedures?"

"Esha has spell-slingers posted at every Woodwall station. Trust me, we were getting checked out before we got within a mile of this place. How else do you think they knew Aebreanna was coming before they could even see it was her?"

The divine baroness led her entourage across the bridge, her pure-white Sylvai pony taking up a bouncing trot that pulled the glowing Sylva away from her dim associates. Stick and Urge, who normally reveled in the attention their riders shunned, became surly as attention was so fervently showered on another mount.

Aebreanna guided Mayva toward the center of the courtyard and the raised platform usually reserved for award ceremonies, promotions, and other important functions. The Sylvai pony effortlessly leapt to the stage with a flourish of her snowy mane and tail that matched the joyous flaring of Aebreanna's own wintery mane. Tomas and the other ignored males were abandoned at the gate. Had they even wanted to join with their teammate, there existed no path to do so. The Woodwall soldiers surged towards the stage, the mob eager to pay homage to the visiting hero and her sidekicks. So while their Sylva companion reveled in the well-deserved worship of her glory, the men simply sat astride their horses, ignored.

Once Mayva had finished a series of spins and prancing hops, Aebreanna held out her hands to a pair of soldiers she graciously selected with a crocking of her fingers. These joyful men stumbled forward, trembling in the presence of the Baroness Tressalon, offering her assistance in dismounting the white pony. Each of the warriors was rewarded with a kiss on the cheek that made the hardened soldiers swoon. Another pair was blessed by their Sylva mistress by being allowed to take charge of her pony, and were similarly rewarded. Striding to the center of the platform, the Sylva turned her back to the crowd and let her fur-trimmed cloak slide off her slight shoulders, revealing the leather skirt and halter she had dressed in that morning in defiance of the bitter cold. She turned to face the crowd and posed in a sultry manner that highlighted her long legs and wicked opalescent eyes. If possible, the soldiers went even further insane.

"I wondered why she dressed like that," Tomas noted.

"She's been to these forts before," Rogan pointed out. "The Sisters of the Lady of Light make a lot of morale visits out here. Aebreanna makes a point of joining some of them."

"Can't imagine why."

The knight shrugged. "It's good for the men here; let's them blow off some steam." Besides, Rogan added with a mildly-relieved look, "After the village, she could use a little…"

"Positive attention?" The squire shivered slightly despite the thick cloak wrapped around his lean body. "Isn't she cold?" he asked.

A soldier younger even than Tomas began climbing the platform without need for the steps that were only a few feet to his left. Aebreanna smiled at his enthusiasm and, with a suggestive sway of her hips, walked over to where her admirer was climbing. Placing the tip of her steel-toed leather boot on his forehead, the sensual baroness gently ran her foot along the edge of his face and down to his chest before shoving him off her stage. The young soldier's comrades caught and cheered him for his courage.

"Right now that woman is being warmed by adoration," Rogan said.

Beraht summed his feelings up as only he could. The Uldra spit on the ground and muttered, "Sylva witch."

"Come on," the knight replied while dismounting. "She's going to be at this for a while so we might as well—" Rogan's words were cut short as he found himself surrounded by a half-dozen Woodwall personnel. All of the new arrivals, Tomas noticed, were women.

"Greetings, your Highness," an older woman dressed in the blue robes of a Guild wizard said. Her auburn hair had only the barest of grey at its roots and her face was touched only lightly with wrinkles, these more likely from a lifetime of study than the passage of years. Normally, her formal Guild robes would have concealed much of her body's attributes, but the blue garment had, no doubt mistakenly, been left open to reveal a form-fitting shift of grey and light blue, one that emphasized curves and cold alike. She smiled at the prince and breathed deeply. "I am Effemy, senior wizard of Fortress Constan. I would like to welcome you."

"I'll bet."

"Shut up, kid," the knight growled. Rogan gently took the wizard's soft hand in greeting but took a deliberate half-step back. "It's a pleasure, Waylan Effemy."

A look of pure equine innocence on his face, Stick bumped his rider, knocking him into the flushed wizard. Rogan stumbled forward but easily maintained his balance. In doing so, however, he startled Effemy, who stumbled back and would have fallen but for the chivalrous Rogan who still held her hand and caught her in midair with a strong arm around her waist, pulling the trembling adept straight towards into his powerful torso. Effemy made no effort to resist as she was pulled into Prince Rogan's thick arms, instead staring into the knight's green eyes and feeling the power of his broad chest pressed against her own. The collection of females surrounding them all drew a unified breath, and two even fainted at the thought of being pressed so tightly against the hero of the Northlands and champion of House Calonar.

After a look of unrestrained hatred toward his horse, who maintained one of total innocence, Rogan turned a softer gaze back to the trembling adept. "Are you all right?" the knight asked softly.

Effemy made only a small squeak of a noise and nodded slightly, her own eyes locked on the lines of Rogan's lips.

The prince gently, but firmly, disengaged the enthusiastic adept and picked up his fallen saddlebags, trying his best to ignore the whispered comments made when he was forced to bend over by his clowder of admirers. Mustering what dignity he could, Rogan told Beraht to find their quarters and deposit their bags while he and Tomas saw to their mounts. The knight then pulled his snickering squire out of his saddle and headed toward the stables.

"Why'd you call her 'Waylan' Effemy?" Tomas asked.

"Title," the surly knight replied. "Or rank, I guess. She's the lead spell-slinger attached to this regiment."

"So, what is it with you and magical girls, anyway?"

"Shut up, kid."

In the small stables, the heroes found an older soldier brushing down one of the horses. The veteran wore the triple chevrons and diamond insignia of a senior sergeant and had the look of a man who had seen many more miles than years in his life but had never let this fact do more than spur him toward ever more miles. The veteran noted their arrival and smiled. "I wondered how long it would take you to get in here," he chuckled with a voice marred by decades of yelling.

"It took a while to get past the welcoming committee," Rogan answered, leading Stick into a free stall. "I take it there hasn't been a morale visit in a while?"

The old sergeant shook his head and put away the brush he had been using. "Last one was late summer," he replied. The veteran exited the stall his horse rested in and walked to the center of the stables. Drawing himself to stand as tall as he could, the sergeant saluted his prince. "Welcome to Fortress Constan, your Highness," he said.

Rogan stood tall and returned the salute. Tomas led Urge to a stall adjacent to Stick's and started pulling the saddle off his warhorse.

"Sergeant Steinn, right?" Rogan asked from Stick's stall.

"I'm surprised you remember," he answered. The soldier retrieved a ration of oats for their horses. "We've only met once."

Rogan laughed and saw to feeding his irascible warhorse. "Little hard to forget," he pointed out. Rogan glanced at Tomas and said, "The last time I was out here, Sergeant Steinn was yelling at some poor soldier so loud we heard him from over a mile away."

"You must have been pretty mad," Tomas observed.

Steinn handed the squire a brush and nodded his head towards where the rest of the stable supplies were stored. "Not really," he replied. "I just needed to make sure

I was understood." The sergeant walked to where Rogan stood and jabbed a thumb toward the central tower across the courtyard of the castle. "I've had a room set up for you, and a meal is being prepared. The Major wants to talk to you as soon as convenient."

"Where is he?" the knight asked.

"She," Steinn corrected. "The Major has quarters on the same level as the room I set up for you. We've also set up a cot in her quarters for the Baroness whenever she gets done."

"Thanks," Rogan said. "We can take it from here."

After tending to their horses, Rogan and Tomas made their way around Aebreanna's adoring crowd to the center tower and climbed up to the level that held their room. Tomas briefly went inside the small chamber to grab Aebreanna's personal things before returning to Rogan's side. The knight moved down the small hallway to the adjacent door and knocked, declared himself, and asked permission to enter.

The commander's quarters, while still as spartan as the assignment demanded, nonetheless carried a sense of slight comfort. The two chairs had deep cushions, and the small fireplace was complemented by several candles that brought a welcoming light and warmth against the winter cold. While the small desk was filled with various reports and dispatches, there was also a small pot of wildflowers and a tiny mirror. The major herself was not what Tomas was expecting. The woman was tall, very nearly as tall as Rogan. Her dark hair had been cut very short, and she wore the same blue and gray uniform as did every officer in Calonar's House Guard, with her rank insignia as the only adornment. Her face, while attractive enough in a rough sort of way, was marred by a light scar that ran down between her eyes and by a deeper one that stretched along her jaw. When the major stood, she squared her shoulders and raised her arm in salute.

"Thank you for seeing me, your Highness." The commander's voice held cold steel in it that betrayed no weakness, no hesitation. It was a voice that gave orders and expected them to be obeyed with no argument.

"Your house, Major," the prince replied, answering the salute. "Seemed the least I could do." He nodded towards Tomas. "My squire, Tomas Fidelis of Pelsemoria."

The major glanced at where Tomas stood, noticing the bags, and nodded her head towards the cot opposite her own. The squire put down Aebreanna's bags with relief before crossing back and standing at Rogan's shoulder. The knight continued standing in front of the desk, waiting patiently for the major.

The commander gestured to the empty seat and waited until Rogan sat before sitting herself. Tomas glanced around but, not finding chair, contented himself to lean against the wall with his arms crossed over his chest. "So what did you need to talk to me about, Major…?" Rogan left the question open, not knowing the officer's name.

"Ryka, your Highness," she supplied. "Formerly of the Ubelheim Regiment. I just took command this summer."

Rogan was quiet for a moment. "I didn't realize you'd been cleared to return to duty, let alone for another hardship tour."

"I requested it, your Highness." The major reached down and retrieved a bottle of wine from the floor. She poured a cup for herself and Rogan before returning the bottle to the floor. "I prefer to be on assignment rather than at some administrative job back at the Keep." The scarred commander raised her cup. "No offense."

Rogan grinned and raised his own cup. "Some taken," he replied. They both drank. "So was the drink all you needed?" he asked. "We've been on the road for a while now, and I feel a nap coming on."

Major Ryka lowered her cup and shook her head. "Unfortunately, no, your Highness. I was hoping you could tell me why I haven't received any dispatches or supplies from the Keep recently."

"The blizzard shut us down pretty effectively," Rogan answered. "And now with winter in full force, we're having trouble letting the outlying posts know what's been going on. Plus, we've been hearing about some disruption to magic."

"Forgive me, sir," the major interrupted, "but we haven't had a supply convoy or messenger for over three months."

"Three months?" the knight sat forward. "What about your adept?"

"Effemy has been trying, but as you said, the blizzard kicked up some kind of interference. She's only been able to contact the closest Woodwall installations."

"So you're totally cut off?" Tomas asked.

Ryka shook her head. "Effemy and the other adepts have set up a relay system. One wizard sends a message to the next, who passes it to the next, and so on. Woodwall is still intact, and coordinating, but we've lost contact with Wildelves Wood. The Sylvai had to hunker down for the storm, and we haven't seen any since."

"What about the Uldra?" Rogan asked.

"They're fine," the major snorted. "They barely noticed the storm. Woodwall's still getting supplied from the neighboring clans, so we won't starve."

"Did you try sending a messenger to the Keep?" Tomas suggested.

"Yes," Ryka said, "The other commanders and I put together a twelve-man force that was supposed to return to the Keep and reestablish communications. They left three weeks ago, and we haven't heard from them since."

"The mercenaries," Tomas said to his knight.

"What mercenaries?" Ryka asked.

Rogan nodded. "I hate to say it, Major, but your team probably didn't make it back to the Keep. We've had reports that a large force of mercenaries has been building up in or near Crossroads. We also have reason to believe that the warlord Vagris has taken command of them. The Keep itself came under attack during the Harvest Festival."

"They're cutting off communications," the major deduced.

The prince nodded. "If I had to take a guess, I'd say you've got more than a few teams of mercs in the woods making sure that nobody out here interferes in whatever the bad guys are planning. We were attacked multiple times on our way out."

"Do we know what they're planning?"

"That's one of the things my team is trying to find out," Rogan said. "But this answers a really big question."

"It does?" Tomas asked.

"There's only one reason to cut off someone's communications, kid."

"Preparation for attack," Ryka added.

Rogan nodded grimly.

They were silent. Finally, Tomas asked the question on all their minds. "Do we go back?"

The heir of House Calonar thought. "No," he answered, shaking his head. "We're only four people. Killdare, Remm, and Rashid have the entire House Guard. Four more bodies won't make that big a difference." He gave is squire a meaningful look. "And our mission has priority."

The major said nothing, only looked at her prince. Rogan returned the look and nodded. "Commander's ears only," he ordered. "Relay to the other Woodwall commanders but keep this information secure."

"Understood," she said simply.

Rogan took a deep breath. "The King's been poisoned. He's dying."

Ryka's cool manner, her unflappable discipline and military bearing, nearly broke. "No," she gasped.

"The Queen's keeping him alive, but only just. During the attack on the Keep, he tried to used his magic and collapsed. He's powerless."

"A cure…?"

"That's what we're doing," Rogan confirmed. "We've got evidence Theodorico Balshazzar of Tordenia either arranged all this, or at least helped make it happen. We think he knows how to find the poisoner and, thus, the antidote."

"That sounds like a lot of guessing," Ryka said, her neutral tone becoming almost accusational.

The knight shrugged. "Not much choice. Right now, it's our only lead. We're heading into the Western Empire, we'll confront Balshazzar and find out what he knows. Then we'll hunt down the antidote and get it back to the King."

Major Ryka was silent, her eyes lost in thought. "If the Keep's coming under attack, should Woodwall intact the contingency?"

"No," Rogan said firmly. "The Keep has enough forces for its defense. Besides, the last thing we need is for a Druug helter to form because you weren't out here keeping a lid on things." He paused then. "But. Start drilling on the contingency, just in case."

"We would need to inform the Uldra. The contingency calls for them to assume control of Woodwall if we left."

The knight shook his head. "Everything but. Drill, make sure your people can move if the worst comes, but keep a lid on everything. Tell the soldiers you've gotten word and that I've ordered a series of drills."

The prince sat quietly for a few moments, an unwanted and distasteful thought playing out on his face. He took a deep breath and locked eyes with Ryka. "Major," he said in a voice mixed equally with quiet resignation and grim resolution, "it is absolutely essential that you get a messenger through to the Keep. By any means necessary."

The officer was silent. She sat staring at her prince for some time before finally replying. "Sir," she said, "if there is a significant enemy force lying in wait, the only way to ensure a messenger gets through is to either send a large force or multiple messengers to overwhelm the blockade. If we're ordered to maintain Woodwall and drill for the contingency… there's no way to send an overwhelming force."

"Time is of the essence, Major. We don't know when the enemy is going to move. The Keep MUST know that they're being blockaded."

"Then that leaves just the one option. Do I understand your orders, sir?"

"You do, Major. Use whatever means you have to, but you must get a message back to the Keep, warning them about what's happening."

Ryka stood and saluted. "Yes, sir. I will ensure a messenger reaches the Keep, by any means necessary.

Rogan stood and returned the salute. "I'll make several copies of a dispatch for the King and General Killdare and have them in your hands by morning." The prince turned and left the commander's quarters with Tomas following.

"What was all that about?" Tomas asked as the two warriors returned to their quarters.

"All what?" Rogan replied.

"All that 'by any means necessary' stuff?"

The prince stopped and took another deep breath. "I just ordered her to send several of her people on a one-way mission," he finally said.

Tomas stopped in place and stared at Rogan. "You don't know it's one-way," the squire insisted.

"The Wood is crawling with mercenaries attacking everything that moves," Rogan said flatly. "Major Ryka can't afford to organize a large-enough force to ensure they can punch their way through, so she and the other commanders will send out a swarm of messengers. Most of those people are going to get attacked. Most of them won't survive."

"There has to be another way."

Tomas stood staring at his knight. Rogan returned the look. "Something about this doesn't feel right," the squire noted.

"It isn't supposed to, kid," his knight said in a quiet voice. "I pray to God the day never comes when it gets easy for me to send people to their deaths."

"What about that 'contingency' thing you two kept mentioning?"

Rogan resumed walking. "In the event the Northern Keep is in danger of being overwhelmed or of a massive attack from the South, the Woodwall regiments will abandon the Western Fortresses, organize into a single army, and respond to the threat. The Uldra will assume responsibility for securing the Ulheim foothills."

"And we're not there?" the squire asked.

"Not yet."

Chapter 13

Although offered a private dining room for the evening meal, Rogan insisted that he and his companions would eat in the main hall used by all those assigned to Fort Constan. As with their initial arrival, Aebreanna was the center of attention among the fighting men. The beautiful baroness had changed before the meal, entering the hall wearing a blue dress in the style of the Sisters of the Lady of Light. Attached to Aebreanna's wrists and ankles, she wore small bells that sang a soft accompaniment to her sultry movements as she danced barefoot from one table to the next.

Ignoring her companions, Aebreanna shared the meal with the common soldiers, joining with their jokes and toasts and singing for them whenever asked. The Sylva listened in rapt attention as the soldiers attempted to outdo one another with stories of their battles against the Druug and never hesitated in showing her admiration for and gratitude towards the defenders of the Northlands, even going so far as to grant a kiss on the lips to one soldier after it was revealed he had risked his life to save several of his squadmates in an attack weeks earlier.

Through imperious command supported by the cheers of the defenders of Fort Constan, Aebreanna even convinced Rogan and Beraht to join the festivities with their own tales of adventure. Tomas had expected his knight to refuse, knowing how much Rogan hated being the center of any attention, but was surprised at how quickly he agreed, joining the soldiers and telling stories of his many adventures. Beraht also surprised the young man by restraining his usual inclination towards violence and sharing with the warriors of Woodwall his stories instead of his fists. Even Tomas himself was included when Rogan insisted the squire relate his own tales of Pelsemoria and the squire's quest to find Cyras Darkholm. Tomas was also pressed to discuss the recent struggles against the Death Mage. The soldiers cheered at his description of the warehouse battle, in which they first defeated Anninihus' monstrous creations, and they all rose in solemn recognition of the terrible battle in the Keep's gardens, in which so many fell.

Tomas learned much that night as he enjoyed the company of the soldiers of Fort Constan. There was a strong sense of brotherhood to the men and women who served together so far from home. Even when Ulhe occasional fight broke out and was almost immediately stopped by the ever-present Sergeant Steinn, the two combatants inevitably ended up joined in drink and song. Having been included in the group, even if only superficially, gave Tomas a strong sense of belonging that he had not felt for as long as he could remember. Here was a place that lines of class and culture blurred. Noble and peasant joined with the wealthy and the poor. All were a part of this extended family, and all were cared for. The young man learned why a man or woman could spend years amidst these cold hills and love it so much that they would return again and again. Here was a place to belong.

With their meal more or less concluded, Sergeant Steinn gave permission for the ale barrels to be opened that night in celebration of so noteworthy a guest and her companions. Again and again, Aebreanna was asked to dance, and never once did the radiant Sylva refuse a request. She leapt from the top of one of the hall's long tables to another and danced for as long as the soldiers could supply music or song or even just the clapping of hands. Some of the more courageous warriors were even allowed to dance with the beautiful baroness, enjoying a series of caresses and movements of hands, legs, hips, and heads that could weaken even the strongest of men. Aebreanna was loved by all and in turned loved them all, giving each soldier the attention he or she deserved for their service.

Beraht gave the warriors of Woodwall the chance to prove their worth, accepting every challenge offered. Through the night, every soldier present tried arm wrestling the barbarian, and each was defeated; the warriors even went so far as trying to have three men at a time try to pull on Beraht's immovable arm, but of course, the three were sent laughing to the floor. A lesson in axe throwing left a door in splinters but caused much cheering, as did the soldiers' various attempts to out-belch a true son of Uldron. Beraht toasted the bravery of Fortress Constan and sang their songs.

Rogan spent the evening with the common soldiers. It seemed the knight was more at home here among these Guardsmen than he could ever be in the comfort and luxury of Castle Calonar. At no time during the night was Rogan alone as each soldier wished for a chance to speak with their prince. Rogan was happy to accommodate each of them, sharing a drink when offered and talking about any issue the soldiers wished. The men and women of Fort Constan learned that no subject was taboo to their prince, from their duty to the Northlands to their pay and concerns for the family in the most remote of villages. The prince of the Northlands even spoke to his warriors about events going on around the world and their place in those great matters. Rogan treated every soldier with a level of respect that eliminated the class structure so common in other armies.

Even the gathering of Fortress Constant's handful of women was included in this camaraderie. Initially, Rogan had needed to fend off the amorous attention of Effemy and her assistant-mage, the support staff and other few females. This he did with polite efficiency, being kind but firm in his loyalty to his wife. As the night proceeded, these unwanted advances faded. Though the vast majority of soldiers were men, still Rogan treated the women assigned to Fortress Constan equally. No matter if a member of the castle joined in patrols or prepared meals, no matter if they maintained the garrison's equipment or waged battle against the Druug, all those assigned to the fortress received equal respect from the heir of House Calonar.

As the evening drew to a close, Tomas was reminded of why his companions were so important to the people of the Northlands. More so than ever before, Tomas was reminded of why Rogan Eigenhard inspired the loyalty of an entire kingdom: he was first and foremost a man of the people, and there was never any question about where his loyalties lie. The very presence of these heroes was enough to lift the spirits of the defenders of Woodwall. The men and women who served as the first line of the Northland's defense looked at Rogan, Beraht, and Aebreanna as something akin to gods; heroes of the old times who could do no wrong and would never suffer defeat. It was an awful burden the squire felt pulling at his heart when he realized that he too was being included with the heroes of House Calonar.

The young man left the warmth of the main hall and climbed up the steps of the central tower to its parapet where he looked out at Ulheim. The jagged peaks glowed with the light of Vaeta, now waning in the night sky, and the mountains seemed to claw at the sky like some impossible titan. The stark cold of those foreboding peaks seemed to chill Tomas, and he drew his thick cloak tighter around himself. He saw two great mountains, larger than their fellows and isolated, as though they had absorbed their siblings to enlarge themselves. Even the clouds that forever obscured Ulheim like a misty veil retreated from the Parent Mountains. Something sinister waited there, something… someone, so impossibly vile that the world itself recoiled from her.

Rogan appeared behind his squire with a cup of something warm in his hands. "What's bothering you, kid?" he asked.

"Just thinking about what's ahead," the young man replied. "Or… who."

The knight stood beside his apprentice and sipped at his drink. "There's always a point when you stop and think about what's coming," he said. "There's that quiet moment when the… reality of what you're doing, what you're heading into, rolls right over you."

"It's not that," Tomas objected. "I'm just afraid of—"

"Of what?"

The squire maintained his gaze on the moon-bathed Parent Mountains. "How do you live with their expectations?" he finally asked his knight.

Rogan took another drink before answering. "The soldiers?" he asked.

Tomas nodded. "It seems like they look at you like you can't lose, that you'll never fail them. How do you live up to that?"

The prince sighed. "Don't forget that most of what we do gets exaggerated all out of proportion. Most of what these soldiers hear are just stories only slightly based on reality."

"You were the one telling the stories," the squire reminded his knight.

"Exactly. Stories. I was telling them stories. If we told them the truth about what happened, they'd be really boring stories. Think about it, over the past two weeks, what have we done that was so interesting?"

Tomas shrugged. "A few fights," he mused. "That thing from Otherworld. Other than that, just a lot of riding."

"Exactly, so we leave that out. When I tell the story about how we beat the Zafael from Otherworld, I don't mention that it beat the crap out of me and Beraht before you finally managed to sneak up behind it and get in a lucky hit. I just skip to the interesting part."

"But we still saved her," Tomas noted. "All your stories end the same way. We stopped the Zafael. We survived the Lamashti. We beat Anninihus. You saved those slaves being sold in the City of All Sins. You defeated the Greysoul. When we first met, you saved me from those Druug."

"How could I not? You were so cute and helpless standing there. You were like a puppy barking at a burglar."

"You really know how to inflate a guy's ego."

"Kid, you have to understand that everyone makes mistakes."

"When have you ever failed spectacularly to measure up to someone's expectations?"

Rogan stared silently at his squire for some time before finally answering. "How about the Madness?"

Tomas stiffened.

"That was a failure, kid. Not just any failure. The Madness was a spectacular failure. We realized almost immediately how bad we'd screwed up, and do you know what we did? We ran. We saw how bad it was getting in Pelsemoria, and we ran. We left, and your people had to suffer the consequences for a decade because of what I did. I knew I couldn't save the city and would have lost my own people trying, so I had to run."

"How did you get over that?" Tomas asked. "How do you keep going?"

"What makes you think I got over it?" Rogan demanded. "I never got over it. I never got over the things I had to do while I was with the Bellonari. And I damn well never got over letting Anninihus…" The knight breathed deeply and glanced towards the constellation of the Huntress. "Letting him kill Hannah," he finished.

"You told me once that Kyla helped you get over the death of her."

"She helped me get past it, kid, but you never forget your first…"

"Love?"

"Your first anything. Your first everything. Your first love. Your first kill. Your first… everything."

"If you've done so much that's so bad, how is it that people still see you as the invincible hero?" Tomas asked.

"Because they have to," Rogan answered.

"I don't understand."

The knight turned his back on Ulheim and leaned against the stone battlements, already covered in a light dusting of falling snow. "The average person lives their life without ever really doing anything amazing," Rogan said, as his eyes drifted back towards Wildelves Wood. "The average person doesn't save anyone's life or defeat a great evil or witness any miracles. Average people are just average. They live normal lives and die normal deaths. But they still need to feel connected to something special, and that's where we come in."

"We?" the squire asked.

"Oh yes," the knight laughed. "Don't think you're going to miss out on this. Already your legend grows. Those soldiers down there are going to tell others about Tomas Fidelis of Pelsemoria, who protected Cyras Darkholm from rampaging Druug and singlehandedly slew twelve of the monsters before the arrival of Rogan Eigenhard. Together, the heroes turned back the monsters and studied at the feet of the Trickster Mage, learning from him the secrets of Creation.

"They'll sing songs about Tomas Fidelis and his journey north, slaying a terrible agent of the Xeshlin and saving the life of the King of Alvaro. They'll whisper the horrible story of his arrival in Wildelves Wood, where he banished a horde of Lamashti back to the spirit world. They'll cheer his terrible battle against the villainous Death Mage, Anninihus, and his legion of horrors. In that earth-shattering conflict, the noble Tomas stood alone in defense of the good King Cylan.

"The story will spread about how the courageous squire stood valiantly against an invasion of Zafael as they spilled out from Otherworld with only his trusted blade, Steelheart to hold the monsters back as his comrades lay fallen on the battlefield and the virtuous Aebreanna Tressalon was held in vile bondage."

Tomas stared at his knight. "That's not even slightly how any of that happened," he pointed out.

"Doesn't matter, kid," the prince replied. "That's what they'll remember. And each time they tell the story, your bravery will get greater, the Druug'll get bigger, Cyras will get less annoying, the monsters will get more powerful, and Aebreanna will get more... virtuous."

"But that's my point, Rogan," the squire insisted. "How do you live up to their expectations? How are you able to keep giving these people hope? What happens when I fail?"

"Ah, the point emerges. You're scared you won't live up to people's expectations?"

"How can I?"

Rogan straightened. "First of all, don't worry about anyone's expectations. History forgives and forgets a lot. And at this point, if you don't fall out of your saddle more than two or three times, you'll live up to mine just fine."

"Gee, thanks."

"I'm a giver," the knight shrugged. "Second of all, you can't let yourself get all tied up in knots over what anyone else thinks you need to accomplish. At the end of the day, you just do the best you can and things work out."

"But what if that's not enough?"

Rogan put a hand on his squire's shoulder. "Well, then you've got me and Beraht and Aebreanna there to cover you."

"What happens when that still isn't enough?" Tomas asked. "What happens when I… when it all goes bad?"

"Then you learn. You keep living. You pick yourself up and keep trying. And you make damned sure you never make the same mistake twice."

"Does that work for you?"

"Mostly," the knight replied. "My problem is I keep finding new and more interesting ways to screw up."

"I bet I could come up with something bigger," the young man noted.

"Oh yeah, that's a goal you want to set." The prince took another drink.

"What is that?" Tomas asked. "It smells like apples."

"It is," Rogan replied, offering his squire a drink. "Warm cider."

The young man glanced at his knight. "I thought you were drinking ale?"

"Nothing better on a cold night than a warm mug of cider," Rogan insisted.

Tomas took a long drink and almost immediately started coughing violently as his throat felt as though it had caught on fire.

"Warm cider mixed with some other things, that is," Rogan finished as he calmly took back his mug and continued drinking.

Chapter 14

Rogan and Tomas rose early the next day, unable to sleep longer through the deafening snores coming from Beraht's cot. Less snores, the thunderous noise coming from under the Uldra's blanket was more like the dying roar of a dragon falling into a bottomless chasm. After dressing, the knight led his squire to the dining hall, helping themselves to breakfast and sitting alone so they could complete their correspondence. Rogan had told Tomas to write his own interpretation on the events their team had witnessed while in Wildelves Wood and information they had gained, which the knight would forward along with his own reports to the king. King Cylan preferred multiple perspectives of the same events so as to gain a better picture of something, or so Rogan had told his apprentice. Since both men needed to complete the same chore, neither had any excuse but to do it.

While he wrote, Tomas held in his other hand the soft white ribbon that had been her gift to him on the day of the joust, now almost a month ago. Although it may have just been his imagination, the young man could swear that the small piece of cloth still carried a hint of his Mary, some slight scent that would fill his lungs and soothe away any turbulence in his soul. Once his official correspondence was done, the young man took a blank piece of parchment and began writing a letter to his lady, filled with all the love he felt and his sorrow over their separation.

Rogan glanced at the letter and firmly took it, crumpling the parchment and throwing the unfinished letter into the fire. "What the…!" Tomas was livid.

"No," his knight said firmly. "Never." He held up his left hand, emphasizing the missing ring from his finger. "Our enemies can't know about them." He reached under his tunic and pulled free an iron chain, from which hung a small gold ring. "We keep them close, and deep. But we don't let the bad guys know about them."

"Everyone knows you married Kyla!" Tomas insisted.

Rogan level an intense stare at his squire. "And she's suffered for it. She's been attacked. She's been in danger. Because of this," he again held up the ring. "You want to keep Mary a secret for as long as possible… to keep her safe as long as possible."

The squire, who had half-raised from the bench, sat back down. He mulled the thought and understood. "But," he tried to object. "I feel like I need to…"

Rogan returned the chain, settling the ring so that it once again rested against his heart. "Keep the words here," he said, pointing towards the ring. "Keep them safe until we get home."

Once finished with his correspondence and his meal, the squire saw to his duties, brushing down each of their horses, applying a little more care to Urge, something his warhorse allowed but did not award with anything more than only a single, casual attempt to bite his rider. Tomas then carefully checked the hooves of each horse, from Urge and the other warhorses to the pack animals before giving them all their feed. As he exited the stables, Tomas realized that the garrison chapel was located just next door and decided to take advantage since God only knew when he would next get the opportunity.

The chapel was small, with only three rows of pews and a simple wooden altar upon which rested a small candle floating in an iron bowel. After kneeling before the altar and saying a few prayers not only for the continued success of his mission but also for the safety of his beloved Mary, Tomas stood in preparation to light a candle before leaving but was stopped short when he saw Rogan kneeling before the small collection of candles.

"Morning, kid," the knight said without turning.

"How did you know it was me?"

"Who else would be in the chapel this early in the morning?" Rogan asked, standing.

"You, apparently," the squire pointed out.

Rogan chuckled. "True enough."

"Don't take this the wrong way, but what are you doing in here? You always told me you never had much use for church."

The knight stood and sighed. "I was just saying hello to an old friend."

"Are you going to explain that or just stay mysterious?"

The prince sat at one of the pews and rubbed his eyes. "I keep forgetting what I have and haven't told you about my past," he said softly.

"Don't forget the stuff that's apparently none of my business," Tomas reminded him.

"Do you want to hear this or just stand there making smartass remarks?"

Tomas held his hands up in surrender and sat down on the same pew as his knight.

Rogan took another deep breath and stared into the soft light of the altar candle. "Once upon a time, kid. Once upon a time. I told you how I left home and was eventually recruited by the Bellonari?"

"Yeah," Tomas replied. "And you eventually broke away from them when you found out how they really operated."

"Well, the man that recruited me was named Beckett. We all called him Silverhorn because of this streak of gray hair that ran along the top of his head. Anyway, Beckett ran into me while I was soldiering for House Calexto during their border skirmishes with the Velaross nobility that the Republic did such a good job of ignoring. Beckett was on a mission for the Bellonari in that area, and we got to know each other. Of course, at the time, I had no idea who he was, but apparently he thought I had some potential because he offered to train me."

"As a Bellonar?" the young man asked.

Rogan shook his head. "That's not how the Brotherhood works, kid," he replied. "When a Bellonar wants to recruit a new member, they put the recruit through training for over a year before they even hear the word Bellonari. It's only after you prove yourself during the training that you're allowed to know the Brotherhood exists."

"What was the training like?"

"Do you remember the days you spent training with Beraht and Remm?"

Tomas rubbed his neck in painful memory. "Are you kidding? I'm still sore."

"Training with Beckett was like that only all day, every day."

"Why did you stay with him?"

The knight shrugged. "Why did you hang around?"

"I don't know. I was learning new things every day."

"Same reason for me. Even as a total novice, I realized that I could learn more from Silverhorn in just one year than I could in ten years with anyone else. Plus each night, he would teach me things like the warrior philosophies of Tramaya. Besides, Silverhorn told me that I could only train with him for a year before each of us would have to decide if I could progress to the next level."

"Which you did."

Rogan nodded. "After that first year, Silverhorn and I sat down and had a long talk about what I wanted and where I was heading in life. He really made me realize some important things about myself."

"Sounds like the King," Tomas noted.

"I wish I could have put Silverhorn and Cylan Calonar in the same room, kid. From what the King's told me, they'd met once or twice but only in passing. With the possible exception of Cylan Calonar, Silverhorn was the wisest, more honorable man I've ever met."

"What was he doing with the Bellonari?"

"There's something you have to understand about the Bellonari, kid. What they are now is not what they're supposed to be. Originally, the Brotherhood was a group of… I guess warrior-philosophers is the best description. They looked to the more abstract nature of war." Rogan let his eyes roll to the vaulted ceiling, trying to explain. "You see, the core of the Bellonari is the worship of Bellonar, the old Sylvai goddess of war…" He grimaced. "'Worship' isn't really the right word. The Brotherhood looked to her for inspiration, for an example. Originally, she was venerated as honorable war, as martial discipline, as strength used to protect and lead. A Bellonar would study the goddess, learning to fight only as a method of perfecting his mind and body. The pursuit of war was only one aspect of what was supposed to be a journey of the mind and body. We were also supposed to learn skills, trades, crafts. Music, dance, poetry, art, philosophy. A Bellonar was supposed to perfect all the aspects of himself."

"Art," Tomas mused. "Like what you were supposed to do with House Eigenhard?"

Rogan nodded. "I think that's what won me over with Silverhorn. I wanted to be a fighter, but I was also a half-decent painter." The knight laughed ruefully. "He had me spending as much time with a paintbrush as he did a sword. But that was the point of the Brotherhood: to find truth in yourself, through exploring many disciplines."

"Sounds more like a religion than a mercenary group."

"In a lot of ways, the Bellonari are a religion. Or, they're supposed to be."

"So Beckett explained all this to you?"

"Oh, God, no," Rogan laughed. "The Bellonari don't tell you their secrets until you join up. And even then, you're only given the information you need as you progress through the Order. Only the Twelve Generals know the whole story."

"And they are?"

"The leaders of the Bellonari. The Generals are our most experienced members. The twelve men that have served a lifetime of war and know the greatest secrets of Bellonar. Silverhorn was one of them."

"Wow. So you got recruited by the top guy."

"Well, he wasn't First General, but he was one of the Twelve. When I agreed to travel with him to the Mother Temple, Silverhorn shared with me some of the truth about the Bellonari. I spent five years under the tutelage of another master to prevent any chance of favoritism. After that, I was given my first assignment."

"The kidnapping with Vagris," Tomas recalled.

The knight nodded. "There were problems leading up to that though," he admitted. "Once Beckett got me back to the Mother Temple and my training began in earnest, I saw that most of the men being recruited were nothing like Beckett; most of them were like Vagris. Silverhorn told me later that he'd been away from the Brotherhood for years prior to bringing me back, and that the Bellonari had changed while he was gone."

He sighed then, and rubbed his eyes. "The old First General had died, and his successor was moving the Brotherhood in a new direction. It comes down to your understanding of Bellonar, I guess. On one hand, she is a goddess of war; she's a warrior and killer. On the other, she's a goddess of creativity, of expression and introspection. For centuries, the creative aspect was most venerated by the Brotherhood. Over time…"

"They swung the other way?"

Rogan nodded. "Traditionally, the Bellonari waited until a war broke out and then hired themselves out to one or both sides, pretending to be regular mercenaries. The conflict allowed the Brotherhood to learn new techniques of war and test their training on the battlefield. Between conflicts, Bellonari would hire themselves out as bounty hunters, tracking down the worst, most dangerous scum in the world, or travel in search of new masters to learn new skills.

"But, under the new First General, the Brotherhood became more… proactive."

"They started causing wars," Tomas guessed.

"And helping criminals escape only to hunt them down after they scored a few more atrocities and the price on their heads went up. More importantly, the new First General started revealing the existence of the Brotherhood to certain individuals to better advertise our services."

"What people?"

"Tienel Greysoul, for one. That's partly how I got caught up in that whole mess. Many of the most powerful noble lords were also told, as was the Emperor, the Elector Lords, and some of the less scrupulous Lords Cardinal."

"I don't know for sure, but Silverhorn and I both guessed that anyone that didn't fit in to the new First General's new way of doing things was going to disappear. A lot of the brothers started having accidents or drawing really dangerous assignments."

"So that first assignment of yours was a setup?" Tomas asked.

"I don't know for sure, but it makes sense. In the whole history of the Bellonari, there have only been three members that have successfully gone rogue. I was the last. The first was Silverhorn, who disappeared about two years before I did. The second was Hahn T'shan."

"Let me guess, your second master?"

"And a former student of Silverhorn's," Rogan confirmed.

"Stands to reason they'd assume you'd go rogue too," Tomas noted.

"When my first assignment came, I figured that they were trying to get rid of me, so I went ahead and saved them the trouble."

"So which one is buried here?" the squire asked. "Beckett or Hahn T'shan?"

"Beckett," the knight replied.

"Did they find him?"

"No. Actually, Beckett never even hid. He all but dared the Brotherhood to send someone for him."

"Was he crazy, suicidal, or just that good?" Tomas asked.

"A little of all three, kid. Silverhorn was the greatest fighter I've ever met, and there wasn't a single man in the Brotherhood that wasn't terrified of the thought of having to fight him for real. There was a death mark put on Silverhorn, but the Bellonari never tried sending anyone to claim it. He ended up dying of natural causes, and since he was originally from a small village near here, I asked the King to have him entombed here. This way, Beckett gets the respect he's due, and I don't have to worry about the Bellonari desecrating his grave."

A strange sensation had started pulling Tomas' attention toward the nearby altar. Within moments, the young man could make out no noises as it felt as though the blood from his entire body had surged into his head, and a horrible chill rose from the stonework floor to seep into the squire's entire body. Even when Rogan called out to his apprentice and tried to grab Tomas by the arm, the young man could sense nothing but the terrible pressure building his mind and the cold that had wrapped itself around his heart.

Rogan had stood when his squire did and repeatedly tried to get Tomas's attention. The young man could make no reply but a gargled choke that cut the knight's breath short. Tomas felt his body take several jerking steps to the front of the altar where he collapsed to his knees. In the instant Rogan took a single step to aid his squire, a sudden blast of air colder than any winter erupted from Tomas. The doors into the chapel slammed shut, and all light was extinguished, save for the single altar candle that steadily burned as through there was no wind at all.

Talon leapt from its sheath as Rogan spun in a circle with his longsword at the ready. Spotting no spell-slinger, he moved towards where Tomas knelt, constantly scanning the bitterly cold, dark room with Talon ready for any target. His squire tried to call out, tried to warn his knight, but he remained locked within his body, unable to act.

The wind stopped as suddenly as it had begun. A deathly calm filled the chapel that pressed against the weary knight. From beneath him, deep in the earth and muffled by the grave, came a voice from Rogan's past that chilled Tomas' soul the way that no evil wind could. "Rogan," the voice said.

Awareness passed through Tomas. Information entered his mind and left. He was aware of things in one instance and ignorant of them in the next. His knight turned toward the altar where, silhouetted against the single candle, the darkness had gathered itself together into the form of a man now almost ten years dead. Silverhorn Beckett, dressed in the robes of a Bellonari General and holding the sword that had seen him through countless battles, faced the man who was once his apprentice with the empty eyes of the dead.

"Rogan," the phantom said again.

The northlands prince had seen horrors aplenty and magic in all its forms during his many adventures, so the shade of his former master did not rob the warrior of his strength nor his readiness for battle. "What business do you have here, Beckett?" Rogan demanded. "Why have you attacked my squire?"

"I made no attack on the student of my student," the shade replied. "His power called me from my rest."

"What power?"

"An ancient power rests within the boy. A power that came to him through the Veil and calls to those who have passed beyond but found no justice."

"Does he know of this power?"

"He will," the shade said, growing more distinct from the dark mists that spawned him and gaining greater animation.

"What justice do you seek, Beckett?" Rogan demanded. "Why have you come back?"

"Why have you not avenged me?" the spirit of Beckett demanded. "You, who were my hope for the future of the Brotherhood, why have you not brought me my justice?"

"What justice, Beckett?" the knight snapped, still holding Talon ready. Although not enchanted, Rogan's longsword had seen him through countless battles, against countless horrors. "You died a natural death! There was no call for vengeance!"

"You are wrong," the wraith replied, its dead eyes beginning to burn with the green wrath of the dead. "My death was the work of neither Time nor Fate, nor the White Lady, sister to our Mistress. My death was ordered by my brother Generals. My death was the price for your former partner to assume my rank."

"Vagris!" Realization burned the cold from Rogan's bones. Hatred for his enemy rolled out from the knight's body in waves that crashed against Tomas' awareness, nearly pushing back the darkness holding his squire frozen. "He was made a General for killing you!"

"Poison, Rogan. The coward had not the courage to meet me through combat nor open challenge, but through the cowardice of poison. I call for vengeance."

"You'll have it, Silverhorn," the knight swore. "Once my business with Balshazzar is complete, I swear I'll take vengeance on Vagris and all the Twelve Generals in your name."

The darkness reached out to reclaim the spirit of Beckett, pulling his spirit back to its place of rest. "Balshazzar is but one arrayed against you, my student," the spirit called out. "And the true face of your enemy is not his."

"Who?" Rogan demanded, reaching forward to try and hold his master's spirit in place. "Who's behind all this?"

The knight's words were in vain, though. The spirit of Silverhorn Beckett had returned to the darkness, and Tomas collapsed to the floor with a sigh, exhausted by the ordeal placed upon him.

Chapter 15

"What do you remember?" Rogan asked.

"Not much," Tomas admitted. He was lying on a cot in Effemy's small chambers. Rogan had carried his squire there and sent a messenger for the castle's wizard and Aebreanna. Both had arrived and, after a brief explanation from Rogan, began a detailed examination of Tomas. "We were talking about how you joined the Bellonari and your old mentor was entombed under Woodwall. Then... here."

Aebreanna put a wet cloth on the squire's forehead. "This is not the first indicator we have had of late. Some power stirs within our young friend."

Effemy was kneeling beside the cot. In one hand she held a large crystal, round and flat. This, she was slowly passing over Tomas' body. She held another, similar crystal up to her eye. "There is something here," she mused. "Something very deep."

"You'd been out for over an hour," Rogan said. "Aebreanna said you were just exhausted, so we let you sleep."

"That wasn't sleep!" the squire snapped. "Something attacked me."

"I'm not so sure, kid."

"What are you talking about?"

"Interesting," Effemy interrupted, mostly to herself. The crystal she was passing over Tomas had paused, held over Alexia's golden rose. The wizard leaned a little closer, then set aside the lens and made to touch the small pin, fashioned in the shape of a rose mid-bloom. The young man's hand shot up, faster than lightning, catching Effemy's hand before it could touch the golden pin.

"Why did you do that," the wizard asked gently.

"Do what?" Tomas asked. When she nodded to his hand, clutching hers, he dropped it immediately.

"Very interesting," Effemy said.

"You told me that Alexia did something to you before she died," Rogan pointed out.

"So?"

He shared a glance with Aebreanna. "I think she gave you some of her power."

Tomas sat up and looked at Rogan. "What makes you think that?" he asked.

The knight sighed. "When you blacked out, Beckett's spirit appeared and told me some things. One of which was that a power inside you is what called him back." Rogan sat in the small chair at Effemy's desk and rubbed his eyes. \

"Have you ever raised the dead before?" Aebreanna gently asked. "Or communicated with them?"

Tomas mutely shook his head.

Rogan sat back. "That's what I thought. Calonar told me once that his aunt could speak with the dead."

Aebreanna stood and adjusted her skirt. "Alexia knew she was dying and, with her Truthsight, knew some of what was going to happen to our young companion. She may have transferred some element of her power before passing through the Veil."

Rogan nodded. "If she knew what was going to be happening, and that she wouldn't be here to help any more…"

"Her only means of aiding us through these difficult times," the Sylva agreed.

"I don't really call blacking out and having the spirit of your dead teacher possessing me help," Tomas snapped.

"What he told me was helpful," Rogan argued.

"Which was?"

The knight related his conversation with Beckett's spirit, trying his best to keep an even temper as once again he was forced to think about the death of the man most directly responsible for his path in life.

"You're handling the news rather well," Tomas observed. "All things considered, I don't think I'd be able to stay as calm."

"Trust me, kid," the knight grumbled, "I'm putting on a good show."

"Regardless," Aebreanna interrupted. "The question remains of what to do." She opened the door and whispered to Beraht, who had been standing outside to prevent any unwanted listeners. The Uldra nodded and left.

"What can we do?" Rogan asked.

"Little, I fear," the Sylva admitted.

Effemy returned her devices to a small wooden box. "If this power is not native to his body, he'll have trouble controlling it."

"Can you do anything?"

The wizard shook her head. "Maybe Parden Esha. This is far beyond my experience."

"We're not going back," Tomas said flatly.

The other looked at him, surprised. The squire shook his head. "What you said before was right, Rogan. Our quest is too important. And you said there'd be… distractions."

"One serious distraction," the knight grumbled.

Beraht returned, opening the door and leaning down to pass Aebreanna one of her bags. The Sylva retrieved a small pouch and added a pinch of the mixture inside to a cup of water. This, she gave to Tomas. "Drink."

The squire was about to refuse the noxious-smelling brew, but a stern look from Aebreanna convinced him. He drank and fought the desire to gag. "Your young apprentice is correct," she said. "We must continue, and now, at least, we will know to be alert for other manifestations."

"If it happens again," Rogan mused, "could you do something?"

The Sylva held up her hands and shrugged.

Rogan let out an explosive breath and stood. "Alright. We go on." He turned to Effemy. "Do I have to say…?"

The wizard smiled and shook her head. "Confidentially is key. Wizards are good at keeping secrets."

Aebreanna and Beraht went to gather their bags in preparation to leave. Rogan led Tomas to Major Ryka's quarters to inform the commander of their early departure. "Are you going to need help?" Tomas asked suddenly.

"What?" his knight asked.

"What you said to Beckett, about hunting down Vagris and the other Generals."

Rogan stopped and stared at his squire. "Do you know what you're saying, kid?" he asked. "When I do this, it isn't going to be clean. I usually use Beraht for this sort of thing."

Tomas returned the look his knight gave him. "I can't promise I can do what needs to be done, but I can promise to help however I can."

Rogan nodded, resuming their course to the regiment's commander. "I'll think about it kid."

Chapter 16

The small party left behind the safety of the Woodwall fortresses, moving further into the foothills of Ulheim. The terrain was steep and imposing. Most of the hills were formed by steep cliffs of hard granite, as though some malicious deity had drawn a finger across the world to gouge the great furrows. Their passage was limited to the narrow ravines that ran between the cliff faces. The snow had been cleared along a certain route, not quite a road but more than a simple path. Their horses trudged up the steep ravines, needing frequent rest and casting hateful looks at their riders. Mayva, Aebreanna's white Sylvai pony, was particularly ill-suited to the hard passage, though Sus, Beraht's Uldric shire horse, treated the rough ground as though it were the gentlest hillside. The air grew colder and the weather shifted from light snow to freezing rain. The group grew increasingly discontent in the hours-long climb, all but Beraht.

Fortunately, with winter now in full force, the Druug were effectively trapped within their territories with little ability to encroach into the relative safety provided by the Uldra and the Woodwall patrols. In point of fact, the party was well into the hills, virtually into the mountains themselves, before the slightest sign was spotted. Fortunately, the sign they came upon was a cluster of Druug heads driven through stakes planted into the unyielding ground.

Beraht absently pulled on his braided beard, looking around with an air of professional criticism. "Anyone you know?" Rogan asked as they continued up the steep valley.

"Looks like Dradjek's work," the Uldra replied. He took in the gaping black tongues of the Druug heads, the ichorus spittle having long frozen. Each head was large, even larger than Beraht's own boulder-sized skull. The curving horns had all been removed, not by cutting, but by having been torn out by the root.

"What's a Dradjek?" Tomas asked.

In response, a thunderous bellow came roaring out from the cliffs above. There was such force, such impossible hatred in that roar that the snow and ice dislodged, showering down on either side. One particular clump of wet, filthy snow, fell on Aebreanna. The beautiful Sylva, having grown even more sullen than the Humans as they drew ever closer to the mountains proper, shook her head and sighed, sending her opalescent eyes to the heavens in resignation. "Uldra," she nearly sobbed.

Once the echoing roar had subsided enough that Tomas's hearing had somewhat returned, Beraht took a deep breath and responded with a bellow of his own. Sus joined with his rider, emitting a sound that could not possibly come from even the hulking shire horse, but should rather have come from some angry mountain bear. The other horses reared and thrashed as the air around the group of adventurers erupted in the most horrendous noise to ever cross the lips of any creature. Mayva tried desperately to turn and run, though not from fear but from head-shaking disgust. Only Aebreanna's reluctant coaxing kept her pristine white pony in place. Several loose stones were shaken free and sent rolling down the steep valley the group had been climbing, no doubt fleeing from the horror around them. The few birds that had bravely thought to remain to that point now took flight, eagerly wishing to escape the auditory assault. Tomas feared that he felt blood running from his ears but could not spare a hand to check as all his strength was required in holding on to Urge's saddle as the warhorse tried to throw him.

Just as suddenly as the noise Beraht and Sus had created began, it ceased. All was calm and still in the valley. Not a single creature dared make a sound, and even the normally strong mountain winds seemed to have been stunned to silence. Every living thing, Human, horse, and hill alike, was frozen in terrified anticipation of what may come next. The only motion came from Aebreanna's white pony, which continued to thrash about.

Without further warning, the hills erupted with Uldra. More than a dozen of the mountainous warriors appeared all around the tense heroes in an avalanche of armor and weapons and beards and fists. Each of the thunderous barbarians stood at least a head taller than any Human, and most were taller still. Their bodies were impossibly thick, but as a mountain was thick: beyond muscle or fat, as though the stones themselves had stood up on powerful legs. No Uldra was missing a beard, some reaching their owner's knees, and each showing signs of meticulous care and adornment. The Uldra were violence incarnate; a steady rumbling of hoarse laughter and thinly veiled insults came marching ahead of the mountain men, cutting into the intruders as cleanly as any weapon of steel the barbarians could forge. Fearing the worst, Tomas reached for Steelheart, uncertain of what good any act of defiance would do against such a fearsome collection of open hostility.

Seeing his squire's reaction, Rogan barked, "NO!" Tomas looked and saw his knight shaking his head emphatically. "They'll kills us all if you draw a weapon! Beraht can handle this."

As the young man looked on in frightened confusion, their towering companion dismounted and, roaring such curses that the air around them nearly caught on fire, advanced on the surrounding Uldra. Beraht made no gesture of timidity as he stormed forward with his great waraxe held ready. In response to Beraht's attack of belligerent words, one of the Uldra, somewhat taller than Beraht but not as large in the shoulders and carrying a massive steel mace adorned with spikes stomped forward, his own curses befouling the air. The two Uldra advanced on each other, hefting their weapons and doing their best to kill each other with insults in both Uldric and the common Velish. Upon finally reaching each other, they stood silent for a few heartbeats before dropping their weapons, knocking each other's horned helmets from their hairy heads, and grabbing one another in a bone-crushing bear hug.

Tomas's fear of a confrontation seemed justified until he noticed that the two Uldra were laughing and begun pounding on each other's shoulders with such force that the squire thought his own bones might break from just the sight and sound.

"Behold," Aebreanna said with utter contempt after regaining some measure of control over her distraught pony, "the ancient Uldra Rite of Greeting."

"Are you serious?" Tomas demanded.

"Oh yes. Whenever two warriors meet on neutral ground, they must prove how unafraid they are and how happy each is to see the other."

The three watched as horns of ale were brought forward to the two Uldra, which they poured down each other's throats while laughing. "What's that?" Tomas demanded. "The ancient Rite of Getting Reacquainted?"

Rogan shook his head. "No, that one takes blood loss. This is the Rite of Respect, performed once two warriors have agreed not to kill each other."

"Now I know you're making this up," the squire said.

"Believe it or not, kid, the Uldra have a deep, profound system of beliefs that stretch back to the beginnings of their race."

"Of course, to all non-Uldra," Aebreanna sniffed, "this is merely drunken violence."

With the various Rites apparently satisfied, Beraht led the other Uldra over for what Tomas hoped would be a less violent introduction. "This is Dradjek. He's the local boss."

"Boss?" Tomas asked with a raised eyebrow. "Is that an official rank?"

Rogan laughed. "Unlike Sylvai and Humans, Uldra don't go in for titles. If a Uldra runs things, he's the boss." The knight leaned forward in his saddle. "Well, Boss Dradjek, was this a Druug helter that you rearranged?"

"Nah," the brute replied. "Just another roving pack. When we got word that Beraht here was leading some *rodeks* through our range, we decided to make sure you encountered no trouble."

"Rodeks?" Tomas asked Aebreanna quietly. "I don't recognize that word."

"A term for races other than the Uldra themselves," she explained. "Loosely translated as: 'soft-bodied and weak.'"

"Well, as long as he's not being insulting."

"Actually, the term is often used as a one of endearment between an Uldra and someone he feels is deserving of protection."

"I really don't know how to feel about that," the squire said.

Aebreanna grimaced. "Few do."

Rogan was still speaking to Dradjek. "Does that mean that we won't encounter any Druug during our trip through the mountains?"

The Uldra boss shrugged. "We've cleared a lane through our range to the *Tarad Adelit*." Although the Uldra leader spoke effectively in the Velish tongue, his accent was nearly thick enough to stand on.

"We appreciate the help," Rogan told the Uldra.

"Don't worry about it," the boss replied. "You're Calonar's boy, so you get the same help he gives us. Just don't forget us when the next war rolls around."

The knight laughed. "Don't worry, if things keep going the way they have been, there'll be war enough even for you."

"Come!" Dradjek laughed, or perhaps roared, Tomas was unsure which. "You will enjoy our village's hospitality! We can give you a proper send-off before the witch Vara kills you!"

Rogan glanced at Aebreanna, whose sudden loss of color and violent trembling betrayed just how she felt about spending any extended time in the company of a gang of Uldra. She said nothing, but only sat astride her trembling pony, her head either shaking an emphatic denial, or succumbing to a spasm. Rogan sighed. "Ah, as much as I would love to experience a true Uldra send-off, I'm afraid our mission is critical, and time is of the essence. We can't afford the weeks a village such as yours would use to properly toast us."

"Very diplomatic."

"Shut up, kid."

Dradjek shrugged. "Oh, don't worry!" he barked as several of his warriors stomped forward to take the reins of their trembling horses. "We won't keep you more than a single night. We've been hoping for a reason to have a proper celebration!"

"No doubt the celebration of the mountains being tall and the sky blue was growing somewhat stale," Aebreanna muttered.

Tomas was unsure of what he had expected from an Uldra village. Most of what the Republic had taught its youth had been based on how the Uldra had lived while as slaves to the Sylvai Empire and then during the world-shattering Uprising. The Elector Lords never considered it worth their time to learn how the mountain clans lived in modern times. The more civilized people of the Republic commonly believed that what went on in Ulheim was of little, if any, interest to good and proper Humans; so long as the Uldra caused the Republic no serious problems, it was best to ignore the barbarians. For the majority of Lanasia, the strange mountain clans were little more than an oddity.

Having spent so much time in the company of Beraht and Remm Stonebearer, two rather extreme examples of the Uldra, Tomas could not help but feel that the assumptions of the Republic's people had been correct. The barbarians of Ulheim were a short-tempered, often violent people with only the most tenuous grip on civility. No doubt, or so the squire assumed, their communities would reflect the rough speech and temperament of the Uldra. After all, so many in the Republic justified, the Uldra had not built any cities in hundreds, perhaps thousands, of years; since the destruction of most of their civilization, first by the Khepri and then the Sylvai, the Uldra had taken to living in small villages surrounded only by the members of their respective clans.

When the party was led by Dradjek and his warriors into a nearby valley, Tomas was struck dumb by what they found.

The village was of moderate size, its streets and buildings conforming to the twisting valleys in which it was built. Dozens of houses and places of work radiated out from a large center, in which was a great hall that could likely serve as either a place of worship or for community gatherings. Smoke poured from innumerable workshops and the streets were bustling with activity. Each home was tall and wide, reflecting the people who lived within, with granite walls and carved wooden roofs that demonstrated great care in both design and construction. Although a thick blanket of snow surrounded the village, each porch and street showed signs of meticulous sweeping, and any excessive mounds had been cleared from the yards and gardens surrounding each home. A smoking chimney rose from each roof with the smells of baking bread and meat being carried by the mountain winds across the miles that separated the village from the ridgeline upon which Tomas and his friends traveled.

As the group approached and proper recognition was given by their escorts, many of the Uldra children ran out to greet them, happily jumping into the arms of their fathers and filling the air with laughter and unending questions about the new arrivals. Their delighted chatter came in a combination of Velish and the Uldric tongue, blurring together in the oddly harmonic accent of the mountain people. Once the identity of the visitors was revealed, the children, many already as tall as Tomas, gathered around Beraht with great enthusiasm, tugging on his scalemail armor and speaking so quickly in Uldric that Tomas was unable to make out much, if any, of what they said.

"Beraht seems popular," the squire observed.

Rogan nodded. "He's sort of a celebrity to the younger Uldra," he said.

"Because of the drinking or the violence?" Tomas guessed.

"Both," his knight replied with a grin. "Plus he carries that waraxe." Rogan pointed toward the weapon that rode, as always, on Beraht's belt. Watching carefully, the squire noticed that the surrounding children, despite their enthusiasm over having the chance to talk with such a celebrated member of their race, took great care not to touch the great waraxe.

"What's the story with that thing anyway?" Tomas asked. Following his knight's lead, the squire dismounted and led Urge by the reins as they followed along behind Beraht's slow moving parade of youthful enthusiasm. "Aebreanna once said something about it being an Uldra relic."

"It's holy," Rogan answered. "That waraxe is one of the most important artifacts in the Uldra religion."

"Why does he carry it then?" the young man asked. "Shouldn't it be in a shrine or something?"

"You have to understand how the Uldra think, kid. To an Uldra, something is only important if it's useful. They don't believe in having purely ceremonial objects. If that weapon couldn't be used for something, then it wouldn't be important and couldn't be holy."

"How'd Beraht get it?"

"Long story."

"He was hit by lightning," Aebreanna said from where she still rode on her pony. The Sylva was holding a kerchief to her face as though wiping it clean, yet obviously trying to block an unpleasant smell. Mayva was not so subtle, though. The white pony was thrashing her head and grumbling at her surroundings.

"Hit by lightning!?!" Tomas replied, stunned by the implication.

Aebreanna nodded. "Oh yes. He had entered a ruined shrine to the Uldra Allfather. As we waited outside, the sky suddenly grew dark and a bolt of lightning crashed into the building. When we entered, Beraht was standing in the middle of the room with smoke pouring from his body and that weapon in his hand."

"Was he all right?"

"Compared with what?"

The squire had no answer to that. "What's so important about the waraxe?" he asked. "Other than it can get you struck by lightning?"

"The Uldra believe it's the weapon of the Nameless," Rogan answered.

Tomas nodded. The Nameless was what history called the unknown Uldra who had appeared in Pelsemoria in the wake of the Disaster at Nassinalia. Stories varied from race to race and place to place, but the most common ones said the Nameless led his people out of Sylvai lands and back into Ulheim, returning centuries later to wage the great Uprising against their former enslavers. After the end of that terrible war, the Nameless disappeared.

"No wonder he's so popular," the squire noted.

"Sir Beraht's popularity has little to do with what he carries," Aebreanna sighed.

"Then what is it?"

The Sylva sighed and dismounted as their procession approached the village's well and the collection of gray-bearded Uldra waiting there. "Observe and learn."

The village children retreated away from Beraht as he approached the collection of elders. Their barbarian friend removed his helmet, letting the mountain wind catch at the few strands of his hair that had escaped his purple headband. Beraht nodded in respect to the gray-beards, a nod the elders did not return. Although Uldra mannerisms were very much a mystery to Tomas, it seemed to the young man that the elders not only shared none of the enthusiasm the children had felt over Beraht's arrival in their village, but in fact behaved with indifference, almost hostility.

Beraht spoke with no hesitation in his native tongue to the gray-beards. If their barbarian friend noticed the chill in the elders' response to him, he gave no indication of it.

Rogan leaned in close to his squire. "Kid, you speak Uldric," he said. "What are they saying?"

"I'm pretty sure Beraht's telling them we're on a mission for House Calonar, and he's asking for their help."

One of the gray-beards, the eldest with a stout cane supporting his movements but still possessing strength enough to shatter stone, stepped forward and looked at Rogan, ignoring Beraht completely. "*Utar bagjorsun Rogan benhel Calonar cukhaver vehbikt*," he said with a voice deep but withered with age. "*Ajorgunnu yu lori kazik hirvorfsoi.*"

"They're greeting you as the son of Calonar," Tomas translated for his knight. "They're calling you a friend and ally, but they're mad about you bringing a Sylva into their village and something called a *vorfsoi.*"

"Outcast," Rogan muttered darkly. "They're talking about Beraht."

"Do they realize you don't speak Uldric?"

The knight shook his head slightly. "They're not talking to me, kid. They're talking *at* Beraht."

"So what do you want me to say?"

"Nothing. Let Beraht handle this."

Their companion began speaking in a low voice that, while it carried respect for his elders, nonetheless held within it the tone of command. Tomas had spent enough time with the barbarian that he had grown accustomed to Beraht's mood and could tell that it was only with sheer force of will that he was keeping his temper in check against the now-blatant disrespect of the gray-beards.

"He's telling them that as friends of Calonar they have to help us," Tomas translated. "That they're bound by their oaths to Calonar and something called *hayvut.*"

"Religious obligation," Aebreanna explained. "This must be Shinbetak."

"What's shinbetak?" the squire asked. "They used that word before."

"The Day of Rest. All Uldra are required by their religious law to not only take a day off from their labors but also to give aid and comfort to at least one other person or group in need."

Beraht's words had clearly struck a chord among the village elders. The gray-beards had retreated to the far side of the well to speak in hushed voices that did little to hide how little they liked the situation in which they had been placed. Their discourse lasted only a few minutes before a hush fell over the assembled villagers as another Uldra entered the small square. The new arrival, though unbowed by age or infirmity, walked with a staff made of iron with numerous copper runes engraved along the shaft and a stylized well at the tip made of what looked to be the purest silver Tomas had ever seen. The assembled Uldra stood aside reverently, making slight nods of respect as they allowed this new Uldra to pass. Even the gray-beards, clearly used to having the respect of the younger Uldra, stepped away from the well to allow the new arrival a place alone in a position of authority.

"Who's that?" Tomas whispered.

"The Keeper of the Well," Rogan answered in a soft voice. "The village leader."

The Keeper of the Well moved to stand directly in front of the village well, holding his staff before him and surveying the assembled Uldra with dark, unflinching eyes. He wore the same heavy leather tunic so popular among Uldra men but was unburdened by armor or weapon, and his beard flowed freely in the cold breeze, without the gold and silver adornments his people favored. His long black hair was kept in place by a simple leather headband.

"*Beraht benhel khamjorn ruden kupallakt hirmarun,*" the keeper finally said. "*Shinbetak yuir chekt.*"

"Beraht, son of a grave-builder, speaks with the wisdom of something called a *marun,*" Tomas translated.

"Teacher," Aebreanna supplied. "The closest thing the Uldra have left to a priest."

"He says that Shinbetak must be honored," Tomas continued. As the Keeper of the Well addressed the assembled villagers, the squire kept translating for his knight. "The Keeper is calling for someone to step forward and provide a meal and place to sleep for—"

"For what?"

"I'm not sure, but I think he just called us children."

"Probably just a bad translation.

"Hey, I'm doing my best here."

"Don't do your best," Rogan instructed. "Just do better."

An Uldra wearing a scorch-stained leather apron and carrying a massive hammer stepped forward. His scarred face and hands betrayed the danger of his profession, and he walked with a noticeable limp. "*Rohr benhel Rolst chekt Shinbetak,*" he said.

The keeper nodded. "*Rohr benhel Rolst. Ek chekt helka dak.*"

"We're being introduced to Rohr, son of Rolst," Tomas explained. "I'm pretty sure he's volunteering to take us in for the night."

Apparently satisfied, the Keeper of the Well turned and left the village center, as did the gray-beards and most of the assembled Uldra. Their host, Rohr, stepped forward with a grin that stretched the skin on his weathered face. "*Beraht benhel khamjorn,*" he said.

Their Uldra companion faced Rohr with an equally large grin on his ugly face. "*Rohr benhel Rolst,*" he replied. The two shared a rough embrace before Beraht turned to the rest of the party. "Rohr," he said in Velish, "my friends can't speak the true language."

Rohr walked forward to stand less than a breath from Rogan. To his credit, the knight did not allow any sign of the discomfort he felt at such proximity to show. "No worry, my friend," the metalsmith said in broken Velish. "I say Human words." To Rogan, he said, "Welcome, son of Calonar. My home yours for Shinbetak."

Rogan clasped the Uldra's offered hand and let only a muffled gasp of pain escape his lips as every bone in his hand was reduced to powder. "Thank you, Rohr," he said through clenched teeth. "We are honored by your generosity."

The knight gestured to where Aebreanna stood beside her pony. "This is Aebreanna, daughter of Calonar." The Sylva gave an exquisitely graceful curtsey that did not match the look on her face.

"Sister?" Rohr asked.

"By deed more than blood," Rogan explained. The knight then gestured with his barely functioning hand to Tomas. "My student, Tomas."

"Student?" the smith remarked. "Very lucky." The squire's heart started thundering in his young chest as the hulking Uldra stepped up to him and extended his hand in greeting. Several excuses flashed through Tomas's agile mind, but a single look from his knight quashed any hope of escaping the pain to come, and the young man clasped hands with the Uldra.

For the remainder of his life, Tomas was convinced he had developed a slight muscular twitch from that greeting that never properly healed.

Chapter 17

Once the introductions had been completed, Rohr led the visitors through the village. The Uldra community seemed even stranger to Tomas up close. Most of the buildings used the traditional wattle and daub method so common in eastern Lanasia. Wood frames supported the plaster-like walls, and thatched roofs offered cover over what appeared to be stone floors. But a few of the homes and shops were different. These larger buildings, the ones most noticeable from a distance, were newer. These had stone and mortar walls supported with thick timber columns and roofs of heavy oak, carved with intricate designs of looping knots. Tomas politely called their host's attention to these larger newer buildings as the group made their way through the wide, unpaved street.

"New build," Rohr shrugged in answer to Tomas' question. "New ways. Better."

Beraht pointed to an older building they passed. Its walls were crumbling and its frame splintering. A team of three Uldra were pulling the wattle and daub apart, and a large pile of newly-quarried stone rested nearby. "As the old buildings wear out," he said, "instead of repairing, we're replacing."

Rohr's home was easily discernable from the other buildings in this part of the village by its open-air forge. The fire still burned, though low. Three great anvils surrounded the fire, and a long workbench held an array of neatly-organized tools of the metalsmith's trade. To the side of the forge was some great collection of steel and copper, partly covered with a great sea of canvas. Like the rest of the newer houses, Rohr's home was tall and wide, a house built of mortared stone. The wooden roof was carved with more of the strange, intricate decorations, the ones on the smith's home forming icons of his trade. The large, fenced yard held no animals, but several children of varying ages played happily under the stern supervision of a female Uldra who looked to be in her late teens. Of course, Tomas knew Uldra aged slightly slower than Humans, which could easily have put her at close to thirty or forty years. Their host opened the tall wooden gate, which to him barely reached his hip, and formally invited the guests into his home.

The children, upon catching sight of their father, immediately stopped their game and rushed to try their best to tackle the patriarch. After some good-natured rough-housing, Rohr eventually let his children know the identity of their visitors, and just as quickly as the young Uldra had forgotten their previous game, their father was forgotten in favor of attacking Beraht.

The Uldra warrior took the children's game as equally well as Rohr had. Being at last allowed to regain his feet, Beraht walked with Rohr to where the Uldra maiden stood waiting with a blush on her cheeks and her breath coming in short gasps. She was tall, of course, but shared little of the thunderous heft of Uldra males. She was not lean by any measure, but instead had a full-figured, well-proportioned body. Her blonde hair reached to her back and was tied into twin, looping braids adorned with silver. She wore the homespun dress common to the Uldra females and heavy half-boots.

A brief introduction was made in Uldric, and Beraht gently took the girl's hand in his own. Rohr's sister Dagna, as she was introduced to Rogan and the others, barely glanced at the non-Uldra during the introductions, instead taking every opportunity to steal quick looks at the oblivious Beraht. Finally freed of the necessity of courtesy, Dagna was sent inside the house to inform Rohr's family they would have guests for the Shinbetak dinner.

Within moments, during which Rohr had time only to show his guests where they could tie up their horses, his matronly wife appeared in the doorway. She was, of course, as tall and muscular as any of her race, but Tomas was struck by how bright and friendly her smile was. Rohr's wife had not a single hint of a frown blemishing her round face and the several loops of her blond braids were adorned with brightly-polished steel and gold.

"Friends," Rohr said proudly, "my wife, Annfrid."

Annfrid wiped her powerful hands off on the spotless apron she wore around her broad hips, then warmly embraced her husband before greeting each of their guests individually.

"And this Tomas, student of Rogan," Rohr gestured to the squire who nodded in greeting. The reference as Rogan's student was declared more as though it was the squire's status or rank than his employment.

Annfrid enfolded his hand in both of hers and bathed him in another warm smile. "Welcome, honored student," she said, again making Tomas's position sound like a badge worthy of the highest respect.

"You speak Velish very well, ma'am," the young man replied.

"My father is merchant," she explained. "He trades with Calonar often. As a girl, I would go with him. I learned Human words."

Rohr looked up to where the sun was dipping lower in the sky, already grazing the tips of the western peaks. "Is meal ready, wife?" he asked.

Annfrid turned and began moving back toward the house. "Nearly," she answered. The lady of the house pointed to where one of her daughters had brought out a large basin of steaming water and several towels, placing them onto the porch. "Wash." Her words, while still carrying the warmth and kindness that seemed to push back the bitter chill of the mountains, nonetheless allowed for no misunderstanding of being a request.

Aebreanna was ushered into the house by Annfrid's daughters, who wasted no time in tying an apron around her tiny frame so large it had to be wrapped three times around. Rohr led the men to the steaming basin and stripped off his leather apron and tunic and proceeded to wash himself. Shivering slightly in the sharp wind, Tomas was hesitant in following suit even as Beraht stripped and also cleaned himself.

"Couldn't we do this inside?" the young man asked rather plaintively.

Rohr and Beraht paused in their washing to stare at the squire for a moment before the metalsmith leaned over to Beraht and muttered something in Uldric.

"I do *not* have to sit down when I pee!" Tomas objected.

Rogan grabbed his apprentice by the collar and half dragged him to the basin where the knight started stripping off his cloak and tunic. "Kid," he grumbled, "just shut up and wash."

After the test of manhood was complete and just barely passed, Rohr led Beraht and his shivering companions into the blessed warmth of his home just as Annfrid and Aebreanna, with the help of Dagna and Rohr's daughters, were bringing the food from the kitchen. The sight of their Sylva friend in so domestic a situation brought any number of remarks to Tomas's lips, but a single burning look from Aebreanna's seething opalescent eyes brought the young man up short. Rogan noted the silent exchange and grunted. "So that's what it takes to shut you up," he noted.

Rohr led his guests to a large table that sat very low to the floor, with a large meal was arrayed upon it that smelled so delicious it nearly made Tomas swoon. After so long on the road, the young man had nearly forgotten what a warm, home-cooked meal smelled like. Even as Dagna led each of them to their appropriate place at the table, taking extra care to ensure Beraht was comfortable, Tomas could not help but wipe his mouth of excess drool as his eyes roamed the table from the platter of steaming meat to the cauldron of gravy and mounds of fresh vegetables. His stomach began angrily reminding the young man of just how long it had been since their last decent meal.

Annfrid's oldest daughter set an unlit candle in front of each place at the table just before her mother arrived with a candle of her own, this one lit. Seeing Rohr and Beraht stand, the others followed suit. Annfrid went round the table, using her candle to light the others one at a time and saying a brief blessing with each lighting. Once done, the matriarch returned to the head of the table and brought forward a small barrel of what Tomas assumed was ale. Rohr said a blessing over the barrel as he opened it, and everyone else passed their cups forward. One by one, Rohr filled each cup and passed it back down the table, filling one extra and giving it to his wife who placed the cup at an open place at the table's far end.

Once each person had their drink, Rohr turned to face his family and guests. The metalsmith smiled and said, "*Barukaba Shinbetak.*" Each person repeated the phrase, and all sat down. Annfrid stood and sprinkled a small portion of salt over the great loaf of bread before offering it to her husband and retaking her seat. Rohr tore the bread into several pieces and distributed them equally to his family and guests. Following the lead of Beraht and their hosts, Tomas, Aebreanna, and Rogan waited until the bread had been distributed, including one piece that was put at the empty place; this done, all present took a single bite of the bread, and the meal began in earnest.

It took all of Tomas's control not to gorge himself as quickly as possible. The meal was a simple one but made with obvious care and tasted better than anything the squire could recall. Even the ale, though strong enough to make him gasp a bit at each swallow, was delicious, with a hint of fruit easing the bite.

It surprised the young man at how much courtesy Beraht and the Uldra were demonstrating, with great care in the consumption of the food and drink and the conversation remaining on unimportant topics. No one spoke out of turn, and even the children sat patiently and asked for permission before speaking. Compliments were made to Annfrid but not embarrassingly so. Most surprising of all was the lack of belching, which Tomas had thought to be vital to any Uldra meal.

Rogan noticed his squire's confusion and smiled. "What's on your mind, kid?" he asked.

"I'm just a little surprised at… well, everything," the young man admitted.

"Not-Uldra think they know us," Rohr said after swallowing his food. "Few learn how Uldra live."

"I mean no offense," Tomas insisted. "It's just that the Uldra I've seen are so different from the people who live here."

"Uldra know how to behave in proper times," Annfrid said. "Unlike Sylvai, we know when relax and have fun. But unlike Human, we know when is time for quiet and peace."

Rogan and Tomas shared a look across the low table.

"No offense," Annfrid insisted with a mischievous smile.

"I guess there's still a lot we just don't know about the Uldra," Tomas admitted. "No matter how long our two races have been friends."

"Even friends not know everything," Rohr replied. "What you want to know?"

The young man thought for a moment, taking another bite of the delicious potatoes. "I honestly don't know where to start." The squire glanced at the empty place at the table. "Why did you set a place that wasn't going to be used?"

Before Rohr could answer, his wife stopped him and gestured to one of her daughters. The young Uldra maiden smiled and answered Tomas in a tone that suggested she was reciting a lesson. "We leave place open for the one who will come."

"One who will come?" Tomas asked.

"The Nameless," Rogan guessed.

"No," Annfrid corrected. "Nameless is gone. We set place in hopes of next one that will come."

"You mean the next prophet of the Allfather?" Tomas asked.

"Last prophet," Rohr said. "One that comes next will be last and greatest."

"So you set a place for the next prophet," the young man mused.

"Actually, squirt, we set a place for the one that will reveal him," Beraht grumbled. "A great warrior will reveal the next prophet. We set a place for him so that he knows how much we'll appreciate what he does."

"What about the prophet himself?" Rogan asked.

"The Nameless said that the next prophet would need neither bread nor ale. That he will come to bring comfort and wisdom to the whole world. We won't try and hold him to one house."

"It hope of each family they be honored by visit from one that reveals prophet," Rohr said. "To give meal to one so blessed would be great honor."

The squire nodded and glanced at Dagna, who sat quietly beside Beraht, still blushing and trying very hard not to be caught looking at the warrior. "You said Dagna is your sister?" he asked Rohr, not wanting to interrupt the younger Uldra's obvious concentration.

The metalsmith nodded.

"Why does she live with you instead of her parents?"

"They left village for *Karadak Boran*. She stay here until adult."

"*Karadak Boran?*" Tomas repeated, trying to translate the words. "The Allfather's Throne? I thought going to that mountain was forbidden."

"Except when parents are going through *Hayvut Althai Ferkrus*: the Rite of the Holy Path," Beraht said quietly.

"You know Rite?" Rohr noted in surprise. "Rare. Not many know."

"What is the Rite of the Holy Path?" Tomas asked.

"When child is born wrong, parents are blessed," Annfrid replied.

"Wrong?"

"Deformed," Rogan supplied. "Or sick, or any other serious problems."

"The parents take the child to the Allfather's Throne?" the squire guessed.

Rohr nodded. "Child taken to Allfather. If they survive journey and climb, Allfather heals child, and parents return home. Great blessing to be called to Allfather."

"What do you mean 'if they survive'?"

"The Allfather's Throne is in the middle of Druug territory, kid," Rogan told him, "near the ruins of Uldron. The parents would have to fight their way through hundreds of grey-skins to even reach the mountain, let alone trying to climb the tallest peak in the world."

"Great honor to be called," Annfrid said. "Greater honor to succeed. If they return, whole clan celebrates, and child is holy."

"Holy?"

"Child is touched by Allfather," Annfrid explained. "Destined for great things."

"What happens if the parents don't make it?" Rogan asked.

Rohr shrugged. "Family goes to Allfather. This life or next."

"Has anyone ever succeeded?" Tomas asked.

"Few," Annfrid replied. "Very few, but some. Those that do are meant for greatness."

Following the meal and cleanup, which everyone assisted in, Aebreanna was shown to Dagna's room where she would be allowed to sleep. The Sylva made no objection but was clearly relieved when the girl left her alone to sleep with the children. Rogan, Beraht, and Tomas were given what spare blankets and cushions the family had and made comfortable in the main room around the fireplace before their hosts retired for the night. Beraht was asleep very nearly before he finished falling, but Rogan and Tomas had some trouble getting to sleep due to the rather extreme noises coming from their host's bedroom.

"How long can they keep that up?" Tomas demanded irritably.

"From the noises he's making," Rogan mused. "I'd say not much longer."

"Are we leaving tomorrow?"

"Beraht wants to attend services with the village," the knight replied. "And Rohr's willing to put us up for another day, so I figure why not take the rest while we can."

"How long do you think it'll take to reach the Parent Mountains?"

Rogan thought about it. "No idea," he admitted. "Never been there before, so I can only guess. The Uldra'll guide us, so hopefully we won't have to spend too much time in the mountains."

"… And then… Vara," the squire whispered.

"Yeah."

Chapter 18

The cold sun dawned on the day of Shinbetak to find only a light snow falling and a halt to the cutting wind that had made the trip into Ulheim so unpleasant. The various fires started the day before by the Uldra of this mountain village continued to burn cheerily through the night, making it all the more difficult to rouse oneself from sleep. Tomas, serving as both apprentice and squire to Rogan, typically had little trouble rousing himself since he knew he had work. His knight was, by no means, a harsh taskmaster, but the young man had a deep-seated sense of responsibility forged by the years of hard living in the ruins of Pelsemoria where, if one did not work, one did not eat. Although Godsrestday was mandated by the Adamic Church, the survivors of the old capital could not afford the lost time. Tomas had naturally assumed that the Uldra, living as they did in Ulheim, surrounded by the monstrous Druug, would also be forced to compromise on the adherence to a religious day.

It came as something of a surprise when the day arrived, however, and Tomas could not find a single villager at work. Throughout the community, children played games in the fresh snow while the elders sat around fires talking of days and deeds long past. Families gathered and enjoyed each other's company, while those who preferred solitude sat in quiet reflection of life and their place in it. Beraht, once able to pry himself from the warm blankets he had enjoyed so much through the night, joined Rohr's family in their day of rest, playing with the children and spending time talking with the adults.

"The Uldra take their religion seriously, kid," Rogan explained, while he led his squire through a lesson in swordplay in Rohr's yard.

Tomas followed his knight slowly through the various forms, letting his muscles memorize how to move, while his mind drifted to other matters. "I know," he replied. "I just thought the mountains wouldn't allow them to have the day."

"Allow?" the knight replied with a snort. "I've seen Uldra in the middle of a war take the day off."

Tomas brought Steelheart up to a high guard position and rolled his shoulder to sweep the shinning blade around and down to a low guard. "What about Beraht?" he asked. "He hasn't stopped to observe a day of rest this entire trip."

"Watch your balance," the knight advised. "Never lose your center, no matter what your arms are doing." Rogan seemed to have the ability to observe his squire's every movement, even when not looking at him. Even a conversation was never enough to prevent the knight from making sure his squire learned the lessons properly. "Beraht wouldn't let his personal religious obligations interfere with a mission for the King."

Tomas tried to follow his teacher through the next series of new movements but could not seem to make his feet follow along. "I didn't get that," he admitted. "If Shinbetak is so important, then why does he compromise?"

Rogan moved to stand in front of his apprentice and repeated the last pattern at a greatly reduced speed, nodding in approval when Tomas completed the series. "You've got to get in the head of an Uldra, kid," the prince said.

"No thanks," the squire replied with a shudder.

The knight nodded to his squire and sheathed Talon. "Very funny," he said while drawing two wooden practice swords out from the bags and tossing one to Tomas. "Seriously though, never forget that, if you're going to fight someone, you have to get inside their head. If you can think like your enemy, you can anticipate their moves and more easily counter-attack."

"Were you planning on fighting the Uldra?" Tomas asked.

"God, I hope not. But it works for life in general, kid. To understand why someone does something, you have to get in their head." Rogan held his wooden sword at the ready, facing his student.

"Explain," Tomas said, holding his own weapon at the ready.

Rogan launched a series of attacks on his squire, nodding in satisfaction as the kid blocked each of them and send a few of his own attacks the knight's way. "What's the most important factor in Uldra life?" he asked when they had a brief pause.

Tomas struck low at his knight's legs; and after being countered as he expected, the squire rolled his shoulder in one of the patters he had just practiced and launched an overhead strike at Rogan's head, which the knight parried at the last moment. "Beer?" the young man suggested.

"Seriously," the knight grunted in annoyance before making two quick strikes to the young man's head before making a mirrored series that landed a blow on the squire's leg. "Think about the waraxe Beraht carries. It's a religious relic, but he still carries it into battle."

Tomas gritted his teeth, more in annoyance at his own inability to block the strike than the minor pain in his leg. "Everything has to have a purpose," the young man grunted. "Everything has to be useful."

"Exactly," the knight replied. "If the day ever comes that Beraht doesn't think he's useful to us or to the King, he'll probably retire... maybe even..." Seeing his squire recover and bring his weapon back to the ready, Rogan made a few more idle strikes and counters before launching the same attack that had scored a hit on his squire. Tomas blocked the attack this time and even parried, spinning on his uninjured leg and making a quick strike that landed just above the knight's tailbone with enough force to bring a bark of pain. "Easy," Rogan said through gritted teeth.

Tomas grinned. "Sorry," he said insincerely. "Too much for you, old man?"

Rogan blinked and then slowly narrowed his eyes and his student. The knight leaned back slightly and slowly brought his weapon into a low guard. Tomas had time enough only to think, "Uh oh," before his knight launched a blurring series of strikes that battered aside the squire's weapon and landed several ego-shattering blows to the young man's arms, legs, and buttocks.

"OK! I give! I GIVE!" The squire went so far as to throw his weapon into the snow to demonstrate his surrender.

"Good," Rogan said with an evil grin. "We should get cleaned up anyway. The village elders have invited us to their services."

"Us?"

"All right, me. But if I have to go—"

The squire shook his head. "I know, I know." Tomas shook his head as he picked up their remaining gear and followed his knight into the house. "You know," he mused loudly enough to ensure his teacher heard him, "I sighed up to learn how to fight like you, O mighty hero. I don't remember volunteering for diplomacy lessons, though."

Rogan turned and raised an eyebrow at his smart-assed apprentice. "Well, guess what," the knight said with irritation, "you volunteered. That means you get the same lessons in diplomacy King Cylan shoved down my throat."

Tomas and his friends, accompanied by Rohr and his family, traveled the small distance to the center of the village and the large stone lodge located there. Despite his earlier protests, Tomas made the trip with idle curiosity, wondering how similar an Uldra worship service would be to an Adamic one. Many academics shared a common theory that the Adamic faith had its origins with the worship of the Uldra Allfather. The theory stated that, turning their backs on their hedonistic worship of the Sylvai so many thousands of years ago, primitive Humans had turned to their Uldra allies to teach them monotheism. There were many religious scholars and historians who argued both sides of the belief that the Father Creator worshipped by the Adamics and the Uldra Allfather were one and the same. This argument, though never resolved, was put to rest, however, when the Lords Cardinal declared such ideas to be heretical three centuries ago. Despite the prohibition, there were many, especially among those with regular contact with the Uldra, who could not avoid speculation.

The building that served as both village assembly hall and center for worship had apparently been rebuilt in the same new style the Uldra had developed. It was now made of the same granite as the rest of the village, with shuttered windows and large doors at the center that rose tall, even for a Uldra. These massive iron doors carried the same intricate carvings that adorned the wood roofs and doors of the newer homes: twirling lines that formed great beasts and monsters, mountains and forests, seas and sky. In the center of each door, however, were great icons. On the left door was a chalice of gold held by an Uldra maiden, on the right was a silver waraxe held by an Uldra warrior, the mirror of Beraht's weapon.

Looking at these icons, Tomas asked Beraht of its meaning. "The Nameless," the barbarian replied. "We have no runes to write his name, so we use those: his cup and his axe."

The squire nodded his understanding. A thousand years ago, The Nameless had united for the first and only time all the Uldra clans and set the laws under which his people were expected to live. As much a high priest and prophet as he was a general or king, the Nameless had been revered forever after by the Uldra for what they credit as the creation of their society and restoration of a culture nearly destroyed by the invasion of the Khepri and enslavement by the Sylvai.

There seemed to be a strange inconsistency to the doors. They were partly open, allowing the villagers to enter, but the decorations along the inner edges, those that would meet with the door was closed, seemed irregular. While Rogan and Beraht spoke with Rohr, the young man curiously moved from side to side, trying to form in his mind what the doors would look like closed. In a few moments, his inner eye at last formed the picture. Together, the doors would form the image of a great open book.

"What is that?" Tomas asked. "The book?"

"*Knuuston*," Beraht said softly.

The young man glanced up at him and then back to the strangely-compelling image. "Knuuston…?" The word was close to his understanding, but just out of reach, like the scent of a beloved dish that invoked a treasured memory, nearly forgotten. "Wisdom? History?"

"All," Beraht replied softly. "More." His voice carried a tone that was at once utterly alien to the thunderous barbarian, and somehow indelibly part of him. "The great book of the Nameless. His laws. Our history, our present, our future."

"Your holy book? Like the Teachings for Adamics?"

"The holiest book." Beraht put a gentle hand to his waraxe and closed his eyes, raising his chin to the southern sky. "But not just for Uldra. For all of us." His head dropped then with a sigh. "Lost."

"The Uprising?"

The great Uldra nodded. "The Nameless had the last of our priests assemble all his words into one great book: *Knuuston*. But it was lost."

Rohr and Beraht led their group to one of the great oak benches at the front of the hall where they sat and waited for the rest of the villagers to find their seats. Tomas noticed that, although the entire village had arrived, the Uldra were in no great hurry to be seated, instead taking the opportunity to talk with the other members of their community about matters ranging from important to trivial.

Beraht sat down between Tomas and Aebreanna, to the Sylva's obvious irritation since that placed her beside Rohr's sister, Dagna, who had given the strange visitor little peace since their arrival. Dagna had taken an instant and unreturned fascination with Aebreanna, sharing with the stoic Sylva all the gossip of the village and her personal opinions on a wide range of subjects. The Uldra maiden had also tried to help her newfound friend prepare for the service by putting her long mane of wintery hair into a proper Uldra braid, looping and adorned with clasps of silver and gold. To her credit, Aebreanna had yet to draw one of her many thin, iridescent Sylvai blades, though her annoyance, with the Uldra in general and Dagna in particular, was clearly rising. Beraht had tried to keep Aebreanna and Dagna together as often as possible, the amusement it provided him to annoy his Sylva teammate being obvious.

Tomas took the opportunity to look around the great hall. The benches, like so much of Uldra architecture, were intricately carved with decorations and runes. This beautiful woodworking continued in the massive pillars supporting the vaulted ceiling. The young man at first did not notice, but then a beam of golden sunlight floated in through one of the narrow windows. The light drifted across the hall, drawing a line to a nearby bench. Tomas blinked, then saw that the carvings and runes were imbedded with gold. The squire looked around, now understanding for what he was searching. Gold adorned everything. Tiny, delicate spirals and streams, so subtle as to be nearly invisible, shone with craftmanship of skill far beyond Human imagination.

"The irony is," Rogan noted, "they don't have to mine any of it."

"They don't mine the mountains?"

"Sure they do," the knight nodded his head back out the large doors. "Remember that Rohr is a metalsmith. The Uldra extract stone, metal, gemstones, all kinds of resources from these mountains. The trade they maintain with the Keep is a large part of House Calonar's wealth." He looked around the gold-laced hall. "But they don't bother trying to find gold."

"Why not?"

"Remember what I told you about Human gold-hunters?"

Each of the surrounding Uldra started chuckling in deep, sinister voices. The hair on the back of Tomas's neck stood on end at the looks and laughter coming all around from the Uldra.

"The clans have come up with a game they like to play with anyone stupid enough to try and pull gold from their mountains," Rogan explained. "It's called..." he glanced at Beraht. "What was it?"

"*Girshoguir hirarkjuiram.*" The Uldra replied with an eager gleam in his dark eyes.

Tomas thought for a moment, making the translation, but convinced he was mistaken. "Kick the gold-hunter?"

"Pretty much their cultural pastime."

The squire looked to Beraht for confirmation, clearly in disbelief but somehow unable to dismiss the possibility. The barbarian nodded. "Each year, we get dozens of you stupid *ayner* that try to sneak into the mountains, hoping to make it back out with gold." He shrugged. "Druug get most of them."

"What about the rest?" Tomas asked incredulously.

"Well, we let them gather the gold," Beraht explained. "Then we catch them and take them to where we play the game."

"Each clan has their own slope," Rogan added.

"That's right," their barbarian friend agreed. "There's a lot of pride in which village has the best slope. Anyway, we take the *ayner* up to the top of the slope and let him jump off."

"You make them jump off a cliff?" Tomas demanded.

"Of course not!" Beraht insisted. "It's more like a steep hill. If they survive the fall, we let them go home. We keep the gold, of course."

"Wait, why do you keep the gold?"

"That's what you have a problem with?" Rogan asked.

"We trade it to Calonar's people," Beraht answered. "They give us goods we can't get or make on our own."

Tomas rubbed his temples with his forefingers, trying to avoid the headache he felt approaching. "So let me get this straight," he said. "You wait until the gold-hunters get through the Druug and gather as much gold as they can carry. Then you catch them and make them jump off a cliff... excuse me, a steep hill, and if they survive, you take the gold they found, send them home with nothing, and trade the gold to the Northern Keep?"

"And we bet on jumps," Rohr added from behind them.

"Bet?"

"Sure," Beraht nodded. "We bet on how far he'll roll, how many pieces he'll land in, whether he'll jump or have to be pushed, how long he'll scream, if he'll beg. Pretty much anything can be bet on."

"Why would people keep coming into these mountains?" Tomas demanded.

Rogan shrugged. "Every now and then, someone gets in and out with a huge amount of gold," he explained. "Even if only one person in a thousand gets through, that's enough for the desperate or stupid to think that they can make it too. After all, if someone does make it, it's a big payoff."

"That's terrible."

"The really funny part is when they get repeat players."

"Auris Venator," one Uldra said with a profound tone of respect. This name was picked up by others, and a happy conversation broke out amongst the mountain people. Tomas looked to his knight. "Famous gold hunter," he said. "Probably a legend. Kept coming back and getting caught and coming back again."

"True," Rohr insisted. "Six times he came and six times he was caught and made the jump."

Beraht nodded. "And on the seventh time, he was allowed to keep a portion of his gold."

"The same guy was thrown off a cliff seven times?" Tomas asked incredulously.

"Steep hill."

By now, the Uldra had more or less taken their seats, and the service had begun, with the Keeper of the Well dressed in the same clothes as Tomas had seen the day prior but this time holding a large leather-bound tome instead of his staff. "I thought your holy book was lost," the squire whispered to Beraht.

"Most," the barbarian whispered back. "Parts survive. Over the years, Keepers have added their own teachings and explanations of the Nameless' words."

The Keeper placed the great book on a stone altar bearing the symbols of the Nameless and stepped back, taking a seat to the side of the altar and being replaced by one of the gray-beards who had confronted Beraht and his friends the day before. The elder stepped up and opened the great tome with a grunt, struggling a bit with the size and weight of it.

"So is that still the *Knuuston*?" Tomas asked in a whisper.

"*Visdojom*: the Book of Sayings," Beraht answered in a whisper.

"Is that gray-beard the village priest?"

"There are no priests anymore. Our priests were wiped out during the Uprising. We call him the *marun*, the teacher."

The *marun* began reading out of the Book of Sayings in Uldric, using words Tomas could not translate, nor even guess at. The squire leaned over to Rogan and muttered, "Isn't it nice to be included?"

"Can you understand any of it?"

"Not really," the young man admitted. "He's reading about something that happened at the end of the Uprising. He keeps talking about something called the *Enirsobt*."

"Ah." The knight clearly gained some insight into what was happening.

"What?"

"How much do you know about the last years of the Uldra Uprising?"

"Just what the Republic historians recorded," Tomas replied. "The Sylvai and Uldra, on the verge of extinction, met in one last battle on the shores of Lake Tragedy and annihilated each other. After that, the Humans took over."

"Before that," Rogan grunted, "about the Uldra themselves."

"Not much," the squire admitted. "Human history talks mostly about what happened in Velaross, Kordenel, and Frostfront."

"In the last years of the war," the knight told his apprentice, "the Uldra had lost nearly all their people. Not just warriors, but everyone. They all knew their race was on the edge of extinction, so a few of the clan leaders got together and tried to convince the Nameless to abandon the war against the Sylvai and return to Ulheim. When he refused, one of the leaders tried to kill the Nameless and take his place."

"So what?" Tomas demanded. "Uldra fight over leadership all the time."

"You're not hearing me, kid. The clan leader didn't challenge the Nameless to a fight. He tried to assassinate him. When the Nameless found out about it, he slaughtered the leader's entire family, sparing only one grandson but putting a curse on the entire family. Ever since then, that family has been marked. The Uldra still call them traitors."

"How do you know so much about this?"

"The one survivor of the clan leader's family?"

"Yeah?"

Rogan nodded his head toward Beraht. "You're sitting next to his last descendant."

Tomas looked dumbly at his Uldra friend. Beraht sat silently, watching with dead eyes as the gray-beard before the altar read off the list of crimes his family had been accused of for over a thousand years. For the first time since he met the barbarian, Tomas thought he saw a look of mute suffering showing on Beraht's ugly face and the slightest of tremors running through his scarred hands. Looking around the room, the young man noticed that, from time to time, the eyes of each Uldra was drawn to where Beraht sat; those Uldra of advanced years held looks of accusation and disgust, while the younger villagers looked at the him with pity. Even those Uldra who had been friendly to Beraht still could not hide the disappointment on their faces as they spared glances at the last descendant of an assassin, the worst type of coward in the mind of the Uldra. Of them all, only the youngest of the Uldra, those not yet grown into their beards or braids, who looked to Beraht as though he were something other than the inheritor of a curse.

At the conclusion of the *marun*'s history lesson, the elder looked directly at Beraht, not even bothering to hide the contempt from his face. The gray-beard continued to speak in Uldric with accusation clear in his voice.

"It is important to stay in the roles of your life," Tomas translated quietly. "If the Allfather makes you a worker of metal, then you must work the metal. If you are made a hunter of beasts, then you must hunt the beasts. And those who have been marked with shame should admit their shame."

The squire stopped his translation and again leaned in to his knight. "Why are they so hot on Beraht?" he demanded.

"Beraht's a problem for the gray-beards," Rogan answered. "He was born with this black mark on him and was supposed to live a life of suffering and service to his clan and village. Instead he turned his back on his people, left his village, and joined the Legions."

"Is that why they're so mad?"

"Not exactly. If Beraht had gone off and gotten killed somewhere, then the family would have died off, and as far as they're all concerned, so much the better. But Beraht left the Legions and joined up with House Calonar, saving the world a few times and generally making a huge name for himself as great warrior. If that wasn't enough to make these guys mad at him, Beraht's also become a hero to a lot of the younger Uldra.

"Being so popular with the next generation is a problem for the old guard. Because Beraht's not only violated pretty much every rule the gray-beards have established but also carries one of the greatest artifacts in their religion, the young Uldra that are coming of age are starting to question the rules of the gray-beards."

"They're afraid of losing control," Tomas guessed.

"They're afraid of being proven wrong," Rogan corrected.

"And for that, these dried-up bastards are trying to what? Make Beraht cry? Why are we just sitting her listening to them?"

"Because we have to," the prince grimaced. "The clans are important allies to House Calonar, and we're agents of the King. We've been invited to an official function, and we have to sit through it even if it's just an excuse for the gray-beards to complain."

"This is stupid," the squire insisted.

"Welcome to diplomacy."

After a few more minutes of the *marun*'s lecture, Tomas was on the verge of responding, diplomacy be damned. It was only Rogan's rock-solid hold on his squire's arm that kept the young man in his seat, though the look on the knight's face showed that he too was losing patience. Finally, an end came from the most unlikely and, yet somehow, most appropriate source.

Aebreanna gracefully stood atop the great oak bench, planting her delicate hands on her sensuous hips, stared at the gray-beard until finally he stopped speaking. Looking with undisguised contempt at the assembled elders beside the altar, the Sylva spoke with a voice of soft steel. "Do you understand me if I speak in the language of the Humans?" she asked.

Another of the gray-beards stood and nodded. "We all know the words of the Humans."

"Good," she replied flatly. "My Uldric has never done justice to your inflexible minds."

"*Khazik* may not speak here!" the *marun* insisted. "This is a place for only the faithful to speak."

Rogan stood and put his hands on his belt. "Aebreanna Tressalon is a daughter of Calonar," he said in a booming voice. "You will hear her words." The knight took his seat without waiting for a reply.

Aebreanna again scanned the gray-beards. "Never before in my life have I witnessed so gross an injustice," she nearly spat. "You sit there and accuse *Beraht benhel khamjorn* of crimes committed a thousand years ago. You accuse him of cowardice and betrayal, while in truth you fear his courage and loyalty. When the Human Republic came under attack by Tienel Greysoul, there was no army of Uldra to challenge him, no grey-beard who could kill him; it was *Beraht benhel khamjorn*! When I was taken from my home, gravid with my children and stripped of my honor, no Uldra came to my rescue, except *Beraht benhel khamjorn*! When children were taken from their parents and forced into dumb slavery, the mighty warriors I see before me did not save them, nor even concern themselves with such dishonor! Instead, only one hero slaughtered the beasts and returned the saddened children to their weeping parents: *Beraht benhel khamjorn*! Most telling of all, when your Allfather choose the most worthy among the Uldra to bear the weapon of the Nameless once again, none of you, fearful and weak, were chosen. The Allfather's champion is *Beraht benhel khamjorn*!"

That last may have been too far, Tomas thought, as the gray-beards roared in fury and reached for weapons. The squire reached for his own blade but was stopped by Rogan, who just watched with a neutral expression. The gray-beards looked like they meant to move on Aebreanna and strike her down for her insolence but came to abrupt stop when Beraht stood and stepped in front of her. The look on the champion's face allowed for no misunderstanding. To attack the Sylva would require going through him.

"Even now you fear him," Aebreanna relentlessly continued. "You fear what he has accomplished with his entire life before him, while you fear the White Lady breathing upon your necks and have accomplished nothing. His name tower amidst the highest peaks long after yours have crumbled to dust. All that will ever be said of the elders of Clan *Aphek* is that, when the time came to support *Beraht benhel khamjorn* on his holy mission, they were too weak and fearful to do naught but shout accusations at him as a dog would bark at a bear while retreating from its fangs."

Without another word, Aebreanna dropped from the bench and swept from the hall, leaving the gray-beards standing and staring after her in shock. Beraht stood, staring at the elders for a moment more before turning and leaving as well. Rogan stood and straightened his belt. "I must apologize for my Sylva sister," the knight told the crowd more than the gray-beards. "Her people tend to let their emotions overrule their reason, letting all kinds of unpleasant truths run free." The knight bowed slightly to the village elders and led Tomas out of the hall, the two warriors catching up to their friends as they walked back to Rohr's house.

When at last they reached the home of their host, Beraht paused before opening the door. Turning to Aebreanna, the barbarian grimaced. "You couldn't have spoken up ten minutes earlier?" he demanded.

The Sylva raised an eyebrow at her lumbering friend. "You should consider yourself lucky I deigned to attend at all," she replied. "The smell in your 'holy place' very nearly drove me into the night."

"Like you've never done any night-walking," Beraht accused.

"Whatever needed to get away from your misbegotten kind!"

The two continued their argument inside where it was warmer. Tomas stared after them for a few moments before turning to his knight. "So do they like each other, or hate each other, or what?"

Rogan shook his head. "Kid, I don't think they even know."

Chapter 19

Rogan clasped hands with Rohr and bowed to Annfrid before mounting Stick. The warhorse snorted and pawed at the snow in his eagerness to continue their mission.

"Have care at Parent Mountains," Annfrid warned. "Even Druug fear evil who sleeps there."

"Isn't that why we're going?" Tomas muttered and climbed onto Urge. The squire's own warhorse, like his combative sire, was trembling not from the bitter cold of the early morning, but in anticipation of the battles that awaited them all in the days ahead.

Annfrid stepped forward and held up her right hand. "*Ruirchek enirkaradak denektem,*" she said, making the traditional blessing of her people upon departing warriors.

"*Ruirchek enirkaradak alktpotek helka,*" Beraht replied, bowing in his saddle.

Without another word exchanged, Beraht led his friends down the wide street that to the edge of the village. In the cold grey of the early morning, the Parent Mountains loomed large and undeniable, staring down on them as though in silent warning. Tomas looked back at the Uldra community that had sheltered them these past two nights and marveled at how easily the eye slipped over the snow-covered gray stones. Only the warm smoke floating up and away from the numerous chimneys gave any evidence of inhabitation. Not a single light could be seen escaping from any of the tall buildings, and no sound at all carried across the deep snow. With a deep breath that filled his young heart with resolution, the squire turned his face resolutely to the road ahead.

"We go no further," Dradjek said firmly. The hunter and his group had escorted them for the two days it took to reach the valley surrounding the Parent Mountains. As promised, the Uldra had cleared a path away from their village. The heavy snow had been cleared and scattered patches of Druug heads marked the passage. Dradjek and his hunters had left only a few hours head of them, and yet made much better time. The Uldra's massive bodies, their thick legs and thicker skin made movement through the Ulheim less of a hinderance. The smaller, shorter-legged Humans and

Sylva, to say nothing of their smaller mounts, could not possibly have made meaningful time through the mountains, especially with winter weather a constant threat. Thanks to the Uldra, though, the passage was fairly quick and without incident.

Rogan reached up an took Dradjek's hand. "I understand," he said.

"We will wait there," Dradjek was saying, pointing back to the far end of the valley. Most of the Uldra hunters were behind the mountain, refusing even to get this close. They kept their eyes averted and muttered prayers for the dead as Tomas and his friends had passed. "We will wait six days. If you have not returned, we will go home."

Rogan nodded and jerked his head to the rest of his team, nudging Stick forward.

Tomas could not take his eyes from the peaks ahead. The Parent Mountains were indistinguishable from each other. Both reached taller than any other mountain in sight. They were both bare of any vegetation. The sky was clear in a circle around the twin peaks, and no birds circled. There were no roads or paths in the surrounding valley. No ruins or signs of any habitation, present or past. "Do we know where exactly we're going?" the squire asked.

Rogan grunted. "Got a feeling finding her won't be hard."

Within hours of leaving the Uldra hunters behind, Rogan and Tomas were forced to dismount and begin breaking a trail into the heavy snowbanks' filling the valley around the Parent Mountains. While Stick and Urge greatly appreciated their efforts, the knight and squire went to their blankets that night with trembling legs and burning muscles.

"There has got to be an easier way to do this!" Tomas growled the next day as he and his mentor took a rest. The squire was sitting on a rock his efforts had exposed, one that, if left uncovered, could have spelled disaster for one of the horses. His breath came in steaming gasps as he worked through the breathing techniques Rogan had taught him that slowed the heart.

"If you've got an idea," the knight spat, "I'm all ears!"

Stick walked up and started shoving at his rider, encouraging him on without a thought for the knight's weary body. Rogan forcibly shoved the warhorse's head away irritably. "I'm trying to rest, you overgrown mule!"

Stick sighed impatiently. "God, I hate that horse," the knight sighed.

"Where did you get him anyway?" Tomas asked.

"The Endless Sands," the knight replied.

Tomas barely glanced up as Aebreanna knelt down beside him. She reached up, under the sleeves of his long tunic and began rubbing a flowery smelling ointment into his arms.

"I did a favor for the Padishah of the Shamashi a while back, and he gave me Stick as a reward," Rogan continued.

"You should have asked for money."

Rogan just grunted, unable to form words as Aebreanna's ministrations began ono him.

Tomas glanced up at where Beraht was standing watch from a small rise. The Uldra warrior's normally casual demeanor had been replaced upon their departure from the Uldra with a steady awareness that never wavered. Beraht's eyes scanned the area around them constantly, letting nothing go uninspected.

"How do Uldra move through this snow?" the squire asked as he absently rubbed his neck, adjusting for the partially open golden rose pinned as always to his collar.

"Used to, we didn't," the warrior replied, never wavering in his scans of their surroundings. "Winter came, we stayed home. Now, things change."

"What do you mean?"

"New inventions," Beraht said. "Machines with steam and wheels, of steel and copper. They melt the snow, keep the paths open."

"What?" Tomas snapped. "Why in Underworld didn't we bring one?"

"There's only one in the whole village," the Uldra shrugged. He jerked his thumb towards Sus, where his great shire horse was idly chewing on a tuft of exposed grass. "And it takes four of those to move it."

"Oh," the squire blinked.

Tomas looked along the steep mountain slope they were approaching. The mountains towering above them rose so sharply that it was very nearly a cliff to one side and a ravine on the other whose bottom was obscured by the ever-present fog no amount of snow-heavy wind could move. He sighed heavily and stood, grabbing his shovel. The squire glanced past the rising slopes of the Parent Mountains. "Is it my imagination, or do the mountains get thicker past here?"

Rogan stood as well, bending backwards to elicit a crack from his spine. "Yeah, that's Grief's Chasm. Thick mountains around it."

"Grief's Chasm?" I don't remember anything like that in my geography lessons of Ulheim."

"It is new," Aebreanna said softly. "Relatively." She put away the salve she had been rubbing into the two Humans. "Best to keep your mind on the task at hand. Focus and preserve as much of your strength as possible. Remember, we still must confront the Witch of the Mountains."

"I thought Sylvai didn't like calling people 'witch.'"

"Normally, we do not," the Sylva confirmed. "But in this case, that particular descriptor is accurate. Every negative connotation you Humans associate with the term 'witchcraft' can be applied to the sorceress Vara with great accuracy. In point of fact, her crimes against you Adamics and your church pale in comparison with the various grotesqueries inflicted upon the *Sy'lva'n*."

"And the Uldra," Beraht added with a growl.

"You know," Tomas mumbled happily, "it may just be the ointment talking, but I think I'm starting to follow your sentences all the way to the end."

"You're just too tired to care, kid," Rogan noted. "Well, at least it'll only be another day or so before we start the climb."

The squire nodded and looked again at the deep mounds of snow ahead of them. "There has got to be a better way of doing this," he almost wept.

His knight retrieved the pair of small shovels they had brought along from the Keep for just this reason and handed one to his apprentice. "Shut up and shovel," he grunted.

As the sun dipped behind the peaks overhead, they realized that the snow was thinning. Somehow, not even winter could maintain a firm grip on the Parent Mountains. Their pace increased and whichever of their group was shoveling had an easier time of it as the slope grew higher. Finally, while Aebreanna maintained security and Rogan rested, Beraht stopped his shoveling. "That's far enough," he said.

Rogan roused himself. "We've got another hour or so of light. We should get as far as we can before night to have the whole day to find her cave."

Beraht turned and looked at his Human friend. "That's far enough," he repeated without a change to his voice or manner.

"Right," the knight agreed. "Probably best to conserve our strength."

Their two small tents were erected, and a campfire started. Tomas saw to their horses as Rogan began pulling out their armor. Beraht went back to a small stream downslope while Aebreanna prepared a warm meal. Once the chores were complete they devoured the food.

"Do we have a strategy?" Tomas yawned through a full mouth.

Rogan cracked his neck and glanced up to the massive peaks. "We go straight at her. Nothing clever."

"What's wrong with clever?"

The knight shook his head. "No point," he replied. "She knows we're here. As powerful as she is, there's just no way to sneak up on her. Hopefully, she'll be in a mood to talk."

"Oh yeah," Tomas agreed. "Because that's what evil, soul-stealing witches are known for. Conversation."

"You have a better idea?" Rogan demanded.

"No," the squire admitted. "But I'm not the world-renowned hero feared by evildoers everywhere."

"Let us assume Vara does know of our arrival," Aebreanna interrupted, "and there is no reason to believe that logical assumption is incorrect. Assuming also that she has power enough that, had our deaths been her desire, she could have achieved them while we were still some distance from the Parent Mountains, then we can maintain the hope that she has not only allowed us to approach but is also curious enough to allow us to address her."

"What happens if we don't say anything interesting?"

"Then we do what should've already been done," Beraht grumbled. "We end the Witch of the Mountains."

Tomas looked across the fire to Rogan. "I guess we'd better have something interesting to say then."

The knight shrugged. "First time for everything, kid."

"If we do have to fight her," the squire asked, "how do we do it? You've said Vara is on the same level of power as the King and Cyras Darkholm."

"Honestly, kid, I have no idea."

"Fighting individuals with that degree of power is like fighting a force of nature," Aebreanna said. "To ask how one goes about defeating Vara is to ask how one might defeat the tides or the winds."

"How did you beat Tienel Greysoul?" Tomas asked. "He was one of those impossibly-powerful wizards, right? How did you do it?"

"Luck," Rogan snorted. "Blind, stupid luck."

Aebreanna sighed. "Sadly, chance does have an oversized influence on such confrontations. We can do our best, fight our hardest, but Fate will decide the outcome of our encounter with one such as Vara."

"You're not really helping, Aebreanna," Tomas muttered.

"Kid, the last thing you need to do is worry about it," Rogan advised. "Worry will only cost you sleep. If the battle comes, then we'll fight it, and we'll win. Vara wouldn't have let us get this far if she was feeling squirrely. Have you noticed how we haven't hit one serious snowstorm the entire time we've been in these mountains?"

"Sure."

"And have you noticed that, despite all the avalanches that roll down these mountains, there hasn't been a single one that's come down near us?"

"Now that you mention it."

"She wants to see us," Rogan concluded. "She's been making sure that we get through."

"Why?"

"Who knows?" The knight stood and moved toward the tent he shared with his squire. "Regardless, we know that she wants to talk to us, and that gives us a chance."

Tomas stood and entered the tent behind his knight. "So you're not scared?" he asked.

"Are you kidding?" Rogan laughed. "I'm on the verge of wetting myself."

The squire sat on his blankets, staring at his mentor. The knight just shrugged and grinned at his apprentice. "Hey, if it makes you feel better, just remember that the soul-sucking Queen of Evil is probably scared of us too."

Tomas sat back and laughed in derision. "Why would the witch who stained the Velaross basilica red with the blood of a hundred innocent children be afraid of us?"

"Like you said, we took down Tienel. The Greysoul may not have been as powerful as Vara, but he was definitely up there in the evil masterminds club."

"Well, that's great for you, but what about me?"

"You beat a Zafael, remember? And you helped beat a Death Mage. Your survived the Lamashti. That's nothing to sneeze at."

The young man thought about that for a few minutes, letting the fact of their previous successes fill him with hope.

Chapter 20

The team rose with the predawn light barely appearing in the eastern sky and made ready for battle. No words or instructions were necessary. Each of the heroes knew that, although there remained the hope that the sorceress Vara would allow them to approach and talk, there was the very real possibility of battle against one of the greatest, most feared arcane adepts in all Arayel.

Tomas helped Rogan into his splintmail, and the knight aided his squire into the chainmail, each pulling the armor over their blue and grey long tunics and securing them with the thick leather belts that would carry their respective swords. In the bright morning sun, the crossed diamond regalia the two warriors of House Calonar wore seemed to glow with an inner power that pushed back the bitter cold around them. Although he had spent most of his life hating House Calonar and everything the family stood for, after learning the truth only a months ago and spending time with the heroes who made up that noble group, Tomas had developed great pride in wearing the crossed diamonds representing the greatest champion to ever fight for the people of Lanasia.

Rogan drew Talon and checked its edge, swinging the longsword a few times before again sheathing his weapon. Tomas mirrored his teacher by drawing Steelheart and making the same checks, though the flawless blade had no need of inspection; and as always, its balance was perfect. Rogan pulled his long red hair back and secured it with the leather headband Beraht had given him years ago, twisting his head back and forth to make sure it was secure and insuring the Uldra rune was centered on his forehead.

"What does the rune mean?" the squire asked.

"*Akh*," the knight replied. "Brother. Beraht gave it to me after Tienel kidnapped Aebreanna, and we went after him."

Tomas, also needing something to hold back his growing hair, brought out the white ribbon his beloved Mary had given him on the day he had won the Harvest Festival tournament in her name and pulled back his increasingly-shaggy locks, tying them in place with the fabric and letting the scent and memory of his beloved warm his heart.

Rogan saw this and raised an eyebrow at his squire. "A ribbon, huh," he mused. "Nice."

"Mary gave this to me," Tomas pointed out defensively.

"Your girlfriend gave it to you, huh?" the knight mused. "Nice."

"Yeah, well, what about your…" the young man looked over his knight's gear but had trouble finding anything as questionably effeminate as the ribbon his betrothed had given him. Seeing Rogan waiting with a raised eyebrow, Tomas finally just said, "Shut up."

Finally drawing out a pair of thick leather gloves, Rogan first pulled out the small golden ring that rode on an iron chain against his heart. He laid a quick kiss on the ring before replacing it and pulling on his gloves. "Aww, that's sweet," Tomas quipped.

"Shut it, ribbon boy."

Beraht replaced his old scalemail with a new suit Rohr had gifted to him the morning they left the Uldra village. He secured it in place with the massive leather belt on which rode his waraxe. The towering warrior drew a thumb along one sharp edge of his weapon, bringing a crimson line of blood that he smeared down the length of the shaft, muttering an Uldric invocation of the Allfather's power as he did so. Beraht then pulled the purple ribbon he kept tied around his head free and readjusted his thick hair before retying the ribbon and placing his horned helmet onto his head, saying without words that he was ready and eager for what lay ahead.

Aebreanna dressed in form-fitting black leather, folding away her cloak despite the deep cold and stretching her arms and legs. The lithe Sylva drew several thin Sylvai blades from her bags, tying them to her arms, legs, hips, and waist with great care. The spy's thick mane of winter-white hair was tied back in a tight braid that made Aebreanna's beautiful features predatory, with a silver band around her throat that had attached to it a blue and gray gem fashioned into Calonar's sigil. Seeing the boys around her watching and waiting as she finished her preparations, the playful baroness blew them a kiss and grinned wickedly.

"Everybody ready?" Rogan asked. Nods around, except for Tomas. A lassitude had fallen over his mind as the cold surrounding him seemed to dim, being replaced by a subtle warmth that moved around him like water. His hand absently went to the golden rose, its pedals half opened, that rode against the pulse of his neck. The warmth in his mind drew Tomas's eyes up, to the southern of the two Parent Mountains, and it seemed to the squire that he could see through the stone of both peaks. A cave as obvious as the mountains themselves rested only part of the way up the steep slope of the southern peak.

"There," the young man said softly, pointing toward the cave.

"What? Where? What?" Rogan asked. The knight looked up to where his squire was pointing but saw nothing.

"There's a cave right there," Tomas said. He could not understand how his friends could not see it.

Rogan turned to Aebreanna. "Do you see anything?" he asked.

The Sylva narrowed her opalescent eyes and scanned but finally shook her head. "Beraht?"

The Uldra took a step forward and stared hard at the spot Tomas was pointing to. "I don't see a cave, but the way the mountain looks, there could be one."

Rogan thought about it for only a few moments before deciding. "Fine," he said. "As good a place as any."

The four heroes untied their horses but left them with the camp, seeing little purpose in trying to ride up the jagged slope just to leave them outside a cave they only hoped was there. With the passes all blocked with thick snow and any possible predators trapped outside, Rogan and the others reasoned their mounts were as safe in the valley as anywhere and unlikely to be able to stray very far.

The climb was not an easy one. Encumbered as they were by their armor and weaponry, the men struggled with each outcropping of rock. The group was frequently forced to adjust their course to take wide detours around deep crevasses and jagged cliffs. The ice and stones frequently rolled from beneath their feet. The nimble Aebreanna frequently danced away from such a sudden slide, but the Humans frequently crashed to their hands and knees. Only Beraht, whose people had an instinctual knowledge of how to move among rugged slopes of Ulheim, remained upright for their entire climb. The Uldra had to catch each of his friends several times over the ensuing hours, making a last-second grab as one of them was about to tumble into razor-sharp rocks. He took each opportunity to criticize their carelessness.

"I get it!" Tomas exclaimed as Beraht pulled him up from the deep hole that had suddenly appeared under the squire. "You are great, and I am nothing!"

Although Beraht had made a quick grab, snatching the young man out of thin air, the mountain-man had not as yet pulled him up. Instead, Beraht had taken the time to describe to Tomas all the myriad ways in which Uldra were superior to Humans. "If I have to pull you up one more time," the Uldra barked as he finally pulled the squire up, "I'm going to use that ribbon of yours to tie you to my belt!"

Once back on steady ground, Tomas looked at his Uldra savior with irritation. "Hey, you're wearing one too!" the young man pointed out.

Beraht grabbed the back of the squire's chainmail vest and leaned him over the edge of the hole. "What was that?" the warrior asked calmly.

"Oh, nothing," Tomas replied in an equally calm voice.

After another hour of missteps and last-second saves, the party finally reached the spot Tomas felt drawn to. "You realize that this is, of course, a trap," Aebreanna pointed out.

"Yeah," Rogan agreed. "But what choice do we have?"

"There's something here!" Beraht called out. The Uldra was kicking packed snow away from a narrow crack in the side of the mountain.

"Cave?" Rogan asked.

"Looks like."

"Well," Rogan said, "if it is a trap, she'll be springing it right about—"

The snow, stone, and ice surrounding the cave entrance exploded all around Beraht, forcing the warrior away from the cave entrance until he lost his footing and fell backward, down the rough slope. Tomas jumped forward and grabbed his Uldra friend an instant before he would have gone over the edge. Yanking him back, Tomas laughed. "Ha! See, you fall too!"

Beraht just pointed behind the squire with an irritated grimace.

The snow, stone, and ice that had exploded outward now coalesced back together, forming several lumbering shapes more than twice the height of a Human and thicker than three Uldra. Each creature roared with a great mountain wind from a gaping mouth in the center of its body, and, although they had no eyes, none of the monsters seemed to have any trouble locating their prey.

And one of the creatures was reaching a massive hand towards Tomas and Beraht.

Swearing in Uldric, Beraht grabbed his young friend and pulled them both over the edge and down the slope, continuing the fall until they landed in a deep bank of snow several dozen feet below. The Uldra's cursing continued even after they had landed until Tomas finished pulling his friend out of the snow. Beraht stared hard at the squire, who could only smile meekly in return.

Above, three of the creatures advanced on Rogan and Aebreanna, lumbering forward with the unavoidable lethality of an avalanche.

"What in Underworld are these things?" Rogan demanded.

"Elementals!" Aebreanna replied tensely. "Spirits of the Wyld given form and purpose!"

One of the elementals swung a massive arm overhead and brought an icy fist down towards the two heroes. Rogan and Aebreanna leapt in opposite directions, avoiding death by inches.

The knight darted forward and ducked under the swing of the nearest elemental. Rogan slashed with Talon, swinging the sword out and cutting the elemental straight through the middle. The creature paused for a moment and then brought both of its arms up and back down, nearly pushing the knight into the center of the world. "How do we stop them?" the knight roared, trying to be heard over the frozen wind each monster emitted.

"Steelheart is hardened against magic!" Aebreanna yelled back. "It can destroy their bodies! Beraht's axe! His faith can disrupt them!"

Rogan rolled to his feet and squared his shoulders. "Great," muttered.

Tomas reached out for a handhold to pull himself back up to the ledge on which he could hear Rogan and Aebreanna fighting the creatures. Finding nothing but snow, the squire could only struggle for a firm handhold.

"Will you hurry up?" Beraht roared. Although strong enough to easily bear the squire's weight, having Tomas squirming around while standing on his shoulders while he himself was trying to climb back up the mountain was proving more difficult than expected. "Just grab something and pull!"

A giant white hand reached down, grabbed the squire, and pulled, flinging him up and over, slamming into the snow above the cave entrance. "Ouch," he grimaced.

Fortunately for the young man, Tomas's vision cleared just in time to see one of the elementals, most likely the same one that had assisted him in his climb only moments before, reach back and send another frosty fist flying straight towards him. With a yelp, the squire rolled down and scrambled away from the towering monster above him. The creature, though momentarily confused by Tomas's evasion, quickly located its young target again and, having cornered him against a stone wall, reached both arms up to crush the squire.

The creature's torso suddenly exploded as an Uldra fist erupted from behind. Beraht roared in fury as he lifted the elemental above his head and threw the monster over the edge, sending it howling to the distant ground.

"Behind!" Tomas barked as another of the elementals tried to attack Beraht while the Uldra's back was turned.

He spun as the blow came down and, pulling his waraxe free, swung the weapon low, destroying the elemental's legs with one swing of the brutal weapon. Using the momentum of his initial attack, Beraht swung his great weapon up and brought the blade down in the middle of his enemy's chest. A heartbeat passed, and then the creature exploded in a hail of snow, stone, and ice.

Rogan was chopping at another of the elementals. Talon was not hardened as was Steelheart, nor holy like Beraht's waraxe, so the knight resorted to sheer brutality. He swung Talon, lopping off one arm, then another. Seeing the first appendage regenerating, Rogan swung again. He maintained his assault, trying to stay ahead of the monster's ability to restore itself. "Little help," he growled.

Tomas shot forward and swung Steelheart in a great vertical slash. The elemental was bisected. The two pieces fell to either side and exploded.

"At any point in which you men would care to lend assistance," Aebreanna snapped. "I would like to remind all those present that I have no weapons with which to harm these creatures!" As she spoke, the lithe Sylva danced between the two remaining elementals, punctuating each word with another dexterous move that only barely avoided an attack.

As one, the three men charged toward their besieged friend. Aebreanna leapt behind the boys just as Rogan and Tomas swung their swords low, separating the last two elementals from their legs. Beraht roared and swung his waraxe in a wide arch, destroying the two monsters.

A roar from behind pulled their attention. The last elemental, the one thrown over the side, was pulling itself back up. Tomas and Beraht charged forward. The squire swung Steelheart low even as the Uldra warrior swung his waraxe high. The last of the elementals exploded.

"Anybody see it?" Beraht called out from where he was leaning over the edge. Following the battle, the Uldra had demanded that everyone help him find his missing helmet. When he had been forced to save Tomas by hurling them both down the slope, his horned headgear and slipped off. Although hesitant to lean over the side, after being threatened with being thrown over instead, both Rogan and Tomas gladly offered to help.

"I hate to say it," Rogan said carefully. "But as thick as this snow is, we might never find it."

Beraht gave the knight a flat look of cold hostility. "Or we can keep looking," he suggested.

The Uldra's scowl deepened until finally he exclaimed, "There it is!" Without the slightest hesitation, Beraht stepped off the edge and dropped down into the fog below.

Rogan and Tomas darted forward in startled fear. "Beraht!" they called out.

"What?" he grunted, sticking his head up.

In startled confusion, both Humans leaned over the side and sighed in irritation when they saw the narrow ledge their Uldra friend was standing on. Both warriors walked away, grumbling to themselves. "Hey, somebody help me up!" the Uldra called.

Rogan and Tomas joined Aebreanna at the cave entrance, waiting only for their reckless companion to finish climbing back up and join them. Rogan sighed as he stared into the cave before them. "Well," he said, "now that the easy stuff is over, let's go see Vara."

The knight drew his sword and advanced into the waiting darkness.

Chapter 21

After only a brief disagreement over who would lead their party into Vara's cave, one Beraht ended by shoving Rogan aside and walking in, the four heroes entered the lair of the sorceress Vara. The cave, a narrow tunnel really, could accommodate only a single person at a time, forcing the adventurers to advance in a single file with their mound of Uldra muscle in front and Rogan close behind, ready to assist his friend when the inevitable danger revealed itself. Aebreanna followed behind the knight with their only torch held aloft, casting long shadows in the cold tunnel that Tomas in the rear tried not to imagine could hide any number of horrors. Not a single sound could be heard as they made their way down the gently sloped tunnel, ever deeper into the heart of the Parent Mountains. Neither light ahead nor hint of wind behind gave any indication of when their course would end and their confrontation truly begin with the Witch of the Mountains.

Tomas followed behind Aebreanna resolutely, refusing to allow the near terror that threatened to overwhelm him to abandon his duty. The squire held his sword low, noticing with wonder at how the torchlight reflecting off his weapon seemed to make Steelheart glow. Tomas took comfort in his weapon's presence, knowing that he was only the latest of a long line of warriors who had wielded the blade in a righteous cause. Frequently turning back as Rogan had instructed him to cover their backs, the young hero maintained his courage. Alexia's rose seemed to beat against his neck in time with his pulse, lending Tomas the support of his departed friend for the coming confrontation.

A strange, gentle warmth radiated from the cave ahead. Once the heat of battle had passed, Tomas had once again felt winter's cold fingers reaching under his armor and tunic. But now, as he followed his friends into the lair of the Witch of the Mountains, that wintery grip retreated. The squire found his shivering had stopped. He even noted a slight sheen of perspiration on his forehead.

"Aebreanna," Rogan whispered.

The Sylva extinguished her torch. The darkness that fell upon them lasted only a few breaths. Then, a soft light of bluish-green drifted up through the narrow tunnel. Music traveled with the light, soft and melodious. It was the music of winds and strings, of a gentle drum and an indistinguishable voice. Tomas could not make out words or even specific notes, but he did feel the welcoming pull of the kind voice and the placid music.

Beraht glanced back at Rogan, who grunted and nodded. The Uldra squared his shoulders and moved forward.

The tunnel opened into a very large cavern. The ceiling far overhead was lost in the shadows. The walls were distant, only barely visible. The ground was covered in a thick carpet of moss, soft and yielding to their feet. A path of smooth, flat stones led forward, to a staircase of beautifully-carved marble. The stairs curved around and up a great stone pillar, thicker than the greatest trees of Wildelves Wood. Beside the pillar was a small wooden cottage, whose walls and roof were carved in a bizarre amalgamation of Sylvai and Uldra styles, with swirling glyphs blending with images of nature. All around the cavern were tiny pinpoints of light. These lazily floated about, casting their inviting glow across their home. A few of them drifted towards Tomas and his friends. The squire looked closer and noted that the pinpoints of lights were, in fact, tiny creatures, as though Human or Sylvai but impossibly small, with fluttering wings of kaleidoscopic gossamer.

The four heroes paused at the entrance, taking in the sight. Finally, Rogan squared his shoulders. "Alright," he said firmly, "cottage or stairs?"

"I await you here." The voice, one of hearthfires, of kitchens and freshly-baked bread, floated down the marble staircase.

The knight sighed and shook his head. He then nodded to Beraht to lead the way.

The staircase had a curved banister of matching marble. The slope was gentle and the steps evenly-spaced, so that neither Beraht nor Aebreanna, with their vastly-different gaits, had difficulty with the climb. They drew higher and the air grew warmer. It did not become uncomfortably hot, but rather gained greater comfort; it became more inviting. At the top, a simple arch made of multi-colored roses allowed entry.

They moved through, weary.

At the top of the great stone pillar was a hot spring. An outer ring of uneven, moss-covered stones bordered the pool. The water itself steamed pleasantly and carried the faint scent of eggs. In the center of the pool was a gathering of stones, and against these rested a woman. She was half-submerged and half-obscured by the rising steam. The music filling the cavern did not come from her, for Tomas could hear her softly humming. She was facing away, yet still greeted them the moment they passed through the rose archway. "Welcome, dear sister," she said in a melodious voice that harmonized with the cavern's song. "I apologize for the rude greeting; I had honestly forgotten the sigil was there." She reached up and waved a hand forward. "Why wait there? The spring is a lovely now as when we first discovered it."

All three men turned their heads to look at Aebreanna, each carrying a question that needed no words. The Sylva returned their looks with a shrug of uncertainty. Finally, Rogan dismissed the words with a slight shake of his head and patted Beraht on the shoulder, signaling the Uldra warrior forward.

As one, the party pushed forward. Beraht and Aebreanna moved to the right, while Rogan and Tomas went left. The woman in the hot spring kept humming to herself, seemingly indifferent to their approach. They paused when on opposite sides of the pool. The woman sighed then. "I suppose you'll insist on making this as difficult as always, dear sister." She rose from the water, standing a little more than waist deep, and walked slowly through the pool, to a far edge. There, she ascended natural stone steps, emerging from the spring. She raised her hands slightly and the water rose with her, wrapping itself around her body, flowing and changing into some impossibly-smooth and delicate fabric. Her gown of blue and white conformed to her figure, emphasizing narrow hips and a small chest, dipping very low on her back and settling on her thin shoulders. Tomas realized she bore the Wyrdmark, just as did Aebreanna. Her body reflected the cold season, just like their Sylva friend's: her skin was the same alabaster, and her hair that flowed down to her bare feet was the same luminescent white. She turned to Rogan and Tomas.

She was a Sylva. Opalescent eyes with an azure glow regarded them for only an instant before widening. She gasped, her gaze fixing on the squire. She was clearly shocked at his presence and looked closely at the young man, her eyes finally stopping on the golden rose pinned on Tomas's collar. "She's dead," she said, not making it a question.

The squire nodded silently.

Sparks of blue power shot through Vara's opalescent eyes, and Tomas could feel a surge in his mind. A great pressure swelled in his head and the air seemed to be pulled from his lungs. Vara's hair rose in a gale of invisible power. Her small body rose above the stones and she raised her hands, outstretched towards the squire like claws. Hissing in rage, the Witch of the Mountains lashed an arm out, crushing Beraht and Aebreanna against the stones at their feet. Rogan was flung back with bone-jarring force, his body spasming with arcs of blue rage clawing at him. As Vara lashed out, Tomas blinked, the pressure in his head easing and his thoughts clearing. He made to attack the Witch of the Mountains, but she made a wide, sweeping gesture with her arms and the water of the hot spring surged, grabbing the squire's legs and pulling him to the ground. The water raised up, mirroring the sorceress' gestures, and thinned into whipping tentacles that lashed at Tomas, beating at his armored back.

As Vara attacked Tomas with her power, Beraht and Aebreanna leapt forward, trying to intervene, but were both stopped in midair as though they struck something solid. The Stealer of Souls, still hissing curses in a language not spoken in Lanasia for a thousand years, extended an arm toward Rogan and arched her fingers, forming her hand into the appearance of a claw. The knight had recovered and was moving forward, but had not escaped the notice of the Witch of the Mountains. In response to the sorceress' gesture, the knight dropped his sword and clutched his chest. All color drained from Rogan's face, and only a chocking gasp escaped from his lips as the knight fell.

Tomas roared and rushed forward, swinging Steelheart in a wide arc, not at Vara, but at the space between the Witch of the Mountains and Rogan. There was a flash of light, and the squire stumbled back, blinded by the disruption of magic. His knight gasped and relaxed, released from Vara's torment.

Aebreanna jumped onto Beraht's shoulders and vaulted into the air, flipping and launching a pair of her Sylvai blades at Vara. The sorceress made a negligent flick of her hand and the weapons were sent flying away. She then pointed at Aebreanna, and arcs of blue magic sent her spasming to the ground, her scream of agony tearing the air.

Beraht roared in mindless fury and brought his waraxe down, crashing through the invisible barrier. He barreled towards Vara, incapable in his rage of even snarling a challenge. Seeing this, Vara released her mystical grip on Aebreanna and turned, swinging her arm wide and pulling a white mist free from Beraht's chest that brought the Uldra warrior's charge up short.

"Do you see, mighty Uldra?" the Witch of the Mountains demanded. "I have your soul!"

With an anguished cry, Beraht dropped to his knees, his waraxe slipping to the floor from numb fingers and his tearful eyes locked on the glowing mist draped around Vara's fingers.

But just as he had seen happen to King Cylan during the battle against Anninihus months ago, the blue fire in Vara's eyes fluttered and died even at the height of her magical power, and the Stealer of Souls collapsed to the cavern floor with a trembling sigh. The mystical arcs dragging their horrid claws across Aebreanna's body vanished. The color returned to Rogan's face. The white mist around Vara's fingers snapped back into Beraht like a released bowstring.

Tomas did not hesitate to take advantage. He leapt forward and brought Steelheart up, ready to end this threat to his friends. "Wait!" Rogan barked, even as squire raised his sword. Rogan intercepted his apprentice midswing and, upon a demanding look, gestured toward Vara. "I think this was a misunderstanding," the knight said.

"She ripped out Beraht's soul!" Tomas snapped. "She's down, and I'm making sure she stays down!"

"Kid, do you trust me or not?"

The squire snarled in frustration but finally backed away.

Rogan approached Vara and knelt down beside the sorceress. "Are you dying?" he asked.

The Witch of the Mountains weakly snorted. She lay on the stones, crumpled and wilted like a discarded flower, her drab white hair hanging around her shaking body.

"Do you taunt me, prince of heroes?" she demanded. "Do you make sport before slaying me."

Rogan knelt and looked into her dim, opalescent eyes. "Calonar was poisoned."

"I know."

"He looked like this."

Again, Vara weakly snorted. "This is what comes to an adept from overexertion." She snarled at him. "I am only weak. Had you come mere weeks later…"

Rogan took a few steps back and looked closely at the sorceress. "What happened to you?" he asked.

Aebreanna was taking a closer look at Beraht, who had not moved, even after Vara's illusion had been revealed. "The storm," she deduced while inspecting her Uldra friend. "Manipulating the weather depleted her power."

The sorceress looked at Aebreanna with cold indifference. "I see you have not completely abandoned the gifts your father's blood grants you," she snapped. With a sigh, the Witch of the Mountains sat back, against one of the taller stones, taking deep breaths.

Aebreanna stiffened and blushed deeply but said nothing more.

Tomas stepped up behind Rogan and noticed that he too could sense something missing in Vara. It seemed as though she was hollow, almost transparent in the squire's eyes. "Watch it, kid," Rogan advised. "Seeing you was what set her off."

"Why do you delay," she said wearily, a hand covering her opalescent eyes. "Claim your prize and go."

"Prize?" Tomas asked.

Vara snared at the squire and made as though she would rise, but collapsed back to the stones, gasping. "Just do it," she nearly sobbed. "Kill me as you did her," the sorceress' opalescent eyes went to the golden rose.

Rogan glanced at Alexia's pin, then back to Vara. "Yeah," he said softly.

"What?" Tomas asked.

The knight shook his head. "She thinks we killed Alexia."

"What?" the young man was shocked at the accusation. "I didn't kill Alexia!"

Vara snorted her disbelief. "Your words are betrayed by the smell of her, Adamic. My sister's aura is all over you! You stink of her death!"

Tomas sheathed his sword and stepped forward, ignoring the warning from Rogan. Vara flinched away when the squire knelt beside her. "I was with her when she died," the squire said softly. "Just before, she gave me something. She passed some part of herself to me."

Vara stared at Tomas through her limp hair, letting her eyes drift from the partially open rose at his collar to his eyes and back. "She must have seen something special in you," the sorceress whispered.

"She saved my life."

"Are you here to kill me?" Vara's voice went small and weak.

Rogan put a hand on his squire's shoulder, pulling him back The knight knelt down beside Vara. "We don't know yet," he admitted, "but we do need some answers from you."

"And my answers decide whether or not my life is forfeit?"

"Yes."

Vara glanced once again at Tomas before returning her gaze to the knight. She weakly sat up. "Very well. Ask," she finally said, "and let us see where the conversation takes us."

Rogan stood and sheathed Talon but kept his hand close to the hilt, ready to react instantly. "Why did you attack the Keep?" he asked.

"Why should I speak honestly, knowing the answer may result in my death?" she asked.

"You want something," Aebreanna noted.

"Many things, Daughter of Fate. But only some of which you can provide."

"What do you want, Vara?" Rogan demanded.

The sorceress looked again at Tomas. "How did Alexia die?" she asked.

Tomas looked to his knight who nodded. "We were in a small town on the edge of Lake Tragedy," the squire said. "A warlord named Vagris had attacked the town a few days earlier and killed a lot of the people. He stole most of what little they had, including the virtue of their women."

"I know that name," Vara admitted. The sorceress glanced at Rogan. "And its history."

The knight said nothing.

"Vagris had threatened the people he spared that if they gave any comfort or aid to the agents of House Calonar, he would return and slaughter them all."

"Was Raven with you?"

Tomas took a deep breath and shook his head. "Raven had died earlier in a fight with the Praetorians. Alexia was taking her body to the Sylvai Vale when I met her. I'd agreed to escort her home."

"Why?"

"As penance for sin," the squire replied. "I had aided in Raven's death and, as penance, agreed to help Alexia take her home."

Vara said nothing; she just sat and stared at Tomas.

"When we entered the town," the squire continued, "the people realized that Alexia and Raven were in service to House Calonar. They attacked us. We fought the mob, but they overpowered us, beating us nearly to death and throwing us into the lake. The mob burned Raven's body and left us for dead. I pulled Alexia from the water and passed out. While I was unconscious, Alexia used the last of her power to save me."

"Where is her body?"

"She asked that I bury her in a small grove of trees beside the lake."

Vara nodded. "So my promise is kept," she said softly to herself, wiping a single tear from the soft wrinkles around her eyes. "I outlived you."

"You said she was your sister," Tomas pointed out. "I saw a genealogy of House Calonar."

"And my name was not upon it," the Witch of the Mountains finished. "I was the unwanted daughter of a Calonar matriarch. She was violated and forced into fertility."

Aebreanna gasped. It was a soft sound, strangled and cut quickly. Tomas glanced over and saw his friend looking away, trembling slightly.

"Indeed," Vara said softly, with the barest hint of sympathy. "Rare, but known to happen to Sylvai." She saw confusion in Rogan and Tomas. "We can control our fertility," the sorceress explained. "We decide when we may produce children. But, this choice can be taken from us by... hardship... by suffering. We can be forced into a fertility cycle and made to conceive." Vara glanced again at Aebreanna. "Such children are looked upon with pity, normally. Still, they are marked for life." She again looked to Rogan and Tomas. "As was I. My mother shunned me. Even my name is barely a grunt in the music of our language." The sorceress wearily rubbed her eyes. "My sister though, she was wanted, celebrated. We discovered our powers at nearly the same time. We have been... rivals for most of our lives."

"What about our questions?" Rogan demanded.

Vara sat, staring at Tomas for a long time before turning to the knight. "I am still at a loss as to why I should answer at risk to my life?"

"Your life's at risk either way," Rogan said darkly, with his hand resting on Talon's hilt.

"Oh please," the sorceress replied, waving the threat away. "I have information you desperately need and am helpless besides." Vara looked directly into Rogan's eyes. "I know you, heir of Calonar," she said. "I know you better than you know yourself. Darkholm and Fak'Har are not the only ones who know what is to come. My sister and her progeny are not the only ones who can peer into the truth of things. I am no longer a threat to your people and am helpless. You will never spill my blood unless I give you reason."

"You gave me a reason when you attacked my people," the knight reminded her.

"I harmed none of your people," the sorceress pointed out.

Rogan looked at Beraht, who was still kneeling, his eyes blank and his mouth agape.

"The Uldra will recover," Vara shrugged. "There was no lasting damage."

"To his body," Tomas countered.

"And yet," the Stealer of Souls argued, "he lives. I am, in the current moment, no threat. The designs of Anninihus' master are a clear, imminent danger, and you know it."

Rogan said nothing. He stared hard at Vara until finally taking his hand off his weapon with a low growl.

"Good," the sorceress smiled darkly. "I want a few things from you in exchange for the answers to your questions."

"What?"

"I will tell you everything you want to know, heir of Calonar. I will tell you who Anninihus' master is and what he plans to do. I will tell you how to cure your king, who the traitors are in House Calonar, and how to protect your family from what is to come."

"And in return?"

Vara looked at Tomas. "I want him. Or to be more precise, I want what Alexia put inside him."

"No," Tomas snapped.

"You've got your answer," Rogan added. The knight turned to leave, motioning for the others to follow.

"Would you be amenable to a compromise?" Vara called after him.

Rogan turned back and crossed his arms over his chest. "You can't have the kid," he said flatly.

"Fine," the sorceress replied agreeably, "but neither will I give you all the information you require."

"Then what?"

Vara smiled. "Three questions. I will answer any three besides those I offered."

Aebreanna narrowed her opalescent eyes. "In exchange for what?" she demanded.

"I want an oath from the hero of the Northlands that neither he nor any agent under his command will attack me now or in the future."

Rogan shook his head. "No permeant protection," he said flatly.

"Very well, an oath that, so long as I take no further actions against you, you will take none against me for a period of five years."

"Why five years?" Tomas asked.

The Witch of the Mountains shrugged. "After five years, none of you will be of any further concern."

"Is that all?" Rogan demanded.

"One matter more," Vara said with a dark smile. "I also want a vial of your blood, Daughter of Fate."

The Sylva stiffened in surprise but said nothing. Tomas looked at his Sylva friend. "What do you want her blood for?" he asked.

"Although your friend is unwilling to embrace her parentage, I am not so weak," Vara replied. "Her blood holds great power. I can use that to hasten my recovery."

The knight looked to Aebreanna. "It's your decision," he said.

The beautiful spy stepped forward. "Fine," she snapped. "One vial." Aebreanna pulled a blade from her hip sheath and drew it along the palm of her left hand. Vara held out a small vial she seemed to conjure from nothing as the Sylvai blood began to trickle out. It took only a few moments for the vial to fill, and Aebreanna turned away, tying a small piece of cloth around her hand. The sorceress looked at Rogan.

"I swear that neither I, nor any person I command, will cause you harm for the next five years," he said, "provided you don't attack us, either directly or indirectly."

"Three questions," Vara said as she stoppered the vial.

"Why did you attack us?" Rogan asked.

"I was hired by the master of Anninihus to create a storm powerful enough to ensure that you and your companions would not leave the Northern Keep on your little adventure until a time he specified."

"Why did he need to delay us?"

"You enemy wasn't ready for you yet. Apparently, Anninihus was not supposed to attack you as early as he did, and his master needed you delayed a little longer before you went looking for him. I imagine that, had you not killed the Death Mage, his master would have."

Rogan stared hard at Vara, putting several things together in his mind before asking the final question. "You put yourself at great risk draining yourself of all your magic to hit us with that storm," he pointed out. "Even if I didn't come and kill you, the Uldra might have."

Vara just sat and waited.

"What did you get out of this?" he asked. "What was your payment?"

The sorceress raised a hand to Rogan. "Assist me, and I will show you."

The knight hesitated a moment, then helped Vara to her feet. The Witch of the Mountains walked back to the pool and entered. As she did, the mystical material of her dress seemed to melt away, rejoining the steaming water of the hot spring. The sorceress waded to the center of the pool, to the collection of stones there. She reached into a nook and withdrew something small. Vara then waded back to the edge of the pool and held the object up, allowing Rogan and Tomas to see, but out of their reach.

It looked similar to the reading lenses Tomas had seen Esha use. It was perfectly round, fitting in the palm of Vara's small hand. The object had a frame of gold and bronze and silver, entwined like the vines of a plant. This frame enclosed a lens of glass or crystal, perfectly smooth and with the barest hint of blue light contained within.

"Is that…?" Rogan asked through clenched teeth.

"Yes," Vara said with a knowing smile. "After your battle with the Greysoul, Anninihus recovered it for his master. He traded it to me for the storm."

"Why would you want one of those?" Aebreanna asked. She had been helping Beraht to his unsteady feet, and somehow was supporting his massive weight. The Uldra was barely responsive to her touch, and his eyes remained unfocused.

"Why would I not?" The Witch of the Mountains countered. She held the lens up and looked at it. "This particular one will become very useful in the coming years, very sought after." She then leveled her opalescent eyes at Rogan. "And now I have it."

For a moment, the briefest instant, the knight seemed as though he would draw Talon, that he would violate his oath. Tomas saw him clenching and unclenching his jaw, tensing his sword-arm, fighting against his very nature. "Let's go," Rogan finally said, turning to leave.

"One thing more," the sorceress called out just as Rogan had reached the rose arch.

The knight turned back but refused to look at Vara or the strange lens.

The sorceress was staring at them, her opalescent eyes drifting from one to the next until finding Alexia's golden rose. She was biting her lip, clearing fighting against herself much as Rogan had just done. Finally, the Witch of the Mountains sighed. "Anninihus' master has laid traps for you in the foothills," she said with a resigned voice.

Rogan's eyes snapped to hers. "What!?!"

Again the sorceress sighed. "He wants to hold you in Ulheim until the war in Jarek has already begun, until you can no longer prevent the bloodshed." She sighed again and shook her head. "He wants to keep you out of Frostfront, since he believes you might be able to convince the Triumvirate to at least pause the fighting."

The knight stood for a few moments, saying nothing. Finally, "Why?"

Vara looked again at Alexia's golden rose. "Just go," she said with a hint of near disgust, but more with herself, Tomas thought, than anything else. "Go and be… what she no doubt hoped you would be."

Chapter 21

As the sun slipped behind the Parent Mountains, they gathered around their campfire in silence. Beraht had followed them, but said nothing. Their course was slow without his guidance and support. They needed hours to reach their campsite, so many that the sun had long retreated behind the mountains by the time they reached the questionable safety of their tents. Once there, Aebreanna mixed a drink for the Uldra that she said would put him into a deep sleep. "He will need time," was all she said.

They ate in silence. Finally, Aebreanna gave voice to what they all had been thinking. "We have only her word of this enemy force to the east," she pointed out as she picked absently at her food. The Sylva had been greatly shaken by Vara's words and, upon their return to the camp, had changed back into her warm traveling clothes. Despite the fire, Aebreanna had her thick fur cloak pulled tightly around her narrow shoulders.

"Why would she lie?" Tomas asked. Although greatly relieved when he and Rogan had removed the armor they had worn into Vara's cavern, the squire found the chill that wrapped around his sweat-covered body greatly unpleasant. No amount of clothing or fire could banish the chill that had settled into his young bones.

"Any number of reasons," Rogan grunted. "She's been her own agent for centuries."

"Like Cyras Darkholm," the squire pointed out. "Or Fak'Har, or Tienel Greysoul." His fingers rubbed the golden rose. "Like Alexia?"

Rogan shook his head. "Big difference there, kid."

"Indeed," Aebreanna added. "Alexia dedicated her life to helping House Calonar. The others…"

"It's a problem for later," Rogan insisted. The knight had finished his rations and now sat staring deeply into their campfire. "Right now we have to figure out what we're going to do next."

"We ran into all those mercenaries in the Wood," Tomas pointed out. "But never enough to stop us."

"Just slow us down," Rogan agreed.

Aebreanna gathered their wooden plates. "Our unknown adversary seems intent on controlling our progress."

"Suggesting we need to disrupt that," the knight decided.

"The question remains, how?"

"The tunnel," Beraht interrupted. They all turned and saw the great Uldra standing in front of his tent. His face was grim, but once again filled with unshakable purpose.

"What tunnel?" Tomas asked, taken aback.

Rogan looked to Beraht. "Could you find the entrance?" he asked.

The Uldra joined them at the fire, sitting and staring into the flames. "Some memories don't fade."

Aebreanna cleared her throat, handing Beraht food. "The entrance is beyond the ruins of Uldron, on the slopes of the Allfather's Throne," she reminded him. "To even reach the tunnel, we would have to go around through the worst of the mountains, into the heart of Druug territory, in the heart of winter." She stared hard into his eyes. "And we would need to pass through the village. Besides, there can be no guarantees the tunnel still stands."

"What tunnel?" Tomas asked again.

"Are you sure you find it?" Rogan asked his Uldra friend again.

"Rogan, you know through where we would have to pass in order to reach the entrance," Aebreanna insisted. "You are asking too much." Although she did not stand too near him, nor put a hand on him, there could be no mistaking her protective bearing.

"I can do it," Beraht said softly.

"Still waiting for an explanation here," Tomas said almost to himself.

Rogan glanced at his squire. "Come on, kid," he said. "As big a history buff as you are and you never heard of the tunnel under Ulheim?"

"The Uldron-Frostfront tunnel? I thought it was just a myth."

"When Frostfront allied with the Uldra, they built a tunnel connecting the Free City with Uldron. They used it to move supplies, the wounded, anything that had to be moved safely. And it's still there."

"Possibly," Aebreanna corrected. "No one has attempted to travel its length in centuries, let alone confirm it even still exists."

"But if we can get to the tunnel and use it to reach Frostfront, we can bypass the traps and make up a lot of time. Not to mention we could get into the Free City and talk to the Triumvirate. Maybe we can head off this damned stupid war."

"What would be the problem in reaching the entrance?" the squire asked.

Rogan pulled a map of the Northlands from his pack and showed it to Tomas. The knight drew a finger along his suggested course, through areas marked off by the Uldra as too dangerous to enter.

"That looks like some nasty terrain," the squire noted.

"Not for us," Beraht said grimly.

"Even with Uldra guiding us..." Tomas objected.

"The Ways," the mountain man interrupted. He looked to Rogan. "Another new invention. The clans have been using machine-diggers to build new tunnels connecting the villages." He stood and crossed to Rogan, pointing at the knight's map. "There's tunnels connecting Aphek, Merom, and Rephedim. We go back to the village and take the Ways south. We only need to cross from Rephedim to Uldron."

"Why not take these tunnels all the way?" Tomas asked.

Beraht shook his head. "They don't go that far. Someday, but not yet. The southern Way ends at Rephedim."

Rogan was staring at his map, his lips pursed in thought. "It might work. South to Rephedim. Only a few days through the valleys to Uldron. Then through the tunnel to Frostfront. We'd gain real ground."

"Rogan," Aebreanna said with rising heat. "To approach the ruins of Uldron, you know where we must first pass."

Beraht stood tall and glanced back at the Sylva. "I can do it, Aebreanna," he said almost gently.

"No," she insisted. The Sylva stared hard at Rogan. "You cannot…"

"Do we have any better options?" the knight asked.

She said nothing, only retreated to the tent she shared with Beraht. The Uldra himself grabbed a thick chunk of tack and entered the tent as well, where Tomas and Rogan tried not to overhear their heated exchange.

"Aside from the obviously-suicidal problem of going into the ruins of Uldron," Tomas asked. "What's the problem?"

Rogan stood and collected the field plates. "Beraht's home village is in the approach to Uldron."

Tomas joined him, helping with the cleaning. "Bad home life?"

"The village was destroyed. The people are all dead."

The squire stopped. "Oh," was all he could think to say.

His knight nodded. "This won't be easy on Beraht but, like I said, there's no other way."

They were quite as they cleaned. the plates were put away and the fire built up against the night. "Hey, Rogan," Tomas said.

"What?"

"What was that lens-thing that Vara had? It looked like you recognized it."

"Yeah," the knight said with a deep exhale. "That was the Mind's Eye, one of the Seals of Stalline."

Tomas dropped the wood bundle he had taken from a pack horse. "A Seal of Stalline?" he gasped.

Rogan helped gather the wood and build up the fire. "Yeah," he almost whispered. "We've seen them before. The fight against the Greysoul? It was over the Seals. He was trying to gather them."

"But that's forbidden!" Tomas gasped. No matter one's race, no matter one's House or position. The entire world knew of that greatest of taboos. "They MUST remain separate."

"Do you remember that time we were in Esha's tower?" Rogan asked, sitting beside the warm fire. His eyes floated into the flames, lost to time. "We were finding out about Anninihus' movements?"

Tomas sat as well. "Yeah," he said. "She'd conjured that map of Lanasia."

"Do you remember when she pointed out where Tienel's tower had been?"

The squire nodded. "It was near that giant crater, the one you said…" His eyes went to the knight.

Rogan nodded. "That's what happens when the Seals of Stalline are gathered in one place. Afterwards, we lost track of them. Rashid's been trying to figure out where they went for years." He glanced up to the Parent Mountains. "I guess we found one."

"A Seal of Stalline," Tomas mused in wonder. "Unstoppable magic." He looked at Rogan. "What does the… what did you call it, 'The Mind's Eye?' What does that one do?"

The knight shrugged. "I'm not sure, exactly. It's the Seal of Wind."

"Knowledge," Tomas finished. "Wind Magic is insight and discovery." He blinked. "And now Vara has it."

"Yeah. Good news."

Chapter 23

They finally exited the Uldra Way. The mountain air, though frigid, was a sweet ambrosia. The mist-shrouded valley, though grey and threatening, was an open paradise. The evergreen pines, though a foreboding screen against any number of potential threats, welcomed them back to the surface world. Like a group of souls, damned to Underworld but suddenly paroled back to life, Tomas and his friends emerged from the Uldra tunnel with an eagerness that bordered on mania.

There was no way of knowing how long they had spent underground. The Uldra miners told them they had only been traveling for three weeks. Although they had no reason to deceive their honored guests, still Tomas doubted. In his heart, they had spent years, perhaps eternities, trapped under Ulheim. Day and night were the same in the eternal twilight of the Way. Their eating and sleeping schedule were determined entirely by the Uldra miners, who told them when to stop and rest, when to take a meal, and when to carry on. Tomas had felt helpless during their interminable journey.

The worst of it had been the terrible noise. The digging-machine, which the miners had called an *auger*, had roared like a thousand, thousand lions. The great metal thing had carved a passage through the stone, grinding the unyielding rock to rubble and passing that back, onto an impossibly-long belt. The *auger* had moved slowly, but steadily, rumbling along on its iron wheels as though the mountain-roots were no more a hinderance than the open air would be to ox. Journeymen miners bellowed curses and orders to one another, manipulating levers, running wheels, and feeding coal into the great burning belly of the unnatural machine. Apprentices sorted the stone their digging-thing extracted, moving common rocks to another in their great relay of conveyors, while extracting valuable minerals and gemstones. Even miles back from the active work area, Tomas both heard and felt the incredible power of the Uldra and their machine as it carved a new Way under Ulheim.

There had been no sleep during their passage. The ground shook endlessly. The roar of the digging machine never stopped, never quieted. The Uldra miners moved constantly, clearing castoff stone and sorting minerals, relaying fuel for their digging-thing, barking instructions to each other and to their guests. The air was thick with dust. They made a point of stopping at each of what the Uldra called breakthroughs. The miners periodically adjusted their digging-machine, pausing its forward movement and sending a spiraling probe up. That long, spinning metal arm cut a channel straight up, to puncture a hole. At these points, for a few holy minutes, direct sunlight could breathe through, and a teasing hint of fresh air could be tasted. But even in these blessed spots, they could do no more than doze.

At last, in just one more of their endless, sunless days under Ulheim, the roar of the digging-machine had stopped. Tomas had, at first, thought he was hallucinating, imagining the sight, but ahead he saw daylight. This had not been the dim greenish light of the strange glass cylinders the Uldra miners carried, the heatless torches they had traded minerals for from the adepts of the Northern Keep. This had been true, radiant daylight. Tomas had rushed forward, but been beaten by Aebreanna, who had thrust him aside in her maddened charge into the open air.

Their Sylva friend had not done well during their subterranean passage. She had wilted into herself. When they rested, she curled into a tight ball, like a young kitten suddenly bereft of her mother. While they rode, her arms were crossed over her chest and her chin tucked in, opalescent eyes firmly closed. Her vibrant hair had grown limp and her shoulders slumped, as though she were carrying Ulheim on her very back. The welcome return to the open-air rejuvenated Aebreanna, though. She had charged out of the tunnel, riding atop the equally-eager Mayva with arms spread wide, her head thrown joyously back, and her mouth open as she eagerly drew in lungful after lungful of fresh air.

As tempted as he was to join the Sylva in her ecstatic return to the living world, Tomas instead joined Rogan. The knight was speaking to the miners, offering his thanks, and to a delegation of Uldra who had ridden up from the nearby village. They had exited less than a mile from the village of Rephedim, a stunning feat of underground navigation. Without stars or sky, the Uldra had maintained an accurate course south, digging their new Way with incredible accuracy. At one point, Tomas had asked the miners how they were navigating, and the Boss had opened what he called a map. This was, to the squire's eyes, only a bizarre diagram of triangles, strange numbers and letters, and straight-line arrows that connected nothing and led to nothing. Tomas had become increasingly convinced they were lost, until they emerged and found their target almost exactly where the miners said it would be. What was more, the villagers from Rephedim approached, having been expecting them to emerge on the day that was forecasted.

"We can't thank you enough for the help," Rogan was saying to Boss Koreh, who had led the construction of the Way.

The Uldra shrugged, shaking the knight's hand. "You Calonar-son" he said in broken Velish. "You ask, we help." Koreh was short for an Uldra, only a little taller than Rogan. He was even broader in the shoulders, though, which made him look a bit top-heavy. His knowledge of his trade was unsettling, though. He often glanced at an unpolished stone and identified it without error. He knew the digging-machine as intimately as a lover, interpreting unheard changes in vibration or tempo, making subtle adjustments, and keeping his crew working with tireless efficiency.

The village representative, a smiling grey-beard Uldra named Lehban, also took the master-miner's hand. "Welcome in our village," he said in similarly-broken Velish. "You team welcome as long as need."

Koreh shook his head. "We stay night, then back working."

"The tunnel isn't finished?" Tomas asked.

The master-miner shook his head. "Much work. Support arches, vault ceiling. Runes. Much work."

Lehban turned to Rogan. "What you, Calonar-son?" the grey-beard asked. "You stay?"

Rogan glanced at Aebreanna, who was kneeling at a small patch of flowers with white pedals and yellow stems that had somehow bloomed in the cold of winter. She had a revenant look on her beautiful face, and seemed to be revitalizing even as they watched, now that she had been freed of the Uldra and their tunnel. "Ah, no," the knight said thoughtfully. "Our mission is critical. We've got a long way to go and time is short."

The grey-beard glanced at Aebreanna and nodded. He then waved a group of young Uldra forward. These were carrying stacks of supplies, from foodstuffs to extra blankets. "Then you take gifts," Lehban said.

Tomas and Beraht accepted the supplies and organized them on their pack horses while Rogan offered the necessary courtesies to Lehban. Within an hour, the Uldra were making their way back to the village, Koreh and his miners leading the grumbling, steam-spewing digging-machine. Rogan sighed deeply, breathing in the cold, fresh air himself.

"So, which way," Tomas asked.

His knight shrugged and looked to Beraht. "Well?" he asked.

The Uldra nodded his chin in a seemingly-random direction. "West," he said.

A month after their departure from Rephedim, a month of frozen travel and unending tension, Tomas and his friends finally came within view of the lands once held by Beraht's clan. A narrow valley, heavily forested, stretched out ahead of them. To the north stretched an impossibly-large lake that stretched around Ulheim's peaks. Thick clouds overhead sent snow falling gently onto the heroes as they descended along an easy slope that differed from the rugged terrain that had plagued their journey thus far. Little sign could be seen of nearby grey-skins, adding to the sense of peace that each of the adventurers felt as they left the harsh mountains for this place of shelter.

For days, as they drew closer to Beraht's homeland, a single mountain peak came to dominate the western sky. The Allfather's Throne, greatest of all mountains, not just in Lanasia, but in all the world, towered above all its siblings. There could be no mistaking that peak, that mighty heart of Ulheim. Nor could there be any mistaking why the Uldra believed that incredible mountain to be the home of their Allfather. In the mornings, when rosy dawn was just waking from her slumber, already the tip of that impossible peak shown with the sun's first rays. In the evenings, long after twilight had drawn her curtain across the sky, still the Allfather's Throne remained backlit with the last embers of the day. The mountain wore the highest clouds like a royal mantle. And the great stone pyramid looked down on them as they passed, an ever-watchful, all-seeing king of Ulheim.

"What's that lake?" Tomas asked.

"The Lost Sea," Rogan said.

"I didn't know Ulheim had an inland sea."

"Not really an inland sea," Aebreanna corrected. "The Lost Sea is more accurately called a series of large lakes, the largest in Lanasia, in fact."

"Why, 'The Lost Sea?'" the squire asked.

"This was our home," Beraht said softly. "All Uldra. The Nameless tells us our people were born here. The Lost Sea was the heart of our culture." The mountain-man grimaced. "Until the Khepri, the Sylvai, the Druug." Beraht had grown increasingly withdrawn the farther they drew to that serene valley. Since they had finally caught sight of it, the warrior had solidified, nearly to stone. His friends knew that Beraht's homecoming could not be an easy one, but only Aebreanna remained unsurprised at how sullen their Uldra friend became as they approached the frozen lake. Although he continued to lead the team on their course, Beraht did not join his friends in their conversation, nor even rise to the bait as Aebreanna repeatedly tried to goad her troubled companion into yet another of their heated fights. An occasional sigh was the only sound Beraht made and then only when his eyes caught sight of something familiar.

They needed three days to reach the edge of the frozen lake. The gentle breeze drifting through that gentle valley allowed the snow to build into great mounds. This forced Rogan and Tomas to return to their hated task of breaking a trail. They dug a channel, frequently diverting around discovered stones, sudden dips, and newly-exposed roots. They continued to break a trail in the direction Beraht indicated, trusting to his memory and the growing sorrow displayed on their mountainous friend's large face. They rested often, falling into their pattern from the approach to the Parent Mountains: two dug, one rested, and one maintained security. They ate cold rations and collapsed to their blankets each night. They drudged on, digging their way to the shores of the Lost Sea. Only the sudden end of any trees marked where the lake began.

"Are we sure this is safe?" Tomas asked as he eyed the ice nervously. Having been raised in the warm South, the squire's knowledge of and trust in traveling on ice was minimal.

Beraht let his eyes drift along the lake with any number of emotions clearly playing out on his hairy face. "It's safe," he replied softly. "We'll have to lead the horses, but this time of year, it's always safe to cross."

"How much farther to the Allfather's Throne?" the young man asked, his eyes going as they often did to the great mountain dominating so much of the sky.

"Not long," the Uldra shrugged. "Once we cross the lake, we'll follow it west for just a few days before we reach Uldron." Beraht's eyes followed the lake south, towards an area bordering the shore where a few piles of stone could be made out through the thick mounds of snow.

Aebreanna followed his gaze. "We can spare the time if you wish," she told him gently.

Beraht nodded without looking away.

The spy glanced at Rogan. "Set up camp," she instructed. "We will not be long."

The knight nodded and started unpacking their equipment, and Aebreanna and Beraht moved towards those half-obscured ruins. Tomas glanced at Rogan and then turned to watch their friends. "It's their business," Rogan said, noticing his squire's interest. "Tie up the horses and find us some wood."

"You want to build a fire?" the young man asked. "Isn't that risky?"

The knight shook his head. "Minimal," he replied. "No Druug winter here, so this must be a disputed area. They don't usually fight in the winter, so we're as safe here as anywhere in these mountains. Might as well take advantage to thaw out a little and get some warm food before we make our run for the tunnel."

"What's over there?" Tomas asked dully as he started tending the horses.

Rogan shrugged. "The ruins of Beraht's village. He wants to pay his respects."

The squire nodded absently and struggled to focus on his task. Seeing his trouble, Rogan walked up and put a hand on his squire's shoulder. "You all right, kid?" he asked.

Tomas put a hand to his throbbing head. "I don't know," he replied. "I've been feeling strange ever since we got into these trees."

"Strange how?"

"I don't know. Detached, I guess. It feels like I'm here but sort of disconnected."

"We've been pushing hard," the knight told his squire. "You're probably just tired. Let's get that fire going and a decent meal. Then I want you asleep."

"No argument here."

Chapter 24

Aebreanna and Beraht returned after an hour or so and joined the Humans at their fire. The meal was simple but warm, which made it delicious. Although still somewhat withdrawn, Beraht was clearly in a better mood after visiting the ruins of his home and even joined Rogan and Aebreanna in their idle conversation. Tomas found himself dozing as they sat around the comforting warmth and quickly retired to his tent, only vaguely hearing Rogan as his mentor told him that the others would handle the watch. The squire was asleep almost before he had finished lying down.

Tomas's return to consciousness was partial at best. He had no memory of how he came to be standing outside, staring at the bright moon overhead with Beraht trying to get some kind of response from the young man. The squire was only dimly aware of the deep cold around him and the gentle glow of their fire, nor was he aware of why his eyes were locked so firmly on the sky overhead. Even when Rogan, roused by Beraht, tried shaking his squire and yelling at him, the only thing Tomas could do was continue staring at Vaeta.

"What in Underworld is wrong with him?" Rogan demanded once Aebreanna had emerged from her tent.

She pulled her thick cloak close to ward off the deep chill and crossed their small camp to look closely at the distracted young man. Placing a soft hand on the side of Tomas's face, Aebreanna gently pulled the squire's gaze down to meet her own. "Tomas," she said very softly, "can you hear me?"

"Yes," he replied dumbly.

"What is wrong?"

"It didn't happen here," the squire replied.

"What didn't happen here?" Rogan demanded. "What in Underworld is he talking about?"

Aebreanna held her other hand up, demanding silence, while keeping her opalescent eyes locked with Tomas's and never removing her hand from his face. "Where did it happen?" she asked.

"Can't you feel it?" the young man asked.

"No," the Sylva replied. "I cannot."

Without knowing how he did it, nor even why he was doing it, Tomas reached out his own hand and placed it on Aebreanna's face, mimicking her touch. The Sylva gasped as Tomas opened his mind to her, letting the strange tides in which he was caught flow into her mind as well.

"Wait!" Beraht snapped, putting an immovable hand on Rogan's shoulder as the knight made a move to separate them. "Watch."

Tomas and Aebreanna remained locked, each unable or unwilling to remove their hands from each other, nor even pull their eyes away from the locked gaze they shared. After endless moments, Aebreanna gasped again and pulled away from Tomas, nearly stumbling into the small campfire but saved by Beraht's quick reaction. Rogan stared at the spy as she struggled to regain control of her breathing until he could wait no longer and again moved to his squire. "Dammit, kid, wake up!" he shouted.

"Can't you feel it?" Tomas asked, raising his hand up toward Rogan's face.

"No, and I don't want to!" the knight barked, slapping his squire's hand away. For lack of any better idea, Rogan grabbed Tomas by the front of the young man's tunic and reached back in preparation to slap the besieged squire.

"Wait!" Aebreanna gasped. A questioning look from Rogan brought a gesture from the Sylva for patience. With Beraht's help, Aebreanna stood and moved back to Tomas. "He is not being attacked," she declared.

"Then what?" Rogan demanded.

"The power within him has sensed the tragedy that befell Beraht's village," the beautiful spy replied. "The spirits here are calling to him."

"Great," Rogan growled as he stared at his squire. "More dead people." The knight turned to Aebreanna with an angry look. "Is this going to happen every time we're around dead people?"

"I have little understanding of just what was done to our young friend," Aebreanna admitted. "I thus have no means of anticipating any future incidents."

"How do we snap him out of it?"

"We must accede to the wishes of the spirits." The lithe spy took Tomas's hand and once again looked into his eyes. "Tomas," she said softly, "can you take us to where it happened?"

The young man nodded and led the others through the trees, toward the ruins of Beraht's village. Aebreanna glanced back to Rogan. "Bring Steelheart," she said softly. The knight nodded and retrieved his squire's blade.

Despite the uneven ground, Tomas moved with a calm certainty, supporting Aebreanna when her small feet slipped on the snow or tripped over an unseen obstacle. Rogan and Beraht followed closely behind, trying their best to remain close without hindering their young friend. At last, Tomas stopped on a small rise that overlooked what remained of the village.

"He stood here," the squire said. Tomas's eyes drifted over the crumbling stone walls, pausing only briefly a large mound of snow, taller than any of the ruins.

"What's that?" Rogan asked in a tense whisper.

"My family's burial mound," Beraht replied flatly.

A stern look from Aebreanna silenced them both. She followed Tomas's gaze, and maintaining her firm grip on the young man's hand, the graceful Sylva leaned in close to whisper into his ear. "Who stood here?" she asked.

"He was looking for someone," Tomas replied.

"Who was he looking for?"

"The Heir's companion. He's supposed to live in this village, but I can't sense him." The squire's face darkened, and a bleak snarl curled at his lip. "He's supposed to be here."

"The Heir's companion?" Rogan asked, then looked at Beraht.

The Uldra glanced at his Human friend, then turned to stare at Tomas. "He came here looking for me?" the warrior demanded.

"Darkholm," Tomas muttered darkly. As the others watched in tense fear, darkness filled the squire's eyes as his expression twisted to one of complete hatred. Aebreanna gasped in sudden pain as the squire's hand clenched into a fist, threatening to crush her small fingers. She tried to jerk away, to free herself, but Tomas' grip was too strong. "He moved the companion before I could kill him!" Tomas raised his free hand and, making a strange gesture, summoned a ball of black light from the darkness surrounding him. With a muttered word in the arcane language, the squire sent the power lancing out toward a ruined building, destroying it utterly. "I will find him, Darkholm!" Tomas snarled as he used the darkness to destroy yet another ruin. He cursed in a language he could not know, a language dead in Lanasia for ten thousand generations. He snarled and cast Aebreanna aside, lifting both hands to lash at the ruins with shadowy bolts of sinister magic.

Tomas's three friends were all sent stumbling away from the young man as lance after lance shot out from his hand, destroying what little remained of Beraht's home. "Stop him!" the Uldra roared.

Rogan leapt to his feet and lowered his shoulders, clearly intending to tackle his squire to the ground but was blocked by a thunderous wind that sprang up all around Tomas, knocking Rogan to the ground and sending clumps of snow flying in all directions. "Where is he, Darkholm?!?" Tomas roared as he continued his mad destruction of a long-dead community.

When Tomas's eyes settled on the burial mound of Beraht's family, the Uldra leapt forward, heedless of the burning wind and stinging ice, to intercept any attack the squire might launch. With a snarl of contempt, Tomas clenched his fist and raised it up high. In response, Beraht was caught by some unseen force and lifted into the air. Despite the howling wind, Rogan and Aebreanna could still hear the gasps as Beraht desperately tried to breathe against the constricting magic being used against him.

"They are linked!" Aebreanna screamed over the wind. "Use the sword!"

The knight grimly raised Steelheart and advanced on his squire.

"No!" the spy screamed again. "Between them!"

Rogan launched himself against the wind and swung the blade into the space between Tomas and Beraht. There was a clap of thunder and a flash of pure white light. The Uldra was released from the magical attack and fell to the ground, unmoving. The knight then turned on his squire, anticipating his own attack and trying to prepare himself for it.

Before Rogan could take another action, though, Aebreanna also threw herself against the wall of freezing wind Tomas had summoned to keep them away. The graceful Sylva twisted with the wind and rolled midleap to land behind and slightly beside her possessed friend. Aebreanna reached around and pulled Tomas's shirt open before slapping her right hand against his exposed chest. Rogan was forced to look away as a blinding golden light exploded from both Aebreanna's and Tomas's eyes, filling the whole valley with a gentle warmth that banished all darkness.

"What was it?" Tomas asked as he sipped at the tea Aebreanna had given him.

The Sylva looked up from her examination of Beraht's ribs. "A memory," she replied before returning to the hairy torso of her Uldra friend. "The person who destroyed the village held power so great and so dark that the memory of the event imbedded itself in the land. When your mind was opened to the spirits here, that darkness possessed you, forcing you to relive the evil."

"I couldn't stop myself," the squire said in a weak voice. "I was there, and I kept trying to stop, but it was like I was stuck in a corner of my own mind, watching as I attacked you."

"That is, in fact, a very apt description of what occurred. The evil overwhelmed your mind and took possession of your body."

"Can it happen again?" Rogan asked from his seat beside his shaking squire.

Aebreanna began wrapping a bandage around Beraht's chest despite his objections. "Unlikely," she said. "Conditions must be right for the channeling of spirits, and with those past, the dark memory will fade again."

"We'll have to warn Frostfront and the Uldra about what's going on here," Rogan declared. "Hopefully, one of them can do something about it." The knight turned to Tomas. "Can you tell us anything about the guy that attacked Beraht's village?" he asked.

Tomas took a long drink of the warm tea and thought. "I don't know," he said. "I could hear his thoughts at the time, but it was so confusing. He wanted to find and kill Beraht before he could meet someone called the Heir."

"Rogan," Aebreanna supplied. "Darrell's prophecy refers to the Heir; we believe this person is Rogan."

"Because he's heir to House Calonar?"

The Sylva shrugged and finished with her Uldra patient. After putting her medicines away, Aebreanna washed her hands thoroughly as Beraht stood and twisted, grumbling various complaints and idle insults.

"What else, kid?" Rogan asked.

"He knew Cyras," Tomas added. "And he hates the Trickster Mage more than anything."

"Information which does not narrow our possible suspects," Aebreanna insisted. "Everyone who has met Darkholm has a distaste for him."

"It's not like that," the squire replied. "This guy's entire soul is filled with hatred for Cyras. Not just the man himself but everything he stands for. It's like his only reason for living is to not just kill Cyras but to beat him at something, to defeat him. To prove him wrong."

Rogan shared a look with Aebreanna and Beraht. None of the experienced heroes looked happy at this revelation. "What?" Tomas asked. "Do you guys think you know who it was?"

"Maybe," Rogan replied. "Do you have any idea what this guy looked like?"

Tomas shook his head. "I never got a feeling for what he looked like. Just that he's really old and really powerful. And you know, evil."

"There exists a not-insubstantial possibility he would be working to counter Darkholm," Aebreanna noted.

"But he's never made a move this blatant," Rogan argued.

"Who?" Tomas asked.

"Fak'Har," Beraht growled.

"The Shadowed Mage?" Tomas started. "Another of those ultra-powerful adepts?

Rogan took Tomas's cup and cleaned it out before putting it away. "Fak'Har is a very long story, kid," the knight said. "But you're right. The Shadowed Mage is one of those guys like Cyras and King Cylan. He's been around for a long time and has enough power to rip these mountains down around our heads."

"You've met him?"

"Not me," the prince replied. Rogan nodded his head toward Aebreanna.

"I have had the misfortune," the Sylva admitted. She mixed various herbs with warm water and gave the cup to Beraht who eyed it suspiciously. Aebreanna rolled her opalescent eyes. "Just drink," she sighed.

"Could the Shadowed Mage be the one who Anninihus was working for?" Tomas asked.

Rogan shook his head. "Doubtful," he replied. "It's just not his style to act so aggressively. Fak'Har is a manipulator. He doesn't make moves that are so blatant."

"Nevertheless," Aebreanna argued, "the evidence points to his implication in the destruction of Beraht's clan."

"Fine," the knight conceded. "But that's a problem for later."

"You're getting pretty good at postponing things," Tomas noted.

"We've got enough problems that are trying to kill us right now," Rogan snapped. "Let's worry about the things that will try to kill us later… later." The knight looked at Beraht. "I can image what's going through your head right now," he said.

"You really can't."

"Fair enough, but I need you now."

The Uldra picked up his waraxe and drew one of its edges along his right hand. Beraht did not allow a single look of discomfort cross his face as a thin line of blood dropped to the snow. "I swear that Fak'Har will die for his crimes," the Uldra warrior growled. "I will tear open his chest and eat his heart while it still beats. My clan *will* have their vengeance."

"Beraht," Rogan said softly, "I need you now."

The Uldra hefted his waraxe over his shoulder and nodded. "If I see the *basar*, then I will have vengeance. But until this mission is over, I will not hunt him."

Rogan nodded, and Beraht returned to his tent. Tomas stood and intercepted the Uldra before he entered. It was clear from his expression that the young man wanted to apologize but lack the proper words.

"Beraht—" Tomas began.

The Uldra held up a meaty hand to stop the squire before Tomas could become uncomfortably emotional. "The bent-wand's magic made you do those things," he said flatly. "There was no shame for you. When I find Fak'Har, you can join me in the kill and a portion of his heart is yours."

"Uh… thank you?"

Beraht patted his young friend on the shoulder and punched him in the stomach, sending Tomas gasping to the ground. "Don't do it again," the warrior advised.

Rogan turned to Aebreanna. "Will he be all right?" he asked, nodding toward his squire.

The Sylva nodded. "The damage to your squire was more emotional than physical. He will recover."

"And Beraht?"

Aebreanna snorted in derision. "You know as well as I just how much damage that barbarian can take. While a day's rest would be advisable, riding will not exacerbate his injuries."

"Good, at first light, we need to get out of here."

"Why?" Tomas asked. "I thought you said there weren't any Druug here."

"First of all," Rogan corrected, "I said probably. Second, that little light show that Aebreanna had to use to save your butt has alerted every grey-skin for a hundred miles that there's something interesting here, and I'd rather be gone by the time they get here."

"What was that light?" the squire asked, turning to where Aebreanna sat.

"I believe you have already been informed as to the degree of power my heritage can afford me," the Sylva replied.

"Wow," Tomas remarked. "No wonder Vara wanted a vial of your blood."

"I would consider it a favor on your part if you did not continue to place me in situations forcing me to employ a power granted by a person for whom I have no great affection."

The squire lowered his head and dropped back to his seat beside their campfire. "I'm sorry, Aebreanna," he said. "I'd give anything to take back what happened."

"Your encounter with the King's aunt has clearly granted you some form of arcane sensitivity," the Sylva pointed out. "Upon the successful completion of our mission, I would highly advise you to seek out instruction in the control of whatever power has been passed to you."

"Do you know what I am?" Tomas asked in a small voice.

Aebreanna's face softened at the squire's tone. She crossed the fire and sat beside Tomas, putting an arm around his slumped shoulders. "You are a just and honorable young man," she replied. "And you are the squire to Rogan Eigenhard. Keep these facts always in your mind. No matter what the future holds, nothing can change these facts without your allowance."

Chapter 25

Only part of the Allfather's Throne was visible below the thick clouds stretching without break across the sky. The titanic mountain appeared to be perfectly white, with not a single rocky blemish marring its wintery mantle. Unlike its lesser siblings, the Allfather's Throne was not pressed on all sides by mountains, instead towering over a great valley dotted with numerous trees, streams, and the ruins of Uldron, the great city of the Uldra, center of their nation and religion.

"The Explorer's Guild once tried to mount an expedition to study the ruins of Uldron," Tomas related to his friends as they followed the remains of a road that had long since returned to the forest. "They disappeared without a trace."

"Some places keep their secrets," Rogan said in a low voice. "Some places aren't meant to be visited." The knight's eyes were everywhere as they continued down the ancient road; he never stopped scanning the trees around them and overhead for any danger.

"There are all kinds of legends surrounding the ruins," the squire continued in a soft voice. "They say the Uldra hid a great treasure under the city when the Khepri invaded. They say the Uldra had secret knowledge that was lost in the ruins, and that's why the Nameless ordered his people back here, to try and rediscover it."

"Other than its cultural and religious history," Aebreanna argued, "Uldron holds little real value. The only reason the Khepri destroyed the city and the Uldra tried to rebuild it was because Uldron was at the heart of Uldra society and was thus the key to their unification."

Beraht held up his hairy fist, bringing his friends to an immediate stop. Tomas realized he was holding his breath as the warrior dismounted and moved on silent feet through the snow toward a threat only his Uldra senses could detect. Following his knight's lead, the squire loosened Steelheart in its sheath, letting all his senses reach out in anticipation of attack.

Their Uldra friend approached a thick cluster of trees and reached into the snow between two of the larger trunks, drawing out something dark and sinister. Beraht was shaking his head in annoyance as he walked back, holding the evil thing up for Rogan and the others to see. "Druug club," the warrior grumbled.

Tomas looked closely and confirmed his friend's identification with a shudder, his mind going back a year to his first encounter with the grey-skinned monsters and his close brush with death. "What's that tar covering it?" the young man asked quietly.

"Druug blood," Beraht growled again.

Rogan swore venomously and rubbed his bearded chin in deep thought. Tomas realized the ichorus blood meant something, but could not understand what. The squire looked to Beraht for an answer.

The Uldra shook his head. "They're hunting each other," he answered. "They're awake, and hungry."

"I don't understand," the squire admitted. "Why would they hunt each other?"

"Thanks to Vara," Beraht replied, "winter came early. The Druug were caught unprepared, and they're starting to go hungry. The ones that couldn't hibernate will be hunting."

"How many do you think didn't hibernate?" Tomas asked.

The Uldra shrugged and tossed aside the club, cleaning the viscous Druug blood from his hands with snow. "Not many," he said. "In a pack of a hundred, maybe a dozen of the weakest will stay awake."

"A HUNDRED!" the young man gasped. "Druug packs don't get that big!"

"Not normally, squirt, but the packs are big around the Lost Sea."

"So dozens of Druug are running around these woods, and they're getting so desperate for something to eat that they're starting to eat each other?"

"Normally, the Bull would stop that kind of thing, but with winter so early and so strong, the pack would've been caught unprepared. The Bull would've driven the weakest off. Those've been eating each other to survive. Only a few will be left; the meanest, most desperate."

"Decision time," Rogan said grimly. "We weren't expecting this."

"Indeed," Aebreanna agreed. "We expected to be able to pass through as the Druug hibernated. That any are active is unexpected and dangerous."

"Can't go back," Beraht muttered. "Too much time."

"Besides," Tomas insisted to Rogan. "I've seen you take on three Druug by yourself. The four of us should be able to handle a couple of the weakest that have been starving all winter."

"All right, Mr. Hack-and-Slash," the knight growled, "Let's tone down the motivation, all right? We wouldn't be taking on three Druug that probably got run off by their pack. We'd be taking on the ones that have been able to survive an Ulheim winter. Cannibalizing each other."

"So do we turn around?" Tomas asked.

The knight shook his head. "Beraht's right. It would take too much time."

"Is there another way to the tunnel?"

Beraht shook his head definitively.

"Then what?" the squire demanded.

"Your apprentice makes excellent use of logic," Aebreanna pointed out to Rogan. "If we cannot go back, cannot go around, and certainly cannot remain, there is but one course left to us."

"Why can't we stay here for a few days and wait for the Druug to find something else to eat?" Tomas asked.

Rogan shook his head. "If they're not tracking us yet," he said, "they will be soon." The knight glanced at this Uldra friend. "Well?"

Beraht looked around the trees and the mountains surrounding them. "My parents found a frozen river that led straight through the ruins and up the mountain," he said. "It's near. If we really push through the night, we could reach the mountain proper by dawn. Once we start the climb, the Druug will give up."

"Why?" Tomas asked.

The Uldra looked up at the towering mountain. "The Allfather keeps his Throne. The Druug can't touch the mountain."

A howl full of rage and hunger thundered through the valley from the south. Each of the heroes found their eyes drawn in that direction as another howl joined the first then another. Tomas lost count after a half-dozen monsters joined in their chorus, declaring the hunt and their intent to pursue it. A chill that had nothing to do with the omnipresent wind ran down the young man's spine, settling finally in his stomach.

"Well," Rogan said grimly, "I guess the decision's been made." The knight gathered Stick's reins and dug in his heels. The dark warhorse reared and answered the monstrous challenge still echoing through the trees with one of his own. "Let's ride!" Rogan barked as Stick launched off toward the west, deeper into the lands of the Druug.

Within a few minutes of dodging amid the large trees, the group emerged from the menacing forest into a clearing that led straight to the Allfather's Throne. Once away from the shelter of the woods, however, the vicious wind that had torn at the heroes for their entire journey through these accursed mountains returned with full force, ripping at their cloaks and burning their faces with merciless fury.

And the adventurers charged headlong into it.

Only a strong walk could be made against the wind that worked tirelessly to push them back. Tomas and his friends could barely see as snow and ice were jabbed into their eyes each moment they risked looking ahead. Breath was impossible, and every gasp of air felt as though it was ripped from their lungs even before they could finish drawing it in. Tomas could not even tell if he was shivering in the terrible cold, as his entire body shook with the force of the wind that threatened constantly to force him from Urge. Even the warhorse beneath him could do little against the wall of air before them but lean forward and battle for each step.

Fury built within the young man's chest. Tomas grabbed on to the heat of his hatred for their cursed luck and let it fill him, bringing warmth that the squire had nearly forgotten in the bitter cold of these evil mountains. *Just a little good fortune*, Tomas thought while trying to shield his face from the worst of the wind. After weeks of digging through the intractable snow, after climbing one knifelike peak after another covered with razor-sharp rocks, after one enemy after another trying nothing more than to break the young hero's will, Tomas Fidelis was finished. *This damned wind will not fight us as well!* The squire grabbed on to his rage with the full force of his mind and hurled it back at the wind before them. Weeks of cold! Weeks of struggling! Weeks of misery! Enough! *Enough*! "ENOUGH!!!" Tomas words were lost on the howling fury of winter's wrath, but his will would not be denied.

Just as Father Konrad often told his young student, sometimes a prayer is answered no matter in what form it is made.

The bitter wind that had been such an enemy to the party in the many weeks since their emergence from the Uldra Way suddenly and without warning shifted its allegiance. An explosion of air shoved at the party from behind, very nearly lifting their horses off the ice and hurling them forward. No longer did the flying ice sting their eyes or tear at their skin; instead, it cleared their path of all obstacles. The helping wind lent its great power to the heroes and continued to aid them as the horses, with Stick and Urge in the eager lead, raced down the frozen stream with joyous abandon.

"Will this hide our scent?" Tomas yelled to Beraht, struggling to be heard over the cheering wind.

"Some!" the Uldra replied. "But they know where we are!" Beraht sent the squire's eyes to the left and right with a gesture and several foul oaths. Tomas struggled in the diminishing light of dusk to see the threat, finally spotting several dark shapes running with even greater speed than their mighty warhorses through the trees on either side of their slick highway. "They're boxing us in!" Beraht roared.

Rogan said nothing. The knight just lowered his head even further, giving Stick the least resistance to their flight.

Something large rocketed past Tomas's head, missing him by only a hair's breadth. "What in Underworld?" the squire sputtered and looked to see the point of origin of the deadly missile. Several more stones came flying from either side of the river, catching the four heroes and their terrified mounts in a rocky crossfire. "Heads up!" Tomas yelled to his companions.

"Heads down!" Rogan corrected, ducking a rock larger than his head.

"The wind's helping, but they're going to get lucky!" Beraht roared.

A terrified whinny came from behind, drawing Tomas's eyes back to see where a rock had brought down one of their pack horses. Before the unfortunate creature had even stopped sliding along the ice, several Druug were on it, tearing the horse apart with brutish muscle that no amount of dark fur or grey skin could hide. Tusks and massive jaws ripped the horse's flesh free from its thrashing body in bloody chunks as the pack animal kicked desperately at its attackers to no avail. Even a direct hoof strike to one thick head resulted in nothing more than the crack of the horse's leg. Tomas looked away as the horse was ripped apart, praying that the release of death would come quickly for the poor animal and desperately trying to ignore the smell of gore that was carried on the wind.

With the smell of fresh meat on the air, their attackers were briefly distracted from the rest of the party. Rogan wasted no time in exploiting the sacrifice the pack horse had made, leading his team farther down the stream as fast as Stick could carry him. "Faster!" the knight barked, more to his own irritable steed than any other. In response, Stick lowered his head and shot forward at tremendous speed. Of the other horses, only Urge could keep up, matching the pace of his sire stride for stride.

With the snow and wind and deepening darkness concealing much of the terrain around them, Tomas was unsure when exactly it was that they had crossed into the ruins of Uldron. As time passed and the moon began to cast its ghostly glow on the frantic chase, the squire noticed that many of the hills they passed had unusual shapes. Rising like the bones of some great monster, walls and collapsed buildings could be seen through the snow. But time had been brutal to the stonework of the Uldra, with ancient houses reduced to little more than caves, and the monuments of forgotten heroes broken down to rubble. With their thoughts resting solely on survival, it was not until passing under a series of crumbled bridges that Tomas and his friends realized they had truly entered the lost city of the Uldra.

It eventually became clear that, although Stick and Urge had some chance of putting enough distance between them and the pursuing Druug, the other horses simply could not. The pack horses were too burden with their supplies. Beraht's shire horse, Sus was powerful but lacked endurance. Aebreanna's graceful Mayva was speedy, but the pony lacked the stride and strength. Rogan glanced back at the ever-growing gap between him and Tomas and the rest of the party. With a snarled curse, the knight reined Stick in and began desperately looking around for some alternatives.

Aebreanna pulled her gasping pony beside Rogan's and looked at the knight gravely. "We cannot reach the mountain ahead of the grey-skins," she declared. "Our mounts cannot maintain such a pace for very much longer. We need another course of action."

Rogan looked at Beraht. "How did your parents make it?" he asked.

The Uldra shook his head. "We didn't have horses," he replied. "They just ran along the river up to the mountain."

"Surely your parents could not outrun an Druug," Aebreanna objected.

"They weren't this hungry," Beraht insisted. "They only came after us once, and we gave them enough of a fight that they knew it wouldn't be worth bothering us anymore."

"Could we do that?" Tomas asked. "Give them enough of a fight that they wouldn't think it's worth the effort?"

"Did you see what they did to that horse?" Rogan demanded. "They're so hungry they'd charge through fire to get a squirrel!"

A howl echoed along the river from ahead of them, answered quickly by another from behind.

"It would appear our options are swiftly expiring," Aebreanna pointed out.

Rogan swore again and looked around. "We need a place," he barked.

Beraht pointed farther up the river, toward a raised area heavily broken by jagged rocks. "There!" he grunted. "We get high and hold!"

Rogan and Beraht led them up into the rocks, finding the ruins of an ancient fortress bulging with toppled walls and crumbled rooftops that formed a maze of twisting paths and great potential for concealment. The wind, now calming somewhat in baited anticipation of the battle to come, had blown clear most of the loose snow and ice that blanketed the bones of Uldron. This made the top of the crumbling fortress accessible, though just barely, by climbing over and around the many boulders that were all that remained of a once mighty Uldric building. A narrow cave that could once have been a great hall provided some protection for their animals, while their riders would engage the Druug. "Shouldn't we stay mounted?" Tomas asked as he and Beraht forced the horses into the sunken cave. "Rogan says that fast and mobile is better than slow and stationary."

"Pointless," the Uldra grunted as he finished forcing the last hesitant horse into the cave. "Druug are faster on foot than a horse carrying a rider," he said while rolling a massive boulder into place, sealing the echoing hallway.

Tomas followed his mountainous friend up into the rocks above, joining Rogan and Aebreanna at the top. As the four looked on, they could see two groups of Druug, each numbering around a half dozen, join up at the frozen river and start following the horses' trail up into the nearby hill where the heroes waited to greet them. "They're bigger than I remember," Tomas noted calmly.

"You fight them the same way," Rogan replied, equally as calm as his squire. The knight removed his cloak and tightened his gloves. "Go for the soft spots," he said. "Throat, bend of the arm and leg, back of the skull, anyplace you can get to something important. Don't try to stab them in the chest or cut off their heads."

"I bet Beraht could do it," the squire pointed out as he also removed his cloak and readied his gear.

"Sir Beraht could topple a tree with his breath," Aebreanna replied as she let her thick cloak fall from her supple shoulders. "Use the gifts you have and think not of the burdens others must endure." The baroness checked her various blades and stretched her arms and legs in preparation for the many gravity-defying maneuvers that were her trademark.

Their Uldra comrade slowly rotated his head sending a series of cracks and pops so loud his Human friends winced at the sound. "Just don't slow me down," he said with a menacing grin as he hopped across a narrow hall that time had reduced to a deep ravine. Beraht drew his great waraxe from its resting place on his belt, taking a few practice swings as he eagerly watched the Druug reach the base of the fortress ruin.

"Will they go after the horses?" Tomas asked as he and Rogan descended into the narrow corridors below.

Rogan drew Talon and shook his head. "Druug like meat and violence together," he replied. "There's nothing they love more than food that fights back."

"Hope they're hungry then." The squire drew Steelheart and turned to face down one direction, while his knight faced the other.

The first Druug hauled itself up the rocks with great speed, leaping over the corridor that concealed the Humans in favor of more dangerous prey. Only when the monster reached Beraht and finally caught sight of the waiting Uldra did it pause. The Druug's last sight was of Beraht's waraxe swinging low and up, sending the monster's head flying with great speed into the sky, while its accompanying body fell limply among the Druug moving about below.

Two Druug leapt onto the stone ledge Beraht had claimed for his own on either side of the waiting Uldra. In a surprising act of coordination, the two monsters charged the warrior with clawed hands outstretched and gaping mouths eager for Uldra meat. Beraht swung his waraxe wide to the left and down toward the left Druug's leg, crushing it utterly before spinning and planting the axehead into the beast's neck. Before the second monster could finished its charge, Beraht then dislodged the waraxe and sent the weapon arching over his head and down into his target's shoulder, carving a great chunk from the Druug. Beraht contemptuously kicked the brute free of his weapon and off his rooftop.

Knowing full well they could never match the brutal power of their Uldra friend, Rogan and Tomas made no attempt at standing firm and holding a piece of territory against all attackers, instead moving amidst the twisting corridors and cavernous chambers of the fallen Uldra castle. The two men knew that the moment this battle truly began, they could separate only by a few feet; survival meant staying together. Each trusted the other with an unshakable faith that the other would keep any of the monsters from hitting them from behind. Death came quickly to the lone warrior.

The attack came with a great roar that sent stones tumbling down from above. A Druug dropped down in front of the steady warriors, while others of its kind gathered along the walls above for their part in the slaughter to come. Rogan and Tomas reacted instantly to the threat, heedless of the grey-skin's attempts at intimidation. Rogan met the Druug's charge with one of his own, darting forward with a quick thrust that brought the monster's hands up to protect its hideous face before spinning quickly on one foot, and swiping his trusted blade across the back of the monster's knees. The Druug yelped and collapsed in pain as its legs became useless, unable to take more than the briefest of breaths before Tomas leapt forward the moment his knight was clear and drove Steelheart's point deep into the creature's throat before ducking low and rolling under the attack of another Druug that had dropped from above.

Aebreanna prowled on the highest platform of the rocky hilltop, watching calmly as Beraht continued to engage the monsters all around them, waiting for an opportunity that the Sylva knew her Uldra friend would provide. One of the Druug charged the warrior, eager for its meal but stunned in confusion as Aebreanna leapt from the stones above and sent a pair of iridescent blades into the beast's eyes; the grey-skin's pain was ended abruptly by Beraht's waraxe. Another Druug, thinking the Uldra vulnerable from behind, barreled toward Beraht the moment it had gained a foothold on the irregular platform but was brought up short as Aebreanna dove between the brute's massive legs and rolled, stabbing two daggers back into the knees of the Druug without bothering to look first. Aebreanna wrenched her Sylvai blades free, twisting the knives as she did so and dancing to the side as a Druug fist slammed down into the ground on which she had stood only a moment before. The spy twisted and sent two narrow blades flying into the throat of a Druug that was threatening Beraht as the Uldra warrior slaughtered both beasts with mighty strikes of his waraxe. Once more leaping into the air, Aebreanna continued her nimble evasions even as Beraht renewed his brutal attacks.

More of the monsters came. Far more than the paltry dozen that had begun the attack. More fell to the weapons, their skill, and their teamwork. And yet, still more came.

"I thought there would only be a few!" Tomas grunted as he dove under a Druug's club. The squire rolled on the ground and spun, slashing Steelheart across the small of the monster's back.

"I know!" Rogan snarled, stabbing Talon over his squire's head and into another Druug's throat. He pulled his longsword free and spun it in a wide circle, deflecting another Druug club. Tomas stabbed Steelheart up, under the brute's ribs and into its heart. "There's too many! This isn't right!"

Still more of the monsters appeared, clambering over the ruins walls of the Uldra fortress. "Where in Underworld are all these coming from!?!" Beraht roared as he swung his mighty waraxe, decapitating a pair of Druug. These were much larger than the first few, threatening even the great size and strength of Beraht himself.

"They are summoned!" Aebreanna gasped leaping and twisting in midair. She landed with a single hand on Beraht's massive shoulder and pushed off, gaining even greater altitude. The nimble spy sent another of her blades flying, slashing the throat of an oncoming Druug. "Someone has awoken the Bull! We face the entire pack!"

Confronting an overwhelming Druug tide, the two Human warriors below moved with fluid precision through the maze of ruined halls and forgotten chambers, using the twisting paths to confound the Druug's primitive attempts at a massed attack. Time and again, Rogan and Tomas would let a group of the monsters catch sight and scent of them, only to disappear into the skeletal labyrinth, forcing the Druug to split up where they could then be engaged and eliminated one at a time. Attack from above was impossible since each time one of the beasts would climb up to the pillars and uneven pathways overhead, the knight and squire would disappear into a tunnel only to reappear as though by magic some great distance away. Rogan led his apprentice with the confidence only desperation could produce, choosing their paths at random and hoping for the best but burning the layout of the stone maze into his memory as the two Humans made quick slashes at their attackers when possible and retreating when not. At long last, knowing their strategy of evasion could only hold so long against the sheer numbers and tenacity of their enemy, the Northlands prince spotted a collapsed column providing access to the roofs above and climbed with his apprentice only a step behind, hoping to link up with the rest of his team for a more concentrated defense.

Still holding his rooftop with the tenacity for which his people were rightly feared, Beraht faced off with several Druug, supported by Aebreanna, who was employing the dexterity for which her people were rightly renowned. One of the monsters leapt toward Beraht, greeted in midair by a thunderous blow that sent the Druug into the ground where an immediate strike to the back finished the job. Another of the grey-skins, using the distraction of its fellow's death, wrapped its apelike arms around Beraht's massive chest, lifting the Uldra off the ground and pinning his arms. Aebreanna flipped through the air and landed on the Druug's shoulders, drawing two Sylvai blades across the monster's neck and sending a flood of dark blood washing over Beraht.

Once freed of the beast's crushing attack, the Uldra swung his waraxe over his head toward another monster's shoulder as it made a grab for Aebreanna but growled in surprise when the Druug suddenly grabbed his waraxe in one meaty hand. Without hesitation, Beraht swung his fist down, snapping the restraining arm but losing his grip on his beloved weapon in the process as Aebreanna made a flying retreat to try and regain the initiative. A second Druug barreled into Beraht before the warrior could recover from the last attack, shoving the Uldra warrior into the side of a cracked stone pillar upon which Aebreanna was standing, sending the deadly Sylva rolling away as two more grey-skins pursued her. Beraht leaned back against the rock and struck out with both stubby legs, planting two kicks into his Druug attacker's head, either one of which carrying enough force to shatter metal. The Druug's tusks broke free of the beast's mouth, and blood flowed freely from the monster's pug nose. Beraht reached up and, clasping his fists together, swung into his attacker's torso, crushing the Druug's bones and destroying its organs.

Beraht turned with the intent of assisting Aebreanna, who could not escape the pursuing grey-skins, but was prevented as a Druug leapt on his back from behind. With titanic strength, the beast forced Beraht to the ground and beat at the Uldra with its fists. Beraht twisted under the monster and grappled with it, each hulking brute trying to outwrestle the other as they rolled amid the ancient stonework but neither winning before the two combatants went tumbling off the edge and into the darkness below.

Rogan and Tomas, sprinting across the stone platform and leaping among the many crevasses twisting everywhere, had spotted the trouble their friends were having and made a desperate attempt to reach the closer of the two but were too late. "Beraht!" Tomas called desperately, seeing his friend vanish into the hungry darkness and sprinting forward with all his youthful energy, heedless of the danger.

"Behind!" Rogan called.

It was too late, however. A Druug pulled itself up onto the rocky platform Tomas and Rogan had been crossing and swung its arm wide, catching Rogan in a bone-jarring strike that sent the knight slamming into a nearby boulder. Rogan's mouth exploded with blood; he could do nothing as the Druug raised both fists high in the air to finish the kill.

Aebreanna leapt from the rock that had so brutalized Rogan and flipped in midair, landing on the advancing Druug's shoulders. The Sylva screamed her fury as she jabbed two blades deep into the beast's neck on either side of its massive head and flipped to the ground. Spinning backward and lashing out with the steel tip of a booted foot, Aebreanna sent the monster back into the darkness whence it came.

The Sylva dropped to her knees beside Rogan and quickly checked his chest and head. "Can you fight?" she asked tersely.

Tomas tried to shout a warning but failed and could only look on as another of the Druug leapt from the rocks above, pinning Aebreanna to the ground. The monster grabbed the stunned Sylva in one hand that wrapped completely around her lithe body and slammed her into the stone above Rogan with a sickening crunch.

Tomas could spare only a quick glance at the fate of his friends while being attacked by four of the Druug. The squire backed away, putting his back to a large stone and saw that more shapes were appearing in the shadows. *So this is it*, the squire thought. *Well, they're going to earn their meal.* With a roar of fury and hatred, defying Fate and celebrating his life, Tomas Fidelis of Pelsemoria charged into the teeth of his enemy, swinging Steelheart with all the strength he could summon. Two Druug fell to the venerated sword of House Calonar before the squire made the briefest pause to identify new targets. A high sweep of a Druug fist caused Tomas to duck low, where he cut viciously into one monster's hip before spinning to thrust Steelheart up into the throat of another. Two of the beasts tried to attack the enraged squire from opposite directions but met nothing but air and each other as Tomas ducked and rolled away, coming back up to his feet and stabbing a Druug in the groin before twisting and reversing Steelheart to thrust it up into the skull of yet another attacker.

No matter how greatly the rocks beneath the squire shook with his fury, no matter how many times his strikes would knock loose the ancient stonework under his feet, no matter the rivers of ichorus Druug blood that now flowed down the ruined stones of the Uldra fortress, even one trained by Rogan Eigenhard must inevitably fall to the furious onslaught he now faced. An unseen attacker hurled a stone that caught the squire in the temple and blurred his vision. A swarm of grey surrounded Tomas as he desperately continued to swing Steelheart in the patterns drilled into him by his knight. Some of his attacks made contact; others sliced nothing but air. Pain filled his mind, and at some point, Tomas lost his grip on Steelheart.

"Mary," the hero whispered as he fell into darkness.

Chapter 26

A feeling of warmth and well-being slowly filled Tomas's mind, gently raising it from the depths of unconsciousness. Muffled sounds pressed against the young man's peace but gained little headway against the soothing bliss that cradled Tomas and gently encouraged him to remain still and silent. Even the pain that had stabbed at Tomas's whole body eased until it was little more than a vague memory. Nothing could disturb the young adventurer as he drifted through eternity on gentle waves of light.

The sound of humming pulled at Tomas's mind, filling his heart with gentle compassion. Ghostly hands that radiated love wrapped themselves around the squire's chest, and soft lips pressed themselves against his cheek as luminous hair brushed against Tomas's head. The scent of spring and everything the season carried floated through Tomas's senses, and without opening his eyes, the young man knew he lay in the arms of his beloved Mary. His fiancée's soft song continued to soothe what little ache remained in her lover's body, while Tomas lazily ran his hands along Mary's arms, reveling in the feeling of her soft skin. Again, a soft kiss was placed on the squire's face, but this time was met by Tomas's lips, holding fast the soft bow. The young hero turned in Mary's arms, easily ignoring the faint objections of his wounded body, and wrapped his own arms around his heart's truest love. Tomas reveled in the feeling of Mary's bare flesh against his and continued the kiss that carried with it all the passion of true love. Neither lover opened their eyes even after the kiss ended; Tomas and Mary simply floated together in that warm eternity, wrapped in each other's arms and whispering their love for one another.

If this is a dream, the squire thought, *then let me never wake. If this is White Lady, come to claim me, then I welcome her eagerly.* At some point, the squire felt pulling at his arms and legs, but again the disturbance of his body was barely noticed by the soft waves that cradled his mind and soul.

Unwelcome consciousness returned with chest-ripping force. For the first few moments, Tomas could not form thought, and his entire reason for living was clearing the warm water from his lungs with painful coughs that jarred his entire body. Eventually, the young man became aware of gentle hands holding him steady, while the squire struggled to clear his lungs of fluid. Finally, Tomas rolled onto his back, only vaguely aware that his head rested in a warm lap, and worked to steady his hoarse breathing and clear his unsteady vision.

Tomas gradually became aware of pain. His entire body ached. His head throbbed, and the steady trickle of sticky warmth that ran along his face told the squire that he was bleeding. The pain kept building and would not stop. The young man felt a cold numbness spreading from his crooked fingers down along his bruised arms despite the comforting warmth that wrapped around his ravaged body. At each moment, Tomas hoped the pain had reached its upper limit, only to dismay at its continued increase. He could not even pray, since the pain robbed him of thought.

The chainmail Tomas had been wearing was gone, leaving tattered shreds of his clothes and his mauled torso exposed to the gentle fingers that probed as carefully as possible, looking for mortal wounds. Even the squire's boots had not been spared the violence that had brought him to this unenviable fate; one was missing altogether along with much of its accompanying foot, and the other had a gash that ran the length, leaving the bloodied and gnarled limb visible.

A gargling roar that was suddenly cut short drew Tomas's attention to his right. Rogan, looking much like Tomas felt, was pulling Steelheart from the throat of a Druug whose misshapen body gave mute testimony to a brutal fall that had come to a sudden and awkward end. The knight's clothes were torn and soaked in both his blood and that of his attackers. His face was a broken ruin, with his nose bent at an ugly angle, numerous gashes crossing his chiseled face and one eye so swollen it looked as though the orb could explode from the hero's face. The leather headband Beraht had gifted to his friend was missing, letting Rogan's long red hair fall limply from his head, several patches of it soaked with the knight's blood. Red flecks dripped from Rogan's grimly set lips with each wet breath, and a tremor ran without stopping along the chiseled muscles of the warrior's exposed chest. Tomas could not imagine the pain that must accompany the injuries through which his mentor suffered.

Looking about through the mist of pain, Tomas noticed several more Druug scattered across the massive dome-shaped chamber into which they had fallen. The large pool in the center of the ancient structure was, the squire realized, an underground hot spring. The water emitted a faint pink glow, filling the dome around them with a light that blended perfectly with the soft moonlight floating down from the jagged hole far above their heads. All around the chamber, naturally embedded in the dark green stone of which this chamber was made, were bright red crystals that either created the pink light or perfectly reflected and amplified it, giving the illusion of a thousand red stars. The uneven remains of a wide stone walkway ringed the chamber with several large platforms leading out into the steaming spring, many of which showed signs of recent Druug impacts. A bench of polished stone or the crumbled remains of one sat in the center of each platform with a gentle ramp before it leading into the water. Although some had surrendered to the siege of time, and those that had not were still marred by long cracks both ancient and recent, several in what had once been a network of great stone arches rose along the walls to intersect each other far overhead where Tomas could hear the frustrated roars of the Druug. In the center of the great pool was a single pillar of the same stone of which the chamber was made, its simple elegance marred by the impaled Druug, whose blood ran down the rough surface of the ancient structure.

Rogan, having finished his grim work with the few enemy survivors of their fall, staggered over to where his squire lay, finally letting Tomas's sword fall to the ground and dropping to his knees himself. "How is he?" the knight asked in a hoarse voice.

"He lives," Aebreanna replied as Tomas realized that his head was resting in her soft lap, "for the moment."

Although it caused him even more pain, the young man twisted his head slightly to look up; and even in his condition, Tomas was shocked at the sight of his friend. Aebreanna had been spared none of the violence of their attack. A large clump of her normally lustrous hair had been torn free of her scalp, leaving a bloody mess in its place. The remaining mane that normally held such life hung limply across the right side of the Sylva's face, concealing what may lie beneath. The spy's nose had been crushed, twisted into a horrific mockery of itself and blood ran freely from it to join the crimson lines that dripped from the corner of Aebreanna's full lips. The nimble Sylva sat with one leg stretched to the side, an ugly discoloration and odd protrusion giving mute testimony that Aebreanna would be unable to use it for some time. Denied even the comfort of dignity, the baroness's armor and clothes had been shredded just as Tomas's had, leaving her body exposed and giving the young man an ample view of the numerous places along her body in which a Druug had sampled the taste of her flawless pale flesh.

"Even mauled, your young eyes cannot avoid feminine curves," the spy said with a half-hearted smile.

"Sorry," the squire croaked. Tomas closed his eyes and tried to sit up but was forced back down as the world began to violently spin, and his lungs suddenly refused to draw breath. Blood resumed its flow from the many wounds on the young man's body, and he began to tremble with a chill that belied the comforting warmth coming from the spring. Aebreanna held a cool hand against her young friend's forehead and said a few words in the musical Sylvai language that unfortunately did little to ease his pain.

Rogan sat down on the stonework floor the remnants of his team rested on and looked around with his one good eye. "Will he make it?" he asked dully.

Aebreanna did not answer, but her downcast gaze and grim expression were response enough. Tomas had seen the same look others in the long years of Pelsemoria's decline. Victims of the Xeshlin, of bandits, of each other had been knelt over by people with the same look now upon Aebreanna's beautiful face. "How're you?" the knight asked her.

"I feel little pain," the Sylva replied grimly. "Which in and of itself is not a good sign given the severity of my injuries. I am employing all my gifts and discipline to maintain consciousness. I suspect I will not be long behind our young friend."

Rogan coughed and spat some troublesome blood out of his mouth before looking up at the irregular crack whose opening had granted them entrance into this forgotten chamber. The knight grimly looked at the several Druug that were crawling around the hole, obviously unwilling to give up on the meal that had temporarily eluded them. "It won't take them long to find a way down here," he growled.

"Yes," Aebreanna agreed, holding a hand to her head.

"Where in Underworld did they all come from?" the knight demanded. "Druug are supposed to hibernate in the winter! There should've only been a couple of them, not the whole damned pack!"

The Sylvai spy took a deep breath that brought fleck of blood to her full lips. "Although there is… little means of determining with… certainty," she whispered, "I would suspect that.. they were roused from their winter sleep by our… unseen adversary."

"Any sign of Beraht?"

Aebreanna shook her head slightly. "No," she replied. "Even if he lives, there is… little… chance…"

"How long have you been awake?" Rogan asked.

"I am unsure. My… perception of time has been affected by… my injuries." Aebreanna's head was starting to droop, and her breath was growing shallow.

The squire glanced again at the spring, and some quiet part of his mind, still functioning despite the pain and Death's approach, tried to call out. Only the slightest groan, the barest whisper of words escaped Tomas' lips.

Rogan stared at his squire with dead eyes. "What did he say?" he asked grimly, leaning in as best as his wounds would allow.

Again, Aebreanna put a hand on the squire's head to try and bring the young man some peace, if not relief from his pain. "He is fading," she said in a very soft voice. "The White Lady comes."

The knight shook his head slightly, wincing from the pain even that small movement brought him. "Damn me," the hero whispered.

"Self-recriminations are … counterproductive," Aebreanna said as she struggled to draw deep breaths. "We are alive… our mission… remains unchanged."

"Mission?" Rogan demanded. "Beraht's gone, and we've lost our supplies. We're surrounded by Druug and we're too busted up to fight." The knight shook his head. "Why did I bring us here?"

Tomas's eyes fluttered open briefly as his breath became more labored. Again, that quiet part of his mind called out something vitally important, some salvation. The squire tried to say something to his friends but lacked the strength.

Rogan turned his head despite the obvious pain it caused him to look at his squire with his one good eye. "I'm sorry, kid," the knight whispered.

Aebreanna put a firm hand on Rogan's less-injured arm and locked eyes with the knight. "Your guilt serves no purpose but to hasten our deaths!" she hissed. "You must... not allow despair to claim you! Think!"

Rogan looked around the dome-shaped cavern for some inspiration. "No horses," he muttered to himself. "No backup. No magic. Dozens of Druug against three critically injured warriors. What would Calonar do?"

Tomas reached out with a limp hand, which Rogan grasped gently. Again, his squire tried to say something that the knight could not make out. "What's he saying?" Rogan asked. Getting no response, the prince looked up and saw that Aebreanna had put her hands on the ground to either side of her and was working to stay upright, unable to muster enough strength to speak.

The knight leaned in when his apprentice made another attempt at speech. "*Bjorgatkin*," he struggled to say.

Rogan looked down in helpless confusion. "What does that mean?" he asked.

In response, Tomas freed his hand and shakily pointed at the softly glowing water. "*Bjorgatkin*," he said again.

The knight looked at the spring and down at his squire. Realization dawned in his pain-riddled mind; and without a word, Rogan stood and dragged Tomas, ignoring his friend's painful outcries. Putting the squire on his shoulder, Rogan staggered into the warm water, ignoring his own pain and praying aloud that he understood. Once reaching knee depth, Rogan unceremoniously dumped the now-still Tomas into the water, taking care to keep only his head above and waiting anxiously for a miracle.

At first, nothing happened. Tomas slipped down, letting the darkness reach up for him. Then there was light. A soft light of blue and green surrounded him, entered him, energized him. Tomas drew a deep breath and felt peace. This was not the peace of Death, though, for the White Lady had passed him by. Instead, this was the peace of comfort, of freedom from pain. The young man felt his body knitting, healing, restoring. His bleeding slowed, then stopped. His flesh gently regenerated. He opened his eyes and looked at Rogan. The knight's own wounds were also closing, albeit with agonizing slowness.

Rogan, again praying aloud, submerged his squire fully into the healing waters. Despite the lack of air, Tomas was comfortable; his chest drew in what felt like air. He floated for a moment, then rose, or was lifted, to float on the surface.

A muted cry drew Rogan's attention back to the stone platform in time to see Aebreanna collapse. The knight wasted no time, leaving Tomas to float and heal and rushing back out of the water to grab his Sylvai friend and carry her into the spring. As with Tomas, the water's magic began to work almost immediately on Aebreanna.

The soft green and blue light surrounded her small body and began the work of healing her: closing her many wounds and bringing color back to her beautiful face.

Rogan laughed. A warm, almost hysterical laughter began in his belly and radiated outward. Rogan flung his arms out to either side and fell backward into the water, continuing to laugh even as he sank down, needing no air as the water covered him. Only after several minutes did the knight surface and even then very reluctantly and only to check on his friends.

"We're going to make it!" he roared in joy as the healing process continued on his friends.

A thunderous roar echoed from above, answering the knight's joy with rage. Tomas looked up as an impossibly-thick figure jumped from the uneven ledge high above and plummeted into the water below, on the other side of the monolith in the center of the spring. A massive wave surged out from the creature's impact point, slamming into the cavern walls and briefly knocking Rogan off his feet. The water settled, and the following silence was deafening.

A massive brute of muscle and horror slowly rose from the water. The Druug bull stood more than three times the height of the tallest Human. Shoulders wider than a wagon led to arms that stretched all the way to the water, even when the monster stood tall. Two long, curved horns poked out from a forest of long, matted black hair crowning a head that seemed too large for even the bull's beastly torso. A tongue longer than a man's leg stretched out from the monster's cavernous mouth and wrapped around the swordlike tusks as the creature stared at its prey with eyes that were solid black. The monster carried no weapon other than its massive paws, each individual digit capped with a scythe-like talon that promised pain and death.

Rogan sent an irritated glance to the sky above. "Really?" he asked in annoyance. The knight looked about and calmly grabbed Steelheart, the sword that had served the heroes of House Calonar for generations. Squaring his shoulders, Rogan strode deeper into the water, shaking his head to clear his still-blurred vision to face the Troll. "We're not going out like this," the warrior growled angrily. Tomas tried to rouse himself, to follow his knight into battle, but lacked the strength. He could not even raise a hand, so drained he was. The squire could only look on as Rogan Eigenhard marched forward to face the brutish monster in an impossible duel.

The bull suddenly threw its massive arms out to either side in surprised pain and turned in place, revealing an Uldra waraxe imbedded in the beast's broad shoulders. Tomas blinked in surprise and looked past the writhing monster at the far end of the dome. Standing at the mouth of a jagged tunnel on the opposite side of the forgotten spring, Beraht snarled an oath in the Uldric tongue and roared a challenge to the beast that threatened his friends. The monster roared in fury and charged.

Beraht waited until the Druug bull was within arm's reach, then thrust his fist straight into the brute's face. The monster's pug-nose was crushed in a bone-shattering collision that rocked its head back and flipped the monster backward through the air. Beraht did not hesitate a moment in launching himself onto the monster's shoulders. He tore his great waraxe free and kicked the Druug bull as it tried to stand. Beraht reached back with his waraxe and swung down, but missed as the beast rolled to the side. Moving with impossible speed and agility, the Druug bull regained its feet and hurled itself at Beraht, knocking aside his weapon. In response, the Uldra wrapped his massive arms around the monster's neck and twisted again, planting the brute face down into the water.

The Druug bull swung its huge arms, trying desperately to grab the vicious Uldra holding it. The monster beat at Beraht's face and chest, bringing explosions of blood from the Uldra's mouth and tearing free fistfuls of beard. Still Beraht held the bull beneath the water. At last, the monster found a large, loose stone and crashed it into the side of Beraht's head. The Uldra stumbled backwards, dazed, as the Druug bull again regained its feet.

Despite his wounds that the magic of the ancient spring worked even now to heal, Rogan swung Steelheart with all his strength and the speed his lifetime of training and war had granted, cutting brutal gashes into the Toll's back with rapid strikes. The Druug bull swung its massive arms backward, striking at the Northlands prince in a rage that grew by the second. Rogan dropped to one knee and rolled through the water, trailing blood from his reopened wounds and growling in pain. The knight tried to quickly regain his footing but was slowed by the warm water, giving the Druug bull enough time to recover and launch itself at him.

A sudden attack from behind sent the monster tumbling into the water away from Rogan as Beraht came to his friend's defense and roared another challenge. The Druug bull did not refuse, charging toward the son of Uldron, swinging its fists with terrifying force. The warrior ducked low as both stone-crushing attacks swung in and threw his shoulder into the monster's waist, grabbing the monster's legs and pulling back with all his amazing strength. The beast fell backward, sending another wave surging against the cavern walls that caught Rogan even as the knight was trying to reposition for another attack and sending the Northlander tumbling.

In one fluid movement, Beraht rolled along the Druug bull even as it fell into the water, spreading his legs to straddle the monster's chest and pummeling the beast's face with mighty blows of his fists. The bull quickly halted the attacks by grabbing Beraht around the throat and twisting, forcing the warrior down into the water for only a moment before picking the Uldra up bodily and slamming him back down into the shallow water. Again and again, the powerful monster slammed its Uldra prey into the walls and the water, trying to crush Beraht with sheer force.

Finally weary of the amusement it gained from beating the Uldra into the surrounding stone, the Druug bull reached up and slammed Beraht down one last time, holding the weakly struggling warrior under the warm water and drooling its pleasure at the meal to come. A blur of steel flashed, and the monster's hand was separated from its wrist. Rogan roared and lunged forward with all his strength even as the monster tried to reorient toward the threat, plunging Steelheart into the beast's chest. The monster roared in pain and rage but was not brought down by the desperate attack, instead reaching back and, with one brutal swing of its remaining hand, sent Rogan skipping across the water like a small stone thrown by a child.

Using the desperate distraction his Human friend had provided, Beraht kicked the Druug bull's knees with both legs, sending a loud crack echoing through the cavern. The beast roared in pain and fell back into the water, roaring in fury and writhing in agony. Once freed from the monster's grip, Beraht circled around behind it and with grim determination wrapped an arm around the bull's neck, grabbing the beast's head with his other arm and slowly pulling the massive skull to one side. It gasped and weakly struggled but could only emit a strangled grunt as a series of cracks and pops preceded one massive snap. The monster went limp, and Beraht threw down the dead monster's body.

The warrior looked up with a snarl of hatred at the watching Druug. The son of Uldron then reached down and took the bull's horns, one in each massive Uldra fist. Beraht, champion of the Allfather, then planted a foot into the back of the dead monster's head and pulled, leveraging all his titanic strength. There was a wet tearing, a cracking like stone in the unrelenting winter faced with the heat of a thunderous volcano. The son of Uldron snarled a primal roar and tore free the horns of the Druug bull. The monsters were silent as they stared back, having clearly watched the entire battle and its shocking conclusion. Beraht took a deep breath and, raising high his prize, roared in victory, shaking the gore-dripping horns at the creatures above. The air shook with the son of Uldron's victory cry, and several stones above were dislodged, falling down into the water below. Needing no other motivation, the Druug fled from sight, their frantic retreat and howls of despair sending several more stones falling from the ceiling overhead.

Chapter 27

"How're you feeling, kid?" Rogan asked from beside his apprentice, banishing a wonderful vision of Mary from his apprentice's mind and heart.

Tomas slowly opened his eyes and glancing at his mentor with resignation. "Next time," the squire said with a grimace, "listen when I'm trying to tell you something."

Rogan grinned. "Cut back on the sarcasm," he replied, "and I'll think about it."

Tomas and Aebreanna, though conscious, had been unable to move for hours. The wonderous magic of the spring was healing them, but slowly. All the friends had discarded whatever shreds of clothing and armor were left to them, and sank gratefully into the blessed waters of the Allfather's treasure. They all floated in the healing spring, silent and relived as life was gradually replenished within their broken bodies. Aebreanna had, at some point, drifted away from the men, swimming lazily as far from the rotting carcass of the Druug as possible, while her companions rested near the tunnel Beraht had used to find them.

"Is it my imagination or is the water not working as well as it was at first?" Tomas asked, rubbing a hand across the vicious scar running along his leg. As the hours slipped away, the soft glow of the spring had gradually paled. The green and blue light surrounding them had faded so that now it was barely visible. The red light from the walls had also dimmed, so that they were now in near-darkness. The squire ran his hands along where he felt there should be gaping wounds leaking his lifeblood and grunted in pain when his hand reached a spot on his ribs that, while having mostly healed, now seemed to remain sore and unresponsive to the powers of the spring. A quick inspection of his other wounds revealed that, although greatly improved, most of these areas were still very tender to the touch and showed ugly bruising and scars that would not fade.

"I think we used it up," the knight said. "There were too many contaminants in the water for it to take full effect anyway. Still, it kept us from dying."

"Contaminants?" The squire glanced at the many dead Druug. "You mean them?"

"And us," the Northlands prince added.

"You're not supposed to bring anything into the water that isn't alive and purified," Beraht confirmed. "We went in wearing armor, carrying weapons, and dropping rocks and Druug."

"Is the spring destroyed," Tomas asked, "or used up?"

"It will come back," Beraht said, sitting up in the water. "Once we're out, and the spring isn't using all of its power to try and fix us, it will recharge. Could take a while, though."

"What about the Druug?"

Rogan glanced around at the rotting bodies. "We got them out of the water before it could heal them and made sure they stayed dead. If we had the time, I'd say we clear them out, but we just don't."

Beraht shook his head. "The mountains will take care of the cleanup," he growled. "Once spring begins, the animals will handle the mess."

"I'm sorry we did this to your people's holy place," Tomas told his Uldra friend.

"What do you mean?" the Uldra replied with a confused expression. "This was glorious!" Beraht pointed to the Druug that had been impaled on the center obelisk. "There can be no better way to purify the Allfather's waters than with the blood of an enemy. These Druug have been stinking up Uldron for generations, and we've finally started cleaning them out!"

"So how'd you know about this place?" Rogan asked, edging away from his overly excited friend. "And why in Underworld didn't you say anything earlier?"

Tomas shrugged. "Well, we were a little busy in the ruins, and after the fall, I wasn't thinking all that clearly what with the mortal wounds and all." The squire looked around the chamber, again marveling at the glittering red crystals surrounding them. "Do you remember I mentioned the legends about the treasure the Uldra supposedly hid under their city after the Khepric invasion?"

"Not really," Rogan answered. "I'm not listening when you start in on one of your monologues."

"Anyway," the squire continued, "I read once that the Uldra called their treasure *Bjorgatkin*."

"You kept saying that word," the knight remarked. "What's it mean?"

"It's from a language called *Adikahdt*, the language spoken by the Uldra when they lived in Uldron."

"Protection against weakness," Beraht translated.

"You know ancient Uldric?" Rogan asked in surprise.

The Uldra shrugged. "When my father built a burial mound for someone, it was traditional to list the family's accomplishments in the old tongue. My father taught me and my brother."

"I didn't know you have a brother," Tomas remarked.

"Had," Beraht corrected.

"Oh," the squire realized the implication and felt renewed guilt from his personal experience at the ruins of Beraht's home village and the burial mound of his murdered family. "Most people thought the legend referred to some kind of treasure," Tomas continued, changing the conversation back to a happier subject. "But I noticed that I felt a lot better in the water before you pulled me out, so I guess I just made an educated guess."

"It was a little more than that," the knight insisted. "You seemed to know."

Tomas shrugged. "What did we have to lose? We were dead anyway."

"Good point."

"So how long are we going to stay?" the squire asked.

Rogan rubbed the back of his neck, feeling the many miles they had traveled as well as the ones before them. "I don't suppose there's any reason to linger," he grudgingly admitted. "Those Druug won't stay away forever." The knight turned slightly in the water and called out to where Aebreanna floated by herself, clearly basking in the feeling of warmth and cleanliness afforded by the spring. "Time to go!" he barked.

Tomas looked and, in the soft moonlight filtering down from the new opening overhead and the fading glow from the crystals around them, could easily make out where the spy was moving slowly through the water. Even from the distance that separated Aebreanna from the men, Tomas could hear the Sylva saying something, though her soft voice and low tone prevented the squire from making out specific words. "Who's she talking to?" the young man asked.

Rogan shrugged. "Herself, I guess. Just give her some time, kid. We've all been through a lot."

Tomas glanced at Beraht. "How did you find us anyway?" he asked Beraht.

"I just followed them," the warrior replied, jabbing a thumb over his shoulder at where their horses waited patiently on the nearest platform. "Turns out that crevasse we stuffed them into was a tunnel that led straight here. After I took care of the Druug that grabbed me, Rogan's horse started making all kinds of noise so I decided to check on them. Him and that horse of yours led me here."

"So we owe our lives to Stick and Urge?" Tomas asked.

"SHUT UP!" Rogan hissed. The knight looked over at the horses to ensure that they had not heard his squire's damning admission. "Don't let them hear you say that!" he snapped.

"Are you afraid of Stick?" the young man asked.

"Are you afraid of Urge?" the prince demanded.

The two Humans stared at each other for a minute without speaking. "So we can use that tunnel to get out?" Tomas asked, changing the subject.

"Easy," Beraht replied.

"What about the Druug?"

"Beraht killed their bull," the knight replied. "Take them a while to pull themselves back together."

"I thought they were too hungry to think straight or act normally," the squire pointed out.

"Gave them plenty to eat," Beraht laughed.

"How long to reach the tunnel?" Rogan asked, glancing skyward and noticing the predawn glow.

The son of Uldron glanced at the obelisk and the Druug rotting on it while he thought. "Weeks," he said. "A month, maybe. We don't need to climb the whole way, only about half."

"And the climb won't be easy," Rogan grimaced. "I've scaled a few mountains. Even with gear, it's hard."

"There's a path," Beraht pointed out. "Hard, but passable, even for your horses."

"When do we leave?"

Rogan moved to the short ramp that led out of the pool and up to the nearby platform. "As soon as Aebreanna's ready," the knight answered.

"I am prepared." The spy's voice appeared beside Tomas with no warning, startling several years off the young man's life in the process. The beautiful Sylva slid gracefully through the warm water towards the platform on which their horses were waiting and lowered herself one last time into the comforting waters of the spring. Tomas could not help but stare as the sensuous baroness emerged slowly and climbed the stone ramp with infinite grace, letting the warm water stream down her generous curves as her soft hips swayed in a perfect counterpoint to her every movement. Once reaching the top of the platform, the dangerous Sylva slowly ran her delicate hands up along her stomach while turning and, with her long hair covering the right side of her angelic face, glanced at Tomas with a wicked smile on her soft lips.

A small part of his reason exploded into Tomas's mind, and the squire realized he had been holding his breath. The young man spun quickly and sank deeper into the water, trying desperately to think of battle and death and other safe things.

Rogan had already pulled on his pants and undershirt before he noticed that his squire was still in the pool and not making any move to leave. "Let's go!" the knight barked.

"I… uh… need a minute," the squire said in a shaky voice.

Rogan threw an irritated look at Aebreanna, where the spy had retrieved new cloths from her bags and was slowly bending over to pull on her leggings. The knight just growled in irritation and continued dressing.

Chapter 28

Rogan and Tomas pressed against opposite sides of the crumbling tunnel that had provided their team with an escape from the ancient spring. The two warriors looked out of the tunnel's opening before them in overlapping scans, searching for any sign of danger. The sun had risen during their short trip through the dark tunnel that had once been a grand hallway. Although little vegetation survived outside the warm chamber that housed the forgotten treasure of Uldron, time had done its damage to the ancient stonework, with uneven stones jutting out from the floor and walls. No light could be risked for fear of detection, forcing the team to lead their hesitant horses forward with careful steps that could detect threatening stones before they could cause harm to their remaining mounts. Although the slight breeze brought the promise of fresh air and open skies to the weary heroes, it also brought to them a renewed sense of danger.

"Anything?" Rogan asked.

Tomas shook his head. "It looks clear."

"DON'T say that!" the knight snapped.

"What?"

"Never say 'it looks clear!' That's just tempting Fate!"

"You really are an old woman, did you know that?" the squire snorted.

"I'm sorry," Rogan grumbled. "How many Vaeyen have you fought?"

"Well—"

"Then shut up and stop bringing bad luck down on us."

"I'm bringing bad luck down on us!" Tomas demanded. "How many times have you said, 'don't worry, it'll be fine?'"

"That's different!" Rogan insisted. "I've gotten almost killed enough times to know what brings bad luck!"

"That's not exactly a good point, you know," the squire replied flatly.

"You know, for just five seconds, would you shut up? Just five miserable seconds. That's all I want."

"Children!" Aebreanna hissed. "If you are quite finished?"

Rogan sneered at his apprentice and looked out again on the ruins surrounding the tunnel entrance. "Fresh snow," he grunted. "Could hide signs, but I don't see anything nearby. Looks safe enough."

Tomas nodded. "One might almost say it looks… clear."

The knight turned back to his squire. "You know, I could cut you right now, and nobody would care."

"I will conduct a reconnaissance," Aebreanna interrupted, moving between the bickering Humans.

"I'll go too," Beraht grunted, pushing past his friends and disappearing into the surrounding stones with an ease that belied his usual lack of dexterity.

Rogan and Tomas were quiet as they waited for their teammates to return, continuing their watch while scanning the nearby ruins for danger. "Did you notice the scar?" the squire softly asked.

"Aebreanna?" Rogan replied.

Tomas nodded.

"While she was dressing and you were looking everywhere but her face, I caught a glance," the knight replied while trying to warm his hands with his breath. With one pack horse eaten and another missing but presumed eaten and the clothes and armor they had been wearing effectively destroyed, the party had been forced to improvise winter clothing from what little remained with only the most minimal success. Rogan had been forced to dress in a light tunic and hose that was meant for summer, with only a wool horse blanket Stick was none too happy about loaning wrapped around the knight's shoulders to ward off the deep cold of the Ulheim winter. "She's trying to hide it, but it's pretty obvious that it's bothering her." The prince glanced at his apprentice. "How'd you know about the scar?" he asked.

The squire shrugged and pulled his cloak closer about his shoulders. Despite having a large tear up the side, Tomas's cloak was still the best protection he had left against the cold. "She's been going out of her way to keep her hair covering the right side of her face."

"I'm a little surprised you noticed," Rogan admitted before giving his squire a knowing glance. "Or do you just spend that much time staring at her?"

"What?" the young man sputtered. "No! I… that is—"

"Relax, kid," the knight smiled again breathing into his shivering hands. "Just having a little fun with you."

"Did you see how bad it is?" Tomas asked.

Rogan nodded.

"How bad?"

The knight shook his head. "Bad. I don't think she can use the eye. I think it's still there, but…" Again, he shook his head. "The scar is deep and runs from her crown to her chin."

"Why didn't the spring heal it?"

"You should have seen the wound before she went into the water. The eye was all but gone. Maybe if we had stayed for a few more hours or even a day or two. Or maybe if the water hadn't been drained fixing us all."

"Do you think the clerics will be able to heal it once we get back to the Keep?" Tomas asked.

Rogan shrugged. "Not my specialty," he replied. "For her sake, I hope so."

"You think it'll affect her that much?"

"Kid, God only knows how she'll react. I've seen beautiful women get the most God-awful scars and come away with no problems, just going on with their lives as though nothing had changed. I've also seen people get the smallest blemish and go to pieces. There's just no way to predict."

"What should we do?"

The knight shifted Talon where the sword rested against his back in the improvised sheath Rogan had made after losing his scabbard. "We wait until she wants to talk about it, *if* she wants to talk about it. And we be supportive. Other than that, there's not much we can do."

Both warriors spotted Beraht emerge from the ruins before them and wave his friends forward. Leading the horses, Rogan and Tomas joined Beraht and Aebreanna in the ruins of an ancient courtyard adjacent to the frozen river that had originally granted the party access into Uldron.

"The path is clear," Aebreanna declared. "We can proceed."

The party walked their horses down to the road of ice and mounted, each saying nothing as the four friends steeled themselves for the climb ahead. Once mounted, the adventurers all looked up at the titanic mountain that dominated the sky ahead. Rogan gathered Stick's reins and squarely faced the Allfather's Throne. "Let's ride."

They spent a month on the slopes of the Allfather's Throne. The path on which Beraht led them was wide and built of carved tiers, allowing a steady, gradual assent. Great plazas had been carved out at even intervals, set one day's travel from each other. On these, the party rested. With so much of their supplies gone, they had to ration what was left, making for cold, meager meals. "Were these carved only for the ritual climbing?" Tomas asked after the first day.

Beraht shook his head. "The Nameless tells us that we were closer to the Allfather once. When Uldron was first built, before the Khepri and the Sylvai, our priests would climb the mountain. They would commune with the Allfather."

Tomas looked up the great slope. "This was your temple," he mused aloud. "Your holy place."

The days grew longer. The sun rose a little earlier each morning, and gave them more time before retreating behind the mountains. Despite this, the air grew even colder. There was no snow, but the wind was merciless. They covered the horses in all the spare clothing they had left, and used the remaining tent to build a windbreak them. The party huddled together against the bitter nights, overlapping their cloaks and holding each other. Aebreanna fared best in this, surrounded not only by the larger Human men, but by the towering Uldra. She spent each night curled up in the center of layer upon layer of cloth and men, while Beraht remained the most exposed, heedless of the weather upon his hard Uldra body.

As they climbed, the air grew thinner. They had to rest more and more often. Even though the great tiered steps were smooth and even, and the climb should not have been onerous, still their lungs had to work harder and harder with each successive level they climbed. At each of the plazas, which appeared with more frequency the higher they climbed, was a fountain. The water source was sheltered from the wind with great stone shields, and the water itself poured into small pools that gathered and spilled down the side of the mountain. Somehow, this water was not frozen. "Magic," Tomas guessed.

"Uldra magic," Beraht confirmed. "Once, we had magic as great as the Sylvai." He shook his head sadly. "Now, it's gone."

The view was spectacular. They rose higher, above the great peaks of Ulheim. One afternoon, as they turned to begin climbing another set of tiered steps, Tomas happened to glance to the north and gasped. The others looked to see where he was pointing. Far to the north, at the very edge of the horizon, were the twin peaks of the Parent Mountains.

"Think she's watching us?" Rogan asked lightly.

"Perhaps," Aebreanna replied. "But only as a distraction, as entertainment."

"Could she have been the one who set the Druug on us? Tomas asked.

The Sylva shook her head. "Unlikely. Unless our adversary found some other payment to motivate her, Vara would not risk the wrath of House Calonar,"

Onward they continued. They rested often, taking in great lungfuls of the thin air. Their legs burned despite the bitter wind. In the evenings, as they huddled together, sharing their bodies' warmth, they looked for any conversation to distract from their difficult climb. "What was wrong with you?" Tomas asked as they paused at another of the great plazas.

"Nothing's wrong with me," Beraht replied. "It's the rest of the world that has the problem."

"No," the squire replied, realizing how foolish his choice of words was. "I mean, when you were born, your parents brought you here as part of the Rite of the Holy Path."

"That's right."

"So what was wrong with you? Why did your parents have to bring you here?"

The Uldra paused and took a deep breath of the cold mountain air, adjusting his purple headband. Of them all, only Beraht had retained his armor and helmet.

Though, by some miracle, Mary's white ribbon had escaped unscathed and was now wrapped around Tomas' neck.

Tomas looked up at his Uldra friend and realized he may have crossed a sensitive line. "I'm sorry," the squire said softly. "If it's none of my business—"

"It's all right," Beraht whispered. "Rogan and the Sylva already know the story." The warrior sat down in the snow, working his rear end back and forth to fashion a suitable seat. "I was born with the *Levjot Khatud*. It's a disease of the mind and body that makes a child weak and useless to his family and clan. He usually dies young, but only after forcing his family to care for him for many years. It's shown at birth when the child doesn't cry as it should, instead making only a small mewling sound, like a frightened kitten."

Tomas sat down beside his friend, suffering quietly through the cold discomfort until his backside was properly numbed to the snow as Beraht continued his story.

"My mother, while she still carried me, started suffering from pains in her body and mind; she had visions that plagued her dreams. Our *marun* suspected that neither she nor I would survive the pregnancy and told her to take *takafata* to end it. My mother prayed that night for guidance and had a vision of the Allfather, commanding her to follow the Holy Path. She kept her faith and delivered. As the Allfather promised, she gave birth to a child marked with an affliction, meant for the Path. As the Rite commands, on the morning of the seventh day, my parents left my brother with family and brought me here."

"Did they see the Allfather?" Tomas asked.

Beraht nodded. "So did I," he said. "I have clear memories, of the trip and the fights, then of the face of God looking down on me."

"What did He look like?" the young man asked breathlessly.

"Nice," the warrior replied. "Clean, well-groomed."

"Dumb question?"

Beraht only looked at him.

Tomas shook his head and smiled. "So what happened next?" he asked.

"My parents were blessed by the Allfather. I was healed, and we returned home." The Uldra stood and shook the packed snow free of his pants, signaling to his friends that the break was over.

"Isn't any child that completes the Rite of the Holy Path supposed to become a leader of his clan?" the squire asked.

Beraht nodded but said nothing.

"What happened?"

The Uldra resumed their course, letting Tomas fall in behind while the young man waited for an answer. Finally, the warrior sighed and shook his head. "You know what *aduiron* means?"

"Caste," Tomas nodded. "Or job; task. An Uldra's place in his clan."

"My father was a builder of burial mounds, the lowest *aduiron*, like his father, all the way back to the Uprising."

"Because of your family's crimes?" the squire asked hesitantly.

"Yeah," Beraht grunted. "All my life, my parents told me how I was the one that would regain our family honor and restore our name. That it was my responsibility to not fail in our family's chance at regaining honor."

"That's a pretty serious burden."

"I trained constantly. A child that survives the Rite must master each *aduiron* in the clan, especially the traditions of the *marun*."

"Sounds like a lot of work."

"One day, just a week before I was to take the Rite of Maturity, a traveling merchant came into the village. Since that was the only *aduiron* I wasn't trained in, my father told me to wait and made arrangements to go with the merchant on his next trip for the training and experience. I was supposed to only be gone for a few months, then come home and go through the Rite and begin the process of reclaiming my family's honor."

"You never went home." It was not a question.

"The merchant was bound for Pelsemoria. I started learning about the world outside of Ulheim and wanted to know more. I started to think that there might be things worth knowing outside what's written in the Book of Sayings. I wrote my father a letter saying that I was going to stay in Pelsemoria for a while longer, learning more of the outside world, before returning home."

"That couldn't have gone over well," Tomas guessed.

Beraht shook his head. "I never heard from my clan again. It wasn't until years later that I found out about the massacre." He stopped and looked out, towards the valley in which the ruins of his village rested. "I will never know if they even got the letter. I will never know if my father supported my decision. My brother."

Tomas was silent as the implications of his friend's words soaked in. Beraht had, in his own mind, abandoned his entire clan and the expectations they had for him, only to have the village destroyed by an enemy who was after him. The young man could not guess the devastating sense of responsibility that was crushing upon Beraht's broad shoulders, the guilt that must weigh on the Uldra's heart and soul.

"I'm sorry, Beraht," Tomas said, not knowing what else to say.

The Uldra warrior just shrugged and continued to lead his friends up the tiered slopes of the Allfather's Throne.

Chapter 29

Dawn broke one morning and they woke, once again wrapped in each other's arms and their overlapping clothes. Tomas blinked and breathed deeply, only reluctantly stirring to wakefulness. He then looked down at where Aebreanna was, as always, snuggled into the men's arms and legs. The squire could not help but start.

He had seen the Wyrdmark's effects before, of course. Tomas had spent nearly a year in Aebreanna's company and seen her shift with the seasons from spring to summer to autumn to winter. Still, the change was once again so abrupt, so quietly undeniable, that Tomas could not help but stare.

Aebreanna's winter-white mane was now honey blonde. Its faded luster from their desperate battle in Uldron had returned with full force, such that her springtime mane nearly glowed with renewed life. Her fair skin, porcelain to reflect winter's snowy presence, had become cool ivory, flushed with all the potential of spring's return. The Sylva opened her left eye, the opalescence there now shining with verdant power, her right still hidden behind her now-golden mane. She blinked and looked up at Tomas' sensing his gaze. She held up her hands, noting the change, and then quickly drew a light touch to the right side of her face.

She held her fingers there, under what her luminous mane hid. The Sylva sighed then, and her verdant gaze went back to Tomas. "I had hoped…" she whispered.

Tomas realized his arms were around her small body. He pulled into an even closer embrace and whispered, "I'm so sorry, Aebreanna."

"It matters little," she said firmly, though she remained in his embrace for a time. Finally, she sighed again and broke free. "If your boys can endure the absence of my flesh," she said then with a wicked smile, "I will prepare our breakfast."

That afternoon, they reached the tunnel's entrance.

The path upon which Beraht led them leveled and turned, leading briefly back down into a plaza even larger than the previous ones. The Allfather's Throne had seemed to stretch its stone walls to either side, leaving an almost perfectly flat plain that, although untouched by loose snow, was covered by a lake of ice that was so perfect it seemed to be made of flawless crystal. Towering at the end of the frozen platform, seemingly as natural a part of the Allfather's Throne as was the gray stone on which the adventurers now stood, was a sealed gate that would easily dwarf the city gates of the Northern Keep, Pelsemoria, or any other city in the world. The gate was built of some dark stone that seemed to shine with reflected sunlight, showing no sign of rust or other decay despite the many centuries during which it must have sat unused in this frozen wilderness. All along the flawless gate were carved Uldric runes, each taller than a man and made of perfect silver. At the center of the ancient doorway was a massive bronze disk with a representation of the Allfather's Throne engraved upon it, with a replica of Beraht's waraxe on one side, and a great chalice on the other.

"Yes," Aebreanna sniffed, "very nice, I'm sure." Rogan and Tomas, still open mouthed in shock, turned to stare at their Sylva friend. The spy just glanced at them and shrugged. "What?" she demanded.

"Yes," Beraht grinned, beaming with pride for the accomplishments of his ancestors. "They don't build them like that anymore."

Tomas cleared his throat. "So… uh… how do we open it?" he asked.

Beraht did not reply. The Uldra did, however, lose a great deal of his glowing pride.

"Beraht," Aebreanna purred, "how do we open this towering example of Uldra exuberance?"

"Well—" the warrior replied. "That is… we just… uh—"

"YOU DON'T KNOW?" Rogan exploded.

"Not exactly."

"We dragged our sorry assess all the way here!" Tomas watched in concern as his knight continued yelling, his face turning so red and his body generating so much heat that the snow around the Northlands prince began to melt. "We fought through those Druug! We climbed this big bastard of a mountain! And only *now* do you realize that you can't open that door!!"

"I never said I couldn't open it," Beraht insisted. "I just don't know exactly how."

Rogan tried to continue his criticism of his warrior comrade, but most of his words descended rapidly from inarticulate syllables to little more than grunts and growls.

Aebreanna took a deep breath and stared at the massive gate, all the more impressive now that the heroes realized they could not open it. "Keeping in mind the Uldra predilection for simplicity," the Sylva mused. "I have no doubt that the gate has an opening mechanism that can be operated with a minimum of difficulty."

Tomas nodded. "The question is," he added, "what's the opening mechanism?"

Both glanced at Beraht. The Uldra looked at them and shrugged before sitting down in the snow. "Did your people not maintain a history of the operation of this device?" Aebreanna asked.

The Uldra picked absently at his nose. "Sure," he replied. "But the priests were responsible for opening and closing it."

"And they're all dead," Tomas finished with a grimace.

Rogan continued swearing and grunting as he began to stomp across the ridgeline upon which the heroes stood, while Tomas and Aebreanna continued staring at the gate. "We have only to solve the riddle of this machine and entrance is ours," Aebreanna insisted.

"Riddle?" Rogan demanded. "What riddle? The Uldra just forgot how the damned thing works!" The knight waved his arms and jabbed his fists toward the uncaring gate. "God forbid they just write down the instructions!"

Tomas and Aebreanna glanced at each other and then stared hard at the runes carved into the gate. "It can't be that simple," Tomas insisted.

"When dealing with Uldra," Aebreanna corrected, "simplicity should never be immediately dismissed. Can you read the runes?"

The squire shook his head. "I think they're in *Adikahdt*, the ancient Uldra language."

"You cannot read *Adikahdt*?"

"I know some Uldric, but I never learned any *Adikahdt* runes."

Tomas and Aebreanna glanced at Beraht. The Uldra looked back at them with an empty expression. "Well?" the Sylva demanded.

"What?" Beraht replied.

Aebreanna groaned and rubbed at her temples. "Can you read the runes?" she sighed.

"Sure."

"Then please do so."

"It says: '*Kurish Foiryurn Fieft.*'"

"And what does that mean?" the Sylva asked with remarkable patience.

Beraht shrugged.

"I thought your father taught you ancient Uldric?" Tomas demanded in exasperation.

"Not all of it."

Aebreanna sighed again. "Yes," she said. "Well, I just need to stand over here for a while." The weary baroness walked away muttering to herself in Sylvai.

Tomas rubbed his eyes and joined Beraht on the frozen ground. "All right," he said, "we can do this. Let's go through the runes one at a time."

"All right."

"You said the first one was what?"

"*Kurish.*"

"OK." The squire closed his eyes and tried to remember his lessons in the Uldra language. "That sounds a little like '*Kesh*,' which means 'request,' or 'to announce.'"

"Right," Beraht agreed.

"So maybe *Kurish* means 'to request' or, I don't know, 'to knock.' That's a good start, right?"

"Right."

"And *Foiryrn*, what do you think that means?"

The Uldra thought about it for a minute. "Sounds a little like *feyer*," he noticed. "Maybe it means 'before.'"

"All right," Tomas agreed. "So before we can request… what? Before we can request to get in?"

"The last part says, '*Fieft*.'"

"*Eif*?" the young man suggested. "Open? Or opening?"

Rogan stopped his pacing and stared at the runes. "You can't be serious," the knight growled.

"What?" Tomas asked.

"Before opening, knock?"

The three men stared at the runes. "We must have made a mistake somewhere," Tomas admitted.

Aebreanna returned from her Uldra rest. "Have you discovered anything?" she asked.

"No," Rogan replied flatly.

"Maybe," Tomas suggested.

"Knock before entering?" the knight snapped in derision.

Aebreanna stared at the three boys. "I wish to go home now," she declared flatly.

"What have we got to lose?" Tomas insisted.

Beraht stood and walked down the gentle slope before them. As he crossed the ice-covered courtyard, the Uldra pulled free his waraxe and hefted the large weapon over his broad shoulder. Beraht stood in front of the gate before raising his weapon and reached back, aiming the rounded end at the gate.

"This is the stupidest thing we've ever tried," Rogan grunted.

"I very much doubt that," Aebreanna replied.

"Well, it's in the top ten at least."

Aebreanna only stared at her Human friend with a resigned expression.

"All right, fine! It doesn't even rank! But this is still pretty stupid!"

Beraht pounded on the gate three times with enough force to shake the air all the way back to where his friends stood. Within moments, the ground began to shake violently, and huge drifts of snow were dislodged from above the gate, falling down and burying Beraht as the gate split evenly at the center and parted, opening inward to reveal the ancient tunnel within.

Rogan and Tomas struggled to maintain control of the horses, while Aebreanna sprinted to the massive pile of snow and ice that now covered Beraht, plunging her arms into the cold grave and furiously shoveling snow aside. As the shaking subsided and the gate continued opening, the Humans mounted and led their steeds at a gallop down to where Aebreanna still desperately dug.

The three heroes cleared the snow as fast as they possibly could, hoping to reach Beraht before the Uldra ran out of air and fearing their efforts would prove too slow. Finally, Tomas uncovered an Uldra foot and called out to his friends. Rogan and Aebreanna joined the squire and pulled at the foot, putting all their strength into freeing the Uldra connected to it. In an explosion of snow and ice that covered the fearful adventurers, Beraht broke free of his icy prison and rolled over top of Rogan before landing with his face planted in Aebreanna's chest.

At first stunned from the force of his release, Beraht was forced to take a moment, shaking his head and blinking his eyes. In the instant the Uldra realized where his face was, he leapt up and began wiping his face, making disgusted sounds and spitting on the ground. "You are welcome," Aebreanna said with a sneer.

"Are you all right?" Tomas asked, brushing snow off his friend's shoulders.

"Are you kidding!" Beraht demanded, still trying to cleanse himself of the memory of Sylva cleavage. "I was better off in the snow!"

"Next time, we shall leave you buried then!" Aebreanna snapped as Rogan helped the Sylva to her feet.

"Couldn't you have tried to get clear?" the knight asked.

Beraht shrugged while trying to clear the packed snow from his cavernous ears. "It was just a little snow," he insisted.

A massive icicle, larger than a knight's lance, broke free of its base overhead and fell, stabbing into the ground only a few feet from where Tomas stood. "And some ice," Beraht added.

"Let's get in there before anything else tries to kill us," Rogan said, leading the way into the ancient tunnel that would at last take them away from the frozen Ulheim and to the Free City of Frostfront.

Second Interpose

Chapter 30

"Is there anything new from the Lords Cardinal?" Kyla asked Cardinal Tain hopefully during the meetings of the Advisory Council following the Winter Solstice celebration. The holiday that year had been muted or some indefinable reason. The wreaths were bright and the many torches and lanterns shone as always. The evergreen boughs adorning windows and mantles still carried their comforting scent and renewing magic. But something had been missing from what was normally a festive, even joyous celebration in the Northern Keep.

Mary and Kyla had joined in the celebrations, of course. With the Queen dedicating so much of her time with the ailing King, the eldest daughter of House Calonar had taken charge, officiating the multi-faith services and lighting the city's yearning log, commemorating the lengthening of days ahead. Princess Kyla took part in the songs and dances, and she helped deliver the gifts from House Calonar to the less fortunate among their people. She outwardly showed overflowing joy in the company of the citizens of her father's city. But Mary knew this was a show.

Neither of them, princess or handmaiden, took particular joy in the winter holiday. The absence of their men and their friends was only one of the darkening elements to shroud the season. The King was failing, his strength seeming to wane with greater speed every day. The gardens were still a blackened scar that could not be healed until the spring thaw. The aftereffects of Vara's Storm continued to disrupt travel and communication. Little word reached the Northern Keep from the surrounding towns and villages, and travel had become all but impossible. Mary did not know how her mother was faring in the winter, having had no contact with her home in months. For the sake of her princess, the handmaiden kept her mask of festive cheer, and aided Kyla in maintaining her own disguise.

Finally, the holiday had passed. The decorations were being taken down and the festive clothes put away for another year. The business of governance resumed, and with them, the now-weekly meetings of the King's, now the Princess' Advisory Council.

Cardinal Tain had little direct communication with his peers in the Holy City of Velaross since the departure of Prince Rogan and his team and the disruption of Vara's Storm. Between the heavy weather and the arcane interference, the old priest had little success in reaching out to the other Lords Cardinal. Only in the past week had the lingering disruption to the Winds of Magic faded. Messengers still could not penetrate outside Wildelves Wood, and only the strongest adepts could reach outside the Northlands. With Esha's help, Cardinal Tain had, at last, made contact with Velaross. The leaders of House Calonar hoped that Tain could use his influence with the other Lords Cardinal to gain assistance from the Adamic Church in their growing conflict with House Balshazzar.

"No, your Highness," Tain replied gently. The saintly old man was one of the King's most trusted friends and a lifetime ally of House Calonar. Despite the many problems his loyalty had caused him over the many decades, including once being captured and tortured by the Inquisition, the cardinal had never wavered in his commitment to not only House Calonar, but to all the people of the Northlands. It was a common belief that, for all the work King Cylan had done to protect the people of the Northlands from the machinations of the old Electors Council, Cardinal Tain had done just as much with the Lords Cardinal. Now ancient and in failing health, Tain nonetheless continued to serve as best he could.

"I'm sorry," the old priest said, "but the other cardinals refuse to take any provocative action against Emir Balshazzar until definitive evidence is uncovered. Particularly with the worsening situation in Jarek." Tain sighed and rubbed his tired eyes against the bright light of the council chambers. "The split in the Church came as a shock to many of the cardinals." The priest shook his head. "Many of my brothers have a woefully narrow view of the world and never really appreciated just how tenuous our Holy Mother's grip was on the hearts of the people living beyond Ulheim. Despite how many of the upper clergy and knights from those lands severed their ties with Velaross and joined with Balshazzar's new church, there are many among the Lords Cardinal who believe there can still be a reconciliation."

"Can there?" Rashid asked from his normal place at the council table.

"Personally, I don't think so. Those who have gone to Tordenia are among the most conservative, meaning those who typically have the greatest hatred for House Calonar and what we hope to achieve, to say nothing of their bigotry towards Inhumans."

"Couldn't a new Adama call for unity?" Mary asked softly from her place at Kyla's side. Although hesitant as always to speak at the council meetings, the princess' constant requests that her handmaiden speak her mind had brought occasional comments. Much to her surprise, Mary's input into the meetings, few and hesitant though they may be, were as welcomed as any others. House Calonar had a reputation in Lanasia for welcoming talent regardless of class or status. While most of the Noble Houses scorned this, the King and Queen believed this inclusivity was their family's greatest strength.

"A new Holy Father very well could bring them back, daughter," the old cleric replied. "But we are cursed by our own traditions. According to Church law, we must have at least two-thirds of the cardinals in Velaross to elect a new Adama, and more than one-third of the Lords Cardinal have defected to the Western Empire."

"Replace them," General Killdare said bluntly. Never one to mince words, the old veteran offered the most direct approach to any situation, regardless of the theological implications.

Tain smiled sadly. "Again, if only it were that simple. A cardinal can only be replaced after his death or with a two-thirds vote by the remaining brothers. I have tried convincing the others that it may be time to set aside a few of our more stringent rules in this time or crisis, but it seems my advice no longer has the impact it once did."

Kyla put her hand over the old man's. "We still value it. This council would be nothing without you to guide us."

The old cardinal smiled at her attempt to cheer him. Tain had been present from Kyla's birth and throughout her entire life. The cardinal was very much a second father to her despite their different faiths.

From out in the city, even through the shuttered windows, an explosion could be heard. All eyes in the council chamber turned to Esha, whose tendency toward self-detonation had become so commonplace that her repeated detonations did little to surprise anyone. Noticing the attention, the tiny archmage shrugged. "I was not involved. My Tower is observing the Princess' command to suspend experiments until we can overcome the disruption caused by Vara's Storm."

"In that case," Kyla said, "have you learned why your adepts keep blowing up? We're getting complaints."

The diminutive Sylva shook her head. "I have dedicated three of my students to the investigation, but they have, as yet, made little appreciable progress. Although the Winds have experienced a chaotic surge as of late, it seems unconnected with our current tendency toward detonation." Esha was seated in her specially-built chair. Small even for a Sylva, the archmage was a vital member of House Calonar's Advisory Council, but would hardly function in one of the Human-sized chairs. As a result, Remm Stonebearer had, without prompting, constructed a personalized place for the brilliant adept. The chair was formed of a single piece of oak, with intricately-carved engravings of magic and nature. The tall legs meant the Tower Mistress of the Northern Keep sat at eye-level with the other council members, and a simple step, incorporated into the other engravings, offered Esha an easy means of mounting and dismounting her near-throne.

"How is that possible?" Rashid asked.

Chandra nodded. "They must be connected. The Storm hit, magic went crazy, and now wizards are blowing up."

Esha continued looked at the scattered documents she had been examining. "I would not confuse correlation with causation," she said. The archmage glanced up and, noting the empty expressions, she took the large viewing lenses from her tiny nose. "Ah, yes." She cleared her throat. "While these events are quite probably connected, I would not assume one caused the other."

"Well, keep looking into it," the princess replied. "The property damage is starting to be a problem." Kyla turned her pearlescent eyes next to General Killdare for the military report.

"Our peacekeeping force reached Jarek right before the blizzard hit, your Highness," the iron-haired officer said in response to his princess' gaze. The Guard commander's tone reflected his still-frosty attitude towards Kyla. Although the general was fiercely loyal to Prince Rogan and House Calonar, his mistrust of the princess' leadership was little secret. Killdare blamed Kyla for Vagris' escape and the ensuing escalation of the mercenary threat, now that such a dangerous, well-trained man led them.

"Did Vara's Storm reach that far south?" Mary asked.

"Partly," Killdare replied flatly. "They had heavy snow and wind, but the bigger problems were mudslides."

"That storm has kicked up problems all over eastern Lanasia," Captain Rainer added. The general's aide was gaining a reputation as mediator between his irascible commander and the senior members of House Calonar.

"Both the Alvaro and Frostfront forces withdrew," Killdare continued, gesturing with a scarred hand to the large map of eastern Lanasia laid out on the council table.

"Where did they withdraw to?" Kyla asked.

For a reply, the general looked to Rashid. The baron handed the various dispatches he held to his aid, Chandra, and stood to place two small wooden figurines, representative of the two armies, on the map. "The Alvaro force gave every indication of going home," the spymaster said as he moved one of the figurines away from the town of Jarek toward Alvaro. "They got caught by the bad weather, however, and are wintering near Recedo Pass."

"I didn't think the winters were that severe around Alvaro," Mary pointed out softly.

"Normally," Baron Tressalon replied with a gentle smile. Of all the members of the Advisory Council, Rashid had seemed the most receptive to Mary's presence. The spymaster openly welcomed her questions and input, maintaining an encouraging tone with the shy handmaiden. "Vara's Storm has pinned them down. They won't be able to move until the spring thaw."

Kyla looked to Esha. "What will the long-term effects of the storm be, Esha?" she asked.

"Difficult to predict," the archmage responded. "Certainly, this will be a colder winter with strong storms continuing through spring. Hopefully, Sora's Speakers will have the weather stabilized by the end of summer. Of greater concern is the disruption to the Winds."

"But that is abating?" Cardinal Tain asked.

Esha shook her head. "Gradually. I fear the disruption will endure for some time. I have assigned a team of my students to look into historical precedents."

"Have they found anything?" Chandra asked.

"Little," the tiny archmage replied. "So far, the closest we have come is the description of events following the Disaster at Nassinalia."

A tide of worry washed over the entire council. "How long did it take for that to end?" Mary asked softly."

"Centuries," Esha replied. "Some effects remain to this day, most especially in the Zaka Sea and the straits in and around Dagon'ay. Fortunately, I doubt we shall suffer the same disruption for the same duration."

"Why?" Kyla asked.

"Proportionality," Esha shrugged. "The Disaster annihilated an entire city and much of what had been central Lanasia. It shattered our continent, changed our seasons, and triggered a decades-long winter. In our case, we endured a blizzard. A severe one, to be sure, but still only a single storm. Mathematically, though the disruption effect may be similar, it will not be as strong, nor last as long."

The princess nodded and returned her gaze to Baron Tressalon. "What about the Frostfront army, Rashid?" she asked.

"This is the bit of good luck that came from Vara's Storm." The spymaster moved the figurine representing the Frostfront army about half the distance between Jarek and its home city. "The Arcane Guild is suffering from the mystical disruption the same as everyone else."

Killdare stood and nodded. "Frostfront armies have always depended on their spell-slingers," he grumbled. "Without that, even though they have superior numbers, they don't have the same lethal capabilities."

"They don't even maintain archers, cavalry, or skirmishers," Captain Rainer pointed out.

"They'd have to fall back on their spearmen," the general nodded.

Rashid pointed to the figurine. "They made a show of returning home, but my people found them camped in the middle of the Creir Forest."

"Did they get caught in the weather as well?" Kyla asked.

"Yes," Chandra replied. "But only briefly. They had to camp for a week or so, but then had enough clear weather to return home. It also looks like they wanted us to think that's exactly what they did.

"My people have seen the camps," Rashid added. "That army hasn't demobilized. In fact, it's grown with reinforcements dispatched from Klemens."

"Why?" Kyla asked. "What are they doing?"

The spymaster deferred to General Killdare. "There are only a few possibilities, your Highness," the scarred veteran answered. "They could be planning a campaign somewhere else and are using the winter to organize and plan. This is likely since House Calexto has been a constant problem for Frostfront, as have the warlords in the South. The Triumvirate could simply be taking advantage of the fact that they already have an army assembled."

"Esha," Kyla asked the archmage, "have you received any information from the Guild that they could be planning what General Killdare is suggesting?"

The tiny Sylva shook her head. "I have received no communiqués from the Arcane Guild," she replied, "initially, due to the Storm's disruption. However, even as the effects begin to abate, communications from Frostfront have been nearly entirely absent."

"Would they feed you false information?" Rashid asked. "Or shut you out all together?"

"Possibly," Esha replied. "I know there is a growing faction within the Guild that wants to see me removed as Mistress of my Tower. At the very least, I know I am not trusted by the more politically-minded of Frostfront Prefects. If any action was being considered that ran counter to their relations with House Calonar, they would almost certainly not keep me informed."

"Why all the intrigue?" the spymaster asked. "I thought it was Guild tradition to swear an oath of loyalty to the local lord."

"True," the Sylva agreed. "However, Guild tradition also demands that oath should fall second to one's obligations to the Triumvirate and the Prefects of Frostfront."

"How likely is it that the Guild would use their army to start a war?" Kyla asked.

"Given the evidence, I would say highly probable. However, if you are asking me to anticipate their objective, I must admit ignorance. The motivations of the Prefects and certainly the Triumvirate have remained obscure."

"General?" the princess asked.

"Your Highness," the old warrior said, "you don't raise an army unless you plan to use it. It's simply too expensive to maintain a force of any size and not employ it."

"What are the possibilities?"

"They could be planning to build a force to try and occupy the area around Jarek rather than taking the town itself."

"Why would they do that?" Mary asked.

"Frostfront rejected our peace treaty. We can assume their original motivation remains: they want the gold in Jarek. They have an army in the area but are weakened by the mystical disruption. Esha believes this disruption is temporary, and fading. The Guild likely thinks the same. When the effect passes, when Frostfront thinks they once again have the advantage, they'll attack."

"Such a conflict will escalate," Cardinal Tain added sadly. He nodded towards the map and its miniatures. "Jarek lies in the disputed boundary between Alvaro and Frostfront. Traditionally, those communities paid homage to Alvaro. Even without the gold, House Calexto would feel honor-bound to defend the town. With the gold…"

"All-out war," Killdare agreed.

"And worse," the elderly cleric noted. "Alvaro is friendly to the Lords of Velaross and the Church. The Arcane Guild has always been antagonistic towards the Church. If Frostfront becomes aggressive, the Lords Cardinal will call on the Holy Knights and the Lords of Velaross to support Alvaro."

"The Kordenel Counties will get drawn in," Captain Rainer noted. "Klemens has already sided with Frostfront and Gracia with Alvaro. The others are all too close; they'll be forced to take sides, and fighting will likely break out."

"Which will weaken them against the warlords and Xeshlin," Killdare mused. "Ironheartshaven will probably support the Church."

"Doesn't that mean Frostfront will be outnumbered?" Chandra asked.

Captain Rainer nodded. "And they'll look for allies." He pointed to the west, past Ulheim. "Daivic, Oneld, and the Western Empire."

"But that's where Tomas…" Mary bit off her objection, her fear.

"Any large-scale war," Rashid said, "will trigger a general mobilization, right when the Prince and his team are trying to slip through."

Kyla stood and looked at the map spread before her, letting her eyes drift around the area that the Frostfront figurine stood. "When?" she asked softly.

"In all likelihood, spring," Killdare replied. "Give a few months for the magical disruption to pass and wait for the thaw. If I was running a war for Frostfront, I'd pull back to a spot that I thought I could hide in, just like they've done. Next, I'd start calling in as many reinforcements as I could get my hands on, just like they're doing. Finally, the moment magic was reliable again and the ground could support a march, when I had a force that could overpower the King's peacekeepers and the Calexto forces, I'd move back in and take the town. With our small peacekeeping force now caught in the middle," the grizzled veteran grumbled, "I knew that mission would bite us in the butt."

"Gentlemen," Kyla said softly, "this is exactly what we need to avoid. Rogan is seeking a cure for my father. He can only do that if he has relative freedom of movement, which he will lose if there's a mobilization. We MUST maintain the peace to give him time to reach Tordenia, find the cure, and get home."

The entire council was quiet following Kyla's declaration. Finally, General Killdare spoke quietly, returning to his seat and leveling a gaze at the princess with a soft twitch under his left eye. "Peace at any cost?" he asked.

"Yes," Kyla replied evenly.

Mary placed a gentle hand on her princess's arm. "Wouldn't the prince want to protect the people first?" she said in a voice that was barely a whisper. "Wouldn't his Highness want to protect the innocent people of Jarek and prevent an even bigger war?"

Kyla glanced into Mary's eyes and sensed the truth in her friend's words. The princess then turned back to Killdare. "General," she said after a deep breath, "is there any way to prevent this war?"

The old warrior took several deep breaths himself and then looked down at the map, letting a dozen tactical situations run through his mind. The general glanced at his aide. "What do you think?" he grumbled.

Captain Rainer stood and looked down at the map. Finally, he shrugged. "Controlled burn."

Killdare nodded and raised his eyes to meet Kyla's. "With Frostfront locked in their current mind-set, it's only a matter of time before it sets off some kind of war." The soldier's voice carried the undeniable tone of command and experience. "At this point, a conflict is all but inevitable. But we can decide when and where it occurs and how much it escalates."

"How?" Tain asked. "It seems that any conflict will cause all Lanasia to burn."

Captain Rainer handed his general another figurine, this one a soldier with a poleaxe, marking him as a warrior of House Calonar. Killdare placed the figurine at the lower edge of Wildelves Wood. "If we muster a large force and send them south," as he spoke, the general moved the House Calonar figurine until it intercepted its brother from Frostfront, "we can intercept the Guild force in a time and place of our choosing."

"What would be gained by attacking the Frostfront army directly," Esha asked. "Surely such an act would precipitate a full-scale war between the Arcane Guild and House Calonar."

The general gestured for this aid to answer. "We'll wait until the army is already on the march for Jarek," the happy captain replied with a sly grin. "This will pull the enemy army into a tactically vulnerable position."

"I fear I still have little understanding of the wisdom of attacking a superior force on the march," the archmage admitted.

Rainer patted the tiny Sylva on the shoulder. "Don't worry about it," he said. "It's an army thing, trust us."

Killdare cleared his throat. "While the army is moving south, we'll need dispatches sent to House Calexto," he said. "Enough so that it'll be obvious to the Guild that we're communicating with Alvaro."

"My people can handle it," Rashid said.

"Even with the disruption?" Kyla asked. "The mercenaries?"

The spymaster glanced at Esha, who nodded. Rashid then looked back to the princess. "We'll have the adepts send communiques outside Wildelves Wood, to Greenhills. My people will take these south. And we can make sure some are intercepted by Guild agents."

"What is all this leading to?" Kyla asked.

Again, General Killdare motioned for Captain Rainer to answer. "Once Frostfront finds out that we're in communication with Alvaro, they'll get very nervous, your Highness. When the force they thought would be such a surprise gets attacked and they learn about communications between the Keep and Alvaro, this'll reinforce their fear of an impending alliance not only between House Calexto and Velaross, which would be bad enough, but an alliance between House Calexto, Velaross, and House Calonar, which would spell serious trouble for the Guild."

"But what happens if we lose the battle?" Mary asked.

"We don't have to win the battle," Rainer insisted. "All we have to do is hit the Guild force hard enough that they have to halt their march toward Jarek."

"If we time this operation correctly," Killdare added, "Alvaro will realize what's happening and have time to mobilize. They'll get reinforcements from Velaross and maneuver into an advantageous position. The Prefects of Frostfront will be forced to negotiate for a lasting peace or face attack from two forces from two directions. Best of all, the people of Jarek will be spared any bloodshed."

"Where will you get the soldiers from?" Rashid asked.

"The Keep mostly," Killdare replied. "We have two standing brigades here, which I'll augment with Esha's people and elements from the towns and villages surrounding Wildelves Wood. I'll also have a detachment from Woodwall join us. On the way south, the army can rendezvous with forces assigned to Drailia." He turned to Esha. "Can your people get word to the Western Forts yet?"

The archmage shook her head. "Soon. Perhaps another week."

The general nodded. "That's fine. I'll mobilize here and have the Woodwall reinforcements meet me on the march. By then you should be able to reach Drailia and Green Fields, yes?"

Esha nodded.

"Then, you're people will send word to those garrisons as soon as you're able and the combined force will meet up in the foothills of the Sentinel Mountains."

Remm, commander of the City Watch and, with the absence of Beraht, acting representative of the Uldra, jumped to his feet, pounding the table with a massive fist. "That would only leave a single brigade of reserves to defend the city!" he roared. "You can't leave the Keep that weakened!"

"He has a point." Chandra noted, her voice a soft counterpoint to Remm's rumbling growl. Chandra's voice was renowned throughout the Northern Keep as much for its wisdom as for how often it was compared with that of a satisfied cat after a fresh meal. On the rare occasion that Rashid's second chose to speak, it was almost unheard of for those around her to ignore the spy's words. "As long as the identity of Anninihus's master is still a secret, and Vagris remains at large with a force of mercenaries, it would be dangerous to leave the Keep defended by so small a force."

"There's still the Watch," Captain Rainer insisted. "And the Walkers provide a shield from anyone even approaching the city."

"I won't take all the forces from our various outposts," Killdare declared. "But yes, your Highness, it will take the majority of our standing forces to match the army Frostfront has gathered. As for our vulnerability, we'll still have the forest. The Speakers have sworn to protect us. Besides, Tressalon will hear of anything large enough to threaten the Northlands with enough lead time to allow the army to return if necessary. The mercenaries are out there..." he could not hide his anger, "as is Vagris. But, no matter what force the warlord has, he can't possibly threaten the Keep, and seeing our army on the march will encourage some of those mercenaries he's hired to seek employment elsewhere. To be blunt, Princess, wars are never won by keeping your army at home 'just in case.'"

Kyla nodded her understanding. Arguing with General Killdare on any military subject was difficult; as one of the few remaining graduates of the War College, his mastery of war was legendary across Lanasia. The princess turned to Remm and asked, "Will that provide enough soldiers to defend the Keep and Wildelves Wood if we do come under attack?" she asked.

The Uldra thought about it. As he so often did when deep in thought, Remm drew a finger along the intricate tattoos that covered the right side of his face. One of the greatest mysteries of the Northlands was how Remm Stonebearer had been tattooed across the entire right half of his body and all the hair on that side had been turned white. Despite frequent questions though, the Uldra only ever responded with sarcasm, if at all. "It should do as long as none of the warlords come at us in force," he finally replied.

"It sounds as though timing and tactics will be critical for this operation," Esha pointed out, "to say nothing of expediency. Events will not begin until the mystic disruption passes, and that is unpredictable. Much will depend on the field commander to adjust to new circumstances and responding to changing conditions without need for orders from home."

"Absolutely crucial," Killdare agreed.

"Then who will command the force that engages the Guild army?" Tain asked. "Who among your officers has that degree of skill?"

"I've got colonels that can get the job done," the general insisted. "I'll meet with my staff and have a name for the princess by the end of the week."

"No, General," Kyla said sternly. "This operation is too delicate and too critical to entrust to a subordinate. You must take command of our force."

"With all due respect, Princess," Killdare's voice carried an irritation the old soldier did not bother to conceal, "as commander of the army, it's my prerogative to assign who commands what units." Few soldiers, regardless of their combat experience, could stand before General Killdare when his temper was up.

Kyla, however, had steel in her soul that few had ever seen. "Correction, General," she replied evenly, "it is your prerogative to advise who should be placed in command of what units. It is ultimately my husband's decision, and with him gone, it is now mine. As regent, it's my decision that your expertise is needed to bring a swift end to this campaign."

The general hesitated a moment, but then bowed. "I didn't mean to question you, your Highness. I apologize."

The princess took a deep breath and shook her head. "I took no offense, General. But we can't afford to have the army caught up in a long war right now. Vagris may not have a large force, but he is out there. The sooner you can complete this mission and come home to defeat him, the safer we'll all be."

"You're right, of course," Killdare admitted. "This plan is complex and needs close supervision."

"Will it work?" Kyla asked, partially to herself.

Without hesitation, Killdare responded with absolute resolution. "Yes, your Highness. It will work."

Kyla stood, precipitating all others present to rise. "Then I'll consult with my father. In the meantime, make your preparations, General." The princess threw a whimsical grin toward Captain Rainer. "Operation Controlled Burn is approved."

The various members of the Advisory Council slowly began exiting out of the chamber. Rather than following the others as they made their way out of the council chamber, the princess returned to her seat. Mary brought her a glass of water and laid a gentle hand on Kyla's shoulder, drawing the princess's attention to where Baron Tressalon and his assistant still sat at their places at the table.

Without a word, the spymaster threw a pointed look at where Mary stood and to Lukas, the bodyguard who, since the departure of the Archaeknights, had been assigned to the princess' protective detail. In response to Rashid's questioning look, Kyla said, "We have to trust someone."

"The more people who know a secret," Chandra said, "the less of a secret it becomes."

Kyla nodded in concession and looked over her shoulder. "Lukas, would you excuse us?"

The soldier nodded and left the council chamber. Even as the bodyguard was leaving, Chandra cleared her throat meaningfully and nodded at Mary.

Kyla shook her head. "Rashid trusts you, Chandra. I trust Mary. Everyone needs someone."

Rashid and Chandra exchanged brief looks before beginning the report that only the princess could be allowed to hear. "We've done everything we can to uncover the traitors in the service," the spymaster said. "But we've had very little success."

This more than anything else worried Kyla since the Advisory Council relied heavily on Rashid's agency to provide them with the information they needed to make the proper decisions.

"I'm sorry, Princess," Rashid said, "no matter how we try to smoke them out, the moles just refuse to be exposed. Every lead we had has dried up. I'm afraid we've hit a dead end. To make matters worse, we're fairly sure that whoever the traitor on the council is, that person has tipped off the agents he or she has turned that we're looking for them."

Kyla smiled warmly at the chief of intelligence. "It's all right, Rashid. I understand that it must be very difficult to find people who you yourself have trained not to be found."

"Don't go too easy on him, Highness." Chandra said with a sardonic smile. "He hasn't been working as hard as he could. I've seen him several times just sitting at his desk mooning over his wife."

The princess looked at Rashid's second. "So have you had any more success, Chandra?" she asked with an arched smile.

A shadow passed over the woman's face. "No, Highness, I'm afraid not. As you've said, we train these people to infiltrate and disappear into the most difficult and dangerous places, so we really shouldn't be surprised that they've done just that."

"Do you have any way to discern what news you can trust versus the false intelligence we keep getting?"

Rashid shook his head. "I'm afraid not," he said.

"We do know that Frostfront's activities are real," Chandra insisted.

"How?" Mary asked.

"Triple confirmation," the spymaster replied. "Each piece of important intelligence that comes in has two more teams put on it for confirmation."

"For the time being, we'll have to keep deploying the teams this way," Chandra said.

"How long can your agents maintain that?" Kyla asked.

"Not long," Rashid admitted. "The more time passes, the more likely it is we'll miss something important."

"So what are you going to do next?"

The spymaster stood, followed quickly by his second. "I have a few ideas, Princess," he said. "But if it's all the same, I'd rather keep things quiet until I'm ready to act. That way, there's no chance for a leak."

"I told you that I trust Mary," Kyla reminded him.

Rashid gathered up his paperwork and turned to leave. "That's fine for you, Your Highness," he said over his shoulder with a glance that took in everyone present. "But I don't trust anyone."

Chapter 31

After seeing everyone out of the council chamber, Kyla decided to pay a visit to her parents. She tried letting Mary have some time for herself, but the insistent handmaiden kept leveling one excuse after another until Kyla had to demand a private meeting with her immediate family. Mary reluctantly acceded to her princess' request and departed to find Ilse, so the two could have a meal. Lukas, of course, stoically listened to Kyla's instructions and proceeded to ignore them, trailing behind her as always. With her father being as weak as he was, the princess could never even consider forcing him to come to her, and the presence of his daughters was one of the few things that brought some life into Cylan's eyes. Kyla entered the royal apartments without knocking. Lukas remained outside in deference to the royal family's privacy. Hearing sounds coming from her mother's sitting room, the princess made her way over and entered.

"Good morning!" she said brightly. Nora looked up from where she had been teaching the younger Calonar daughter, Karen, how to play cat's cradle. Rising, the old queen met her elder daughter in a warm embrace that neither hurried to end. Karen still stared intently at the maze of string between her hands, bending all her thoughts to solving the problem.

Seeing her sister's intensity, Kyla laughed. "Didn't you learn from me how dangerous it is to teach that game?" she asked jokingly.

The queen smiled at Karen. "I had hoped that one of you would develop the passion for the game I had as a girl. But, I'm afraid Karen has the same problem that you did. She just can't accept that it's meant to be fun."

Nora led her older daughter to a comfortable couch where they both sat. The queen poured them both cups of tea, while Kyla tried to offer her sister some advice on the game. "If you just picture what it's supposed to look like, your hands can figure out where to go."

Karen looked up from the game and shrugged, losing interest. Not even bothering to untangle her fingers, she crossed to the couch and flopped down beside her big sister. "How's my nephew?" she asked brightly.

Kyla made a face, trying to help untangle her little sister's hands. "Well, these cravings are getting a little tiresome. Not to mention the morning sickness. And my breasts are so tender I can barely stand wearing a dress."

"How is that new?" Karen asked.

"Fate can be a cruel goddess," Nora said, putting Kyla's cup where she could reach it without having to stretch.

"What do you mean?" the princess asked, finally untangling Karen.

The queen sipped at her tea. "When I was pregnant with you, I drove your poor father almost to distraction with the odd foods you made me want. And as far as morning sickness, I can say that at least you were regular. Every morning I would have to get up just before dawn."

"What about me?" Karen asked, reaching to the bowl of apples and pears that had been delivered just that morning.

"You, little miss, nearly broke three of my ribs. For a little while, I thought you were going to try and kick your way out."

Kyla took a sip of her tea. "And Rogan thinks battle is hard," she muttered into the cup.

"The best is yet to come." Nora smiled into her own cup.

Kyla rolled her pearlescent eyes. "General Killdare is taking a large part of the army south to intercept a force the Arcane Guild is going to use to try and retake Jarek."

"He's taking the army?" the queen asked in surprise.

Kyla smiled impishly. "Well, he was going to send it with one of his colonels, but I told him to go himself."

"Why?"

"He was acting up in council this morning, trying to bully me into making the decisions he wanted me to make. Besides, he needs to get out more. All the general ever does is stay in the Guard's headquarters issuing orders to the lower officers."

Nora set her cup down and picked up an apple. "That's how the army works, Kyla. The job of fighting is left to the young and brave and foolish. The old soldiers just tell them where to go and who to fight. Besides, that poor man has been serving your father for decades. Killdare came to us as a major and essentially created our army, marching all over Lanasia fighting in more wars than I can remember. I, for one, think he's earned a rest."

"Should I tell him he doesn't have to go?" Kyla asked.

The queen shook her head. "That would only encourage him to act up again. By now, he wouldn't want to stay anyway. He's had more than enough time to get over being angry with you and thinking about all the good times he had fighting alongside your father."

Kyla's eyes moved in the direction of the King's study. "How is he?" she asked in a small voice.

Nora took the half-eaten fruit Karen had deposited next to the tea pot and handed it back to her. "Would you go let Tynae know that we're just about ready for lunch?"

The young girl sighed and took the fruit with her as she went to find their maid.

Nora waited until Karen was gone and the door closed before answering her daughter's question. "Petr and I are still trying various remedies, but so far, nothing is working. Because the poison was brewed with magic, only magic can cure it."

"Have you tried letting Esha search for a cure?" the princess asked.

"She already has. Unfortunately, the only two people in the world who might know about such a cure are Tienel and Cyras."

"I doubt Tienel would help," Kyla huffed.

The queen picked up her tea and took another sip. "You might be surprised. No matter how many times Tienel and your father were on opposite sides, they still stayed friends."

"That doesn't make much sense."

"Men can be bitter enemies and still respect each other, *Kasaya*. Best friends can fight to the death and never lose their love for one another. It's the way they are. Tienel was the wizard who helped get your father inducted into the Arcane Guild, and they did have many adventures together."

"What about Cyras?" the princess asked her hand absently massaging her abdomen. "He and Daddy are best friends. Surely he would help."

"If we knew how to call for his help, we would."

"Daddy knows, doesn't he?"

The queen nodded. "Your father insists that he'll only call on Cyras in the case of a world-threatening emergency."

"Was it easier when Cyras lived in the Keep?"

Nora laughed. "Not really. Cyras always had his own agenda. Even when he lived here, he was never that easy to contact."

"How did you call him when you needed him?" Kyla asked.

"He would always just show up at the right times. Whenever you father really needed him, Cyras would walk into the room with answers and sometimes even a plan."

"Well, Daddy needs him now!" the princess snapped. "So where is he?"

"Perhaps he's here," her mother pointed out. "It really wouldn't be that giant a leap to think Cyras capable of giving help from the shadows and then leaving without telling us he was here. It could be that something even more important is going on that requires his attention."

"What could be more important than his best friend being poisoned?"

"He could be helping Rogan," the queen replied. "As I recall, the last time anyone saw Cyras, he warned your husband that something important was going to happen very soon. If Rogan and Tomas are at the center of what's happening, then Cyras would most likely be giving them his undivided attention."

Kyla shook her head, again shielding her eyes. "Are you saying I should just have faith?"

Nora took her daughter in another embrace. "Yes, *Kasaya*. I'm afraid the only advice that one high priestess can give another is, 'have faith.' Rest assured that whatever is going on in the world, Cyras Darkholm is in the thick of it."

The two stayed that way for a few moments, with Kyla enjoying the feeling of her head on her mother's shoulders, trusting that she was right. Finally, the princess rose and stretched her back.

"You should take a bath and try to get a little sleep." The queen noted.

"I want to visit Daddy first." With one last embrace, Kyla left her mother's sitting room. The princess passed quickly towards her father's study, pausing briefly as she always did in the adjoining chamber in which the king displayed the memories of his past adventures. The various blades he had used in his many battles all rested against one wall, as did several suits of armor. Tokens of appreciation from numerous grateful individuals and communities were arrayed for a lifetime of heroism. Kyla glanced, as she always did, at the opposite wall that held the large family tree of her ancestors going back to the ancient founding of the Sylvai Empire, bearing names that had rocked the world and others lost to the mists of time. And there, standing apart from all the other display cases in the center of the room was the one thing that always caught the princess's sapphire, pearlescent eyes. A single lock or red hair, eternally preserved with a simple plate that read: "Samantha, never forgotten." Kyla never had the courage to ask her parents about the life of the woman who had nearly won her father's heart, instead hearing second-hand stories from others, but curiosity always burned in her whenever the princess passed through this room.

Kyla did not waste more than a few moments among her father's memories. Instead, the princess moved to the entrance of the king's private study. Steeling herself and putting on the face she so often used in the course of her duties, the princess entered.

King Cylan Calonar was seated in his favorite chair, looking out the large windows that provided, Kyla thought, the best view of the city below. The old king's eyes, a match of Kyla's own, were half-closed as the hero dozed in his chair. His lean frame shook slightly and was bowed by the thick blue and gray robes he wore to ward off the chill of winter as the king fought with the poison an assassin had given him weeks ago. Although the graying of his dark hair and the deep lines that crisscrossed his face gave mute evidence of the king's advancing years, it was not until being poisoned by House Balshazzar that he truly appeared to weaken. Kyla could clearly hear the impurities in her father's breath, which was shallow and irregular, and the thick veins growing ever more pronounced on Calonar's neck and wrists showed a discoloration that grew worse each day.

Although there was a cup of tea at the king's shoulder, it had long since cooled without a single drink. The desk behind her father's chair was, for the first time Kyla could remember, free of parchments, dispatches, books, and maps. Even the tall bookshelves that lined either side of her father's study, normally cluttered with books, scrolls, and all number of odd implements and devices Kyla could never begin to guess the meaning of, seemed sterile and much too organized, quietly testifying to her father's inability to continue his arcane studies. There was a quiet feeling in the study, the feeling one gets in a room that has seen brighter days.

Circling to the front of her father's chair, Kyla was surprised to see the king still awake, looking out over his Keep. As still as he had been, the princess was sure he had been asleep. "Hello, Daddy!" she said brightly, leaning over awkwardly in a fierce hug.

"Good morning yourself, little lady," he replied with soft smile.

"How are you today?" she asked, pulling a footstool beside her father's chair.

Calonar took his daughter's hands in one of his own. "I could ask you the same question. How are you and my grandson?"

Making a face, she replied, "I think your grandson is doing just fine based on how much I'm eating. Mother says that it's just Fate's justice for what she had to go through with me."

"I remember," he smiled with a roll of his pearlescent eyes. "There were times when your mother was pregnant with you that I thought she'd been possessed by some kind of demon as erratic as her eating became. She once even demanded raw eggs with fried vegetables. I once called Cyras in just to make sure everything was all right."

"Well, Mother and Cardinal Tain say everything is fine."

There was a knock on the door, and Calonar gave permission to enter without looking back. When the door opened, Remm entered, closing it behind. When he turned back and stomped into the room, the Uldra looked surprised to see Kyla beside her father. "I thought you said you wanted this private," he growled.

"I apologize, Remm. I lost track of time." The king turned back to his daughter. "I'm sorry to cut our visit short, but Remm and I need to talk about some things."

Kyla stood and smiled brightly. "It's all right, Daddy. I need to take a bath and a nap anyway." The princess threw a questioning look at Remm, however.

Noticing the look, Calonar smiled. "You would be surprised at some of the things Remm Stonebearer can be trusted with, young lady. Of everyone in the Keep besides Rogan, your mother, and your sister, Remm is the one you can trust the most."

"What about you, Daddy?" she asked quietly.

The king laughed at that. "As your mother could tell you, a pretty young girl should never trust a dirty old man like me."

By this point, Remm had endured more than enough. "Aw, knock it off you two! Damn! I'm starting to get emotional." The Uldra absently picked his nose.

"Go take care of my grandson," Calonar said, holding a gentle hand to his daughter's cheek. Kyla's earliest memory of her father was that caress. His hands, so strong and sure, yet so gentle in their treatment of her, had been a foundation stone of her entire life. Now, she felt the slight tremor in her father's hand. It was skeletal and lacked any power. "Come by for dinner tonight."

"I will," the princess promised, closing her pearlescent eyes, only one of the many gifts she had inherited from the greatest of the Heroes of Fate, to hold back her tears. She cradled her father's hand against her cheek for a moment, desperately praying that some portion of her strength would pass to him, that at least some of the infinite love and devotion he had given her would earn him a reprieve from this near-blasphemous poison. Kyla sighed and, at last, returned her father's hand to the chair. As she walked to the door, she affectionately reached up and, standing on her tiptoes, ruffled Remm's already-disheveled hair, to which he looked annoyed.

Once out of her father's study with the door closed, Kyla let out a shuddering sigh. *The visits are getting harder*, she thought to herself. The princess loved her father like no other, but for all of her life, King Cylan Calonar had been a man that could stand before the gates of Underworld itself and demand entry. She recalled an early memory, when one of her family's many enemies had tried to kidnap her. Kyla had only needed to call out her father's name, and he was there in a flash of arcane lightning. He had been merciless to the men who had threated his little girl, wielding sword and spell in her defense. Kyla was used to seeing her father as the hero of thousands, leading a nation and harnessing the Winds of Magic at his leisure. To see him now, steadily withering away while she was helpless to do anything but watch, was almost more than she could bear. *Please*, she prayed, *please let him live long enough at least to hold his grandchild one time.*

III

Frostfront

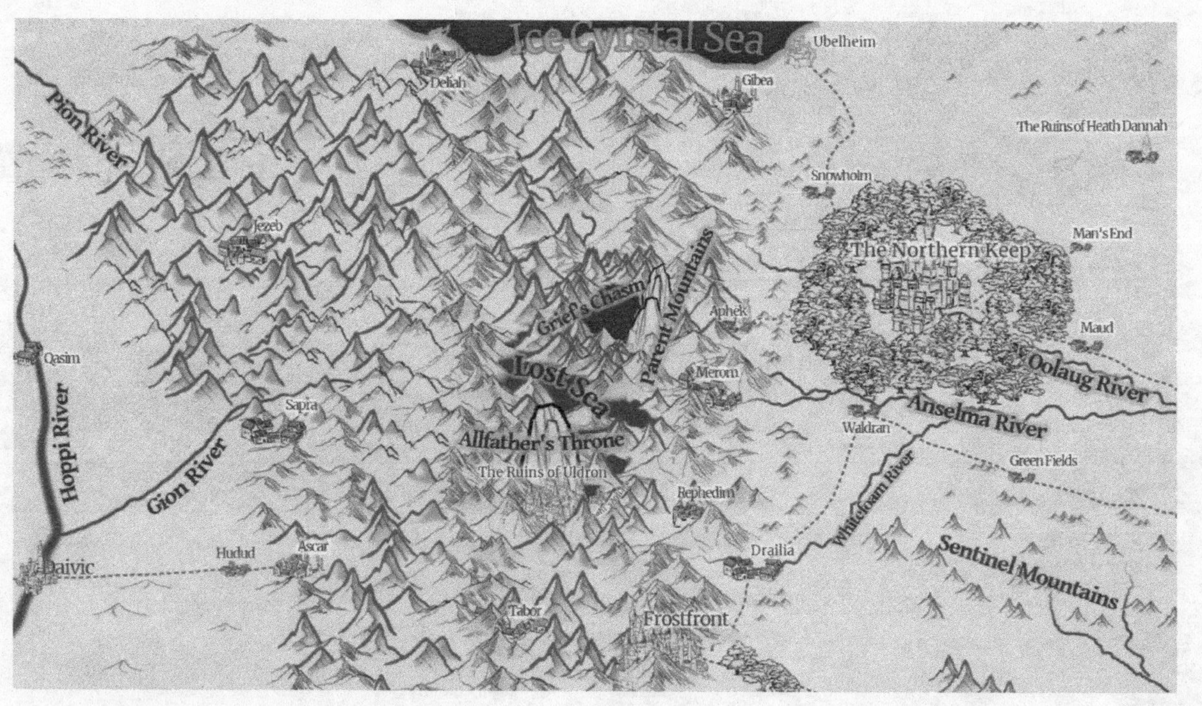

Ice Crystal Sea
Ubelheim
Gibea
Deliah
Pion River
The Ruins of Heath Dannah
Snowholm
Man's End
The Northern Keep
Jezeb
Grief's Chasm
Parent Mountains
Aphek
Maud
Oolaug River
Qasim
Lost Sea
Merom
Anselma River
Hoppi River
Sapra
Allfather's Throne
Waldran
Green Fields
Gion River
The Ruins of Uldron
Rephedim
Whitefoam River
Hudud
Ascar
Drailia
Sentinel Mountains
Daivic
Tabor
Frostfront

Chapter 32

The tunnel was vast, easily wide enough to accommodate hundred men standing shoulder to shoulder and stretched beyond the distance. Despite being formed into a great arch, it so tall that the vaulted ceiling above could only just barely be seen. Stone columns, thicker than a wagon and engraved with the silver runes of the ancient Uldric language, rose up at even intervals as far into the tunnel as Tomas could see. The air itself was old, with only the faintest hint of a breeze pushing outward, gently traveling up the descending tunnel against them from whatever lay at the distant exit, somewhere near the Free City of Frostfront. Some of the greatest moments of the past had taken place within these sacred walls, and Tomas felt awed that God had granted him the chance to see this historic site.

Upon their entrance into the ancient tunnel, the mighty door that granted them access began to close, seemingly of its own will. Even as the dim sunlight was being blocked by the massive portal, silver runes began to glow on the massive stone pillars spaced evenly in a double-row stretching ahead. The oppressive darkness that had been wrapping itself around them retreated, replaced by a gentle white radiance. Stranger still, as the runes began to glow, the runes adorning Beraht's waraxe did likewise.

"Uldra magic," Tomas whispered.

Beraht held up his sacred weapon, his eyes wide and his cavernous mouth agape. The mountainous warrior could only nod.

"Well, that helps," Rogan noted dryly, putting away the torch he had retrieved from their packs.

"A most fortunate circumstance," Aebreanna agreed. As had become her custom, the beautiful spy continued to style her long mane of honey-blonde hair so that it would cover most of the right side of her once-flawless face. "I very much doubt our few remaining torches would have lasted the entire trip to Frostfront," she added.

"How did your people do this?" Tomas asked while closely inspecting one of the glowing runes.

The Uldra, humbled by the history of his people in which he was now standing, shook his head slightly. "The knowledge was lost when the *Kor Kashadak* were lost."

"The priests?"

Beraht nodded. "The Uprising destroyed our knowledge of Uldra magic."

"Maybe someday you'll get it back," the squire suggested.

The Uldra mounted his horse and began the trip down into the tunnel that would lead them out of Ulheim. "Before he led our Uprising against the Sylvai, the Nameless had our priests and wisemen record all our knowledge in a single place. He knew that if the Uldra lost the war or suffered too many casualties, they could forget the lessons of the past. This way, the knowledge could be saved."

"Where did they put the knowledge?" Rogan asked as he mounted Stick.

Beraht shrugged. "Only the priests and the Nameless knew."

"Ironic," Aebreanna mused. "Your people recorded the secrets of your race to prevent them from being lost forever and then lost the secret of their location."

"There's no clue at all?" Tomas asked.

"The *maruns* tell us that the Nameless took the secrets with him to his grave," Beraht replied.

"Where's his grave?"

"We don't know where. The Nameless told us that he didn't want a burial mound that would become an object of worship. He taught us that we needed to worship the Allfather on His Mountain, not the places and objects of people."

Time passed, and the team moved farther into the tunnel. Down through the passage that led under and through the mountains, guided by the glowing runes and cheered by the thought of leaving the hardships of Ulheim behind. After so many weeks of danger and winter, the ease of their passage brought each of the friends a welcome sense of peace that did much to repair the emotional damage of their battle within Uldron. Even Aebreanna, who suffered much during their trip through the Uldra Ways, seemed at ease within the great tunnel. The shadows hid the ceiling and far walls; they seemed, rather than passed beneath the great mountains of Ulheim, to be passing down an evening-shrouded street. Although there was no wind, the cold of the surface eased and was replaced by a comfortable warmth; the farther they went, in fact, the warmer it became. Casual conversation and friendly arguments once again became the norm for Tomas and his friends as they continued on, at last feeling they were making progress on their perilous quest.

The tunnel was very different from the new Ways the Uldra were constructing. Tomas could see similarities: the new tunnels were supported with vaulted ceilings and thick stone arches. The runes, whether in the ancient Uldric language or the modern, were unmistakable for the writings of the mountain-peoples. Still, the differences were profound. The stonework of the ancient tunnel, for one, was flawless. The new Ways showed unerasable signs of toolwork, and the scars on the tunnel walls from the machine-digger added a bizarre texture. The ancient tunnel, though, seemed made of unblemished rock. There were no toolmarks, no flaws; the stonework was perfect, as though the mountains had opened themselves up of their own accord.

At each of their stops, Beraht seemed drawn to the massive pillars and the smooth walls. He frequently ran a calloused hand across the work of his ancestors, and frequently could not help but mourn, "We've lost so much."

Gauging the passage of time as the party traveled quickly under the mountains was impossible. The new Ways relied on ventilation holes dug evenly through each tunnel. These small breakthroughs could offer at least some sense of time, as Tomas could look up through one and see either light or darkness. The ancient tunnel beneath Ulheim had no such holes, no way to distinguish day or night. Where the air came from, neither he nor Beraht knew. They could not spot any ventilation holes or vents, yet there was a perpetual breeze, a circulation of air. When the adventurers grew tired, they slept. When hungry, they ate. On the fourth day of travel, they encountered an underground stream that began running parallel to the tunnel, giving them access to fresh, if odd-tasting, water; it had a strange aftertaste of minerals, of the mountains themselves. The even stonework and gentle sloping of the tunnel put little strain on their mounts, and Stick and Urge led them on eagerly, just as happy as their masters to be free of Ulheim. With only a meager supply of firewood and no way of anticipating how far they would have to travel before exiting the tunnel, they decided early on that there would be no campfires, and their meals would be uncooked. While this brought many casual complaints from Beraht, even the surly Uldra could give little true rancor to their current situation. The group was safe at last from the many problems that had plagued them from the moment they had departed the Northern Keep. Their pace was once again steady with nothing to delay their eager mounts in the canter Rogan maintained on their course, and although limited, the heroes' best estimates concluded that they had more than enough supplies to see them safely through the tunnel. Finally, it seemed Fortune, that most flighty and undependable of gods, had seen fit to bestow some of Her blessings on Tomas and his friends.

The tunnel's midpoint was unmistakable. The stream that had run parallel to the underground highway for so many weeks abruptly plunged into the earth, and the gradually descending road began an obvious ascension. At that same location, a thick line had been carved into the floor of the tunnel and filled with silver, clearly marking a separation of territory.

"One would almost think the Uldra had an issue with boundaries," Aebreanna noted with her typically aloof tone when speaking on the subject of the mountain people.

Tomas turned in his saddle to Beraht. "Is there any way to gauge how far we've come?" he asked.

"Halfway," the Uldra shrugged, his attention clearly elsewhere.

"Thanks," the young man grunted. "That was helpful."

"It doesn't matter how far we've come," Rogan pointed out from his place at the head of their small formation. "We're at the midpoint, so now we know about how long it'll be before we're back in the open."

"Still," Tomas insisted, "it'd be nice to know about where we'll be coming out."

"The tunnel will exit just outside Frostfront," his knight replied.

"How do you figure? Just because the stories say that doesn't really prove it."

"I thought we talked about that skepticism of yours?"

The squire shrugged. "Just staying in practice. You realize, of course, that if we're only halfway out, we've got a problem though."

"Do tell."

Tomas glanced back at their remaining pack horses and grimaced. "My best estimates have us at less than half of our remaining rations."

"Then we go on even shorter rations," the knight replied. "We've got a timetable now. And we can make a pretty good guess on when we'll see daylight."

"If you say so."

"Look, just think about it. The whole point of this tunnel when they built it was to connect Frostfront with Uldron and the clans. The tunnel started just outside Uldron so, logically, it'll open up just outside the Free City."

"Your logic is taking some rather extreme leaps from one point to another," Aebreanna said mildly. "However, your assumption is not unreasonable."

"Thanks."

"You've got to love those Sylvai compliments," Tomas laughed.

The beautiful Sylva turned her head to throw the squire a neutral glance around the hair she used to cover her scarred face. "And perhaps someday you yourself will perform some minor act that will, at last, be worthy of even the faintest praise."

"So… 'shut up' is what you're saying."

An arched eyebrow was the only response Tomas received and more than was needed. The young man cleared his throat and glanced at Beraht, noticing that his friend seemed to be staring intently into the surrounding darkness as through looking for something. "What is it?" he asked.

Beraht's reply was unusually serene, a bad sign in itself. "There's something here," he whispered.

"Rogan!" Tomas barked, his hand going to Steelheart.

The knight glanced back and, seeing both Tomas and Beraht's reactions, quickly moved Stick back to join his friends. On the way, Rogan gestured to Aebreanna to conduct a quick reconnaissance of the area. "What is it?" the Northlands prince asked as he pulled Talon off his back and worked the longsword free from its improvised sheath.

Although maintaining his steady scan of the surrounding darkness, Rogan took a moment to look at his squire and the briefest of frowns on his scarred face gave mute evidence of the mentor's concern for his apprentice. Tomas's hand shook as he slowly drew Steelheart from the makeshift scabbard the squire had fashioned. The squire's breath came in short spurts, and his young eyes were just a little wild as he stared into the darkness. A slight sheen of sweat glistened off the young man's forehead, and the muscles of Tomas whole body tensed in preparation of an attack that may or may not come.

Rogan reached out slowly, in full view of Tomas, and placed a light hand on his squire's shoulder. "Easy, kid," he whispered. "Stay calm, but stay ready."

Tomas took a deep breath and visibly fought to regain control of his body. The young man nodded his head and clearly pulled himself back together but continued to nervously eye the darkness pressing in all around them.

Seeing that there was little he could do for his young friend at this moment, Rogan turned to Beraht. "What's going on?" he asked softly.

Beraht made no reply. The Uldra just sat astride his great shire horse as he let his eyes slowly close. The Uldra's breath came slowly, in deep pulses, and Tomas noticed a slight shiver run along his ugly friend's hairy arms. Beraht gave no hint of danger or even excitement, only serenity.

In moments, Aebreanna returned to the circle of light that surrounded the men. "Anything?" Rogan asked in a low growl.

The beautiful Sylva nodded slowly, a look of concern on her once-flawless face. "There is a door carved into the wall," she calmly replied. "There are markings I could not discern. I will not approach it."

Rogan stared into the utter darkness in the direction Aebreanna indicated. "You ever hear of this tunnel going anywhere other than Frostfront?" the knight asked his squire.

Tomas concentrated, quickly scanning through his extensive knowledge of history for any hint of a door's purpose in this ancient tunnel. Finally, the young man glanced at his mentor and shook his head. "I've only ever heard that the tunnel ran from Uldron to Frostfront."

Without a word or gesture of explanation, Beraht dismounted and moved calmly, but quickly, in the direction Aebreanna had indicated. Seeing this, Rogan jerked his head at Tomas and dismounted himself, raising Talon and following behind his Uldra friend.

Tomas glanced at where Aebreanna had remounted her white pony, saying, without words, that she would remain behind. "If you hear screaming," the squire said, "assume we found something."

The young man hurried to catch up to where Rogan and Beraht continued on into the darkness. As the three warriors approached, two columns, set away from their brethren marking the main passage, began to glow. Unlike the other runes that glowed with a soft blue light when the visitors drew near and faded to darkness again once Tomas and the others had passed, the runes running along these two columns glowed with a deep, dull red. It was the color of ancient fire that fell down on the weary heroes, of the forge and the hearth. The light glowed brighter than the blue runes now behind them. Beraht held his waraxe high, its inlaid runes matching the dull red of the new pillars.

With the strange illumination, Tomas could see the door that had so disturbed Aebreanna, situated between the two red-glowing columns. It was, as best the squire could tell, even more-perfectly constructed than was the ancient tunnel, fitting in with the surrounding stone so flawlessly that only the barest of separations could be discerned and, even then, only after a moment of careful inspection. The door fit Beraht's dimensions perfectly, making it more than a head taller than the Humans and easily wide enough to accommodate an Uldra warrior's broad shoulders. A disk of flawless steel was set in the center of the door, catching and amplifying the glowing red light of the runes on either side. Engraved within the disk were icons similar to the ones Tomas had seen in the doors to the Uldra meeting hall: on one side was a perfect replica of Beraht's waraxe, and on the other was a chalice, with the Allfather' Throne between them.

Beraht set his waraxe on the ground before him. He then dropped to one knee, his head bowed in reverence. Rogan looked first at the door before them and at his Uldra friend's reaction and gestured for his squire to follow as he returned to Aebreanna and the horses.

"Is that what I think it is?" Tomas asked.

"No way to know for sure without translating the runes," Rogan replied. "But I'm willing to bet it is."

"The tomb of the Nameless," Tomas said in a tone verging on awe. "I can't believe nobody ever thought to look here before."

"Maybe they did," the knight suggested. "Those runes didn't start glowing until Beraht got close." He paused, glancing back towards Beraht and the red-glowing pillars. Likely as not, we'd've passed by without knowing it was there if not for the runes.

"Or," Tomas mused, "maybe when his axe got close?"

"Maybe both?" the knight suggested.

The squire stared at his knight. "Are you saying the tomb wanted Beraht to find it?"

"I don't know," Rogan shrugged. "Uldra magic has been dead for a thousand years, and the Sylvai did everything they could to erase all records of it. Nobody knows what it was capable of. There's no way of knowing for sure."

Tomas glanced at Aebreanna, who sat astride Mayva with her face turned firmly away from the red pillars. "Why did the Sylvai go to such efforts to erase Uldra magic?" he asked.

The spy said nothing at first, keeping her gaze averted. Finally, she only mumbled, "Different theories exist."

The squire glanced back at the soft red light that marked the tomb entrance. "Is Beraht going to open it?" the young man asked.

"That's up to him," Rogan replied. "Doesn't involve us."

"I'd give a lot to see what's inside that tomb," Tomas admitted, his academic lust swelling.

"Forget it," Rogan grunted. "That's probably the holiest place in the world to the Uldra. If Beraht decides to open the tomb and go in, he'll do it alone. You and I are the last people that have any right disturbing an Uldra tomb."

"What about Aebreanna?"

The knight thought about it for a moment, a glance towards their silent companion. "All right," he conceded. "You and I are the next to last people that have any right."

Chapter 33

After more than an hour, as best Tomas could estimate, Beraht completed his prayer before the tomb of his race's most renowned member, their lawgiver and liberator, and returned to where his friends had waited on the glowing path. The Uldra made no comment as he took his ration of food from Aebreanna and quickly devoured it, never raising his eyes from the small meal.

"Well?" Tomas finally demanded, unable to restrain his curiosity.

"Well, what?" Beraht growled.

"What are you going to do?"

The warrior stood and walked towards the spot where the small stream disappeared into the surrounding rock. "Urinate."

"What about the tomb?" Tomas demanded.

"What about it?" Beraht asked over his shoulder.

"Are you going to open it?"

"No."

"Why not?"

"Can't."

Tomas deflated and stared back at the red columns. "There has to be a way…" he mused.

"There is."

The squire looked back at his towering friend. "You know how to open it?"

Beraht nodded and hefted his waraxe. "You need the keys."

"The axe and…? That chalice?"

"The Cup of the Allfather," the Uldra confirmed. "Gifted to the Nameless on the eve of the Uprising."

"Let me guess," Tomas said in near disgust. "Lost?"

Beraht shook his head. "Not lost, just not found… yet."

Rogan cinched down the saddle on Stick, absently avoiding the warhorse's teeth. "Let's get ready to move." Rogan turned to Beraht. "Is there any reason to think the tunnel will be longer on the Frostfront side?" he asked.

Beraht shook his head and mounted his waiting horse. "This is the exact center," Beraht replied confidently.

The Northlands prince grunted as he hoisted himself into the saddle. "We've been taking it easy on the horses after Uldron and because we didn't know what shape the tunnel was in," he said, ignoring the irritated grunt from Stick. "I think it's about time we started covering some serious distance. Let's ride."

The tunnel around them was changing, this was clear to them all. The perfectly smooth stone walls and the pillars and arches supporting them became somehow less flawless. Minor imperfections could be detected in the stone surrounding them, and while still impressive beyond words and large enough to accommodate an army, the tunnel seemed to narrow slightly. The blue runes that had led the heroes on their journey took different forms, the ancient Uldric writing being replaced by the mystical glyphs used by the Arcane Guild. The glow from Beraht's waraxe faded, the further they drew from the centerline of the tunnel.

Beraht looked upon these changes with utter contempt, often scoffing at what he perceived as the amateurish attempts at masonry by what must have been the greatest minds and skills Humanity could produce. "I don't know why they bothered," he grunted at one point.

"Who's that?" Tomas asked.

"Those Frostfront fools," the Uldra answered. "Why even bother trying to put up a proper arch if you don't know how?"

The young man looked up at the ancient stonework and tried to spot the flaws Beraht considered so very obvious. "It looks fine to me," the squire admitted. "And it's remained standing for a thousand years."

Beraht snorted again and spit a large glop on the ground. "Big deal. Talk to me when it stands for *ten* thousand. No Uldra worth his beard would put his mark on something like this."

"Well, as long as it stands," Tomas insisted, feeling a need to defend his race from Uldra criticism, "that should be all that really matters."

"It's that kind of thinking that keeps you Humans living in such ugly cities."

Tomas was about to reply when Rogan reined Stick in, motioning the rest of the group to join him at the vanguard. Upon doing so, they sat on their horses for some time, staring at the unfortunate scene before them.

The tunnel ahead had collapsed. From top to bottom and across its entire length, rubble filled the ancient pathway and blocked completely any chance of farther passage.

"I guess they could have done a better job after all," Tomas admitted.

Beraht shook his head. "This was recent," he declared.

"How recent?" Rogan asked.

The warrior considered as he stared in irritation at their newest obstacle. "One year," he finally answered. "No more."

"Then it wasn't Anninihus," Tomas declared.

His knight looked at the young man. "What makes you say that?"

"Remember what Esha told us? Anninihus came to Frostfront after being recruited. But that was about ten years ago." Tomas nodded at the cave-in. "A year ago he was already back in the Northlands, stirring up trouble. A year ago…" The squire's words trailed off as a new thought emerged from the back of his mind.

"What is it, kid?" Rogan asked.

"A year ago," Tomas replied. "You and I met about a year ago."

"More than that," the knight objected. "By now, we were at the Keep, or almost."

The squire nodded. "And do you remember the day we met?"

"Yeah, I saved you from those Druug. You and…" Rogan sighed and shook his head.

"Right." Tomas glanced back up at the piles of stone and sand. "He said he was heading west."

"And will your fascinating story be including us at some near-future point?" Aebreanna asked pointedly.

"Cyras," Rogan said shortly. "He was there when me and Tomas met. After he put the geas on us, he went west." He looked hard at her. "Could this be him?"

The spy faced the cave-in and sniffed slightly, then wretched. "It was him," she said between gags. "He's manipulating us, as always."

"Well," Tomas sighed. "At least we know there's a way out." He glanced at his knight. "I doubt the Trickster Mage would set us up to die."

Aebreanna huffed.

"Is there a way through?" Rogan asked Beraht.

Beraht stepped up and began moving several of the stones aside but gave up after a few seconds. "Forget it," he spat. "That rubble goes on for a while and moving any of it will just bring more down on top of us."

"Well, now what?" Tomas demanded. "We can't just turn around."

"We may not have much choice," Rogan grumbled.

"Death alone awaits us behind," Aebreanna insisted. "Our path must go forward."

Beraht, ignoring his friend's argument, gathered a handful of sand from the floor the recent collapse had deposited and stood, letting the grains fall slowly to the ground and watching intently as they did so.

"Well?" Rogan demanded, having noticed his friend's actions and recognizing when the Uldra was concentrating.

"There's a breeze," Beraht replied. The Uldra nodded his head to the right of the collapse. "An opening is that way."

"Could the collapse have opened a hole to the surface?" Tomas asked hopefully.

Beraht shrugged. "Anything's possible."

"Not much choice," Rogan declared. "Either that or back the way we came, and I've had enough Druug for one trip. Let's try it."

With Beraht leading the way, the party made their way along the collapsed wall of rubble until they reached the tunnel's right side. By the faint light of the blue runes now behind them, the surly warrior quickly located a large fissure in the wall that stretched from the floor up into the darkness overhead.

"Only large enough for us to proceed one at a time in single file," Aebreanna pointed out.

"If we get attacked while we're in there, it'll go very bad for us," Tomas added.

"Something else," the Uldra noted.

"What?"

Beraht nodded toward the fissure. "This wasn't part of whatever caused the cave-in. It was formed at the same time, but separate."

Rogan stared at the large crack in disgust. "Does anybody else get the feeling we're getting led around by the nose here?" he asked.

The others all nodded grimly.

"Any way to know if that thing actually goes anywhere?" the knight asked. "It'd be hard to back out once we're all in."

Beraht just stared at his old friend. "Any choice?"

"No," the sullen prince sighed. "Let's do it."

It finally took blindfolding the already-weary horses to get them into the narrow crack. Even then, Stick and Urge would not be moved.

"Get in there, you overgrown donkey!" Tomas barked as he set his shoulder against the massive rump of his stubborn warhorse and shoved with all his effort, the result being little more than Urge's amusement at the squire's frustration.

Stick, just as stubborn as his progeny, had a much simpler method of objecting when Rogan had tried leading him into the cramped crevasse. "Somebody get this beast off me!" the knight gasped as he struggled to get out from under where Stick had sat on him.

"Perhaps we should be guided by the wisdom of our mounts," Aebreanna suggested.

Tomas gave up trying to force the reluctant Urge into the fissure and instead pulled his knight free from Stick's rump. Rogan, once freed and breathing steadily, walked around to face his horse. "You're going into that crack," he declared.

Stick gave his rider a look of undisguised hostility.

"We'll blindfold you," the knight said with compassion, going so far as to holding up the piece of cloth meant for that purpose. "You'll be all right."

Stick reached out and grabbed the blindfold in his powerful teeth and spat the offensive cloth to the ground.

"Would you rather stay here?" Rogan demanded. "Or go back to Uldron and all those Druug?"

The warhorse thought about it and finally sighed his reluctant agreement. Rogan reached out and patted his evil mount with one hand. "You don't have to like it," he said. "Let's just get through as quick as we can."

Stick nudged Rogan aside and walked toward the fissure, calling Urge over as he walked. Together the two warhorses entered the narrow tunnel and followed behind Aebreanna.

Tomas walked up behind Rogan and gestured ahead. "Age before beauty?" he grinned.

The knight shoved his squire in. "Ladies first," he growled in response.

Chapter 34

Realizing the blue glow of the mystic glyphs could no longer be relied upon once the party had entered the fissure, Tomas had drawn one of their few remaining torches from the packs, along with flint to light it.

"Good thinking, kid," Rogan approved as he spotted the sparks from his squire.

"Well, it's hard being both the beauty and the brains, but I manage it somehow," the squire replied lightly.

"Whatever you have to tell yourself to get through the day, kid."

To the heroes' great relief, to say nothing of their mounts, the detour Tomas and his friends were forced to take through the crushingly narrow fissure was a brief one. The tight tunnel through which they traveled curved almost immediately and ran parallel to the tunnel for only a few hundred paces before opening into a narrow chamber of total darkness.

The air around them was dead. Not a single hint of a breeze could be detected in the wide, low-ceilinged chamber. Stone walls surrounded them, covered in incredibly detailed carvings depicting a variety of scenes ranging from average life to incredible acts of magic. In the center of the chamber was a block of perfectly smooth stone, only a little wider than a man's shoulders but somewhat shorter than his height and featureless but for a line of Sylvai glyphs that ran from one end of the block to the other.

"A tomb," Tomas noted.

"A Khepric tomb," Beraht corrected. "And a Khepric coffin."

"I wonder whose?" Rogan agreed. The knight turned to Aebreanna, who was staring down at the Sylvai glyphs carved into the sarcophagus. "Does that mean this is the tomb of a Sylvai noble?" he asked.

Tomas shook his head. "Sylvai don't entomb their dead," he insisted.

"Indeed," Aebreanna agreed, her eyes never leaving the glyphs. "We leave that barbarism to Humans and Khepri."

"Can you read these glyphs," Tomas asked, clearing as much of the excess dirt as he could from the faded writing.

The spy stared intently at the inscription. "An old dialect," she said after a few moments. "Long unused."

"How long?" Rogan asked.

"Nine thousand years."

"That *would* put it at the time of the Sylvai Empire," Tomas noted, "Before the founding of the Free City." The squire glanced at Aebreanna. "What does it say?"

"'Here sleeps one who had only the future, but never the past.'"

"Well," Beraht snorted, "wasn't that enlightening?"

Tomas looked around at the images surrounding them. Although the squire had no knowledge of modern Sylvai writing, to say nothing of a dialect now millennia dead, the carvings still told a story that he felt was just out of reach. He stared at them, letting their tale wash over his mind and soul. He followed the tales until realization struck him like lightning. "Oh, my God," the young man gasped.

"What?" Rogan demanded.

"It's the Witness."

"Which witness?"

"The Witness. The one who led the Twelve Companions through the desert to Adama before anointing them as the first Lords Cardinal."

"Kid, how in Underworld could you possibly know that?" Rogan demanded. "The Teachings don't say anything about the Witness after he left Adama."

Tomas gestured to the pictographs surrounding them along the walls. "It's all here," the squire insisted. "The whole story was put here by whoever built this tomb." Tomas glanced at where Beraht stood running his thick fingers against the tomb's wall. "Beraht, you're people used to carve images like these into your cities, right?"

"Before the Khepri Invasion," he admitted. "When we still had cities." The Uldra glanced at Tomas. "There were some in Uldron."

"We were a little busy," Rogan snorted.

"How are they supposed to be read?" Tomas asked.

"Starting at the door, from the right side all the way around, top to bottom."

"Look here!" Tomas said excitedly, pointing a finger the space to the right of the sealed doorway.

Rogan, who was struggling to get the horses all out of the crevasse and into the crypt, barely glanced at where his young apprentice was pointing. "I don't see anything," the knight grunted.

"Exactly!" Tomas agreed. "This is a Khepri tomb with Uldra engravings. And look here, where the beginning should be."

"There are no markings," Aebreanna pointed out.

"Exactly! His whole life story but no beginning, no birth. The Teachings tell us that the Witness had no beginning. The first image here is him in the desert with the Twelve Companions, leading them to Adama. I'm telling you, this is the tomb of the Witness."

Aebreanna ran a hand lightly along several of the pictographs. "Perhaps," she admitted, glancing again at the Sylvai glyphs on the coffin. "No loyal servant of the

Empress would be placed in a Khepric tomb like this and surrounded with Uldra carvings. Doing so would be considered a great insult."

"But what in Underworld is the Witness doing buried by the Khepri and the Uldra under Frostfront with Sylvai glyphs carved into his coffin?" Tomas demanded, unable to take his eyes from the beautiful wall carvings.

Aebreanna shook her head slightly. "Assuming my dating of the language is correct, which is by no means a certainty, this tomb would predate the founding of Frostfront by more than five thousand years."

"But why so far from one of the major cities?" Tomas asked. "The Sylvai Empire never built any settlements this far into the mountains. That's why the Free City was built here. This would've been the distant wilderness of the time." He looked at Beraht. "Did the Uldra ever build one of their cities here?"

The mountainous warrior thought. Finally, he shook his head.

"An intriguing mystery," Aebreanna admitted.

Rogan shook his head. "Look, as interesting as this is, I don't really care right now." The knight crossed the wide tomb and climbed the narrow steps that ended quickly at a massive cover stone blocking the tomb's only exit. The knight glanced at his Uldra friend.

"It'll take a few minutes," Beraht replied and motioned for Rogan to move.

"Is there any chance you could avoid doing permanent damage?" Tomas asked, fearful of the history that would be lost to Uldra enthusiasm.

"Look here," Aebreanna called to Tomas, gesturing toward another series of pictographs. "After departing from Adama, your Witness joined with human refugees fleeing the salt and copper mines of Otylia."

Tomas moved up beside his Sylvai friend and peered close at the images. "That might start to explain how he ended up getting buried here," the squire mused. "According to the Teachings, the descendants of those runaway slaves eventually founded Frostfront."

"And if the Witness remained with the refugees into his twilight years, they would very likely have had regular encounters with the southern Uldra clans who could have helped build this tomb for him."

"But why the Khepric design and the coffin with Sylvai writing?" Tomas insisted.

Both squire and Sylva continued progressing through the pictographs, ignoring the riot of breaking stone as Beraht continued to work with what tools he had for their freedom. The scenes revealed that the Witness settled in the mountains with the Human refugees. Life continued in an apparently uneventful manner until the arrival of two new figures who featured prominently for the last third of the Witness' life. The figures were humanoid but totally featureless, one painted white, the other black.

"Who were they?" Tomas asked, staring at the new figures.

"Brothers perhaps," Aebreanna suggested. "Or supernatural creatures. They could have even been beings that crossed from Otherworld."

"They just seem to appear next to the Witness."

"Look here," the Sylva instructed.

Tomas looked and saw the two figures, light and dark, on either side of the Witness. "They're telling him something?" the young man guessed.

"No," Aebreanna corrected. "The Witness is telling something to them. Time passes, and the Witness tells many things to the two beings, and they record it all…" She gasped, her opalescent eye widening and looking back at the coffin. "Darrell," she said in a choked whisper.

"Who?" Tomas asked. "What?"

"This is the Darrell Prophet," Aebreanna said in wonder. "He who revealed the future, the destiny of Ramalech's rise and the destruction of the world."

Tomas looked from the coffin to the two painted figures and back. "Does that mean one of the figures is Cyras Darkholm?"

Aebreanna nodded with a grimace. "And the other is most likely Fak'Har. They are the only two in the world with access to the complete prophecy and have shared it with no other. This is where they first gained their knowledge of what is to come."

Tomas closed his eyes and smiled. "So many theories have come and gone about how Cyras Darkholm gained his knowledge of the future, but nobody ever thought he might have been visited by the same prophet who anointed the original Lords Cardinal."

"To be more accurate, the Prophet did not visit Darkholm. Darkholm visited the Prophet." Aebreanna walked back to the center of the tomb and stared down at the stone coffin with her opalescent eye narrowed in irritation. "I have little doubt this entire tomb is little more than another of Darkholm's idiotic jokes. Bury a man who lived his entire life trying to bring peace to the world in a mockery of the funeral practices of every major culture."

"I don't think so," Tomas objected. "Look here." The squire pointed at the end of the pictographs. "When the Witness… when the Prophet had finished telling Cyras and Fak'Har what was going to happen, there was a great battle." The young man pointed to an image of the light and dark figures locked in a battle of magic that destroyed everything around it. The battle was so great that it attracted the notice of the Uldra, Sylvai, Humans, and Khepri. Together with the figure of light, these groups destroyed the dark figure, transforming it into a shadow that fled.

"All the races of Lanasia coming together to fight a great evil alongside Cyras Darkholm? If something like that really happened, it would have been recorded in history," Tomas insisted. "No matter how long ago."

"When Darkholm is involved, nothing is impossible," Aebreanna insisted. "If the Trickster Mage wished it, he could have easily wiped the knowledge of that battle from history."

Tomas shook his head in wonder. "So a man appears and leads the Twelve Companions to Adama. He guides them in the formation of the Adamic Church, then comes back, helping the freed slaves of Otylia build a new community, which will eventually become Frostfront, home of the Arcane Guild. Then, he reveals the future to the most powerful adepts in the world before dying. Those two so violently disagree over what to do with the knowledge that they engage in a battle against each other that draws in other races who all join together and drive off the evil wizard. They then bury the Prophet, each race honoring him in their own way."

"As fascinating as all this will be later," Rogan called," we're having some problems here."

Beraht grabbed the blocking stone with both gnarled hands and with a roar of exertion heaved but had no success. The stone would not move.

"Wait," Tomas said, walking through the tomb and thinking. "Wait, wait, wait."

"It's not like we're going anywhere here," Rogan snapped.

"This tomb tells the story of Cyras Darkholm, right?" the squire asked.

"Yeah, him and Fak'Har, I guess. So?"

Tomas looked back at the small fissure that had granted them access. "You said that crack was formed by something other than whatever caused the cave-in, right?"

"Yeah," Beraht replied.

The squire turned and looked at his three friends. "That cave-in would have trapped us, maybe even killed us, since we didn't have the supplies to survive the trip back out. That opening just happened to be right where we needed it and just happened to lead us here. You said it yourself, Rogan. Somebody's leading us by the nose. Cyras, probably. The Trickster Mage wanted us to find this tomb."

"So how is this getting the door open?" Beraht asked, jabbing a hairy thumb at the blocking rock.

Tomas closed his eyes, calming his thoughts so that he might better hear that quite part in the back of his mind from which so many insights emerged. "Cyras wanted us to find this place. He opened that crevasse and made sure it led in here. He wouldn't have trapped us." The squire's eyes opened sharply, and he walked to the door. Rogan and Beraht moved aside and watched in weary suspicion.

Tomas took a deep breath and squared his shoulders. To the blocking stone he said, "Open."

Without pause, the stone rolled aside.

"Well, that's just stupid," Rogan snapped.

It took little encouragement to get the horses to leave the cramped tomb, despite how low the staircase was. It was obvious that the party's mounts, even more than the heroes themselves, had long since had more than their fill of underground chambers and yearned for open air. Urge all but knocked his rider aside in his eagerness to exit the tomb.

Once getting a second torch lit, Aebreanna climbed the stairs to join Beraht, while Rogan and Tomas worked to lead the horses up and out of the small crypt. This done, the two Humans also left the ancient tomb behind and climbed the stairs but looked about with a certain dismay as they realized that, rather than finding a passage leading out, the stairs led only to another level of the tomb, again inhabited only by the dead.

"Well, this got old real quick," Rogan noted with annoyance.

The higher chamber bore little resemblance to the smaller one the party had just left. It was much larger than the lower one, but its arching walls had no decorations. Unlike the sole occupant of the lower level, this part of the crypt held twelve sarcophagi arranged in a circle around the center of the room, with the only exits being the stairs leading down on one side and another set leading up. The unrelieved stone sarcophagi, although much smaller than the lone coffin below, could not be mistaken for anything other than the resting places of the ancient dead.

"Well," Rogan grunted, nodding toward the far staircase that continued the climb up, "at least we don't have to worry about getting lost."

Beraht and Aebreanna led the horses forward. Tomas was about to move to join in the effort but paused as his eyes were unavoidably drawn to the faint image carved on the closest sarcophagus.

"Rogan," the squire called.

"Forget the history, kid," his knight grunted. "We don't have time."

"I think I know where we are."

Rogan stopped and joined his apprentice beside the sarcophagus but did not recognize the faded image. "Where?"

"I think we're in the Frostfront Necropolis," the squire noted.

"The what?" Beraht asked.

"Frostfront's Necropolis," Tomas repeated. "It used to be traditional to entomb the greatest citizens of a city in one place called a necropolis, a city of the dead. There's one under Frostfront, and others under Velaross and Ironheartshaven. There were even rumors about a necropolis under Pelsemoria."

"Makes sense," Beraht conceded. "Keep all the dead people in the same place. Saves room."

"It was considered a great honor to be entombed under the Free City with the greatest heroes to have ever lived."

"Well, the greatest Human heroes," the Uldra corrected. "Whatever that's worth."

"How do you know where we are?" Rogan asked.

Tomas gestured to the sarcophagi surrounding them. "These are the Twelve Innocents," the young man replied.

Rogan looked sharply at his squire and back at the sarcophagus before them. The knight reached out and brushed off the layer of sand that obscured the already-faded image and stared at it. Staring intently for a moment, Rogan could begin to discern the image of a boar. "Ebur?" he suggested. "The Boar Nation?"

Tomas nodded and gestured around the circle of sleeping dead. "Folkfardur, Jorg, Ele, Munda. One from each of the original Twelve Nations all entombed together in a hidden place far from the Sylvai Empire."

"Could be them," Rogan conceded. The knight looked around. "And that would mean we're in the necropolis."

"What are they talking about?" Beraht demanded of Aebreanna as the two non-Humans stood among the horses waiting to continue.

"Human history," the Sylva replied. "According to Human myth, Frostfront was originally built by the followers of a group of children called the Twelve Innocents."

"Not myth," Tomas corrected. The young man looked reverently around the tomb and the child-sized sarcophagi. "Not anymore. This is the tomb of the Twelve Innocents, buried beneath Humanity's first Free City after leading their people away from the oppression of the Sylvai Empire."

"Why in Underworld hasn't the Guild told anyone that this tomb is down here?" Rogan demanded. "People have been trying to learn the secrets of Frostfront's origins for centuries."

"Knowledge is power," Aebreanna pointed out. "And the Guild is as unlikely as any group to freely let go of power."

"Whole generations of explorers have died searching Ulheim for this tomb," Tomas said softly.

"We can't be sure this really is the Twelve Innocents," Rogan said. "It may be, but it may not."

"We have to find out for sure," Tomas insisted.

"Next trip. Right now we have to go save the world." The knight gently, but firmly, led his squire away from the twelve sarcophagi and gestured for Beraht to continue up the stairs.

The Uldra quickly stopped and began swearing

"What's wrong?" Rogan asked.

"Another damned rock blocking the stairs! And this one isn't moving when it's told!" Beraht growled. "What is it with you Humans? Do you think the dead are going to get up and wander away if you don't lock them up?"

"Darkholm's enchantment may require Tomas to speak the command," Aebreanna suggested.

"Give it a try, kid." Rogan said.

The squire nodded and took a step forward but stopped. "What was that?" Tomas asked suddenly, looking back over his shoulder.

"What was what?" Rogan asked.

"I thought I just heard whispering."

"I heard something as well," Aebreanna said slowly.

"Beraht!" the knight barked as he freed Talon from its improvised sling.

Without hesitation, the Uldra bounded down the few steps separating him from his friends and drew his waraxe, looking eagerly about for signs of danger. Tomas drew Steelheart without realizing he had done so until the blade bounced off a nearby sarcophagus. The whispering continued and grew in volume, becoming several voices that, while their words still could not be made out, nonetheless promised horror and death.

"Somebody talk to me," Rogan said as he continued to scan the surrounding chamber.

"Can't you hear it?" Tomas demanded.

"Kid, I can't hear anything." The knight glanced at Aebreanna. "What is it?" he asked.

"I do not know," the Sylva admitted. "I sense a change in the Winds but cannot identify the source."

Rogan looked over his shoulder at Beraht. "You hear anything?" he asked.

The Uldra shook his head. "Maybe the Humans had a good reason for sealing this place up," he grumbled.

"Something's coming!" Tomas snapped. "I can feel it!"

"Steady!" Rogan barked. "Back-to-back!"

As one, the party moved together, putting their backs to one another and holding their weapons ready and pointed outward in an impenetrable circle of potential violence. Suddenly, Tomas gasped and stiffened, nearly falling but for Beraht's quick reflexes.

Rogan turned and looked at his squire but recoiled when he saw the young man's eyes had turned completely black and dark shadows crawled along his face, taking the form of arcane marks they were all only too familiar with. "Anninihus!" Rogan snapped.

Aebreanna pulled Tomas from Beraht's arms and took his young face in both of her small hands, staring intently into the squire's eyes while whispering something in the Sylvai tongue. Tomas again stiffened, but this time shook his head and seemed to force the shadow marks off through will alone. Rogan moved to support his slumping apprentice and looked at Aebreanna with a question in his weary eyes.

The spy nodded briefly. "He is free," she answered. "The power had no great hold on him."

"It's not over," the squire said grimly, shaking off Rogan's grip and squaring his shoulders. "The power is still doing something."

Without warning, the whispering stopped. Silence pressed in around them with even greater animosity than the oppressive darkness that battled against the two torches sputtering on opposite sides of the tomb.

Even Rogan sensed the completion of evil magic and growled, "Stand ready."

All at once, the twelve sarcophagi surrounding them exploded, showering the heroes and their terrified mounts with the stinging shrapnel of ancient stone. Suffocating dust and evil darkness filled the chamber, replacing the oppressive silence as the torches were extinguished. Tomas's heart raced in terror as he lost all sense of orientation and could not even find the breath to call out to his friends.

A soft blue light then filled the crypt, shining from behind Tomas. The squire turned and saw with great relief Aebreanna standing with her back to a wall, holding a silver tree branch shining with cleansing light. A hand then softly grabbed the young man's shoulder and forced him to turn. Standing before Tomas was a body, desiccated by time and unrecognizable as anything but death in motion. Although it may have been a trick of the faint light, it seemed the creature's shadow, instead of mirroring the corpse's movements, was guiding them, manipulating the long arms and holding the body upright, leading it through the aggressive movements.

The long-dead body of an ancient child reached out to Tomas and hissed in a voice born from the darkest pit of Underworld, "Be with me."

The squire shrieked and lashed out, not with the lifeless sword in his hand but with his entire soul. Every fiber of Tomas' being rebelled against the horror before him, and the young man reacted in pure instinct, all rational thought erased as his terror and rage took over.

The stone walls surrounding the heroes and the obstructing boulder blocking their escape exploded in yet another shower of rock that tore bloody streaks across all the living. A howling wind roared down from the now-clear passage ahead of the party to tear at all the tomb's occupants, both living and dead, but could still not match Tomas' mindless scream. Pulses of blue light shot from the silver branch in Aebreanna's hand, forcing the Sylva to drop the mystical device with a scream of pain as it came alive and writhed in agony to match that in Tomas' soul. The dead and their shadowy puppeteers convulsed as though they were attacked from within until shattering with great force. The animating darkness was banished back whence it came and the ancient dead crumpled, disintegrating into piles of dust to be blown away.

Even once the magical assault ended, Tomas could not regain control of his mind. The young man threw down his sword and bolted for the exit, screaming incoherently again and again and unable or unwilling to heed the cries of his friends. Blinded by terror and rage and a hundred other emotions that he could not control nor even understand, the squire ran as far away from the source of his panic as his legs would allow, collapsing in sudden exhaustion and huddling against a stone wall, holding himself as tightly as he could and rocking back and forth, a pitiful whimper the only sound Tomas could make.

Chapter 35

Awareness returned slowly to Tomas. At first, only vague sounds dribbled into his mind, taking time to form the actual meaning of his friend's voices. Even after the young squire could make sense of their speech, he had little desire to rise from where he lay, realizing after his first few attempts that his whole body was a series of tender bruises and stiff joints. As Tomas's vision gradually returned, it reveled, at first, only the vaguest blur that was slow to resolve itself. Eventually, through a confused haze, the squire realized he was alone somewhere bearing an unfortunate resemblance to a dungeon cell.

With slow and weak movements, Tomas reluctantly rose from the pile of rotting straw on which he lay to a sitting position and took in his surroundings, confused not just by his current situation but by the odd weakness permeating every part of his being from his skin all the way to his soul. It felt as though all the energy that normally coursed through his young body had been drained, leaving only a withered husk that trembled with every exertion. Even Tomas's heart, normally beating strong beneath his smooth-skinned torso, could now do no more than flutter somewhere deep in his desiccated chest. The boy drew shallow breaths and searched both his cell and himself for answers to where he was and how he had gotten there.

In time, the muted voices of his friends came drifting through the darkness and stale air. Although the distance separating them did not seem great, their words and the echoing walls surrounding them on all sides slurring their speech into an unrecognizable mess of sound that did little to quell the continued sense of hopelessness that threatened to pull Tomas back into the dark pit from which he had only just emerged.

"Hello?" the boy called hesitantly, moving to the solid door of his cell and the small metal grate that offered his only view into the greater prison beyond.

"Kid? Are you all right?" Tomas could now clearly make out Rogan's voice. His knight sounded tired and angry, more so than usual, but his steady tone and solid words did much to calm the growing fear in his squire's heart.

"I think so," he replied. "What happened? Where are we?"

Aebreanna's soft voice, as full of comfort as always, reached out to caress Tomas's ears from the dim light of the hallway beyond the squire's cell. "After our perceived indiscretions with their more sacred unliving citizens were discovered," she said sardonically, "we were invited to stay within some of Frostfront's less-inviting accommodations."

"The Guild's soldiers found us in the necropolis," Rogan translated. "After the mess we made when Anninihus' trap went off, they weren't too ready to listen to any explanations. After they got done slapping us around for a while, the Prefects ordered us thrown in the dungeons while they try to figure out what to do with us."

A deep, rumbling growl echoed through the hall, sending a quiver of dread down Tomas's spine and causing his hands to tremble with weakness and terror. "What's that?" he demanded, his young mind filling with images of terrible monsters summoned by the adepts of the Arcane Guild to exact horrible vengeance on their enemies.

"It's Beraht," Rogan answered. "He's been asleep for a while now."

"How can he sleep at a time like this?"

"Well, they chained him to a wall," the knight explained. "It's not like he can pace."

"Our degenerate associate does seem more relaxed whenever he is incarcerated," Aebreanna noted. "Perhaps, having spent so much time in the custody of various jailors, our good Sir Beraht has learned how to find relaxation in the leather and chains of bondage."

"I thought that was more your idea of relaxation?" Rogan asked their experimental friend.

"I admit to an affinity for the occasional domination of my lovers," she admitted casually. "However, I myself have found little enjoyment at being confined to another person's dominion."

"So you can dish it out, but you can't take it?" the knight asked.

"I can withstand anything any male could ever provide with strength enough to return in kind," the Sylva replied primly. "You asked what I prefer, not what I allow."

"WHAT ARE YOU TWO TALKING ABOUT!?!" Tomas barked.

"Sorry, kid," Rogan said gently. "I guess we should have had that little talk before you started hearing about the weirder things that Aebreanna is in to. You see, when a boy and a girl love each other very much, they—"

"OH MY GOD!"

"Tomas," Aebreanna said gently, "your mentor's weak attempt at humor notwithstanding, Our intention is to simply ignore our situation until we can affect it."

"How in Underworld can you ignore the fact we're in a dungeon?" the squire demanded.

"Well, Aebreanna could tell you about how she first met Rashid."

"Again, and for the hundredth time, I had neither the idea, nor intention, to remove his clothes after we had restrained him. That particular stroke of genius was the brilliant suggestion of the noble Sir Beraht."

"Speaking of being stripped," Rogan noted, "did they ever give you something to wear after they searched you?"

"They did not," Aebreanna replied somewhat indignantly. "And I must confess that the environment of this cell is not a conducive one for nudity."

"Why did they strip you?" Tomas asked.

"After discovering the various tools and resources I keep scattered about my person, the guards had the ridiculous idea that the only way to ensure I would be free of any devices for escape would be to remove all my clothing and make an overly detailed inspection of my person."

"You, naked, alone in a room full of men," Rogan noted. "How is it you weren't made queen or empress or goddess or something?"

"Alas, a female adept was present for the examination," the Sylva sighed. "She was rather inconsiderate of the many possibilities for recreation the situation held."

"So what do you still have?" the knight asked.

"I still possess a tool for opening locks. If you wish, we could be out of these cells and away presently."

"I thought you were naked?" Tomas asked.

"I am."

"Then where could you hide... You know what, never mind. I don't want to know."

"Hold what you've got, Aebreanna," Rogan instructed. "Let's see what the Guild is up to before we do anything permanent."

"I believe our answers are forthcoming," Aebreanna noted as the rustling sound of a jail door opening silenced further conversation between the heroes.

Four men wearing the green and blue gambeson padded vests and open-faced bascinet helmets typical of the Frostfront military walked up the narrow corridor. They carried no blades, but instead had long wooden clubs tipped with copper caps. Two of the soldiers were holding torches over their heads, giving Tomas a clear view as they walked past.

"Alright," one was saying. "We'll start with the two Humans. Drag them out to the edge of the dungeons; make it look like they fought their way to the door before being killed." Though he spoke in the common Velish, he had an accent that seemed vaguely Uldric, as though centuries of proximity to the mountain clans had imprinted on the people of the Free City their manner of speaking. The guard was pulling a ring of keys from his belt as he talked. The group had stopped in front of Tomas' cell door.

"What about the Sylva?" another of the guards asked.

"What about her?" answered the first.

"I know we were told to kill her, but can't we have some fun first?"

The first guard paused, considering. "You know who she is," he warned. "How many men she's killed."

Another guard laughed cruelly. "Yeah but, the Baroness Tressalon? Imagine how she must taste!"

"How many men can say they've had her?" another insisted.

"Hundreds, what I hear!" the fourth insultingly joked.

The first, apparently their leader, considered. "Well," he finally said, "there's no harm, right?" He changed the key he was holding for another. "It's not like she'll be talking about it come morning!" They moved past Tomas' cell door.

The squire moved to the small grill and fought at the door, to no avail. The guards were laughing in their lustful anticipation as they moved further down the dungeon hallway.

"Wouldn't try that," Rogan called out a warning. "Might not be healthy."

The cells were staggered, so that one door did not face another, but Tomas could barely see, from the corner of the small grate at his door, where the guards stopped. One of them turned to another cell door. He pulled the copper-tipped wooden club and beat it against the door in front of him. "Shut your hole!" he growled. "Or we'll do the same to you before we riddle you with bolts!" Tomas thought he saw, in the moment the copper cap on the club made contact with the iron grate, a spark of blue light.

There was the sound of a lock being undone and a heavy door squealing in protest of being moved. There was then the sounds of heavy impacts and men grunting. One of the guards flew back into Tomas' line of sight, hitting the far wall with a curse. Aebreanna's naked body danced briefly into view, tumbling and spinning among the guards. She lashed out with feet and fists, her honey-blonde mane a golden blur as she spun and flipped amidst the guards, pummeling them with her small limbs.

The guard she had apparently flung against the wall stood and wiped blood from his clearly-broken nose. He grabbed the copper-tipped club from his belt. "That's enough out of you!" he snarled and jabbed the club forward. There was an agonized scream and the sound of a body hitting the stone floor.

"Beraht!" Rogan roared. "Save Aebreanna!"

A horrid screeching of metal gave way almost instantly to the thunderous surrender of stone. Some great eruption of rock and wood and metal filled the hallway. Terrible sounds of rage and terror and impossible violence thickened the air even more than could the debris of a dungeon wall. One man was flung bodily into Tomas field of view, impacting against the far wall with a wet crunch. He remained fixed against the stone wall, immobile. Beraht's massive form then came into view, apparently stalking a man who had tried crawling away. The Uldra, his mind lost to rage, grabbed the doomed, squealing guard and lifted him into the air with both hands. "Wait," Rogan called out. "We need…" There was a sharp crack as the body went limp, having been bent backwards beyond a right angle. "Information," Rogan finished, his voice resigned.

"Any of them conscious?" Rogan asked as he stepped out of his cell. When he had finished subduing the four guards, Beraht retrieved the keys and opened Tomas' cell. The squire had moved to help Aebreanna as the Uldra freed Rogan.

"Not sure," Beraht admitted.

"How's she doing?" Rogan asked, looking at Tomas and Aebreanna.

The squire was kneeling beside his Sylva friend, who was lying prone on the stone floor and gasping for air. "Just help me up," she said, though her words were broken by a random spasming of her body.

Tomas gently raised her to a sitting position, noting a circle of reddened skin at the small of her back that had already begun to swell. He left her side only to retrieve the padded gambeson of a dead guard, the man's crushed head stating better than any words could he no longer had need of it. Tomas set the padded shirt around Aebreanna's slight shoulders, settling the garment so that it covered her nakedness.

Aebreanna looked up at Tomas though her left eye, the right covered as always by her heavy mane. "Ever the chivalrous one," she smiled, trying not to let the pain show through on her delicate-seeming face.

Rogan picked up one of the guards' copper-tipped clubs. "New toys?" he guessed.

"Careful!" Tomas snapped. "That's what they used on her."

The knight looked around and found a whimpering guard. "Really," he muttered darkly. He walked over, kicked the cringing man over and held the copper tip of the club only a breath away from the man's face. "Now's when you talk," he said with no emotion and less mercy in his voice.

"We were ordered," he stammered through tears. "Just doing what we're told!"

"Yeah," Rogan said, again without feeling. "Can't tell you how many times I've heard that. He positioned the copper tip just above the man's eye. "Ordered by who?"

"Prefect Niklaus! The Prefect! He ordered us!"

"Ordered you to do what, exactly?"

"Make it look like you broke out, that you were trying to escape!"

"And got killed in the process," the knight guessed, moving away.

"You're not going to kill him?" Beraht asked curiously.

Rogan walked over to Aebreanna. "Not my choice," he replied. The knight knelt in front of his Sylva friend. "Can you move?" he asked gently.

She nodded and stood, with help from Tomas. The unconquerable baroness looked up at Rogan and held out her hand. The knight gave her the copper-tipped club. Leaning on Tomas, Aebreanna limped over to where the guard lay in a growing puddle of his terror. She looked down on him with undisguised loathing. Slowly, terribly slowly, the vengeful baroness raised the club until its copper tip hovered over the man's crotch. "That was... uncivilized." She thrust.

Chapter 36

Rogan and Tomas stripped two of the dead guards. The Humans donned the gambesons and bascinets, taking as well the boots and belts. "Doesn't have to be perfect," Rogan grunted, throwing aside one pair of boots for a larger set. "Just enough for a casual look."

"What's the plan?" Tomas asked, setting the leather belt.

"He said Prefect Niklaus gave the orders. We find him and have a friendly chat."

"We're going to search the entire Free City for one man?"

Rogan glanced at Aebreanna. The spy had tried standing but could only take a few steps before the pain of her new wound overwhelmed her. Seeing this, Beraht simply picked up the tiny Sylva. Surprisingly to Tomas, Aebreanna made no objection, but rather settled into the cradle of Beraht's massive arm, and even rested her head against his mountainous chest. Wrapped in the large gambeson Tomas had draped over her, and now enfolded in one of Beraht's powerful arms, only her head and the very bottom of Aebreanna's legs and feet were visible. "The Barfüsserkirche," she said.

"The what?" Tomas asked.

"Town hall," Rogan grunted. "Government offices. Logical place to start." He looked meaningfully at Beraht. "Guarded."

"Sneak or fight?" the Uldra asked.

"Sneak," the knight said firmly. "Let's look for our gear."

The disguised Humans spent several minutes investigating nearby rooms. They were in a basement. Four hallways, including the one Beraht and Aebreanna remained in, converged in a central room. The other halls had rows of cells similar to the ones in which they had been imprisoned. The central room held tables and chairs, lanterns and weapons racks with more of the copper-tipped wooden clubs. There was also a stone staircase leading up. Tomas stood at the base of this and nodded up.

Seeing this, Rogan shook his head. "Not yet," he said very softly. There had been no other guards, nor any other prisoners. No sounds came from above either. There were no storerooms or other storage in which their equipment might have been placed. The two Humans went back and led Beraht and Aebreanna into the center room. "Ok," Rogan said. "Me and Tomas take point. We walk like we belong. Block by block. Beraht carries Aebreanna and stays out of sight."

"What if there's a fight?" Tomas asked.

"Let's avoid contact as long as possible. We try for the town hall. But if we're discovered, start raising all kinds of attention. Rouse the whole damn city.

"What," the squire asked. "Why?"

Rogan shook his head. "This whole thing stinks of conspiracy."

"Indeed," Aebreanna agreed from her Uldra cradle. "Our capture and imprisonment were public, but our murder was clearly meant to be private."

"So if we're discovered, we raise the whole city and make them aware of what tried to happen."

The knight led his squire up the stairs, walking confidently. Tomas tried to mimic, but was taken aback when they reached the top of the stairs. They were in a cathedral. A wooden door was at the top, partly opened. Pausing only briefly, Rogan walked through, followed by Tomas. The young man stood in numb shock. They had not been kept in a jail or military outpost. Their captors had planned to rape their friend and murder them within the walls of a house of God. "What!?!" he could only demand in a voice choking in outrage.

"Easy," Rogan said firmly, standing in front oof his squire and laying a gentle hand on his shoulder. "They brought us to the Münster, the Frostfront Cathedral."

"How…" the squire demanded. "Why… what…"

The knight breathed deeply, looking into Tomas' eyes and encouraging him to do the same. "Easy now, kid. Take it slow." He kept breathing deeply and talking steadily.

Tomas nodded and mimicked his knight. "How could they use a cathedral for…?"

Rogan nodded. "After Pelsemoria fell, the Guild broke from the Church. All the Adamic clergy were banished. The government took over the Cathedral. They've been using it for…" He glanced meaningfully back down the stairs. "For other things."

"What's happening?" Beraht called up as gently as his thunderous voice could manage.

Rogan patted his squire on the shoulder. Tomas nodded. The knight looked around, "Come up," he said. "It's empty."

Indeed, the cathedral echoed as empty as any tomb. The wooden pews had been moved to one side of the great hall, stacked like so much firewood. Great tables and benches sat in their place, strewn with the documents of government. Only a handful of lanterns still burned, and these very low. All the decorative tapestries, traditional for any great cathedral, had been removed. The stained-glass windows were dark, and many were even covered by large canvas tentcloth. Worst of all to Tomas, the altar was gone; the stone had been chiseled, leaving nothing at the apse except shelves holding scrolls and books. There was no sacred flame, no copy of the Teachings, nothing religious remained. This was no longer a holy place, Tomas decided. It was now just another building.

Rogan jerked his head towards the staircase that should lead to the belltower. Tomas moved to investigate while Rogan moved around the central hall, quickly looking under tables and behind cases. Tomas went to the rising staircase at the corner of the building. The door was slightly ajar and he kicked it fully open. He looked up, but could see nothing in the pervasive darkness. The squire looked back at his knight and shook his head.

Rogan jabbed a thumb at the large double doors. "Keep watch," he told Beraht and joined Tomas. The two Humans climbed the stairs, their copper-tipped wooden clubs held ready. They reached the belfry after a short climb, the trap door open. Again, Tomas could not help but stare.

The bells were gone. The great bronze bells that should have called the faithful to services, that should have played their sweet music for the city each day, were gone. The belfry was empty but for some tattered ropes and rotting wood frameworks. Tomas sighed and shook his head, joining Rogan in looking out over the city.

Frostfront was large, but no so much as the Northern Keep. Ulheim's harsh peeks dominated the western sky and hills and forest covered the east. A great river, the Creir, Tomas realized, divided the bulk of the city in the west from a large facility on the eastern bank. The city's walls were thick, with similar, star-shaped fortresses as were found on the Northern Keep's. Rogan pointed down and to the east of the building that had once been Frostfront's cathedral. "See that?" he asked.

Tomas looked and saw a large building. It was made of red stone or brick, setting it apart from the surrounding buildings. There was a large tower on one end, and few lights shined in any of the shuttered windows. "How far?" he asked softly.

"Half mile or so straight-line," Rogan shrugged. "Give it an hour to get there. We'll be careful, but quick. Stay off the main streets, avoid open areas."

The squire looked up. Vaeta was waning, with only a slight crescent of the moon offering minimal light. "How long until dawn?"

"Hours. We've got time., but let's not waste it."

They moved quickly, but carefully. Rogan and Tomas ranged ahead, walking in the center of the narrow side streets and trusting to their stolen uniforms. Beraht followed a distance behind, staying close to buildings and moving from cover to cover. Despite Frostfront's traditionally-friendly relations with the Uldra, they saw no signs of the mountain-people and did not want to chance Beraht encountering a curious local, especially given his Sylva cargo.

They encountered no townsfolk in their journey, though. The windows were shuttered against the cold night of early spring. The only light came from the crescent moon overhead; the buildings were nothing more than a dark series of low canyons through which they navigated. Only one patrol of three soldiers crossed their paths, and their lantern gave Rogan and Tomas ample time to back into a nearby alley, waving Beraht to hide.

Within an hour, they were looking out at Frostfront's central marketplace. Like the rest of the city, it was deserted. Carts were closed and locked. Shops were shuttered and bolted. There were no guards or late-night pedestrians. Across the cobblestone plaza was the red building, the town hall. "What now?" Tomas whispered.

Beraht, still carrying Aebreanna, leaned out from the dark alley in which he hid. "Strong or sneaky?" he asked.

Rogan grimaced. "Sneaky until we can't," he replied. "Then we do it your way."

They walked up to the doors. Rogan and Tomas stood in front while Beraht moved to the side, out of direct sight. The knight grabbed the knocker and beat them against the solid door. A metal cover slid back from the metal-grated peephole. A man's face looked out before the cover slid back. There was the sound of a latch being pulled and the door opened. "What is it?" the man asked.

Rogan tapped the copper tip of his club against the man's chest. The two Humans rushed in. Tomas grabbed the drooling, twitching man and dragged him to the side while Beraht ducked into the low-ceilinged room. Rogan slammed the door shut and threw the bolt.

The room was empty of anyone else. Rows of book and scrollcases lined the walls. Three scribe desks lined one side of the room and a wide table lined the other. Beraht grumbled and knelt, being too tall for the low ceiling. Papers, parchment, books, scrolls, charts, and dispatches were scattered everywhere. Inkwells and half-finished proclamations sat on every surface. The air carried the heavy taste of writing and governmental bureaucracy.

"All right," Rogan breathed. "Now we start looking."

Tomas was at a bookcase, however, scanning its contents. "Kid," his knight called softly, "what're you doing?"

"Give me a minute," the young man replied. He continued to scan the labels of books and scroll stacks. Finally, he pulled one heavy book from a shelf and laid it on a table, scanning its contents.

"What in Underworld are you looking for?" Rogan demanded.

"This," Tomas said, pointing at a page. "Office assignments." The line he was pointing to said: Prefect Niklaus Meier, West Room 2-11. "Well?" he asked his knight.

Rogan looked and nodded, patting his squire on the back. "Not bad, kid. Not bad." He led them up the western stairs, to the second floor.

Whatever subtlety remained to Rogan, Tomas mused, must have been expended. The knight walked up to the door marked: West Room 2-11 and glanced at Beraht. The Uldra nodded and moved to one side of the door. Rogan nodded to Tomas, and the squire moved to the other. The knight squared his shoulders and kicked in the door, barreling in with Beraht and Tomas on his heels.

"What-?" one of the guards tried to object but was cut short as Tomas thrust the copper tip of his club into the man's chest. His body stiffened and the man collapsed. Beraht had grabbed the only other man in the room by the throat. The Uldra was still cradling Aebreanna in his left arm, having turned his body so that she was further protected by his entire mass. Using his right arm, Beraht lifted the unfortunate guard off the ground by his throat, slamming the choking guard and beating him into the wall until he stopped moving. Rogan stormed up the center, charging with his club raised at the man behind the large desk.

Prefect Niklaus was beautiful. Not handsome, but beautiful. His blonde hair was perfectly styled with fashionable curls. His porcelain skin had no hint of blemish and was highlighted by the perfect amount of rouge. His thin beard had been groomed exquisitely to mold to his aquiline chin. His rich cloths were as equally flawless, molding to his sculpted body like a second skin of impeccable taste.

Despite this outward beauty and perfection, Tomas sensed something in the Frostfront prefect, something… wrong. "Wait!" Tomas tried to call out, but too late.

Rogan leapt at Niklaus. The prefect raised a hand and spoke a word that may have been Sylvai, but was more harsh, more hateful. The wooden club in Rogan's hand exploded, sending the knight to the floor, cradling his mauled hand. Beraht roared in fury and charged, keeping Aebreanna and his left side shielded with his right. Niklaus spoke another hate-filled word and raised his arms. In response, the heavy wooden desk before him lifted from the floor and launched towards the Uldra. Beraht crouched, enfolding Aebreanna in his massive body as the desk hit and exploded against him, sending both Uldra and Sylva to the floor.

In desperation, Tomas threw his wooden club at Niklaus, but the man spoke a hateful word and flicked his well-manicured hand, causing the copper-tipped weapon to spin away, falling to the floor near Beraht's unmoving body.

The squire tensed and sprinted forward, low and intent, as his knight had taught him. Niklaus sneered and spoke another dark word, clenching his fist in the air. Tomas gasped and writhed; dark claws of evil, purple light grabbed him and lifted him into the air. He tried to resist, to find some purchase against the hideous magic, but found none. Instead, his eyes spotted their only hope. "The pendant!" he growled through the horrid pain.

Niklaus was wearing a black pearl encased in gold pinned to his chest. This adornment, Aebreanna attacked. She leapt from behind, reaching around and thrusting the copper tip of a wooden club so that it struck the black pearl pendant.

There was a flash of blue light wrapped in hateful black fire. Aebreanna flung herself back, away from the small explosion.

What was the Prefect Niklaus Meier had changed. His slightly-curled blonde hair was now ghostly white. His beautiful face was twisted in a snarl of hate, further marred by jagged scars running the length of his face. His once-glorious blue eyes were now burning blood. Those eyes seemed filled with pulsing rage. The creature hissed at Aebreanna and pointed a hand, curled like a predator's claw, and spoke words in a language like the breaking of ice.

Aebreanna tried to scream, but her body twisted backwards, her arms and legs splayed in a parody of Sylvai movement, her throat and jaw locked in agony. She was lifted into the air, even as Tomas had been, by claws of hateful magic. Tomas and Beraht tried to rise, to help their friend, but were too weakened by their own injuries.

Then, a group of Frostfront soldiers burst in. They all wore the green and blue gambesons and iron bascinets, and carried the copper-tipped wooden clubs. They looked about in confusion, and gaped at the monster floating in the air and snarling hateful words of darkest magic. The creature that had been Prefect Niklaus hissed at them and flung an emaciated arm, sending waves of purplish lightning at them. The soldiers screamed and scattered.

Gathering what remained of his strength, Tomas lunged at the creature that had been Prefect Niklaus. He wrapped his arms around the monster and heaved, bodily throwing him to the floor and pinning him there. The creature in his arms twisted and writhed, reaching back, impossibly dislocating its own limbs from their sockets to claw at the squire. Despite the pain and the blood and the impossible writhing, Tomas held on. "Little help!" he snarled.

"Tomas!" Rogan called, already leaping. In his hands, he held one of the iron bascinets. Tomas glanced, saw, and understood. At the last moment, he rolled aside, exposing the mystical creature to the knight's attack. Rogan swung with all his fading strength, smashing the iron helmet onto the false Niklaus' head. There was a flash of released power, of magic unchained. A crack of thunder sent Tomas and Rogan both rolling across the floor, to lie near each other, panting and blinking, trying to force their thoughts into rationality.

Chapter 37

"So, what was it?" Captain Luis Brücker was a serious, practical man. After the creature that had been Prefect Niklaus was defeated, the soldiers had taken custody of Tomas and his friends, but only to escort them to a nearby barracks, where their wounds were being tended. The captain had arrived within the hour, time he had spent first examining the site of the small battle.

"Nekalan," Rogan grunted as a salve was applied to his right hand. When the club he held had exploded, that hand had been lacerated with innumerable small, deep cuts. "Xeshlin infiltrator. We found one in Alvaro; it had taken the shape of a Calexto noblewoman and was steering their House to war with you."

"So that's it," Captain Luis mused. "A lot of Alvaro's decisions never really made much sense these past few years." His wrinkled eyes went out of the barracks, towards the town hall. "Like a lot of ours."

"Yeah," Rogan sighed. "I'm guessing these things have been in place since the fall of Pelsemoria. Not making trouble, just making it worse."

The captain looked at Rogan. "So, you came here to expose this infiltrator?"

The knight sighed, not for the first time. "Love to say that was the reason," he admitted. "But we had no idea."

"Then what was your purpose in the Free City?"

Rogan shook his head. "That's a long story."

Luis glanced around the room. Tomas was seated nearby; of them all, the squire was least physically wounded, but still clearly exhausted. Beraht lay where the squad of men who had been tasked with carrying the Uldra dropped him: on a wide table. Although the warrior had tried to rise, to help in the struggle against the Nekalan, the impact of that large wooden desk had done far more damage then was at first obvious. Since the creature's death, Beraht had been still, and silent. Aebreanna had convinced the soldiers to let her minister to the Uldra, and was still applying poultices and bandages to her massive friend. Beraht was breathing, but weakly, and he had yet to regain consciousness. "I don't think you'll be leaving soon," the captain pointed out. "Your team won't been road-ready for some time."

He looked squarely at Rogan. "You are also the heir to a kingdom with which we are essentially at war. I think an explanation is proper."

"What?" the knight asked. "We've been trying to negotiate peace between you and Alvaro. How does that make us at war?"

Luis stared at Rogan for a moment. "I take it you have been out of contact with your city."

Rogan nodded.

"A large army flying the colors of House Calonar has marched towards our force near the Crier River. There have already been a number of skirmishes to the east of Drailia, and a pitched battle is almost inevitable."

"What?" Rogan asked in a flat voice as cold as the night.

"Are you saying you know nothing of General Killdare's activities in the hills to the east. That your arrival here is not some coordinated strategy?"

"Captain," the knight said evenly, "I swear to you that this is the first I've heard of any actions our army has taken against you. The last orders I gave were to continue negotiations toward a peaceful resolution between Frostfront and Alvaro."

"Your peaceful resolution has changed into an open alliance between Houses Calonar and Calexto," Luis said. "A de facto state of war now exists between Frostfront and the Northlands."

Rogan sighed once again. "Are we prisoners of war?"

"Right now," the captain said, wearily rubbing his eyes, "you are prisoners because you destroyed a priceless tomb in the necropolis, assaulted multiple guards, and… well, I don't know how this… Nekalan figures into things."

"You'll also find four dead guards in the old cathedral basement," Rogan added.

Captain Luis looked up. "You admit to murdering four of my men?"

"They started it," the knight replied. "They were ordered by that Nekalan to kill us and make it look like we died trying to escape." He turned to Aebreanna, who was looking at them. "Show him."

She stepped forward, limping, but her gait stronger. She turned and pulled up the tunic the guards had provided. The Sylva showed Luis the burn mark on the small of her back. The captain examined the wound and grunted, "That's definitely from one of our shock-sticks," he admitted.

"Not only that," Aebreanna said with a hard edge to her normally-soft voice. She returned to Beraht's side and lay a gentle hand on his massive shoulder, leveling her opalescent eye at the captain. "Your men planned to violate me before murdering us. My friend was defending me."

"The loyalty of an Uldra can be… destructive," Luis mused. He looked back at Rogan. "What about the necropolis?"

"A trap set by a Death Mage," the knight replied. "We were passing through the tunnel from Uldron but hit a cave-in. There was a fissure that led into the necropolis. While we were looking for a way out, the trap went off."

"Why would a Death Mage set a trap here?"

Rogan raised his hands and shrugged.

Luis sighed and rubbed his eyes again. "Well, we've got adepts investigating. If they confirm your story… well, it's not up to me. The Prefect Council has already convened. I imagine they'll-" The captain was interrupted by the arrival of a messenger. Luis took the parchment and unfolded it, quickly reading. "Well, that's that, I suppose."

"What?" Rogan asked wearily.

The captain straightened. "You've been summoned before the Triumvirate. They will decide what to do with you."

Aebreanna flatly refused to leave. So long as Beraht remained unconscious, she never strayed more than a few steps from his side. Captain Luis tried cajoling, pleading, threatening, and even bribing, but the immovable Sylva would not relent. Finally, a Life Mage was summoned. He was thin and quiet, wearing the pure white band of his school on his blue robes. "Who will offer?" was all he asked, all he said, the whole time he was present.

Aebreanna immediately stood forward, but Rogan forbade it. "You've taken too much damage," he said firmly.

"I'll do it," Tomas said. "I'm just tired, but not really wounded."

The Life Mage drew Tomas to stand beside Beraht. He took the squire's hand and laid it over the Uldra's heart. There was a warmth then, a feeling of heat passing from Tomas to Beraht. The young man felt even more weary, but unharmed. Beraht took a deep breath and his eyes opened. When the Uldra sat up, Aebreanna examined him and, after determining he was stable, began berating her mountainous friend for his carelessness, clumsiness, thoughtlessness, and racial stupidity.

"All right," Rogan said. "We're off to see the wizards."

They were loaded into a large, open-topped wagon pulled by a team of oxen. Captain Luis had offered a proper carriage, but Rogan had refused, jabbing a thumb at the towering Beraht to emphasize the practical difficulty in transporting an Uldra.

Despite their technical status as prisoners, Tomas and his friends were treated with curtesy during their trip through the city, towards the headquarters of the Arcane Guild. Rogan and Tomas were given long tunics and cloaks, while Beraht was offered a large bearskin blanket as an improvised cover. Captain Luis sent two of his men to a nearby house where they purchased a dress similar to those worn in the Northlands for Aebreanna, along with a fur-lined cloak, leggings, and half-boots. The soldiers helped them into the open-topped wagon, taking special consideration for the wounds each had. Tomas and his friends were not bound or otherwise placed in fetters, but instead given thick blankets to protect against the cold morning air. Even the contingent of guards looked more ceremonial then restrictive, their green and blue gambesons replaced with burnished breastplates and gauntlets, and their wooden clubs with gold-inlaid swords.

"We're prisoners of status," Rogan explained, noticing his squire's curious expression. "Over the centuries, there's been a lot of fighting between the various Houses. They've gotten it into their heads that war can be civilized if they follow the rules. One of the big rules is that when you capture enemy nobility, you treat them well." The knight shrugged and settled onto the wagon's bench. "It's better than gagging us and marching us through town while people throw rotten vegetables at us, I guess."

"So all the prisoners get treated like guests and sold back to their homes?"

Rogan snorted his derision. "Of course not," he grumbled. "The rules only apply to the nobles and the wealthy. If your family has the money to buy your release or offer something in exchange, then you're treated well. Peasants are usually just let go. Anyone deemed dangerous or who has a family that won't negotiate…" The knight nodded his head to a raised platform with a headman's block.

"Well, as long as things stay civilized," Tomas said sarcastically.

Rogan leveled a long look at his squire. "You all right, kid?" Rogan asked gently.

"Compared to what?"

"Fair point. We just need to keep our heads today. The Triumvirate can be dangerous."

"People, I can deal with," he said in a weak voice. "It's the monsters and the dead and everything else I can't handle."

"Don't sell yourself short. You've taken on more in the past year than most people do in their entire lives, and you're still standing."

"Except when I crack."

Rogan put a hand on his squire's shoulder. "It happens, kid," the knight said gently. "When you get hit with too much, too fast, it can happen."

"I don't even know…" Tomas said in misery and humiliation.

"You were reacting. One of the dangers of our job is that when the metal meets the meat, you don't have time to stop and think, let alone react to anything, and you really don't have time to feel anything about what's happening or what you're doing. That comes later."

"I don't understand."

Rogan straightened and let his eyes travel over the sharply sloped rooftops of the buildings around them as the party traveled along the wide streets of Frostfront toward the bridge that would grate them access to the towering headquarters of the

Arcane Guild rising above the cityscape. "Tomas, when you're in the middle of a fight and you have to put someone down, what do you feel at that moment?"

The boy thought about it but, sensing the debilitating fear and horror rise up again, quickly changed his line of thinking. "I don't know," he admitted. "I guess I don't really feel anything."

"Exactly. You can't feel anything at that moment because you're too busy. The best warriors are the ones that shut down the part of their souls that feels compassion and doubt and fear and everything else that keeps rational people alive and sane. We shut all that down, and we do what we have to for victory and maybe even survival. The people that can't shut their feelings down are the ones that freeze up in a crisis or just collapse and start screaming."

"Like I did," the squire said.

"Not until the threat was dealt with," his knight pointed out. "I talked about it with Aebreanna while we were in that dungeon, and she thinks that you used whatever it is you got from Alexia to deal with the trap instinctively, before anything else happened. That's what real warriors do: we take care of the situation, and then we feel all those emotions that would've gotten us killed before. You see, that's where the danger lies. If you wait too long before letting all that garbage out of your soul, or if you get hit with too much too fast, then something has to give."

"I still lost control," Tomas insisted.

"We've all lost control at some point," Rogan snorted. "A lot of times it happens more than just once."

"Have you ever lost control like that?" the squire demanded.

"You've seen it happen, kid," Rogan reminded his apprentice. "Do you remember Senen? You had to talk me down. Or when we fought Anninihus? At the end, I completely lost it, and it took you and Beraht and Aebreanna to make sure the Death Mage didn't kill me."

Tomas thought about that, a flicker of hope sparking deep in his young heart. "So it never stops happening?" he asked.

Rogan shook his head. "Sorry, kid. Like it or not, you've got the chance to become a great warrior, and that means you have the ability to close your heart off at times when you need to without even thinking about it. But those feelings you put away in the back of your soul don't go anywhere. They need to be dealt with at some point. Now you've seen what happens if you don't."

The squire looked his knight in the eyes. "So how do you deal with these feelings without letting them overpower you?"

Rogan shrugged. "It's different with everyone," he answered. "What works for one guy may not work for another. Beraht drinks and brawls and celebrates. Aebreanna spends time with her husband and kids. General Killdare writes poetry if you can believe that. You have to find what works for you."

"You paint," Tomas noted, gaining a sudden flash of insight into his mentor's soul.

Rogan said nothing but did clear his throat and look away guiltily.

"All those scenes of battle and ancient wars that you paint. That's how you deal with everything."

"Like I said," the knight replied in irritation, "you have to find something that lets you feel those emotions and release them without ripping your soul to pieces in the process."

"What happens if I never find a way?"

"You've probably seen men like that," Rogan said. "Sometimes they become heartless killers that just go from one fight to another. Sometimes they can't live with what they've become and find a way to die that isn't technically suicide. Sometimes they just fall apart and can never put themselves back together. It's not something you want to risk."

"So how do I find what I need?" he asked. "I'm not all that artistic."

Rogan shrugged. "Go with what you're good at," he replied. "You love the sound of your own voice, so try talking about what you go through."

"To who?"

"Everybody. All those histories that you love to read were written by someone. Try writing about your experiences."

"I'm not an historian," Tomas objected. "I wouldn't know how to record great events."

"Then don't try. Write down what happens to you, what you think about it and how it affects the people around you. Let history make its own decisions."

The party passed through a plaza that joined together several of the city streets into one great boulevard that led onto the single bridge across the Creir River. This passage traveled to the massive, walled complex of buildings that housed the leaders of the Arcane Guild. Scattered around the square were a number of large statues of great figures from Frostfront's past. Tomas looked up at these men and women whose deeds were no longer known and whose faces had decayed with time until no unique features could be made out against the gray stone the statues were carved from. "I wonder if that's how they started," the squire mused.

Rogan looked up at the statues and shrugged. "I doubt anybody knows for sure," he remarked. "Nobody really knows that they're in the middle of some great, historic event until after it's over. And the only way anyone can remember the event is if the people that were there take the time to write it all down."

"Big responsibility."

"Not really," the knight objected. "Don't try to teach a history lesson, kid. Just talk about your experiences. Trust me, history will attach all kinds of nonsense to anything you write until it's more legend than fact."

"Then what's the point?"

"Everybody loves a good story." He looked at his squire. "And sometimes telling is more important than hearing."

Chapter 38

Tomas was silent as the group made their way across the wide bridge to the gold-lined iron gates of the Arcane Guild's headquarters. The squire tried to take in the whole complex but could not. The centuries of added construction by each generation that resided within its walls had taken what must have begun as a fairly simple building and transformed it into a riot of conflicting architectural designs. Large spires competed with a maze of connecting walkways for space along the rooftops of the buildings. Angels jostled with gargoyles along the various parapets that irregularly lined the balconies, some with windows and some without. Massive doors of wood and steel sat beside open portals without even a gate to slow traffic. Banners hung limply alongside flags waving freely in the cold wind, each bearing different colors and symbols for the infinite orders, brotherhoods, schools, disciplines, cabals, and associations that together made up Lanasia's Arcane Guild. Nowhere among the dozens of buildings that together made up the Guild's headquarters could a unifying theme or style be discerned; even the three towers rising above the architectural cacophony were each unique, built of different types of stone in different styles.

In response to the chaos before them, Tomas could only think to say, "Wow."

"Welcome to the best reason in the world why you never want a group of wizards making important decisions," Rogan said derisively.

Upon their arrival, an officious wizard in formal blue robes and bearing the soft blue lining of a Water Mage shuffled forward and tried to take charge of the prisoners but was summarily dismissed by Captain Luis. All it took was the officer tapping the emblem on his gauntlet, and the squat adept stepped aside with a fawning bow. As Tomas and his friends were shepherded inside, the squire noted that all the wizards, and non-wizards who were no doubt responsible for the actual work, gave the prisoners and, more obviously, their guards a wide berth.

"Is it my imagination, or is everyone afraid of our guards?" Tomas quietly asked Rogan.

The knight chuckled. "You're not imaging it." Rogan nodded toward the closest guard with a pointed look toward the insignia on his gauntlet, the same eye and black sun Tomas had noted earlier. "That's the symbol for the Order of the Black Sun."

"I've never heard of them," the squire admitted.

"That's surprising. I thought you'd read everything about everyone."

"Sorry, I guess I need to study harder."

"The Order of the Black Sun is a lot like the Praetorians were to the Legions," Rogan explained. "They're the elite bodyguards of the Triumvirate. Technically, they're part of the Frostfront military but answerable only to the Triumvirate. They're adepts that have been trained to be warriors as well." He snorted then.

"What?" Tomas asked.

Rogan shrugged. "We don't know; nobody's confirmed the story." He glanced at Captain Luis with a knowing grin. "There're rumors that the Order was founded during the Xeshlin Invasion."

"So?"

"It was when Frostfront was under siege, and most of the Guild fled. Rumor is," he emphasized the word rumor, "that Cylan Calonar trained a group of adepts he freed from Xeshlin slavers. He taught them how to fight. They led the relief of Frostfront and began the tradition of a small group of adepts who train in the martial skills, just like Cylan Calonar did."

Tomas looked at Luis, who was looking at them. "I wonder if it's true," the squire mused.

Luis moved forward, leading them down a particular hallway. He paused, though, and glanced at Rogan. "The Order knows its history," he said. Then he paused. Before moving ahead, he added quietly, "and we remember."

Tomas and his friends were escorted into the largest of the clustered buildings to which the Triumvirate's towers were connected. Inside was an even greater collection of chaos than outside, with a riot of murals covering the walls depicting the epic, and somewhat revised, history of the Arcane Guild only to be covered by tapestries depicting equally epic and equally revised scenes. The ceiling overhead rose to an absurd height and, despite being vaulted, was arched with glass panels allowing in ample sunlight, making the randomly-placed braziers and torches redundant. At each intersection of two or more hallways, that all seemed to move in random directions, rose towering statues of bronze, iron, jade, and other metals and stones. These statues seemed better cared for than the ones in the city proper, but like the ones outside, they had no identifying marks, making their significance a mystery. The only common factor among the statues inside the Guild headquarters was that each obviously depicted a master wizard, each robed and bearing various traditional implements of the mystical arts.

"Impressive," Tomas said.

Rogan just chuckled as Beraht snorted in derision at each demonstration of Human skill at traditionally Uldric art forms. Aebreanna said nothing and gave no indication of her personal feelings at their surroundings other than a smile that would have been equally at place had she been watching a puppy chew on its own tail.

Their twisting path through the maze of corridors, each a different design, led at last to a pair of massive doors. As best Tomas could tell, they were made of solid gold with runes and glyphs of silver set within. The squire struggled for a moment as a wave of euphoria washed over him upon sight of the grandiose doors, and a quick look at Aebreanna showed that she too was overwhelmed by the formidable magical defenses set into that portal.

"You all right?" Rogan asked as he supported his squire.

The young man nodded and righted himself. "Just a little light-headed," he replied. "I think the artwork is starting to make me nauseous."

"Well, keep any other comments you have to yourself," the knight warned. "Once we're in front of the Triumvirate, we'll need some careful diplomacy to get out of this."

"So you're letting Aebreanna do all the talking?"

"Smartass."

The doors were opened with great effort by the four guards standing before it, each of them bearing the heraldry of the Order of the Black Sun. Once enough clearance had been made, Rogan and the others were ushered inside, and the doors were closed behind them. It was dark inside, with a single point of light high above shining down onto a circle into which the heroes were led. Once this was done, their guards retreated without a word back into the surrounding darkness.

Stepping forward came three adepts: two male Humans and one Sylva. Each appeared ancient, with hair so gray it was almost white, framing faces lined with heavy wrinkles, and surrounded by the raised hoods of their blue robes. Each wizard held a staff of perfect, unblemished wood that gleamed with reflected light. Their robes of unrelieved blue gave no hint of what specialty each may have once had before rising to their great rank, and no emblem or insignia of any kind differentiated one from the others. Although great age weighed down on them all, not one of the archmagi showed the slightest hint of weakness or frailty, instead standing straight and looking at their prisoners with unflinching eyes. It was the eyes of these adepts that drew the greatest attention, however; all color was gone from the adepts' eyes, even the Sylva. Instead, they looked at Tomas and his friends through solid black orbs broken only by a dazzling collection of tiny lights, as though the night sky was contained behind their faces. Tomas sensed great power emanating from each of these master-wizards arrayed at equal distances around them and knew with absolute certainty that each held the power to tear apart creation itself should they wish. This, then, was the Triumvirate, Tomas realized. These were the leaders of the Arcane Guild and the rulers of Frostfront.

"Rogan Eigenhard," one of them said in a voice that sounded like a chorus, "Heir of Calonar, Champion of Light."

"Aebreanna Tressalon," another said in the same chorus-voice, "Daughter of Fate, Darkness and Light." Aebreanna stiffened at their identification but said nothing.

"Beraht of No Name," the third said, "Son of a Grave-Builder, Herald of the One Who Comes." The Uldra made no reaction.

All three turned to the squire. "Tomas Fidelis," they said as one, "the Final Host."

With a start, Tomas recalled his brief meeting with Cyras Darkholm, the meeting that had set him on his current path, in which the Trickster Mage had referred to Tomas in the same way but had given little explanation. A startled glance at Rogan offered no answers since the knight was staring with a neutral expression at the Triumvir closest to him.

"You walk as always," one of the archmagi continued, "along the path of Prophecy.

The third wizard, the Sylva, said, "You were not expected within the Free City."

"And yet, you are here," the third added, this one with the strange features of a Tramanese man.

"Your path was meant to lead around Frostfront."

"To the east and south, through Otylia and on to the Endless Sands."

"Why have you come here?"

"It was not our intention to violate the sovereignty of your city or the sanctity of your dead," Rogan explained. "Our entrance was an accident forced—"

"By the recent collapse of the tunnel and the exposure of the fissure," the Sylva archmage finished. The Triumvirs looked at one another.

"Unforeseen events," the Tramanese man observed.

"The collapse altered the Heir's path to lengthen his quest," another Triumvir mused.

"The fissure allowed the Companions to bypass the collapse, hastening his quest," the third added.

"This allowed them to view the crypt. It gave them information not meant to be yet revealed."

"The Scions manipulate events to their favor once more."

"Either the Trickster or the Shadow seek to force our involvement in the upcoming conflict."

"And one or both disrupt our Truthsight with the recent storm."

"And the perceptions of our more gifted adepts."

"The Guild was to remain neutral during the Inversion. This was how our adepts would survive."

"Yet we are drawn further into conflict. Even the limited skirmish at Jarek is escalating."

"As the Scions no doubt intend."

Rogan cleared his throat. "Did you know about the Nekalan?" he asked.

"Of course," one replied.

"Xeshlin machinations have been amateurish since the loss of their Dark Empress," another added.

"And increasingly desperate in fear of her return."

"We allowed the infiltrator's schemes since they advanced our own."

"You want war with House Calexto?" Tomas demanded, but bit his lip after a stern look from Rogan.

"We are indifferent to the conflict," the Tramanese Triumvir said.

"The Xeshlin seek civil war to weaken the emerging Lanasian kingdoms," the Sylva Triumvir added. "This will either assist in their slave raids, in the event their Dark Empress does not soon emerge, or expedite her renewed invasion, should she return."

"In either event, Frostfront will not be weakened by irrelevant war."

"And yet," Aebreanna interrupted, "you make war over Jarek."

"The town means nothing."

"The people mean nothing."

"We seek only what lies within the nearby hills."

"The gold?" Tomas asked.

Rogan raised a hand, trying to quiet his team. "If there's something specific you want in Jarek, we can negotiate your withdrawal and the safety of the people."

The Triumvirs looked at each other. There seemed to be a silent conversation. Finally, one spoke. "Your concession to our desire seems unlikely."

"Your master would demand possession of what we seek."

"As he did ten years ago. He would only contain them, rather than employing them."

"What are we talking about?" Rogan demanded. "I can't negotiate or even speak meaningfully unless I understand what you say."

"The Seals," Aebreanna supplied. "They speak of the Seals of Stalline." She narrowed her opalescent eye. "One of the Seals is in the hills outside Jarek."

"It was them," Beraht rumbled, his voice nearly a growl of growing hostility. "They put the Greysoul up to it. They're the reason he knew where to look for the Seals."

Rogan looked from the Uldra to the Triumvirate. "Well?" he demanded.

"Tienel Uskera acted with our sanction," one admitted.

"He approached us with a theory on how to penetrate the Covenant Barrier."

"He sought escape from the coming conflict."

"The civil wars?" Tomas asked.

"The Death of Calonar," a Triumvir corrected.

"The Inversion," another added.

"The Return of the Dark Empress," the third continued.

"The Rise of the Demon-god Ramalech," all three said together.

"Had the Tienel Uskera succeeded," the female Triumvir said, "his process could have been replicated."

"You're going to run," Beraht said, spitting on the ground. "You cowards are going to run from the fight."

"The fight is not ours," a Triumvir insisted.

"It will shatter this world," another added, "regardless of who wins."

"And to Underworld with the people," Rogan said, his voice nearly as dangerous as Beraht's.

"The people are neither or concern, nor our responsibility."

"You will lead the war to come, Heir of Calonar. You will have allies aplenty. Our role is irrelevant, so we seek escape."

Rogan took several deep breaths, clearly mastering his growing temper. "The matter at hand is Jarek," he insisted. "If your war is irrelevant, if all you want is the Seal so you can escape, just take it and leave the people in peace. The Xeshlin want you to fight, to weaken Frostfront. Don't give them what they want."

"The same enemy who has been moving against the Northlands is moving against the Guild," Aebreanna pointed out. "We share this mutual enemy."

"The Daughter of Fate speaks truly."

"But we must not tie ourselves with House Calonar," the Sylva insisted. "The Death of Calonar draws close, and with it, the Inversion."

"Nevertheless, the Scions maneuver for us to become involved despite our designs. We must determine the degree of our involvement in the events now unfolding."

The Triumvirate turned as one to face Rogan. "Heir of Calonar," one of them said, "your quest has been manipulated by your enemy and your ally. Both Shadow and Trickster would adjust your path according to their designs."

"We find this manipulation of Time and Fate unacceptable."

"We will rebalance the Prophecy by expediting your trip through Ulheim."

"I thank you for any help you will provide," the prince replied with a formal bow. "A guide through the mountains will be of enormous help."

"You misunderstand, Heir of Calonar. It is a small matter for us to send you to the other side of Ulheim. Your horses and possessions are even now being assembled outside. In this way will we restore the balance that was skewed by the efforts of the Scions."

"You will not arrive late to Tordenia, as the Shadow desires."

"You will you arrive early to Tordenia, as the Trickster desires."

Tomas had been in close company of Rogan long enough to spot the signs of his knight's surprise, but the hero made no outward move other than to bow again. "Thank you," he said simply.

"Do not thank us, Heir of Calonar. We are merely restoring you to your proper place along the path of Prophecy and undoing the effects our inadvertent involvement has had."

"What of your armies?" Rogan asked. "The conflict between Frostfront and Alvaro is also something that you have been manipulated into."

"You have learned the lessons of diplomacy well, Prince."

"You speak with the half-truths that are the negotiator's greatest tool."

"We were not manipulated into the initial conflict with House Calvino. We sought it for the furtherance of our aims, the recovery of the Seal."

Rogan crossed his arms. "All right, but what about the truce arranged by my agents and agreed to by yours?"

"We will honor the terms of the truce so long as the Seal is retrieved and delivered, but we will not recall our army now that it has already been mobilized."

"What? Why?"

As one, the Triumvirate folded their arms behind their backs, their staves vanishing into the darkness. "The Inversion is fast approaching, and our Guild requires the proper resources to survive it," one explained.

"You can survive it with help, with friends." Tomas felt himself saying the words, but he had no idea from where they came, or why.

The Triumvirate stared at Tomas. "The Host speaks with the voice of youth," one Triumvir pointed out.

"No," the Tramanese Triumvir argued. "The voice of another."

"He carries a dual aura," the Sylva suggested.

"A voice through the Veil whispers through him."

"The Matriarch has laid designs of her own."

"This will be an asset in his confrontation."

"But it is unforeseen. The Scions may be equally ignorant of this move."

"Her actions on either side of the Veil do not concern us."

"Agreed." They turned as one to Rogan. "Rogan Eigenhard, we give you one opportunity to leave in peace with our assistance if you go now."

"Stay and continue your useless words, and you will remain in our custody while we work to divine another means of negating our interference in the current conflict."

Rogan gritted his teeth, forcing back a number of retorts. "We'll leave," he replied stiffly.

With no other word or warning, the Triumvirate vanished into the surrounding darkness.

Third Interpose

Chapter 39

Steam rose from the bath. The heavy clouds drifted up, filling the air and rising to the domed ceiling, where a wide oculus looked up at the cloudless sky. This portal was partially blocked, like an iris looking down upon them. Mary knew from experience that the statue of the Lady of Light was the blockage, that the steam rising from this sacred place would waft up and around the image of her princess' goddess. The cold weather prevented most of the Northern Keep's citizens from enjoying the baths that were central to the Lady's temple, and they were denied a wonderous sight. From the top of the temple, from the public baths in which the Sisterhood of the Lady of Light saw to the physical and emotional well-being of the people, it appeared as though the Goddess was resting on a cloud. There was no statue here, though.

The private baths of the Sisterhood were circular, in contrast to the great rectangular ones at the top of their temple. There were no statues or other decorations; instead, the walls were painted in soft pastels and divans with great cushions dyed in every possible color circled the pool. The Uldra had constructed this private path with a bizarre series of fountains and vents around the edge; a priestess could soak in the peaceful center or let one of the myriad fountains pour down on her from above, or sit against the vent from which hot bubbles emerged, tickling her body. There were no musicians here; instead, the air was filled with the music of feminine laughter and idle conversation. There were no titles here, nor positions of authority, nor responsibility. Here, the Sisters themselves found refuge.

"The explosions are getting worse, your Highness," Chandra said.

For the past few weeks, Kyla had been spending an increasing amount of her time in this sanctuary. Pressured as she was in her duties as regent along with the changes to her body, the princess found that she needed the warm comfort of her Sisters.

"They are increasing not only in number but also in severity," the spy continued. "But at the same time, there doesn't seem to be any predictability to them. Some explosions have the force of a tornado, while others are little more than a flash of light."

Because Kyla wanted to spend more of her time in this sanctuary, this necessitated her advisors to adapt. Men were absolutely forbidden from entering the Sisterhood's private bath. Thus, Rashid's reports came most typically from Chandra now. Even Lukas, as persistent and unyielding as he was in his role as Kyla's bodyguard, was refused entry by the adamant Sisters of the Lady of Light. The sullen Archaeknight-in-training was forced to create a perimeter around the temple and await his mistress.

"How bad are the injuries?" Kyla asked. She was lying near the center of the pool, her back against Mary, who was rubbing her shoulders. Ilse, who was quickly joining the handmaiden as one of the princess' constant companions, was also close at hand. Out of respect for the security of their Sister Superior's meetings, the other priestesses in the bath had remained at the outskirts, well out of earshot. "Has anyone been killed?"

Chandra shuffled through a series of documents. When Kyla had insisted she would begin taking her meetings in the private bath, Remm had engineered a series of floating tables. These coved slabs of wood remained buoyant enough that the princess' advisors could bring the various dispatches, reports and other bureaucratic errata so necessary for governance into the center of the steaming pool. "So far, there have been no fatalities," Chandra replied. "In each case, the practitioner was trying to use whatever form of magic he or she has access to but in the process suffered from some kind of seizure." She had been initially hesitant to join Kyla and Mary in their frequent baths. Rumor suggested she had objected to Rashid, but was overruled. The spy had also tried, on the first such meeting, to remain clothed and outside the water. Kyla saw this and impishly waded to the very center of the pool, where she held court ever since. Chandra had been forced to sullenly disrobe and join them.

Kyla had confessed to Mary her puzzlement over the spy's apparent discomfort. Mary had only shrugged away her princess' confusion. Admittedly, Chandra had nothing to feel shame for, her training with Rashid had gifted her with a firm athlete's body. But then, the handmaiden knew, any woman in the presence of the near-divine Jewel of House Calonar, proudly unclothed, could not help but feel a swell of insecurity. Even as she neared the end of her first trimester, the princess remained an icon of feminine grace and beauty. Her lustrous hair and shining, sapphire-liked pearlescent eyes remained. Her flawless skin seemed somehow even more so. Her already-envious breasts were getting even larger. Even the slight bulging of her stomach only seemed to emphasize her feminine quality. Mary understood how a woman could feel self-conscious around Kyla, even if the princess herself was oblivious.

"Not a seizure," Esha corrected. The tiny Sylva reclined in another of Remm's ingenious inventions. The archmage, as diminutive as an infant, could barely reach the top of the pool here, in its deepest section. She certainly could not use the floating desk invention Remm had made for Chandra. To accommodate Kyla's desired location, the Uldra mastersmith had fashioned a floating chair. It was cushioned and reclined and somehow impervious to moisture. It allowed Esha to dangle her short legs in the steaming water and even, through some manipulation of Uldra engineering, control how far into the warm water her tiny body would settle. Somehow the seat remained steady, as did the wide shelves on either side containing the archmage's notes. Even when the diminutive Sylva moved, twisting or turning to reach for some report, the chair remained constant and level. Resting in her throne-like seat, the tiny archmage was able to soak in the comfort of the steam and the company of Kyla's entourage while contributing her expertise in all things arcane.

"Well, what would you call it?" Chandra asked.

"It's not physical," Ilse said. Because Cardinal Tain could not be present at these meetings, and the Queen refused to leave the castle or her care for the King, Ilse had assumed the role of religious advisor and representative in Kyla's briefings. "Whatever's happening to our adepts is not of the body."

"Since the Princess relaxed her ban on experimentation," Esha added, "at least for the purposes of our research, I have coordinated trials amongst some of our adepts. We can say with certainty that the disruption from Vara's Storm is passing. Our gifts are returning. With this, however, there has not been a corresponding increase or decrease in the number of incidents."

"So, they're not connected?" Mary asked. She offered a glass of water to her princess, who drank eagerly. As the pregnancy progressed, Kyla had gotten increasingly thirsty. As a result, Mary had made a point of always having something close at hand for her mistress to drink.

"Perhaps connected," Esha noted. "But not inexorably linked. The incidents continue even as the disruption fades."

"What exactly happens?" Kyla asked, handing her glass back to Mary for a refill.

"In each case," the archmage explained, "the spell being cast or ritual performed begins without any indication of hazard or imbalance. However, at the moment of activation, when the energy the practitioner has collected within her body is supposed to be released in a specific way to accomplish a specific task, some event occurs that not only magnifies the amount of energy being collected but also its intensity. I have spoken at length with those who have suffered from the phenomena, and each has related to me a similar sensation, that of the magic within them igniting and being released in all directions, without guidance or restriction."

"Could we prevent any more explosions by limiting the use of magic?" the princess asked. "I could reinstate my ban."

Esha shook her head. "In pursuing my investigation of the incidents, I issued such an order to all my students with a similar hypothesis in mind. Only hours after confirmation of my order, there was another incident involving a member of my Tower who, at the time, was not attempting the use of magic. These detonations do not require the adept to be actively tapping into the Winds."

"An incident that, incidentally, destroyed an entire warehouse," Chandra pointed out. "It took the City Watch four hours to put out the fire." The spy lifted a map of the Keep. "Thankfully, it didn't spread to any of the surrounding buildings. Remm was… annoyed, though."

"When is he not?" Mary laughed.

"So how do we keep anyone else from blowing up?" Kyla asked. The princess absently rubbed her throat. Mary quickly retrieved another glass of water from a priestess at the perimeter of the pool and brought the filled glass back. After draining the water in only a few moments, Kyla handed her empty glass back to Mary who refilled it and offered more to her princess. As her mistress's pregnancy had progressed and her demand for water increased, Mary had taken the expedient measure of always having at least two or three pitchers close at hand.

Esha removed her reading lenses and rubbed her opalescent eyes. "I fear, at the present time, there is simply no way to implement effective preventative measures. Until I, or one of my students, can identify the source of this phenomenon, or its purpose, we must continue to suffer its effects."

"There's another problem," Chandra said. The spy handed a dispatch to Esha, careful to keep the parchment well above the water. "Read this," she said.

The archmage quickly scanned the report and sighed. "Oh, dear."

"What is it?" Kyla asked.

Chandra raised the city map and pointed to one of the armories on the eastern edge of the city. "There's been another explosion," she said grimly.

"Someone in the armory?" Kyla guessed.

The spy shook her head. "The armory itself."

Kyla glanced at the map and back at Chandra. "I don't understand."

"The building exploded."

"More accurately," Esha pointed out as she replaced her reading lenses and continued the report, "several objects inside the armory detonated."

"I thought only adepts were blowing up," Kyla objected. "How could a building explode?"

Esha leaned back in her floating chair and closed her opalescent eyes, dangling her reading lenses in the warm water. In contrast to Chandra's objections, the archmage seemed more focused in the bath. Her tiny body seemed to absorb the steam and the quiet company, the freedom from distractions that came with the world outside. Freed from her burn-scarred and frayed robes, Esha's entire body seemed lighter, as though she could float in the hot air. Mary often noticed the archmage smiling to herself and tracing droplets of sweat along her bare flesh, even as she offered complex lines of thought. "That assumption may have been in error," she admitted. "There may have been any number of incidents, particularly before my investigation, when it was not an adept who detonated, but rather something she carried."

Chandra grimaced. "Whatever this… effect is, it's gotten much worse than we originally feared." Although the rest of their small group took great comfort in the bath, Chandra did not. The steam seemed to avoid her and, even in the water, she stood upright, never floating or reclining, with barely half her body ever inside the water.

"What could be happening?" Ilse asked quietly. "And why now? Could it be another attack?" The young priestess often seemed just a little distracted during their watery meetings. Although no specific rule limited the use of the private bath to the Sisters of the Lady of Light, the clergy of the Harvest Mother had never requested to do so. So far as anyone knew, Ilse was the first, and the priestess reveled in the opportunity. Frequently drifting towards one the powerful vents shooting ticklish bubbles up along her body.

"That's a good question," Chandra replied. The spy turned to look at Esha. "When did this start?"

The tiny Sylva glanced up at the domed ceiling. "As best as I am able to recall," she mused, "the first incident was reported within a week of the departure of Prince Rogan and his party."

Chandra nodded. "And they've been getting steadily worse ever since."

"*Could* it be another attack?" Kyla asked. "Could it be Vara again or someone like Anninihus?"

Esha shrugged. "Although a distinct possibility, I rather doubt that is the case. Any attack that not only took this long to build up to sufficiently-dangerous levels while causing only minor damage in the process, but also gave us such obvious warnings of its presence, would not be of much use in an offensive capacity. There are any number of far more effective methods of attack.

"I have also sensed no malicious spells targeting anyone or anything in the vicinity of the city since the dispersal of Vara's Storm." Esha glanced back down and looked straight at Kyla. "I have, however, detected a steadily-building force of natural magic."

Chandra and Ilse followed the archmage's look. "Almost like something natural is growing?" the priestess asked without looking away from Kyla.

The princess looked from Chandra to Ilse to Esha and back, none shifting their gaze away. "What?" she demanded.

"Have you used any of your magic since the prince left, your Highness?" Ilse asked carefully.

"I don't think so," Kyla shrugged.

"Are you sure?"

The princess crossed her arms under her swelling breasts and narrowed her pearlescent eyes at the spy. "What are you accusing me of?" Kyla was already made irritable by her bouts of morning sickness and the constant urge to drink water, to say nothing of the inevitable side effect of taking in so many fluids, and they were all drawing dangerously near to invoking the fiery princess' wrath.

Mary floated up beside Kyla and place delicate hands on her princess's shoulders. "Your Highness," she said soothingly. The handmaiden was growing apt at diffusing Kyla's increasing number of outbursts. Mary's voice worked to ease the princess's mood and cool the heat that Kyla was directing toward her advisors. "Perhaps we should take a break?" the handmaiden suggested.

There were times, however, when Kyla was unwilling to let go of a good dose of anger. "I don't want a break," she said with a low growl. "I want to know what they're accusing me of!"

Several eyes in the group, to say nothing of the scattering of priestesses also using the private bath, were drawn to Esha and the smoke now coming out of the Sylva's ears. Esha looked down at her hands and noticed a number of blue sparks leaping between her fingers. "Oh, dear," she noted calmly.

Ilse noticed this. "Princess, you really need to calm down." Even in the face of such danger, the priestess said in a tone Mary had heard when soothing someone lost to hysterics.

"I will not calm down!" Kyla exploded.

And then Esha exploded.

The burst was thankfully contained. A blast of heat pushed at Kyla's advisors. A wave rushed away from where Esha had been relaxing in her floating chair. The chair itself was reduced to splinters and small flakes of the strange spongy material Remm had used in its construction. The angry wave of mystical energy Esha's detonation released pushed outwards, forcing a sudden gush of steam up and through the oculus.

The tiny archmage herself had been rocketed across the bath and into the domed marble wall, into which she was suddenly imbedded. "Ouch," the little Sylva said calmly through gritted teeth and clenched eyes.

Mary and Ilse rose from where they had leapt upon Kyla, hoping to shield their princess from whatever was happening to Esha. The bath was enveloped in a crushing silence. The vents had paused in their cheery bubble-making. The steam had fled up and out. The priestesses were huddling with one another along the outer wall. Chandra emerged from where she had finally submerged into the warm water.

Medaka, an Elder Sister of the temple, ran in. She was dressed as always in bright purple with a red sash. Her face was pale and she trembled in fear. Ilse pointed to where Esha had been imbedded in the far wall.

The mature priestess hurried over and pried the tiny Sylva free, her hands running over Esha's body with a soft, golden glow, her magic working to heal the damage and soothe the pain.

Chandra emerged from the pool, grabbing a nearby towel to wrap around herself. She moved carefully up to where Medaka was propping Esha into a sitting position.

"Are you all right?" the spy asked, waving away some of the smoke that clung to the Sylva.

Esha blinked up at the spy. "WHAT?" she yelled.

Kyla, Mary, and Ilse swam up to Esha, climbing onto the marble edge and hurrying to their friend. "Oh, Goddess!" the princess exclaimed. "Esha, are you all right?"

Esha nodded and waved off Medaka, who was still trying to mystically heal her. "Certainly," the archmage kept blinking and working her jaw. "I have suffered through many explosions far worse than that." The moment Medaka released her, Esha fell back to the floor.

Kyla stretched out her hands to the Sylva's tiny chest. "Here," she said softly, "let me heal you."

Everyone in the bath yelled, "NO!" Every hand present shot forward to prevent the princess from tapping into any magic. Even Esha, dazed and reeling from the explosion, flinched away from Kyla's hands and the thought of another outburst of emotion.

Mary took her princess' hand and helped her rise. "Perhaps we should let someone else tend to the Parden," the handmaiden suggested.

Chandra nodded and helped Medaka lift Esha from the floor. "Why don't you take the princess back to the castle while we get the Sisters to fix Esha?"

Chapter 40

Kyla was lying on her bed, using all her concentration to control her emotions. The princess had been greatly withdrawn since the incident in the private bath, saying little as Mary and Ilse escorted their distraught mistress to her quarters and accepting no visitors, banishing even the persisting Lukas to the outer rooms. Even hours after the incident, Kyla remained very pale and occasionally shook with barely-contained grief.

Queen Nora stood over her daughter, using all her power to help Kyla. Nora's hands moved a hair's breadth above Kyla's body, emitting a soft golden glow that seemed to seep into the princess. The queen's aging eyes remained closed in deep concentration. Although dedicating most of her time and effort to holding off the poison that threatened the King's life, Queen Nora joined her daughter in Kyla's quarters immediately after learning of the princess' new condition. Everyone hoped the queen would be able to help Kyla gain at least some control over the emotional outbursts that were apparently the cause of so much damage and so many injuries to the magic users of the Northern Keep.

Princess Karen was lying beside her older sister. The girl had come with the Queen and, without prompting, climbed onto the bed and placed her head on the first daughter's shoulder. The little princess said nothing as her elders worked and worried, she only lay beside her sister, holding hands.

Rashid had arrived only moments after the Queen and Princess Karen. This was the only time the younger Calonar daughter left her sister's side. The princess crossed to Rashid and leaned on her tiptoes to whisper something in the spymaster's ear. He nodded and took Ilse aside, who, after a brief whispered consultation, left. She returned an hour later with Medaka, who joined Queen Nora in the mystical examination of Kyla. The two older priestesses whispered strange words to each other, things Mary could not understand. Such was the bizarre nature of their consultation that the handmaiden could not even be certain they spoke in Velish, the common tongue.

"Why did you bring Medaka?" Mary whispered to Ilse. The two women stood to the side, powerless to help their princess. In answer, Ilse glanced at Rashid.

The spymaster noticed their gaze. "She's had some… experience," he said in a tone that clearly said he would say no more.

Mary glanced at Princess Karen. "Does her Highness know…?"

Rashid just shrugged.

Medaka and the Queen continued their strange discussion and their mystical investigation of Kyla. Time passed and little seemed achieved. Finally, Mary's concern for her princess overrode the patience she was trying to maintain. "Do you know what's wrong, your Majesty?"

Nora let her hands fall to her sides and sighed. "No," she quietly replied. "I can detect nothing out of the ordinary." The queen opened her eyes and looked around for a place to sit. Mary moved one of the chairs near the balcony over to the bed.

Kyla sat up and swung her legs over the edge of her bed. Karen clambered over and sat beside her big sister, again resting her little head on Kyla's shoulder. "There must be something, Mother," the first daughter insisted.

"I agree, *Kasaya*. But I sense nothing strange about you or the child."

Mary sat down beside her princess, putting a small arm across Kyla's shoulders in support. "Then what do we do, your Majesty?" the handmaiden asked.

"I don't know." Queen Nora sat down in the large chair. Seated so near to one another, Mary marveled again at how the women of House Calonar resembled one another. Although Nora's blond hair was heavily streaked with gray and her blue eyes were deeply wrinkled, still there could be no mistaking from whom Kyla and Karen had received their beauty. Kyla, even pregnant, radiated grace, while her little sister, only at the beginning edges of womanhood, showed signs of equal glory. Indeed, seeing the three so close together, Nora, Kyla, and Karen greatly appeared to be the same person, but in different stages of life. The only discernable difference was not in the features, no matter how obvious the Queen's Human eyes were against her daughters' Halvan ones. The real difference was behind those eyes. Kyla shared her mother's great magic, her affinity for the divine. Karen, though, had wisdom in her pearlescent eyes, and a gaze that, like her mother's saw beyond the surface and the present.

"You delivered three children," Rashid pointed out to his queen. "Did you ever go through anything like this?"

Queen Nora shook her head. "There are some significant differences between my pregnancies and Kyla's."

Rashid sat down in a chair in the far corner of the room and steepled his hands in front of his mouth. "For example?"

"I'm a Human woman," Nora pointed out. "Both my parents were Human. I delivered Halvan children by a Halvan father. Kyla is a Halvan woman and will deliver a Halvan child by a Human father."

"Halvan mother instead of Halvan father," Rashid mused. "Son instead of daughters." The spymaster leaned back and steepled his fingers in front of his face.

"The Queen did deliver a son," Ilse pointed out, very quietly.

All eyes went briefly to the young priestess, who blushed. Discussion of Kyle Calonar was not forbidden in any formal way. However, the topic of the Queen's first child had, in the years after his tragic death, become an informal taboo.

"Indeed," the queen said with the shadow of sadness in her voice.

"Majesty," Rashid began, his voice as soft and gentle as silk. "I must ask…"

Queen Nora nodded. "There were no incidents like this when I was pregnant with Kyle," she answered a question to which none wished give voice. "Other than the extra time a Halvan pregnancy takes, there was nothing unusual about it." She thought a moment. "But then," she used, turning to Kyla "Your brother was not an adept."

Seeing Kyla beginning to search for some water, Mary rose to get the water herself. "Could her Highness's magic be causing the problem?" the handmaiden asked.

Medaka shook her head. "I doubt it. Kyla has the same amount of magic as the Queen, lacking only the Truthsight."

"What about Daddy?" Kyla suggested. "Did his mother have anything like this happen?"

Nora shook her head. "His mother was Human, and if she had any of these side effects, he never said anything about it. Nor did Alexia, who midwifed."

"What about the Matriarch?" Medaka asked. "She mothered a child, and carried the blood of House Calonar, the same as Kyla. Were their complications in her pregnancy?"

The queen shrugged. "She never spoke of any. Though," Nora sighed, "she spoke little of her son."

The door opened without a knock, and Esha entered. "You may be overestimating the effect the princess' gravid state is having on her powers," the archmage said. The tiny Sylva had changed into her scorched and frayed robes and had a large bruise on the side of her head but spoke clearly, leaning only slightly on her staff.

"How are you feeling?" Rashid asked.

"Much as one would expect after detonating and being hurled with great force into a marble wall." This she said with a smile.

Kyla stood and took a few hesitant steps toward Esha but stood helplessly with a stricken expression on her beautiful face. "Esha… I…" Words failed the princess. Karen stood and took her sister's hand.

The archmage laughed happily. "I suffered no permanent damage, your Highness. And when compared with the various explosions I have inflicted upon myself over the years, this latest incident hardly seems worth any particular attention." Esha's tone was eager, as though excited at having enjoyed a great new experience.

"But I'm so sorry—"

Esha waved the apology away. "To be honest, Princess, I should thank you."

Kyla blinked. "Thank me?"

"Indeed." Her bright, opalescent eyes shone with excitement. "After receiving reports from the several individuals that have endured the same effect, I was very curious. Had I not exploded, I would most likely have tried to simulate the effect to satisfy that curiosity. You have saved me a great deal of time and effort, and granted me an invaluable insight that may be the key to discerning a solution."

Kyla glanced down at her little sister, who shrugged. "You're… welcome?" the first daughter of House Calonar said.

Esha laughed again and took a seat near Rashid, setting her staff on the floor.

Rashid leaned over and grinned. "So how was it?" he asked.

"So invigorating," Esha replied with delighted laughed, nearly a giggle. "I was truly energized, as though I could harness so much more of the Winds. Despite the smoke, there was very little heat. I felt only a growing pressure. The explosion itself was really quite pleasant," she continued happily, "since it relieved that pressure." The archmage considered a moment. "I wonder if a means could be found of the same catalytic effect without the detonation…The impact against the wall was unpleasant, however."

They were all silent for a moment. Rashid then looked away saying, "Moving on, then."

Mary guided her princess to a large upholster chair, helping Kyla to sit and laying a blanket over her legs. As the elder Calonar daughter took up only a portion of the great chair, her little sister sat as well.

"You were saying something about a solution, Esha," Queen Nora pointed out. "What is it?"

The archmage glanced back at the queen, clearly having been lost in her memory her most recent explosion. "Sorry?"

"The solution, Esha," Rashid said while hiding a grin. "You have a solution?"

"Esha was saying that Kyla's pregnancy may not be the cause of her condition," Karen said. This was the first thing the little princess had said since her arrival. Mary, who was offering Kyla a glass of water, blinked at the younger daughter of Calonar. "What?" Karen asked.

"Nothing."

"Ah yes," Esha sighed happily. "I was considering the situation as the clerics tended my wounds." The tiny archmage glanced up at the ceiling as he struggled to focus his brilliant mind. "I believe we may be focusing too much of our attention on the Princess."

Rashid shook his head. "The explosions didn't start until she got pregnant."

"Not to mention the massive coincidence it would be if she just happened to get pregnant at the same time her magic started sparking," Rainer added, entering the room.

"Sparking?" Ilse asked.

"What else should we call it?"

"The term will suffice until a more accurate one can be assigned," Esha agreed. "I agree that the probability of a coincidental pregnancy is infinitesimal. However, in our zealous investigation of the Princess, we have neglected one other suspect."

All eyes turned to Kyla's abdomen. The expectant mother put a protective hand over her expanding stomach.

Medaka knelt and stared with a cocked head at Kyla's middle. "Hm," she pondered. "Unusual," she glanced at Queen Nora. "But not unheard of."

Mary and Ilse stood protectively at Kyla's shoulders. "What are you talking about?" Mary demanded.

"Normally," Esha explained, "an adept manifests her power with maturity. *Sy'lva* adepts manifest upon *shey'iel'enim'or*, their capability to initiate fertility. Human females manifest with their first bleeding. One would assume Halvan females would be similar."

"Kyla first manifested at that time," Queen Nora confirmed.

"My age," Karen agreed. The little princess held up her hands and started wiggling her fingers. She then looked up and shrugged.

"Khepric females manifest upon their first molting," Esha continued. "Historical records are silent about the possibility of Uldra females manifesting."

"The Queen says this will be a boy," Ilse pointed out.

"And Halvan," Mary added.

"Which complicates matters," Medaka agreed, walking to the balcony window.

"Indeed," Esha agreed. "And what further complicates matters is the nature of these outbursts."

"What do you mean?" Rashid asked.

The archmage leaned back in her chair. "I could not identify the nature of the mystical assault. From what school of magic it derived."

"And that tells us what?" Rainer asked.

"I have mastered all the doctrinal schools," Esha pointed out. "I can identify, quite easily, from which school a manifestation derives. Since I could not identify the outburst, it must have derived from one of the forbidden schools."

"Forbidden schools?" Mary asked.

"Time and Fate. The few acolytes of Time Magic were all killed in the Disaster at Nassinalia; and the Arcane Guild has maintained the *Sy'lva'n* taboo against it. As for Fate…"

Mary and Ilse looked at each other and shrugged. They looked to the Queen who explained. "Fate Magic is too powerful, girls, too uncontrollable. Only two men in history have gained any measure of control over it."

"Cyras Darkholm and Fak'Har," Esha added. "The Trickster and the Shadow."

"How can this be?" Kyla gasped, her hands clutching at her abdomen. "It's not possible!"

"Please remain calm, your Highness," Medaka said. "If your child is tapping into unknown magics, then he will sense your emotions and respond."

"Indeed," Esha agreed. "If we were to track the various incidents, I believe a pattern would emerge of the Princess experiencing a sharp spike in emotion. The baby, his mind unformed and unable to distinguish a mere annoyance with a genuine threat, responds instinctively, protectively."

"He's protecting her?" Mary asked, her eyes wide and her mouth open in shock.

Kyla looked down and caressed her abdomen. "Are you protecting your mommy?" she whispered, unshed tears shining in her pearlescent eyes.

A sparkling mist formed in the bedchamber. Twinkling bits of gold and silver and colors unimagined appeared and solidified. The points of love danced in the air, swirling gently around Kyla and the gathering of women around her. Mary reached out to one of the gleeful sparks and the light brightened then solidified, revealing a perfect, tiny female with butterfly wings and a shift of green mist.

"*Fael,*" Esha gasped. "The Hidden Ones."

"The Children of Otherworld," Medaka said, equally shocked at the sight. One of the tiny Fael flew to the Elder Sister's face, lighting a tiny foot on the very tip of her nose and blowing the priestess a kiss.

"What?" Rainer said.

"How?" Rashid added.

"Spirits of light," Queen Nora said, holding out a hand onto which a dozen Fael landed. They chimed a song to her sounding like a chorus of tiny, tinkling bells. "Guardians. They respond to protective love."

Lukas entered the room suddenly, his weapon drawn and his eyes hunting. "What?" he started.

The Fael's song changed, then. It grew agitated, even angry. The tiny, kaleidoscope-winged females rose in the air and began swarming around Lukas. The bodyguard took a step back and raised his sword.

"No!" Mary snapped. "Don't hurt them!"

"They're friendly!" Ilse added.

"They don't look friendly to me!" Lukas snapped. The Fael were swirling around him, pushing him out of the room. He swung his shortsword, slashing at the creatures, but they nimbly dodge the metal.

Kyla put her hands on her abdomen. "It's ok," Mary heard her whisper. "It's ok, we're safe. I'm safe."

Karen looked at the swarming Fael and back to her sister's abdomen. She placed a hand on Kyla's and closed her pearlescent eyes. "Send them back," she said in a voice that belied her youth.

The Fael vanished. Their song lingered a few moments, but also faded back to Otherworld.

They were silent for a time. The men looked at each other and the women all looked to Kyla and Karen. Lukas was breathing heavy, his sword still in a shaking hand. "What...?" he demanded.

Captain Rainer approached him slowly, his hands raised and his voice calm. "It's ok, son," the veteran said. He reached the trembling bodyguard and put a soft hand on the younger soldier's sword-arm. "It's over now. Put it away."

Lukas swallowed and nodded. "Sorry, sir," he said. The bodyguard then straightened and bowed to Kyla. "Forgive me, your Highness."

"It's alright, Lukas," the princess said. "Why don't you take the rest of the day?"

"No, ma'am. I'll get back to my duties." the Archaeknight-in-training turned on a heel and resumed his post outside Kyla's door.

Rashid took a deep breath. "That could have gone very badly," he muttered.

"I don't think so," Medaka argued. "The Fael were only responding to a potential threat, an armed man near the mother. So long as Kyla remained calm, the Fael were placid."

Esha nodded. "The same with the detonations," she mused. "Any incident can be prevented so long as the Princess remains at peace."

Captain Rainer snorted. "So we only have to worry about a pregnant girl getting emotional. No problem." He flinched, though, with a room full of leveled female eyes boring into him. "I'll be good."

"The point remains," Queen Nora insisted. "If Esha and Medaka are correct, then the baby will react any time it senses Kyla's distress."

"So what do I do?" the princess asked, tears in her eyes.

"I believe the Princess may be able to exert control over this phenomenon," Esha suggested.

"How?" Rashid asked.

The archmage looked directly at the spymaster. "You will recall a similar situation, in which an expectant mother was possessed of a powerful magic that was independent of her wishes, and yet she could exert a measure of control for the duration of the pregnancy."

Rashid leaned back in his chair and nodded. "But Aebreanna..."

Esha held up a hand. "I believe the two situations are similar enough for a plan of action."

"Which is what?" Kyla asked in growing exasperation. As the conversation involved her and her unborn son, without either of their participation or input, the princess was growing increasingly agitated.

"During Aebreanna's pregnancy," Queen Nora said, "she studied the Songs of the Lady of Light."

Kyla nodded. "That's when she decided to join the Sisterhood." She looked to Esha. "But I already know all the Songs."

"Perhaps not all," Medaka murmured. "Some secrets remain shrouded in our archives."

"But with everything else…" the princess said, her eyes going a little wild, "How can I…?" There was a small explosion outside. Rainer went to the window and looked down.

"Well?" Rashid asked.

"Wizard," the captain said.

"Is she alright?" Esha asked.

The aging veteran shrugged. "They're still trying to fish her out of the moat."

Kyla moaned and put her face in her hands.

The queen glanced up at where Mary was standing behind her daughter's chair. "I seem to recall that our House recently gained a new archivist."

Mary knelt by her princess. "You're not alone," she took Kyla's hand.

Ilse knelt on the opposite side. "We can help."

Karen put a hand on her big sister's face and smiled at her. Kyla looked at her little sister and could not help but return the smile.

"I can help with the archives," Medaka offered. "At least, I can point you towards the areas we haven't explored in a while."

Rainer cleared his throat. "I think we can step up a little too," he added. The soldier glanced at Rashid, who nodded.

"I will assign several students to researching our Tower records, as well," Esha added. "This may be the first manifestation of either Time or Fate magic in generations. I recall some mention of other instances, long ago. We shall investigate."

"And I'll get a couple of agents to go through the Calonar family records we have here in the castle," Rashid added. "All of this data can be directed through the family's archivist." This, he said looked at Mary. The handmaiden glanced at him and nodded.

Queen Nora stood and walked to her daughters. She drew Kyla and Karen into an embrace. "The most important thing," she said, "is to remember that we are never alone."

IV

The Endless Sands

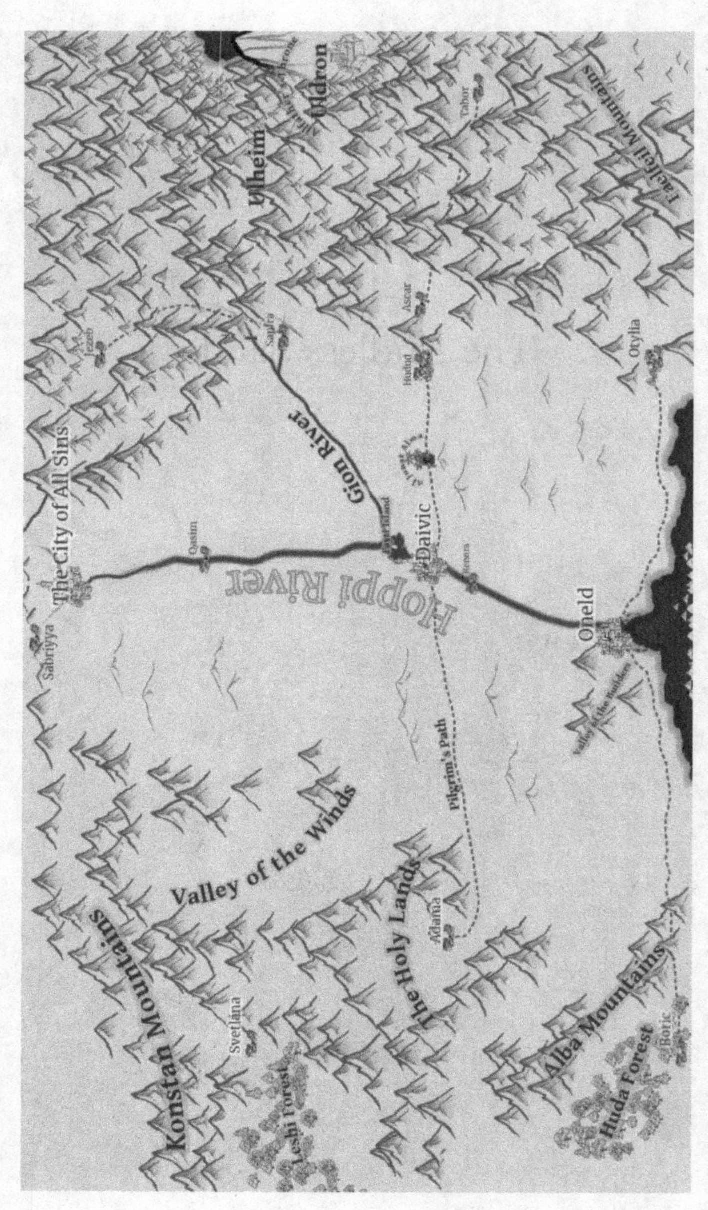

Faciethil Mountains
Ulheim
Uldron
The City of All Sins
Gion River
Hoppi River
Daivic
Oneld
Qasim
Sabriyya
Konstan Mountains
Valley of the Winds
The Holy Lands
Alba Mountains
Hinda Forest
Leshi Forest
Svetlana
Pilgrim's Path
Orylla
Boric

Chapter 41

In a scream of arcane fire, Tomas and his friends arrived in Ulheim's western foothills. They were standing with their horses in the center of the dirt road connecting the western Uldra clans to the Human communities of the Endless Sands. Despite his prior experience with arcane movement under the tender mercies of Esha, Tomas felt a wave of nausea at the sudden alteration of the world around him. In one moment, the squire and his friends were standing in the courtyard of the Arcane Guild headquarters, surrounded by the vigilant Order of the Black Sun, and in the next, the young man was kneeling on a road, his stomach heaving.

"Bastards," Rogan growled as he leaned against Stick. The knight was wiping the sweat from his brow with the back of his hand. "They didn't even try to make the trip easy on us."

Aebreanna showed little sign of discomfort at their abrupt departure from the Free City, instead looking about with calm detachment as she absently made sure her long mane of honey blonde still covered the right side of her face. "Did you really maintain any expectation of courtesy from people who would callously order the destruction of a town just to avoid some nebulous future conflict?" she asked.

Rogan grunted.

Beraht spat a small glob of blood. "Looking for courtesy from wizards is like looking for courage from Sylvai," he rumbled. The Uldra was making a great show of indifference to his recent injuries. Despite this, his breathing was hard and his ugly face was tight in unexpressed pain. The magical relocation was hard physically, feeling as though one was being jerked without warning from one place to another. As relatively unharmed as Tomas was physically, the translocation still made him sore. What Beraht must be suffering brought a tear of sympathy to his young eye.

The knight straightened and helped his squire to stand. "Let's just get to town before dark. It would be nice to get a decent night's sleep for once." Rogan made a point of neither helping Beraht, nor giving any indication he noticed the Uldra's pain. Tomas spotted his knight, though, glancing at their mountainous friend with concern.

"I haven't been to Hudud in years," Beraht said. "They always keep a good stock of Uldra spirits at their inn."

Rogan looked down the road at the random collection of flat-roofed brick buildings that Tomas assumed was the town in question. "Well, I've got bad news for you," the knight said. "It's going to be even longer before you get to see the tavern."

Beraht actually grew pale. "What do you mean?"

Rogan shook his head. "We're looking for information, supplies, and some rest, not a fight."

"Oh, come on!" the Uldra insisted. "What's the point in visiting a town if you're not going to start a fight?"

"Tomas will come with me, Beraht. I need you buy us supplies and clothes, while Aebreanna meets with the local agent. And see if you can find replacement pack horses."

"I'm on shopping detail!" he roared. The Uldra could not help but grab his side when a spark of pain shot through him. Beraht winced but tried to pretend as though he was not hurting.

"That's right," Rogan said, still ignoring his friend's injuries every bit as much as the Uldra himself was trying to do. "Every merchant in the world knows better than to try to cheat an Uldra. Now go."

Without another complaint, suspicious in itself, Beraht mounted his horse and started toward the town marketplace.

"Oh, and Beraht?" Rogan called after his friend.

"What?" he replied sourly.

"We need supplies. And when I say supplies, I mean food, new clothes, things like that. Not beer."

"But I need *something* to pass the miles."

"Beraht, get food, get supplies. Leave the beer."

Grumbling to himself, the Uldra continued toward the market.

Aebreanna mounted her white pony and took up the reins. "I will need at least an hour to make a full report and have it forwarded to Rashid," she told Rogan.

The knight grunted. "Me and Tomas will head to the local bazaar. We need to replace our equipment, and we'll try to get a feel for the road ahead. We'll get rooms after, so meet us at the inn."

"I will seek whatever information the local agent has uncovered."

"Try not to get distracted while you're uncovering things."

Aebreanna laughed and led her pony towards an unassuming corner of the town. Rogan turned to his apprentice. "Come on, kid, let's go shopping."

Tomas and Rogan were disappointed by the available gear. "Where's the Ulheim steel?" the knight demanded of the town's blacksmith.

"Use up." The blacksmith's accent was heavy and his words broken. "Steel no more. Uldra stop send."

Knight and squire had arrived to find the town's bazaar nearly empty. Shops were open, but lacked merchandise. Shelves and tables were bare. Merchants busied themselves with housekeeping, when they were present at all; many shops and stands stood empty. Food vendors offered only local goods: dates, goat and poultry, some vegetables. Cloth-sellers had only local cotton. Leather was scarce. Any goods from beyond Hudud were entirely missing. Tomas had found a pair of scabbards that imperfectly fit Talon and Steelheart, but were a far improvement from the makeshift sling Rogan had been using and the squire's near-destroyed sheath. Any hope of replacing their destroyed armor, however, was quickly fading.

When they had arrived at the forge, they found the smith scavenging old horseshoes for iron. A pile of cookware lay nearby, ready for melting. There were no weapons or armor of any kind. Instead, the metalworker had only a small collection of pots and pans, some small tools, and a handful of patched horseshoes. Even the smith's hammer looked chipped and in desperate need of replacing.

Rogan began speaking to the blacksmith in a rolling language. His words seemed to blur together into a string of extended vowel sounds Tomas could not distinguish from each other. The town's blacksmith replied, his town sorrowful. "The Uldra have stopped trading," the knight translated. "There hasn't been a caravan in or out of Ulheim since last summer." He spoke again, asking questions in that strange tongue.

The blacksmith answered in his native language and gestured around the near-abandoned market. "With no more Uldra goods," Rogan translated, "merchants from Daivic and the City of All Sins have stopped coming." The blacksmith gestured helplessly. "They're getting desperate," Rogan continued to translate, but paused at a certain word. "People want to move away, but Parano's mercenaries won't allow it." The translation continued. "The soldiers loyal to House Parano have all been reassigned and replaced by foreign mercenaries. The soldiers were escorted by recruiters who also took all the able men. They were accompanied by a priest-inquisitors from Tordenia. The mercenaries claim to be taking orders from Daivic, but the people fear the real commands come from the Western Empire."

The blacksmith again gestured to the empty stores. "Even though the inquisitors have forbidden anyone to leave the town, the herders have been moving their flocks at night, a few at a time. Anyone with money enough has smuggled their way south to Otylia. Only the poor are left; families are starting to starve."

Rogan demanded something of the blacksmith, his tone angry. The blacksmith huffed and pointed to the west, matching the knight's angry tone. "House Parano does nothing to help them," the knight translated.

The blacksmith pointed to a building at the far end of the empty bazaar. It was blackened, the wood burned away and the brick charred. The man spoke solemn, fearful words.

"What is it?" Tomas asked.

"Tax collectors," Rogan nearly spat. He nodded to the burned building. "That family didn't have anything to pay, so the tax collectors burned their shop." The knight asked the blacksmith something, which brought a choked sob from the man, whose answer was filled with sorrow. Rogan shook his head. "His son was taken by the recruiters."

The blacksmith looked around, then leaned in, speaking quietly. Although Tomas could not understand the words, the squire did recognize "Calonar." Rogan thought a moment, then nodded. The man spoke then to Rogan, softly and with frequent glances towards the tallest building in the town, from the top of which flew the flag of House Parano: a field of green with a white strip below and a scarlet crescent moon above.

The blacksmith went into the building behind his empty, open-air forge, and returned with a large bundle of studded leather. He handed this to Rogan, who accepted with a short bow.

Nothing more was said, and Rogan led his squire away, handing Tomas the bundle. "Well?" he asked his knight.

"A gift," Rogan said. He led Tomas back to where they had tied the horses. "House Parano was never all that popular, especially out here. Now, with Tordenian inquisitors taking all the young men and tax collectors taking everything of value…" the knight shrugged. "The people used to secretly support the Shamashi, hoping the Bedouins would one day defeat Parano. Now, the desert-people have retreated west of the Hoppi River and have stopped fighting. He implied that there's a hope House Calonar will help them." He then nodded to the bundle in Tomas' arms. "It's all he had."

Tomas looked closely at the gift. The leather felt strange in his hands, and was covered in iron studs. "This doesn't feel like normal leather," the squire noted.

"Goat," the knight grunted.

They reached the waiting horses, and Tomas stored the new studded vests in his saddlebags, handing Rogan one of the new scabbards. "What was that language?" the squire asked.

Rogan pulled Talon from its improvised sling and sheathed the longsword in the new, ill-fitting scabbard. "Lugha, the language of the Shamashi."

Tomas pulled Steelheart from its own nearly-useless sheath and settled his sword in its temporary home. The two men then freed their mounts from the hitching post and, remaining dismounted, walked Stick and Urge down a side street. "I thought everyone spoke Velish," the squire said.

"It's the official language, the one House Parano uses," Rogan replied. He led them away from the empty market, to the western edge of town. "Most people know at least some Velish, but it's not really used outside Daivic, except along the borders for trade." The knight nodded to the western horizon. The vast desert that made up central Lanasia spread away from Ulheim's foothills. "This land belonged to the Shamashi long before House Parano showed up. The people still speak the desert tongue, and most of them still honor the Bedouins."

The squire looked at his knight closely. "Is it my imagination," he asked, "or are you taking this a little personally?"

Rogan sighed and rubbed his eyes. "Maybe," he conceded. "The time I spent out here, I got to know the Shamashi. They're… they've suffered a lot from the Paranos."

Tomas glanced around. The people seemed fearful, not doubt the memory of Parano's recruiters fresh in their minds. "Are they Shamashi?" he asked.

Rogan shook his head. "Descendants of the eastern settlers from the first century. There was some intermarriage for a while, but House Parano put a stop to it when they took power after the Xeshlin Invasion."

He stopped then, and looked around, ensuring privacy. "Kid," he said softly. "The blacksmith especially warned us about the mercenaries. When the recruiters came through and took the Parano soldiers and most of the young men, they left behind a small detachment of mercenaries to keep order."

"So," the squire said, "what do we do?"

"We meet with Aebreanna and Beraht at the inn and get on with our mission."

Despite the growing struggles of the town, Hudud's inn was a well-maintained and clean place at the western edge of the town. The road leading out of Ulheim and into the Endless Sands stretched out from the inn, through the low foothills, and vanishing into the shimmering dunes beyond. The building itself stood somewhat apart from the town-proper, as though its purpose in hosting foreigners made the community shrink away. The common room was mostly open-air, with most of its tables and benches on a large porch surrounding the front half of the building. Among these seats were a gathering of Parano mercenaries.

Rogan saw this and swore. The knight paused and squared his shoulders. "Keep your head on straight," he muttered to Tomas.

The squire nodded.

"Keep to yourself," he continued, walking forward at a steady, but unhurried pace. "Don't talk unless I tell you to, don't look anyone in the eye, and don't put your hand on your sword."

"They don't look local," Tomas noted.

Rogan shook his head. "Parano doesn't hire local talent. Too big a risk. His mercenaries come mostly from the east." He led his squire to the hitching post and tied up Stick.

"We're still going in?" Tomas asked softly, tying Urge.

The knight thought, looking around the area. Finally, he nodded. "Let's at least try to get out of sight."

He led his squire to the short steps that led into the inn. "Just remember, if you don't look that tough, most of these guys won't bother with you. Don't make eye contact, and for God's sake, don't call me Rogan while we're in there."

"Why not?"

Rogan rubbed the back of his neck in embarrassment. "When I was here, before joining House Calonar, I got… involved with one of the strongest Shamashi tribes. I fought with them for a while and I… helped them. I built a reputation out here, and that's like waving a flag at a bull. The warriors in the Endless Sands are always looking for a chance to build their own reputation. Best way to do that is take down someone well-known. If anyone in there realizes who I am, they'll want to pick a fight, and the last thing I want is get in a bar fight. It's just too damn cliché."

"They'll start a fight just for the chance to beat up the legendary Prince Rogan Eigenhard?" Tomas asked jokingly.

"Look, smartass, just do what I say and let's try not to cause a scene. I'll be real happy if we can make it out of this town without incident."

Before the knight could explain further, his path was blocked by a man who was something akin to an ambulatory mound of upturned earth. Rogan looked into the face of this mass of muscle and flesh. "Excuse me, I didn't mean to run into you," the knight said humbly.

As Rogan tried to move around him, the overly-large man reached out a hand that could quite possibly have strangled an ox and pushed the knight back. "Just a second," he rumbled.

Rogan took a step back and tried to be reasonable. "Look, I don't want any trouble. If I did anything to upset you, I apologize."

"So much for not getting into a fight," Thomas said grimly, eying the three other men who had moved up to flanking positions behind the behemoth. "We didn't even make it into the bar."

"Shut up," the knight hissed.

The mountain spoke again. "You look like a man I know."

"I don't think that's possible," Rogan assured him. "I don't lift weights much."

"I was serving as a mercenary for Amuna up at the City of All Sins four years ago," the fighter told his friends. "Prince Rogan of House Calonar came through and broke up a black-market ring that had been set up selling slaves. It didn't matter if you were one of the merchants or just the muscle; he got all of us thrown in the dungeons!"

"That sounds like a horrible thing to happen to anybody," Rogan said, putting his hands up and trying to back away. "I hope you meet up with that prince someday."

The huge man grabbed the knight by the front of his tunic and pulled him in close saying, "You think I'd forget your face Eigenhard?"

"Well I was kind of hoping," he said lamely.

"So," Thomas said, "fight now?"

"Kill 'em Bok!" one of the very drunk mercenaries cried out.

As the knight threw his squire a dirty look, the huge creature started shaking Rogan. "I just got out of the dungeons last month and here you are Eigenhard!"

"And I know you're ready to lead a law-abiding life now that you're out."

"Do you know the type of rats in that place!?! They were as big as dogs!"

"At least you ate well!"

In response the somewhat swollen gentleman tossed Rogan like a doll into the street. Thomas immediately rushed to his knight's side, helping him to his feet.

"Well Eigenhard?" Bok roared, attracting an even larger crowd than had already gathered. "Are you man enough to fight?"

Without a word, Rogan turned to leave.

The belligerent mound of man took Rogan's retreat as a sign of weakness and decided to press his advantage, shadowing the knight's movements. "Well," he roared to the crowd, "look at this. The great Prince Rogan Eigenhard of House Calonar. Feared enemy of evildoers everywhere. Hero of the people. Defender of the weak. I never thought I'd see the day that such a great man would show what he really is: a sniveling coward riding a mangy nag!"

As the overly muscled mercenary went around behind the warhorse, all the better to continue harassing Rogan, Stick suddenly and without warning kicked out a rear leg, landing his attack firmly in Bok's chest and sending the huge man sprawling into the dirt of the street. Unfortunately, none of the onlookers or even Bok himself had been paying attention to Stick; thus, when Bok managed to pick himself up, the first view he had was of Rogan with his leg back, the knight having instinctively dropped into a fighting stance. Bok naturally assumed the worst.

Rogan looked at his innocent-appearing horse. "Dammit St—" his sentence was cut off as the monstrous Bok hurled himself at the knight. Seeing Tomas move to help his mentor, several of Bok's associates jumped the squire.

Kicking his knee into Bok's gut, desperately trying to get the bigger man away from him, Rogan furiously yelled, "Great! This is just great!" As Bok doubled over in pain, the knight jabbed his thumbs into the giant's eyes, temporarily blinding him. "All I wanted was to get through one town without getting into a fight!"

Ducking an awkward punch by one of his assailants, Tomas countered with several rapid jabs to the man's stomach, sending the attacker to the ground. "At least we didn't get into a bar fight!"

Rogan kicked one man charging him and, using the momentum, continued the kick into Bok's head, insuring he was out of the fight. "Oh yeah, this is much better!"

As another mercenary leapt at him, the knight used the man's forward motion to send him tumbling into the street. "Instead of getting into a bar fight, we've gotten into an 'in front of the bar fight!' This is much better!"

Tomas was grabbed from behind, his arms pinned to his back. Another mercenary was moving forward, ready to take advantage, but the man holding the squire's shoulders was forced away by a powerful kick. Tomas jabbed a thumb into the eye of the mercenary in front of him before sparing a glance behind. The man who had grabbed him was doubled over on the street, a fountain of blood pouring from his mouth. Tomas glanced at Urge, but his irascible warhorse was just glancing around innocuously.

The battle continued for a few more minutes, with Rogan and Tomas incapacitating a few more mercenaries with the occasional assistance from Stick and Urge. Finally, after the fourth attacker lay unconscious at the knight's feet, Rogan showed what looked like utter terror.

Knocking out another mercenary, Tomas looked at his knight. "What's wrong?" he called.

Ducking what had to be one of the clumsiest kicks Tomas had ever seen, Rogan called out, "This fight just got a lot worse!"

Distracted as he was, the squire did not notice the mercenary until he already had Tomas in one hell of a headlock. "What do you mean?" he said with some effort.

Unable to speak because of a mercenary punching him in the face, the knight just pointed up the street. Tomas shoved his elbow into his attacker's middle and then flipped the man over his shoulder, looking where Rogan had pointed. Coming down the road at a full gallop, his face showing what looked to be almost religious hysteria, Beraht charged right at the brawl, roaring in joy at the chance to hurt something.

Rogan and Tomas, now under attack by over a dozen men, shared a mutual look of horror before being swarmed.

Chapter 42

An hour later, the three warriors stood, somewhat unsteadily, in the private office of the town's magistrate. Rogan was nursing a broken nose and what felt to be no less than three cracked ribs. Beraht was obviously suffering from several blows to the head, and his eyes were having trouble focusing; Tomas, leaning against the Uldra, could feel the muscles in his legs informing him he had pulled some things he really should not have, and one of his eyes had blackened and swollen shut. All in all, as Beraht had put it upon their arrest, it had been a pretty good fight.

"I can't believe we're getting kicked out of another town," Rogan finally said, wincing with the effort to draw in enough air to speak.

Beraht laughed, spitting out a tooth. "At least I managed to buy the supplies before you two started that fight."

The knight shook his head and regretted it. "Things would have ended fine if you hadn't said that any man that wouldn't fight you had no need of their codpiece," he accused.

"You were the one insulting their mothers!" Beraht shot back with another tooth.

Tomas, whose head was aching before the argument, held his hands up, trying to hold off any further yelling that would only serve to increase his pain. "Can we at least show some dignity now that the fight is over?" he asked.

Rogan and Beraht both sighed and turned back to their patient observation of the magistrate's desk, waiting for his arrival. "I can't believe we're getting kicked out of another town," the knight said again.

After a few pain-filled minutes, the office door opened, and the magistrate, a tall thin man of middle age, entered, followed closely by a woman wrapped in a long, flowing tunic dyed a deep green. She was very short, and had a veil covering her face. Upon entering the room, Tomas did a double-take, shocked to see it was Aebreanna. The loose, flowing garment gave almost no indication of her body shape and was utterly opaque, a radical shift from the Sylva's normally tight-fitting and revealing clothing. In the same motion with which she removed the veil over her face, Aebreanna also adjusted her flowing mane of honey blonde to ensure it still covered the right side of her face. The Sylva then gave the three males a look saying plainly she was, in no way, pleased with recent events. The three warriors looked down like reprimanded schoolboys, shuffling their feet and wincing at the pain the motion caused them.

The magistrate sat behind his desk, pushing aside stacks of parchment for a clear line of sight. "My name is Qadin," he said in accented, but clear Velish. "The Baroness has already told me your identities, so there is no need for pretense, your Highness."

Rogan glanced at Aebreanna, who nodded, moving to stand by the small window that displayed a view of the mountains, never taking her stern gaze off her troublesome boys. Now silhouetted against the midday's light through the window, Tomas could see through the surprisingly thin material of her flowing tunic. She had baggy-looking trousers over her lower body and a very thin shift with a cord of some kind supporting her breasts. Tomas could even see that the spy had even secreted several of her thin Sylvai blades to carious places on her arms and legs.

The magistrate held up a scroll and smiled ever so slightly. "I received this order from Daivic only last week," he told them, but then grimaced just slightly. "Rather, I received this order marked from Daivic, but relayed through our new inquisitorial… guests. I am ordered by our masters to maintain peaceful trade and relations with the east for as long as possible." Qadin leaned back in his chair. "However, I am also ordered to report any contact with the agents of House Calonar. I must obey, of course." He leaned forward and glanced at a map of the Endless Sands spread before him. "The next envoy from Daivic is expected in two weeks. I will send a dispatch, informing my superiors of your arrival, along with the other pile of official paperwork. That envoy typically takes two weeks to return to Daivic, though I expect they will hurry when informed of Calonar agents within the Endless Sands." The magistrate looked meaningfully at Rogan.

The knight nodded. "We'll be well gone by then."

"The Baroness Aebreanna and I have spoken at length about this," the magistrate said. "She has made some very convincing arguments on your behalf. She has especially promised that your presence in the Endless Sands has no purpose regarding either my town or the Shamashi."

"I can't tell you what we're doing," Rogan said. "But I can promise that we're just passing through."

Qadin nodded, but then he sighed. "There are a great many rumors," he said. "Things are stirring in my home." The magistrate leaned back again and glanced out the window. "Have your spies told you of the western Uldra?"

Rogan shook his head.

"They've vanished. Ascar, the closest village, is empty. All the reports I've seen, which are only a fraction of the truth, of course, all say the same thing: the western Uldra are gone."

"Where?" Beraht asked, too calmly.

Qadin shrugged. "We don't know. The last anyone saw them was before the snows fell. When the passes cleared and our merchants went for trade, they found the villages abandoned. There is nothing now, except empty buildings. No food or supplies, no metals or gems, no tools or weapons, and no people."

Rogan shared a look with Beraht. "Why?" the knight asked.

The Uldra only shrugged. "No reason I can think. And the eastern clans are all in place."

"When I sent an inquiry to Daivic requesting information and instructions, the Inquisition told me, in no uncertain terms, that I would not attempt further investigation, and that there would be no further contact with the Uldra."

"They know something," Tomas mused.

"But they say nothing," the magistrate countered. "When strange events begin," Qadin added, "the agents of House Calonar often follow close behind. I just assumed your arrival was linked."

Rogan shook his head. "We can't be sure. Our mission has nothing to do with the western clans.

The magistrate stood and nodded. "I would wish you well, Prince, but as I do not know, and do not want to know your goals…" he shrugged.

Qadin had his local cleric waiting to treat their minor wounds, an Adamic priest who had objected to the order at first. He was perfectly willing to heal Rogan and Tomas, but the prospect of being in close proximity to non-Humans made the holy man nearly gag. Qadin reprimanded the priest and forced him to comply. Beraht received the barest minimum of healing magic before the priest left to purify himself.

"He will send his own message to Daivic," the magistrate warned after the cleric was gone. "Our Adamic priests are utterly loyal to the Inquisition. Those who were not are gone."

"I understand," Rogan said, rotating his newly-healed shoulder. "Will this be a problem for you?"

Qadin laughed ruefully. "My town is dying. The people will soon begin to starve, the Shamashi are somehow pacified, the Inquisition dominates us, and our Parano fathers do nothing. My problems are becoming as grains of sand in the desert."

The magistrate saw them to the street where their mounts were already saddled and waiting. In addition to their own horses, new pack horses were waiting, loaded with fresh supplies, all compliments of Qadin. As Rogan climbed onto Stick, the magistrate took his hand one last time. "Are you sure you will not at least stay the night?"

The prince shook his head. "Best we leave before anyone else recognizes us," he replied. "We can make a few miles before dark, and we've still got a long way to go."

"Peace be with you, then."

"Peace be with you, your Lordship, and your town." With that, Rogan spurred Stick forward and led the party out of Hudud.

Once they were a good distance down the road, Tomas pulled Urge next to Aebreanna. The Sylva had pulled the veil free and was letting the air flow through her long hair, though she now wore a green, two-piece cap that fixed her mane so that it would not reveal the right side of her face. "So what did you say to convince the magistrate not to throw us in jail?" Tomas asked.

"Never mind," she said with uncharacteristic bluntness. "I really am trying to maintain my philosophy regarding those with whom I am condemned to associate."

"It couldn't have been that bad," the squire insisted.

"Let it go, kid," Rogan called from ahead.

Aebreanna smiled sweetly at the knight. "Fear not, Mighty Prince," she purred. "I have ample time to properly repay you for making me rescue both you and the noble Sir Beraht... again." The last was said without any trace of smile or even emotion.

"I take it that bailing the guys out is a regular occurrence for this team?" Tomas asked.

"Drop it, kid," Roan said bluntly, turning back to face front.

"Oh, come now, Rogan," the spy said innocently. "We can easily speak about this topic while continuing our journey." Turning to Tomas, the Sylva smiled again. "You see, Tomas, Rogan and Beraht may receive all of the blame for their various misadventures, but they also acquire nearly all the credit. People, in fact, do remember that our two great heroes saved Frostfront from an evil cult just as they do, in fact, remember the two warriors getting the Free City banished to Otherworld. What none of the historians mention is my efforts to find an adept powerful enough to bring the city back."

"So why don't you ever set the stories straight?" the squire asked.

"Ordinarily, I could care less what the general public perceives as regards to who the heroes of our various adventures are and which of us basks in the adulation of the masses. As long as the task is successful and we all return home with our lives, I feel my duty was done properly. However," her voice lost all hint of warmth, "every once and a while, I need to remind the boys of just who repeatedly frees them from the dungeons into which they always seem to find themselves thrown."

Beraht scratched his head. "Hey, wait a minute, Aebreanna," he argued. "You only broke us out of three dungeons that I remember."

"Shut up, Beraht," Rogan grunted.

The frosty Sylva turned her gaze, which could probably have cracked a boulder at that point, to the earthy Uldra. "Well," she said with a smile that was not in any way friendly, "your beer-soaked memory notwithstanding, I recall five dungeons. And let us not forget the time you two were captured by the Inquisition. Tortured for three days, was it not?"

"Well, if you count that."

"And the time the Greysoul was going to kill you both, but I distracted him long enough for you to escape. That was when he captured and almost killed me, was it not?"

"Well, we did rescue you," the Uldra replied lamely.

"Yes, you did," she snapped. "You and Rogan attacked the Greysoul's tower, alone, to save me. And I had to use the damned power my father gave me to block his magic long enough for Rogan to stab him!"

"Well, it was team effort."

Aebreanna started counting the incidents on her fingers. "And then there was the time you tied Rashid up and stripped him naked because you thought he might attack us. I cannot count the number of apologies that incident has required."

"Well, you two weren't married yet—"

"And then there was Reydia."

"Well—"

"And the City of All Sins."

"But—"

"And that Vaeyen you just had to wake up."

The listing of Beraht and Rogan's sins took up most of the rest of the afternoon, lasting into the night. At the very least, Tomas learned a great deal about their adventures before he had met them. All in all, it was a very interesting day.

Chapter 43

Morning came. Tomas climbed out of his bedroll just as the sun was rousing herself from shimmering dunes ahead. The young squire had pulled the first watch and so had enjoyed a long, restful sleep. As Tomas stretched, trying to work the sleep from his muscles, he was shocked to find that Aebreanna's lecture still had not ended.

"And really, was it completely necessary to set fire to the ship as a distraction?" the Sylva demanded. "Could you two not have found a better way to get the warlord's attention?" To their credit, both the knight and the warrior were weathering the assault well, although neither showed signs of having slept during the night.

The squire vaguely remembered Aebreanna speaking to the two warriors the night before during his watch but had thought little of it and left them to their conversation. With the unending stress and danger of their passage through Ulheim and Frostfront now past, Tomas was dimly aware that his body was finally relaxing to the point of allowing sleep despite Aebreanna's verbal assault on Beraht and Rogan. To say Tomas was surprised at the tenacity Aebreanna showed at continuing her diatribe throughout the night would be an understatement. "Don't Sylvai need sleep?" he asked.

Turning to Tomas, the squire was surprised to note that as soon her gaze left the two warriors, it almost immediately softened. "No, Tomas, *Sy'lwa'n*, as a general rule, do not need to sleep." Any trace of the obvious irritation Aebreanna felt toward Rogan and Beraht could not be detected in her voice as she answered. "We do, however, require at least a few hours of deep relaxation to rest our minds and bodies, but that can be neglected for a few days, perhaps a week, without ill effect."

The squire rolled up his new blankets and stowed them on the back of his saddle. "Then you can't sleep at all?" he asked.

Aebreanna laughed. "No, we have evolved to the point at which we have little need for shutting down our bodies for so many hours." As she spoke, the Sylva changed the flowing, long-sleeved tunic for another, this one of black.

Tomas flushed. "Well, then when you and your husband are… together. I mean… afterward. What do you do while Rashid is sleeping?"

Again, Aebreanna laughed. "If you have slept with a woman, Tomas, there really is little need or reason to be so uncomfortable in talking about it. After all, sex is a perfectly natural activity every living creature does. You never see a lion blushing while talking to another lion about mating, do you? But to answer your question, while Rashid is sleeping, I just snuggle up to him and relax, enjoying the feeling of being so close to the man I love."

The squire shook his head. "But if you only need an hour or two of relaxation, and Rashid sleeps for six or eight, then you must get really bored." He pulled some new clothes from his bags, loose trousers and a flowing tunic of white.

"Not really. You see, once you Humans get over this preoccupation you seem to have toward avoiding casual physical contact, you will discover just how comforting a good snuggle can be. Given the option, there have been many times I would have been just as happy to snuggle up to Rashid without being physically intimate. I required a few years, but I finally got that idea through his head, and now we frequently have nights where we just lay in each other's arms, taking comfort and pleasure in the close contact of our bodies."

The young man struggled a bit with the strange, flowing garments. "And Rashid doesn't have a problem with you two not...?"

"Being physically intimate at every opportunity?" Aebreanna finished, helping Tomas settle into the new clothes. "Believe me, Tomas, my husband has all the intimacy he can handle without my hurting him."

Beraht laughed. "From what I hear, he gets plenty of hurting from you."

Rogan looked at his friend with such hostility that, for a moment, Tomas thought the knight might draw a weapon. Aebreanna immediately looked back at the two warriors, who had been attempting a discreet exit from the campsite during the conversation between the squire and spy. Unfortunately, Beraht's complete inability to remain silent drew the irritated Sylva's attention back.

"Well," she said with a smile that withered every male creature for miles around. "I certainly hope my love life has not, in any way, made you think less of my husband. After all, you do have such an unblemished reputation, my good Sir Beraht. Especially since you have never been seen in any kind of house of ill repute, such as, for example, one of the innumerable brothels in the City of all Sins. And you certainly would not have been seen frequenting such an institution in the company of the honorable Prince Rogan."

That immediately got Tomas's attention. "Brothels in the City of All Sins?" he asked, throwing a questioning look at his knight.

"Drop it," Rogan growled.

"Oh no," Tomas laughed. "I understand you two have probably been getting yelled at all night, but you can't let something like that be said and just let it go."

The knight looked at this squire with undisguised hostility. "Look, you people know how uncomfortable I am with this whole prince thing, but there is one benefit. I'm in charge, and when I put my foot down, that's it. Discussion over."

"But, Rogan," Tomas said innocently, "you said I should learn as much about House Calonar and its people as possible. You said I should stop listening to what other people say about you and start hearing your side of things. Well, here's your chance. I'm sure Aebreanna wouldn't mind telling me what happened."

"My duty as a mother is, most importantly, seeing to the education of the young," the angelic baroness said with a sweet smile.

"You weren't even there," Rogan replied in a growl that his squire noticed was getting to be a habit.

Aebreanna shrugged. "Word travels fast, and we did have an agent there at the time."

"Figures," the surly knight grunted. "Fine. You win. I'll talk. About four years ago, Rashid got word about a slave ring that was delivering young girls to the brothels in the City of All Sins."

"Rashid was going to send a team to look into it, but Prince Rogan tends to take the degradation of women especially poorly," Aebreanna interrupted.

"I wasn't doing anything special at the time, and yes, it really sticks me when I find out that young girls, and none of them were more than twelve by the way, are being abused by a bunch of scumbags that have nothing better to do than torture children.

"Anyway, Beraht was in town, and I thought I might need some backup so I grabbed him up and headed over to Ironheartshaven, where the slaves were being imported from. Once we fixed things there, we went to the City of All Sins."

Aebreanna put on a mockingly serious expression. "Our magnificent leader is leaving out the rather significant fire he and Sir Beraht caused when they, shall we say, intervened with the lord who was arranging for the kidnapping of local girls."

"Yeah," Beraht said with a deep smile, reveling in the memory of unleashed chaos.

"The two great warriors arrived in the city and started subtly investigating," Aebreanna continued. "In other words, Tomas, they immediately went to the nearest tavern and started a fight."

"Like Hudud?" the squire guessed.

"Oh my, yes, except this particular bar fight erupted into a city-wide riot. From what I was told, an entire district was set on fire, and hundreds of people ended up in chains before the watch could reestablish order. Our two heroes managed to escape capture, of course."

Rogan threw the saddlebags he was preparing to place on Stick to the ground. The warhorse snorted his objection to the mistreatment of his property, but Rogan was beyond caring. "All right, let's just set the record straight, if you don't mind. First of all, it wasn't a tavern. It was a wine shop. Second of all, the only reason we went there was because you told us that the local agent could be contacted there. And as far as the fight, word of our arrival in the city had somehow gotten out, and bounty hunters hired by the Inquisition decided to show up and try to arrest me and Beraht. It was no wonder a riot broke out. The Inquisition isn't exactly popular among the people that live there."

"What about the fire?" Tomas asked. "Come to think of it, why do so many of your stories involve fire?"

In answer, both Aebreanna and Rogan looked at Beraht. "What?" the Uldra demanded. "You said we needed a distraction, so I made a distraction."

"You set fire to an entire district?" the squire asked in shock.

"Of course not, I just set fire to a warehouse."

"That was filled with supplies for the local Arcane Guild!" Rogan yelled.

"That probably made a pretty big explosion," Tomas noted.

"It could be heard all the way across the Hiltia Sea," Beraht said with pride.

Aebreanna looked back at Tomas. "Now do you see what I have to live with?" she asked. "These two are a constant source of destruction and mayhem to anyone with the misfortune of close association and any place that must suffer a visit. One cannot help but wonder how they have managed to live so long."

"Definite proof of Fate," the squire agreed. "Luck could never last so long."

Rogan picked up the saddlebags and, finishing his preparations, mounted his indignant warhorse. "If you two philosophers are finished analyzing my destiny, we do still have a mission."

"Of course, Mighty Knight," Tomas said with a grin, bowing deeply before moving to Urge.

"We live to serve," Aebreanna agreed, curtsying and going to her own pony.

Chapter 44

As the party continued their journey west, the desert wrapped around them. The road they followed seemed nothing more than a stretch of solid ground in a sea of sand. The dunes around them shifted ceaselessly, in some bizarre replication of the tides. There were no clouds, nor even a hint of moisture in the air. Every breath drew an inferno into the chest, and every exhale seemed to expel all the body's water. Tomas had wondered at the many casks of the life-giving liquid Magistrate Qadin had given them. Now, as they rode deeper into the parched landscape of the Endless Sands, the squire understood. Rogan called halts every few miles; he and Tomas watered their horses liberally, and only then drank themselves. The knight even made them eat large portions of salt with each meal. Despite these efforts, still a constant thirst had possessed the young man. He sweated constantly, and yet his clothes remained dry, for the moisture his body released was burned off almost immediately by the unrelenting sun. The strange new clothes, Tomas admitted, helped considerably. The loose, flowing tunic held back the worst of the sun's piercing rays, and somehow the fabric insulated him against the oppressive heat of the desert's air.

Something occurred to Tomas as they made their way across the highway as it wound its way towards the great Hoppi River. Pulling Urge beside Aebreanna, the squire asked, "While we were in Hudud, did you have enough time to talk to Rashid's man there?" Not for the first time, the squire had to adjust the strange hooded cloak he now wore. It was striped and flipped about his torso as they rode, and the hood was attached to a thick cord tied around his head. Even with Rogan's instruction on how to wear it, Tomas simply could not adjust to the bizarre, foreign clothing.

"Actually, it was a woman," the spy replied to his question. "But yes, I did manage to talk with her for a few minutes before word reached us of the trouble you boys were in."

"A woman?" the squire started. He then thought. "You know, I can't remember seeing any women in Hudud."

"You wouldn't have," Rogan answered. "The outlands follow the Shamashi way. Women don't go out in public unless escorted by a relative, and they wear veils when they do."

"Is that…?" Tomas gestured at Aebreanna's flowing tunic.

She nodded. "When traveling through Shamashi territory, one must accede to their cultural peculiarities."

"Anything interesting from the spy?" Beraht asked from where he rode with the pack horses.

"Apparently, we have finally earned a little good fortune," she replied. "The agent currently assigned to Hudud is Naya."

"No kidding," Rogan said with a smile on his face. "I didn't know she was an agent."

"After the trouble with Tienel Greysoul, she started doing partial training with Rashid in addition to her duties in Esha's Tower. Once her training was complete, my husband put her on the active list."

Tomas cocked his head. "Why would Rashid emplace a woman here if they're so restricted?"

"My husband believed a woman would have the most success gathering intelligence in this area."

"But if women can't go anywhere without an escort, how does she...?"

"Naya was placed here with another agent, and the two behave as man and wife. Hafiz was recruited many years ago by Rashid, but he has only ever been a legitimate spice and perfume merchant. Since women are all but ignored, so long as there are veiled and escorted, you would be quite surprised at how much is said within our earshot. Additionally, Naya employs her mystical training to further disguise herself and obfuscate her actions."

"Did you have time to draft any dispatches?" the knight asked.

"I also secured us disguises Naya had available, that of mercenaries," she replied. "While I bathed and searched through Naya's supplies for some suitable traveling clothes and equipment, I dictated my reports, and she wrote them down. Fortunately, Naya and I share similar proportions. She has promised that, after we have left the area and any chance of suspicion is past, she will gather her things and personally deliver the reports home."

"They're abandoning this post?" Rogan asked.

"There seems little point in remaining," Aebreanna said with a shrug. "Her husband's cover as a spice and perfume merchant cannot endure with the imminent collapse of the local economy. Further, the same disruption of arcane communication plagues this area, as much as it has Frostfront and eastern Lanasia. Between the Triumvirate's machinations, the discovery of the Nekalan in the Free City, and now the disappearance of the western Uldra, Naya and I agreed that the Keep must be informed."

Rogan grunted. "Things do seem to be accelerating."

They spent weeks traveling across the eastern desert. With Ulheim and Frostfront safely behind them and the bitter cold of winter long forgotten within the spring of the Endless Sands, the trip away from Hudud brought a great sense of relief to Tomas and his friends, despite the rising heat. Rogan adjusted their routine, so that they rode in the late afternoon and evening, once the heat of the day had passed. They sheltered in the morning, erecting the tents Magistrate Qadin had provided. It was nearly a pavilion, really, made of heavy material that seemed more like carpet than canvas. The interior of their shelter was so large, in fact, they could shelter their horses as well as themselves, and still had space aplenty.

This was a restorative time for the four friends. The day's heat was great and growing, the wind carried particles that could never be removed, infiltrating everything they ate and drank, and every crevasse of their bodies. The nights were strangely quiet, but for the sound of hoofbeats on the hard road. Despite all this, they drew strength from the peace of the desert. They were alone, isolated for as far as the eye could see in all directions. Rogan assured them that there were animals aplenty, but hidden among the dunes. Still, this strange solitude was comforting, healing. After the horrors of Ulheim, of Vara's cave and the stifling Uldra Way and the Druug and the Nekalan and all the other hardships of their mission, serenity had at last found them. Their bodies healed, as did their spirits.

When they crested a low hill, nearly three weeks after departing Hudud, Rogan paused, letting the rest of the team catch up to the knight. Tomas blinked in the steel-grey light, and shook his head. "I'm seeing things, right?"

Ahead, in the vast valley stretching before them, was a great gathering of green. Trees stood tall, with narrow trucks and branches only at the very top. Bizarre plants unseen anywhere else in Lanasia flourished in this impossible paradise. Even from the miles separating them, Tomas was sure he could smell water, could feel its coolness on the suddenly-renewed and welcoming breeze. A single road, the one upon which they traveled, crossed through the lush island in this sandy ocean, moving through the mirage and into the shimmering horizon.

"Al Junat Alma," Rogan said. "The Paradise."

"Rogan," Aebreanna said sharply. Beraht was also pulling his great waraxe free. Noting this, Tomas put his hand on Steelheart, but did not draw, his eyes everywhere.

"Damn," the knight grumbled, his own hand going to Talon.

"What," Tomas demanded. "What is it."

"Nothing, and no one," Aebreanna said.

"What?"

"There's no people," Rogan pointed out. "This is the only water for days in any direction. It's why the road moves through here." He jerked his chin at the oasis ahead. "There should be tents, caravans, people moving around."

Now aware of what he was seeing, Tomas spotted only the gentle swaying of the strange trees. There was no other sign of habitation. "What do we do?" the squire asked.

Rogan sighed, glancing at Aebreanna. "We'll have to take care of it," he said, jerking his head to Tomas. "Any woman alone will attract way too much attention."

Knight and squire moved ahead, assuming the role of scouts, normally filled by Aebreanna. The pair rode ahead, quickly but carefully, their eyes everywhere. They needed little time to find their answer.

A caravan, or the remains of one, was just inside the green border of the oasis. Carts were overturned. Animals were slaughtered. Some few bodies, here and there, lay on the ground, all women. A collection of tents had been burned days ago, the ashes long cold. "Guessing it's like this throughout," Rogan grunted. He had not bothered to dismount, only sitting on Stick and looking at the massacre.

"Was this Shamashi?" Tomas asked, covering his nose from the smell of decay and horror. "I've heard the desert raiders can be this... brutal."

Rogan shook his head. "No. If it was Shamashi, they'd have killed the men, burned the tents, and taken the women and goods." The knight nodded at the nearest overturned cart. Jars and baskets had been overturned and smashed, with piles of fruit and nuts scattered everywhere. A single woman and young girl were hunched over the cart, having been cut down. "The men are gone. I'm guessing any weapons and armor, and field rations, anything that will be of use to the army is gone." He looked sadly at the bodies of the women. "Anything useless was... destroyed."

Tomas knelt, then, and pulled a large piece of cloth free from a dead woman's clenched hand. The material was dyed a deep red that matched the drying blood smeared across the body. Rogan saw the cloth and cursed. "Inquisitors," he grunted.

"How can you be sure?" his squire asked.

"Shamashi don't wear red; it's the color of the Adamic Church. Most common people in the Endless Sands have adopted the practice." He nodded at the torn cloth. "Inquisitors wear red sashes tied to black robes."

Tomas dropped the hateful thing and wiped his hand on edge of his long tunic. "Should we move on?" he asked.

Rogan shook his head. "We'll find a shady spot. We need a day to rest the horses."

Most of the day was needed to find Rogan's shady spot. A large spring rested at the heart of the oasis and seemed untouched by the violent passage of the Western Empire's inquisitors. There were a number of open areas with evidence of frequent, but temporary, occupancy. A small village with a handful of now-empty buildings was just out of sight. This offered the friends not only shelter from the heat of the Endless Sands, but from the growing injustice of its masters and their brutality.

"Was wondering why we hadn't run into any caravans," Rogan noted as he and Tomas erected their pavilion.

"Should there be a lot of traffic?" the squire asked.

His knight nodded, settling the heavy material in place. "This is a major road, connecting the western Uldra to Daivic. This time of year, there should be all kinds of trade happening."

Tomas stretched his back before going to bring in the bags. With water so near, they had tied up the horses in the open air leaving most of their large pavilion empty for once. "Do you think the western Uldra left because of what's happening here," he asked, "or is it the other way around?"

Rogan pulled free his long Shamashi tunic with a sigh. "No way to know," he answered. "Remember what I told you about distractions?"

Tomas pulled his own light clothes free, relishing the relatively cool breeze on his bare torso. "So, we stay focused on our mission?"

The knight nodded and led his squire out to the cookfire Aebreanna and Beraht were building.

"Never miss a chance, do you?" Rogan half-joked as Aebreanna let the males continue setting up their small camp to gather her bathing instruments and head towards the nearby spring.

The Sylva stopped and threw a leveled gaze back at the weather-beaten knight. "Although you may have little care as to how you smell," she said with a sniff of the air, "I have a greater sensitivity. Once I have finished, perhaps you boys would have the wisdom of washing some of your more manly areas?" Without another thinly-veiled order, the baroness went to her bath.

Beraht lifted an arm and smelled under it. "It doesn't seem so bad to me," the rugged warrior noted. "A good stink just means that a man has earned his pay." Also freed of most of his clothes, the mountainous warrior glittered as though he were covered in tiny jewels. The beads of sweat adorned his massive, hairy torso like the most priceless of gemstones.

Although Tomas was starting to feel the weariness of their trip catching up with him, now that Aebreanna had brought their attention to it, the squire was forced to admit that the smell of his body was becoming rather strong. With his movements becoming harder and harder, Tomas finished watering the horses. Urge was so tired, in fact, that he made only the most perfunctory attempt at biting his rider, more interested by far in his meal and a good rest. Once seeing to the animals, the squire dug in his own bag for a piece of soap and a coarse towel.

"Turning Sylvu on us, kid?" Rogan asked from where he was preparing a meal.

The young man laughed softly. "I wouldn't have bothered, but now that she's pointed it out, I would feel better once I got some of this stink off. Besides, I feel like I've got half the desert caked on me."

"Cost of adventuring, kid," the knight said sagely, warming several pieces of flatbread. "You have to accept being dirty."

Tomas sat down by the fire, waiting for Aebreanna's return before he, himself, would bathe. "Then you won't mind listening to more of her remarks about something foul in the air?"

Glancing back to where the spy was bathing, Rogan sighed. "Now that you mention it, I think I could use a little washing up."

Beraht laughed from where he was pulling his bedding from the back of his giant saddle. "I tell you, there's nothing sadder than seeing two warriors whipped into submission by a Sylva, or any female."

The Uldra may have had more to say but was interrupted by a bucket of water being dumped on him, the bucket itself then being dropped on his head. Looking up from the rim of the bucket, Beraht seemed unsurprised to see Aebreanna, having returned from her bath on silent feet and wrapped tightly in her small towel, standing over him with a kind smile and twinkle in her opalescent eye.

"Now then," she said with the sweetest of voices, "you can either bathe here, one bucket at a time over the next several hours, or you can roll around in that spring for a few minutes."

The Uldra muttered some of his favorite insults in his native tongue about the Sylva's backside.

"That is very sweet of you to notice, Beraht," she said, dropping a piece of soap onto his lap and going over to her bags to pull out her bedroll.

After the three warriors returned from their bath, where there had been only a minimum of horseplay, they went about cooking up a portion of rations and settling in for their well-deserved rest. Taking his small meal and settling down near the fire, the squire looked over at his Sylva friend. "Aren't you going to dress?" he asked between bites. Aebreanna had not taken the opportunity of their absence to retrieve fresh clothes, instead still wearing only the small towel wrapped around her curvaceous body.

She paused in brushing her long mane of honey blonde to point up at the early evening sky. "*Vaeta* is full tonight," she noted as if that explained everything.

Looking up, Tomas noted that the moon was indeed full. "So?" he asked.

"It's a Sylvai thing, kid," Rogan noted from where also ate. "They feel some kind of connection to the moon."

"*Sy'lva*, actually," Aebreanna corrected emphasizing the feminine form of the word. "All the females of my race know that gentle *Vaeta* governs the cycles of life, including the cycles of the body, be she Human, *Sy'lva*, or even Uldra. Any night in which the moon is full, looking down on us to ensure all is well, we honor Her by casting off any barrier to Her inspection."

"You sleep nude," Tomas guessed, not really understanding.

The spy continued her efforts with her thick hair, making sure the right side of her face was never exposed to their view. Smiling she said, "On the night in which Vaeta is full, every *Sy'lva*, if able, sleeps with nothing to block her view of the moon and vice versa: outdoors and skyclad. Our mission has thus far provided me few opportunities to practice those traditions meaningful to me, so with this pleasant pause in our typically frenzied pace, I am taking full advantage to renew my bond of sisterhood with *Vaeta*."

"So, tonight you'll sleep outside in the moonlight?"

Aebreanna nodded, finishing with her hair and unrolling her blankets. "A tradition as old as the *Sy'lva*."

"Won't you get cold?" Tomas asked. Although the days were impossibly hot, even within the safety of the oasis, the nights seemed nearly as impossibly cold.

"I will survive one night, Tomas," she replied. "And the chill air on my flesh will be neither unpleasant nor unwelcome."

They were all silent for a while, the four of them looking up into the sky and its collection of moon and stars. Despite the danger of their situation, they could all feel the same contentment that comes only from being clean, fed, and happy. It was then Tomas realized that he was happy. They were moving through land controlled by hostile forces that would inflict all manner of pain upon them should they capture the party, and still Tomas was happy.

"What're you thinking, kid?" Rogan asked.

"I'm happy," his squire replied.

"Happy about what?" Beraht demanded.

"Everything."

"You sound surprised," Aebreanna noted.

"I am. All my life, I've lived in Pelsemoria, just living. Until now, I don't think I've ever been really happy."

"It's not happiness you're feeling," the knight said, poking a stick in their fire.

"It feels like that," his squire objected.

Rogan shook his head. "Happiness comes in pulses. A good meal, a fun party." He glanced at Tomas. "Winning the tournament. These are moments."

"Then what...?"

"Purpose," Aebreanna offered. "Fulfilled purpose."

"Meaning," Beraht added. "Doing what you have to, what you know is right."

Rogan nodded. "You're on a mission, doing the right things for the right reasons, and you're making progress. It's the feeling that comes when you find what you're good at and get to do it."

Tomas considered. "Is it always like this, when you guys are…?" he gestured around the open sky.

"Yes and no," his knight replied. "Think about Mary."

The feeling Tomas had did not go away, but it did lessen with the memories of his love. "So how do you get both?" the squire asked.

"An excellent question," Aebreanna mused. "And one we would be most grateful for an answer to, should you happen upon it."

"There's a cost, kid," Rogan admitted. "For everything, even purpose and meaning."

"You have to find balance in life," Beraht advised. "The Allfather makes this an imperfect world so that we learn to appreciate what comes, and what passes, and how to live with all imperfect things." The mountainous warrior stood and retrieved a box from one of his bags. He lumbered over to Tomas and dropped the box into the squire's lap. It was large, but not overly heavy, made of polished wood with brass hinges. Tomas looked up curiously at Beraht before opening it. Within rested several sheets of blank parchment, as well as a stoppered ink bottle and a pair of quills. The squire looked back up at his Uldra friend, who only shrugged. "We all need something," was what he said before entering their pavilion and collapsing onto his blankets.

"I almost forgot…," he said.

"Beraht didn't," Rogan noted. He stood and walked over to his squire, laying a hand on the young man's shoulder. "Meaning and purpose, kid. No story really exists until it's told," was all the knight said before also retiring to his blankets.

Tomas looked at Aebreanna, who smiled encouragingly. The young man pulled free a quill and stirred the ink. He thought for a moment, letting his mind go wherever it would, then, he began.

Every day, he wrote, *no matter the grey veil covering this fallen world, nor the bleak sight of my decaying home, I spent most of my time sitting and staring at the ruins of Pelsemoria…*

Chapter 45

A week later, they stopped atop a low hill as soon as they came within sight of the Hoppi River. It was massive, allowing easy passage for the dozens of ships sailing its calm waters. Farmland hugged either bank of the great river, with occasional trees and villages similarly adorning the length of the Hoppi. In the distance, the city of Daivic rose like a displaced relic. The city's architecture did not match the other buildings in view, instead possessing a riot of outdated styles from eastern Lanasia meshed with strange, bulbous towers. There were walls, but these had great arched entries standing open. Massive bridges blended in with the city itself, to create a continuous urban blight across the peaceful Hoppi River.

About midway between the hill on which they stood and the city of Daivic was a customs station. Normally, the arrival at civilization would be welcome after almost a month amidst the shifting dunes of the Endless Sands. Even from miles away, Tomas and his friends could make out the voices of travelers and workmen, of soldiers and citizens. Much less welcoming, however, was what they saw flying from the top of the largest building.

The customs station was a complex system of buildings straddling the highway ahead. On the far side awaited a small sandstone fortress flying the green and white banner of House Parano. Most distressing of all: beside the flag, flying at equal height, was the banner of the Western Empire, the golden Adamic flame surrounded by a wave of the midnight sea on a crimson field.

"The reports are true," Aebreanna noted as she dismounted.

"Doesn't change anything," Rogan grunted, also climbing down.

"Why would they allow it?" Tomas asked.

"Only one reason," Beraht spat, tying his great bay horse to a nearby tree. "Parano's joined with Balshazzar."

Rogan gathered close with his friends. "Alright," he said in a firm voice of command, "we stick with Aebreanna's plan. We're not random travelers, we're mercenaries, looking for work. No names, no heraldry, no distinguishing equipment." He moved to his packs, removing the clothes given to them by Magistrate Qadin.

Tomas followed the instructions that Aebreanna gave, exchanging his desert clothes and armor for the equipment the Sylvai had acquired back in Hudud and scavenged from the looted convoys in the Al Junat Alma oasis.

"What kind of power will the Inquisition have here?" Rogan asked Aebreanna.

She shrugged out of her voluminous clothes, folding them neatly and placing them back into her packs. "After the Inquisition was disbanded, the surviving leaders fled to Tordenia with whatever priests would follow them. Nearly a third of the Holy Knights defected, forming a new order that swore loyalty to the Western Empire and House Balshazzar. After Daivic joined with the Emir, approximately one hundred knights were assigned to its defense and the enforcement of Balshazzar's law throughout the Endless Sands. The Inquisition sent forty of their priests to assist the knights and counter any arcane threats from Frostfront or the Keep. Wizardry is forbidden in the Western Empire, but the Inquisition is using the research materials stolen from Pelsemoria to use arcane magic in addition to their divinely based powers."

Tomas picked up the splintmail shirt Aebreanna had acquired. "I thought divine magic was basically asking God to do something for you?" he asked Aebreanna.

The spy pulled a black silk shirt over her head. "Essentially, that is the process," she replied. "A cleric says a prayer to whatever goddess he or she worships, asking that deity to perform some minor miracle." The new blouse was nearly transparent around the midriff and sleeves.

"Then how is the Inquisition still casting spells?" the squire asked.

"What are you getting at, kid?" Rogan asked, working his way into his metal shirt.

Once his knight's chainmail was in place, Tomas started changing his own clothes, careful to ensure that the half-opened golden rose, Alexia's final gift to him, remained safe.

"That has to be hidden," Rogan said, nodding toward the pin. "And the ribbon."

The squire glanced at his knight and then down at both the golden rose and the white ribbon that was, as always, tied around Steelheart. Tomas nodded his understanding. "Everyone used to think the Inquisition was ordained by God to root out all nonbelievers and heretics," he noted, wrapping the white ribbon around the golden rose. "There was no question whence their magic came. But if they abandoned Velaross, turned their backs on the Teachings and the Lords Cardinal and their priestly oaths, how are they using divine magic? Who's granting their prayers?" Tomas tucked the small package containing his two most priceless possessions under his shirt, to ride against his heart.

Rogan put Talon away, instead replacing his preferred blade with a broadsword having no crests or identifying marks. "Like Aebreanna said, they ransacked the Guild Tower in Velaross and stole the secrets of casting arcane magic," he said. "God isn't granting them spells anymore, so they use arcane magic to convince people that they still have God's blessing."

Aebreanna dug into her bags, pulling out a pair of black leather pants. "No. All our agents in and around Daivic have reported the inquisitors are still casting divine magics in addition to the arcane spells they stole."

Beraht, being far too large for anything Aebreanna could procure, did not change. His own gear was relatively undamaged from their encounter in Uldron, so of them all, the Uldra had needed the fewest replacements of lost equipment. "You mean there's a difference?" he snorted.

The spy straightened her outfit and added steel bracers and a new pair of steel-toed boots. "Yes, Beraht, there is a difference," she sighed, rolling her opalescent eye. "Divine magic and arcane magic have subtle differences in how they are manifested and their effects in the world. The Service is trained to distinguish not only the difference between types of magic but also schools and even specific spells. Our agents assure us that the priest-inquisitors are employing both types of magic and many spells the Arcane Guild assured us were destroyed."

"You just can't trust a spell-slinger," Beraht spat. The Uldra was carefully wrapping a cloth around his waraxe and stowing it with one of the pack horses.

"Why are you hiding your it?" Tomas asked, settling his new armor in place.

Beraht shrugged. "A priest might recognize it if he got a good look."

"What if you need it in a fight?"

In answer, the warrior grinned and walked several feet away from the horse. Without a word, Beraht raised his right hand. Just as Tomas was about to question the Uldra, the great waraxe suddenly flew out of the packs and hurled itself into Beraht's outstretched hand.

"Wow," Tomas said.

Beraht grinned and retuned the waraxe to its hiding place, instead retrieving a large mace.

The squire shook his head. "Back to the question at hand. How is the Inquisition still casting divine magic?"

Finishing her small touches, Aebreanna pulled a leather vest out of her bags and put it on. "They must have found a new god to answer their prayers, one of whom the general population is unaware."

Rogan pulled out a leather thong and tied back his unruly mane of red hair. "If we could get proof of that and release it to Duke Parano, it could be just what we need to get him to break with Balshazzar."

Aebreanna shrugged. "The Service has been trying for years, but we can find no evidence of another god the Inquisition worships."

"What about the Padishah?" the knight asked as he settled his unfamiliar gear. "Has anyone tried to make contact with the Shamashi?"

The Sylva shook her head slightly. "The Bedouins remain as elusive as ever," she replied, "both with their Parano overlords and with their Khepri cousins to the south. We have had no meaningful contact in more than five years."

"Cousins?" Tomas asked.

"Indeed," the spy replied. "Were you not aware?" When the squire shook his head, she continued. "Ages ago, the Khepri took Human mates, even as some Sylvai did. Whereas the intermingling of Sylvai and Human produced the Halvans, Human-Khepri parings yielded the Shamashi. The Empress of the time outlawed such cross-species mating, and the prejudice against Halvans has endured. In contrast, the Khepri tolerated the new race and the desert-peoples thrived, even with the decline of their originators."

"What's keeping the Shamashi from attacking Daivic now that the Legions aren't there to hold them back?" Tomas asked. "I doubt Balshazzar has given Parano all that much military support."

Aebreanna was silent for a moment, staring at Rogan with a typically-inscrutable expression. Finally, the spy took a deep breath and answered. "Parano forces captured both the Padishah and his daughter two years ago," she said. "The desert people will not attack the city for fear of the harm that would come to them."

Rogan stiffened at the news and turned, very slowly, to face his Sylvai friend. "House Parano has Safiyya and her father?" he asked quietly.

"Yes."

"And they've been held for two years?"

"Yes."

"And I wasn't told?"

"Rashid believed, as did I, that, had we informed you of the princess' capture, to say nothing of her father's, you would have either mounted a military expedition to free them or simply gone off by yourself. Either of these options presented an unacceptable risk."

"So your husband decided not to report something this vital to me because he decided that I couldn't be trusted with the information." It was not a question.

"If you will recall," Aebreanna said carefully, "you were in final preparation for your mission in the South with Alexia. Rashid thought it best to wait until after you had completed that mission before telling you of the Padishah's capture and then help you plan your inevitable rescue mission. This would have given us more time to develop better intelligence on the situation. Unfortunately, Tomas's arrival and Anninihus' attack precipitated this."

Rogan stared hard at his trusted friend for some time. "Did the King know?" he finally said in a tone empty of any emotion.

Aebreanna shook her head slightly. "Had Rashid informed the King, Cylan would have felt obligated to tell you, defeating the intention of—"

"Controlling my reaction."

"Rogan, our intentions were—"

"I really don't care, Aebreanna," the prince said flatly. "When we get home, your husband and I are going to have a long talk about who's in charge and if the spymaster has a future with House Calonar."

Rogan turned away from Aebreanna toward Beraht. The Uldra had said nothing during the exchange. "Change of plans," the knight said. "We're not going around Daivic. We're going in."

"Is that a good idea?" the warrior asked carefully.

"They saved my life, Beraht. I owe them."

Chapter 56

Surprisingly, their passage through the customs station went

without incident. The mercenaries, unshaven and filthy, accepted a minimal bribe and a reasonable lie to allow them access.

"Why was that so easy?" Tomas demanded as they rode away.

"The only two things border guards are worried about are armies and caravans," Rogan answered. "We're not smuggling enough of anything in to be dangerous or worth a decent bribe. And we're not a big enough force to start raiding. Those guards are more than happy to let the Watch worry about what we do once we're inside the city."

"That doesn't seem right."

"Don't knock a lazy guard," Beraht laughed. "If he'd done his job right, we'd probably have had to kill him."

Once through the customs station, as they began the approach to Daivic itself, the tone of their journey changed. The occasional passerby kept his head down and his eyes away from them. There were no merchants or other travelers from distant lands, besides the ever-present mercenaries. Farmers moved heavy carts of produce towards the city, their bones sticking through their skin and their ragged clothing hiding little of their starvation. It took less than one hour before the first patrol stopped them. Fortunately, since the lands through which they now traveled were so flat and featureless, the general lack of anything to hide behind meant that no force of any size could move from place to place without being spotted a good distance away.

As it was, Aebreanna's Sylvai eyes had no difficulty spotting the armored group approaching them, giving her friends more than enough time to double check their disguises before the knights were upon them. As the armored warriors approached, Rogan began hissing curses.

"What's wrong?" Tomas asked.

"Those knights have an inquisitor with them!"

"Is that a problem?" the squire asked.

"If he has any degree of power, this is most definitely a problem," Aebreanna said.

"What do we do?" the squire asked.

In response, Rogan loosened his sword in its sheath. The others followed his example, discreetly readying themselves for a possible fight.

The Holy Knights and their inquisitor overseer rode up, not stopping until the leader was within an arm's reach of Rogan. Raising his visor, the knight looked down his nose at Rogan, which did little to endear himself. "Your name, mercenary?" the knight demanded.

Bowing in his saddle, albeit stiffly, Rogan tried not to sneer. "I am called Derrik, Sir Knight. I lead this band."

"Your business in these lands?"

"We have accepted a commission to protect caravans moving from Oneld, through Daivic, to Frostfront."

"You have documentation proving this?" the knight demanded.

Rogan looked back at Aebreanna, who produced a small bundle of parchment from her bags. She was keeping her head down in a humble pose. Taking the parchment from the spy, Rogan handed them over to the waiting knight.

As the lead knight looked through the falsified contracts, the priest-inquisitor, dressed in black robes with a scarlet sash tied around his waist, was looking at Beraht with undisguised suspicion. In his effort to remain inconspicuous, the Uldra looked very piously at the priest and then crossed his eyes.

Tomas, trying desperately to think of a way to kick Beraht without attracting attention, noticed an unusual pressure in the back of his skull. At first attributing it to his intense desire to choke his companion, after a few moments, the squire dimly realized that the odd sensation was, in fact, emanating from the inquisitor. Looking closely at the priest, Tomas spotted the man gesturing subtly and moving his lips as if speaking quietly. Throwing a questioning glance at Aebreanna, the spy nodded slightly.

The lead knight handed the documents back to Rogan. "This contract appears to be in order. May God guide you in your endeavors." As the knights made ready to move on, the priest-inquisitor rode up beside the group's leader. "A moment, Sir Knight. These people are not as they seem."

Here we go, Tomas grimly thought to himself.

The inquisitor pointed at Beraht. "That one is not a mercenary. He is a priest of the heathen Uldric god."

Desperate to stave off the nearly inevitable conflict that would result as soon as Beraht realized the priest was trying to insult him, Rogan held his arms up. "If you please, Holy Inquisitor. I can assure you that this creature is not a priest of any heretical gods."

The creature comment appeared to mollify Beraht somewhat. Rogan continued. "In point of fact, noble priest, this Uldra has served me for many years, and I can assure you that he lacks the intellect to be anything other than the barbarian he is."

The lead knight turned to the inquisitor. "You must admit, this thing does lack any apparent intelligence."

The inquisitor did not appear to notice the slow rage building in Beraht. The priest ignored everyone but the knight he spoke to. "Despite this beast's obvious lack of intelligence, I sense within him a great divine power."

The lead knight turned to Rogan for an explanation. Beraht, obviously having had more than his fill of being insulted, slowly moved his horse toward the priest. Tomas and Aebreanna, spotting the warning signs, desperately tried to alert Rogan to the danger.

Rogan, to his credit, was still trying to talk their way out of the situation. "Sir Knight," he nearly pleaded, "we are licensed soldiers for hire. How on earth could someone like my Uldra here come to possess any kind of divine power?"

"It is unlikely," the knight conceded.

"It is not your decision, knight," the inquisitor thundered. "All contracts for the service of mercenaries within the influence of the Western Empire have a clause that allows any inquisitor at any time to detain any person for questioning they deem necessary to further their duties." The priest pointed at the now dangerously close Beraht. "This stinking mockery of creation will be arrested and taken in our custody back to Daivic for interrogation."

During the priest's rant, Rogan had finally noticed the look on Beraht's face and, surrendering to the inevitable, moved Stick back out of danger. Beraht, by now right in front of the inquisitor, looked into the fool's eyes very calmly.

"What did you call me?" the warrior asked gently.

The inquisitor turned back to the knights. "One of you gag this ape. I will not listen to his heretical—" the priest was unable to finish his sentence as, once he had turned back to Beraht, his face was intercepted by an Uldra fist in midflight.

The knights slammed down their visors, drew their swords, and charged Beraht. Rogan and Tomas, drawing their own blades, intercepted all but two of the knights. The fight was short but brutal. The horses the knights were riding, of lesser breeding than their enemy's mounts and burdened by men in full plate armor, could not keep up with Stick and Urge. Rogan and Tomas thus were easily able to literally ride circles around the knights, wearing them down and eventually unhorsing them all.

Beraht was another matter. The Uldra lacked the skills at mounted combat Tomas and Rogan possessed, thus could not outride the two knights coming straight at him. As the first knight made a wide swing, Beraht intercepted the swipe by grabbing his target's wrist and head-butting the helmeted man, causing the both of them to fall from their horses. As the Uldra rolled to his back, he found the knight already on his feet with his sword at Beraht's throat. The knight smiled, anticipating the prestige he would gain for having defeated so great an adversary. Unfortunately for the knight, he failed to notice Beraht's right hand, raised as if reaching for something. With enough force to shatter his spine, Beraht's mighty waraxe slammed into the knight's back, hurling him dozens of feet away. The second knight, seeing his comrade's fall, spurred his warhorse, intending to ride the Uldra down. As the horse thundered up to him, Beraht swung his weapon in a massive overhead strike, splitting the animal's head and sending the paladin flying out of his saddle. Before his enemy could regain his feet, Beraht rushed him and swung his weapon again, sending the knight's helmet, with the knight's head still in it, flying from his shoulders.

Despite being unhorsed, the knights were holding Rogan and Tomas at bay, the two warriors weary to attack a group of fully armed and armored knights in close formation. The brief stalemate was ended, however, when Beraht, deep in the throes of berserker fury, hurled himself at the knights, roaring and frothing at the mouth.

The fury of the Uldra was so primal, so vicious, that the knights were simply unable to hold their ranks and fell before Beraht like wheat falls to the scythe. Within seconds, he reduced the knights to pieces of armor and broken, lifeless, bodies. Standing in the midst of this carnage, the warrior was breathing heavy, hefting his waraxe as if eager to keep fighting.

Tomas started to move, wanting to help his friend, but was held back by Rogan. When the squire looked questioningly at his knight, Rogan shook his head lightly, pointing at Aebreanna. The Sylva, walking toward Beraht very slowly and keeping her hands in plain view, was speaking softly, trying to reach her friend's mind.

Finally, after what seemed an eternity, Beraht dropped his great weapon and collapsed to his knees, looking as exhausted as he should have been. Aebreanna held the Uldra in her arms, supporting him until he could rise on his own strength.

"She has a lot of love in her heart, doesn't she?" Tomas asked.

Rogan nodded. "It's easy to overlook it when she's being stubborn or vindictive, but in reality, Aebreanna is one of the most loving, gentle people I've ever met. There's nothing she wouldn't do to help someone she loves. She may not give her love easily, kid, but when she does, it's forever."

Looking over at the inquisitor, Tomas called out, "Our friend is coming to."

Swimming out of the darkness that Beraht sent him to, the priest-inquisitor found himself tied up, with a pair of heretics looking down at him.

Chapter 57

"Why is it that no matter how good our disguises and how careful our preparations, you always seem to find a way to force us into a fight?" Aebreanna was standing over Beraht, berating the Uldra.

He was wearily cleaning the gore off his waraxe, the Sylva's words doing very little to sour the happy glow he clearly felt after such a wonderful little fight. Rogan and Tomas, taking advantage of the time Beraht needed to recuperate after his outburst, had tied the priest-inquisitor up and searched him, insuring that he had no surprises for them.

"What are we supposed to do with him?" the squire asked his knight.

"I don't know." Rogan was taking this latest incident a little worse than usual. The knight looked over at Aebreanna. "Any ideas?" he asked.

"I assume you have no problem with simply killing him and leaving him with the others?" the spy looked over at where the bodies of the knights had been stacked behind a low hill that offered fair concealment from the road.

"Not much choice, I guess."

"You're not seriously considering this, are you?" the squire asked them both.

"Practicality, kid," Rogan muttered, looking at the shaking priest. "Not like we can take him with us."

Aebreanna left Beraht to his cleaning and joined the two men. "If we leave him behind, another patrol will eventually discover him, and our presence in this area will be revealed."

Tomas jerked his thumb to where the bodies were haphazardly hidden. "Those are bound to be discovered after too long anyway. I'd say that the chances of our sneaking into Daivic evaporated as soon as Beraht punched the priest."

"Calm down, kid," Rogan said, rubbing his temples. "We need a plan."

"The longer we stand here discussing, the greater the chance of another patrol encountering us," Aebreanna insisted.

"All right look," the knight snapped, "Aebreanna, put the priest to sleep. Put him down for as long as you can, and we'll leave him with the bodies. By the time he comes to, we'll have enough of a lead to make it to Daivic. If another patrol does find them, they'll assume we headed into the mountains, not deeper into enemy territory. For now, our story stands, and we just concentrate on avoiding more confrontations, assuming Beraht will let us, of course."

Aebreanna shook her head. "Your plan has a serious flaw, I fear."

"Now what?" he demanded.

"The materials I use in the forcing of sleep were lost at Uldron."

"I didn't know that," the knight said. Rogan turned and walked off some distance. "That would have been good to know," he said ruefully.

Tomas felt an odd lassitude cover his mind. Although he heard Aebreanna and Rogan talking, their words seemed to make no meaning to the young warrior. The last thing he could clearly remember hearing was his knight saying he needed someone asleep. It seemed to Tomas as though he was standing in water. He could feel currents pulling and pushing him this way and that. As Aebreanna walked past him, possibly toward Rogan, the squire could feel the displacement she generated as she moved, the currents that Tomas felt being slightly disturbed as she moved.

Knowing what to do, without knowing how he knew, Tomas looked at the priest-inquisitor. Walking over to the prisoner, careful to walk slowly to cause as little disturbance to the currents as possible, the squire knelt and picked up a small handful of sand. As he stood before the inquisitor, words came to Tomas's lips; an entire language seemed to flow, not from the squire's mind, but from his soul. Words of power flowed from the young man, words that called to the currents all around him and gently shifted them so that, instead of flowing around the priest without reason, they flowed into him with purpose.

Looking back at his squire, Rogan was shocked to see the young man standing over their prisoner, sprinkling sand over the priest's head and chanting in the arcane language. Seeing the knight's shocked expression, Aebreanna glanced over at Tomas and was very nearly as startled as Rogan. Before either of them could call out, the inquisitor's eyes fluttered shut, and his entire body went limp as he fell into an obvious deep sleep.

As the lassitude that Tomas had fallen into lifted from his mind, the squire blinked and looked around. Seeing the shocked expressions on Rogan and Aebreanna's faces, Tomas shrugged. "Don't ask me," he said.

"Where did you learn how to cast spells?" Rogan demanded.

"I didn't."

"Have you ever done that before?" Aebreanna asked intently.

"No, I don't think so."

"What does it mean?" Rogan asked the Sylva, his eyes never leaving Tomas.

"Spontaneous manifestation," she replied. "Magic without study. Extremely rare, but it does happen, and we have seen ample evidence suggesting he has talents lying in that direction."

"You mean he's an adept?" the knight asked.

"No, an adept must study the nuances of magic to properly harness it. His abilities are sorcerous."

Rogan stared hard at Aebreanna. "You mean… like Vara?"

She nodded.

"Is he dangerous?"

"Excuse me," Tomas snapped. "I hate to interrupt, but I'm standing right here!"

Ignoring the squire's outburst, Aebreanna shook her head. "From what I understand, sorcery is only dangerous when the budding adept experiments with his abilities."

Rogan looked over at his squire with a grin. "I hope we can trust you not to experiment with blowing things up until we can get you back to the Keep."

"I'll try to control myself."

Rogan shook his head. "Well, I'm not the sort of person to question a blessing, so let's throw the priest here in with his friends and get out of here."

"What about Beraht?" Tomas asked. "The whole reason this happened is because the inquisitor said he sensed divine power coming from Beraht."

"That would be his waraxe," Aebreanna noted. "It is blessed with the power of the god of the Uldra."

"Is there any way to hide it?" the squire asked.

"No. As long as Beraht is within proximity of it, the weapon radiates divine power. Our only hope is that any inquisitors we encounter lack the skill to discern the artifact's nature."

Tomas shook his head. "Let me guess, our odds on that happening are slim."

Rogan turned to head back to Stick. "There's no help for it. Let's just hope we have some luck coming our way."

"That would make for a wonderful change," Aebreanna laughed.

Their luck did hold. The road leading to Daivic's eastern gate was full of traffic but patrolled only by more mercenaries, who were more interested in expediting the travelers than inspecting them. The group encountered only one more patrol that was too busy searching a large caravan and could thus do no more than spare the party more than a passing glance before sending them on their way.

Of greater interest was the large group of Bedouins visible across the river. The Hoppi narrowed around Daivic, allowing Tomas his first clear view of the desert people.

"Are those Shamashi?" Tomas asked directing his knight's gaze across the river. He had spent most of his young life reading of other lands and other races, so this first meeting with living members, not just the drawn representatives, of the Shamashi was an important moment for Tomas.

Rogan glanced back at the lean, dark-skinned men, wrapped in thick robes against the desert sun and bearing the curved swords of the Endless Sands. "That's them." The knight stared for a moment at the small group, no more than a dozen, and then looked up and down the river. "What're they doing?" he mused to himself.

"Scouts perhaps?" Aebreanna suggested.

"But scouting what?" Rogan countered.

"They don't seem interested in the city," Beraht noted. "Just the people."

"The people coming out," Tomas pointed out. "They're not exactly like I was expecting," the squire admitted. The soldiers, matched the description of the Shamashi from his books, with wiry bodies showing little muscle and an oddly extended frame that stood more than a head taller than Rogan. They sat astride learn horses that looked much like Stick and Urge, and radiated an intensity that was discernable even from across the river. The Bedouin warriors gave only the most casual of glances at Tomas and his friends, clearly uninterested another group of foreign mercenaries.

Rogan shook his head and sighed, facing back towards the city ahead. "Distractions," he muttered.

Tomas looked ahead of the queue, the long line of frail peasants pulling at heavy carts, the richly-garbed functionaries and priests, and the assortment of foreign mercenaries. The squire tried to take in the great city of Daivic, often called by the government in Pelsemoria the beating heart of the Endless Sands, the only hope of civilizing the savage desert. The gates were massive, but wide open, and seemed more decorative than functional. The wood was rotting and the iron rusting. The battlements above seemed mostly unmanned. Only a handful of House Parano soldiers manned the gates, clearly overburdened with managing the traffic. The buildings beyond the near-useless gates were an array of low brick in the lower areas and great marble palaces in the neighborhoods beyond. Above all towered the great Mari Palace, conquered home of House Parano. "So," the squire said, his eyes drifting from the harried Parano soldiers to the palace, "I'm still not sure I understand why the Parano military is obeying the orders of the Inquisition." He nodded towards the gate guards in their green, white, and red livery and the conspicuous priest with them dressed in the red, gold, and black of the Western Empire. "I thought the army was supposed to be independent from the Church."

Rogan grimaced. "House Balshazzar is trying to convince everyone in Lanasia that he wants to reestablish the Republic as it was; but it's pretty obvious he plans a few changes."

"Like inquisitors leading the military?"

Aebreanna laughed as she continued to scan the horizon. "Although your Legions were, by Republic law, independent of Adamic authority, under Balshazzar, an inquisitor is placed in command of most military units, especially ones comprised of non-Tordenian citizens. The emir has also insisted that his new church headquarters be located in his capital. Within the Western Empire, there is simply no distinction between Church and State. Religious law and secular law are one and the same."

"Will he name a new Adama?" Tomas asked. "The Lords Cardinal haven't appointed one in so long, Balshazzar could really benefit from offering the people a spiritual leader."

"Other than the Inquisition, there are no special church agencies or ranks. Even the position of Lord Inquisitor has been removed."

"So how does Balshazzar's church function?"

"All orders come out of Tordenia, kid," Rogan replied. "It doesn't matter if the orders are for the church, army, or a work crew. Balshazzar is the absolute master of the Western Empire. All the decisions are his."

"Does that include Daivic?" the squire asked.

Aebreanna shrugged. "Duke Edmondo Parano still claims to rule over his lands, and his House Guard still wears his colors, but church knights have seniority over all Daivic military, and the inquisitor assigned to each unit can override any officer, at any time. So you tell me, Tomas, who do you think is in control of these lands?"

The young man shook his head. "How could Duke Edmondo allow this?"

Beraht laughed. "Parano has been scared witless for a decade now that House Calonar will take over his lands. Balshazzar is willing to protect him."

Aebreanna nodded. "The true irony is, before now, the Human Church never really had much presence in the Endless Sands. The Shamashi tribes hate Adamics, and the Paranos never gave much support to Adamic missionaries. After the Republic collapsed, Parano expelled all the priests. He figured that his new kingdom could get by just fine without any kind of religion, but one of the conditions of their alliance with the Western Empire was the admittance of Balshazzar's new church."

"But House Balshazzar is taking over the country," Tomas pointed out, "not House Calonar. I mean, wouldn't the King offer real protection and assistance without taking control?"

"Definitely," Rogan grunted.

"Then why is Duke Edmondo letting House Balshazzar take over his country?"

"He thinks I killed the Emperor," the knight grimaced. "I'm sure it started with Parano siding with what he felt was the lesser of two evils. After all this time, I'd be surprised if Edmondo even could break away from the Western Empire." Rogan turned in his saddle to look at Aebreanna. "How much information has Rashid gained on the Balshazzar-Parano alliance?"

"Minimal."

"Who or what's stopping our agents?"

"Opportunity," she replied. "To say nothing of the Inquisition's interference."

"Could you find out what's happening?" Tomas asked.

Aebreanna shook her head again. "Difficult and dangerous," she looked at Rogan. "Especially given our current focus and the likely attention it will draw,"

The knight straightened in his saddle. "What if you had some help?" he asked with an evil grin.

"Rogan," Beraht grumbled, "our descriptions have been posted in every barracks in Daivic. As soon as we get to those guards, we'll be arrested and tossed in the deepest hole Parano can find."

"Don't forget," Tomas reminded his knight, "our mission is to reach Tordenia and find out who poisoned the King so we can track down a cure. After everything else that's happened, we really don't have the time for all this."

"Why sneak?" Rogan mused.

"I don't understand," the squire admitted.

"He's got an idea," Beraht grinned. "I just love it when he gets an idea."

Aebreanna raised an eyebrow and sighed.

Tomas looked from Rogan's somewhat malicious grin to Aebreanna's look of resignation. "Why do I suddenly have a very bad feeling about this?" he asked.

Chapter 58

"Did they really have to leave us naked?" Tomas asked, rubbing at the manacles that were cutting into his wrists. After riding up to the city gate, Rogan, Beraht, and Tomas had politely introduced themselves and requested a meeting with Duke Edmondo of House Parano. After the sergeant's near-trance had passed, the three emissaries of House Calonar had been stripped and chained in the holding cells just inside the city's eastern gate. There they had been left, under guard, for several hours. How many hours was difficult to tell as their accommodations lacked a window, and the guards outside their cell refused to engage in even the most harmless conversation. "You know, I really hate this plan," Tomas said, trying to ease the discomfort in his wrists.

"Don't you worry, kid," the knight said, stretching against his bonds, "I'm in complete control of the situation."

"Isn't that what you said that time we got surrounded by those Druug and almost got eaten?" Beraht asked.

Rogan looked over at the Uldra. "Why are you always bringing up the past?"

"All I'm just saying is that sometimes your plans don't always work out the way you plan them."

"Well, this time everything will be just fine," the knight insisted.

"Isn't that what you told Aebreanna right before the Greysoul captured her?"

"You know," Tomas said through clenched teeth, "that's it. I quit."

"Now calm down," Rogan said soothingly. "Just relax. All we have to do is wait here, and the bad guys will come to us. What could go wrong?"

"Isn't that what you said right before—"

"Would you please shut up?"

Before Tomas could proceed with his growing hysterics, the cell door was opened, revealing the black robes and red sash of an inquisitor. With barely a glance at Beraht and Tomas, the dark cleric walked to Rogan, taking obvious pleasure in the knight's incarceration. "Well, Sir Rogan," the priest sneered in a guttural, rolling accent that was unmistakably of Velaross, "how should we execute you?" Somehow it surprised Tomas that the inquisitor was from the east, hoping deep down that the reports of the renegade priests had been false, sand all of the clergy who made up the Western Empire's new church were natives of that land. Now, though, the squire was forced to accept the truth; his Church really was divided upon itself.

"Just like that?" the knight replied with an innocent smile. "Won't you at least torture us, gaining all the secrets of the Keep before redeeming our souls through fire and death?"

The inquisitor pulled back his hood, revealing a shaved scalp that was extensively decorated with tattoos. His soulless black eyes regarded the knight. "You should know, Mighty Prince, that our questioning of you and your minions is a foregone conclusion. The only matter that requires any deliberation is the method of execution."

Tomas cleared his throat. "Um, excuse me. Just out of curiosity, if we go ahead and answer all of your questions, could we skip the torture and death?"

The inquisitor and Rogan both threw Tomas identical looks, answering the squire's question. "Don't ask stupid questions," Beraht grunted.

The priest turned back to Rogan, absently gesturing to the door. "Your servant seems to have little understanding of how things work," he noted as the door opened, and a guard brought in a chair.

"He's new," the knight explained.

"It would be a shame to waste such raw, untapped potential. After his interrogation, I should arrange to have him sent to Tordenia for reeducation."

Tomas's hair stood on end at the priest's idle suggestion. "Why are you being so calm about all this?" the squire demanded.

"There will be time enough for anger and harsh words during your formal interrogation, young man," the inquisitor replied without turning away from Rogan.

"So what's this?" Beraht asked.

"This, you retched thing, is merely a casual conversation, while the proper interrogation facilities are prepared. You two have earned quite a reputation in the last decade, and I must admit that I have been quite curious to learn as much about you as possible before matters take a darker turn."

"I don't suppose you'd be willing to answer our questions in exchange for our answering yours?" Rogan asked.

"Do you have so very many questions for one of my order?"

"You'd be surprised how much I'd have to talk about with a higher-ranking member of the Inquisition these days."

"How do you know this guy is a higher-ranking inquisitor?" Tomas asked his knight.

Rogan nodded his head at the tattoos on the priest's head. "Only the top priests in the Inquisition are given those marks," the knight replied. "The stories say that the tattoos have some kind of protective spells placed on them."

"The stories are true," the inquisitor replied. "Those few who are blessed with the sacred marks are protected against heathen magics."

"Define heathen," Beraht grumbled.

"Heathen is what you are and I am not."

"You know," Rogan noted, "I don't think I've ever heard a better definition."

"How is it that you know so many details of my order that most of the faithful do not?" the inquisitor asked Rogan.

"Rashid has always done a good job of keeping me up to date on how our opponents operate."

"The Baron Tressalon? Word has reached us that he is a formidable spymaster. His wife is another matter. What of the Baroness Tressalon?"

"Aebreanna? Well, she sure can dance."

The priest smiled. "Her skills at entertainment notwithstanding, I was actually more interested in her role on the Black Duke's Advisory Council."

"Are you people still calling Calonar the Black Duke?" Rogan demanded. "He was crowned a decade ago."

"The Inquisition and the one true Holy Mother Church have allied with Emir Theodorico of House Balshazzar, and the Emir does not recognize the kingship of the Black Duke."

"Isn't that just a little ridiculous?" Tomas demanded. "Velaross not only recognizes the King's authority but has also allied with him. If you serve the Church, how can you oppose King Cylan?"

"The heretics who currently control the Holy City shall not endure. Of all the petty warlords and tyrants that abound in Lanasia in these dark times, it is only Emir Theodorico Balshazzar who still follows the one true faith. Thus, it is he who will, through God's grace, one day ascend the Redwood Throne. If the Lords Cardinal would rather bow down to blasphemous half-breed than endorse a loyal child of God, then they are no better than the Sylvai cancer that sickens the land."

As caught up in his tirade as the inquisitor was, he failed to notice the look shared by the three adventurers, conveying the horror they all felt when confronted by the priest's closed-minded bigotry.

"So I take it Sylvai really aren't your favorite people," Beraht noted slowly.

"Please don't misunderstand me," the priest asked of Rogan. "We of the Inquisition and Holy Mother Church understand that the sub-Humans cannot help how they are born. It is a shame that God would not allow all creatures of speech and thought to be born Human, but they simply cannot be allowed to continue their pagan ways."

"So you're trying to help the non-Humans?" Rogan asked, his voice dripping with sincerity.

"I doubt very much you would see it thus, mired as you have been since your arrival in Lanasia in the evil of the Northern Keep."

"King Cylan has had some influence on me."

"Were you at least a member of the Church in you homeland?" the inquisitor asked.

"Don't you know? I thought Balshazzar was going out of his way to find out everything there is to know about everyone that serves House Calonar."

The inquisitor smiled in a warm, disarming way. "Although the Emir's intelligence service has learned a great deal about you and your companions, there are a great many things we do not yet know about you."

"So what do you think you know about me?" the knight asked curiously.

"We know that you appeared in the company of Aebreanna Tressalon and this Uldra twelve years ago and immediately swore allegiance to the Black Duke."

"Almost immediately," Rogan corrected. "The King didn't force the issue so I had plenty of time to think about it."

"We also know that you were a mercenary, traveling throughout Lanasia, apparently fleeing from a number of other mercenary bands that you had managed to aggravate over the years. You spent time here in the Endless Sands, amongst those primitive Shamashi mongrels and that you were instrumental in destroying Pelsemoria and killing nearly every high-ranking nobleman in the Republic."

"Don't you just love that story?" Rogan asked Beraht.

"How is it that you came to be in the service of the Black Duke?" the inquisitor asked.

The knight shrugged. "How does anyone find work? A job became available. I heard about it and was qualified for it. I really wasn't doing anything better at the time, so I took the job."

"And that eventually led to your marrying the Black Duke's daughter and becoming his heir?"

Rogan laughed. "Do any job well enough, and you're bound to get rewarded."

"So the Dark Priestess was simply compensation for services rendered?" the priest asked, nodding.

"Don't you have perks for your job?" the knight asked.

"I suppose I do. The fear I instill and the unquestioning obedience from everyone around me are comforting."

"Not to mention being able to cast spells as wizards do and still wear the robes of a priest."

The inquisitor smiled and nodded. "It is satisfying to have such power at my disposal. Are the priests of Velaross still limiting themselves to only those powers granted by God?"

Rogan shrugged. "How would I know? I know about as much about magic as I do about knitting."

"Still, they use magic, and it cannot be granted from God. I must admit that I am curious where they could be getting their powers from."

"They're probably asking the same questions about you," Tomas noted.

"No doubt they believe that they still follow the true faith. No doubt they have fallen in with the worship of some false god." The priest looked back at Rogan. "Tell me, how is it that you came to live in Lanasia? Emir Theodorico has had no luck in discovering your country of origin."

"I got here the same way as everybody else. I walked on the land and rode a ship on the sea. I thought the Emir had huge files on all of us? You don't even know where any of us came from?"

The inquisitor sighed. "Of course, we know that Aebreanna Tressalon hails from Pelsemoria, and your Uldra bodyguard is from one of the tribes in Ulheim, and the Baron Tressalon hails from Sabriyya. You, however, are a mystery. Where do you come from?"

Rogan thought about it for a minute. "I suppose that if I had to claim any one place as my home, it would be the Northern Keep."

"I don't mean the place you consider your home. I would very much like to know where it was you were born." Tomas noticed a slight edge in the inquisitor's voice. "The slight accent in your voice that you have obviously taken great pains to conceal would suggest you are from the Gwyndd Islands, as does your adopted name of Eigenhard. Of course, that House has foreworn any knowledge of you and denied any kinship. Your mannerisms and fighting style are more consistent with a man hailing from the Southern coast of Lanasia with training from the oriental lands. You have claimed that you entered the Black Duke's service as a common mercenary, and yet you somehow, miraculously, have risen to become one of Calonar's most trusted advisors and married his daughter, the Dark Priestess."

Again, the knight shrugged. "What can I say? I've done a lot of traveling."

"Emir Theodorico has had contact with House Eigenhard of the Gwyndd Islands, but that family is composed almost entirely of artists and musicians. There are no warriors, reinforcing the evidence that you cannot be of that noble family."

"I really can't say that I'm all that familiar with them myself," the knight admitted.

"And yet you vaguely resemble Baron Dwyer Eigenhard of Grania." He narrowed his eyes. "What caused your split with your real family?" the priest asked suddenly.

"What?" Rogan said flatly.

The inquisitor smiled and leaned back in his seat. "Your family, Rogan Eigenhard. Tell me about your real family. Why is it that, rather than living in the Gwyndd Islands with those who share your blood, you live in the Northlands with the relatives of your wife?"

"It was a better opportunity."

The priest shook his head slightly. "You were first born," he corrected. "You would have inherited the position as Baron of Grania. And as I recall, House

Eigenhard, while not the biggest or strongest, is certainly the most influential in the Gwyndd Islands."

Rogan said nothing. Although the inquisitor did not notice, the knight made a subtle motion with his hand, signaling his squire.

The dark priest looked to the ceiling of the dungeon cell. "I find it interesting that, although you readily claim a position in House Calonar, you still hold the name Eigenhard. I have never once seen any report of you changing your name to Rogan Calonar. You claim the Black Duke as your father. You claim House Calonar as your true family. And yet the Dark Priestess remains Kyla Calonar, and you remain Rogan Eigenhard. Why is that?"

"A man's name doesn't matter," Rogan replied. "His actions matter."

"Oh, I think a name does matter, Rogan Eigenhard," the inquisitor said, standing up and stepping in front of the sneering knight. "I think you can't let go of that name. Why is that, Rogan Eigenhard? Why can't you let go of your real family?"

Rogan glanced past the priest's shoulder. "Would you shut him up please?" he snarled.

A chain wrapped around the inquisitor's throat, and Tomas pushed against the dark priest's legs, forcing him to the floor. The squire continued to apply his advantage of leverage to the inquisitor's throat and back until their captor stopped twitching.

Once ensuring that the priest was dead, Tomas rose and, using the picks Aebreanna had given him, began working on Rogan's shackles. "I'm really glad she taught me that wrist trick," he whispered.

"I guess we finally found a good use for that mouth of yours." Rogan whispered back.

Tomas snorted. "For a minute I was afraid these things were going to poke a hole in my tongue."

"Wouldn't that have been a shame? Good thing you've got those girlish wrists," the knight noted. "You might not have gotten your first hand free."

"How long do you think we've been here?" Tomas asked, opening Rogan's restraints.

"Don't know," the knight replied, rubbing his wrists. "Hours, at least."

Once freed, Beraht dragged the inquisitor's body to his former set of chains.

"What's the plan?" Tomas asked in a hoarse whisper.

Rogan began stripping the inquisitor's robes off the body. "We call the guards in, jump them, and take their gear. Then we walk out."

The squire looked at his grinning knight. "That is a terrible plan."

"Exactly. It's too crazy to try, so who would think to? Besides, we've done it before."

Beraht was about to say something, but Rogan interrupted him. "That time doesn't count."

"What about, Beraht?" Tomas asked. "I don't remember any Uldra-sized guards out there."

"You're not leaving me here," Beraht said flatly.

"Well, you're not exactly decent!" Rogan snapped.

"Is he ever?" Tomas asked.

"Once we kill the guards," the Uldra suggested, "why don't we just go find our gear?"

Rogan, feeling a headache coming on, could only shake his head. Tomas patted the warrior on the shoulder. "Uh, Beraht," the squire said, "we're in the middle of a detention center in a hostile city filled with soldiers, knights, and inquisitors who all want us dead. Maybe we should try something a little less likely to draw a lot of attention."

Beraht snorted. "Oh, sure. If you want to do things the easy way, just go ahead. But whatever we do, it needs to be fast. One of those guards is going to come and check on holy boy over there sooner or later."

"All right." Rogan snapped, trying to head off any more arguments. "We take out the guards and wear their gear. We get Beraht dressed as best we can and then pretend he's our prisoner and try to just walk out of this detention area."

"You know," Tomas noted, "I'd swear I've heard this somewhere before."

Rogan grew red-faced. "Could you please, just for a minute, give me a break?"

"Hey," Beraht noted, a thought entering his mind, "didn't we try a plan just like this that time we tried to break out of—"

"Shut up, Beraht!"

"For a second there, I thought these idiots were going to knock each other out for us!" Beraht laughed, dropping an unconscious guard to the floor.

"The Paranos really need to set up a better training program," Rogan noted, also letting the guard fall who he had slammed into a wall.

"That's all right," Tomas snorted. "As long as we're fighting them, I'll be just as glad that they stay incompetent.

Within minutes, Rogan and Tomas were dressed in the Daivic uniforms and managed to even use the inquisitor's robes to fashion a prisoner's smock for Beraht. As this meant rubbing his more fragrant anatomy against the holy symbols stitched into the garment, the Uldra found the manacles they put on him more acceptable.

Once their disguises, such as they were, were ready, the heroes boldly made their way out into the halls of the small military compound. Even with the late hour, the halls of the small detention building were surprisingly deserted; even the doors were unlocked.

"Is anybody else getting that 'too easy' feeling?" Tomas asked.

"Don't jinx it," Beraht replied. "It's about time we got some luck our way."

The front barracks, the last room they found on the way out of the building, held their missing items. This too was deserted. "I hate it when things go this well," the prince growled.

"So… trap?" Tomas asked.

The knight just shrugged. "At this point, who knows?" Rogan identified his sword and armor. "Let's just gear up. If they do try something, at least we'll be armed."

Accustomed as they were to getting in and out of their gear every day, Rogan, Tomas, and Beraht were dressed, armed, and set within a quarter hour. Even that added time without interruption only added to their growing anxiety, though.

"We should have had to kill somebody by now," Beraht insisted.

Rogan narrowed his eyes. Looking at Tomas, he asked, "Kid, can you pick up any magical effects in the area?"

The young man shrugs. "How in Underworld would I do that?"

"Just relax," the knight instructed. "Deep breaths. It's all about gaining focus by not concentrating, remember?"

"Yeah, all right. Just give me a minute." The squire sat down on the floor and began breathing deeply, focusing on the movements of the muscles in his chest and abdomen as Rogan had taught him. Tomas relaxed his mind and reached out, sensing the currents he had felt before.

"What do you feel, kid?" Rogan asked.

Keeping his eyes closed, Tomas could feel the same strange currents. As he concentrated, it seemed to the squire that, rather than flowing about randomly as they had before, the currents were moving toward the streets outside with a specific purpose.

"Just relax," Rogan said, placing his hand lightly on his squire's shoulder. "Let the magic do the work."

Taking his mentor's advice, the squire took a deep breath, feeling the currents of magic flow into his body as readily as the air. After a moment, Tomas discovered that the currents seemed to have different flavors depending on how he turned them in his thoughts. "I can feel what's happening," he said quietly.

In his mind's eye, the young man let himself flow along the currents, letting them pull his thoughts outside the building and into one of the central plazas scattered throughout the city. Gathered in the plaza were hundreds of people, all paying rapt attention to an inquisitor who was standing atop a recently constructed platform, giving a speech. As the priest spoke, Tomas could feel a number of the dark priest's associates, inconspicuously scattered throughout the crowd, forcing the same currents on which Tomas rode into the minds of the people gathered. As the young man moved about the plaza, trying to understand what was happening, he became aware of the attention of the inquisitors; although they had not located him, they were aware of his presence. Deciding to act upon the better part of valor, Tomas left, instantly opening his eyes and looking about the barracks room he was still sitting in.

"Well?" Rogan demanded.

"I was in a plaza outside," Tomas explained. "Everyone has been called outside to listen to the inquisitors talk. I got the feeling they do this a lot. I can't be sure, but I think the priests were using magic on the minds of the people."

"Could that be why nobody around here is questioning the priests?" Beraht asked.

"It's possible," Rogan grunted. "Either way, we can't fix every problem in the world as we go. If everybody is stuck in a meeting right now, it will make our job all the easier. So let's take advantage of the situation and move."

Tomas nodded enthusiastically. "That'd probably be a good idea. I think one of the inquisitors sensed me. I think they know we've escaped."

"That settles it, then." Rogan decided. "Aebreanna is waiting for us near the palace. Let's move."

Chapter 59

After seeing the boys safely captured, Aebreanna slipped away from the city gate through which she had entered earlier. After stabling their horses near House Parano's ostentatious palace, the agent decided to make use of the time she had to gather a little information.

Very quickly, Aebreanna noted an unusually large number of inquisitors moving throughout the city. She absently fingered the ring Esha had assured her would temporarily not only mask her opalescent eye, but also conceal her magical heritage from any but the most direct probe. Passing a small cluster of priests, Aebreanna noted that they took very little interest in her, which, while putting the baroness at ease as to whether or not they could sense her natural magic, still piqued the spy's curiosity since it truly is the rare male who could resist letting his eyes play along her body.

Deciding to test her theory, Aebreanna scanned the street she was on until she spotted a young woman wearing a rather pretty red dress. Changing course to start walking up behind the young girl, the spy waited until she turned a corner and was temporarily out of sight. Sprinting up behind the oblivious girl, Aebreanna drew a small silver needle from her boot and plunged it into the girl's neck. The chemical worked quickly, and the spy pulled her target deeper into the alley, well out of view of any passerby. Working quickly, she stripped the girl of her clothes and money, leaving as if by accident a small piece of jewelry that would more than compensate for the clothes and inconvenience. Stripping quickly out of her own clothing and packing it into her shoulder bag, Aebreanna then put on the red dress and shoes, securing the girl's thin veil and arranging her long hair. Wanting to add more to the outfit, the spy pulled a long red silk scarf out of her bag and tied it around her waist, enhancing her hips. Next, she carefully cut a line up the dress that would easily expose her shapely leg and modified her makeup to match the clothes and enhance the allure of the thin veil so common among the women of the Endless Sands. Wanting her arms free, Aebreanna stripped the sleeves off at the shoulder and, realizing the dress was a bit too small, removed the top three buttons of the dress to allow for easier breathing and a better view of her breasts. Seeing her preparations nearly done, the baroness took one last step, replacing her dark traveler's cloak with the girl's lighter, soft-red one, covering her victim with her heavier cloak so that the sight of a young girl clad only in her undergarments would not be available to any passing men who might try to take advantage of the girl's predicament.

Her costume in place, Aebreanna climbed nimbly up the side of the building and, vaulting from rooftop to rooftop, made her way back to where the inquisitors were standing. Ensuring there were no witnesses, the spy climbed down into the nearest alley and, making one last inspection of herself to ensure all was ready, boldly stepped out onto the street. Noticing the looks she was drawing from several passing men, not to mention looks of envy and hatred from more than a few women, Aebreanna was satisfied at the sensuality of her appearance.

Adopting a humble pose before the priests, which incidentally would allow them to look straight down the front of her dress, Aebreanna bowed awkwardly to the inquisitor whose red sash was adorned with a gold Inquisition symbol, marking him as the ranking priest. "Excuse me, holy one," she said softly, "I seem to have lost my way and was hoping such a strong man as yourself would help me home." The spy made sure to breathe deeply and showed more than a little leg to the priest.

"If you need assistance, find a soldier," the inquisitor barked, giving the beautiful woman barely a glance. "We have little time for children."

Somewhat taken aback, Aebreanna let her cloak fall back, revealing her very shapely body. "Surely, great priest, you would not force so young and vulnerable a girl to walk the streets without an escort?"

The inquisitor put his hand on her shoulder and forcibly shoved her away. "Be gone!"

Acting cowed, yet seething on the inside, Aebreanna moved away from the priests and back toward the alley from which she had come. Before reaching it, the spy noticed a young couple walking toward her, arm in arm. Walking up to the young man, Aebreanna pulled him into an embrace and kissed him passionately, grabbing his hand and placing it on her chest. The young man offered little resistance that ended quickly. Breaking the kiss, Aebreanna stepped back toward the alley, throwing a look of wicked invitation back over her shoulder. His companion forgotten, the young man rushed to the spy's side.

"Never mind," she said, putting a hand up. "Just checking." Then she pulled her cloak shut and walked back down the alley.

The spy next moved across town until she found the headquarters for the local garrison. Noting a cluster of officers at the main gate, the spy walked by them and turned a corner, stopping as she dropped her bag to recollect her things. While slowly repacking, she overheard the officers mentioning that their commander had just received a promotion and would be leaving soon for Tordenia and a higher position;

they were greatly interested in doing something for him as a farewell present and as a means of gaining his pleasure for possible advancement.

Pulling her cloak tight about her shoulders, she brazenly walked up to them. "Excuse me, gentlemen," she said, opening her cloak to reveal what lay beneath. "I am looking for the commander of this place."

Each of the officers took some time to gaze up and down the *Sy'lva*'s beautiful body. Finally, one of them spoke up. "You have business with the commander?" he asked, sweat glistening on his forehead.

"The boys on the gate thought to give their leader a farewell gift, referencing something about his being promoted," she replied. Pulling back on her hood while still keeping her veil in place as well as the hair covering her right side.

The officers were still in rapt appreciation of the *Sy'lva*'s features. Growing impatient, the spy snapped her fingers just in front of her breasts. "Boys, I do not receive my pay based on an hourly rate but on individual performances. The soldiers on the gate paid for a single transaction and did not pay all that much. So I would be just as happy to complete my business in an efficient manner."

The one officer that was capable of speech thought for a moment, a sly look appearing on his face. "Just how much did they pay for?" he asked.

Aebreanna shrugged, making sure to let more skin appear briefly. "They paid for the usual services; nothing especially special."

"Would you give us one moment?" the leader asked. The group had a whispered conference at the end of which the leader collected a fair amount of money from the others. Returning to Aebreanna, he bounced the purse suggestively. "What would thirty-five gold zeris buy?"

The spy blinked. "When did they start paying you officers in the coin of the Western Empire?" she asked. "The guards are still getting shekels."

"Does it matter?" one of the other officers asked. "It's still gold. What does it matter if its Balshazzar's or Parano's sigil stamped on the coin? It all spends the same."

"True enough," Aebreanna conceded and took the purse. The spy bounced the pouch in her hand for a moment, a thoughtful look on her face. "Thirty-five zeris? For that, he can do nearly anything he likes."

The leader smiled. "Then why don't you go ahead and pay the commander your respects? Just make sure you pay him ours, as well."

Aebreanna smiled and put the purse in her shoulder bag. As she walked past the officers, the spy let her hand slip beneath the leader's belt. "Try not to allow your duties to take you anywhere distant," she breathed. "Once I am finished with the old man, I will surely have strength enough for all of you."

"All of us?" one of them demanded in awe.

The agent shrugged. "All at once or one at a time," she replied. "For the right price, I would allow you to make the choice."

"We'll be here," he stammered.

"Make sure you have plenty of money, boys," she called back as she entered the building. "I feel like having fun tonight."

After a brief search of the building, Aebreanna found the commander's office. Opening the door silently and moving inside, the spy devoutly prayed that she would not have to push her performance too far to get the information she sought. Although prepared for nearly any contingency in the performance of her duties, Aebreanna had little desire to perform the same tiresome seduction to an endless parade of soldiers. It seemed on this mission, however, the Goddess had chosen to smile on Her child and kept the hallways clear until Aebreanna located her prey.

The commander's office was sparsely decorated, with few awards on the walls and no memorabilia of previous campaigns. His desk was free of any paperwork and looked relatively unused. The commander himself was one of the fattest Humans Aebreanna had ever seen. The folds of his flesh very nearly oozed out of his stained and unadorned uniform. His bald head was decorated with only a few wisps of gray hair and a series of unhealthy-looking warts that grew out of the side of his neck. The smell coming from the man was so truly offensive that the spy had great difficulty in fighting back the urge to vomit.

"What is the meaning of this?" the commander demanded, his voice broken by a wheeze full of some kind of fluid.

Forcing her revulsion aside, Aebreanna moved toward the slug, her hips swinging sensuously and her hands playing about her body. "A few of your officers wanted to get you a going away present," she explained.

The commander looked confused. "What present?" he asked.

The spy stopped. Pulling the right strap of her dress down to expose the top of one breast said, "This present. The boys downstairs thought you could use a little entertainment this evening."

Realization and lust dawned on the putrid commander's face, and he began waddling over to Aebreanna with his hands outstretched. Dancing out of his grip, Aebreanna laughed. "Oh no! Your men wanted you to have a very good time! You get the full treatment today!"

The spy led her target back to his chair and forcibly shoved him down into it. Grabbing up her bag, Aebreanna pulled out a pair of thin scarves and proceeded to tie the commander down.

"I like this game!" he drooled.

Turning her back to him, Aebreanna looked back over her shoulder. "I thought you might."

Seeing that the commander was unable to move, Aebreanna moved the other strap of her dress down, holding it over her breasts with her hands. "Your men said something about a transfer," she purred.

The commander nodded dumbly. "Several of us are going. We just got the orders to move to Tordenia."

Aebreanna began rhythmically swinging her hips, moving her bottom up against the commander. "You must be very good to get a job in the Western Empire," she noted.

His eyes boring into Aebreanna's figure, the commander's face went from an unhealthy pale to an even more unhealthy red. "They finally noticed me. I knew someday they would."

The spy let the front of her dress slip down to her waist, turned and leaned over far enough to put her breasts just out of reach of the commander's lips, much to his gasping frustration. "You were not always a big strong commander?" she asked, each syllable enhanced by a pulsing forward toss of her chest.

His breath now coming in ragged gasps, he shook his head. "I spent years as a clerk. It wasn't until the Duke signed his treaty with Emir Balshazzar and allowed the Inquisition into the city that we started getting the respect we deserved."

Aebreanna put her right foot up on the commander's groin and pushed in ever so softly. "We?" she asked.

The commander's eyes rolled back in his head. "The clerks," he gasped. "Supply, bookkeepers, all of us that keep the military running. We finally started getting the positions we deserved."

Aebreanna moved her hands slowly down her leg, caressing each muscle until she reached her shoe and pulled it loose. The spy then put her foot down on the floor and turned, bending over and messaging her other leg as she had the first, letting the commander see that she wore no undergarments. "I thought it was the Inquisition that ran the military now," she said, pulling off the other shoe.

"That's just a rumor. I may have a few inquisitors that offer suggestions from time to time, but I'm still in command."

Still dancing slowly, the beautiful spy ran her hands up and down her body, caressing her breasts, hair, and between her legs. "What happened to the old commanders?" she asked.

The commander was straining against his restraints now, becoming more and more desperate to satisfy his lust. "Gone. They're all gone to command training centers outside Tordenia. That's where they're sending all the army leaders."

Aebreanna began pulling slowly on her dress, exposing more and more of the smooth flesh beneath her stomach. "I hope these transfers have not left the army vulnerable."

Before he could answer, the commander's eyes went, if possible, even wider. Aebreanna paused her dance. "Are you all right?" she asked.

The fat commander continued struggling against the restraints, his face changing from bright red to blue. Suddenly, he opened his mouth with a gurgling gasp, his tongue sticking out, and let out one last breath. All sounds over, the commander's head tilted back and to the side. An even more putrid stench forced itself into Aebreanna's nose as she realized his bowel and bladder had released.

"Oh, dear," Aebreanna said. She checked for a pulse but found none, briefly satisfying herself with muttering some *Sy'lva'n* curses.

Realizing that, should her luck return to its usual path, one of the commander's aides would surely be coming to check on him at any moment, Aebreanna decided to make only the briefest of searches before taking her leave of the departed commander. During her cursory investigation, she happened upon an official decree from the Mari Palace under Edmondo Parano's signature placing every inquisitor at the top of the chain of command for all his military. The spy stared at the document for a moment, stunned at the implication, but then compared it to other decrees from the Duke of House Parano. They were close, but did not match. The most recent orders had been signed by another, forging Edmondo's script. Aebreanna pursed her lips and began digging even deeper into the commander's desk, seeking more intelligence.

"What in Underworld?" The same officer who had hired Aebreanna as a present decided at that particular moment to enter without asking. Standing at the door, looking at the obviously-dead commander tied to his chair with his vacant eyes staring in accusation at his murderer and the topless Aebreanna rummaging through his desk, the spy could only imagine how such a scene must appear to the casual observer.

"Should you believe it or not," she said calmly, "there exists a perfectly logical explanation."

Turning toward the hall, the officer yelled, "Guards!" Unfortunately, because he had turned, he failed to see Aebreanna vault over the commander's desk and launch herself at the young officer. On a positive note, however, he did get an excellent view of the beautiful spy's chest and her well-formed legs, not to mention her foot as it impacted his face. Using the reverse momentum to flip back into the office, Aebreanna dove to her bag and, taking only enough time to replace her shoes and grab her cloak, sprinted out the door, nearly forgetting to pull her dress back up on the way out.

Replacing the cloak about her shoulders, Aebreanna tried walking calmly toward the front exit, hoping her disguise would hold for only a few more moments. Just as the front doors came within view, however, a shout of "Stop that woman!" rang through the building.

"Of course," she sighed as two orderlies jumped at her.

Dispatching the two men with a series of jabs and kicks, the spy flew across the room toward the doors and freedom. The three guards who tried to block her escape proved to be no problem as she simply flipped over their heads and neutralized the middle one with a spinning back kick. As the other two guards spun to face her, Aebreanna drew their daggers from their belts and, doing a flawless split, drove the small blades through the soldiers' knees. Running toward the gate, the spy pulled a tiny pouch from her bag and opened it, flinging its contents into the faces of the two guards moving to intercept her. The powder burned at their eyes and set them to coughing violently, giving Aebreanna more than enough of a lead to disappear into the population of the city.

Chapter 60

There were multiple alerts out, which Aebreanna could honestly not tell if they were due solely to her actions or if they had something to do with whatever mayhem the boys were no doubt up to by now. The agent glanced up at the setting sun and knew she still had several hours before their prearranged meeting, but the increase in patrols meant she was unlikely to accomplish anything of value other than avoiding capture. Already, she had noted several individuals bearing only the most vague similarity in body type to her being accosted by Parano soldiers. The time for stealth and evasion had come.

"You there!" a shout came from the opposite end of the alley in which Aebreanna was standing.

After sending an irritated glance skyward, the baroness sent an irritated blade into the soldier's throat and leapt upward, climbing the wall opposite her. Climbing quickly before the dead man's comrades could respond, Aebreanna reached the rooftop and left the area. *Accidentally kill one fat man*, the spy thought as she vaulted from one roof to another, *and everyone behaves as though it were the greatest cultural loss this city had ever experienced*. Somehow, Aebreanna knew, once the boys escaped they would not receive even a small percentage of this kind of pursuit.

An arrow shot past her head, forcing her down to roll along the current rooftop. Without pause, Aebreanna reached the limit of the roof and, grabbing the edge, flipped and quickly scaled down the wall. Having had no time to look before she leapt, however, the spy failed to notice the squad of Shamashi soldiers waiting at the base of the building when she landed.

"*Fal'elesh'a*," she snarled at the soldiers.

"Submit, whore!" one of soldiers, an officer, shouted from the safety of the rear.

"None of you *leph'en* have the prowess to force me into submission! I will have each of you kneeling before me, begging for release!"

Encouraged by the presence of more than a dozen of his soldiers, the officer stepped forward; he stayed a distance he hoped was safe from Aebreanna's blades, however. "You are surrounded," he declared. "We have archers on every roof. Throw down your weapons, and we will spare your life, woman!"

Aebreanna blazed in growing fury. "Throw down your weapons, and I will only cut off a small piece of your body… man!" she promised.

The officer paused and gasped, his face going pale and his legs moving back. The other soldiers all similarly withdrew, their eyes widening. Confused, Aebreanna looked about. Mutterings of 'witchcraft' began growing through the assembled men. The spy paused and looked down at her ring. The metal was cold and lifeless, its enchantment spent. Her hand involuntarily went to her left, exposed eye, realizing her race and her unwanted aura of magical heritage was apparent.

"Sylva!" one of the soldiers yelled. Others picked up the chant. The officer drew his sword and growled. "You will die here, Sylva whore!" he snarled and spit in Aebreanna's face.

Before she could react, the officer dropped his sword and screamed in sudden pain, grabbing his stomach and dropping to the ground. His scream continued, finally changing to a squeal. The man squealed again as Aebreanna looked on in confusion and the other soldiers watched in horror. The officer held up his hands and in dismay saw that they were changing into hooves. His nose became round and flat. His ears pointed out and a curly tail erupted from his pants. Throughout the change, the creature that was once a man continued to squeal in horror.

When it was over, the pig shook itself and stepped out of the clothes it once wore. Looking down at itself, the creature squealed again and ran down the alley, its horror echoing off the walls.

"*Sharsihr*," one of the soldiers said, using the Lugha word for witch.

"*Sharsihr*," another repeated the word, looking at Aebreanna in hateful suspicion. Having made a study of many languages, the spy was unfortunately familiar with the word and the implication of a crowd of superstitious Humans gathering around a woman, accusing her of witchcraft.

An invisible force barreled down the alley, knocking all of the soldiers off their feet but leaving Aebreanna untouched. In her mind, the spy heard a single word. "Run."

She followed the invisible force as it shoved through the remaining soldiers, hurling the last of them with incredible force across the street. Once free of the deadly alley, Aebreanna paused only briefly, spotting the doors to an Adamic cathedral, decaying from lack of use, open of their own volition. The agent sprinted in just as a series of swirling dust clouds descended on the street, throwing clouds of debris into the air and obscuring her escape.

Aebreanna entered the old church and closed the heavy doors with little effort, leaving her back to the room and breathing heavy, her heart racing not from the threats to her life nor from the flight, but from who she realized was within this sanctuary. She did not need to see him. She never needed sight to recognize his presence. She could feel him, not only in her mind, where his fingers always had a light hold, but also in her soul.

"I did not call for you," she said evenly.

"You never do," he replied. "You never have to."

"Then why do you always interfere?"

"Why do you?"

"No!" she snapped, beating a fist against the door. "None of your games! None of your tricks! None of your madness! You are here for a purpose. Reveal it and leave!"

"I thought I already did."

"Oh, please. You would not have come here and expended any amount of energy to resolve that small confrontation."

"Would I not?"

Aebreanna straightened but still faced the door. "You have another reason. You probably arranged that conflict just to resolve it."

"That does sound like something I would do."

"Answer me, damn you!"

"Ask a question."

Aebreanna screamed in frustration, beating on the heavy door. It was not just the frustration of the moment, but the frustration of her entire life, a lifetime of absence and disappointment. A lifetime of unwanted blood and a hateful heritage. She screamed and beat her fists and wanted to change the past.

He just waited, as patient and undeniable and perpetually present as the blood in her veins.

At last spent of her outward rage, Aebreanna stopped screaming and beating at the door that suffered for all the helplessness she suffered due to this man. She took several deep breaths, trying desperately to regain her *Sy'lva'n* calm. There was no one in the world who could affect her this way; none but this one. She finally turned and faced him.

Darkholm was, of course, the same as always. From the first moment she had seen him to this one, he was the same. He still appeared to be a middle-aged male, though Aebreanna knew that to be a lie; Darkholm used the form of whatever race would cause him the least chance of being bothered. When he appeared to her as a little girl, he was a noble Sylvu. When he appeared to Rogan, the Trickster was a Human. His wizardly robes were wrinkled and patched, with frayed edges and the signs of some half-hearted patching. No indication of rank or specific school of magic decorated them, nor did anything resembling a spot of cleanliness. His bright eyes still held the glow of madness, and his beard could still use a wash and at least the occasional visit of a comb. His heavy leather belt had a number of pouches and a small case on one side, which Aebreanna knew could hold anything from scrolls to a live animal, depending on the Trickster Mage's mood. He carried no staff as most wizards did, instead standing with his thumbs tucked into his belt, calmly waiting on her.

"And where is you manservant?" she asked calmly. "Nek is the one with whom I can at least count upon for decency."

"With me," the Trickster Mage replied.

Aebreanna rolled her opalescent eye. "I suppose pointing out the fact that you are standing before me while he is not would be superfluous?"

"And yet you said it anyway."

"What do you want, Darkholm?"

"You know what I want."

"And you know my response!" she snapped, putting her hands on her hips.

Darkholm shrugged. "Patience is a virtue, or so I have been told."

"What is your purpose here?"

"Asked and answered."

"What are your other purposes here, then?"

"Do you want them all?" Darkholm grinned. "That might take a while."

Aebreanna sighed and shook her head. "I tire of this," she said. "I tire of you. Rogan and the others find you so very useful in their endeavors, so why is it you do not pester them?"

"They were not the ones about to get lynched."

"So suddenly you care?" she demanded. "Suddenly you want to help? Suddenly you feel protective?" Aebreanna pulled back the hair from the right side of her face, revealing the terrible, monstrous reality she was trying so hard to ignore, to hide from the world. She stepped forward, her one remaining eye blazing with her hatred, her bitterness, for a lifetime of neglect culminating in the ruination of her flesh. "What of THIS!?!" she roared.

Darkholm took a step back and averted his eyes.

"Look!" Aebreanna commanded and demanded. "What of this!?! Where were you when THIS happened!?!"

"If I could have prevented-"

"NO!!!" She let her honey blonde mane fall back into place, almost unconsciously adjusting it to hide her great shame. "No. You knew it would happen! You let it happen! Just like you let my mother be raped and murdered by your brother!"

"There are some events that cannot be prevented," Darkholm said feebly.

"Your artificial attempts at attention are far too late to be of any interest to me. If you truly wanted to come to the rescue of someone, perhaps it should have been my mother! Perhaps it should have been before the Druug mutilated me!"

A shadow crossed Darkholm's face, exactly as Aebreanna had hoped.

"How long are you going to hate me for what I have to be?" he asked.

"How long are you going to live?" she replied venomously.

Darkholm laughed suddenly. "Funny you should ask that." The Trickster Mage shook his head somewhat sadly and turned, walking toward a side door. "The way you came may not be safe," he warned. Darkholm reached the side door, and it opened for him. "Oh, and keep Rogan's squire safe, he will be the key to…" He glanced back at his daughter. "He can help you avenge your mother." The Trickster Mage entered the room, and the side door began closing behind him.

Aebreanna hurried forward and intercepted the door before it could finish closing. She pulled it back open and entered behind Darkholm, finding the room beyond empty. Instead of her despicable sire, there was instead a hallway leading into a mausoleum. The Sylva entered and looked about, noting in surprise that each of the coffins had been recently opened and the bodies removed.

From within the cathedral, Aebreanna could hear the sounds of a patrol entering, no doubt continuing their search for her. Quickly, Aebreanna searched through the church's mausoleum and found a second exit leading out, behind the old building. The street beyond appeared to hold no soldiers, so the agent once again slipped into the city.

Chapter 61

With what seemed to be the entire city drawn to its many marketplaces by the insidious magic of Balshazzar's inquisitors, their trip to Parano's palace was uneventful but very tense. Leading the way, Rogan moved Tomas and Beraht from one back alley to another, slipping from shadow to shadow on silent feet as his veteran eyes scanned the surrounding buildings constantly for any hint of danger. Beraht watched their rear, moving with absolute certainty as though daring anyone to block their path or try to attack from behind; the Uldra moved without sound with his mighty waraxe resting on one shoulder, eager for a chance at violence. All around them the city was still; a dry wind made the only sound to accompany the droning speech of the inquisitors, which only added to the tension that each of the heroes felt as they drew ever closer to their goal.

Between his nervous glances into the surrounding shadows cast by the bright moon shining her light on the tall brick buildings between which they stalked, Tomas was bemused by the growing sight of the Mari palace, conquered home of House Parano. Built of flawless marble inlaid with gold, the palace belied the poverty implied by the hovels of the lower city and even belittled the more ornate houses of the wealthy surrounding it. Strange teardrop-shaped domes adorned the building at several points that towered over the city, casting long shadowy fingers that grasped at the wealth Daivic was said to hold. Great balconies jutted out of the palace's upper levels to loom over the gardens surrounding Parano's seat of power to look out on the desert over which the Noble House ruled. A great wall rose up to separate the city's rulers from the people who sustained them, pushing away the homes and shops whose endless toil made such splendid luxury possible. The palace was a monument to noble arrogance and haughty superiority.

Rogan motioned for his team to stop when he reached the end of an alley that looked out on the walls surrounding Duke Parano's palace. A low growl rumbled from the knight's throat as he looked at the towering monstrosity denying them access. Only one gate could be seen from the alley in which they stood and, true to his team's luck, the soldiers were still at their posts, rather than being carried away by the speech of the inquisitors.

"Your growling carries far in the night," Aebreanna said.

The three men jumped.

"A little warning, next time!" Tomas snapped in a hoarse whisper.

"Well?" Rogan demanded in a low whisper.

"Each point of access is guarded by at least four Parano soldiers," Aebreanna replied calmly. "Any one of which can raise the alarm by the time we can approach."

The knight looked up at the crescent moon that cast a damnable amount of light on the large open area that had long ago been cleared around the wall to prevent exactly what the heroes planned to do that evening. "Can we go over?" he suggested.

The Sylva shook her head slightly. "While I, and perhaps your young squire, could scale the wall without need of grappling equipment, you and Sir Beraht would be unable."

"Could you distract the guards at one of the gates?" Tomas asked.

"Possible," she replied. "I would not recommend it, however. Setting aside the unavoidable consequences of such a diversion, there is always the possibility that at least one of my intended targets would be . . . uninterested."

"Uninterested?" the squire remarked. "How could any man be uninterested?"

"They didn't have men that liked to cross swords where you come from, kid?" Rogan asked while staring at the distant gate and its surrounding guards.

"Cross swords? What does..." Tomas blinked. "Oh," he said, suddenly understanding.

"So," the knight continued, "we can't scale the wall since we don't have the equipment. We can't sneak up on the guards since it's too bright. We can't just rush them since they would have too much warning. We don't know how long the city will be busy with whatever the inquisitors are doing so we have to hurry."

"We can't sneak," Tomas mused. "We can't fight. We can't hide. What does that leave us?" Then the squire had a thought. "Hey, Beraht, how strong are you?"

"Come here, and I'll show you."

"What are you thinking, kid?" Rogan asked.

"Well, Aebreanna and I can get over that wall, and if Beraht gives you a boost, the two of us can pull you up and over."

"What about, Beraht," the knight asked. "How does he get over?"

"I don't," the warrior replied. "You three go get the prisoners. I'll get the horses and meet you at that gate."

"Once we have the princess and her father," Tomas continued, "we'll signal Beraht and rush the gate from both sides. At that point, they can call for all the help they want since we'll be mounted and heading out of town anyway."

"With a huge contingent of soldiers in close pursuit," Aebreanna pointed out.

"Can't the princess and her father help with that?" Tomas asked.

Rogan nodded. "There are those Shamashi we saw outside the city walls," he mused. "Their tribe would be close. If Safiyya and her father are with us and they call for help, the warriors'll cover our escape."

Aebreanna threw a weary glance at the knight. "Please do not suggest we actually attempt this ridiculous plan?" she pleaded.

"I don't have a better idea, and it has the advantage of us moving right now so why not?"

The Sylva shook her head. "This will not go well," she sighed.

As is so often the case, Beraht's friends seriously underestimated the Uldra's strength. Once free of his armor and clad only in the padded vest and pants he wore under his chainmail, Tomas was able to, with only a slight boost from Rogan, scale the wall beside Aebreanna. The two crouched low on the narrow wall and reached down to receive Rogan's outstretched hands once Beraht had lifted the knight up. Unfortunately, their Uldra friend was never a person of great patience; and rather than stand with Rogan's feet in his hands while his two weakest comrades tried to pull the knight up, Beraht simply gave Rogan a greater boost than anyone was really expecting.

With a startled yelp, Rogan vaulted over his squire's head, while Aebreanna sighed and shook her head. By a great stroke of luck, there was a large stack of canvas bags on the other side of the wall that provided a convenient place for Tomas and Aebreanna to climb down. In a great leveler of luck, Rogan had landed right beside the soft bags on a stone path. The two were able to collect their friend and move into the shadows of some nearby trees until Rogan could regain his senses.

Once awake and finished with the series of curses he felt Beraht deserved, Rogan dusted himself off and drew his blade, leading Tomas and Aebreanna through the dark garden surrounding the palace. "Any idea where the princess and her father will be?" the squire asked in the barest of whispers. It took some effort not to let the exotic scents of the myriad flowers in the palace gardens overwhelm him.

The knight jerked his thumb at a wide balcony that overlooked the expansive garden, facing toward the south. "That's where high-ranking prisoners were usually kept," he replied. "Parano will want to keep Safiyya and the Padishah safe and relatively happy so that the Shamashi won't rise up."

"If that is the case," Aebreanna whispered, "then our only dilemma is a stealthy approach to their quarters and a safe extraction."

The small group exited the garden and reached the palace itself, pressing into the side of the building. "There's a servant's entrance into those rooms that's away from the main corridors," Rogan said while moving carefully along the wall. "We'll get up there that way."

"How do you know so much about this place?" Tomas asked.

"I've been here before," the knight replied, then held his hand up for silence and stillness.

Two Parano guards approached from the opposite direction the three adventurers were moving, engaged in casual conversation with their curved swords sheathed and their spears held casually.

Rogan nodded to Aebreanna and pressed even closer against the curve of the building, motioning for Tomas to do the same. By the time the guards drew close enough to spot the warriors waiting in ambush, it was too late. Rogan shot forward in a blur of controlled violence and jabbed his elbow into a guard's stomach. The knight then spun around behind the gasping man and pressed his forearm across the guard's throat while simultaneously pushing his knees into the back of the man's legs, forcing him to the ground where Rogan continued to squeeze against the man's throat. Aebreanna moved even faster than her Human friend, seeming to leap into the soldier's arms while, in the same movement, seizing the arm with which the guard was holding his spear with both of her hands and grabbing the poor man's head with her legs. The momentum of Aebreanna's leap forced the guard to the ground, where the Sylva pressed her legs tighter against either side of the man's head; and with a slow gargle from the guard that ended with a sickening snap, the man stopped moving.

Rogan looked up from where he continued to lie on the first guard, limiting the man's weakening struggles, and glanced at his squire. "Put on that armor and grab the gear," he whispered, indicating with a jerk of his head the guard from whom Aebreanna was unwrapping herself.

"What about that one?" Tomas asked.

"He'll be done in a minute," the knight grunted.

Once both guards were safely dead and their bodies stashed in the surrounding trees, Rogan and Tomas donned the odd scale armor common to Parano soldiers but kept their own swords, leaving behind the unfamiliar curved blades in favor of their own weapons. The squire noted that even with his lean frame, he did not fit into the armor very well. "Won't these attract attention?" the squire asked.

Rogan settled the pointed helmet onto his head and grimaced when he realized it was slightly too small. "The people in there don't pay any attention to servants and less to soldiers," he replied. "Besides, we only have to walk in a door, turn left and we're up the stairs and into the prisoners' chambers."

Moving confidently, Rogan led Tomas forward, while Aebreanna trailed behind, staying in the shadows and trusting to her nimble and deadly skills to avoid detection. Just as the knight had said, only a short walk brought them to an inconspicuous door that, upon entry, revealed a silent kitchen and a narrow stairway. The party's luck held as they climbed up to the higher levels where Rogan had guessed Princess Safiyya and her father were being held; no guards and few servants were seen at this late hour. Tomas kept his eyes straight ahead as he followed Rogan but used his peripheral vision to track each of these few individuals as long as he could.

The stairs led to a vast hallway with a domed ceiling that arched high overhead. The marble pillars were adorned with intricate carvings of nature, while the walls seemed to be covered in the strange spidery script of the Shamashi language written in golden characters. The floors were polished so bright that it seemed the heroes were walking across a frozen pool. Everywhere there was the smell of burning incense and the spicy perfume so popular in the Endless Sands that made the air so thick Tomas feared he would gag. Although it was late and there were few people about, the strange, long-necked oil lamps used in the Endless Sands abounded throughout the hallway, bathing them all in a soft, golden light that made Tomas uneasy in his efforts to remain invisible.

Moving with a confidence that his squire prayed was justified, Rogan led them to a set of large wooden doors inlaid with gold. A pair of guards stood outside the doors who eyed the approaching group wearily. As Rogan and Tomas approached, it became obvious they were imposters and the guards drew breath to shot an alarm. He never had a chance to make a sound; Aebreanna, unseen until then, jabbed a small needle into the guard's throat. At the same time, Tomas leapt forward to keep the armored man from falling to the ground in a great clatter, and Rogan moved alongside his squire to grab the second guard's shoulders, cutting the man's throat in a flash.

Aebreanna snatched a key from her victim's belt and unlocked the door. Moving quickly, the Sylva held the door open, while Rogan and Tomas dragged the bodies inside. With one quick check for signs of violence, Aebreanna quietly closed the door and secured it behind them.

"What is the meaning of this?" a light voice thick with the Shamashi accent demanded from within the room.

Tomas dropped the dead guard and turned, ready for further threats but saw none. The wide chamber opened out to the large balcony the squire had seen on their approach through the gardens below. Like most of the rest of the palace, the floors were made of polished marble with divan-like couches scattered throughout. A low table with an arrangement of untouched fruit rested beside the central couch on which was reclining, the young man guessed, Princess Safiyya.

The Shamashi princess leaned back on her seat, looking at the three intruders with weariness but little, if any, actual fear showing in her round, overly large, dark eyes. Her soft brown skin seemed to complement the gold furniture surrounding her just as the diaphanous blue dress Safiyya wore complemented her youthful curves. Rather than a dress or even one of the flowing long tunics of the Endless Sands, the princess wore a strange satin halter that, while concealing the bare minimum of what modesty demanded, left her abdomen and very long arms exposed to the warmth of the desert night. The princess' feathery mane of black hair was tied with a series of blue ribbons so that the tail spilled down, along her body like a wave of night. With a start, Tomas realized that Safiyya was still a fairly young girl, only just entering into womanhood.

Rogan pulled off his borrowed helmet, letting his mass of red hair free, and grinned at Safiyya. "Hello, Princess," he said.

Safiyya's large dark eyes widened in shock at the sight of her rescuers. "Rogan?" she said breathlessly. Then, with a squeal of joy, the Shamashi princess leapt from her divan and threw herself into the knight's arms, covering his weathered face in kisses as she began to weep in joy. Despite her youth and clearly not being fully grown, the Shamashi princess was nearly as tall as the knight.

Tomas watched calmly at the spontaneous, yet familiar, display of enthusiasm before commenting. "What is it with you and princesses?" he asked.

"It's not like that," Rogan replied as he fended off Safiyya's joyful reunion.

Tomas looked at Aebreanna who stood with a neutral expression. "It isn't?"

The spy shrugged. "Prince Rogan's time among the Shamashi is not one with which I am familiar," she admitted. "Only after he left the Endless Sands did our noble prince finally encounter and join House Calonar."

"So we don't have any way of knowing what really happened while he was here?"

"Will you two shut up?" Rogan demanded while finally succeeding in pushing Safiyya off him. He held the Shamashi princess off the ground without strain. Even with his great strength, the knight should not have been able to hold up Safiyya, and yet it seemed as though the princess had very little weight. "It wasn't like that! Safiyya was kidnapped by a tribal leader that was at war with her father, and I rescued her. And she was only four at the time, by the way!"

"What took you so long this time?" Safiyya demanded, hitting the Northlands prince in the side of the head. "I have been held for two years!"

Rogan threw an angry expression at Aebreanna. The Sylva sighed and lowered her gaze. "I'm sorry, Princess," the knight said. "I only just found out. Where's your father?"

Tears formed in the girl's great eyes, causing them to swirl with color like black pears exposed to moonlight. She buried her face against Rogan's broad chest and whispered, "Gone." "Parano said he had taken ill, but I believe that the demon had my father killed for not giving in to his demands."

The knight was quiet for a moment, holding Safiyya close as a flash of grief crossed his face. "Why did Parano take you?" Rogan asked. "How?"

"Edmondo Parano declared that all the Shamashi were to serve him," the princess replied, pulling free of Rogan's arms and straightening, collecting her composure. "That we were his children now. By the old laws, Parano took a wife from each of the tribes and called on all sheiks to come to Daivic and swear loyalty."

"But what about your father? He was the padishah. The sheiks were loyal to him. The tribes could have fought."

"What's a sheik?" Tomas whispered to Aebreanna.

"Their name for a tribal leader," she replied. "Usually the elder with the most wealth and influence."

"Father had united the tribes, but the Paranos had gold and great magic. He brought soldiers and priests from the Western Empire to fight for him, and many tribes sold themselves to him. Other sheiks led their people north to Qasim and Sabriyya to escape his power or west to the Valley of the Winds to hide and build strength to one day fight."

"What about your tribe?" Rogan asked.

The princess pointed out to the surrounding desert. "They wait outside the city. They will not leave me but will not be made unclean by this place."

Aebreanna stepped forward and bowed slightly to the Shamashi princess. "Your Highness," she said. "What is happening to the people of this city?"

Safiyya hugged herself as though to ward off a chill. "There is great evil here," she replied. "Priests from the Western Empire came with great magic and made slaves of the people. Their minds are made weak, and they cannot fight the Paranos."

"That agrees with what I saw for myself today," Aebreanna confirmed.

"Is your tribe affected by the inquisitor's magic?" Tomas asked.

Safiyya shook her head. "Only those inside the city's walls are slaves to the priest's magic. My people are still free."

"We have to do something about this," Tomas insisted.

"Like what?" Rogan demanded. "We're four people against all of Parano's soldiers, the forces Balshazzar has sent here to support him, and whatever else the inquisitors can throw at us. We don't have the strength to stop this."

"What about Duke Edmondo himself?" Tomas suggested. "If this is his palace, maybe we can find him here and, I don't know, kidnap him and give him to the Shamashi."

"The demon is not here," Safiyya said. "He has gone to the City of All Sins to negotiate the terms of their joining the Western Empire." She looked at Rogan. "That is… the Inquisitors say he has gone. Many Paranos have left the city in recent months."

"When is the last time you spoke with a member of House Parano?" Aebreanna asked. "When is the last time you saw one?"

The Shamashi princess thought. "Many weeks," she admitted. "There have been public appearances, but always from a distance. I have no spoken to one of the demons since… The winter. The new year."

Rogan shook his head. "This is too much," he declared. "We've still got a job to do, and we're getting pulled in too many directions."

"Agreed," Aebreanna said. "We must withdraw and readdress the situation when the odds are more favorable."

"What of my people?" Safiyya asked softly of Rogan. "Will you leave them helpless?"

"We're heading into the Western Empire to deal with Balshazzar," the knight replied. "If we're successful there, then a lot of the power Parano is depending on will vanish."

"Then you must take me to my people," the princess demanded. "If the Paranos can be made weak, then I must take my tribe to Valley of the Winds and join with the other Shamashi."

"If we get you out of the city, can your people get us away from Parano's forces?" Rogan asked.

The Shamashi princess nodded. "The desert is our ally," she said confidently. "There is none that can deny the Shamashi the freedom of our home."

Safiyya retrieved a pair of slippers and a cloak of blue satin. She placed these on her slight shoulders and pulled up her hood, securing a veil across the bottom half of her face. Once covered and ready, the princess led Rogan and his team back into the palace and into a hidden staircase that brought them out near the gardens. "Do you know a way out of the city?" Rogan asked in a tense whisper.

The princess shook her head. "If I knew a such way, I would be with my people already."

"Then I guess we do it Beraht's way," the knight grimaced.

"Goddess, help us," Aebreanna prayed.

Rogan and Tomas led the way toward the southern gate and the Human guards who manned it, pausing in the shadows to prepare for the inevitable disaster. "How do we know if Beraht is in place and ready?" Tomas asked.

"He has had more than ample time to retrieve our mounts and return," Aebreanna noted. "We must simply trust that our Uldra associate is ready."

"How do we signal him?"

"Leave that to us." Aebreanna rose and motioned for Safiyya to join her. Over Rogan's chocked objections, the two women stepped out onto the stone path and walked boldly forward, toward the guards. Hissing oaths in several languages, Rogan motioned for Tomas to approach the guards from one side, while the knight moved around to the opposite.

The guards quickly spotted Aebreanna and Safiyya. One of them, the leader by the marks of rank on his armor, stepped forward, flanked closely by a pair of his men and barking orders in the Shamashi tongue. Princess Safiyya continued walking forward and responded to the soldier with an imperious retort. While Tomas had no idea what the words were, there could be no doubt from the princess's tone and gestures that she was giving orders with an expectation of obedience. The guards looked less sure of themselves but held their ground. The leader stepped forward and grabbed the tall princess roughly by one long, slender arm.

An Uldric waraxe spun through the air and planted itself into the leader's back, throwing him past Aebreanna and Safiyya. With a roaring battlecry that shook the walls, Beraht charged the party's horses directly at the gate, showing no indication that the guards would serve as any kind of obstacle. Assuming that would serve as a signal as well as anything else they could have come up with, Rogan and Tomas charged out from either side of the soldiers, felling three of the guards and causing a debilitating shock that froze the soldiers in place. Stick and Urge, free of any control, ran these men down, stomping their screaming, broken bodies into the dirt. Those few men who were not killed outright by the stampeding warhorses were quickly finished off by Rogan and Tomas as Beraht reined in and turned the mounts, retrieving his waraxe and cleaning it with a contemptuous shake.

Tomas ran to Urge and quickly mounted his eager warhorse, noting that the others were also climbing onto their mounts. Safiyya needed no urging to climb onto Stick, holding tight to Rogan. The knight led them all out, away from the palace and back into the city toward the southern gates and the freedom that the desert beyond promised.

A number of shouted alarms rang out from several points in and around the palace. The alarm was relayed to the palace walls where a signal fire was lit, letting the alert spread within minutes throughout Daivic all the way to the city walls, far faster than Tomas and his friends could move. There was no doubt that soldiers throughout the city were mobilizing, and any chance at a swift escape from the city was growing smaller with each passing moment.

With the thought of an imminent pursuit, the adventurers galloped through the streets. Finding them empty for now, Aebreanna led the small group through the urban maze toward the southern gate and, they all hoped, the safety that could be found with the Shamashi tribe. Unfortunately, their luck was not, as usual, to last.

Even as the gate came within sight, Tomas spoke those most damnable of words. "I think we're going to make it!"

Before the squire could even close his mouth, eight inquisitors emerged from the gatehouse even as an iron portcullis slammed down to block their exit from the city.

Rogan reined in Stick and threw a hard look at his apprentice.

"Surrender now!" the Inquisition leader called.

"That's a good idea," Rogan noted.

"It's the sensible thing to do," Tomas insisted.

"I guess they got us," Beraht sighed.

With grins so dark they could freeze the blood, the three warriors raised their weapons.

"On second thought," Rogan sneered.

"Where's the fun in surrendering?" Tomas finished.

Roaring promises of pain and death, all three of the warriors leapt at the inquisitors as Aebreanna dismounted and bolted down a side alley, leaving Safiyya safely back with their pack animals. Beraht, using traditional Uldra battle tactics, barreled into his enemies with little finesse and no hesitation, beheading one priest and, without slowing, cleaving a second in two. Rogan followed closely in his friend's wake, jabbing his sword through the chest of one priest while Stick bit down on another inquisitor's shoulder and tore free a hideous amount of flesh. With the lesser priests engaged, Tomas could sense one of the ranking inquisitors trying to harness the currents of magic to use against them; to prevent this, Urge nearly danced past the clumsy thrust of an attacking priest and charged the adept. The ranking priest, caught off guard in the middle of trying to summon his magic, was unable to defend himself as Tomas buried his blade in the man's chest.

Two of the inquisitors, stunned by the ferocity of the attack, leapt to either side of the melee, desperately trying to remain free of the death that was being handed out so freely by the warriors. One died without ever seeing Aebreanna, his throat opened from behind as the Sylva emerged from the shadows. His comrade on the other side of the street saw this with horror and raised his hand in preparation to summon his magic, but before the inquisitor could utter even one world in the arcane language, a Sylvai blade imbedded itself in his throat.

Safiyya came forward with the pack horses as Beraht rode up to the winch that controlled the portcullis and, with only a few pulls, raised the barrier enough to allow them all escape. Seeing the last of their enemies, still alive and cringing in terror, the Uldra saved the dark priest any further indignity with a quick swing of his waraxe before rejoining his friends. The party then rode hard out of the gate before any further pursuit could be mustered against them.

Chapter 62

Less than a mile from the city, Rogan reined Stick in. "Where are you people camped?" he asked.

Safiyya pointed to the other side of the Harun toward a distant collection of trees and the dim lights of campfires. Rogan looked at the camp and shook his head. "Why is nothing ever easy?" he demanded.

"Is there a place to cross the river?" Tomas asked.

"Sure," Rogan snorted. "There's a bridge inside the city and another one to the north. The only other crossing is by boat or all the way down at Oneld."

"Then how are the Shamashi going to help us?"

"Damn fine question. I don't suppose you have a damn fine answer."

"Me? This was your idea!"

"Gentlemen," Aebreanna interrupted, "perhaps recrimination can wait for a time when we do not need to be actively fleeing for our lives."

Rogan nodded. "Let's ride."

As the eastern horizon began to glow, bathing the desert around them with the eerie glow of predawn light, Aebreanna glanced back and grimaced.

"How many?" Rogan called over the noise of their horses.

"Twenty," she replied. "There are, perhaps, more behind. They are most likely common soldiers and a single priest. Among them are four knights."

Rogan swore but continued to ride, urging Stick on.

For more than an hour, the pursuit continued. It was clear that the force from Daivic was gaining. Finally, Rogan reined in and turned.

"Everybody, get ready," the knight said. "It looks like we've got to fight this out."

A shrill whistle from a nearby hill drew the party's attention. Dozens of warriors, clad all in black in defiance of the desert sun and bearing the curved swords of the Shamashi, poured over the sand dunes. Without a command, the horsemen turned sharply away from Tomas and his friends to charge the enemy in a remarkable display of horsemanship. The Shamashi warriors collided with the approaching soldiers and made very quick work of them. The lean horses of the desert people danced around the slower mounts of the soldiers from Daivic, and the curved blades of the Shamashi severed limbs and heads, while the awkward thrusts and desperate counters of their opponents could not find a single unarmored target.

The pursuit force was cut down to a man; and their horses ran off into the desert before the Shamashi tribesmen turned and, with their weapons still ready, wearily approached Rogan's team.

The group of warriors stopped some distance away, and a single rider continued the approach, stopping once he could clearly make out their faces. Even for the Shamashi, he was tall, and the thick hair of midnight black that all his people had, this warrior kept cut very short. Dark eyes took them all in, and a scarred face grimaced at what he beheld. The Shamashi warrior sat very comfortably in his saddle, as though born to ride a horse, and his long limbs, though lacking the muscles even of a Sylvai, still showed signs of a weary readiness should the newcomers before him prove to be a threat. Rogan nudged Stick forward but stopped several paces from the Shamashi man.

"*Kar hadan*," the knight said in the Shamashi tongue. "*Jay alet fee mor halan alet.*"

"I speak you words, outsider," the Shamashi warrior said in thickly accented Velish. "Why were you hunted by the Parano-slaves?"

"We stole something Parano prized," the knight replied. "Something you also prize."

Rogan nodded back toward Safiyya, and the princess moved her horse forward, removing her veil and pulling back the hood of her satin cloak. Safiyya had a delighted grin on her young face at finally being reunited with her people. "*Kar hadan Timear,*" she said impishly.

"*Safiyya?*" the Shamashi said in wonder. "*Bah felee malan, Safiyya?*"

"Yes, it is I. Once again, I am with you."

The Shamashi covered his face with both hands in what looked like a ceremonial gesture before turning and calling the rest of his people forward. Each of the Shamashi, upon seeing their liberated princess, made the same gesture as their leader had and spoke in hushed whispers as they surrounded Safiyya. Like the princess, these desert warriors were tall and lean, with great, round eyes of midnight and limbs that seemed too long for their torsos. They moved with an impossible grace, a lightness that spoke of little mass beneath their flowing black robes. A few of the Shamashi tribesmen pulled their hoods free and Tomas noticed that what he had thought was hair on the princess' head was actually a long tail of small feathers, unbound on the men.

The princess raised her hands in a benedictory gesture to her people, who lowered their heads. "*Shey at orih kah at alet halah ou,*" she said in the manner of prayer or blessing. "*Shey felee.*"

The Shamashi all let out a trilling whistle that echoed across the desert and raised their swords, cheering in great joy. Safiyya was crying openly, unashamedly.

After the princess was transferred to what the Shamashi called a proper horse, Safiyya and the leader of her tribe, Timear, led Rogan and the others out into the sands towards a collection of tents around which a herd of horses and camels were gathered. On the way, Timear explained that he had divided his tribe into two halves on either side of the Harun to be ready for the day Safiyya was brought out of Daivic, and they could attempt a rescue no matter on which side of the river the princess appeared. "But now we will gather," the Shamashi leader said as they all dismounted and entered one of the larger tents. "Now is the time to plan."

Tomas was relieved to enter the shade of the tent. Even with the cooling breeze from the river, the sun was almost unbearably hard. The squire could not imagine how hot it must become in this great desert in the summer nor how anyone could live in it. Inside Timear's tent was a welcome cool that made Tomas's weariness grow stronger by the minute.

Timear led Safiyya to a number of cushions and helped the princess to sit, then dropped to the floor himself and clapped his hands together, summoning servants with food and drink. Seeing no chairs and taking his lead from Rogan, Tomas also sat down on the floor, surprised at how soft and comfortable the carpets and cushions were.

"It has been much time since we had reason for joy," Timear was saying to Rogan. "Now we have not only the return of a great hero and friend but also the return of Safiyya."

Rogan nodded and took the offered bowl of meat and bread. "How are things with the tribe?" the knight asked.

"Our herds grow large and our sons strong," the Shamashi leader replied. "Our daughters are beautiful and our wealth great. Once we lacked only our princess, and now we lack nothing."

"What of the other tribes?" Aebreanna asked.

Timear stared at Aebreanna. "It has been much time since we have taken a Sylva," he mused. "And much more since so beautiful a one."

Safiyya leaned forward. "She is my rescuer," the princess reminded him. "She is our guest and friend."

Timear nodded and sighed. "Of course. It is a shame, but it is right." To Aebreanna, the sheik said, "Most tribes are weak and broken. Those with no herds go north, to Sabriyya and Qasim, to beg for Kessian scraps and be dogs for better men. Those with herds but no courage go west to the Valley of Winds to hide. I fear the time of the Shamashi has passed."

"Are there any other tribes still near the Harun?" Rogan asked as he ate.

"No," Timear replied with a shake of his head. "No others stay to fight. The only tribes that stay take Parano gold and become slaves."

"We must plan, Timear," Safiyya said. "We must gather the tribes."

"The time of your father is done," the Shamashi argued. "The days of the Padishah are done. Now each tribe must survive alone."

"The time of the Shamashi is not done yet," Rogan insisted. "Would the other sheiks recognize Safiyya?"

Timear considered it. "Some would not," he finally said. "But most would."

Rogan set aside the bowl and cleared his throat. "Timear, you have your princess back but it isn't enough. House Parano will push until they have her back, or she and your tribe are all dead."

"The Paranos will not follow us," the sheik argued. "We will use the desert. We will kill his men and take his horses."

"Parano has the Western Empire," Rogan pointed out. "He can bring in enough men to fight you. And he has enough money to buy the Kessians to hunt you. Your tribe can't stand alone."

Safiyya leaned forward. "You said before that you go to end the power of the Western Empire," she said to Rogan. "What will this do to the Paranos?"

"I don't know for sure," the knight sighed. "House Parano is getting a lot of money and soldiers from Balshazzar, but if we're successful, then the money is going to stop."

"No more gold means the Shamashi slaves will serve no longer," Timear pointed out.

"But he'll still have enough to hold Daivic and the Harun," Rogan noted. "If the Shamashi are to survive, you must finally retake your city."

Timear shook his head. "Daivic is strong," he said. "The Paranos are strong. All the tribes would be needed to retake the city."

"Then we will use all the tribes," Safiyya insisted. "We will go to the Valley of the Winds and unite the Shamashi. When the northern tribes learn of the gathering of the Shamashi, they will come. When the Paranos' gold is gone, the *abd-at-fasala* will come home. Then the Shamashi will be strong again, and we can take back our home."

Timear slowly nodded. "It will be as it was," he agreed. "Before the Paranos. Before the Republic. The Shamashi will rule the Endless Sands."

"The Shamashi will need allies," Rogan pointed out.

"Who would help the tribes?" the sheik demanded.

"We would," Tomas said.

Rogan glanced at his squire with a grin and nodded. "House Calonar will help you," the knight offered. "A war is coming, and King Cylan is preparing to fight it."

Safiyya shook her head. "The tribes will not fight another man's war again."

"They won't have to. Unite the tribes and ally with the Northern Keep. House Parano will have enemies on both sides, and when Tordenia stops sending its gold and soldiers, Edmondo Parano will fear you. All we ask is that you unite the tribes and, if you can't take the city, then just hold Parano forces in Daivic until we finish with the Western Empire. If we win, then I swear to you by the friendship I shared with Safiyya's father, we will send you help in retaking your lands. If we lose, then you can still retreat back into the desert."

Safiyya and Timear looked at each other and held a brief whispered conversation in the Shamashi language. Finally, the princess straightened and nodded. "You are a friend of the desert, Rogan," she said. "Your words are true. We will wait for seven days while you go south, then travel to Valley of the Winds and unite the tribes. If you stop the Balshazzar gold from coming, we will attack the Paranos and take back our home. We will be allies."

Chapter 63

Safiyya and Timear needed little persuasion to convince Rogan to allow his team to rest for the day under the watchful protection of the Shamashi. The knight knew full well that their misadventure in Daivic was only the beginning of what would no doubt be an increasing number of difficult situations as his team penetrated the territory of the Western Empire. Travel during the daytime was inadvisable in the Endless Sands in any case, and the presence of the Shamashi meant that, for once, each of the four heroes could get a full rest and be ready to continue fresh.

As the sun set and the growing heat of the day gave way to a clear evening, Rogan and the others emerged from the tent that had been provided for them to see that Stick and Urge had been joined by a new team of horses, nearly as sleek and powerful as the two warhorses and all bearing fresh supplies. Of their mounts, only Stick and Urge, beside Beraht's Uldra shire horse Sus and Aebreanna's Sylvai pony, Mayva, remained.

Rogan threw a questioning glance at Timear, who stood with a wide grin beside Stick. "Gifts for the return of our princess," the Bedouin sheik explained. "Those beasts you rode may pass in the barbarian east, but in Shamashi lands, noble warriors have noble horses."

Stick tossed his head in agreement.

Rogan approached and warmly clasped the hand of his desert friend. "Thank you," the knight said simply. "You honor us with your gifts."

Timear stood back. "We will await your victory," the Bedouin said. "We will be ready to take back our desert."

"Until we fight beside each other again, may God watch over you."

Safiyya stepped forward and said a benedictory prayer over each of them. Saving Rogan for last, the princess offered something wrapped in cloth to the knight. Rogan firmly closed Safiyya's hands over the small package and took a step back. Tears were standing in the Shamashi princess's great dark eyes as she held the bundle against her heart and silently stared at the Northlands prince.

Rogan mounted his warhorse and motioned for his team to do the same. Nodding to Timear, the knight drew Talon and raised the blade in salute.

Timear touched his hand to his forehead before raising it in a benedictory gesture. "Go with God, my friends."

Without another word, Rogan led his team out into the desert, following the Harun River south. Tomas pulled Urge up alongside his knight. "What was that all about with the package?" the squire asked.

"Nothing," the knight grumbled.

"Nothing-nothing or nothing-something?"

"Nothing, shut up and get away from me, nothing."

"Oh. You know, it's funny because I remember reading once that, in the Bedouin culture, when a girl gave a present to a boy that she really liked what it meant was—"

Rogan looked at his apprentice with a sneer. "If you tell Kyla I will kill you until you are dead."

"So what is it with you and princesses, anyway?"

The knight growled and searched for something to throw at his comical squire.

"Well, you're a better man than most," the young man conceded.

"How do you figure?"

Tomas shrugged. "An exotic princess is infatuated with you," he replied. "Your wife is a thousand leagues from here and would never find out about it. You could have done whatever you wanted with that girl and probably gotten away with it."

"Are you kidding?" the knight demanded. "First of all, I knew Safiyya when she was four years old, and I was good friends with her father. Second of all, that girl wasn't much more than a child. I wasn't about to take advantage of her infatuation. Lastly, and most important, I'm married. It doesn't matter where my wife is. I would never betray her, period."

The squire nodded. "So like I said, you're a better man than most."

Rogan looked over at his apprentice. "So are you saying that if, given the chance, you would have—"

"Betrayed Mary?" Tomas asked in shock. "Are *you* kidding? Do you know what she would do to me?" the young man shuddered in horror at the thought of his fiancée's reaction and the ensuing torment.

"What's next?" Tomas asked Rogan as they continued south, hoping to change the subject.

"We're going to head south to a village called Renora," the knight replied. "We can hire one of the barges there to take us downriver to Oneld. Once we get there, we'll link up with the ship that'll take us to Tordenia."

"How long will we stay in Renora?"

"We'll get on the first barge sailing. There isn't much reason to stay. Renora isn't much of a town. It's more of a commercial enclave. It's mostly just warehouses and storage dumps for merchants moving along the river."

"Riverboats stop there?" the squire asked.

His knight nodded. "Any farmers, herders, or traders that aren't bound for Daivic and don't feel like paying those dock fees usually board at Renora." Rogan turned to Aebreanna. "Any House Calonar agents there?" he asked.

The spy shook her head slightly.

After thinking about it for a few minutes, his gaze passing over the countryside, the knight nodded. "Well," he said, "I guess we can still give the whole mercenary thing one last try."

"Sure," Tomas laughed. "It's worked great so far."

"Shut up, kid."

Rogan called a halt when they caught sight of Renora. Each of the heroes made their minor adjustments, returning to their dubious disguises as mercenaries.

Like every other town dedicated to the avoidance of taxes, Renora was so shabbily built that most of its buildings were left unfinished, with the missing pieces filled in with canvas, tree branches, or whatever else the economical people could find that would cost them as little as possible. As far as Tomas could tell, there was only one road in the village, running along the river, that was present only to provide access to the wharves, docks, and surrounding storage areas. The entire town, in fact, seemed only to consist of the wharves, warehouses, a collection of ramshackle houses, and the obligatory inn with its tavern.

"Is there some law that I don't know about making it mandatory for every town, no matter how ratty or isolated, to have an inn and tavern?" Tomas asked to no one in particular as the party stopped just outside of town.

"Not so much a law," Aebreanna replied, "as more of a tradition dating back to the very beginnings of the Human and Uldra races."

Dismounting Stick, Rogan glanced over at his beautiful friend. "Please don't tell me that you Sylvai are still telling that joke?"

"What joke?" Tomas asked as he got down off Urge.

The knight adjusted his sword belt and took Stick's reins in his hand, leading the great warhorse on foot. "Oh, it's one of the first things every little Sylvai is taught by his parents, kid," the knight laughed.

"One must educate the young on the realities of history, no matter how tragic they may be," Aebreanna replied piously.

"Will somebody please just tell me the joke while there's still the slightest chance of it being funny?" the squire demanded.

"Well—" Beraht began.

"Anybody but him?" Tomas pleaded.

"What's wrong with my jokes?" the warrior demanded.

"They're never funny," Rogan snorted.

"They also abound with nudity, debauchery, and a complete lack of believability," Aebreanna added.

"What's wrong with that?"

The spy shook her head in resignation. Despite the seemingly randomness of her movements, Tomas was sure that Aebreanna's eyes were everywhere, scanning for any possible threats.

"How did we get on this subject again?" the squire asked.

"Aebreanna was about to tell her joke that nobody thinks is funny," Rogan answered.

"Not a joke," the spy replied indignantly, "simply a story been passed down the *Sy'lva'n* generations since your two species first appeared."

Tomas stopped in the middle of the street. "That's it. I'm not moving from this spot until someone tells me this damned unfunny joke, or story, or whatever it is!"

Aebreanna took the squire's arm in her own, resuming the party's course toward the wharves. "The story is very simple, Tomas," she said soothingly. "The *Sy'lva'n* race is very old, far older than either the Human or Uldra. When the *Sy'lva'n* were already a developed people, but there were not any Humans or Uldra as yet, there was a young maiden. This maiden went for a walk one day into the forest, curious to see what animals lived there. During her walk, she happened upon the first Human, who was just climbing down from his tree. The Human, upon reaching the ground, looked around and asked the maiden where he could find some beer. The maiden could only stare in confusion as an Uldra crawled out from under a rock carrying a barrel. Walking over to the Human, the Uldra said, 'Here ya go.'"

The squire looked blankly at his friend for a few moments. Finally, he took a deep breath. "Is that the whole story?" he asked.

Aebreanna nodded.

Tomas thought about it for a few more moments. "That wasn't funny."

The spy shrugged.

"No, really. That wasn't even a little funny."

"The story loses a great deal of impact with translation. It is much more amusing when conveyed in the music of *Sy'lva'n*."

Looking over at Beraht, the squire asked, "So do you know any good jokes?"

In response, the Uldra bent over and put his hands together, between his legs and sticking out. He then clapped his hands together while saying, "Blah, blah, blah."

"I don't get it," Tomas admitted.

"That's Beraht's imitation of a Sylvai." Rogan supplied.

Seeing the look in Aebreanna's eyes, Tomas knew better than to laugh. Satisfied as to his submission, the spy left Tomas's side to kick Beraht in his Sylvai impression.

With their approach to the wharves, the party straightened their equipment and clothing, slipping into their roles as mercenaries. As Rogan handed Stick's reins to Aebreanna and belligerently walked over to the harbormaster, Tomas sent out a silent prayer that their disguises work at least this once.

"We're looking for work," the knight thundered at the harbormaster in a good approximation of the local accent.

The Renora harbormaster, a lumbering, vicious-looking man himself, was an old hand at dealing with the mercenaries that abounded in his domain. With barely concealed contempt, the older man looked Rogan up and down, making no attempt at hiding his displeasure at what he saw. "Fighting, guarding, or working?" he asked with a sneer.

"I'm no sailor or dockhand," Rogan growled.

The harbormaster looked meaningfully at Rogan's sword. "Can you use that?"

"I'm not wearing it for decoration."

"Wearing one doesn't mean you know how to use it."

"Have you got work or not?" the knight demanded.

The harbormaster grunted and looked down to his records book. After a few moments, he looked back at Rogan. "How far are you willing to go?"

"Oneld."

"I've got a barge heading downriver tomorrow morning that's looking to hire some muscle. Talk to Hadi over at dock 4."

"What's the pay?" Rogan demanded.

"Standard. Twenty a day with food and water or thirty without. Your choice."

The knight huffed. "I think we'll bring our own food. I've tasted what sailors think is stew."

The harbormaster shrugged. "It doesn't matter to me. Talk to Hadi."

Rogan led the group along the wharves until they reached dock 4, where a large flat-hulled boat sat, half-filled with various boxes. All around the boat, a dozen or so deckhands and crew worked at a slow pace to finish the loading while ignoring the shouted commands of an evil-looking man dressed all in canvas and wearing a leather patch covering his left eye.

"Wait here," Rogan instructed the others. The knight handed Stick's reins over to Tomas and marched to the dock. Upon reaching the overseer, Rogan held a brief conversation with him and, upon reaching an agreement, returned to the others. "We meet him here at dawn. The barge will sail as soon as we arrive and get settled."

"Will he allow our horses onboard?" Aebreanna asked.

The knight nodded. "We have to clean up after them, care for them, and I had to cut a few silver off our price, but Hadi agreed. Let's get some rooms and a good night's sleep. That crew of his doesn't look too trustworthy, so we'll probably have to sleep with one eye open the whole trip."

The group moved through the crowded town, ever watchful for any inquisitors. Upon reaching the run-down inn, Aebreanna bargained for two rooms while the men took their horses to the stables and Beraht let the stablehand know exactly what would happen to him if he let their animals disappear. Once the bags were moved into the cramped rooms and they had all changed, the group gathered in the common room to enjoy the feast of overcooked meat and water-thin gravy with rock-hard bread.

"How long will the trip down river take?" Tomas asked, forcing down the flavorless meat.

"About a week," Rogan answered while also fighting to eat his dinner. "It depends on how strong the current is right now and whether or not the captain will stop at night."

Tomas looked over at Aebreanna, whose displeasure at the meal was apparent. "Will our ship be there?"

The beautiful spy nodded, taking a long drink of water to drown the taste of the meat. "Ahmed is very reliable. If he was told he had to be here and ready within a certain time, he will be. My only concern is that we may have a reception waiting for us in Oneld."

Rogan looked around the common room, again ensuring that there were no listeners. "We've been making good time, and the Shamashi will have blocked any conventional messengers. We should be all right."

"Maybe we should have left a false trail that led in another direction," Tomas suggested, nearly breaking a tooth on his bread.

The knight shook his head. "It would have taken too long. If we keep moving, we'll stay ahead of any messengers. Besides, of all the places we could be going, I doubt that any of Balshazzar's people would suspect that we're heading straight to his capital."

"Do not expect the ordinary on any stretch that remains of our journey. If what I witnessed in Daivic was any indication, there are evil goings on in Balshazzar's lands that we could not normally imagine."

Rogan called to the serving girl, ordering a round of ales for the men and more water for Aebreanna. Noticing this, Tomas asked, "Sylvai don't drink ale?"

"Not as a general rule," she replied. "The taste is too harsh for our constitution. Given the option, most of my people would rather drink water or wine."

"I've heard that Sylvai wines were the best," the squire noted.

Aebreanna nodded. "Human vineyards share the same impatience that is so characteristic of you race. The grapes are harvested too soon, the wine is pressed too quickly, and the vintage is never allowed to age properly. I have tasted Human wines that were quite good and many winemakers that showed a great deal of promise, but the *Sy'lva'n* simply have a better mind-set for the craft."

"I suppose every race has its own tastes."

The spy nodded. "My people favor old wines, while Humans tend to drink beer or ale, and the Uldra live to sample that horrid brew they call spirits."

Tomas looked over at Beraht, who had cleaned his plate and was demanding another. "I've heard that Uldric spirits were strong enough to eat through steel."

The warrior nodded. "Once, only the greatest of the lords of Uldron held the secret to creating the finest of spirits. Those secrets were lost long ago, but a few of us have either held on to family recipes or have relearned the ancient ways. Any warrior that can pick up an axe can mix up some spirits for you that would do a fair job of putting any Human on the ground and any Sylvai in the earth, but to get the best, most deadly spirits, the kind that set your throat on fire and send the greatest of warriors to their ancestors, you have to find an Uldra that's got a deep understanding of God's will. It's only through the Allfather that a warrior-priest can harness the rage that's needed to make true spirits."

"Have you ever had the good stuff?" Tomas asked.

Beraht patted a small waterskin on his belt. "Remm has a small barrel in the Keep. Only once, after we beat the Greysoul, did he let me have some, and he gave me a little more for an important day."

"How was it?"

The Uldra shrugged. "I don't remember anything after raising the cup to my lips. But it was a night worthy of song."

Rogan leaned back as the serving girl brought their drinks. "As I recall, the two of you ended up swimming in the moat naked, singing old love songs."

Beraht pulled thoughtfully at his beard. "Like I said, a night worthy of song."

Shaking his head, the knight made sure that the serving girl was out of earshot. Turning to Aebreanna, he said, "Now's as good a time as any. What did you find out in Daivic?"

The spy took a long drink from her cup. "I fear that we have a more serious problem with House Parano than any of us originally thought." She related nearly everything that happened to her during her misadventure through the streets of Daivic.

"So who in Underworld is running House Parano?" Rogan mused.

"If the orders aren't coming from the Paranos," Tomas wondered, "then who...?"

"Tordenia seems the most likely suspect," Aebreanna offered.

A commotion at the entrance to the tavern drew their attention, and just as quickly, each of them turned away. Eight men entered, forcibly shoving aside any that stood in their way. The men found a table opposite in the common room from where Tomas and his friends were eating and cleared the man that was already there by the simple means of picking him up and throwing him to the floor. Seven of the warriors wore identical armor, and all looked around the tavern as though sizing up anyone that dared to make eye contact. The eighth was a gentleman of quality, unburdened by armor or weapon and as well-coiffed as any Tomas could ever remember seeing. He had an expression on his face that said plainly that he did not approve of his surroundings nor even of his companions, despite the fact that they were, no doubt, protecting his life.

They were also all wearing the red and gold heraldry of the Western Empire.

"We just can't catch a single break," Rogan hissed.

"A most unfortunate development," Aebreanna agreed. "I believe the well-groomed one in the center is wearing the medallion marking him as a *pasha*."

"What's that?" Beraht grumbled, sinking a little lower in his seat.

"Military governor," Tomas explained. "The Western Empire doesn't traditionally use ranks of nobility. It's mostly based on the military. A *pasha* is in charge of a large area."

"So what in Underworld is he doing here?" Rogan demanded. "The nearest one should be way down in Cahtara or Boric, not in the Endless Sands." The knight looked at Aebreanna. "Doesn't Parano have his own governors?"

The Sylva nodded.

"Why don't we ask him?" Tomas suggested.

Rogan snorted. "A *pasha* would have the intelligence reports to recognize us on sight."

"Yes, but he only has seven guards."

"Do we have to have the talk again?"

The squire leaned forward. "We need information, right?" he insisted. "Don't you think a *pasha* might have some?"

Rogan sighed and glanced over at where the *pasha's* guards were accosting the serving girl. The knight looked at Aebreanna.

The Sylva shrugged. "If we can lure them into the night and do it quietly, the reward may justify the risk," she said.

Rogan looked to Beraht.

The Uldra laughed. "Are you seriously asking if I want to get into a fight?" he asked.

"Sorry, lost my head for a second." The Northlander rubbed his eyes. "All right, how about we have Aebreanna seduce him, get him into her room where we're waiting, then we sneak him out the window?"

The seductive spy shook her head with a delighted smile. "There is, I think, a problem with that most tried and true of tactics," she said with a nod toward the *pasha*.

The three men looked over. The Western Empire noble was, at that moment, standing at the bar, talking with the tavern keeper's teenaged son, leaning in very close and smiling.

"I believe the tastes of our target run towards other meats," Aebreanna said, stifling a laugh.

"Well, I guess we'll have to try something else," Tomas said.

"Oh, I don't know," Rogan mused, turning back to his squire.

Chapter 64

"What do you think's taking so long?" Beraht asked. The Uldra glanced up to Tomas's window. "It never takes Aebreanna this long."

Rogan shrugged. "It's his first seduction," the knight explained. "Be patient."

Aebreanna stepped forward and crossed her arms under her chest. "I must admit to a curiosity as to what goes on while I am busy with this part of the plan," she confessed.

"This is it," the knight replied. "We stand around waiting for you to open the window and—"

The window to Tomas's room opened and an unconscious body fell out.

"Interesting," Aebreanna said.

"Was it everything you dreamed it would be?"

"Honestly… yes."

The squire, making gagging sounds the entire time, climbed down the wall.

"Will you keep quiet?" Rogan snapped.

Tomas looked at his knight. "No," he replied. "I won't. If you don't like it, go in the tavern and make kissing faces at one of his guards."

"It's all part of being a man, kid." The knight reached down and, with Beraht's help, retrieved the *pasha* and moved down the road.

Tomas stared after them. "What?"

The team quickly moved out of town and down to the edge of the river, well away from any inhabited areas, so that any incidental screams would go unnoticed. By the time the *pasha* was regaining consciousness, he found himself surrounded by nothing but darkness, the nearby river, and four armed warriors that looked upon him as nothing more than a waste of air.

The *pasha* briefly tested the bonds Aebreanna had used to bind his hands and feet but found no purchase. The gag was also as without mercy as his captors.

Rogan crouched down to look at the cringing nobleman. "Do you speak Velish?" he asked.

The *pasha* did not respond.

The knight drew his dagger and put it against the nobleman's stomach. "Let me put it this way," he said reasonably. "I have to assume you speak Velish and are just refusing to. Now, you're going to talk, and you're going to tell me everything I want to know. What shape you're in after that is the only thing you have any control over.

You may have this feeling that's telling you to be strong and resist. Ignore that feeling. That feeling will leave you with no fingers, no toes, no tongue, no eyes, and no ears." He pushed the point of the dagger slightly into the *pasha's* stomach, not enough to penetrate, just enough to be understood.

"Do you speak Velish?" Rogan asked again.

The *pasha* nodded.

"Good. We're going to remove your gag. If you make any sound that's louder that a whisper, for any reason, our questions end, and you take a swim in the river. Do you understand?"

The *pasha* looked over to the dark waters of the Hoppi. Even from that distance, and under the light of the stars with no visible moon, still the dark shapes and sounds of the river's great predators were clear. He nodded.

Rogan nodded to Aebreanna. The Sylva removed the gag and stepped away to maintain watch during the questioning with Tomas, while Beraht loomed over the cringing pasha.

"Name," Rogan instructed.

The Western Empire nobleman worked his jaw a moment before answering. "Kerem," he replied.

"Where are you coming from, Kerem?"

"I was assigned to Tordenia."

"Was?"

"I've been reassigned to Daivic."

Rogan narrowed his eyes. "What about the Paranos?"

The *pasha* said nothing.

"Oh, we're back to that." Needing no instruction, Beraht covered Kerem's mouth while Rogan cut a slice of skin off the pasha's arm. The Uldra continued holding the man down until he stopped thrashing. Once Kerem stopped trying to scream, Rogan nodded and Beraht removed his hand from the *pasha's* mouth. "When I ask a question, you answer it," the knight said. "If you don't, you lose a piece. Do you understand?"

Kerem said nothing and so lost a piece of skin on his other arm.

When his screaming and thrashing again subsided, Rogan and Beraht released him. "Do you understand?" Rogan repeated.

"Yes," the *pasha* whimpered.

"You said you've been assigned as the *pasha* of the Endless Sands," the knight continued. "What about Duke Edmondo Parano?"

The Western Empire official answered immediately this time. "He's dead."

"How?"

"I don't know. I don't care. The Emir told me to come here and assume control."

Rogan thought about that for a few moments. "How long ago did Parano die?"

"I don't know," Kerem said, crying. "Months. His whole family. All the Paranos are dead, even the bastards. All the orders have been coming from Tordenia, through the inquisitors."

"What are the inquisitors doing?" the knight asked. "What magic are they using on people's minds when speaking to the crowds?"

"It is some new power they have learned in the capital. It is a means of keeping the people in obedience. It is meant to make the change in authority more acceptable to the rabble."

"What about kidnapping the Shamashi princess? Was that Parano or you guys?"

For a moment, it looked as though the pasha would not answer, but when Rogan made to grab him again, the nobleman complied. "Parano!" he gasped. "But it was our order! He did not want to do it, but we made him as part of the alliance. He did not understand why we wanted it and last year threatened to let her go to appease the Shamashi."

"What about her father? Who gave the order to kill him?"

"Tordenia. Parano refused, so we sent an inquisitor. That is also when…"

"When you guys killed Parano and his whole House," Rogan finished. "You realized you were losing control. What was the point? What was it all about?"

"The Shamashi," Kerem said. "The Emir knows that you can't control the desert until you control the tribes. The Padishah was a friend of yours. He would ally with House Calonar."

"Then kill him. Why imprison him and Safiyya? Why persecute the outlands? What's your part in all this?"

The nobleman breathed heavy a few times, trying to hold his nerve not to answer, but one look at Rogan's dagger was all it took to break his courage. "Parano was never going to last," he whimpered. "He was objecting to the Emir's orders more and more, especially after orders arrived for the project."

"What project?"

"Something having to do with the dead."

Beraht glanced at Rogan. "Aebreanna said something about them taking the dead out of the crypts," he said

The knight nodded and looked back at their captive. "Why?"

"We don't know. Only the Emir knows. He and…" the nobleman's mouth shut like a trap.

Rogan leaned in, waving his dagger in a summoning motion towards his ear. "He and…?"

"I… can't…" the pasha actually seemed to be choking on the words, as though the very effort of speaking caused his throat to clench.

"Stop!" Tomas snapped.

All eyes went to him. The squire breathed deeply and closed his eyes. He was not sure how he knew, how he sensed it, but the young man reached out with his mind and saw, without his eyes, a menacing shadow twisting in the air around the cringing Tordenian. "He's enchanted," Tomas whispered, his eyes now only half-open.

Rogan looked from his prisoner to his squire and back. "Can you tell by who?" the knight asked.

Tomas shook his head. His hand dipped into his shirt and retrieved the small package that had been riding against his heart. He rubbed his fingers, feeling the golden rose within the white ribbon, tracing a light touch against the nearly-open pedals. He did not recall moving the hand, and was only vaguely aware of what he said. "Shadow," the squire's voice whispered. "Darkness." Tomas felt the currents of magic, felt as they moved around the cringing nobleman. "Control. Deception." He blinked then, shaking his head and returning to his sense of self. "It feels a lot like whatever was at Beraht's village."

Rogan grunted. "Can you get rid of it?"

His squire shook his head.

The knight glanced at Aebreanna, who similarly shook her head. Rogan sighed and returned his gaze to the pasha. "Alright, we won't talk about the shadow-dark-control-whatever. Why were you sent here?"

"Once we killed the Paranos, I was supposed to replace him. I go to Daivic and release the Shamashi princess to her people and ease their suffering."

"Making them love you," Rogan guessed. The knight shook his head. "You set all this up just to get the loyalty of the tribes. It wouldn't be enough, moron. They wouldn't follow an outsider."

"Unless I married the princess," Kerem corrected.

Rogan froze.

"The condition of my releasing her was that she and I would marry. As a wedding gift, Tordenia would make people think Edmondo Parano returned control of Daivic to the Shamashi and took his family to the Western Empire. It would form an alliance that would unite the Shamashi tribes under House Balshazzar."

The knight stood slowly and looked down at the *pasha*, his face blank.

Beraht walked away from Rogan, joining Aebreanna and Tomas.

"You can't kill me!" Kerem insisted. "I'm too valuable as a hostage! I can get you safe passage!"

Rogan moved around behind the weakly struggling nobleman and grabbed him.

"I can pay you anything!" he begged. "I can give you whatever you want!"

"You already did," the knight said calmly. With a heave, Rogan sent the squealing Tordenian rolling into the reeds growing along the river and walked away.

At first confused, Kerem struggled to rise until he heard the first hiss. His screamed in terror as the river predators closed in on their bleeding prey.

The Western Empire

Fourth Interpose

Chapter 65

A storm of late spring was rumbling outside. The people of the Northern Keep, long accustomed to their homeland's weather, were shuttering windows and closing shops, preparing for what was to come. The castle was closing, and its occupants taking shelter. The storms of the Northlands were unpredictable; the lightest, most innocuous clouds could unleash stone-sized hail while the most vile, threatening sky could do little more than a pleasant cleansing mist. The clouds now gathering above Castle Calonar were dark and rumbling, threatening a terrible storm that could rage against the fortress for some time. So, the people of Castle Calonar and the Northern Keep assumed and prepared for the worst. All was made as ready as possible.

Leaving instructions that she wasn't to be disturbed except under the direst of circumstances, which was enforced by the overprotective Lukas, Kyla retired to her quarters. Feeling only a slight pang of loneliness, the princess sat down at the desk which Rogan normally used and unrolled another of the scrolls containing the histories of her predecessors within the Sisterhood of the Lady of Light. For weeks, Mary and Ilse had been discovering lost diaries, histories, and poetry from the long line of Sister Superiors, going all the way back to the Sylvai Empire. The two women worked night and day to sort the great knowledge, distinguishing works that, while interesting, offered little insight into her son's mystical abilities. Kyla had taken to studying the works her friends discovered, hoping each new discovery would be the one most hoped for.

The light of the heatless lamps the Uldra were creating was complimented by the occasional flash of lightning. The crackling fire was joined by the odd crash of thunder. The storm, Kyla realized, was gaining strength. A part of her wished to go to the balcony, safely inside, but looking out, to relish the power of her homeland. As a girl, she had loved thunderstorms. The lightning and the thunder, the wind and the rain, these had all stirred her young heart. Now, reading the ancient records of her sisterhood and absently rubbing her swelling belly, Kyla only wanted her husband.

As engrossed as she was in her newfound studies, the princess was barely aware of Lukas entering the room, accompanied by another flash of lightning. "I'm fine, Lukas," Kyla said without looking up. With her eyes locked on the ancient mysteries of her faith, the High Priestess was unaware of any danger until the needle had already entered the soft flesh of her neck. Mary and Ilse, under the guidance of Medaka, had been uncovering fascinating material. Before the rise of the Inquisition, dating far into the mists of forgotten history, the records of the previous Sisters Superior hinted at great power. The priestesses of old had abilities now lost, that was clear. There was something in the old records that called to Kyla. Some hint and warning of a great and terrible power that could be hers, if she could survive its mastery.

Kyla gasped and jumped to her feet, knocking her chair aside and stumbling back, away from her attacker. To the princess' astonishment, emphasized with the roar of thunder and the breaking storm, it was only Lukas standing before her. The bodyguard stared with dispassionate eyes as he calmly put a needle like the ones Kyla had seen Aebreanna use back into his belt. The princess put a hand to the pulse of her neck and stared with wide-eyed shock at the single point of crimson betrayal that decorated her finger.

"Lukas?" she tried to gasp, but found that her voice failed.

"I really wouldn't have preferred to do it this way," he said softly, the words almost lost with the eruption of a terrible downpour. The guard advanced on his princess very calmly, straightening the blue and grey doublet he was, at that moment, betraying. "But, an order is an order, and my master has ordered your death."

Kyla blinked and shook her head, desperately trying to clear her vision as the world began to spin.

"Don't bother fighting it," her bodyguard advised. "No woman could resist that poison, let alone one as weak as you."

Kyla's eyes snapped open and she flung her arms out to either side. In the same instant, all the heat and light in the room shot into the High Priestess' body. The study went nearly dark, save for the flash of wrathful lightning. With a single, silent prayer, Kyla called to the Lady of Light and her mistress responded, burning the poison out of Kyla's body without harming either mother or child.

Lukas blinked at the flash of divine magic and grimaced at its implication. "I see," he calmly noted. "Plan B, then." The assassin pulled a silken cord from his sleeve and advanced towards his target.

Kyla regarded him calmly and smiled. The Sister Superior of the Lady of Light clasped her hands in front of her expanding stomach and drew a deep breath. "You don't want to do that," she said. Her voice was still Kyla's but more, infused with a divine choir of all the Sister Superiors. A line of women stretching back to antiquity answer their newest sister's distress and lent their voices to hers. A chorus of seduction, of persuasion, of feminine command, reached out to this threat with teasing fingers.

Lukas stopped. "I don't want to do this," he repeated.

The princess nodded. "That's right," she said softly, never losing his eyes. "You want to come with me."

"I want to come with you."

"Everything will be alright."

"Everything will be alright."

Kyla approached the traitor and held out her hands to take his. Lukas held out his hands.

The room shook, feeling as though the entire castle was rocked by the terrible power of the storm. Lukas grabbed Kyla's hands and pulled her down, forcing the princess to her knees. "Nice try," he said with a sneer. "But I came prepared." The assassin drove his boot into Kyla's chest.

Kyla was forced back, gasping for breath and struggling against a surging terror. As Lukas approached, the princess rolled onto her back and struck with her foot as Rogan had shown her countless times, driving with all her strength into her attacker's knee. Kyla was rewarded with a growl of pain as Lukas dropped.

Kyla did not loss the precious seconds her desperate attack had won. She climbed to her feet, ignoring the pain that lanced through her body and the pounding rain at the windows. She ran for the door as fast as her expanding body would move. Nevertheless, Kyla was caught before she had taken more than a step. The assassin caught her long hair in one hand and yanked back with all his strength, pulling the princess to the floor again. A cord was looped around Kyla's throat and tightened before she could do anything more than blink her terror.

The traitorous soldier put his padded knee against Kyla's back and pulled the cord he had wrapped around her throat as tight as he could, all the while maintaining a death-like calm, ignoring Kyla's weak attempts to move as he held her. "I must admit being glad that I won't have to tolerate any more of your nonsense. Why my master waited so long to order your death is a mystery. I suppose he lost patience with this fool curse of his. Better to just kill you and have your fool husband seed another."

Kyla stopped struggling, but Lukas was not fooled. He knew it took much longer to strangle someone. A soft golden light appeared around the assassin but vanished as it drew closer to him. "Typical woman," he snorted. "Never learning from your mistakes. Well, let me spell it out for you in simple terms. Your witchcraft won't work on me for at least another ten minutes." Although all movement from Kyla had stopped and she had apparently stopped trying to breathe, Lukas was taking no chances. He continued to pull.

A gasp drew Lukas's startled gaze to the door. Mary had entered unobserved and now stood, staring in shock at what she saw, her eyes flashing with the lightning outside. "Damn!" the traitor swore and released the princess to deal with this new problem.

Without pause, Mary spun and ran for the front door, screaming for help with such force that it shamed the storm's fury. An instant before the handmaiden could reach the outer door and any possible assistance, Lukas intercepted her and shoved Mary against the solid wood door with bone-jarring force. The assassin stepped closer but was startled again when Mary suddenly spun and hit him in the head with a small vase that had been resting on a nearby table. The gentle handmaiden did not pause in her desperate attack, but grabbed Lukas' doublet and drove her knee into his groin with all the strength she could summon. The killer before her tried to curse but could find no time before Mary released his doublet and began viciously raking her fingernails into his face, drawing a series of crimson lines in her quest for Lukas' eyes as she continued screaming an endless alarm emphasized by roaring thunder.

The assassin growled at the pain and distraction of Mary's attack but was not deterred. Instead, he clenched his fist and struck a brutal blow into Mary's stomach, forcing the air out of her body. "You forget your place, bitch!" he snarled and, grabbing Mary by the front of her dress, slapped her with such force that blood welled in the handmaiden's mouth. Lukas then calmly bolted the door behind Mary and, with one hand gripping the front of her dress and the other pulling at her long hair, dragged the struggling handmaiden into Prince Rogan's study.

Even more than her own pain, seeing her princess lying on the floor filled Mary with rage. She stomped on Lukas' foot and drove her elbow into his middle, twisting and pulling at the traitor to try to break from his grip, hissing her own rage that matched the driving rain.

"Damned whore!" Lukas snarled and released Mary's hair only to use the freed fist to hit her across the jaw. He angrily threw her against a small table, knocking it over and scattering the tray and fruit resting on it across the floor. "Months of you and that slut princess!" the assassin growled. "Months of orders and humiliation!" Lukas drew his dagger and advanced on Mary with a limp as the young woman desperately crawled backward along the floor trying to clear her vision and regain her breath. "Now I teach you a lesson," he said through clenched teeth.

A sudden pounding on the outer door briefly drew Lukas's attention away from Mary. "Damn," he swore. "It looks like I don't have enough time for a proper lesson," he noted as he turned back.

A flash of lightning illuminated the silver serving tray an instant before it struck his face. A fountain of blood, mirroring the rain outside, shot from his crushed nose, bringing stars to his eyes and causing him to drop his dagger.

"Oh, you bitch!" Lukas snapped and tried to raise his left hand to ward off Mary's next blow.

The handmaiden altered her next attack though. Even as she reached back to hit the traitor on the face again, she instead swung low, delivering her next strike with the straight edge of the gold-lined silver tray to Lukas' stomach. Mary then stepped back and delivered a sharp kick to the groin of her princess' attacker.

The handmaiden reached back to once again strike the traitor's face, but Lukas leapt forward and tackled her to the floor, pinning the serving tray down. Lukas balled his fist and delivered several blows to Mary's face and stomach. "Who do you think you are!?!" he demanded between blows. "I'll kill you, bitch!" He stood and brutally kicked Mary before retrieving his dagger. "You and your whore of a princess! To Underworld with the master's plans! I'll kill you all!" he screamed, wiping away the blood from his eyes.

A roar of thunder tried to shake the castle, but was dwarfed to meaninglessness. The outer door exploded inward, revealing Ilse. The priestess' eyes were closed and her hands clasped before her. Prayerful words spilled from her small mouth and her entire young body was suffused with a soft white glow that was somehow strengthened by the flashes of lightning. Ilse did not walk in, but instead floated, buoyed by her faith and the power of her goddess. When the priestess looked up, she saw her princess lying on the floor and her best friend bloodied. Ilse's pretty face twisted into a snarl and her prayers grew harsh and vengeful.

Tendrils of light grew from Ilse's aura, flashing to echo the lightning. They bowed out with each crash, forming themselves into claws. These reached, seeking, hungry for a man's blood. Lukas smirked when these ghostly tendrils drew within a breath of him and then flashed, dissolving. "You women and your magic," he sneered. The traitorous bodyguard pulled a small dagger from its sheath at the small of his back and reached to throw it at Ilse.

"NO!" Mary's scream was enhanced by a crash of thunder. The handmaiden leapt, grabbing the traitor's arm and heaving with all her strength.

Lukas snarled again and reached back to strike the handmade, but was intercepted once more, this time by Ilse, who followed her friend in lashing like the lightning outside, wrapping the assassin's other arm. The three thrashed and tumbled to the ground. Lukas cursed and spat, but could not dislodge the women; though stronger than one, he was no match for both at once.

Karen ran into the room, then. The girl looked briefly at where Lukas was being held by Ilse and Mary, then sprinted to where her sister lay. The young princess put a hand on Kyla's abdomen and whispered something. She then turned her head to Mary and Ilse. "Move!" she yelled.

The two women obeyed, released their hold on Lukas and rolling away. The assassin regained his feet and drew his shortsword, his eyes aflame with murder, but a soft chorus of tiny bells stopped him. He looked around as a sparkling mist formed in the study. Twinkling bits of gold and silver and colors unimagined appeared and solidified. The points of love danced through the air, swirling gently around Kyla and

Karen and the unborn heir of House Calonar. The younger daughter of Calonar pointed a finger at Lukas and said, "Him."

The lights expanded and brightened, revealing perfect, tiny females with butterfly wings and shifts of red mist. In their hands, each of the tiny, exquisite female spirits held an equally tiny, exquisite rapier. The tinkling chorus of unseen bells changed then, the song growing deeper, more menacing. The Fael grew agitated, their kaleidoscope wings writhing in harsh tones of red, brown, and black. The tiny female spirits swirled and surged, spinning around Lukas.

The traitorous bodyguards lashed with his sword, swinging fearfully at the swarming Fael. His attacks may as well have been on the air itself. The Fael swirled around him, pushing him away from the women. Tiny, impossibly tiny cuts appeared across his face and hands, Lukas screamed as thin lines of red slashed across his body. His clothes were shredded in seconds. His hair was shorn from his scalp. He dropped his sword as his hands were reduced to a bloody mess. He tried to shield his eyes, but too little of his forearms remained to do more than wave helplessly against the Fael. His eyes were shredded. His ears and nose dissolved under a thousand, thousand cuts. When he opened his mouth to scream, his tongue and teeth were destroyed. His body was rendered and his scream did not stop, only growing more wet and helpless.

The bleeding, ruined mass that was Lukas dropped to what had been his knees. "Please," he seemed to beg, but could only emit a gargling croak of blood and gore.

Karen placed a hand on Kyla's abdomen and said, "That's enough. Send them back."

In the space between one heartbeat and the next, the Fael were gone. Mary and Ilse, huddled together in a corner, enfolding each other in their arms and wide-eyed in horror at what had happened, could only stare. Kyla breathed, but did not wake. Karen stayed with her sister, her hand not moving from Kyla's stomach and her dreaming nephew.

Rashid and Chandra burst into the room, weapons raised and murder in their eyes. Mary and Ilse flinched back, not knowing who to trust. Karen held up her other hand and said, "It's ok."

Somehow, impossibly, the thing that had been Lukas stood. It raised the stumps that had once been arms and shambled towards Kyla. A sound that was some horrific blend of plea and threat came from a hole in the center of what had been the thing's face.

"No, wait!" Rashid barked, but too late.

Chandra threw one of her blades with deadly accuracy, severing what remained of the Lukas-thing's throat. It collapsed to the floor, showering Kyla and Karen in a horrific spray of gore.

"Damn it!" Rashid barked at his lieutenant.

"Would you rather I let him kill them?" Chandra demanded. "Who knows what that thing could do."

The spymaster grunted and moved to check on Kyla. "Check the body and call for some clerics," he ordered.

The intensity of the storm had passed. The thunder grudgingly gave way, withdrawing for a time. The rain eased, but did not stop. The people of the Northern Keep knew more was ahead.

Mary walked into her princess' bedchambers with a meeting already taking place. "We found this in his quarters," Captain Rainer was saying, handing a crystal half sphere to Baron Tressalon.

Rashid took the object with a grunt. "Communication device. Once the disruption ended, he was relaying back to someone everything we did."

Mary crossed the room, pausing to curtsey to the Queen, before taking her place at Kyla's side.

Kyla said nothing, but only reached up and took her handmaiden's hand. Relief, gratitude, and love shown in the princess' pearlescent eyes. Mary kissed her princess' hand and smiled back. The clerics had healed the damage to her body, and she was working very hard to hide the wounds that went deeper, unwilling to add to her princess' suffering.

Karen, who was lying beside her big sister, reached over and took Mary's hand as well, joining the three of them. The younger daughter of Calonar said nothing, but she looked at Mary through a level gaze that belied her youth, a gaze that echoed that of the Queen, seeing straight into Mary's heart. The handmaiden did not allow tears to emerge in her eyes, but only just.

"What about the princess?" Rashid asked. "Any lasting injury?" The spymaster's voice was level, but when Mary glanced at him, she thought she sensed a great bitterness. Rashid, as House Calonar's chief of intelligence, felt himself responsible for identifying any threat to that noble family. That an assassin had nearly eliminated two generations of Calonar heirs must have weighed heavily on Rashid's soul.

The queen did not bother looking up as she continued to apply a salve to her daughter's neck. "Nothing permanent," she answered. "Thanks to Mary, Kyla here was saved from any grievous injury. To say nothing of Ilse and," the mother look to her younger daughter, "and others, of course." Karen smiled impishly. "A few days of rest, and they'll all be fine."

Kyla looked at her mother in concern. "What about..." Her small hands went to her expanding abdomen.

Nora smiled. "He's fine," she replied. "In fact, he's doing better than you are right now." The queen finished her treatment and handed the small jar over to Ilse, then took Kyla and Karen into her arms and held them very close.

"Any chance of getting any information from the assassin?" Rainer asked quietly.

Rashid shook his head. "Not much. He took a great deal of trouble to erase any signs of his past. I've got Chandra ransacking his quarters, but I doubt she'll report anything. This guy was a professional."

"And patient," Rainer added. "He waited months to do this."

"He was ordered," Kyla said.

"What do you mean, your Highness?" Mary asked.

"He mentioned a master. That's the one who was making my magic go crazy," she said, letting go of her mother and lying back, but keeping her little sister close. "Something about a curse. Lukas received orders to abandon the plan and just kill me."

Rashid nodded. "Once the princess' magic stabilized from her study, he must've needed a back-up plan."

"What about this?" Rainer said, holding up a small talisman they had retrieved from Lukas's body.

"A protective charm," Queen Nora said, pouring several cups of tea. "Meant to negate any magic used against the wearer."

"Then how did…" The spymaster glanced towards the study, where the ruined mass that had been Lukas still lay, awaiting his permission for the castle staff to begin cleaning.

"The Fael and their blades may be mystical," the queen replied, "but they're still blades."

"Is there any chance of tracing this charm back to whoever made it?" Rashid asked.

"How do we know Lukas didn't?" Rainer suggested. "After all, he was already working the curse against the princess. Maybe he was an adept."

The spymaster shook his head. "Possible, but I don't think so. If he had that kind of magic, he would have used it to kill her Highness and the girls. My guess is that he was just using something someone else made." Rashid took the charm from Rainer and stared at it. "I'll have Esha take a look at this and see what she can find out."

"At least now we know who the traitor on the council is," the captain said.

"No, we don't," Rashid argued. "Lukas wasn't at all the meetings and only began to have access after the Archaeknights left. Whoever the traitor on the council is, he or she has been there for a while now."

"What do we do?" Kyla asked of everyone and herself.

They were at a loss. The room was silent, but for the storm that had begun.

V

Tordenia

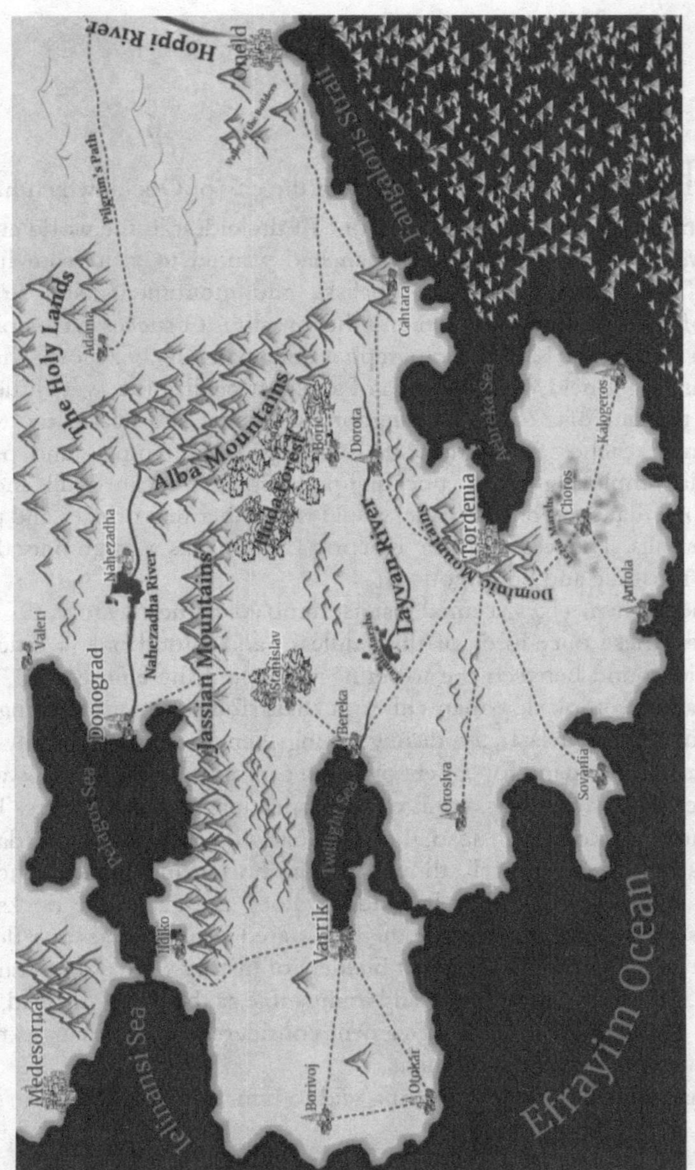

Hoppi River
Ojeld
Fangaloris Strait
pilgrim's Path
Adama
The Holy Lands
Cahtara
Alba Mountains
Botik
Muda Forest
Dorota
Aebreka Sea
Kalogeros
Choros
Nahezadha
Nahezadha River
Velta Marshes
Tordenia
Anfola
Dominate Mountains
Valeri
Jassian Mountains
Layvan River
Donograd
Pelagos Sea
Stanislav
Bereka
Orosiya
Twilight Sea
Sovantia
Idiko
Varrik
Medesorna
Telmansi Sea
Boriwoj
Otokar
Efrayim Ocean

Chapter 66

They had spent only a single day in the city of Oneld, which had been too long for Tomas. The city of the Khepri, one of the oldest in the world and saturated with history, was a place the young man had wanted to visit from his youngest childhood. The ancient sandstone obelisks and monuments still stood despite thousands of years of desert weather and the invasions of successive empires, though the secret to reading the Khepri pictograph writing had long been lost. The crumbling ruins surrounding Oneld, once beacons of a mighty civilization, were little more than the skeletal remains of a forgotten kingdom, clutching at a near-forgotten past like drowning man reaches for driftwood. Even the great temples and palaces were hollow, staring imploringly at the uncaring passersby like vacant skulls moaning their desperate hope that someone, anyone, would remember that princes and priests once walked their halls. The lesson of the Khepric Empire was a harsh one: that all great civilizations must die and be forgotten.

The Khepri themselves seemed just as humbled as their history. Of all the non-Human races, these once-lords of the Endless Sands stood only a little taller than Rogan, a midground between the towering Uldra and the elfin Sylvai. The Khepri were of a darker complexion than either of their sibling races, matching the darker sands surrounding their last city, distinguishing them from the typically-pale Uldra. What Tomas, like so many foreigners over the centuries, had believed was a flowing mane of utterly-black hair was, upon closer inspection, downy feathers. The Khepri, Tomas learned, had no hair; instead, the males had a long crown of very dark feathers. The females had these, as well, though much shorter and firmer, tending to rest around the angular jaw. As they had ridden along the expansive docks of Oneld, Tomas had seen two males begin arguing, and stared in surprise as their flowing black feathers rose up in agitation. The great builders of history were not so frail-appearing as the Sylvai, but in no way as broad and immovable as the Uldra. Instead, the Khepri moved with a jerking grace, each movement considered and seeming as though they would leap into the sky at any moment.

"They had wings, once," Aebreanna said to him, noticing the squire's fascinated stare.

"What?"

"Ages past, when the *Sa'kai* first created the Elder Races, they divided the world between us. The mountains were given to the Uldra, the forest and plains to the *Sy'lva'n*, and the seas to the Xiana. To the Khepri, they gave the skies."

Tomas stared at the small groups of Khepri, moving about as though unfamiliar with walking. "What happened?" he asked.

"*Ethroi'sa'kai*, the Adversary. The Khepri were the builders and planners of the *Sa'kai*, and they faced the worst of the Adversary's wrath. Their flight was torn from them, and they were banished from their home in the Valley of the Winds. They tried for centuries to replicate the wonders of their former home, but they have been a dying people ever since."

"That's so…" words failed the young man.

"Tragic?" Aebreanna suggested. "Their fate is even worse than either your or I can imagine." She directed Tomas' eyes to a young Khepri, who sat alone on a pile of boxes and stared into the sky. "They remember," the spy said. "The memory of flight and their beautiful city in the Valley of the Winds passes from one generation to another. Each is born remembering the glorious freedom they all lost."

Of all the mighty cities of the Khepri, only Oneld remained. It stood on the coast, watching the merchants of younger powers pass through. The sprawling docks were filled with the ships of other nations but worked by the Khepri. This once fabulous metropolis was now reduced to a crumbling collection of sandstone hovels, pressed together by the city walls from which flew the red and gold banners of the Western Empire. No Khepri citizen was allowed to carry a weapon; only the soldiers of House Balshazzar were under arms, and their brutal mastery was everywhere. Even the dignity of the traditional Khepri dress was taken from this once proud people; their white robes replaced with the black of the northern desert. They were a people descended from rulers who now lived as little more than slaves in their own city.

The Khepri themselves looked defeated under the lash of being ruled by yet another conqueror. The Western Empire had forced the subjugated people into service as laborers, clearing the streets they once ruled and repairing the docks from which they once sailed. Each exposed Khepri back, burnt even darker by the unrelenting sun, was marked by a Tordenian whip. Their black-lidded eyes had held neither joy nor even the will to resist. Once possessing the mysterious Mind Magic that had won them Lanasia's first empire, this great power was now a forgotten trick that could do no more than amuse passing foreigners for a few coppers. Khepri beggars guessed names and histories, conjured small illusions only their audience could see, and restored memories once lost. These minor skills they could do for others, but never for themselves. The Khepri had lost all hope.

Tomas had feared what fate would lie in store for the great monuments resting in the Valley of the Builders. Stories abounded in Lanasia that within that nearby region rested the tombs of ancient priest-kings, each a trove of lost relics and fabulous treasure. Since the collapse of their empire millennia ago, the Khepri had tried defending these monuments to their great leaders and creators, but this was a losing battle. First the Sylvai, then the Republic, sent groups they named explorers to raid the Valley's treasures. Now, Tomas saw many groups of so-called explorers from Tordenia, all with eyes agleam for the wealth to be claimed. And the dying Khepri could do nothing to protect their treasured history.

When Ahmed had greeted Tomas and his friends on the docks of Oneld, the squire had shocked his knight by offering no objection to boarding the ship immediately and sailing on the next tide. Rogan had no doubt anticipated having to drag his academically-inclined apprentice out of the cradle of Lanasian civilization. The reality, however, had left an unpleasant taste in Tomas's mind.

Once aboard King Calonar's flagship and out of sight from that crumbling ruin of history, Tomas had spent nearly every moment on deck, staring out at the coastline of the Western Empire as it slid past on their way towards House Balshazzar's capital. For days the squire had tried to find some flaw, some distinguishing characteristic that would set these lands apart from the nations of the east to better show the world all the evil that had come out of the Western Empire. So far, Tomas had found nothing.

The eastern coastline of the Western Empire was no different than any other series of cliffs and beaches around Pelsemoria. Trees still rose up in the distance and rivers still emptied into the same kind of sea. Fish still swam in these waters just as boats still gathered them up in the same kind of nets. The people were olive-skinned and speaking in a strange language that, while similar to Velish, was just different enough for the squire to notice as the *Blue Lady* slid past the fishermen on its way west. Once again, as had so often happened since the young man's departure from his childhood home so long ago, Tomas was disappointed at how different reality was from his preconceptions. He sighed.

"Problem?" Rogan asked, walking up beside his squire.

"Just surprised at how unsurprised I am," Tomas replied without turning.

"You thought the Western Empire was going to be some decaying wasteland?" the knight grinned, knowing the kid's habit of forming his ideas based on old stories. "An evil land filled with monsters and monstrous men?"

"Something like that. Just once, I'd like the bad guys to live in a place that looks evil. These people are just—"

"People?"

The squire nodded grimly. "The Western Empire has seen so much blood over the centuries," he noted. "The Monster War, the Unity Army, Emperor Populus, the witch Xellveya, so many evil people and evil times came out of this land, but it looks so normal."

"That's the way things are," the knight replied. "All those wars and all that horror may have happened here, but those are just small pieces of the history of this place. Mostly, the Western Empire is filled with people the same as anywhere else, people that just want to live their lives in peace. Once we deal with Balshazzar, hopefully, this land will have some of that peace. God knows they've earned it."

"Have they?" Tomas asked. "King Cylan brought peace to the Northlands, but he fought for it, and the people of the north struggled to earn it. Velaross and its lands live in peace, but again, they worked hard for it. If these people want their peace so badly, if they deserve it so much, why won't they fight for it?"

"That's not an easy question to answer," Rogan admitted. "Peace is something that takes a lot of war to earn and a lot more to maintain. People born to it have no appreciation for it, and people that have never had it want it more than anything.

"The people of the Western Empire want peaceful lives and to live free but have never been able to. Through their whole history, every time someone has stepped forward to lead them, telling them they'll bring peace and justice to the land, it's always ended the same, with a new tyrant ruling over them and a new set of laws keeping them in misery."

"Emperor Populus," the young man noted.

"And Xellveya, and the Unity Army, and House Balshazzar. Every one of their liberators has just been another tyrant in training."

"So they've given up hope?"

"I don't know," Rogan shrugged. "Maybe you're right, and these people just need a strong ruler to keep them in line. Maybe they just aren't ready to be free. Maybe they just don't know how to be."

"Would getting rid of Theodorico Balshazzar really help them?"

The knight looked at his squire. "What do you mean?"

"We get rid of House Balshazzar and give these people the chance to live free, but then what happens? Do they just fall apart, waiting for the next warlord to come along? Do they start fighting among themselves and destroy each other? What's the long-term effect of our eliminating House Balshazzar? What's the point if it just opens the door for yet another tyrant?"

"I've got no answers for you, kid," Rogan admitted. "If I had to guess I'd say that once Balshazzar is gone, the Western Empire will break up like the Republic did after Pelsemoria fell. Maybe the Kessians will come south and take over. Or there might be one of the smaller groups, the Varreki maybe, or the Lezians might assume control. The Western Empire isn't as monolithic as the Republic liked to think. There're a lot of different cultures here, all under the dominion of Tordenia. Without House

Balshazzar or some other dominant power, they might just break up into their cultural boundaries. There's just no way of predicting what's going to happen."

"Then why remove Theodorico Balshazzar at all?" Tomas asked. "Why not just weaken him but leave him in power?"

"That's what we hope to do with this trip. Don't misunderstand, our job here isn't an assassination or revolution. Our best-case scenario is that we find out who poisoned the King and how to cure him. Second to that, we find out who this mystery shadow is who's been giving Balshazzar aid and remove that threat but leave the Emir in power. He'll be weakened so much that he won't be a threat to us anymore, and hopefully his own people will rise up against him."

"And we would help them?"

"Absolutely. If a coherent rebellion ever took shape, they'd get as much aid from us as we could provide. But a revolution started, led, and accomplished by a foreign power isn't really a revolution, it's a conquest. A revolution must be started and fought by the people."

"How likely is it that we leave Theodorico Balshazzar alive?" Tomas asked.

Rogan said nothing for a time. Finally, "That's a hard question, kid?"

"Should it be?"

"What do you mean?"

The squire was silent, a doubt lingering in his heart surging once more and finding voice. "The guards, Rogan. The guards and the soldiers and… and that *pasha*, Kerem."

"Kid, what're you talking about?"

Tomas looked at his knight. "You really don't see it do you?"

"Don't see what?"

The squire's eyes drifted back out to the sea, and back through their months-long quest. "Anninihus was an immediate, on-going threat, so we… so I killed him. The mercenaries kept attacking us, so we defended ourselves. The Druug were trying to eat us, so we defended ourselves. That Nekalan in Frostfront, the knights and inquisitors in Daivic, the men who were going to rape Aebreanna… all of them were threats and we were only just defending ourselves or our friends."

Tomas looked again at Rogan. "But the guards, Rogan. When we crept into Parano's palace, we murdered those guards. They weren't attacking us, they weren't threatening anybody. And we murdered them. Because it was confinement. We could have tried knocking them out, we could have tried bribing them or threatening them or even just scaring them off." He stared hard at his mentor. "But we didn't do any of that. We just murdered them, because it was the most convenient thing to do."

"I didn't hear you objecting at the time," the knight pointed out.

"What is it you said?" his squire asked. "Deal with tomorrow, tomorrow? It's tomorrow, Rogan."

"Kid, there's any number of reasons that we had to do what we did. If we'd knocked them out or scared them off, they couldn't come back with reinforcements."

"Would that have really changed the way things went?"

Rogan took a deep breath. "Kid, what you're doing now... the second-guessing, that's natural. In the moment, a decision has to be made. After, with the benefit of hindsight, it's easy to question, to say, 'why didn't we do something else.' Do you think I don't replay Uldron in my head, again and again?"

"I'm not talking about bad decisions or just bad luck, Rogan. I'm talking about how easy it is to just murder people for no good reason." The squire gestured towards the west, towards Tordenia. "You've already got it in your head that killing Theodorico Balshazzar, of ending his House, is a tactical possibility."

"He's an active, on-going threat to the people we love."

Tomas nodded. "That rationale could let us do a lot of really horrible things, you know." He looked back towards the Endless Sands. "And what about the *pasha*?"

"What about him?"

"Was he an active, on-going threat?"

Rogan said nothing, so his squire pressed. "Was he a threat at all? The princess was free. The Shamashi are going to be united. House Parano is gone. We can expose the magic of the inquisitors. What about that *pasha* demanded his death, other than he had planned to do something disgusting to a person you cared about?"

"That's a pretty big oversimplification," Rogan said evenly.

"I don't think so," his squire objected. "He had planned to force Princess Sabriyya to marry him. That offended you, but there wasn't any threat to her. You didn't like the man, so you threw him to the... what were those things, anyway?"

"Crocodiles. River predators."

"Crocodiles." The young man stared at Rogan. "I saw your face as he was screaming. You weren't angry or relieved or anything. I've seen more emotion in you when discussion philosophy. It scared me, Rogan."

They were quiet, watching the fishing boats slide by. The sea was calm, though storm clouds marred the southern horizon. Ahmed had warned them that the waters of the Fangaloris Strait, through which they sailed, suffered a lot of unexpected weather, but the storms seemed, for the moment, to be holding back. Rogan's eyes considered all this before he spoke. "I think I've talked to you about the dangers of our... work."

The squire nodded.

"The best of men can be... corrupted. You can go in with the best intentions, and still be turned into something else. The world will do everything it can to pervert your ethics. I can argue that the *pasha* was a threat, that he could've come back and haunted us later. Maybe he would've, maybe not." Rogan sighed and rubbed his eyes, as though fighting a soul-deep weariness. "Hardest thing in the world is to fight for your loved ones and stay uncorrupted. Violence gets to be easy. There are times when I think I default to it, just because it's so easy, so comforting in the moment."

"You said that Beckett, your Bellonari mentor, that he tried to teach you a form of just war?"

"Yeah."

"What did he say?" Tomas asked. "How did he stay on the righteous path?"

Rogan laughed then, and shook his head.

"What?"

The knight nodded and glanced at his squire. "Beckett once told me that I was what was keeping him on the path. That having someone look at him as an example…"

The squire shook his head ruefully. "If you're suggesting that I'm supposed to-"

"No. I think we're supposed to help each other."

They both looked out, again letting their eyes and their thoughts drift towards Tordenia. "So," Tomas said, "Will we have to kill Balshazzar?"

"I can't tell you, kid. That depends on him. But hey, look on the bright side. Odds are we won't even get close to him before their guards find us and throw us in—"

"Yet another dungeon," the squire sighed.

"That does happen to us from time to time," the knight admitted. "Is that why you're always up here staring at the water? Trying to enjoy the open air while you can?"

Tomas shook his head. "The sea has a life of its own, Rogan. I really feel relaxed out here."

"You're starting to sound like Ahmed," Rogan noted, glancing at the veteran seaman as he approached his passengers.

Ahmed, though an admiral and commander of House Calonar's small navy, was a greatly unassuming man. When Tomas had first met him last year in their crossing of the Zaka Sea, the squire had been surprised at the lack of resemblance between the sailor and his younger brother, Rashid. Although there could be little doubt the two were brothers, their different lifestyles had caused such massive differences that confusing the two was nearly impossible. Rashid had fairer skin, for one, a byproduct of his nocturnally-based occupation, no doubt. Ahmed's skin, in contrast, had long since seen enough sunlight to be nearly bronzed. While Rashid, having been a spy for so long, had developed a soft step that allowed for easy sneaking, Ahmed's pace could be heard from one end of his ship to another. The spymaster's hair, dark to the point of black, lent itself to the occasional need to blend in, while the admiral's hair had been bleached almost blond by the sun. The most telling difference between the two brothers, though, was in their great loves: while Rashid had given his heart to Aebreanna, Ahmed had eyes only for his *Blue Lady*.

To the unenlightened, the *Blue Lady* would appear as just another of the new caravels designed by the Uldra and built in the new Arianwen shipyards. These larger, sleek ships were increasingly popular for their reliability and maneuverability, to say nothing of the speed their odd triangular sails provided. Close inspection, though, guided by Ahmed's prideful explanations, revealed deeper secrets to his beloved *Blue Lady*. Nowhere on the ship, from stem to stern, could be seen any symbol or regalia that would identify her as a ship of House Calonar. The customs inspector at the Oneld docks, a squinty-eyed, distrusting man from Daivic, had made a detailed inspection of the entire ship but was unable to uncover anything more suspect than a few swords and daggers that, after a quick exchange of coins, Ahmed assured him were simply for self-defense. The irony of this being that Ahmed had enough hidden compartments on his ship to hide a great horde of treasure, or the weapons, armor, equipment, and hunted members of Rogan's team. There were also, Tomas noted, numerous emplacements for large weapons.

The aging sailor nodded to the southern horizon. Barely visible, a speck peaked just above the waterline. "Is that Dagon'ay?" Tomas asked.

"No," Ahmed laughed. "We're a few days north of the first islands. That's a ship."

"Do we know who?" Rogan asked.

"The lookout already spotted a signal." The sailor handed Rogan a spyglass and guided them both to the left rail, guiding the knight's gaze.

"Huh," Rogan grunted. "But what does it mean?"

"It's flag-code," Ahmed explained. "We set it up a few years ago as a way to communicate between ships at distance." He nodded to the distant vessel. "She's carrying Ward and the Archaeknights."

"How?" Tomas asked, squinting his eyes at the ship.

"They commandeered a Tordenian galley to the south, my guess would be at either Antola or Kalogeros. They've crowded sail and rowed hard to intercept us." He looked at Rogan. "Not hard to meet and transfer Ward's team here."

"Do it," Rogan said, breathing a deep sigh of relief. He glanced at his squire. "Reinforcements," was all he said, turning to take the news belowdecks to Aebreanna and Beraht.

As Tomas turned to follow, a sudden dizziness overcame him, and the young squire could have fallen overboard if not for Ahmed grabbing him and pulling him back from the rail. Instinctively, the young man's hand went to the golden rose pinned to his collar, feeling it pulse in time with his heartbeat.

"Not a good place to dance, land lubber!" the sailor barked.

Tomas was unable to hear the admiral's words though. With a suddenness that caught him completely unaware, the squire found himself caught up in the tides of magic. In the few times he had tried to sense them, the currents had been slow and gentle. In this case, Tomas felt as though he were caught in a raging flood, all of it rushing ahead. Unable to resist, the squire felt his thoughts being pulled across the ocean towards Tordenia, or more specifically, the city's great cathedral. With no warning, the currents pulled Tomas down, beneath the hallowed building, into a complex network of both natural and artificial tunnels.

At long last, his thoughts were pulled to whatever it was that was drawing in the currents of magic. Within a massive underground cavern were dozens of inquisitors kneeling before a black altar to some forgotten evil. Near the altar stood two men, unknown to the squire, one an obvious nobleman with long gray hair adorned by a gold crown and built as a warrior would be, the other so deeply robed and cowled in black that he appeared to be no more than a shadow. A great trench ran the width of the cavern in which stood row upon row of unmoving warriors, each wearing hideous distortions of the armor of a Holy Knight, enameled black and bearing the worst sigils of unspeakable evil. A simple rope bridge spanned the trench, offering access across to the other platform where a single tunnel led into the subterranean maze that wound beneath the Western Empire's capital.

On the altar itself rested the point to which the currents surged. Tomas looked upon a large crystal sphere, nearly the size of a man's head. It was perfect, as round and seemingly delicate as a soap bubble. The sphere seemed to radiate its own soft glow, casting long shadows throughout the evil place. Even had Tomas not been one with the churning currents of magic, the squire would have known that this was an object of the greatest mystical power.

One of the kneeling inquisitors was speaking to the man garbed in shadows. "Master, Eigenhard and his servants are less than a week from the capital. Our efforts to delay them, sending our mercenaries and the beasts of the mountains to hunt them, diverting patrols to search for them, even collapsing the ancient tunnel, nothing has succeeded in halting his approach. You must use your power to destroy them before they arrive!"

The muscular nobleman nodded, his hand going absently to the curved sword belted at his waist. "I agree. If Eigenhard manages to infiltrate my city, my soldiers may not be able to find him. We cannot allow any of Calonar's agents to see what we have done here."

The black cloaked and hooded figure held up a gloved hand for silence. Raising its head, the figure seemed to sniff the air and, turning suddenly, looked right to where Tomas was watching. A deep, rasping voice emerged from the dark hood. "Eigenhard's whelp!" it snarled. Dipping its hand into the cloak, the gloved hand emerged holding a small blue gem. "Come to me, boy," the voice commanded.

The currents around Tomas suddenly shifted, pulling the squire's thoughts with increasing force towards the gem. Desperation burned his thoughts, but within that inferno, there was a single point of cool serenity. This storm's eye whispered knowledge to Tomas, and the young man acted. He called to the currents, drawing as much of their power to himself as possible before focusing it on the gem the wizard held.

The cloaked wizard swore in several languages as the gem he was holding burst, and tiny crystalline shards were imbedded in his hand and arm, drawing a steady flow of blood. Tomas had time enough only to see a set of pale blue eyes and the vaguest hint of a gnarled face that betrayed a snarl of hatred and frustration before the squire used the remaining power within him to fly back to the *Blue Lady* and the safety of his body.

Chapter 67

Tomas opened his eyes to Rogan and Ahmed bent over him with

worried expressions on their faces. Seeing his squire's eyes open, the knight's relief was obvious. "What in Underworld happened?" he demanded.

Tomas sat up with Ahmed's help and leaned against the railing. "I'm not sure," he confessed. "I felt something powerful. It pulled me so hard, I couldn't control what was happening."

"Are you all right?" Ahmed asked.

The squire nodded. "I think so."

Rogan helped him to his feet. "Come on, kid. We'd better talk with Aebreanna about this."

The two men went back to the rear cabin, finding Aebreanna and Beraht in the midst of a heated debate. "I'm not going to wear it, and that's final!" the Uldra roared.

Aebreanna sighed. "Beraht, unlike in Daivic, there will be no one in the whole of Tordenia who will want to take you alive. Rogan, they may wish to capture for interrogation, and Tomas they may to wish reeducate for the Inquisition, but they will simply execute you and me on sight. Uldra and *Sy'lwa'n* are never allowed to roam free in Tordenia, unless they are accompanied by their owners."

"Owners?" Tomas asked, his eyebrows going up.

Rogan crossed the room and poured himself a cup of wine. "Balshazzar has taken some of the old Republic laws literally. In the Majestos Dynasty, non-Humans were 'lesser citizens with modified rights.' Back when the Republic was up and running, Sylvai and Uldra had to get special permits to work in certain jobs, move from one place to another, and own things like homes and weapons."

Aebreanna laughed. "Unfortunately, the noble Emir Balshazzar takes 'lesser citizens' to mean slaves. Under his rule, non-Humans have few rights, if any. They must be owned by a Human and escorted from place to place."

"What do you mean by escorted?" Tomas asked.

In response, Aebreanna held up a leather collar and leash.

"You can't be serious!" the squire exclaimed.

"I'm not going to wear that!" Beraht roared again.

Rogan slammed his cup down. "Then you're not going. I doubt Aebreanna likes it any more than you do, but we've got no choice. If we're going to get into the city, then we need to blend."

"Why isn't Aebreanna wearing one?" the Uldra demanded.

"Because she knows how to BE QUIET!" Rogan roared. "She knows how to sneak around, and you know, I can't remember the last time you even tried to sneak!"

"Hey, I tried to sneak into that brothel."

"You knocked one of the walls down!" the knight yelled in exasperation.

Tomas laughed. "That is how Beraht sneaks."

"Shut up, kid. Look, Beraht," Rogan said, calming down, "we need you to come into the city with us, but we can't do it unless you play the part of mad Uldra barbarian. I know it's a stretch, but you have to try."

Beraht mulled it over for a few moments. "I'm bringing my waraxe," he said flatly.

Tomas walked over and put his hand on the Uldra's shoulder. "Beraht, if you're playing the part of a slave, then you can't be armed."

"Besides," Rogan added, "Tomas here can carry it, and if there's any trouble, you can call it instantly."

"Can't I at last wear my armor?" he asked somewhat plaintively.

Rogan looked over at Aebreanna. The Sylva shook her head. "He rattles," she explained.

The knight turned back to his mountainous friend. "Sorry, no armor. But if it makes you feel any better, Tomas and I can't wear our own armor either. We have to wear that leather armor Aebreanna bought for us in Oneld."

"Dead cow is not armor," Beraht snapped. "Armor is made of metal. No self-respecting warrior goes into battle with a dead cow wrapped around his body."

"You wear leather boots, don't you?" Tomas asked.

The Uldra rolled his eyes. "Well, you can walk on a dead cow. Who cares? But no warrior can wear a cow into battle and expect to be taken seriously."

Rogan rolled his eyes and sighed. "Look, we'll carry your armor and helmet tied to one of the packs, Tomas will carry your hammer, and Aebreanna will rig the leash so that you can snap it off in a second. Other than that, you'll just have to endure it and think up a couple great drinking songs to immortalize how much you suffered on this mission."

"So long as we are not forced to listen to them this time," Aebreanna muttered.

"Look, we have bigger problems anyway," Tomas insisted.

"And these problems are what?" Aebreanna asked.

Tomas relayed to his friends what happened to him. When he described the crystal sphere, Rogan stopped him. "Wait, what did you say it looked like?" he demanded with an intense look.

The squire held his hands up, about a foot apart. "It was a perfect sphere, about this big, made of solid crystal."

"Did it radiate its own light?" Aebreanna asked. "A soft white light?"

Tomas nodded. "Do you know what it is?" he asked.

Beraht, Aebreanna, and Rogan shared looks of surprise and hope. "What?" Tomas demanded.

"So now we know where another of them went," Beraht noted.

"Another of what?" Tomas asked.

"The explosion was very powerful," Aebreanna added. "It could have been hurled all this way."

"Or Anninihus found it," Rogan mused.

"What are you guys talking about?" the squire insisted.

"Cyras said that once you came to Tordenia you'd know what to do next," Beraht smiled.

Rogan laughed. "I love it. Balshazzar has the King poisoned and the whole time is holding on to what we need to heal him."

Tomas slammed his fist on the wooden table that sat in the middle. Glaring at the three smiling heroes, he snarled, "If one of you doesn't talk in three seconds, slapping faces."

Rogan patted him on the shoulder. "Easy, kid, we're just enjoying some good news for a change."

"Which is?" the squire demanded.

"If the crystal you saw is what we hope it to be," Aebreanna explained, "then you have found the one thing in the entire world that could save the life of the King."

Tomas's eyes narrowed.

Rogan refilled his cup and poured one for his squire. "It's called the Seal of Life, kid, or the Healing Sphere. It's one of the Seals of Stalline."

"You mean like the one Vara had?" he asked. "The…?"

"The Mind's Eye," Rogan supplied.

"The Seal of Wind," Aebreanna added.

Tomas sat on one of the small chairs and leaned back, his eyes lost in thought. "Strange coincidence…" he mused.

Rogan sat as well. "What do you mean?"

"Vara has the Seal of Wind," the squire said, following his thoughts without knowing their destination. "Balshazzar as the Seal of Life. The Triumvirate has located another Seal outside Jarek." He looked at his knight. "Three Seals suddenly in circulation. When just one appears, whole legends are born. Now we've encountered three in just a few months?"

"The coincidence would be extreme," Aebreanna agreed.

"There's no such thing as coincidence," Beraht countered, almost automatically.

"Ever since our battle with the Greysoul," Rogan noted, "Rashid's had teams searching everywhere for those damned things. Now, suddenly, they're just appearing."

"Not just," Tomas argued. "Remember, Vara was given her Seal as payment, from the same person who, we think, is aiding Balshazzar. Esha told us that, before he attacked the Keep, Anninihus was combing the world." He looked to Rogan. "Could that have been what he was doing? Searching for the Seals of Stalline? How many Seals are there, anyway?"

"Eight," Aebreanna said, "each representing one of the fundamental elements of magic. Each of the Seals of Stalline is unique in both form and function, but each is supreme within its own magical tradition."

"Stalline?" Tomas mused aloud. "Wasn't she the Sylvai goddess of magic?"

Aebreanna shook her head slightly. "That is the general opinion of many, including the Arcane Guild, but that is only partially correct. The true race of Stalline is unknown, for her life predated the *Sy'lva'n* Empire by millennia. She was a servant of the *Sa'kai*, or possibly one of them in mortal form. She led the war against the Adversary and defeated its mortal servants. What little is known of her is that Stalline was a practitioner of magic, perhaps the first in *Ar'ay'el*, and established most, if not all, of what we know of magic: the various schools, prohibitions against trafficking with demons, crafting of staffs, and so on. Her last, greatest act was to create the eight Seals that, legend says, together created a barrier around the world that banished the Adversary and prevented its return."

Rogan handed Tomas his cup. "That's the real danger in what the Greysoul was attempting," the knight explained. "Tienel was trying to assemble all eight of the Seals for himself, to penetrate Stalline's barrier. He had most of them, but we'd managed to beat him to a couple. Tienel kidnapped Aebreanna and offered to exchange her for the Seals we had. Me and Beraht went to his tower. If the Greysoul had managed to pierce the barrier…"

"The rise of Ramalech," Tomas whispered.

"We stopped him," Beraht grumbled. "He tried to kill Aebreanna, so Rogan threw the Seal of Fire at him, forcing him through that incomplete door. It exploded, and the Seals were all flung away."

"The rise of Ramalech…" Tomas whispered again.

"Like Beraht said," Rogan assured his squire, "we stopped it."

"No," Tomas argued, "you delayed it."

"What?"

The young man started ticking facts off his fingers. "Remember what the prophecy says: the Greysoul gathering the Seals, the Death of Calonar, the Inversion, the return of the Dark Empress, and the rise of the Demon-god."

"Two brothers," Aebreanna mused aloud, her opalescent eye half-shut and her tone deep. "One of light, the other dark. One who would thwart the prophecy, the other fulfill it."

They were quiet for a time. Then Rogan said, "Cyras told us we'd know what to do when we got to Tordenia."

"This Seal of Life can cure King Cylan?" Tomas asked.

Rogan moved to a cupboard and retrieved a small bottle of wine. He filled his friend's cups and raised his own. "The Healing Sphere can heal any wound and cure any disease."

Beraht raised his cup. "We take it."

Tomas raised his. "We get home and prevent the death of Calonar."

Aebreanna raised hers. "We thwart the rise of the Demon-god."

They all drank.

"So we're not bothering to break into the palace anymore?" Beraht asked.

The knight nodded. "This changes the mission completely," he decided. "We're getting that Seal. If we have the time or an opportunity presents itself, we'll face down Balshazzar, but our priority is the Healing Sphere."

"I don't think it's Theodorico Balshazzar we have to worry about," Tomas said quietly.

"What do you mean?" the knight asked.

Tomas relayed the rest of his experience, including his confrontation with the wizard. "You got lucky, kid," Rogan declared.

"Indeed," Aebreanna agreed. "If this wizard is as powerful as we fear, he could have easily destroyed your mind."

"Then why didn't he?" the squire demanded.

"Who knows?" Beraht grunted. "Maybe the kid just surprised him. Maybe he wanted him to escape. Who cares? Let's go find him and kill him and stop him."

"Another brilliant example of Uldra tactics," Aebreanna murmured.

"He does have a point," Rogan pointed out. "If they know we're coming, then there's no point in trying to sneak."

"Not as long as you don't mind fighting your way through every guard and soldier Balshazzar has," Tomas said sarcastically. He cast a meaningful look at his knight, who nodded.

"Bring them on," Beraht grinned.

"If I might interject a note of common sense into this discussion?" Aebreanna sighed, rolling her eye. "I believe Tomas has a point. If we wish to recover the Seal and escape, then obliterating the army of House Balshazzar may not be wise."

"You have a better idea?" the barbarian demanded.

The beautiful spy smiled sweetly at her companion. "Have you not learned after all these years, Beraht? I always have a better idea."

"Let's hear it," Rogan said.

Aebreanna poured herself more wine and sat down. "Considering everything your squire experienced, we can safely assume Emir Theodorico and his ally are aware of our approach and intentions. Now that the enemy knows that we know of their activities beneath the cathedral, we can logically assume that all the emir's preparations, which he will most defiantly be making, will be dedicated to the defense of the cathedral."

"That's what I'd do," Rogan confessed.

"Then we need to give our enemy a better target," she replied with a smile.

"She's got a plan," Beraht groaned.

"Is that bad?" Tomas asked.

"Yes! I like Rogan's plans better. Anytime Rogan makes the plan, we get into some great fights and barely escape with our lives. All of Aebreanna's plans involve sneaking and not fighting or almost dying. Where's the fun in that?"

"Thanks, Beraht," the knight replied sourly. Turning to Aebreanna, Rogan sighed. "So let's hear the plan."

She told them.

After thinking about it for a few minutes, the knight was forced to agree. "You know, that might just work. Unless anyone has a better idea?"

Beraht raised his hand.

"Except Beraht."

The Uldra lowered his hand.

"Well, I guess we'll be getting an even earlier start than we thought. Aebreanna, tell Ahmed what we're going to need. We've got some preparations to make."

Chapter 68

Emir Theodorico of House Balshazzar stood on a balcony of his palace, looking out over his city, wondering where the attack from where would come. After his newfound ally had warned him that Eigenhard would most likely make his attempt that day, the emir had spent hours going over his plans to capture the mercenary and his minions. Even now, with the sun slipping behind the Dominic Mountains, Balshazzar sent frequent messages to his garrison commanders, modifying his plans as he felt was needed. *It will be soon*, he thought to himself. Eigenhard has campaigned enough to appreciate the value of darkness and was most likely waiting for night to fall.

Theodorico was, by nature, a man of deep ambition. His father had insisted that he serve in the Legions as all the men of his family had since earning their status as a Noble House so many centuries ago. Theodorico found obeying the orders of men so obviously inferior to himself to be greatly distasteful and so had played at the military game with the sole intention of reaching a point in which his will alone would rule. After commanding the Darez battalion during the Reydia Uprising and battling Xeshlin during two separate campaigns, Colonel Theodorico had been more than ready to resign his commission the moment his father died. It was only the threat of his father's displeasure that had forced the younger Balshazzar to endure the constant orders from the fools at Pelsemoria as long as he had anyway. It was one thing to risk one's life, Theodorico believed, but he would never again risk his acting on absurd orders that put his own life in danger, issued by lesser men whose petty schemes would produce no real benefit to the Republic.

Theodorico really had no great love for his father anyway; the man had, after all, been abusive and demanded much more from his son than he was willing to give himself. So it was that once his father had passed on, the younger Balshazzar had retired immediately from the Legions, mourned for only the minimum time custom demanded, and then quickly adapted himself from the military arena of advancement to the political. Theodorico found that his strategies for advancement through the ranks of the Legions worked equally well among the even more treacherous Elector Lords. Through blackmail, gossip, and the occasion accident befalling the appropriate opponent, the emir quickly found himself appointed by the Emperor himself to the Elector Council, a position his family had not held for centuries, despite being the rulers of the Western Empire.

It was his day of glory, that first meeting of the Council. True, nothing of any significance had been accomplished, but it was still Theodorico's fate to be sitting there, among the highest-ranking nobles in the Republic. It was also at that meeting that Theodorico met the man he would come to hate more than any other: Duke Cylan Calonar. Calonar had a popularity with the common people that Theodorico found distasteful. No true leader of men, the emir believed, could be loved by men. The best rulers were the ones who made decisions leading to the death and suffering of the common people for the good of the Republic. Theodorico's suspicion of Calonar was quickly confirmed in that first meeting as the Northlander opposed every proposal any man put forward that would bring any kind of hardship on his precious peasantry.

Seeing the man Theodorico himself would come to label the Black Duke as the greatest threat to the future stability of the Republic, the emir frequently tried to enlist the support of other nobles in forming a coalition that could stop Calonar. With disgust, Theodorico had learned that he alone, of all the Elector Lords, was unafraid of what the Black Duke could do to them. Nowhere the emir looked could he find an ally against the man, until the day he met the wizard Tienel Greysoul.

Even at the time, before the wizard's true plans came to light, the emir knew that the magic user was more than he appeared. Balshazzar had hoped that, with a man as obviously ambitious as himself and with the resources of the Arcane Guild to support them, the emir could, at last, take a stand against Calonar and cast him out of the Elector Council, stripped of all rank and position. The Greysoul had assured him that, once they had brought evidence before the Emperor of Calonar's treasonous actions, whether such evidence existed or not being irrelevant, the Emperor would reward them both with titles and land that would secure them for the rest of their lives.

The Greysoul had betrayed him, of course. Only a fool would trust a wizard after all, and Theodorico was no fool. At an appropriate time, the emir had planned on turning on his ally as well; he was simply beaten to it. The tactician in Theodorico knew that not every contest could be won, and he really hadn't lost anything of great value. True, the Emperor and most of the Elector Lords had been killed and Pelsemoria laid waste, but Theodorico's had expanded. The Western Empire now spread from the Aebreka Sea to the Efrayim Ocean, and from the Jassian Mountains to the Nassinal Sea. The Varreki, the Lezians, the Orosh, and the Hudish all once again swore fealty to Tordenia, to House Balshazzar. To make matters even more satisfactory, he even had a real chance to take the Redwood Throne for himself and rule all Lanasia.

And here he was, once again allied with a wizard in the hopes of finally defeating Calonar. *This time would be different*, he swore. *This time, when the wizard betrays me, as he is surely planning to do, I'll be ready and waiting. This time, the game Calonar and I play is for much higher stakes.* There was little doubt in anyone's mind, least of all Theodorico, that of all the minor nobility still clinging to their lands and titles, only Houses Balshazzar and Calonar had any real chance at the claiming the Redwood Throne. Once one of them was dead, the other would be left to rule a new Empire and begin a new dynasty.

What so few people knew of Theodorico was that he really did not mind the danger of his game. To the emir, it was just that, a game. It was a game a decade ago when the Emperor was killed and Calonar crowned himself a king before Theodorico could think to do it, it was a game when Theodorico had agreed to the Black Dukes poisoning, and it will be a game when one of them finally defeats the other. If the truth were told, the emir was greatly enjoying their game, reveling in planning his next move and trying to anticipate Calonar's. Unfortunately, the needs of Lanasia must override any personal entertainment. The continent was suffering, in need of strong leadership, so Theodorico must soon make his final moves to beat Calonar and claim the victory he had so patiently worked toward over these many years.

Everything was nearly ready. Within a few more days, a week at most, the wizard's project would be complete, and Theodorico would have an unbeatable army at his disposal. Within a few months, six at most, Calonar would succumb to the poison that had cost most of House Balshazzar's treasury to create. Within a year, Theodorico would be able to lay waste to Calonar's city and eliminate every member of that damned House once and for all. Now was the critical point when the plans of a decade and more were reaching their most vulnerable point. The emir could easily berate himself for not anticipating Calonar's countermove of trying to sneak Eigenhard's team into his city to ruin everything, but there was nothing productive in doing so.

Straightening his shoulders, made strong and broad from his military training and maintained so through strict exercise, Theodorico shrugged off such thoughts. A good strategist does not cry over mistakes. He learns from them and minimizes the damage they can cause. The emir smiled; a good strategist also turns them to his advantage. *Let Eigenhard come*, he thought. *Let him come into my city, within my grasp.* According to the emir's ally, who gained his information through a member of Calonar's own council of advisors, Eigenhard was bringing with him the two other of his most dangerous agents. *The Northern Keep will fall all the faster with the Black Duke's best field commander, his deadliest assassin, and his most erratic weapon rotting in my dungeons.*

As Theodorico watched the sun set behind the Dominic Mountains, the emir's smile turned vicious. These were the moments that he relished most, waiting for his opponent's next move. Everything was on the line this evening. Theodorico entire strategy rested on his ability to beat Eigenhard, to find him in the city and stop him before the mercenary could reach the project. The emir's blood raced throughout his body in excitement; this would be a game to remember.

So far, everything had gone well. The emir had left orders that morning for Tordenia to be closed by midday, and no caravans with non-Humans were to be admitted at all. Several platoons of soldiers had made sweeps of the countryside, rounding up a number of deserters, runaway slaves, and even a few criminals. After being informed that a number of Uldra, likely more refugees from the Alba Mountains, were now being held in the city dungeons, Theodorico had ordered the Inquisition to start checking the prisoners, one by one, to see if any of them were Eigenhard's agents. The emir thought it unlikely that the mercenary would divide his small force, but Theodorico knew that Calonar's minions often made a point of doing things that any other tactician would consider insane and somehow still achieve victory. Eigenhard was out there, of that there could be no doubt; but where would he come from?

Just as the sun finally dipped completely behind the mountains, Eigenhard made his opening move. One of Theodorico military advisors called out, "My lord, a ship approaches the harbor." The emir moved beside the general to see for himself. Indeed, coming around the edge of the cliffs that surrounded Tordenia's large harbor, a ship was approaching.

"Were my orders relayed to the fleet commanders?" Theodorico asked.

"Yes, my lord," the man replied. Earlier that day, the emir had ordered that no ships be allowed within a league of the city. Even as Theodorico and his men watched, the half-dozen ships securing Tordenia's harbor moved to intercept the intruder.

"My lord," an older advisor exclaimed, looking up from the spyglass he had been using.

"What is it?"

"The ship that approaches appears to be one of yours."

"What?" Balshazzar snapped. The emir pushed his commander out of the way and looked through the device himself. The ship was flying the red and gold banner of the Western Empire.

One of the advisors looked down at the harbor. "I believe your *yuzbashi* have noticed the mistake, my lord. They are returning."

"Do we have any ships due back within the next two days?" Theodorico asked.

The harbormaster consulted his notes and shook his head. "No, my lord. But you have several ships patrolling the Fangaloris Strait. One of them could have come back early."

"Sink it," the emir commanded.

"My lord, that is one of our ships!" Any further arguments from the functionary were cut off at the sight of the emir's scowl. One of the advisors called to the runners below to open fire on the ship. Within a quarter of an hour, well before the approaching ship came within arrow-shot of the city, the catapults lining the cliffs on either side of Tordenia's harbor let loose. With flying boulders and burning pitch raining down on them, the approaching galley turned sharply and headed back out to sea.

"Order a pursuit," Theodorico instructed. "But only two ships. Keep the others back." His advisors issued the appropriate commands.

"Congratulations, my lord," the emir's senior councilor said, bowing. "It looks like you defeated Eigenhard before he even entered your city."

"Did I?" Theodorico asked, his gaze sweeping the city. "Have the gates all been shut?"

"Yes, my lord," the senior councilor replied. "As you commanded, the gates were closed at midday."

The news did little to comfort Theodorico, who kept looking throughout his city. "It was a distraction," he declared. The emir turned to his advisors. "Order my troops to round up every man who has entered the city with any non-Humans. I want them thrown into the dungeons until I personally authorize their release."

The advisors bowed and again barked orders to the runners. Almost immediately, a rider came up to the palace gates. "Emir!" he cried.

"Is that one of your messengers?" Balshazzar asked.

The senior councilor shook his head. "No, my lord. It appears to be one of the soldiers assigned to the city gates." The aide leaned over the stone wall. "Report!" he bellowed.

"Sir! A group of people, both non-Human and Human, tried climbing the city walls while the catapults were firing! One of them carried a gem fashioned in the symbol of the Black Duke!"

"It looks like you were right, my lord," the senior councilor confessed. "Eigenhard did attempt a diversion."

Theodorico narrowed his eyes. "Send someone to view these prisoners. There should be two Humans, a Sylva, and an Uldra. I want confirmation as soon as possible."

The youngest advisor bowed and left. It was nearly an hour later when his report came back by runner. The young man tried desperately to collect his breath as he was escorted into his emir's presence. Bowing, the runner made his report in a gasping voice. "It is as you said sire. Two Human men accompanied by both an Uldra and a Sylvai. The commander sends his assurances that we have captured the criminal Eigenhard and his companions."

"Did you see the prisoners yourself?" Theodorico asked calmly, sipping on the wine he had brought up during the wait.

"Yes, my lord. The commander made sure that I saw with my own eyes. Two Humans and two non-Humans."

Theodorico put his wine glass down, not bothering to look at the servant. "Did they confess after being captured?"

The runner gave a breathless laugh. "No, sire. The leader claims that he is a buyer and seller of pleasure-slaves, and that the non-Humans are his property. He claims that he has no idea of how the Calonar symbol came to be on his person, and that he is your loyal subject. He claims that he does not remember trying to climb the city walls."

Theodorico drew his curved sword, holding it idly in his right hand. "If the man claims to be a buyer and seller of pleasure-slaves, why is he traveling with a male Uldra?" he calmly asked.

The runner looked confused. "My lord, the Uldra accompanying the Humans was not male. Both non-Humans were female."

Theodorico nodded absently. "Was I not clear that I sought a team of two male Humans, one male Uldra, and one Sylva?"

"My lord," the runner's words were cut off, along with his head. With the young man dead at their feet, the surrounding advisors and commanders trembled, fearing their emir's wrath.

Theodorico calmly wiped his blade off on the runner's tunic and resheathed it. Picking up his wine glass, he turned to his trembling military leaders. "Eigenhard is within the city. I want an immediate curfew set. Place archers on the top of every tall building in the city. Any and all persons on the street by the end of one half-hour are to be shot on sight. I want a platoon of your finest soldiers placed around the cathedral. No one is to be let in or out. Order the inquisitor at the gate to use every resource to determine how that flesh-peddler acquired an emblem of the Black Duke. Once the archers and platoon are in place, conduct house-to-house searches beginning with the those closest to the harbor." The emir put his hand on his sword hilt. "Are my orders unclear?" he asked. "Are there any questions?"

One commander hesitantly raised his hand. "Why the harbor, my lord?"

Before Theodorico could reply, there was a series of explosions coming from the harbor. Rushing to see what the source was, every man on the parapet with the exception of the very still Theodorico was stunned to see the four remaining military galleys in the harbor were on fire, their crews desperately jumping overboard.

"Why the harbor, you ask?" the emir said, raising the wineglass to his lips. "Simple, that is where Eigenhard entered the city."

Chapter 69

"Well," Tomas said from his lookout position on the roof of the stables where Rogan was hiding in, "it looks like everything is going according to plan. Balshazzar's troops are moving toward the harbor, and they're clearing the streets as they go. They should reach us in about a half an hour. What now?"

Rogan took another look down both sides of the street in front of the stables, ensuring it was still clear. "Now," he replied, "we keep going with Aebreanna's plan. Get down here. We need to go. Beraht should be in place by now."

The squire nimbly climbed down from his oversight, taking care not to slip on the wet stonework. Upon reaching the ground, Tomas rejoined his knight, who had been stripping off the Tordenian mantle Aebreanna had provided them for sneaking through the city and was replacing it with the new splintmail suit Ahmed had provided. Tomas quickly pulled on his armor and belted Steelheart on place.

Rogan glanced at his squire and nodded. "Come on," he said, "we're starting to run late."

As the two moved down the back street, Tomas whispered to his knight, "Is this really going to work?"

Rogan shrugged. "Aebreanna's plans do tend to work somehow. If nothing else, trust to a Sylva's winning streak."

"Why?"

"Because I have yet to meet any woman willing to give one up."

The spy's plan had, in fact, proceeded exactly as she had lain out, so far. An hour before daybreak, the four adventurers had been taken ashore some distance from Tordenia, Ahmed giving his assurances that his *Blue Lady* would be in place at the proper time, and that Ward's appropriated Tordenian galley would also be ready. Once on a beach that was several miles south from the gates of Tordenia, the party had split up, Aebreanna joining the caravan of a flesh merchant bound for the city, Beraht moving down the beach toward the cliffs surrounding the city, and Rogan and Tomas using a longboat to carefully move parallel with Beraht's land-bound course, using the many reefs and rising cliffs as concealment for their approach.

After seeing the Uldra had been safely captured and taken away by Tordenian forces, both knight and squire had spent most of the rest of the day gathering a large pile of seaweed, driftwood, and other flotsam to disguise their small boat. Tomas had worried constantly at the decision to split up but had been repeatedly overridden by his knight. Rogan had insisted that Aebreanna's plan would work, with each of them infiltrating the city by a different route and meeting up at a prearranged location and time. For their part, Tomas had to admit that he and Rogan had been remarkably successful. After decorating their boat to the point that he himself could not recognize it, the two warriors then spread on their hands and faces a black paste that Aebreanna had mixed together to dye their skin dark enough to match the murky sea around them. By the time the afternoon sun had begun its decent toward the western mountains, the two men were swimming with the disguised boat between them through Tordenia's large harbor.

With perhaps an hour until sundown, the arranged time at which they would cause their distraction, Rogan had led his squire and the boat to the first of the galleys still sitting in the harbor. The thick, oil-based gel they had spread unto the hulls of the ships was disgusting, and the vapors that came off it frequently made Tomas light-headed. "What is this stuff?" he had whispered to Rogan as they smeared it unto the hull of the second ship.

In response, the knight put his finger to his lips, demanding silence. Once they had finished and moved on to the next of Balshazzar's ships, Rogan whispered an answer. "Beraht mixed it up. He swears that it won't come off in salt water and that the slightest spark will ignite it."

"Where did he get it?" the squire asked.

Rogan shrugged. "I think he drinks it."

Tomas sputtered as he accidentally swallowed some seawater. "That stuff is thicker than sap! I think it was eating through the hull of that last ship! How could he drink it?"

Rogan smiled. "There's an old Uldra myth that, the more a warrior drinks, the closer he gets to understanding the mind of the Allfather. The Uldra believe that if a warrior can get drunk enough, their god will imbue him with divine power."

The squire narrowed his eyes, casting Rogan a suspicious look. "Are you serious?" he demanded.

The knight shook his head. "Sometimes, kid, I wish I wasn't," he replied.

"And Beraht believes this?"

"With all his heart and soul. Believe it or not, Beraht is one of the most pious men you'll ever meet. Of course, for an Uldra, drinking and fighting are religious practices."

The rest of the operation proceeded well. By the time the sun had touched the mountains to the west, the two warriors had spread Beraht's sludge on the hulls of each ship and were making their way towards one of the piers. As they swam, Rogan had left a trail of the slime in their wake. Tomas had prayed frequently that none of the soldiers on the docks noticed the thick streak of rainbowish light sitting on top of the water. As soon as Ward's captured galley rounded the cliffs and made for the harbor, Rogan and Tomas were ready.

"Right on time," Tomas had noted.

Rogan shrugged. "Ward always was punctual."

By the time some of Balshazzar's ships had raised anchor and made ready to leave, the knight and squire had beached the boat and pulled their gear out. As Tomas checked their armor and weapons and cleaned the coloring off himself, Rogan had pulled out his flint and tinder. Hearing the catapults fire, the knight created just enough sparks to start a small flame and threw it into the slick trail that led back out into the harbor.

Tomas stood, watching a line of blue fire make its way out among the waves. If not for Rogan hitting him on the shoulder, snapping in a hushed voice to follow, the squire may have still been standing there, watching the small flame slide along the water. Fortunately, the knight had enough sense of purpose to ignore nearly anything except the mission at hand. Tomas hefted the heavy sack holding their armor and weapons onto his shoulder and followed his knight into the city-proper. The two left the beach as the sky turned red and, wearing the loose mantles common among the people of Tordenia, mixing into the onlookers along the harbor.

When the Tordenian galleys had started exploding, the unavoidable result of that small blue flame reaching them, Rogan and Tomas had reached a local stable and hid there until the confusion of the soldiers trying to clear the streets passed to another section of the city. Once the knight had thought it safe enough to move, he had sent his squire up to look around and opened the packs, lifting with reverence Talon, the sword that had served him so well so many times before.

Once the unwanted leather armor and robes had been removed and replaced with the welcoming embrace of their splintmail, the two warriors began to move from alley to alley, heading toward the cathedral in the center of Tordenia. The narrow alleys and long shadows cast by the many balconies among Tordenia's buildings made their stealthy movement easier. Both warriors made a constant effort to avoid the squads of Tordenian soldiers that were moving through the area in waves, their bright red robes and odd turbans doing little to conceal their presence in the light of the evening's three moons.

"It looks like our luck is holding." Tomas noted as yet another patrol passed while the two warriors hugged either side of their alley. "They're not even glancing down the alleys."

Rogan grunted. "They will."

"What do you mean?"

"Balshazzar is sending most of his soldiers toward the harbor, probably figuring that's where we entered the city. Once the troops get there, they'll probably start doing searches of all the buildings and alleys."

"But by the time they all get to the harbor, form back up, and start the searches, we'll have had more than enough time to make it to the cathedral."

"Balshazzar isn't trying to find us," the knight said grimly. "He's trying to drive us."

"I don't get it," Tomas confessed.

In response, Rogan pointed to the rooftop of an inn across the street from where they hid. "What?" the squire demanded. The oddly conical construction of Tordenia's buildings confused Tomas, making it difficult for the squire to see what it was that his knight was pointing at. In a moment, though, movement drew his young eyes, and Tomas finally spotted the archer that had leaned over for a brief instant before disappearing out of view again.

Rogan shook his head. "The man is good. I'll give him that."

"I still don't really get it."

"Balshazzar thinks that if I see all these soldiers moving around behind me, I'll be forced to speed up and risk the open streets. He's probably got archers covering every street from here to the cathedral."

"So what do we do?" Tomas demanded.

Rogan grinned. "We wait here for a few minutes until another patrol comes by."

"And then what?"

"And then you let them see you running down this alley back toward that big, empty warehouse we just passed and we get ourselves a couple of those red and gold surcoats."

As often as he was captured and thrown into a dungeon, one would think that Beraht would have become used to it. However, no matter how many times or how convincing the Sylva was in explaining her plans, it always struck Beraht as distasteful whenever he found himself jumped and knocked unconscious, only to awaken once again behind bars. His capture had gone well, though; he had ridden up to the catapults lining the cliffs around Tordenia and said some rather unflattering things to one of the officers walking around. The Uldra frequently found amusement in just how poorly most Humans took idle insults. It was common practice among more enlightened people that bantering was simply a way to pass the time and even show some affection; but leave it to a Human to blow a comment as idle as "Was that your mother I saw entertaining the guys on the next catapult?" all out of proportion. Beraht had to admit to himself that he was flattered the officer had thought it necessary to have his entire squad attack him, so naturally he would never be so disrespectful as to just let them capture him without at least a small fight. Damned fragile Humans though, they just could not hold their own in a fight and were so timid that after seeing five or six of their compatriots taken down so quickly, it finally took aiming one of the catapults at the city to force them to attack him again. Beraht was somewhat ashamed to admit to himself that he got a little carried away with putting up a fight before letting them capture him, but he did not kill anyone; that alone should show how hard he was trying to stick to the plan.

Beraht had been carried, with some difficulty, to the city dungeons where he was placed in one of the special cells constructed to contain the legendary skill and worth of the Uldra. He noticed on his way in that most of the cells were filled with a number of his brethren from the Alba Mountains, each of them looking to be in a sorry state of sobriety. Once in his cell and having regained full consciousness, Beraht settled in to enjoy a good nap, figuring it would take Rogan and Tomas most of the day to hold up their end of the plan. The Uldra's contentment was quickly shattered, though, as he realized that those damned Humans had not only taken his weapons but his alcohol as well! What kind of savage takes a prisoner's drink? Beraht thrashed around the cramped cell, cursing the descendants of his jailors for a thousand generations.

"Looking for something, Uldra?" one of the guards had asked upon entering the room, idling tossing around the small skin that held the good stuff.

That anyone, even a Human, could treat the good stuff so disrespectfully filled Beraht with such righteous fury that he hurled himself unto the bars, pulling on them with all his strength.

The guard laughed. "Forget it, Uldra," he snarled. "Those bars are solid lead with steel fittings. It would take a team of wild horses over an hour of pulling to loosen even one." The guard spit on Beraht's face and worked the stopper of his skin loose. The warrior's rage was growing to unbearable heights, his strength insufficient to free himself even to throttle this Human for his disrespect.

Then the Human made a mistake that would cost him dearly.

Having pulled the stopper free of the skin, the guard sniffed at it and, retching, made to pour the sacred liquid into a floor drain. Beraht's eyes went wide as the first drop of the viscous gel dropped from its home and fell through the grate. Seeing the precious gift from his life-brother, Remm, lost forever, Beraht gave himself to the will of his Allfather.

Filling the air with a blood-searing roar, Beraht ripped the cell door from its hinges and hurled it at the guard, who barely ducked it in time. Not waiting to see the result of his initial attack, the berserker launched himself at the prey in front of him, all capacity for rational thought gone. Beraht impacted the guard squarely in the chest, flinging him against the far wall and forcing the man's breath out of his lungs. In one fluid motion, Beraht caught the skin as it fell from the guards hand, stoppered and placed it gently on the floor, then grabbed the guard's groin in one hand and his throat in the other. Planting himself on the ground, Beraht picked up the doomed guard and lifted him into the air. Because the son of Uldron was such a strong proponent of true justice, there was only one possible resolution to this engagement.

The guard's sight cleared just as he was forced, head first, into the same drain into which he had tried to pour the good stuff. Unfortunately for the guard, Beraht was having some trouble planning at that moment and so had forgotten to remove the grate first. Feeling some resistance to the guard's trip, the Uldra put that much more anger and energy into seeing him safely down the drain. Beraht did not stop pushing until only the guard's feet were sticking out of the small drain, long after any wiggling had stopped.

Hearing the roars and cheers of the other Uldra from their cells, Beraht returned as close as he could to rationality. Looking about, the son of Uldron returned the good stuff back to its honored place at the front of his belt and looked around in contempt.

"Are you Sylvai?" he demanded of the imprisoned Uldra. A shocked silence filled the jail. "Are you some holier-than-thou, wine-sipping, shiny-eyed Sylvai that will sit here all comfy while the world goes to Underworld all around you?" he spat.

Curses and roars of fury were Beraht's response.

"Then why are you sitting here when that damned Balshazzar is ruling this city?"

Roars of "Damn Balshazzar!" and "Death to the Sylvai-spawn!" echoed throughout the building.

"I'm going to burn this city to the ground and kill every last Human in it!" Beraht roared. "Who's with me?" The Uldra cheered and swore their support. Beraht could hear the guards responding to the noise he had started, so he knew his time was running short. Raising his right hand into the air. After only a second, the wall behind him exploded into rubble. Once the dust settled, the Uldra prisoners witnessed Beraht standing with the great waraxe of the Nameless held aloft.

"The Thunder of God," one whispered in awe. Others spoke in a hushed voice. "He is a Chosen of God." "He wields the Thunder." As one, the Uldra dropped to one knee before one of the holiest symbols of their race.

"Let any Uldra that would stand with the Allfather in his war against the Demon-god stand with me now!" Beraht roared. With battle cries and a holy fury rising in them all, the children of Uldron forced open their cells. A troop of Balshazzar guards poured into the dungeon then stopped, panicking at the sight of the near-rabid Uldra. Beraht leveled his waraxe at them and roared, "KILL THE HUMANS!!!" The holy warriors hurled themselves onto their startled jailors and tore them apart with nothing but their fists and their fury.

Across town, at the guard house beside Tordenia's North Gate, the interrogation of the prisoners caught trying to scale the city walls continued. The inquisitor who had been assigned to the questioning sat on a small stool, while the *shawish*, leader of the guard, roared questions at the man claiming to be a slave merchant while repeatedly striking him. "Are you spies?" the *shawish* demanded, beating the prisoner.

"I swear I am not!" the man cried, blood pouring from his mouth.

The interrogation had achieved little. The prisoners had been in custody for several hours, and even after the inquisitor had arrived, the *shawish* had learned very little. The flesh-merchant held to his story that he had no memory of climbing the city walls. When the guards had found and detained him, he had not put up any kind of fight, instead staying very passive until nearly a quarter-hour after his capture when he suddenly began protesting his detainment. His protests had been cut short once the *shawish* had begun questioning him.

The *shawish* held up the small gem, cut into the shape of two crossed, four-pointed diamonds, the well-known symbol of the Black Duke's forces. "Then why do you carry Calonar's insignia?" he roared, raising his fist again.

"Please!" the slaver whimpered. "Please, I don't know how that got into my pouch! I swear I serve the Emir loyally!" The *shawish* hit the prisoner again, sending him crashing to the floor. Once lying on the cold stone, the soldier placed several kicks to the man's middle.

Finally, the inquisitor raised his hand and ordered the soldier to stop. The *shawish* was no fool and stopped immediately. Standing up from his chair and smoothing his black robes, the inquisitor straightened the blood red sash tied about his waist and walked to where the prisoner lay, putting a hand in front of his face. The slaver started babbling senselessly, begging for mercy from the merciless priest until the inquisitor lowered his hand and very quietly ordered the man silent. Once the prisoner's sniveling was ended, the inquisitor raised his hand back up and concentrated with closed eyes.

Finally, the dark priest opened his eyes and sneered at the slaver. "This man's memory has been tampered with. The weak-willed fool was forced to act as another wished," the inquisitor declared. "That same someone has altered his thoughts and then erased his presence in the slaver's mind. If we are to uncover the master of these events, we must free his mind." Again, the inquisitor closed his eyes and concentrated, his fingers and words calling forth his magic. Within moments, the slaver's eyes widened as his memory came back to him.

"It was that Sylva bitch!" he exclaimed.

"Who?" the *shawish* asked, his gaze going to the female Uldra and Sylva who wore the chains and flimsy outfits marking them as property bound for one of the pleasure-houses. The two females had been captured with the slaver but had kept silent and did as they were told, standing in a corner with lowered heads and eyes while the Humans were talking.

The flesh-merchant threw a contemptuous glance at the two non-Humans. "Not them!" he spat. "Those are just my property. A Sylva! She was beautiful and graceful and evil! She put some kind of spell on me! She gave me the medallion and told me to climb the walls with my stock!"

"Tressalon," the inquisitor mused. "Why did she want you to scale the city walls?"

By now, the slaver was shaking more from rage than fear, though he still reeked of that as well. "I don't know, holy one! She told me to release all my property except those two and take them to the walls. Once there, we were to try and climb over them!"

The *shawish* cleared his throat. "Perhaps she wanted him to be captured, holy one," he suggested hesitantly.

"Still the question remains. Why?"

"Why did she free all of the slaves but these two? They certainly couldn't have been the best of his stock."

The inquisitor walked over to them and said, "Let us find out." The priest stood before the female Uldra and, holding his hands before him, spoke the words of magic. The air rippled around the Uldra and passed through her, causing the creature to disappear. "Illusion," the inquisitor sniffed before turning to the Sylva. "Perhaps, they were meant to—" the dark priest stiffened suddenly.

"Are you all right?" the *shawish* asked.

In response, the inquisitor turned, his mouth open and a Sylvai blade in his throat. The holy man's eyes rolled back, and he dropped, lifeless, to the floor. The slaver gave a pathetic shriek, crawling to a far corner and tucking himself into as tight a ball as he could manage. Looking in shock at the Sylva, the *shawish*'s eyes widened, until another thin Sylvai blade sliced into one.

Aebreanna retrieved her weapons and, wiping them off on the front of the late soldier's tunic, replaced them in their respective sheaths. The spy then turned to the nearly hysterical slaver. "You know," she said with a cold smile, "you should consider a different vocation. This one seems much too stressful for you."

The slaver continued his panicked babbling from before.

Hearing a commotion from outside, the spy retrieved the small bag holding her things and slid to the window. Outside, a mounted soldier was yelling up, the golden helmet and silver braiding on his shoulder marking the rider as an officer. A soldier came out of the gate house and held the reins steady while the officer dismounted.

"Where's your *shawish*?" the officer demanded.

"With the prisoners, sir," the guard replied. "He and the inquisitor are questioning them and have left orders for no interruptions."

"Well, this is an exception," the officer snapped. "The prisoners in the dungeon have broken loose, and I need every possible man to help."

"With a few loose prisoners?" the soldier asked.

The officer pushed past the guard. "I've got a full-scale riot breaking out! The people are hearing the worst possible noises coming out of that jail. God only knows what those savages are doing to the men." Whatever else the officer was saying was lost to Aebreanna when he entered the guard house.

Sir Beraht has begun his distraction, she thought with a roll of her eye. Hearing the officer walking up the stairs, a sudden idea came to the spy. When the officer entered, he saw the two bodies on the floor, but before he could do more than open his mouth in shock, Aebreanna stepped from behind the door and cut his throat, leaning his body over so that a minimum of blood would get on the uniform. *Oh yes*, Aebreanna thought as she eased the corpse to the floor, *this should do just fine*.

After a few minutes, the guard outside spotted the officer's return. The soldier straightened and saluted as the visitor came out of the guard house and, without a word, remounted the horse. Taking the reins, the officer spurred his horse toward the center of the city at a dead gallop.

Goddess, Aebreanna thought as she rode off, *this armor is killing my breasts*.

Chapter 70

Tomas ran down the alley at a dead sprint, a five-man squad hot on his heels. *If this doesn't work*, the squire thought, *I'm going to kill Rogan*. Fortunately for the young man, just as he ran through the doorway leading into the abandoned warehouse in which his mentor was waiting, Rogan pulled on the thin rope he had tied off on the opposite side, tripping nearly every man chasing his squire. Dropping the rope, Rogan drew his sword and fell on the one soldier who had avoided the trap, sweeping past the man's defenses and beheading him with ease. Before the rest of the soldiers could react or even rise, Rogan and Tomas were on them, swords swinging and bodies falling.

Panting a bit from the exertion, more so than his squire, Rogan sheathed his sword. "All right, kid, pick one."

"Won't the archers be able to tell that we're not wearing the same kind of armor as the rest of them?" the squire asked as he pulled free a relatively bloodless red and gold surcoat.

Rogan shook his head, selecting his own uniform. "From the roofs, they'll only be able to tell that we're wearing armor and Balshazzar's colors. Should be enough to get us to the cathedral."

Tomas threw the loose red robe over his shoulders and belted his sword across it. "How do you think the others are doing?" he asked.

The knight shrugged. "By now, Aebreanna should be making her way to the cathedral, and Beraht should be moving."

"Do you think he can manage a big enough distraction to pull all the soldiers to him?"

"If anyone can, it's Beraht."

Fortunately for Aebreanna, her husband, the legendary spymaster Rashid Tressalon, had long ago taught her the secret of altering one's voice. Using this skill, along with her recently acquired uniform, the spy was able to not only ride at a comfortable pace toward the cathedral but even sow a little confusion among the enemy's ranks. She issued conflicting orders to units searching for Rogan, redirected key messages, rerouted reinforcing units trying to help with Beraht's growing riot, and generally made a minor nuisance of herself. Truthfully, Aebreanna was rather enjoying herself.

Although she frequently made a point of reminding the boys that, despite the many adventures that she had shared with Rogan and Beraht, it was their names that seemed destined to live on in immortal history, Aebreanna was *Sy'lva'n* enough to admit—to herself at least—that her relative anonymity was more often an asset than not. Many and various had been the times in which the spy had been able to extract herself from a dangerous situation with relative ease due directly to the fact that her enemies knew very little about her. There were perhaps only a half-dozen people in the entire world who knew and could pick out the face of Aebreanna Tressalon in a crowd.

But of course, Fate, that most whimsical goddess who took such fiendish delight in tormenting Aebreanna anytime she traveled with the boys, decided at that moment to take full advantage of her lack of knowledge as to the exact workings and traditions of the military. As the Sylva turned a corner of one of the larger markets in the city and started what she hoped would be the final leg of her trip toward the garish Adamic cathedral easily visible from anywhere in Tordenia, she noticed an officious-looking officer giving what to her ears sounding like conflicting orders to a group of confused looking soldiers.

Please, Goddess, Aebreanna silently prayed, *do not let his eyes wander to me.*

"You there, *yuzbashi*," the officer called.

The spy cast an annoyed look to the heavens.

Seeing as two of the soldiers who stood with the officer were armed with those bizarrely-recurved Tordenian bows, Aebreanna could not simply make a break for it. Thus, she decided to try and bluff her way through the confrontation. Riding right up to the short officer, the *Sy'lva'n* looked down her nose from behind the helmet at the men, hoping her rank was greater than his since she had never learned how to read the military rank insignia used by the Western Empire. "Yes?" she asked in what she hoped was a convincing baritone.

"Have you forgotten how to salute, *yuzbashi*?" the senior officer snapped.

Aebreanna raised her arm in what she felt was the correct salute, fighting the urge to swear.

"That salute needs a lot of work, *yuzbashi*," the small officer noted, returning a snap salute.

"Yes, sir," she replied slowly, trying to hold any number of retorts in check.

"What is your business in this sector?"

The time for fast thinking had arrived. "I am under the direct orders of Emir Theodorico, sir. I have been coordinating the efforts to locate Aebreanna Tressalon."

The short man looked Aebreanna over, forcing the spy to draw her cloak closer about her shoulders in an attempt to cover her feminine hips and legs. She kept her helmeted head turned slightly away, hiding her right side. "Your unit, *yuzbashi,* what is it?" he asked suddenly.

"Sir," she replied, her mind racing, "I have been detached from my unit temporarily to act as the Emir's envoy." That sounds believable.

"If you are a messenger from the Emir, then what is the password that accompanies all of his orders?"

Password!?! "Um, sir, there is no password."

The officer paused, looking at her. "Very good, *yuzbashi.* Only a real messenger would know that. Carry on." The short officer walked off towards the closest barracks.

Once he was finally out of earshot, Aebreanna could not help but note, "What an idiot."

"You have no idea," one of the soldiers muttered.

"Anything?" Rogan asked.

Tomas leaned over the rooftop he had climbed onto for a look around. "Well, I think Beraht's broken out of jail," he replied.

"Why?"

"Because every building in that area is on fire. I'm also pretty sure I can hear sounds of looting and smashing and... singing?"

Rogan muttered a few choice oaths.

"Well," Tomas reminded his knight, "we did tell him to create a distraction. What did you think he was going to do?"

"What about that archer?"

The squire looked down at the limp form of the soldier he had encountered on the roof. The man was breathing, but would likely not awaken for some time. "No problem. He thought I was one of them."

"Told you it would work. How many more are there?"

"They're all over the place. There's at least another ten between here and the cathedral, maybe more."

The knight nodded. "We anticipated that. If Beraht's little distraction proves enough, they'll get pulled to put down those riots and fires."

"What if the guards don't get pulled?"

Rogan shrugged. "Aebreanna said she'd take care of any soldiers still guarding the cathedral. Now get down here. We still have about a half-dozen blocks to cover."

Aebreanna was planning how exactly she would keep her promise of making sure the cathedral was safe to approach. Fooling small groups of soldiers and one dim-witted officer was relatively simple; putting on the uniform, stuffing her hair into the helmet, and pulling the cloak around her shapely body had been enough for that. Unfortunately, there were fifty or so men stationed around the massive cathedral. If everything was going according to the spy's plan, which would be a first, the boys would be closing on the building soon. She had to get those soldiers away or those sword-swinging simpletons would be forced to make their entrance as nosily and messily as possible. Aebreanna was really very fond of her boys, perhaps even Beraht, but Goddess knew they needed to learn how operate with at least some degree of subtlety.

As the spy watched, a messenger rode up to the officer who was barking orders to his men. The soldier dismounted and saluted the leader, handing him several dispatches before remounting and riding off. The officer looked through the multiple sheets of parchment before relaying the orders contained in them to the men that would actually carry them out. An idea suddenly presented itself to Aebreanna. Turning back to her horse, she pulled some parchment and ink from one of her bags and began to write in a script not her own.

The distraction was going well, Beraht decided. After breaking out of the jail and setting fire to it, the Uldra had led his warriors from house to house, pillaging, burning, and slaughtering any and every soldier that had the unfortunate lapse in judgment to think he could stop them. Now their ultimate objective lay before them. The warrior took a moment to look upon the beauty of the city's brewery. It was well constructed, Beraht admitted. All too often, he was disgusted at the kinds of hovels Humans thought were suitable for the brewing of good alcohol. Beraht thought it quite odd that those people went out of their way to make their churches beautiful but never put that kind of craftsmanship in a building as important as the brewery. Whoever built this one, though, had a true sense of aesthetics. Properly humble signs, large open windows so the people could watch their liquor being created, and solid stone construction to withstand any incidental detonations. Beraht devoutly hoped the Humans would not make him burn this building; it deserved to stand.

Ordering his warriors forward, Beraht personally led the charge through the front doors, fully intent on running until he sampled a barrel of the city's finest beer. With his Uldra right behind, it was only through an epic feat of strength that Beraht stopped the wave of pious violence from breaking. When the son of Uldron had burst through the doors, he immediately spotted dozens of Tordenian soldiers that were hiding within, recurve crossbows leveled and ready.

They fired, sending a solid wall of iron bolts flying at the Uldra.

Once Beraht has set himself upon a course of action, it takes a great deal to convince him to make any adjustments. So it was that when the bolts flew, the warrior ordered his brothers and sisters forward, deflecting several missiles with his waraxe and barely grunting when one of the bolts caught his left arm. Roaring in fury at the five or so Uldra that fell to Human treachery, Beraht hurled himself on the soldiers that had dropped their crossbows and drawn their pitiful blades. Pushing the sword of the first soldier aside with his waraxe, Beraht put his shoulder into the man's gut and followed up by slashing with the axe, cleaving the man in two. His Uldra were quick to follow Beraht's example, falling on the Tordenians with roars and joyous laughter. *This was good*, Beraht decided. It was hard to properly enjoy good alcohol unless some blood had been split beforehand.

As Beraht beheaded another soldier with a sneer, he heard the leader shouting orders over the roar of battle. Spotting his enemy, the son of Uldron stomped toward the fool, shoving friend and foe alike with his gaze firmly set. The officer saw his death approaching and, drawing his puny sword, backpedaled through the doors behind him, into the distillery itself. Beraht stormed through the doors and hefted his waraxe, smiling an evil smile. The officer crouched low, unwilling to make the first move, waiting to see what the Uldra was capable of. Finally, bored to exasperation, Beraht leapt at his target; the man smiled and, dropping his sword low, spun and kicked out with his off leg, sending Beraht spinning off the catwalk and hurling toward the floor below. The Tordenian officer watched as his opponent plummeted into a vat below containing one of the local brews.

The officer turned his back on the distillery and made ready to lead his men in the ongoing effort. After only a few steps, he stopped, noticing an odd sound. Turning, he went back to the edge of the catwalk, looking down at the vat into which he had sent Beraht. The vat was shaking and draining.

Suddenly, the vat exploded, and Beraht flew up at the Tordenian officer, a look of religious euphoria on his ugly face. The officer flung himself back towards the door, clearly unable to believe his eyes. Beraht stood, somewhat unsteadily, on the catwalk with waraxe in hand. The son of Uldron felt no pain; in fact, he felt nothing but a joyous union with his Allfather, and His blessing on this most devout of His children.

Putting aside his shock, the officer slightly bent his knees and turned to present his opponent with as small a target as possible. the man seemed to have trouble choosing a target, though, as the world swayed like the gentle rocking of a mother's arms, and Beraht swayed with her, a soft, nearly forgotten lullaby of his lost mother returning to his pious mind. Finally, the officer darted in with a low thrust, planning to stab Beraht in its shoulder. Faster than eyes could follow, the son of Uldron deflected the strike with its waraxe and, spinning, hit the Tordenian in the back with his fist. The officer was barely able to keep himself from falling into the same vat from which Beraht had born anew.

The officer tried dancing out of Beraht's range, clearly surprised that he had failed to follow up the attack. Trying again, the officer tried darting in and spinning to the side at the last instant, hoping to slice Beraht's back open. Again, the son of Uldron moved with the divine speed, pushing aside the Tordenian's sword arm and swinging his great waraxe in a mighty overhand strike, severing the limb. The officer screamed in agony as his arm fell into the vat below. This time, Beraht pressed its attack, crushing the officer's right knee with the flattened end of his waraxe and then slamming the flat of the axe blade against the man's shoulder, forcing him down to the catwalk floor.

The officer rose to his one good knee. "Mercy," he sobbed.

Beraht showed his enemy Uldra mercy with a mighty strike from his weapon, sending the two halves of the man's body falling to the vat below and raining gore through the area. Beraht swayed a moment, honoring his enemy that had fought well, and then moved back to the fight outside. There he saw that his people had disposed of the remaining soldiers. Raising his two weapons, the son of Uldron roared in victory, his people echoing his piety. *This would be a battle worthy of memory*, Beraht decided.

Balshazzar grimaced as his attendants adjusted his armor. His newly-forged breastplate bore the great western wave over a golden flame. Red-dyed leather straps covered his upper arms and legs, appearing as though his enemy's blood flowed freely, as it soon would. His bracers bore the black-enameled flame of his new Church, matching those upon his eastern-style greaves. "What is the status of our forces?" he asked the two generals standing at the base of his throne. The emir had come down from the balcony nearly a half-hour ago, ordering that his weapon and armor be made ready and a horse and detachment of guards prepared.

One of the commanders consulted his dispatches. "We are still trying to retrieve the crews from the sea, my lord," he answered. "The light is fading, though."

"Leave them," Balshazzar grunted, reaching for the gold-etched, conical helmet another of his aides held for him. "Move those men to assist with the house searches. I want those completed as soon as possible. What of the riot?"

"The company we sent to put down the escaped Uldra has not reported in, my lord. We must assume a complete loss."

"Do we have any units left that can defeat the Uldra?"

The senior councilor shook his head. "No, sire. Between the fires in the harbor, the riot breaking out in the eastern quadrant of the city, the searches that are now turning into crowd control, and the guards around the palace and the cathedral, we have nothing left."

Balshazzar smiled. "An excellent plan, Eigenhard," the nobleman said to himself. "But I know where you are going." To the commanders, he said, "Take all the guards from the palace and tell them they are to put every building containing an Uldra to the torch."

"What of the people who are trying to flee the city, lord?"

The emir shrugged. "Let them flee. Eigenhard will not try to leave the city until he reaches the project. The fewer peasants we have underfoot, the better. Once this matter is resolved, they will return. Order the units trying to manage the crowd to let them pass and concentrate on moving as quickly as possible in their searches."

"We can only move so fast and still perform a decent search, sire," another commander reminded as the first gave instructions to a messenger.

"Don't worry about making thorough searches," the emir commanded, putting on the helmet. "Eigenhard won't corner himself in a house."

"Then why bother with the searches at all?"

"I'm not trying to find Eigenhard. I'm trying to drive him."

"Where?"

Balshazzar drew his curved sword and swung it a few times, insuring the armor would not inhibit his movements. "The same place I am going, to the cathedral. You still have men set there?"

The senior advisor nodded. "Yes, my lord. There is still a full ten-man squad standing guard."

The emir froze. "I ordered fifty men," he said very quietly.

"My lord," one of the younger advisors objected, stepping forward, "you sent word to move most of those men to help put down the Uldra riot. As you instructed, only a squad was left to guard the front door."

"How did I send that order?"

"I was there at the cathedral, sire. A *yuzbashi* rode up with signed orders."

Balshazzar held his sword against the man's throat. "Where is this *yuzbashi* now?" he asked calmly.

Stammering against the sword's point, the officer tried swallowing. "Sire, the orders said to leave that same officer in command of the squad while—" Balshazzar drew his blade across the fool's throat.

Kicking the useless body off his blade, the emir turned on his remaining advisors, murder burning in his eyes. Taking a moment to calm himself, he sheathed the sword and muttered to himself, "He hasn't beaten me yet." Balshazzar raised his chin and gave his men an icy stare. "I have been very disappointed in your performances thus far, gentlemen," he noted. "I assure you that certain positions and personnel will be reevaluated once this incident is resolved." The emir mounted the steps of the dais upon which his throne sat. Standing before it, the ruler of the Western Empire pointed at the trembling military men. "Take my personal guard and seal the cathedral," he commanded. "Eigenhard has most likely already gained entrance. Do not allow him to leave that building, but do not enter. Alert the inquisitors that the project is threatened. The burden of its defense is now theirs. Tell them that if any man fails in his duty from this moment on, he will answer to the wizard."

"Where will you be, my lord," one of the commanders asked in a shaky voice, fear of the black-shrouded spell-caster nearly unmanning him.

"I will be taking a more active part in this operation," he replied with a cold smile.

Chapter 71

Tomas looked around at the bodies of the guards who had tried to stop them at the base of the cathedral. He sighed and shook his head. Seeing this, Rogan said, "It's always the common grunts that pay the hardest."

Aebreanna pulled off the constrictive armor with a welcome sigh, cradling her breasts in her hands. "I cannot tell you how much I detested wearing that," she breathed.

"The burdens we bear," Tomas said piously.

"I will never understand why you men so adore wrapping yourselves in steel," she said archly.

The squire shrugged. "It's better than dying."

"And the ladies love it," his knight added.

"This one does not," Aebreanna noted with a raised eyebrow.

"Well, you are one of a kind, Aebreanna," Tomas said.

"How nice of you to notice," she sniffed.

"Anybody see Beraht?" Rogan asked.

The three adventurers looked around. Finally, Aebreanna pointed out their approaching comrade. "Here he comes." She said with a resigned sigh.

The two warriors turned and spied Beraht staggering down the street towards the cathedral. He was barely able to stay on his feet and covered in something Tomas was trying very hard not to identify, a mug in his off-hand and an old drinking song on his lips. "What in Underworld happened to you?" Rogan demanded.

Beraht lifted his waraxe and laughed, swaying wildly on his feet. "I liberated the brewery," he declared.

Aebreanna shook her head. "I was not aware the alcohol had been captured."

"Well, I couldn't just let it burn," the Uldra protested. "That would've been criminal." He fell.

"Can he still fight?" Tomas asked, unsure if any of the blood covering Beraht was the Uldra's own.

Aebreanna rubbed her eye, being careful to keep her hair in place. The sight of her lumbering companion trying to get to his feet and stumbling up the steps to the cathedral doors was almost more than she could bear. "Although it pains me to admit, I must confess that Sir Beraht is, in fact, a much deadlier fighter after he has had a large dose of alcohol."

Rogan straightened his shoulders and drew his sword again. Turning to the huge double-wooden doors, the knight closed his eyes for a moment. As the knight stood there, the other three fell in beside him and readied themselves. Opening his eyes, Rogan said, "Beraht, open the doors. Let's do this."

Beraht stalked up the grand steps of the cathedral, which led to a set of wooden doors each at least twenty feet tall and inlaid with gold etchings showing scenes from the earliest stories of the Adamic religion, from the Creation of the universe and God's Blessings being laid upon the first Man to the formation of the Church. The doors to every Adamic church had always held great power to those of the Faith. The doors, some said, were watched over constantly by God, letting no creature of evil intent past them. When Humans had inherited control of Lanasia from the Sylvai, the Lords Cardinal decreed that thenceforth any man who truly sought redemption and absolution of his sins had only to walk through the doors of any House of God, letting the Divine Spirit enter him and purify his soul.

As Tomas looked at the doors to the Cathedral of Tordenia, he suffered in his heart, just a small bit. The young squire had always held a special place for all the stories the priests used to tell the children on Godsrestday, and the ones about the purity of any House of God always touched him. It tore at Tomas that this holy place was being used to hide the dark secrets of Emir Theodorico Balshazzar and gave further proof that Balshazzar and the men who willingly served him could never be true children of the Church. Now Tomas, who considered churches to be the only places that could never be unsanctified, was storming into one with an agnostic knight, an Uldra warrior, and a Sylvai assassin. *Life certainly could lead in strange directions*, the squire thought to himself. He and Rogan moved to either side of the doors as Beraht grabbed hold of the golden handles and pulled.

Before the Uldra could even finish opening the huge double doors, an arcane explosion shattered them both and sent the warrior flying away from the doorway, his beard covered in flames. Beraht went rolling down the large flight of steps that led to the cathedral's opening with a steady stream of curses in several languages filling the air and following the Uldra down.

Rogan reacted instantly, diving through the smoldering doors and behind the stone pews lining both sides of the massive chamber for cover as another explosion roared just above his head. "Aebreanna!" he roared. "Check Beraht! Tomas, with me!"

The squire quickly stuck his head around the doorway and spotted the several inquisitors who had arrayed themselves throughout the main chamber. Pulling his head back as an arc of red lightning flew past, Tomas drew his dagger. Jumping through the doorway, the young warrior threw his blade at the nearest priest while diving behind the pews across from Rogan. The squire's attack was rewarded with a scream from his target and another volley of magic from the remaining inquisitors, this time in the form of green flame. The wounded man and his fellows retreated to the altar, gathering together at the base of the grand dais at the head of the cathedral.

"Nice shot, kid!" the knight yelled over the roar of the spells.

"You know, I'm getting the impression these guys don't want us here!" the squire replied with a grin as he drew Steelheart.

"It must have been something we said!" Rogan laughed.

More magic detonated, cracking the pew Tomas was using for cover. "Any ideas?" he asked.

"Working on it," the knight replied.

The cracks widened as more lightning impacted. "Could you think a little faster?"

"Maybe we should ask them to surrender."

Tomas was forced to cover his head as several large chunks of the pew he had taken cover behind were blasted off under the continuous magical onslaught. "Somehow I don't think they will!" the squire shouted.

Rogan shrugged. "You never know until you ask!"

"Why don't you ask?"

The knight rose to his knees and looked out over the huge, vaulted room. "Anybody want to surrender?"

A storm of raw magical energy hit the pew Rogan was using for cover, shattering it into rubble. The knight used the dust from the explosion as cover to leap across the aisle into the next set of pews in front of Tomas.

"What did they say?" the squire asked, tumbling over the rubble to join his knight and barely avoiding another volley of explosions that destroyed the pews behind them.

"I think that was a no."

"You could ask again to be sure."

The knight shook his head. "They don't seem to be in the mood to talk."

"Now what?" the squire demanded, trying to fan away enough dust to allow him a breath.

"Still thinking."

Just then, from the doorway behind the two warriors, there was a roar of mindless fury. In the shattered ruins of the doorway stood Beraht, his beard completely burned off and murder blazing in his eyes. Moving as one, the several priests throughout the room turned their heads and paled at the sight of the beardless, vengeful son of Uldron.

Desperately, the inquisitors attempted a combined assault on Beraht with their magics. With synchronized gestures, balls of electricity appeared in the priests' hands, and the men hurled their balls of energy into one combined point that then lanced out at Beraht. With a sneer of contempt, the Uldra grabbed a long piece of marble from the shattered pews and swung, hitting the lightning back at the casters and sending them running for cover. Beraht then dropped the scarred marble and picked up a large chunk of the blasted door. Holding the oversized piece of wood in front of him and using it as a shield against magical attacks, the mountainous warrior began marching toward the priests who were now cowering behind the front row of pews and the altar.

"I've got an idea!" Rogan exclaimed.

"My hero," Tomas muttered.

The two warriors split up, Rogan going to the left wall and Tomas the right, using the pillars and other stone- and marblework as cover. With all inquisitor eyes locked on the steadily advancing Beraht, the two Humans were able to quickly take up flanking positions on either side of the front row of pews, ready to support Beraht's assault. Once the door was all but disintegrated by the constant magical bombardment, the furious Uldra tossed it aside and roared again his indignant outrage. As all this happened, Aebreanna entered the cathedral and, on silent feet, glided up the center aisle, readying her weapons as she went.

Beraht fell bodily upon the first priest, cutting off the inquisitor's hands even as the dark priest had attempted to call up another spell. Without the slightest hesitation, the Uldra then spun and lopped off his enemy's head. Using the momentum that started with the swing, Beraht then threw his great weapon into the chest of another inquisitor who had been trying to backpedal to better cover while casting a spell. The furious Uldra did not spare the dead priest the slightest glance as he fell, instead turning in rage at the two inquisitors who had just hit him with missiles of golden light, shafts that impacted Beraht's great torso with no effect but to draw the Uldra's attention.

Even as powerful as he was when lost in his fury, Beraht would have quickly fallen to the combined magic of all the remaining inquisitors had his friends not been there to support him. Tomas spun out from behind the cover of a marble column and roared at the nearest priest, drawing the inquisitor's attention away from his friend. The dark priest tried to redirect the spell he had been in the midst of casting at Tomas, but the squire danced to his left, letting the blast of ice crystals fly past his head. Darting in, he lashed out with Steelheart, slicing the priest across the face with the venerable blade and then spun, turning his back to the swearing man and reversed his weapon, driving the sword deep into the inquisitor's middle. Seeing another priest orienting his magic at the squire out of the corner of his eye, Tomas ducked behind the dead inquisitor's body, using it as a shield. The dead priest's body was hit with a lance of absolute blackness. When the darkness passed, the body was gone, leaving Steelheart free. Not allowing the priest to get another chance, Tomas charged him, running the inquisitor through and then kicking the dead body off his blade.

Rogan was having no more difficulty with the inquisitors than his squire. Hopping over the bodies of his first targets, the knight raised Talon as he caught the flash of magic from one of the inquisitors hiding behind the wooden podium that stood in front of the altar. Seeing a pair of daggers made of blue mist flying at him, the knight deflected the attack with his trusted sword and reoriented on his new attackers. The priests were shocked at the speed Rogan demonstrated as he sprinted straight at them, diving to the floor as another magic dagger was launched at him, rolling along the floor and coming up in front of a podium. Raising his sword with both hands, the knight brought his weapon down with terrific force, cleaving the podium in two and sending the priests scampering away. Stomping over to one cowering inquisitor, the warrior dispatched his enemy with a single stroke. Looking around the room, Rogan saw three priests hiding behind the altar itself, casting their spells and then ducking back down. Turning to Beraht, the knight slashed the last priest at the pews across the chest and pointed back to the altar. "Beraht, take out their cover!" he barked.

The Uldra raised his waraxe high. He then spoke In Uldric, seeming as if to call out commands to the very heavens. As Tomas and the inquisitors watched in awe and shock, the great weapon suddenly exploded in lightning without being destroyed. "You want lightning?" Beraht roared at the priests in Velish, "I'll give you lightning!" Rearing back, the son of Uldron hurled the mystic weapon of the Allfather at the altar. There was another explosion of magical lightning as the altar was obliterated.

The three priests were blown back by the explosion but quickly got back to their feet, trying to cast more magic at the intruders. With no warning, Aebreanna vaulted off Beraht's steady shoulders and, flipping in midair, launched two blades, hitting the outside priests each in the chest and sending their lifeless bodies to the ground. With perfect grace, the Sylva landed lightly in front of the last of the priests and jabbed her fist into his middle, snapping her wrist upward at the last instant. The inquisitor instinctively bent over with pain and shock as the air left his body. Aebreanna wrapped her arm around the man's neck with a blur of speed and, without the slightest expression on her beautiful face, lurched back. There was a sickening snap, and the dark priest's body fell limply to the ground.

Looking around, ensuring every priest was dead, Tomas noted. "Well, that was invigorating."

"I hate fighting spell-slingers," Rogan muttered. The knight turned to his Uldra friend. "You alright, Beraht?" he asked.

The Uldra was mournfully rubbing at his now bare chin. "They burnt my beard," he nearly sobbed.

Tomas patted him on the shoulder. "Hey, you look good."

Beraht shook his head. "Aebreanna, be honest, how do I look?"

The beautiful Sylva looked evenly at the ugly Uldra. "Beraht," she said, "you have always been… undeniable."

Beraht's face immediately brightened. "Hey, thanks, Aebreanna."

Rogan finished wiping off his blade. "Well, how do we get into those tunnels?"

The spy kicked aside a small piece of altar debris. "I believe Sir Beraht has already uncovered the entrance," she replied. The three warriors walked up and saw that the entrance had, in fact, been hidden under the altar. Beneath the pile of rubble was a small staircase that dropped sharply down into darkness.

"Well, I guess this is what we came for," Rogan said. "Beraht, lead the way. Tomas, grab one of those candles over there and light a torch."

The squire looked up. "You realize we're walking into a trap."

"On the contrary," Aebreanna said, "based on what we have encountered thus far, I would feel safe in assuming that Emir Balshazzar had been hanging all of his hopes on stopping us here, in front of or in the cathedral."

Rogan patted his squire on the shoulder. "Trust me, kid. Right now, Balshazzar's probably scared witless."

Chapter 72

Theodorico snatched off his helmet in irritation. "You don't seem to understand," he snarled at his ally through clenched teeth. "Eigenhard and his people are already through the cathedral and working their way through the tunnels. They'll be here soon!"

The black-shrouded wizard did not even bother turning around, his gaze instead locked on the Sphere before him. "Their presence is irrelevant," he replied. "The Prophecy told me Eigenhard would breach your defenses and reach this place. It was pointless of you to try and stop him."

Theodorico moved to block the wizard's view of the Seal of Life. The light coming from it cast the emir's shadow throughout the cavern. "I have had more than enough with you and your precious prophecy," he snarled. "My destiny was never written, wizard! I control my own fate, and I rule the Western Empire, absolutely! Fate did not make me the ruler of more than double the lands of my predecessors. Prophecy never made my decisions for me. Predestination never helped me to work my way up to the heights of power I have now and will one day hold." The emir narrowed his eyes as he walked in a small circle around the black-robed wizard. "Perhaps your prophecy is nothing more than a crutch, old man! You have huddled down here in the dark for months blathering on and on about prophecy and destiny, simply as a means of avoiding responsibility!

"Eigenhard is here now, wizard, and no prophecy will summon forth the forces we need to stop him! For once in this alliance, why don't you try living up to your end of it and finally giving me an example of just why it is that Anninihus feared you so much?" Listening to the wizard for so long, constantly blaming every setback and failure they had suffered on that damned prophecy of his had always grinded on the emir's nerves. Now, with the added pressure of Eigenhard's imminent arrival weighing on his mind, it was enough to make Theodorico's blood boil. What was perhaps the most annoying about the old man's words, however, was that thus far, every one of his predictions had been proven true.

"You have thrown every resource at your command against Eigenhard and his companions for months now in an effort to stop them, and still he advances," the wizard countered. "You have killed any and every one of your underlings who has failed to do what I have repeatedly told you cannot be done, and still Eigenhard advances. Your city burns, and your army is in disarray after your efforts to defeat the prince, and still he advances. You have insisted we send every inquisitor I have converted against Eigenhard and his companions, hoping their magic will destroy him, and still he advances. Tell me, Emir, just how many times must the obvious be forced upon you before your mind accepts it? Eigenhard will reach this chamber, and you and I will confront him here. It is useless to waste any further resources in you vain effort to prove to yourself you are better than the man."

"Is it just my imagination," Tomas snapped as he swung Steelheart across another priest's chest, "or did these guys suddenly lose interest in this fight?"

It was not the squire's imagination, though. Since entering the tunnels that had begun at the base of the long staircase beneath Tordenia's cathedral, the party had been under more or less constant attack. Every shadow seemed to hide a few more inquisitors. In the midst of yet another engagement with the defenders of this place, they suddenly stopped fighting and withdrew without a single command being issued. To the rapidly tiring Tomas, it was a blessing that filled him with apprehension.

"What does it mean?" Beraht demanded, more than a little put out at the end of his fun.

"They must be up to something," Tomas insisted, trying to ease the soreness from his sword arm.

Rogan shook his head, suspicion written plainly on his face. "It just doesn't add up. Balshazzar wouldn't have stopped the attacks. He was always big on using superior numbers to wear down his opponent. It's a habit that shows up in every battle he's ever been in. This kind of hit-and-run strategy just wouldn't occur to him."

"Perhaps our shadowy enemy has finally taken charge," Aebreanna suggested.

"You think this was the wizard's idea?" Tomas asked, still rubbing his shoulder.

The Sylva noticed his discomfort and walked over to him, pulling a small pouch of salve from her shoulder bag. "Logical," she replied. "Balshazzar suddenly changing his tactics would be unlikely in the extreme, and the priests' sudden withdrawal is ample evidence that a new strategy is being adopted."

"How did they know to retreat?" Rogan demanded. "I never heard a single word from any of them."

Beraht grunted in agreement. "These new ones didn't even scream that much."

Aebreanna rubbed a small amount of the salve onto her small right hand and slipped it under Tomas's armor, massaging the medicine into the squire's shoulder. "More evidence that the wizard we believed was serving Balshazzar is, in fact, the one giving orders."

Tomas breathed deeply a sigh of relief as his muscles loosened under the Sylva's tender care. "Is that a good thing, or a bad thing?" the squire asked.

Rogan snorted. "If this wizard pulled the inquisitors back because he doesn't think he needs them, then it's probably a good thing."

"Overconfidence in one's enemies is always welcome," Aebreanna noted.

"What if it isn't overconfidence?" Beraht demanded.

Rogan shook his head. "Let's worry about that when we actually find the guy."

"You promised me help when I needed it!" Theodorico snapped at his ally. "I've given you everything you've asked for and nearly bankrupted the Western Empire doing it. It is long past time for you to live up to your side of this alliance."

"Have I not provided you with a legion of wizard-priests to command?" the wizard asked pointedly. "Have I not altered the magics of your knights so that they could maintain their power and remain ignorant of any change?"

The wizard walked over to the altar. He ran his gloved hands along the obsidian platform, tracing the bloodstains and forcing Balshazzar to recall the many victims the emir had put there. "Have I not kept the secret of who your House truly worships from the entire world?" the spell caster asked. "That information would mean your being subjected to the worst tortures the Adamic Church could devise for such heresy, would it not?" The emir's ally grabbed one of the horns rising from a corner of the altar, identical to the four others. "What would happen to your Western Empire, to your Noble House, if it was revealed that your family has spent generations putting the innocent under the knife, a knife that you have often held willingly, to gain power from the Demon-god? I have kept your secret and have even shown you how to improve upon your practices.

"All these things I have done to advance your power, Emir. If your plans are unraveling, look to your own actions. Do not look to mine."

"Are you trying to avoid responsibility for what has happened?" the emir demanded.

"Not at all. I freely accept the responsibility for Eigenhard making it this far and for our enemies being in the state they are. I also accept the responsibility for hiring the men you wanted."

"Men who you command," Theodorico reminded his ally. "All the mercenaries we have hired, all the missions I have sent them on, you also have added on a few orders for them, which never seemed to make sense to anyone but you. Orders I wager truly come from that mysterious ally of yours among Calonar's advisors. I am no fool, wizard. I know you two plan something that does not benefit me. Your ambitions are of little interest to me except for when they could cost me my own. You command those forces, and where are they now that I need them the most? Gone! All of them off on some errand at the one time when I just happened to need them most. Are those men working for my goals, wizard, or do they serve only yours?"

"Those men have furthered your ends, Emir, as well as mine and my accomplice's. Cylan Calonar is poisoned. Eigenhard will soon be thrust into a position he does not want and for which he is not ready. His army is trapped far from the Northern Keep, and his Uldra allies will soon face their own kin in a war of extermination. The death of House Calonar is imminent, furthering the will of the Prophecy.

"How does any of this truly benefit me or my Empire?" Theodorico demanded.

The Shadowed Mage grinned, his eyes gleaming. "With the coming of the next dusk, my dear Emir, you and your family will be eternal. Your sons and nephews will be forever strong and powerful, your daughters and nieces forever beautiful and treacherous. This I have promised you, and this I will deliver, no more, no less."

"What have you truly delivered, wizard?" the emir asked, almost to himself. "I control no more lands than I did when you first approached me. I am no more rich, and my people no more loyal. Calonar is poisoned, yes, but not yet dead, and I notice you never say he, himself will die. Even if he is no longer a king, even if his House is shattered, Calonar will still have more than enough power to deny me. You promised that Eigenhard would no longer be a threat to me after this project your ally sent instructions on is completed. And yet, as you have said, still he advances."

Theodorico walked over to look out over the vast cavern that, until the wizard had revealed it to him, he never knew lay beneath his city. The emir's eyes passed over the vats where his ally had altered the men who served Theodorico as inquisitors. His eyes passed over the ranks of soldiers and knights who had grown suspicious of House Balshazzar's actions and had been reassigned to Tordenia where they now stood, for all appearances lifeless; they did not seem to even breathe. With a growing feeling of despair, the emir shook his head. Somewhere down there were even the handful of his own family, cousins, uncles, and nephews, who had been threats to Theodorico's control over the House. Threats identified by the Shadowed Mage. "Why did I ally with you, wizard?" he asked quietly. "Your words were sweet when I first heard them, but what now? You told me you would help me neutralize Calonar, but in the two years or more you have been here, all that has happened was that Xaemus managed to poison him. You told me your pet Anninihus would attack the Keep and end the greatest threat coming from there, but he died in the attempt. You told me that your ally among Calonar's advisors would sow uncertainty and discontent among the Black Duke's forces, and yet they still hold firm his lands. You have promised me much, and in the blindness of my ambition, I agreed. Look at what you have led me to, wizard, and tell me why I have allowed this."

"Anninihus did attack the Keep," the wizard reminded Balshazzar. "And though he died, he has ended the greatest threat that would ever come out of that place."

"What threat?" the emir demanded, his eyes still looking out at what has become of his dreams.

"The child. The first-born child of Eigenhard and Calonar's daughter is going to be very special, very powerful. That child would have been the end of all your ambitions, and I have ended it."

Balshazzar shook his head. "My spies would have told me if Kyla had been killed. She lives."

"Of course she lives. Her death would not have served my interests, or yours. Calonar's daughter prevents Eigenhard from spending too much time away from the Keep. Her life limits him and thus strengthens us. No, Emir, I will not kill the first daughter of Calonar yet. First I will have her child. That was Anninihus's true purpose at the Keep. His attack meant nothing, my agent's assassination attempt was nothing; they were designed to fail. But, Anninihus' foolishness prompted Eigenhard to leave, to draw out House Calonar's greatest defenders. The assassin has disrupted Kyla, made her fearful. Now, Kyla is alone, and will seek out corruptive magics. Even now a child grows within the first daughter of Calonar, a child that will be corrupted by his mother's fear and her quest for the secrets of her sisterhood."

"All this trouble for a child that has yet to even be born? Eigenhard attacks now, wizard. His child may be a threat in the years to come, but Eigenhard is a threat *now*. What of your promise to me for aid? Where is your aid?" the emir gestured to the cavern floor below. "Is this your aid? These acts of utter evil and corruption? Is this all the aid you will provide me? These half-dead knights who saw through your lies and mine? The soulless inquisitors who spread across my Empire like a disease? Are you truly aiding me, wizard? Are you?"

The Shadowed Mage turned away from Balshazzar, walking up to the stacks of books he studied. "All shall be as I promised. The moment will soon arrive in which the project will be complete. I have worked for much longer than you could imagine to achieve what shall happen this night. I allied myself with someone who sickens me to gain the knowledge I needed. I aligned with the High Priest of the Demon-god, spread his vile gospel, even to you, all for the knowledge he shared. Only one component is left, and the project shall be complete. One act by an ignorant boy, and you and I will have the power we seek. You to be eternal, with unquestioned mastery of your lands and people, I to have the resources I need to claim the child."

"What is so very special about that child?" Theodorico asked.

The Shadowed Mage looked up and out, as the emir had seen him do before, invoking his power to see through Time, into Fate herself. "That child is the culmination of the Prophecy. Eigenhard's first born to a daughter of mystical legacy, whether the daughter of Calonar or another, will be the final step to complete Darrell's Prophecy." He grinned then at Theodorico. "Worry not, Emir. Once the project is complete, from that moment until the end of this world, Eigenhard will no longer be a threat to your or your House."

"What of his companions? I will not be fooled by your half-truths. Speak to me plainly, spell-slinger. If your mighty prophecy tells you everything that is to come, if your ally tells you how Eigenhard will act, than tell me now, how will this encounter end? Will I be victorious? Will this project of yours succeed and bring me to my eternal throne? Will I finally have the power to defeat Calonar? Tell me, wizard, how does your prophecy say this will end?"

The wizard held his hand over a thick scroll bound with black silk thread. "By the time the sun rises, this encounter will be over," the wizard intoned, his eyes rolling back. "A victory will come and, with it, a loss. With them both will come the eternal throne of Theodorico Balshazzar. He will have power over Death and the absolute loyalty of every creature that dwells within his realm. His family shall be agents of the White Lady and inheritors of Her great power." He turned back to Balshazzar, a smile playing lightly across his lips. "Your rule begins with the next dusk, Emir, so be at ease. Eigenhard's sword will not take your life. It cannot. Your existence will never be ended by any blade forged from this world, in fact. Tonight sees the realization of my ambitions and yours. You ask me how this will end? It will end with your undying union to the White Lady."

Chapter 73

As they drew closer to their objective, Tomas' sensitivity to the currents of magic seemed to increase. In point of fact, as the squire and his friends delved deeper into those cold tunnels, he became more acutely aware of the slightest changes in those strange tides. Once the probing attacks of the inquisitors had stopped, Tomas found he could easily make out everything around him once he stopped using his eyes and started using his thoughts and some kind of inner sight that, until now, the squire was unaware he had.

Looking about himself with this new set of eyes, Tomas was amazed at the ambient arcane energy he could both see and feel infusing the rock around them. Noticing the young man's odd expression, Aebreanna moved closer to him.

"Is everything all right?" she asked quietly.

"I don't know," he replied honestly.

"What is it?" the spy asked.

"The rocks, the tunnels, even the air. Everything here is glowing with magic. It's like we're in the center of one of those light shows the illusionists in Pelsemoria used to put on."

Aebreanna looked very closely at her companion. "Can you tap into it?" she asked.

The squire shrugged.

"Try," she insisted.

"What's going on?" Rogan demanded. "In case anybody's forgotten, we've got a mystical artifact to steal."

"Shush," Aebreanna ordered. "This could be useful."

Tomas could barely hear what the two were saying. The squire opened himself to the currents of magic, trying to purposefully tap into the energy he sensed around himself. Recalling before the powerful current that pulled at his mind before, this time the young man was careful not to lose his grip on his body. It was fortunate that he did anchor himself, for the currents were even stronger than before. The energy around them surged toward the main chamber still some distance below, trying to pull Tomas along.

"It's more powerful than last time," he gasped.

"Can you feel where the Winds are going?" Aebreanna asked intently.

Beraht rejoined the group with a look of annoyance. "Are we going to kill someone or not?" he demanded.

Rogan held up his hand for silence. "Let's see what the kid can find out first."

Tomas's breath was coming out in gasps; the difficulty in fighting the currents was almost more than he could bear. "That sphere," he gasped, "everything is rushing towards that sphere. Whatever they're planning, it's almost ready."

"How many guards?" Rogan asked.

Tomas cast his thoughts about, trying to sense the faint glows of sentient minds amid the magical currents, although he could easily sense Balshazzar's mind and the wizard's, both of which glowed brightly in huge cavern despite the small sun that Tomas assumed was the Healing Sphere. "I can only sense Balshazzar and the wizard."

"Balshazzar's here?" Beraht grunted in surprise. "How did he beat us here?"

"He could have a more direct access route from his palace," Aebreanna guessed. "Or perhaps he was issuing orders from here all along."

"Either way," Rogan said, "it means that both our targets are in the same place. I just have trouble believing that they don't have any guards."

"I'm not sensing any other minds," Tomas insisted, wiping the sweat off his brow. "If they have guards, then they don't have any thoughts for me to pick up on."

The knight looked at Aebreanna. "Could Balshazzar have anything like that?" he asked.

The beautiful spy shrugged. "With as little as we know about that wizard, there could quite literally be anything in that chamber."

"Wonderful," Rogan grunted. "Well, there's no sense worrying now. As soon as the kid gets himself together, we'll head down there and finish this."

Just then, Tomas let out a small groan of exhaustion and fell to the tunnel floor. "Tomas!" Aebreanna yelled in concern when the squire collapsed, clutching his head in his hands.

Rogan and Beraht immediately turned and looked about, expecting a renewed attack by the inquisitors. Seeing none, the two warriors gathered around Aebreanna who was holding Tomas's head in her lap and doing her best to sooth his obvious discomfort.

"What's wrong with him?" Rogan demanded in a harsh whisper.

"I cannot be sure," the beautiful spy calmly replied. "But I would think that as we grow closer to whatever it is our enemies are doing with the Seal of Life, the intense magical field being emitted is causing him greater and greater disorientation. He has been struggling against the Winds this whole time and has finally lost the strength to resist."

"Why isn't the same thing happening to us?" the knight demanded.

"We already knew that Tomas had a great deal of untapped arcane ability and sensitivity. I myself have been feeling particularly unwell for several minutes, but I had hoped he would be spared the worst of it."

"Can he go on?" Beraht demanded.

The Sylva pulled a small vial from her pack and emptied its contents into the squire's mouth. "This should take effect in a moment, and then Tomas will be able to continue."

As the three looked on, Tomas's eyes began to refocus, and his breathing steadied. After only a few seconds, the squire was able to stand again, although he had to lean on Aebreanna initially. "Thanks," he whispered to her.

The beautiful Sylva smiled and patted him on the cheek.

"What was that stuff?" Rogan asked.

Aebreanna replaced the empty vial in her sack and retrieved Tomas's sword for him. "The sap from a young tree that grows only in the furthest corners of Wildelves Wood. The Speakers have found that it can dull a person's sensitivity to the Winds of Magic."

"Really?" Beraht asked with obvious interest.

"Forget it," Rogan grunted. "Your senses are dull enough."

Tomas shook his head a few times to make sure he was steady. "How long will that stuff last?" he asked.

Aebreanna shrugged. "The effects vary from person to person. In all likelihood an hour, perhaps two."

The squire looked at his knight. "Is that enough time?"

Rogan squared his shoulders. "Better be.'

"Any side effects I should know about?" Tomas asked Aebreanna.

The Sylva nodded. "So long as you are under the effects of the potion, you will be unable to access the Winds. Until the potion wears off, you will have no magic."

Tomas hefted Steelheart. "Guess that means I'll have to rely on this."

Theodorico was pacing about the ridge that had housed the Sphere of Healing since the emir's agents had retrieved it over a year ago. The Seal had been one of the few tangible rewards of his alliance with the wizard. Over the succeeding years, the tangible rewards had grown fewer and farther apart, before finally disappearing altogether. This fact finally dawned in all its horror to the emir. Theodorico stopped his pacing and glanced down into the lower section of the chamber where the hundreds of imprisoned warriors stood frozen, dressed in a mockery of the armor of the Holy Knights. When the wizard had started the process that drained the minds of the soldiers and knights they had brought here, Balshazzar had been delighted, envisioning these creatures leading numerous assaults on his various enemies. In reality, despite their ever-increasing numbers, the mindless warriors were never declared ready for use by the wizard.

With Eigenhard now only minutes away, the emir thought it an excellent time for the long-overdue field test. "Why don't you activate those things?" he demanded of the wizard who was currently packing away a number of scrolls into a small sack.

"Are you really so feeble that you need the assistance of two thousand mindless knights to defeat one man?" the spell caster asked without turning.

"What's the use of having an army if you don't plan on using it?" the emir demanded.

"But I do plan on using it, my dear Emir. Not here, of course. There would be little point in wasting any of the creatures here. No, my accomplice and I have many plans for those creatures, and I have already wasted more than enough of my resources on this place. I have no intention of losing any of those warriors."

"What do you mean, not here?" Theodorico nearly screamed. "If not here, then where?"

The wizard turned from his workbench and faced the fuming nobleman. "You really have no idea of my motives, do you, Emir?" he asked. "You still have no idea why I helped you. What my goal was this whole time."

The barest hint of understanding dawned on Theodorico face. "You wanted Eigenhard and his people to come here. And you wanted him to get through the city and down into the tunnels."

"Very good, Emir."

Theodorico shook his head. "Calonar. It was your idea to poison Calonar, and that's what drew Eigenhard to Tordenia. You arranged everything. You commissioned Xaemus to poison Calonar, and you sent Anninihus to the Northern Keep with the intention of them defeating him. You wanted Eigenhard to get angry enough that he would come here. And you used just enough magic and monsters so that he would have to bring that bitch-born Sylva and lunatic Uldra with him. You wanted those three to come to this cavern." By now, the emir's face had turned bright red with his rage and frustration.

"But that doesn't make any sense. Why would you want Eigenhard to…" Balshazzar's words broke off as his gaze turned to the crystal sphere that rested on the black stone altar to emir's true god, Ramalech. "You're going to expose me. You want Eigenhard to find out who I truly worship? What in God's name could you gain from that?"

The wizard shook his finger at the emir. "Now, now, Balshazzar. Do you really think it appropriate to invoke the name of a god your family has not worshipped in generations?"

Balshazzar stormed up to the spell-slinger and, grabbing his robes in his large fists, roared at his ally. "Why? Why expose me to Eigenhard? To the world!?!"

The wizard was silent for a moment and then spoke very softly. "I cannot kill you, Theodorico Balshazzar. Fate would not allow it. You still have a part to play in the rising of your god. Be grateful for this, since your insolence has grown tiresome."

"Answer me, damn you!"

"I will answer. I will answer this one last question. What do I have to gain by exposing you? I gain everything. You could have done it, Balshazzar. You could have beaten Calonar and become the next emperor. You could have remade Tordenia into a new imperial capital and ruled all Lanasia. Your descendants could have expanded your empire until it very nearly covered the globe. It could have all been yours, Emir.

"But your crown does not serve my ambition; a united Lanasia would prevent the rise of the Demon-god. This is why the Sylvai Empire had to fall. Why the Lanasian Republic had to fall, why House Calonar must die. Had I not poisoned Cylan Calonar, eventually, his message of peace and tolerance would have spread. He, or more likely, his grandchild, would have united the world in loving acceptance, anathema to the Demon-god. Even if House Calonar failed and their message of equality and fraternity had turned the power-mad to you, still Lanasia would have united and defied the return of Kelinva. Now, once word of your treachery spreads, your fealty to the Demon-god, and it will, the whole of Lanasia will turn against you. The nobles of Lanasia now see House Calonar as too weak, and will soon see House Balshazzar as too monstrous. Neither of you will be the next emperor. There will be no next emperor, only a Dark Empress. The Redwood Throne is forever out of your reach now, Balshazzar. You were one of only three people who could have built an empire that thwarted Kelinva's return and the ascension of her master. With you and Calonar both denied, there remains only Eigenhard's child, and I will soon own that soul. There will be nothing to deny Kelinva's return and her master's ascension. I will not allow it."

As the wizard spoke, Theodorico could feel the truth of his words. As the wizard spoke, Theodorico saw his dreams of empire vanish and his crown slip forever out of reach. With a rage so pure it burned the emir's heart, he reached for his sword. The wizard made only the smallest gesture, and there was a flash of light, hurling the emir across the plateau.

"I'll kill you," Balshazzar snarled as he tried to rise.

The wizard sighed. "As useful as you've been to me, Balshazzar, do not make the mistake of challenging me. I cannot kill you, but I can make you curse your eternal life. You will sit on a throne gifted by the White Lady, but I can pervert that, make it a throne of blood. I can twist the power your House inherits, making it a hateful curse. Besides, you really should save that anger. You'll need it once Eigenhard arrives, which should be anytime now."

Theodorico laughed, rising unsteadily to his feet. "You think I'll stop Eigenhard? You betray me and flaunt it here in the heart of my domain, and you think I'll save you from Eigenhard's wrath? When he gets here, I'll help him. When he gets here, the two of us will be united for the first time ever. The only matter we will argue over is how, exactly, we put you to death."

The wizard turned his hooded gaze to the altar. "Is that all you'll argue about?" he asked.

"Do you really think Eigenhard will care?" the emir demanded. "Once I tell him that you are the one responsible for every misery he's had to endure for the past year, the only thought he will have is commanding that Uldra of his split you in two."

"Will he not at least spare some thought to who poisoned the man he calls father? Will he not spare some thought to he who hired the assassin, threatened to violate his wife, and burn his home? Will he not spare at least the slightest thought to he who it was who trained, funded, and gave orders to the warlords that operate around the Northern Keep? Warlords like Vagris?"

Balshazzar's face fell. The emir realized that his sins were soon to come back to him.

The wizard turned and put his bag over his shoulder. "You see, Emir, I leave nothing to chance. Your enemy will be here in moments and see you standing between him and the only thing in the world that can cure his adopted father. He will see your altar to the Demon-god, and innocent blood still wet upon it. He will see the product of forbidden magics on warriors he will feel kinship with. Rogan Eigenhard is a man of extreme reactions, Balshazzar, untampered by any moderating voice. What do you think he will do when he sees all this? Will he ally with you and help you defeat me? Or will he simply attack and kill you?"

Before Balshazzar could respond, Eigenhard's voice filled the cavern. "Actually, I thought I'd kill the both of you and sort it all out later."

Chapter 74

Emir Theodorico Balshazzar did not take Rogan's sudden arrival well. "Eigenhard!" he nearly screamed. "It's not what you think!"

The knight walked to the edge of the stone outcropping where he and the others had entered and looked down at the ordered rows of warriors, all of them frozen in unlife. "Really?" he asked flatly. "You haven't been hiding a wizard that's tampered with the minds and bodies of knights and soldiers whose only crime was that they wouldn't obey you without question? You haven't been planning on using these men in a war to destroy my father and his family? You haven't been plotting with this damned wizard to kill me and my entire family just so you could be the next emperor?" His eyes went to the altar. "Your family hasn't been worshipping Ramalech by sacrificing innocent people!?!"

"Eigenhard!" Balshazzar sobbed. "Please!"

"I told you he wouldn't be reasonable." the wizard reminded him. The adept looked out over the lower chamber that separated the plateau he and the emir stood on and the tunnel entrance where Rogan and the others were. "As entertaining as this has been, I'll have to take my leave. Feel free to dispose of Balshazzar however you see fit."

Rogan looked across the distance, his eyes following the rope bridge that connected the two outcroppings of rock. "You really think I'm going to let you go?" he demanded.

The wizard laughed. "Are you suggesting you have a choice?"

Beraht was scratching his head with his waraxe. "Is it my imagination or have we heard that voice before?"

Again, the wizard laughed in derision. "Ah, the powers of Uldric observation."

"Who are you?" Rogan demanded.

"You will find out, when I am ready for you to find—" Hopefully, he was ready for them to find out since Aebreanna choose that instant to throw one of her many small blades through the air and caught the very tip of the wizard's hood, snatching it back and exposing the adept's face to the light of the Seal of Life and the cavern's many torches.

"Cyras!" Tomas exclaimed, immediately recognizing the old wizard's battered face and icy blue eyes. Looking closer at the Trickster-Mage, despite the distance separating them, the squire could just make out a number of alterations to the wizard's face, scars that crossed from temple to jaw, a nose that had once been broken and reset, and hair that was kept in a different style, pulled back in a tight knot at the back of his skull. More than anything physical, though, was the soul; even from where they stood, Tomas could see what was in this man's eyes, the hatred and the evil. "No, not Cyras," he said quietly.

"Fak'Har," Beraht snarled.

"They are twins," Aebreanna said in a tight whisper. "Brothers."

"Who…" the squire began. "What is he?"

"Cyras' double, kid," Rogan said, his sword already drawn. "His opposite. The Shadowed Mage."

"We have to fight that?" the squire demanded.

Beraht laughed joyously. "Have to? No, we get to!"

Balshazzar had been edging away from Fak'Har, trying to reach the rope bridge and the relative safety of the party. "We can still beat him, Eigenhard!" the emir called out. "If we help each other, we can rid the world of this spell-slinger forever!"

Fak'Har threw a look of utter darkness at the emir. "Oh, really?" he said flatly. With a sweeping gesture, the wizard summoned a wall of flame that surrounded the entire plateau and destroyed the rope bridge even as Beraht made ready to charge across.

Tomas and his friends all stumbled back against the searing heat, struggling to breath and shielding their faces against the towering flames. Even through the roar of the inferno before them, the heroes could still hear sounds of torture and mutilation, and the agonized screams of a man faced with his horrific destiny.

With a curse, Beraht raised his waraxe, Uldric words of power on his lips. Aebreanna put her hand on his, yelling, "NO! If you use it, you will bring the ceiling down upon us!"

Tomas looked at the flame wall. "We've got to get through there, Rogan," he insisted. "We've got to help Balshazzar."

The knight grunted, his eyes also locked on the flames. "Kid, I couldn't care less about what's happening to Balshazzar. For all he's done, he deserves whatever that wizard is doing to him."

"Rogan," Tomas said firmly, looking his knight in the eye and the soul. "We're the good guys, we MUST be the good guys!"

The knight looked hard at his squire, but sighed and relented. "Fine! But I'll be damned if I'm going to let Fak'Har get away with that Seal!"

"How do we stop him if he's as powerful as Cyras?" Tomas asked. "Can we stop him?" he asked pointedly.

Rogan looked back at the burning wall. "Don't know. But we have to get to him first." The knight turned to Aebreanna. "Any ideas?"

"I believe I can get us across, but the flames must be stopped first," she replied.

Rogan looked at Beraht, whose knowledge of combustion was without equal. "Well?" he demanded.

"It's risky," the Uldra grunted.

The knight shook his head. "Any choice?"

Beraht shook his head. "It's the only fast way."

"Do it." Rogan and Aebreanna pushed Tomas back into the welcome cool of the tunnel entrance as Beraht knelt and began digging at the pouches at his belt.

"What's he going to do?" the squire asked.

Rogan watched as Beraht tapped a small amount of powder into the skin that held the good stuff. "A few years back, Beraht discovered a way to put out large fires. He once used it to stop a forest fire in Wildelves Wood."

"How?" Tomas asked.

The Uldra swirled the large skin with a look of pure concentration. "It turns out that the good stuff is so strong that not only can it eat through lead, but it can also cause a huge explosion. All it needs is something mixed in to ignite it." Beraht, sweat glistening on his forehead.

Tomas shook his head. "I don't understand. How can an explosion put out a fire?"

Aebreanna looked up from where she had been digging in her bag. "Fire needs air just like any living thing, Tomas. With a powerful enough explosion, all of the air can be forced away, suffocating the fire."

"Powerful enough…" The squire's eyes widened. "He'll bring all that rock down on us!"

"Relax, kid," Rogan snapped. "I don't understand it myself, but Beraht swears that he can somehow shape the explosion so that it only moves in the direction he wants it to. We're safe."

"Then why are we cowering in this tunnel?" he asked sharply.

The knight shrugged. "This is Beraht we're talking about."

The Uldra in question had moved to the edge of the outcropping of rock, somehow ignoring the oppressive heat from Fak'Har's wall and looked down. Beraht held out his thumb, carefully taking aim on just the right point. Then, rearing way back, the Uldra hurled the beer skin into the chamber below and then flung himself back onto the stone floor. "Get down!" Rogan barked.

The explosion was horrendous. The entire cavern rocked as smoke and stone debris filled the entire cavern. Despite the rumbling and cracks that appeared overhead, the ceiling did not come down. Once the smoke cleared enough, Tomas and Rogan looked out and saw that Fak'Har's wall was gone, and the soft white light emitted by the Sphere of Healing could be made out. The knight turned to Aebreanna. "Now!"

The beautiful spy darted out of the tunnel and made an overhand flinging motion. From her hands unrolled a bridge of light. Seeing the way across, Rogan picked himself up and drew his sword. "GO! GO! GO!" he thundered.

Beraht and Rogan led the way across, shoulder to shoulder. Tomas and Aebreanna were less than a step behind them, weapons already drawn. "You had this in your bag?" Tomas marveled.

"I like to be prepared, Tomas!" Aebreanna laughed.

Once the party was across the bridge of light, they were better able to see what had befallen Emir Balshazzar. His body lay on the black stone altar of to the Demon-god, a number of lacerations running the length of his body and his once polished armor now a twisted ruin that had apparently provided little protection for its wearer, if any. His ears and nose were gone and his mouth was a bloody mess. Fak'Har stood behind the altar, his hands drenched in the blood of the emir and his black robes showing no signs of violence. The wizard himself seemed fully at ease, the broken man before him summoning no emotion onto his weathered face. He also held the Seal of Life in his left hand.

"Is he dead?" Rogan asked flatly.

Fak'Har laughed. "No, Rogan, Balshazzar still lives; Fate decreed that he would survive this night… but I had some liberty in what form that survival would take."

"I want that Seal," the knight said in a voice that dared refusal.

"So you can use it to heal Calonar?" the wizard asked. "You know, I've never really understood why you were so eager to keep that man alive. He really isn't much of a king, you know. He's far too timid, refusing to perform those acts of cruelty so necessary for a ruler. You, however, you have that streak of viciousness that would serve a king well. If Cylan Calonar dies, you get everything Balshazzar here dreamt of. Why do you want Calonar back so badly?"

Rogan shook his head. "I'm not going to stand here having a philosophical debate with you. Give me the Sphere, and we'll tear you apart."

Tomas leaned over his knight's shoulder. "Don't you mean, 'or we'll tear you apart?'"

Rogan glanced at his squire and then back at the wizard.

Fak'Har turned and placed the Sphere on a nearby obsidian pedestal. From the sides of the pedestal grew clawlike appendages that reached up and locked on to the Seal of Life with an audible click, holding it tight. "I'll tell you what, Eigenhard," the wizard said, turning back to the knight. "If you can get the Seal off that, then you can have it. The spell I've been preparing for the last year is nearly ready, and it only needs one last element concerning the Healing Sphere. I won't do anything to try and stop you. You take the Seal and go, and I take my things and go. What do you say?"

The knight's eyes flicked to the Sphere and back to the wizard. "I have a better idea," he said flatly, raising Talon.

Fak'Har snorted in derision. "You should rethink that," he advised. "You have but two contributions to the Prophecy: you will lead the war against Kelinva and the rise of the Demon-god, and you will sire the One Who Comes to the daughter of a mystical dynasty. You've already seeded the daughter of Calonar, and you can lead without the use of legs, I suppose. I may not be able to kill you, but I can hurt you." The Shadowed Mage's eyes drifted over the others. "To say nothing of what I can do to your little friends." His gaze lingered on Aebreanna, a vile hunger distorting his face and a leer of hateful lust twisting his mouth.

With matching roars, Rogan and Beraht launched themselves at the evil wizard. Tomas followed closely behind, driving Steelheart forward in a low thrust. Fak'Har side-stepped Beraht, ducked under Rogan's attack, and deflected Tomas's sword with a word that summoned a shield of solid shadow over his left arm. The wizard then let the two Human warriors charge forward and threw himself to the side, trying to keep some distance between himself and the Uldra. Speaking quickly in a horrid perversion of the arcane language, the wizard called to his outstretched hands an orb of freezing darkness. Slamming his back into the wall, Fak'Har forced his hands together, shattering the ball and sending a hail of purplish ice into the advancing Rogan and Tomas. Both warriors were forced back, shielding their faces with their arms and grunting in pain as numerous shards pierced their flesh and drew streams of blood.

Fak'Har grinned at the two men's pain and started another insidious chant, waving his hands and summoning more foul magic. Beraht was not about to abandon his friends, however, and so renewed his roaring assault. The Uldra hurled his waraxe at Fak'Har with enough force to shatter boulders. The wizard spotted the attack, though, and held up his hand, halting the weapon in midflight and then launching it back at Beraht, forcing the barbarian to dive for cover behind the altar, calling his waraxe back to his hand.

Aebreanna had watched, waiting for her opportunity. Seeing how distracted the wizard had been by the boys' combined attack, she saw her opening and vaulted over Fak'Har's head, sending a spinning back-kick to his head. The Shadowed Mage easily blocked the kick with his arm and grabbed her by the shoulders, pulling Aebreanna in close. "Ah, my lovely niece," he sneered, firing a blast of dark magic at the approaching Rogan, flinging the knight very nearly over the edge if not for Tomas grabbing him at the last second. "Still have those Daddy issues, do we?" he asked, leaning his head in toward the cringing Aebreanna. "You really should deal with all those misplaced emotions of yours, my dear. They aren't ladylike. Here, let me help you." The wizard leaned in to kiss her but winced in pain as the Sylva drove her knee into his groin. Fak'Har hurled her bodily into Beraht, knocking them both back. "You always were a feisty little bitch," he leered.

Rogan and Tomas advanced on the wizard again, each supporting the other in the hopes of dividing his attention. "Ah, here come the heroes," Fak'Har noted.

"Whatever shall I do?" At the same instant, both warriors attacked, swinging their swords in a lethal series of strikes that should have reduced Fak'Har to a mess of blood and flesh. However, with a speed that would have shocked Rashid, the old wizard ducked, parried, and blocked each attack with his bare hands, his face never loosing that mocking grin. After the first few blocks, Fak'Har began counterstriking the two warriors, responding to each swing of a sword with a casual slap to the attacker's face. Each hit, seemingly light yet carrying the force of iron, very nearly drove the knight and his squire mad with fury, their attacks becoming increasingly less coordinated and efficient. After only a few moments, the once-precise strikes of both warriors were reduced to savage swings with little finesse. Finally, Fak'Har's boredom overcame his amusement, especially with his seeing that Beraht and Aebreanna were about to reenter the fight, so he batted aside yet another of Tomas's attacks, then spun and grabbed the squire from behind and threw him right at Beraht.

The Uldra caught the squire and dropped him to the ground. "Stop throwing people at me, you son of a bitch!" he thundered. Beraht then charged up to support Rogan, swinging his waraxe at the wizard's head. Fak'Har, instead of ducking the Uldra's attack, instead darted in and grabbed Beraht's arms, guiding the blunt end of the sacred weapon into Rogan's chest and sending the knight crashing to the floor. Only Rogan's split-second reaction and well-made armor saved his chest from being crushed by the heavy blow.

Beraht's rage was growing by the second, fed on by Fak'Har's constant laughter. The Uldra's attacks became more and more vicious, any one that hit the stone behind the wizard created cracks that ran to the ceiling far above. Again and again, Beraht swung his great waraxe, and again and again, Fak'Har would duck or deflect the attack, sending the roaring Beraht spinning off only to have him charge back in again. Finally, Aebreanna had recovered from the wizard's earlier assault and threw caution to the winds, leaping in to support her mountainous friend. The two made a surprisingly efficient team: Beraht's strength and direct physical attacks supported by Aebreanna's nimble blade strikes. Putting immediate action to thought, the wizard called upon his magic and created a shimmering dome of purplish light around himself and the Sylva, shutting Beraht out and forcing the Uldra to start beating on the shield with all his fury.

Fak'Har sneered at Aebreanna. "Nowhere to tumble about," he informed her. "What to do now?" The Sylva darted in and spun, driving the back of her left hand into the back of the wizard's head. Without hesitation, Aebreanna pulled a small needle from her sleeve and tried to stab the monster before her, but Fak'Har caught her hand and twisted, snapping her wrist and sending the needle falling to the floor. Aebreanna let out a yelp of pain and tried to back away but was blocked by the shield. His eyes nearly glowing with sinister purpose, Fak'Har advanced on the beautiful Sylva. Aebreanna let him take a few steps closer then planted her back against the shield and kicked both legs up, hooking the left around Fak'Har's neck and striking with the right, kicking the wizard about the face and chest before dropping her legs, driving her right foot again into his groin, then spinning and kicking his legs out from under him.

Moving with that same unnatural speed, the evil wizard rolled on the ground and was back on his feet almost instantly. He charged forward and lashed out with his left hand, grabbing Aebreanna around the throat and squeezing his grip tighter and tighter. Fak'Har pulled her in close so that her face was less than a breath from his. With his free hand, the Shadowed Mage pushed Aebreanna's hair away from the right side of her face. Now exposed, Tomas and the others saw. A hideous, savage scar cleaved Aebreanna's face, from beside her chin, all the way up across her cheekbone and where the brilliant, opalescent eye had been. That ruined orb was a like a shattered gem, barely held together by a jagged crater. The flesh that should have been like cool ivory in the late Spring, was instead shades of angry red. The side of her bow-like mouth was twisted, its once-sensuous lips snarled on the right side into a permanent, grotesque mockery of a grin.

Fak'Har looked at this, turning Aebreanna's face to expose her grievous injury to the others. "Don't worry," he leered, "you're still beautiful to me." He then ran his tongue along the length of the scar.

Seeing this, Beraht roared in pure, holy rage. The son of Uldron and friend of Aebreanna hit the shield with a mighty overhead strike. A great, crackling energy of blue-white force erupted from the waraxe and leapt ahead of the mighty weapon, gnawing on the shield even as Beraht's attack struck. There was a flash of righteous hate, and Fak'Har's spell was shattered, shards of shadowy power fleeing from the mad Uldra. Beraht raised his waraxe again and lunged at Fak'Har.

In desperation, the Shadowed Mage flung the terrified, mewling Aebreanna towards the chasm edge. Beraht halted his attack in mid-strike and lunged after the Sylva, catching her and pulling his friend close.

"We'll finish this later," the wizard promised. He then raised his arms and snarled, "Enough of this nonsense." He pointed at Beraht and Aebreanna, chanting more hideous words of darkest magic. As Rogan and Tomas watched helplessly, arcs of horrid, purplish electricity lashed out from the Shadowed Mage's hands. The insidious attack aimed for Aebreanna, but at the last instant, Beraht turned her aside, shielding the tiny Sylva with his massive body. The cavern filled with the son of Uldra's agonized screams. His flesh was torn and burnt. His armor melted. His body spasmed. His shielding grip on Aebreanna did not waver.

The onslaught ended. Their eyes readjusted to the dim light of the Healing Sphere. They looked and Beraht remained where he was, kneeling and shielding Aebreanna. Smoke poured from his charred, desecrated flesh. His mighty waraxe slipped to the ground with a clatter. The son of Uldron fell without a whimper, leaving his Sylva friend untouched by the blasphemous lightning.

Aebreanna stared for a moment, wide-eyed and nearly slack-jawed at her great friend. He was not moving and barely breathing. Her remaining eye widened and then narrowed in fury, turning its blazing, opalescent gaze at the Shadowed Mage. The glow of that orb brightened, intensified. A wind, unfelt by all others, swirled around the enraged daughter of Cyras Darkholm. Her flowing, honey blonde mane lashed up and out, as though possessed of its own hatred for the evil brother of the Trickster Mage. Aebreanna lifted from the ground, her beautiful face contorting into a snarl of intolerable vengeance. She spoke no words of magic, but only raised a commanding finger. Every Sylvai blade, whether on her person or scattered about the cavern, responded to its mistress, rising into the air and forming a deadly halo about her thrashing golden mane. Aebreanna pointed, and the blades shot out.

Fak'Har spoke and gestured, trying to deflect the missiles. Most were stopped or deflected, but many struck true. Blades impaled his arms, his legs, his torso. The Shadowed Mage screamed in pain and snarled at his mystical niece. He called to his own dark power to rival her light. The two auras clashed, sparks and shards and whips and blades of energy, dark and light, crashed into one another. The two beings of titanic arcane might ripped open the very fabric of the world and pulled from the aether impossible weapons with which to do battle. Arcs and lances of raw magic thundered through the cavern. Tomas and Rogan were forced to dodge them, forced away from where their friend did mystical battle with the Shadowed Mage.

At last, both adepts gathered their power to themselves and struck with onslaughts of pure energy. They wrested against each other, twisting their bodies into a flood of arcane fire. Aebreanna's once-beautiful face twisted past her horrid scar, filled now with an inhuman hatred for the Shadowed Mage. Fak'Har grunted and strained, then his eyes narrowed and he grinned evilly. "I hope you taste as good as your mother," he snarled, licking his lips. "I hope you whimper when I ravage you, just as she did. I hope, deep down, you enjoy having uncle inside you as much as she did!"

Aebreanna, if possible, became more enraged. She abandoned her mystical assault and leapt at this impossible thing of vile evil. She reached with her claws outstretched, hissing her fury. Fak'Har smiled again, but did not call to his magic. Instead, he drove his fist into his niece's face.

"No more!" Tomas screamed and launched himself at Fak'Har. The wizard smiled and flipped his wrist, sending a dagger of ice crystal flying at the squire. Tomas twisted in midair, dodging the missile, and slashed with Steelheart, shattering the shadowed orb the evil wizard tried to summon. There was a blinding flash that even overwhelmed the awesome power and then all was dark.

The Shadowed Mage blinked and shook his head, then clawed to his feet. He looked and saw his niece lying on the ground, her energy spent. He smiled and pointed at her, vile words of forbidden magic once again seeping from his lips. This incantation was suddenly halted, though, as a shining sword erupted from his chest. Rogan leaned over and snarled, "No more of you." The knight tore Talon free and knelt, even as his squire swung Steelheart, removing the dark wizard's head.

Chapter 75

The cavern was silent. Fak'Har's body was still on the ground. His head had rolled away. The light of the Healing Sphere was constant. The air was filled with the stench of burned flesh.

Tomas's looked to his knight.

"You all right?" Rogan asked weakly.

The squire nodded. They both looked to Aebreanna. Whatever magic she had summoned was past. She now knelt by her great friend, her head bowed and tears flowing from her eye. The Humans wearily lifted themselves and walked over, their blades heavy and useless in their hands. "Is he...?" Tomas asked.

A weak, shuddering gasp ripped from Beraht's mouth. Rogan and Tomas both took a step back, but Aebreanna leaned in, her eye wide and her hands probing. "He lives!" she barked. The Sylva then pointed to the Seal of Life. "Now!" she commanded.

The Humans dropped their swords and heaved at their friend's great mass, straining with all they had left to drag Beraht to the obsidian pedestal. Aebreanna accompanied them, lending her own strength and her tiny body belying the great power she summoned to help in lifting the Uldra. When they reached the strange pedestal, Aebreanna grabbed Beraht's impossibly thick arm and raised it, putting his hand to the Seal of Life.

The soft white light of the Healing Sphere brightened then, changing to gold and filling the cavern with its warm, radiating glow. Finally unable to look, Tomas was forced to shut his eyes and turn away. The shining light endured for only a moment before retreating back to its faint, white glow.

Beraht stood. His body was whole, untouched by even the slightest injury. Even the Uldra's great beard was restored, as full and long as ever.

Aebreanna's unabashed cry of joy, of relief and love, replaced the blazing golden light. She sobbed and held Beraht, her small arms seeming even more so against his mountainous torso. The Uldra and Sylva said nothing, only held each other.

Rogan looked around the plateau, trying unsuccessfully to hide the emotions he was still feeling. "Well, looks like everything here is wrapped up."

Tomas smiled and stood beside his knight. "Yeah," he said. "Everything's been taken care of." He then cast a sidelong gaze to his knight. "Have you been crying?" he asked.

"Of course not," Rogan huffed. "I'm just tired, and you know, all this dust in the air too."

Tomas nodded. "It has been a rough day," he noted.

Aebreanna detached from Beraht and cleared her throat, her face flushed and her movements awkward as she fumbled to restore her mane of honey blonde over the right side of her face. She stepped away from the Uldra and turned from them, walking a few steps to gain some slight privacy.

Rogan and Tomas walked up to their lumbering friend. The squire punched him in the arm. "You gave us a scare," he admonished.

"Rogan said to protect her," Beraht shrugged.

The knight blinked. "Beraht," he said, "that was ten years ago!"

The Uldra shrugged. "And?" he asked.

"I apologize for disrupting all this wonderful male bonding, gentlemen," Aebreanna said with a measure of her stoic grace returning, "but I fear Fak'Har has escaped."

All three warriors snapped their heads around. The Sylva was kneeling over the limp body that was once Fak'Har. "What are you talking about?" Tomas demanded. "I cut off his head. There's no escaping that."

Aebreanna lifted the head. The face was that of a man of the Western Empire, of perhaps thirty years with dark hair and eyes. It was, most definitely, not the face of Fak'Har. Rogan looked at the face for some time, then turned and kicked viciously at the black stone altar on which Balshazzar was laying, cursing violently at this newest development.

"How?" Tomas asked.

Aebreanna dropped the head and stood, dusting off her hands. "The Service has suspected something like this was the case, and what we learned in the Prophet's crypt did more or less confirm it."

"What are you talking about?" the squire demanded.

"Fak'Har is a disembodied spirit," she explained. "His original body was destroyed ages ago during that great conflict with Darkholm. Somehow he survived the Trickster Mage's assault as a spirit, possessing one body after another. When Rogan killed this body, Fak'Har most likely jumped into any number of others within a certain distance of here." She looked around. "We are rather fortunate that he did not try to possess one of us."

"It didn't occur to you to tell us he could do that ahead of time?" Rogan demanded.

"This was no more than a theory," she replied coolly. "Besides, we had no idea that Fak'Har was the mysterious adept working with Balshazzar."

Rogan threw his arms in the air. "How many times will we have to kill that bastard!?!"

"As many as is necessary," Aebreanna replied. "Until we can discover some means of imprisoning him in a body and then destroying that body, he will continue jumping from one to another. We can either stand here venting inarticulate rage over the situation, or we can return to the Keep with adequate warning."

"Warning about what?" Tomas asked.

Beraht stomped up to join them. "There's only one thing that Fak'Har will be doing with an army of mindless soldiers," he muttered.

"The Keep," Rogan said. "He's going to attack the Keep."

Balshazzar weakly raised his head from the altar. "That's why he wanted you here," he gasped, coughing up blood.

The four heroes gathered around the altar, trying to hear the emir's words. "What's his plan?" Rogan asked.

The emir coughed up more blood, unable to answer. Rogan made eye contact with Aebreanna and jerked his head in Balshazzar's direction. The Sylva nodded and started rummaging through her bag for something that would help the emir. Quickly mixing together a potion, Aebreanna lifted Balshazzar's head and poured it down his throat, stepping back and waiting until the emir's breathing became less labored. The spy then looked at Rogan and nodded.

"What's Fak'Har planning?" the knight asked again, enunciating each word.

"It's not just him. He has an ally in Calonar's council that has been feeding him instructions," Balshazzar replied weakly. "Fak'Har wants to stop another empire from forming, but not even the wizard knows what his ally wants. They manipulated me, getting me to do their dirty work for them."

"Which you were more than willing to do," Tomas pointed out.

"I won't apologize," the emir said flatly, still unable to move. "I played the game like I thought I should. I lost, but so did Calonar."

"What do you mean? Who's the traitor?" Rogan demanded.

"It was Fak'Har's power, but it was his ally's plan. He wanted Calonar to appear too weak, and he wanted me to appear treacherous. That would leave only your son, Eigenhard. Fak'Har thinks your son is the only one left who can unite Lanasia."

"But what does the traitor get out of it?" Aebreanna asked.

"Who is it?" Rogan nearly roared.

Balshazzar shook his head. "I don't know. Fak'Har wouldn't tell me. I'll tell you this though. Whoever your traitor is, he's the one giving the orders. Fak'Har frequently received orders he didn't understand and didn't agree with, but he carried them out anyway. Even if they do have a partnership, Fak'Har is the junior partner. It wasn't even Fak'Har's idea to attack your Keep. The order came from the man on the council. Fak'Har is just using it as an opportunity to get his hands on your son."

"But we still have time," Tomas noted. "If Fak'Har has to wait until you have a son, then we have plenty of time before—"

"Kyla's pregnant," the emir interrupted. "Fak'Har told me."

They were all quiet then, the shock of Fak'Har's plan hitting them all at once. "He's going after you son," Beraht said flatly. "That's not going happen."

Rogan straightened his shoulders. "Even with that army, he'll have to get through everyone at the Keep to hurt Kyla and the baby."

"Not now," Aebreanna noted. "The entire army has been deployed because of the growing hostilities with Frostfront. Right now, the Keep is weakened."

Tomas's eyes widened. "And with us all the way on the other side of the continent, the army deployed, and the King dying of poison—"

"Fak'Har'll attack the Keep and everyone in it," Rogan finished.

"Eigenhard, you don't get it," Balshazzar coughed. "He doesn't want the Northern Keep. He doesn't want Calonar's life or anything in that city except your son. He wants to own your son. He said he's already got his hands around your son's soul, and soon he'll own it. His ally may want the Keep destroyed, but Fak'Har only wants your son."

Tomas put his hand out to steady his knight. "Like Beraht said," he said through clenched teeth, "it's not going to happen." The squire and Uldra looked at each other and nodded.

Rogan took a deep breath. "Either way, it means the same thing. Fak'Har's going to use that army to hit the Keep and steal my son." The knight looked at his friends. "It's time to go home, people."

As the other three moved about to gather up their things, Rogan retrieved his sword and leaned in, his face very close to Balshazzar's. They looked into each other's eyes for a few moments, something unspoken passing between them. "I could save Lanasia a lot of trouble right now," Rogan finally said.

Balshazzar took a deep breath. "I wouldn't blame you. You've got more than enough reason."

The knight looked at the symbols carved across the altar. "You worship Ramalech, the Demon-God. You sold your soul to God's enemy, and still you're ready for me to kill you?"

The emir nodded. "If I'm bound for the fire, then there's no sense trying to escape it at the last second. Like I said, I won't apologize for how I played the game. I played. I lost. You can still win if you hurry."

"Rogan!" Tomas' voice snapped through the dim cavern. His knight glanced up, locking eyes with the squire. They stared at each other. Tomas said nothing, nor did Rogan. Yet, an entire conversation passed between them, an argument of what their struggles meant, both against the enemies of their House, and those within their own souls.

Finally, Rogan sighed and nodded. He put the tip of Talon against Balshazzar's chest. "Like you said, this is how you play the game." The knight then sheathed his longsword. "But it isn't how House Calonar plays it, and from now on, it isn't how I play it. This is where playing the way you do leads. Stop and maybe you can still avoid the fire. Maybe we both can." Rogan leaned very close to Balshazzar, his eyes boring into the emir. "Don't even think about trying again. If you do, I'll be back, and I'll show you just how dirty I can play the game."

Without another word, Rogan moved to rejoin Aebreanna and Tomas at the pedestal on which the Healing Sphere was locked. The squire said nothing, only put a hand on his knight's shoulder.

Beraht walked up to the altar and looked at Balshazzar. Without changing his expression, the Uldra punched him in the face. When Beraht joined the others, Tomas looked questioningly at him. "I don't do witty," he explained. "I do violent."

Rogan looked from the pedestal to Aebreanna. "Well?" he demanded.

The spy looked up from where she was examining the device. "Do you want this done quickly or correctly?" she asked with a raised eyebrow. "You cannot have both."

"Is there a happy medium?" he demanded.

"Yes, you may keep pestering me as I keep working. The job will still get done, and you will still gain whatever satisfaction irritating me seems to provide you."

The knight turned and stalked away, muttering to himself about the various inconsistencies of women from any race.

Tomas looked over the Sylva's shoulder as she continued her examination of the obsidian pedestal, trying to fathom her process. After a few minutes, the irritable spy stopped and shook her head. "Tomas," she said very simply, "if you must loom over me like that, could you perhaps make yourself useful?"

"What do you need?" he asked.

"A few days' vacation in the City of All Sins should just about do it."

"I'm sorry?"

She sighed. "Nothing, Tomas, just try and get me some more light."

The young man picked up the torch they had brought with them and relit it, holding it over Aebreanna's head as she continued her examination. "Aren't you maybe overthinking this, Aebreanna?" he asked after several minutes.

"Better that than underthinking it as you boys so often do," she replied.

"Why don't we just knock the top of it off with Beraht's waraxe?" the squire insisted.

Aebreanna suddenly stood and put her hands on her hips. "Are you certain you are not part Uldra?" The Sylva cut off Tomas's sputtered objections with a raised hand. "Listen to me, young man. Whatever Fak'Har was doing here involved powerful magics, and the very worst thing we could do is act hastily. The only safe approach to this device is a careful examination and delicate retrieval. If you really must destroy something, Emir Balshazzar is lying right over there." Without waiting for Tomas's reply, Aebreanna moved over to where she had dropped her bag and began rummaging around in it for tools.

Tomas sullenly looked over to where she was kneeling. "Excuse me for making a suggestion," he muttered to himself. The squire put the torch down and touched the pedestal with one finger. "Oh my God, I touched it! Now the world's going to end, isn't it Aebreanna?" Tomas shook his head. Not really expecting anything of it, the squire put a hand on the Sphere and tried pulling it. Much to the young man's surprise, the talons that held the Sphere released, and the Sphere came free with no resistance whatsoever. Catching the Seal of Life before it could fall, Tomas smiled and looked over at Aebreanna. "Hey look! I got it off!"

Aebreanna looked at Tomas and then looked past him with utter horror. Confused, the squire turned and jumped back with a surprised yelp. The obsidian pedestal appeared to be melting, the darkness spreading very slowly away from where the pedestal had stood and across the cave floor. Rogan and Beraht ran up and stared at the spreading darkness. Both looked at Aebreanna. "What did you do?" they demanded.

"What did I do?" she sputtered indignantly.

Tomas lowered his head and raised his hand.

"You set this thing off!" Rogan demanded.

"Hey good for you, kid," Beraht laughed.

"Shut up, Beraht!" Aebreanna snapped. The Sylva turned to Tomas. "We will discuss this later, young man," she threatened. To Rogan, she said, "Seeing as how your squire has most likely doomed the entire city, perhaps we should expedite our departure."

With no other prodding necessary, the party started crossing Aebreanna's bridge of light. Halfway across, Tomas stopped. "They're gone!" he exclaimed.

"What?" Rogan demanded from the opposing side.

The squire pointed down. The wide lower section that had once held the motionless and soulless creatures Fak'Har had created was now empty. The creatures were gone.

"Questions for later!" Aebreanna insisted.

Tomas turned to leave but paused, looking back at Balshazzar who was feebly trying to move off the altar but obviously lacked the strength. "Wait!" he cried. "What about Balshazzar?"

Beraht rushed past the squire. "What about him?"

Rogan returned and grabbed the young man's shoulder. "Sorry, kid, whatever that is, it's spreading too fast, we can't go back, and we sure can't carry him."

The two warriors spared one last look back then turned as one and ran back into the tunnels.

Theodorico could feel the darkness drawing closer. After his battle with Fak'Har, he lacked the strength to rise, let alone escape. It did not really surprise him that Eigenhard had left him; he would have done the same after all. Lying there, with Death approaching, the emir had only one real regret; he did not regret that he was going to die; he had resigned himself to the fires long ago. Nor did Theodorico regret that he had lost the game. It was playing a game that was the fun of it, after all, not the winning or losing. No, the one thing that Emir Theodorico Balshazzar, ruler of the Western Empire, regretted was that he would not get the chance to see who did win the game. It gnawed at him that the Shadowed Mage might win; Theodorico would rather see Calonar win than that damned wizard.

The spreading darkness reached the edge of the altar and touched his hand. The emir did not flinch away, trying desperately to buy a few more seconds. If this was his end, if this was how the White Lady claimed him, then so be it. Never let it be written in any history that Emir Theodorico Balshazzar died sniveling and clawing at the earth like some peasant. As the darkness consumed him, a deep cold clutched at the emir's soul. *Is this what Death is?* he asked silently. *Is the White Lady an eternal, unfeeling cold?* The darkness had now covered most of his body, and still Balshazzar was unafraid. What was to fear, after all? He had already suffered through learning that he had been played a fool by a wizard for the second time. *Well, come what may*, he thought to himself, *once I get to Underworld, that's it. No more wizards!*

That last conversation came to Balshazzar's mind as the darkness spread across his head. "How will this encounter end?" he asked aloud. Just as the darkness wrapped around his face, the answer came to the emir's mind. *It will end with a union to the White Lady.*

Then all was cold and darkness.

Chapter 76

"Move!" Rogan ordered. "MOVE!"

The darkness was picking up speed. The farther the party ran through the twisting tunnels, the closer the spreading darkness seemed to close on them. Now that they had recovered the Healing Sphere, the one thing in the entire world that could cure their king, none of them would accept dying in these tunnels.

Aebreanna, who had been leading them thus far, reached an intersection and paused, looking down each of the four possible choices in turn with a look of uncertainty on her beautiful face.

"Which way?" Rogan demanded.

The spy shook her head. "If I knew which way, do you really think I would be standing here?" she snapped.

"Well, pick one!" Tomas yelled, hearing the hissing sound the darkness made as it moved, growing steadily stronger as it spread.

"Always the easy answers with you," she sniffed. "Never bothering to think things through must be a truly engaging method of living one's life."

"For God's sake, woman!" Rogan roared. "Just pick one!"

Beraht stomped forward to the intersection and stopped, sniffing the air and running his hairy hands along the rock at each tunnel entrance. After only a few moments, the Uldra pointed at one of the tunnels and said, "This one." Without looking back, Beraht ran down that tunnel.

Aebreanna hesitated only a second before following her friend. Rogan and Tomas shared a look of mutual terror before also following. As they ran along, Aebreanna shook her head. "Goddess, help us," she muttered. "We trust our lives on the direction sense of a Uldra."

As the party ran, they periodically reached another branch in the tunnel network. At each spot, Beraht stopped and sampled the air and stone before selecting a new course and hurrying up it. Only the Uldra's complete lack of hesitation that kept the others running along behind him, had he paused for even a moment or had shown the slightest uncertainty, they would have mutinied. Fortunately, Beraht's instincts proved reliable, and the party reached the steep stone staircase leading back up to the cathedral. Beraht saw this and laughed. "Well, what do you know? I found it!"

Tomas looked at the Uldra in horror. "You mean you didn't know!" he demanded as Aebreanna scurried up the stairs.

The Uldra shrugged. "No clue."

"God, I hate you," the squire muttered as he also went up the steps.

Once all four of them were up, they sprinted for the damaged doorway, both hearing and feeling the spreading darkness close on their heels. Each of them skidded to a halt outside the cathedral, though, when they caught sight of a hundred Tordenian soldiers waiting for them with weapons drawn.

"That's it!" Tomas snapped. "I quit! I'm going home!"

A short soldier wearing an officer's rank stepped forward with an air of superiority. "Oh, not this fool again," Aebreanna sighed, shaking her head in annoyance.

"Drop your weapons!" the officer ordered.

Tomas leaned in to Rogan. "Does he really expect us to do that?" he asked.

The knight nodded. "I really think he does."

"We have you outnumbered!" the colonel reminded them. "Surrender!"

"You should have brought more," Beraht said with a sinister grin.

"We have no time for this!" Aebreanna insisted. "We must escape!"

"Well, do you have any ideas?" Rogan demanded.

Tomas looked back at the shattered altar and spotted the darkness spreading up out of the tunnel entrance. "Whatever we're going to do," he warned, "make it fast."

"Well?" Beraht demanded.

"I'm thinking. I'm thinking." The knight roared.

"No time!" Aebreanna insisted.

From the back of the soldiers arrayed before them, there came a sudden yell of confusion, and several of the Tordenians were hurled all the way to the base of the cathedral in a mass of red surcoats. All eyes turned and saw twelve warriors standing tall and wielding an array of exotic weaponry. Every one of the warriors had the symbol of a crossed, four-pointed diamond tattooed over their left eye, marking them as the Archaeknights, bodyguards and elite warriors of House Calonar.

"Ward!" Rogan yelled in recognition of the huge dark-skinned man standing with no weapon at the head of the other Archaeknights.

"In trouble again, Rogan?" the old fighter laughed. Then, his face losing all humor, the warrior thrust his arms out. "Archaeknights, clear a path!"

With practiced ease, each of the Archaeknights spread across the courtyard. The archer among them climbed onto a nearby statue and began launching mystically charged arrows into the formation blocking Rogan's group, each arrow exploding with arcane power that forced the soldiers to scatter for cover. The Tramanese Archaeknight who carried a long staff tipped with a curved blade struck the ground with his weapon and sent a shockwave rolling away from him, knocking nearly half the soldiers off their feet. Another Archaeknight, this one carrying a pair of small wooden clubs, vanished only to reappear behind one soldier, knocking him down, then disappearing and reappearing behind another. Tomas spotted Sarah, the red-headed Archaeknight who carried a very short blade with a long wooden handle, flipping in among the soldiers, incapacitating a number of them, only to leap hundreds of feet in the air and launching herself at another knot of men.

Each of the Archaeknights, with their own powers and weapons, helped equally in clearing the soldiers out of the way of Rogan's team. The illusionist, an older Tramanese woman with long flowing black hair who carried a fan made of blades, confused the soldiers while the dark-skinned Archaeknight carrying a pair of short swords whose blades waved like a serpent's tongue used his control of fire to punish any soldiers brave enough to force their way ahead. One of the Archaeknights, a small man with shaved scalp who threw small stars made of metal, moved among the soldiers with the grace of a dancer; when one of the soldiers got in a lucky thrust with his sword, Tomas started to see the Archaeknight's body explode into a flood of water only to reform and continue the fight.

"They're clearing a path," Rogan snapped. "Let's go." The knight led his team out into the courtyard, their movement covered by the Archaeknights.

Tomas ducked under the clumsy swing of a soldier and drove the fist that held Steelheart into the man's face, sending him falling to the ground. "What are they?" he asked.

Rogan swung his sword over Aebreanna's head, the Sylva dropping and rolling under the swing and continuing on, letting the knight deal with the soldier who had tried to spear her in the back. "When one of them joins the Archaeknights, the King uses his magic to enhance them. They're given a power that reflects their personality. It reduces his magic but you see what they can do because of it."

The squire lightly flicked his blade at the face of an advancing soldier, forcing the man back. "Sounds like a lot of power to just give someone," he noted.

Rogan laughed. "You see the marks over their eyes?"

"Yes."

"Those tattoos are more than badges. When the Archaeknights accepts that mark, they let the King have free access to their minds. Everything an Archaeknight sees, he sees. Everything the Archaeknights know, he knows. The whole team basically has one mind in a fight."

Tomas started. "You mean the King is watching the fight right now?"

"Don't get stage fright now, kid!" the knight laughed.

"Why do they let King Cylan into their minds like that?" the squire demanded, cutting the sword out of a soldier's hand.

"It makes them unbeatable," Rogan explained. "The King has been around a long time, and he knows just about every trick in the book. With those marks, he can direct the Archaeknights from the safety of the Keep.

Sarah landed as if from nowhere just behind Rogan and continued to fight but spoke in a voice that was not her own. "Rogan," she said, "is everyone all right?"

"We're all right, sir," the knight replied. "We found Balshazzar and stopped his plan, but we found out that it was Fak'Har that was working with him."

Sarah's young face took on a thoughtful expression even as the young woman continued fighting back the soldiers. "I see," she said finally. "What of Balshazzar's plans?"

"Balshazzar's probably dead," Rogan reported as he fought. "Whatever Fak'Har was working on, we broke it up, but there's some kind of darkness that's spreading across the city. We don't know what it is, but it's already taken Balshazzar."

"And Fak'Har?"

"Gone. He's a body-hopper now. I killed the body he was in, but he just jumped to a new one. He's on his way to the Keep right now with a thousand mindless warriors."

"To what end?"

"He wants my son. He told Balshazzar something like he already had his hands on my son's soul, and that he was going to take him just as soon as he's born. That was the deal he made with the traitor on the council. Fak'Har gets my son and Kyla."

"What does his ally get?"

"Besides your death and the destruction of the Keep? I don't know."

Sarah stopped fighting when there was a pause in their immediate area and turned, putting a hand on Rogan's shoulder. "Don't worry, son, we'll take care of it. We already found Fak'Har's agent in the Keep, it was Kyla's new bodyguard. Esha is already neutralizing what he was doing to Kyla. Take the Archaeknights and escape Tordenia, everything else is secondary. Just get out of there."

"There's something else," the knight said, turning and fighting off another soldier. "We found the Seal of Life. We're bringing it back. Just hold on until we can get back."

Sarah nodded. "I will hold on for as long as possible, just come home safely. Ahmed is waiting for you at the harbor, Rogan, so hurry." The young Archaeknight blinked, her eyes returning from blue to their customary green, and shook her head.

"Welcome back," Rogan laughed.

She smiled and leapt into the air again, continuing the fight. Tomas returned to Rogan's side, shaking his head. "That really was a little disturbing," he confessed.

"Believe it or not, kid," Rogan said while grabbing a soldier's arm with his off hand and hip-tossing him to the ground, "it still gets to me a little."

"And just think," the squire laughed, "when you become king, that power shifts to you!"

The knight shot his squire a look of pure venom. After a few more minutes, the four heroes managed to fight their way to Ward's side. Upon reaching him, Rogan briefly took his friend's hand in his before turning and breaking into a full run. "Don't be long!" he called to the leader of the Archaeknights. "That darkness has already spread out of the cathedral!"

Ward grabbed a soldier, lifted him, and threw him bodily into the crowd of his fellows, knocking down over a dozen in the process. "Don't worry. We'll be two steps behind you!"

Rogan and his team ran for the harbor just as fast as their legs could carry them. The sounds of the fighting behind them stopped suddenly as the soldiers finally caught sight of the spreading darkness and broke, dropping their weapons and running for the city gates. Once freed from the battle, the Archaeknights overtook Rogan's team within minutes.

"Archaeknights!" Ward barked as he ran past Tomas. "Give them a lift!" Sarah landed next to Aebreanna and let the Sylva climb on her back before leaping again, covering a great distance even encumbered. Ward picked up Beraht, despite the Uldra's objections, and held him up until a young Sylvu Tomas had not noticed before flew over the old fighter's head and grabbed Beraht, flying at great seed toward the docks. The Archaeknight who carried the wooden clubs appeared next to Rogan and took the knight's arm before disappearing again, reappearing several hundred feet down the street only to disappear again. Tomas started when the blond-haired Archaeknight in black landed next to him, then smiled, and laid a light hand on his shoulder. With only a slight gesture, they both took off into the air. Looking back, Tomas saw the rest of the Archaeknights moving, under their own enchanted power or with the help of their comrades, at great speeds towards the harbor. Now that he was, with the help of one of the Archaeknights, moving above the rooftops of the tall warehouses that filled this section of the city, the squire could see that Ahmed's ship was, in fact, awaiting them at the docks, his crew busy fighting off a large group of Tordenian soldiers.

Ward, whose mystical strength helped him jump from rooftop to rooftop, saw the fight. "There's our ride, Archaeknights!" he roared. "Let's give them a hand!"

The fight was short and direct. With Rogan's team and the Archaeknights on one side and the crew of the *Blue Lady* on the other, the soldiers were beaten quickly, most of them opting to jump into the cold waters of the harbor rather than face the combined might of House Calonar's forces. From the main deck of the *Lady*, Ahmed called out to them. "Ho, Rogan!"

"Ready to go home, Ahmed?" the knight called back.

"Of course!" the sailor laughed. "Did we win?"

Rogan pointed back at the darkness that had, by now, covered the cathedral and was spreading throughout the entire city at tremendous speed. "We will if you can get us out of here before that arrives."

Ahmed blinked and then looked at the four heroes with narrowed eyes. "What is it with you people?" he demanded. "For God's sake, could you just once not destroy an entire city?"

Beraht put his arm around Tomas's shoulders and pulled him down, rubbing a knuckle in the squire's head. "Just breaking the kid in!" the Uldra laughed. "Had to make him one of us!"

Rogan shook his head. "Let's get out of here."

Nearly an hour later, Rogan and Tomas stood on the deck of the *Blue Lady*, watching as the sun rose and the last of Tordenia was consumed by darkness. From the noise audible even from the ever-increasing distance between the city and the ship, it was clear that a great many people had been trapped in the city and consumed by Fak'Har's curse.

"What do you suppose is going to happen to the city?" Tomas asked quietly.

Rogan shrugged. "No way of knowing. Over the years, I've stopped trying to guess what the next evil wizard's ultimate spell is going to do. If they're lucky, Balshazzar and his people will just be killed by it."

"If they're lucky?" the squire repeated questioningly.

The knight shook his head. "There are some pretty horrifying things that wizards can do if you give them half a chance, kid. I've seen wizards turn people into undead monsters, soulless husks, and twisted mockeries of life. And Fak'Har's just about the worst of them."

"If you're trying to cheer me up, do me a favor and stop."

Rogan turned and put his hand on his squire's shoulder. "Look, kid, I won't lie to you. Not now, not ever. That thing Fak'Har built was probably designed to do exactly what it did, no matter what we tried. Aebreanna could have worked on that thing for a year and not gotten the Sphere out. Fak'Har is as sick, twisted, and evil a son of a bitch as you'll ever meet, and this kind of thing is what he does. In all likelihood, there was no way for us to prevent this. The day Balshazzar made his deal with that devil, the people of Tordenia were doomed."

Tomas shook his head. "You can't know that," he insisted. "We can't know that this could have been avoided."

Rogan nodded. "You're absolutely right. We don't know, and we never will. Don't make any mistake, kid. You screwed up. You did something that was incredibly stupid and risky. Now you're going to have to live with this for the rest of your life. Just like I have to live with letting the Madness happen to your home, you have to live with this."

They were quiet for a while. The two heroes stood at the railing and watched a city die.

Eventually, Rogan tired of the terror-stricken screams. He tried leading Tomas away, but his squire was determined to stay at the aft rail and watch. From experience, Rogan knew that this would eat away at the kid. The knight was all but inconsolable after Pelsemoria. Only the immediate crisis with Tienel Greysoul had given Rogan something to focus on besides his total failure. They still had a mission, and that would draw his squire's attention, but Rogan knew there would be an emotional reckoning once they were back at the Keep. He turned to the desk of charts where Ahmed and Ward stood.

Rogan glanced up the mast at where one of the Archaeknights stood in the crow's nest. Walking over to the two men, he jabbed his thumb upwards. "Why is she up there?" he asked.

Ward shrugged. "Coranelana controls the winds. If we want to get back to the Keep as soon as possible, then we need her to call up more than this little breeze."

The knight turned to Ahmed. "How much wind can this ship take?"

The admiral shrugged. "Whatever she can call up, my *Blue Lady* can use."

Rogan glanced down at the navigational maps. Looking at the ones for central Lanasia, Dagon'ay, and the South, he asked, "What's our best course?"

The old sailor looked down and rubbed his chin with his hand. "We sail around Dagon'ay until we reach Pelsemoria, then stop there for provisions before continuing on to Janoah. From there, we sail around the Velaross Duchies to Clayton, or you might want to go to Ironheartshaven and pick up reinforcements there. Once I get you there, you strike out cross-country to the Keep. Normally, with the constant strong wind the Archaeknights can give me, I could get you to Ironheartshaven in about six or seven months, but there is a faster way."

"What way?" Rogan asked.

Ahmed grimaced. "Ordinarily I don't like to risk it, but if we turn east as soon as possible, we can cut several weeks off our journey."

"Why don't you like it?" Ward asked.

Ahmed shook his head and pointed at the tight cluster of islands lying in their path. "It means sailing straight through Dagon'ay."

Ward crossed his massive arms over his even more massive chest. "My Archaeknights can handle a Vaeyen or two," he declared.

The admiral raised an eyebrow. "How about ten or twenty?"

"What?"

Ahmed shook his head. "Most of the Vaeyen left in Arayel make their lairs in those islands. Hopefully, most of them will still be sleeping, but you never really know with those things. Still, the Vaeyen aren't the real dangers."

"What are?" Rogan asked.

The sailor jabbed his finger down at the map. "The seas around those islands are peculiar," he said grimly. "Those channels make their own tides, with whirlpools and rapids and corals that you can't see until you're on top of them. Not only that, but some of those islands have some of the tallest peaks in the world, each of which affects the weather in a different way. All kinds of storms spring up there at the damnedest times, completely without warning."

Rogan closed his eyes, breathing deeply. "How much time can we save if we go through those channels instead of going around?" he asked.

"Weeks," the sailor shrugged, "maybe months, depending on how fast we can get through. If that little lady can keep that wind or even put a little more behind us—"

"She can," Ward declared.

"Then assuming we survive the trip through Dagon'ay, I can put your feet in Ironheartshaven in about four months, with another few weeks travel time to the Keep."

"And if we don't go straight through?"

"Six months at least. More, if we hit weather."

"Can your men do it?" Ward asked grimly.

Ahmed nodded without hesitation. "My crew's the best. If it can be done, we can do it."

Ward turned to Rogan. "If we are to get back to the Keep in time to stop Fak'Har, some risks are going to have to be taken."

The knight nodded. "Let's do it."

Fifth Interpose

Chapter 77

Vagris sat in his private tent impatiently. Time was accelerating and any of a hundred details required his attention. The warlord glanced around his pavilion, not for the first time, tapping his foot and repeated looking at the timing candle. His quarters were comfortable, but not luxurious, as was proper for a General in the field. Vagris knew that many of his fellow Bellonari Generals tended to enjoy the luxuries that came with their rank, but he always believed in a spartan lifestyle in the field.

The crystal half-sphere in front of him remained lifeless. Although he could, of course, initiate contact with either of its mystically-linked partners, doing so only ever resulted in silence at the other end. Fak'Har enjoyed making people ill-at-ease, Vagris knew. This was just one more petty act meant to place himself in superiority to the others.

At last, when the timing candle had burnt away an hour of useless waiting, Vagris was ready to terminate the connection at his end. He was hired by that damned spell-slinger to do a job, not to sit around. Just as the Bellonar stood, a soft red mist rose from the flat crystal surface. With a grumble, Vagris returned to his seat.

Instead of an image of Fak'Har's face, the red mist coalesced into an ordinary-looking Human woman. Vagris needed a moment to remember, she was so ordinary-looking, but then recalled. "The traitor," he noted.

She shrugged off the label. "That depends on perspective." Even her voice was plain, Vagris decided. An entirely-forgettable woman, even for a peasant.

"Where's the wizard?" The Bellonari General demanded.

"Delayed. My master has been in contact with him. Eigenhard arrived at Tordenia ahead of schedule. Fak'Har had to... adapt."

"So why am I talking to a servant, instead of your master?"

The plain woman shrugged again. "My master wants to maintain his cover. No one on the Advisory Council even suspects me, let alone from whom I take orders."

"All well and good," Vagris dismissed with a sniff. "If Fak'Har is too busy after his confrontation with Eigenhard, then what is the purpose of this?"

"My master commanded me to send you an update," the woman replied.

"Report, then."

"The assassin has been stopped, and I killed him before he could reveal anything incriminating. Fak'Har's project succeeded. His creatures are under his control and on their way. They'll reach your position before the year is out."

"Good, what else?"

"Kyla has regained control of herself." The woman smirked. "The curse didn't go quite according to Fak'Har's design. Instead of awakening Kyla's latent power, it awakened her child's."

"Interesting," Vagris said dismissively. "And?"

"To regain control, Kyla has begun researching the hidden scrolls of the Lady of Light, just as my master wished. She will soon rediscover Dream Magic."

The Bellonar shook his head. "Enough of schemes and wizard-plans," he grumbled. "What of the siege?"

"It continues as you instructed. The Advisory Council believes the Western Forts are moving to reinforce General Killdare. The army of Frostfront is now fully engaged with Calexto."

"And the Speakers?"

"Scattered. You have succeeded in your maneuvers. The Sylvai are spread across the forest with no way to reinforce each other or the Keep. All potential reinforcements have been neutralized, clearing the way for your approach."

Vagris nodded. "Excellent. You have my compliments, woman. Your master is proving to be a strong ally." The general stood and consulted his maps. "I'll begin burning the nearest Sylvai villages. There are Xeshlin slavers already here, waiting to buy prisoners. I'll be at the city walls by summer's end."

"We'll be ready."

"Are there any changes to the plan?" Vagris asked.

"No. Attack the city, sack it, kill everyone. Leave the daughters of Calonar for Fak'Har."

To Be Continued

The Journey of
House Calonar Continues in:

The Eastern War
Book 4 of the Master of Fate

ABOUT THE AUTHOR

William Price Jr is a teacher of writing and literature. Having published numerous short stories and poems, he still searches for truth amidst his many made up stories. He lives in New Hampshire